爱伦·坡短篇小说选

SELECTED SHORT STORIES OF ALLEN POE

美 国 文 学 卷

中英对照全译本

[美] 埃德加·爱伦·坡 著

Edgar Allen Poe

盛世教育西方名著翻译委员会 译

盛世教育西方名著翻译委员会

主　　任：黎小说　高民芳　杜　毅

本册委员：孙　怡　曹玉华　郝佳庆

　　　　　李文博　王　杭　陈　默

　　　　　梁　恩　张　雪

世界图书出版公司

上海·西安·北京·广州

图书在版编目（CIP）数据

爱伦·坡短篇小说选：中英对照全译本/（美）爱伦·坡（Poe, E. A.）
著；盛世教育西方名著翻译委员会译. —上海：上海世界图书出
版公司，2011.5

ISBN 978-7-5100-3239-4

Ⅰ. ①爱… Ⅱ. ①爱… ②盛… Ⅲ. ①英语－汉语－对照读物
②短篇小说－作品集－美国－现代 Ⅳ.①H319.4：I

中国版本图书馆 CIP 数据核字(2011)第 028066 号

爱伦·坡短篇小说选

[美] 埃德加·爱伦·坡 著

盛世教育西方名著翻译委员会 译

上海世界图书出版公司 出版发行

上海市广中路 88 号

邮政编码 200083

北京兴鹏印刷有限公司印刷

如发现印刷质量问题，请与印刷厂联系

（质检科电话：010-84897777）

各地新华书店经销

开本：880×1230 1/32 印张：13.25 字数：460 000

2011 年 5 月第 1 版 2011 年 5 月第 1 次印刷

ISBN 978-7-5100-3239-4 /H·1105

定价：24.80 元

http://www.wpcsh.com.cn

http://www.wpcsh.com

前　言

通过阅读文学名著学语言，是掌握英语的绝佳方法。既可接触原汁原味的英语，又能享受文学之美，一举两得，何乐不为？

对于喜欢阅读名著的读者，这是一个最好的时代，因为有成千上万的书可以选择；这又是一个不好的时代，因为在浩繁的卷帙中，很难找到适合自己的好书。

然而，你手中的这套丛书，值得你来信赖。

这套精选的中英对照名著全译丛书，未改编改写、未删节削减，且配有权威注释、部分书中还添加了精美插图。

要学语言、读好书，当读名著原文。如习武者切磋交流，同高手过招方能渐明其间奥妙，若一味在低端徘徊，终难登堂入室。积年流传的名著，就是书中"高手"。然而这个"高手"，却有真假之分。初读书时，常遇到一些挂了名著名家之名改写改编的版本，虽有助于了解基本情节，然而所得只是皮毛，你何曾真的就读过了那名著呢？一边是窖藏了50年的女儿红，一边是贴了女儿红标签的薄酒，那滋味，怎能一样？"朝闻道，夕死可矣。"人生短如朝露，当努力追求真正的美。

本套丛书的英文版本，是根据外文原版书精心挑选而来；对应的中文译文以直译为主，以方便中英文对照学习，译文经反复推敲，对忠实理解原著极有助益；在涉及到重要文化习俗之处，添加了精当的注释，以解疑惑。

读过本套丛书的原文全译，相信你会得书之真意、语言之精髓。

送君"开卷有益"之书，愿成文采斐然之人。

Contents
目录

1. Hop-Frog

一. 跳蛙

I never knew anyone so keenly alive to a joke as the king was. He seemed to live only for joking. To tell a good story of the joke kind, and to tell it well, was the surest road to his favor. Thus it happened that his seven ministers were all noted for their accomplishments as jokers. They all took after the king, too, in being large, corpulent, oily men, as well as inimitable jokers. Whether people grow fat by joking, or whether there is something in fat itself which predisposes to a joke, I have never been quite able to determine; but certain it is that a lean joker is a *rara avis in terris.*

About the refinements, or, as he called them, the "ghost" of wit, the king troubled himself very little. He had an especial admiration for breadth in a jest, and would often put up with *length,* for the sake of it. Over-niceties wearied him. He would have preferred Rabelais' "Gargantua" to the "Zadig" of Voltaire: and, upon the whole, practical jokes suited his taste far better than verbal ones.

At the date of my narrative, professing

我从不清楚有人会和国王一样如此醉心于笑话。国王似乎只为笑话而生。谁要讲个笑话之类的有趣故事，娓娓道来，那必定会平步青云。碰巧国王的 7 员大臣在讲笑话方面都颇有造诣，而且长的全与国王相似，个个身材魁梧且脑满肠肥，都是无法媲美的笑话家。人们究竟是通过开玩笑而变胖，还是胖子本身就易于开玩笑，我还真难以确定。但可以肯定的是，一个清瘦的玩笑家倒是比较稀罕的。

国王很少在风雅之事，或他所谓的机智之"鬼"上费心思。他特别崇尚开玩笑，因此往往为此不厌其长。过分精妙优美令他腻烦。他宁愿选择拉伯雷[1]的《巨人传》，也不愿看伏尔泰[2]的《查第格》。总之，实际行动的戏弄比起字面上的笑话更合他的口味。

在我的小说所处的年月，专业

---

[1] 拉伯雷：法国文艺复兴时期人物，被称为世界四大文化名人之一。其代表作是长篇小说《巨人传》。

[2] 伏尔泰：法国 18 世纪启蒙运动思想家、文学家、哲学家。

jesters had not altogether gone out of fashion at court. Several of the great continental "powers" still retain their "fool", who wore motley, with caps and bells, and who were expected to be always ready with sharp witticisms, at a moment's notice, in consideration of the crumbs that fell from the royal table.

Our king, as a matter of course, retained his "fool". The fact is, he required something in the way of folly – if only to counterbalance the heavy wisdom of the seven wise men who were his ministers – not to mention himself.

His fool, or professional jester, was not *only* a fool, however. His value was trebled in the eyes of the king, by the fact of his being also a dwarf and a cripple. Dwarfs were as common at court, in those days, as fools; and many monarchs would have found it difficult to get through their days (days are rather Longer at court than elsewhere) without both a jester to laugh *with*, and a dwarf to laugh at. But, as I have already observed, your jesters, in ninety-nine cases out of a hundred, are fat, round, and unwieldy – so that it was no small source of self-gratulation with our king that, in Hop-Frog (this was the fool's name), he possessed a triplicate treasure in one person.

I believe the name "Hop-Frog" was *not* that given to the dwarf by his sponsors at

小丑在宫廷中还没有完全被废除。欧洲大陆上的几个"强国",始终保有着它们的"弄臣"。他们身着五颜六色的衣服,头戴帽子铃铛,被期待着当御桌上赐下残羹冷炙时马上能妙语连珠,答谢圣恩。

我们故事里的国王,自然保有着他的"弄臣"。事实就是,国王非要看点愚蠢的事情——希望可以平衡平衡他那 7 位聪明的大臣过分聪明的脑袋,更不消说国王自己了。

那位弄臣或称专业小丑,可不仅仅是个傻子。他还是个矮子和瘸子,凭这点他在国王眼中的价值就高了 3 倍。在旧时的宫廷中,矮子与傻子一样寻常。要是既没个小丑陪着笑闹一场,又没个矮子拿来取笑一番,许多帝王就觉得难以度日,时光在宫廷里可比在其他地方难打发呢。但就像我观察到的,这个弄臣真是百里挑一,膀大腰圆、笨手笨脚,所以国王看着跳蛙(就是这位弄臣的名字)一个顶 3 个活宝,简直心满意足。

我相信"跳蛙"这名字绝不是矮子受洗礼时由教父母给他取的,

baptism, but it was conferred upon him, by general consent of the several ministers, on account of his inability to walk as other men do. In fact, Hop-Frog could only get along by a sort of interjectional gait – something between a leap and a wriggle – a movement that afforded illimitable amusement, and of course consolation, to the king, for (notwithstanding the protuberance of his stomach and a constitutional swelling of the head) the king, by his whole court, was accounted a capital figure.

But although Hop-Frog, through the distortion of his legs, could move only with great pain and difficulty aLong a road or floor, the prodigious muscular power which nature seemed to have bestowed upon his arms, by way of compensation for deficiency in the lower limbs, enabled him to perform many feats of wonderful dexterity, where trees or ropes were in question, or any thing else to climb. At such exercises he certainly much more resembled a squirrel, or a small monkey, than a frog.

I am not able to say, with precision, from what country Hop-Frog originally came. It was from some barbarous region, however, that no person ever heard of – a vast distance from the court of our king. Hop-Frog, and a young girl very little less dwarfish than himself (although of

但可能是 7 位大臣看他走路不能与常人相同，才一致赞成用这个外号。其实跳蛙走起路来，是一种令人感叹的步态——一半跳，一半扭——这种姿态给国王带来无尽乐趣，当然也引以自我安慰，因为国王尽管长得腹如牯牛，头如笆斗，宫廷上下还是把国王当做首屈一指的美男子。

可是尽管跳蛙两腿畸形，以致走起路来十分吃苦费力，但是造物主似乎为了弥补他下肢短小的缺陷，赐给了他无穷的肌肉力量，使他能够在树木或绳索等其他可以攀爬的东西上表演不少身手矫捷的绝技。凭着这种运动，比起青蛙来他当然更像是松鼠和猴子。

我虽不能精确说出跳蛙的原籍是哪里，但他确出自于一个无人知晓的未开化之地，距离我们国王十分遥远。跳蛙连同一个比他稍矮一点点的年轻女孩（但那女孩身材异常匀称，还是个不俗的舞蹈家）被当时一位常胜将军从两人相毗邻的

exquisite proportions, and a marvellous dancer), had been forcibly carried off from their respective homes in adjoining provinces, and sent as presents to the king, by one of his ever-victorious generals.

Under these circumstances, it is not to be wondered at that a close intimacy arose between the two little captives. Indeed, they soon became sworn friends. Hop-Frog, who, although he made a great deal of sport, was by no means popular, had it not in his power to render Trippetta many services; but she, on account of her grace and exquisite beauty (although a dwarf), was universally admired and petted; so she possessed much influence; and never failed to use it, whenever she could, for the benefit of Hop-Frog.

On some grand state occasion – I forgot what – the king determined to have a masquerade, and whenever a masquerade or any thing of that kind, occurred at our court, then the talents, both of Hop-Frog and Trippetta were sure to be called into play. Hop-Frog, in especial, was so inventive in the way of getting up pageants, suggesting novel characters, and arranging costumes, for masked balls, that nothing could be done, it seems, without his assistance.

The night appointed for the *fête* had arrived. A gorgeous hall had been fitted up, under Trippetta's eye, with every kind of

家乡强行掳来，作为礼物献给了国王。

在这种情况下，两个小俘虏之间产生一种亲密之情就不足为奇了。甚至不久之后他们就发誓结为盟友。尽管跳蛙大演戏码，但却根本就不受欢迎，因此无力给予屈丽佩塔一些帮助。而她尽管矮小，但却凭借举止优雅，姿色过人，因此人人赞美爱慕，炙手可热，无论何时，只要她可以就会帮助跳蛙。

一次国家盛会——我记不太清了——国王决定举办一场化装舞会。无论何时国王要举行化装舞会或其他盛会，跳蛙和屈丽佩塔两人肯定要被召去表演一番。尤其跳蛙非常善于安排舞会节目，为了能尽情玩乐，提议新奇角色，张罗服装，仿佛没有他协助便什么也办不成。

钦定节日那晚到了。在屈丽佩塔的监督下，一座金碧辉煌的大厅早已被装饰一新，各种类型的装饰

device which could possibly give éclâ t to a masquerade. The whole court was in a fever of expectation. As for costumes and characters, it might well be supposed that everybody had come to a decision on such points. Many had made up their minds (as to what roles they should assume) a week, or even a month, in advance; and, in fact, there was not a particle of indecision anywhere – except in the case of the king and his seven minsters. Why they hesitated I never could tell, unless they did it by way of a joke. More probably, they found it difficult, on account of being so fat, to make up their minds. At all events, time flew; and, as a last resort they sent for Trippetta and Hop-Frog.

When the two little friends obeyed the summons of the king they found him sitting at his wine with the seven members of his cabinet council; but the monarch appeared to be in a very ill humor. He knew that Hop-Frog was not fond of wine, for it excited the poor cripple almost to madness; and madness is no comfortable feeling. But the king loved his practical jokes, and took pleasure in forcing Hop-Frog to drink and (as the king called it) "to be merry."

"Come here, Hop-Frog," said he, as the jester and his friend entered the room; "swallow this bumper to the health of your absent friends, [here Hop-Frog sighed,]

品足以使化装舞会不同凡响。整个宫廷中的人都翘首热盼。至于服装和角色，不难想象每个人在这一点上都已拿定主意。好多人在一星期甚至一个月前，就已决定好扮演什么角色了。事实上，除了国王和他那 7 位大臣，到处都是一副一丝不苟的样子。除非他们开玩笑，我还就真说不清他们为什么犹豫。很可能是因为他们长得太胖，才难以定夺吧。总之一句话，时间匆匆而过，最后的解决办法就是下旨传见屈丽佩塔和跳蛙。

当这对小伙伴奉国王的旨意前来时，发现国王正与 7 位内阁大臣一起端坐饮酒，只是国王显得情绪不佳。国王知道跳蛙不爱喝酒，因为酒精会使这苦命的瘸子兴奋以致疯狂，撒酒疯的感觉可不好啊。可国王就喜欢恶作剧来取乐，于是强迫跳蛙喝酒，照国王的说法，就是"以酒助兴"。

"过来，跳蛙，"跳蛙和他的伙伴刚进来，国王就说道，"先为你那些故友的健康干了这杯！（听了这话，跳蛙叹了口气）再帮我们动动

and then let us have the benefit of your invention. We want characters – *characters*, man – something novel – out of the way. We are wearied with this everlasting sameness. Come, drink! the wine will brighten your wits."

Hop-Frog endeavored, as usual, to get up a jest in reply to these advances from the king; but the effort was too much. It happened to be the poor dwarf's birthday, and the command to drink to his "*absent friends*" forced the tears to his eyes. Many large, bitter drops fell into the goblet as he took it, humbly, from the hand of the tyrant.

"Ah! ha! ha!" roared the latter, as the dwarf reluctantly drained the beaker. – "See what a glass of good wine can do! Why, your eyes are shining already!"

Poor fellow! his large eyes *gleamed*, rather than shone; for the effect of wine on his excitable brain was not more powerful than instantaneous. He placed the goblet nervously on the table, and looked round upon the company with a half-insane stare. They all seemed highly amused at the success of the king's "*joke*".

"And now to business," said the prime minister, a *very* fat man.

"Yes," said the King; "Come lend us your assistance. Characters, my fine fellow; we stand in need of characters – all of us – ha! ha! ha!" and as this was

脑子。我们要扮演角色——角色，伙计——一些新奇的、别出心裁的角色。我们对这些老套的东西已经腻烦了。来，喝吧！酒精会使你的脑袋灵光的。"

跳蛙照例想尽力开个玩笑来回谢御赐，可无奈努力全部白费。碰巧那天是这苦命的矮子的生日，听到为"故友"干杯的命令时，泪水不禁夺眶而出。当他从那暴君手中谦恭地接过酒杯时，大颗辛酸的泪珠就扑簌簌地掉进酒杯里了。

"啊！哈！哈！"国王在矮子极不情愿地将白酒一口喝干后放声大笑，"看看一杯美酒干的好事啊！嘿，你的眼睛已经发亮啦！"

可怜的家伙！他那对大眼睛只是在隐约模糊而非闪耀发亮啊。酒精对他那容易兴奋的神经的作用导致他酒力瞬时发作，实在厉害。他紧张不安地将酒杯放在桌上，半痴半呆地环视着这群人。这帮人发现国王的"玩笑"奏了效，似乎都非常开心。

"现在书归正传。"首相道，他非常肥胖。

"对，"国王说道，"来给予我们你的帮助吧。角色，我的好伙计。我们需要扮演角色——我们所有人——哈！哈！哈！"这绝对意味着玩笑，

seriously meant for a joke, his laugh was chorused by the seven.

Hop-Frog also laughed although feebly and somewhat vacantly.

"Come, come," said the king, impatiently, "have you nothing to suggest?"

"I am endeavoring to think of something novel," replied the dwarf, abstractedly, for he was quite bewildered by the wine.

"Endeavoring!" cried the tyrant, fiercely; "what do you mean by that? Ah, I perceive. You are Sulky, and want more wine. Here, drink this!" and he poured out another goblet full and offered it to the cripple, who merely gazed at it, gasping for breath.

"Drink, I say!" shouted the monster, "or by the fiends – "

The dwarf hesitated. The king grew purple with rage. The courtiers smirked. Trippetta, pale as a corpse, advanced to the monarch's seat, and, falling on her knees before him, implored him to spare her friend.

The tyrant regarded her, for some moments, in evident wonder at her audacity. He seemed quite at a loss what to do or say – how most becomingly to express his indignation. At last, without uttering a syllable, he pushed her violently from him, and threw the contents of the brimming goblet in her face.

国王伴随着他的 7 位大臣齐声笑开了。

跳蛙也笑了，尽管笑得有气无力，多少有些空洞。

"来，来，"国王不耐烦地说道，"你没有什么好意见吗？"

"奴才一直在努力想些新奇的东西呢。"矮子心不在焉地回禀道，因为他被酒精弄得迷迷糊糊的了。

"努力！"这个暴君激烈地喊道，"你这是什么意思？啊，我懂了。你心中郁闷，想再喝点酒。拿去，把这杯喝了！"说着国王又斟了满满一杯，把它赐给瘸子，瘸子直勾勾地盯着这杯酒，喘着大气。

"喝，我命令你喝掉它！"魔王大吼，"要不就见鬼去……"

矮子犹豫着。国王则气得面色发紫。臣子全都在傻笑。屈丽佩塔脸色如尸体般惨白，向前走到君主宝座，面对圣上双膝跪下。哀求国王开恩饶恕她的伙伴。

这昏君瞪着她盯了好久，分明奇怪她怎敢如此大胆。国王似乎也不知说什么才好——如何才能宣泄出他的无名火。最后，国王一言不发，猛地一把将她推开，把满满一杯酒泼在她脸上。

The poor girl got up the best she could, and, not daring even to sigh, resumed her position at the foot of the table.

There was a dead silence for about half a minute, during which the falling of a leaf, or of a feather, might have been heard. It was interrupted by a low, but harsh and protracted *grating* sound which seemed to come at once from every corner of the room.

"What – what – *what* are you making that noise for?" demanded the king, turning furiously to the dwarf.

The latter seemed to have recovered, in great measure, from his intoxication, and looking fixedly but quietly into the tyrant's face, merely ejaculated:

"I – I? How could it have been me?"

"The sound appeared to come from without," observed one of the courtiers. "I fancy it was the parrot at the window, whetting his bill upon his cage-wires."

"True," replied the monarch, as if much relieved by the suggestion; "but, on the honor of a knight, I could have sworn that it was the gritting of this vagabond's teeth."

Hereupon the dwarf laughed (the king was too confirmed a joker to object to any one's laughing), and displayed a set of large, powerful, and very repulsive teeth. Moreover, he avowed his perfect willingness to swallow as much wine as

这苦命的姑娘竭尽全力站起身，连大气都不敢喘，重新站回御座下首。

半分钟的光景里一片死寂，连绣针或羽毛掉在地上都听得到。然而转眼间就被一阵低沉刺耳且响个没完的嘎嘎声所打断，仿佛突然从宫里四角传了出来。

"什么，什么，你在做什么怪声？"国王转身对着矮子，怒气冲冲地问道。

矮子已经从昏昏沉沉中大大清醒了，他冷静地盯着这个昏君的脸庞，只是突然问道：

"奴——才？怎么是奴才呢？"

"声音像是从宫外传来的，"一位臣子观察后奏道，"臣觉得恐怕是窗口的鹦鹉，在笼子铁栅上磨它的喙呢。"

"不错，"国王答道，似乎对此说法极为放心，"可话说回来，以爵士光荣的名誉发誓，我觉得准是这无赖在咬牙。"

矮子听了呵呵大笑，露出一副令人生厌的偌大钢牙（国王是个地道的爱开玩笑之人，一直不排斥任何笑话）。除此之外，矮子还宣布要他喝多少酒，他就愿意喝多少。国王顿时息怒。跳蛙又干了一杯，倒

desired. The monarch was pacified; and having drained another bumper with no very perceptible ill effect, Hop-Frog entered at once, and with spirit, into the plans for the masquerade.

"I cannot tell what was the association of idea," observed he, very tranquilly, and as if he had never tasted wine in his life, "but just after your majesty, had struck the girl and thrown the wine in her face – just after your majesty had done this, and while the parrot was making that odd noise outside the window, there came into my mind a capital diversion – one of my own country frolics – often enacted among us, at our masquerades: but here it will be new altogether. Unfortunately, however, it requires a company of eight persons and –"

"Here we *are*!" cried the king, laughing at his acute discovery of the coincidence; "eight to a fraction – I and my seven ministers. Come! what is the diversion?"

"We call it," replied the cripple, "the Eight Chained Ourang-Outangs, and it really is excellent sport if well enacted."

"We will enact it," remarked the king, drawing himself up, and lowering his eyelids.

"The beauty of the game," continued Hop-Frog, "lies in the fright it occasions among the women."

"Capital!" roared in chorus the monarch and his ministry.

看不出任何醉态，他又开始抖擞精神，说出化装舞会的计划。

"奴才真是不知怎么会想出这个念头，"他不慌不忙地启奏道，好似平生从没喝过一口酒，"但就在刚才陛下打了那个女孩，将酒泼在她脸上——就在陛下这么干之后，同时鹦鹉在窗外又发了怪声，一个绝妙的解闷主意突然出现在奴才的脑海里——一种奴才老家的玩意儿我们常在化装舞会上扮演玩的。但不幸的是，需要 8 个人才行，而且——"

"我们就是啊！"国王对于自己研究发现这么巧合的事，笑着叫道，"8 人小组，朕和 7 位大臣。说吧！什么玩意儿？"

"奴才们称之为'8 个戴铁链的猩猩'，"瘸子回禀道，"如果我们扮得好，倒确是个好活动。"

"我们一定要扮。"国王挺直腰板，垂下眼帘，讲道。

"游戏的精妙之处在于可以吓倒女人。"跳蛙接着奏道。

"妙啊！"君臣 8 人一齐吼道。

"I will equip you as ourang-outangs," proceeded the dwarf; "leave all that to me. The resemblance shall be so striking, that the company of masqueraders will take you for real beasts – and of course, they will be as much terrified as astonished."

"Oh, this is exquisite!" exclaimed the king. "Hop-Frog! I will make a man of you."

"The chains are for the purpose of increasing the confusion by their jangling. You are supposed to have escaped, *en masse*, from your keepers. Your majesty cannot conceive the *effect* produced, at a masquerade, by eight chained ourang-outangs, imagined to be real ones by most of the company; and rushing in with savage cries, among the crowd of delicately and gorgeously habited men and women. The *contrast* is inimitable!"

"It *must* be," said the king: and the council arose hurriedly (as it was growing late), to put in execution the scheme of Hop-Frog.

His mode of equipping the party as ourang-outangs was very simple, but effective enough for his purposes. The animals in question had, at the epoch of my story, very rarely been seen in any part of the civilized world; and as the imitations made by the dwarf were sufficiently beast-like and more than sufficiently hideous, their truthfulness to nature was

"奴才来把陛下和大人装扮为猩猩吧，"矮子继续说道，"一切都交给奴才吧。外表模样惟妙惟肖才会惊人，以致参加舞会的人才会真把陛下和大人当做野兽——当然了，他们不仅惊奇，也会害怕。"

"啊，这太妙啦！"国王喊道。"跳蛙！朕要好好提拔你。"

"铁链是为了通过它们的哐哐响声让大家越发混淆。假设你们从看守所里逃出来。陛下肯定想不出效果有多好：在化装舞会上，出现了8只戴铁链的猩猩，在场的多半人会认为是真猩猩呢。凶猛的叫喊着，在一群优美曼妙，锦衣绣服的男女当中冲撞着。再也没有比这更独特的对照啦。"

"一定是的！"国王道。天色已晚，大臣们匆匆起立，都去执行跳蛙的计划。

跳蛙将君臣一干人装扮成猩猩的方法虽很简单，但足够灵巧以达到他的目标。在我这个故事发生的年代里，文明世界中很难看到猩猩。由矮子仿制出来的假猩猩足以乱真，而且不只是足够令人惊骇，它们与原型的真实性也被认为非常可靠。

thus thought to be secured.

The king and his ministers were first encased in tight-fitting stockinet shirts and drawers. They were then saturated with tar. At this stage of the process, some one of the party suggested feathers; but the suggestion was at once overruled by the dwarf, who soon convinced the eight, by ocular demonstration, that the hair of such a brute as the ourang-outang was much more efficiently represented by flu. A thick coating of the latter was accordingly plastered upon the coating of tar. A Long chain was now procured. First, it was passed about the waist of the king, and tied, then about another of the party, and also tied; then about all successively, in the same manner. When this chaining arrangement was complete, and the party stood as far apart from each other as possible, they formed a circle; and to make all things appear natural, Hop-Frog passed the residue of the chain in two diameters, at right angles, across the circle, after the fashion adopted, at the present day, by those who capture Chimpanzees, or other large apes, in Borneo.

The grand saloon in which the masquerade was to take place, was a circular room, very lofty, and receiving the light of the sun only through a single window at top. At night (the season for which the apartment was especially

国王和大臣们先被裹上了紧身的弹力布衬衣衬裤，然后被浸透柏油。进行到这个时候，这群人中有人提议插上翎毛。但这个提议立刻被矮子驳回，而且他马上就以视觉上的例证使这8个人信服，类似猩猩这种牲畜的兽毛，用麻来表现是最有效的了。于是就在柏油涂层上面黏满了一层厚厚的麻。接着又取来一条长长的铁链，首先缠绕在国王的腰间系紧。然后再绕在一位大臣的腰间，再系紧。然后一一绕过其他大臣的腰间系紧。所有人以相同方式相互连接。当铁链安排完成后，每个人都站得尽可能与其他人远远的，围成一圈。为了使一切接近原型，跳蛙采纳了现在婆罗洲人捕捉黑猩猩或其他大型人猿的办法，将剩下的铁链作为两根直径，交成直角，横贯圆周。

举行化装舞会的大殿，是座圆形大厅，高耸巍峨，只有顶部一扇窗子可以透过阳光。到了晚上（大殿专为夜间设宴作乐打造）主要靠一盏巨型吊灯来照明，这盏灯由天窗正中垂下的铁链吊着，照例靠平

designed) it was illuminated principally by a large chandelier, depending by a chain from the centre of the sky-light, and lowered, or elevated, by means of a counter-balance as usual; but (in order not to look unsightly) this latter passed outside the cupola and over the roof.

The arrangements of the room had been left to Trippetta's superintendence; but, in some particulars, it seems, she had been guided by the calmer judgment of her friend the dwarf. At his suggestion it was that, on this occasion, the chandelier was removed. Its waxen drippings (which, in weather so warm, it was quite impossible to prevent) would have been seriously detrimental to the rich dresses of the guests, who, on account of the crowded state of the saloon, could not *all* be expected to keep from out its centre; that is to say, from under the chandelier. Additional sconces were set in various parts of the hall, out of the war, and a flambeau, emitting sweet odor, was placed in the right hand of each of the Caryaides [Caryatides] that stood against the wall – some fifty or sixty altogether.

The eight ourang-outangs, taking Hop-Frog's advice, waited patiently until midnight (when the room was thoroughly filled with masqueraders) before making their appearance. No sooner had the clock ceased striking, however, than they rushed,

衡锤上下，但（为了美观起见）滑轮通到外面，装在屋顶上。

殿内一切安排本来交给屈丽佩塔监督负责，但有些细节她似乎是按着伙伴矮子从容的意见来处理的。按他的意见，这次将烛灯撤掉了。天这么热，烛泪掉下是在所难免的。大殿内人多拥挤，来宾中肯定有人站在正中，也就是说，就站在烛灯底下，那么烛泪就很可能弄脏他们华丽的衣服。殿内各个角落，凡是不碍事的地方，都额外增设烛台。靠墙有排女神柱像，总共五六十个，右手各执一支火把，芳香四逸。

8 个猩猩听从跳蛙的意见，耐着性子直到半夜（化装舞会的殿内全部挤满了来宾）方始露脸。钟声一停，他们便冲进去，但其实还不如说是一齐滚了进去，因为那铁链碍手碍脚导致他们大多都跌倒了，

or rather rolled in, all together – for the impediments of their chains caused most of the party to fall, and all to stumble as they entered.

The excitement among the masqueraders was prodigious, and filled the heart of the king with glee. As had been anticipated, there were not a few of the guests who supposed the ferocious-looking creatures to be beasts of *some* kind in reality, if not precisely ourang-outangs. Many of the women swooned with affright; and had not the king taken the precaution to exclude all weapons from the saloon, his party might soon have expiated their frolic in their blood. As it was, a general rush was made for the doors; but the king had ordered them to be locked immediately upon his entrance; and, at the dwarf's suggestion, the keys had been deposited with *him*.

While the tumult was at its height, and each masquerader attentive only to his own safety (for, in fact, there was much real danger from the pressure of the excited crowd), the chain by which the chandelier ordinarily hung, and which had been drawn up on its removal, might have been seen very gradually to descend, until its hooked extremity came within three feet of the floor.

Soon after this, the king and his seven friends having reeled about the hall in all directions, found themselves, at length, in

个个都是磕磕绊绊地进到殿里。

化装舞会的来宾异常兴奋，国王满心欢喜。如预期所料，很多人若不把他们看作真的猩猩，也把这些模样凶猛的畜生当做真实的某种猛兽。好多女宾被吓得昏了过去。国王若非早有预防，撤掉殿内一切刀枪兵器，他们这一伙恐怕早已用鲜血来负担这场闹剧的代价啦。事实上，大家已经一齐向门口涌去。但国王一进大殿，就已下旨立即将门锁死，而且按着矮子的建议，门的钥匙全藏在国王的身上。

大殿里简直一团糟，每位来宾都只顾自己逃命（其实，由于这群受惊的人相互挤压，这才是真正的危险呢）。先前撤去烛灯时，吊着灯的灯链给拉了上去，现在被缓缓放下，直到链钩离地不到 3 呎的地方停下。

铁链刚一被放下，国王和他那七个伙伴就在大殿的各个方向上蹒跚而行，终于跟跄地闯到大厅正中，

its centre, and, of course, in immediate contact with the chain. While they were thus situated, the dwarf, who had followed noiselessly at their heels, inciting them to keep up the commotion, took hold of their own chain at the intersection of the two portions which crossed the circle diametrically and at right angles. Here, with the rapidity of thought, he inserted the hook from which the chandelier had been wont to depend; and, in an instant, by some unseen agency, the chandelier-chain was drawn so far upward as to take the hook out of reach, and, as an inevitable consequence, to drag the ourang-outangs together in close connection, and face to face.

The masqueraders, by this time, had recovered, in some measure, from their alarm; and, beginning to regard the whole matter as a well-contrived pleasantry, set up a loud shout of laughter at the predicament of the apes.

"Leave them to *me*!" now screamed Hop-Frog, his shrill voice making itself easily heard through all the din. "Leave them to *me*. I fancy I know them. If I can only get a good look at them, I can soon tell who they are."

Here, scrambling over the heads of the crowd, he managed to get to the wall; when, seizing a flambeau from one of the Caryatides, he returned, as he went, to the

自然是恰恰挨着灯链。矮子最初是悄悄地跟在他们身后，挑动这8个人将这闹剧进行下去。当他们那样一站定，跳蛙就抓住绑在他们身上的铁链那贯穿圆周且相垂直的两直径交叉部分。霎时灵光一闪，将吊灯的钩子插进铁链。说时迟那时快，虽看不见有人在拉，灯链却径自升了上去，高得伸手竟够不到钩子了，因而8只猩猩就被紧紧拉在一起，面面相对。

到这时，来宾才放下警觉多少安下心来，开始把整件事看做巧妙编排的滑稽戏，眼见8个猿人不上不下地陷入困境，便放声大笑。

"把他们交给小的吧！"这时跳蛙叫道，他那尖嗓子在一片喧闹声中也不难辨认，"把他们交给小的。小的觉得我认识他们。只要小的仔细看看他们，就能马上说出他们是什么人来。"

说着他分开众人，费力挤到墙前面，然后在一个女像石柱上取了支火把，重新跳着回到大殿中，来回活像一只猴子。他纵身一跳便到

centre of the room-leaping, with the agility of a monkey, upon the kings head, and thence clambered a few feet up the chain; holding down the torch to examine the group of ourang-outangs, and still screaming: "I shall soon find out who they are!"

And now, while the whole assembly (the apes included) were convulsed with laughter, the jester suddenly uttered a shrill whistle; when the chain flew violently up for about thirty feet – dragging with it the dismayed and struggling ourang-outangs, and leaving them suspended in mid-air between the sky-light and the floor. Hop-Frog, clinging to the chain as it rose, still maintained his relative position in respect to the eight maskers, and still (as if nothing were the matter) continued to thrust his torch down toward them, as though endeavoring to discover who they were.

So thoroughly astonished was the whole company at this ascent, that a dead silence, of about a minute's duration, ensued. It was broken by just such a low, harsh, *grating* sound, as had before attracted the attention of the king and his councillors when the former threw the wine in the face of Trippetta. But, on the present occasion, there could be no question as to *whence* the sound issued. It came from the fang-like teeth of the dwarf, who ground them and

了国王头上，又顺着灯链向上爬了几英尺，拿着火把向下仔细打量这群猩猩，还不停叫嚷："小的马上就辨认出他们是什么人。"

这如今，殿中所有的人（包括猿人）个个笑到抽筋，小丑突然吹了个口哨。灯链猛地升高三十来英尺——拖着那些狼狈不堪死命挣扎的8只猩猩，悬在半空，上不接天，下不着地。随着上升跳蛙抱住灯链，仍然与那8个面具人保持一定的距离，照旧像什么事也没发生似的用火把向下照在他们脸上，仿佛拼命想看出他们是什么人。

大家眼看灯链上升，所有人不禁大惊失色，现场一片死寂。持续了半分钟后，才被响起的一阵低低刺耳的嘎嘎声所打破，就像之前国王将酒泼在屈丽佩塔脸上，引起国王跟7位枢密大臣注意的声音一样。不过，现在这声音从何而来倒是毋庸置疑。那是来自于矮子那犬牙般的牙缝间，他唾沫四溅，咬碎钢牙，怒气冲天，狠狠瞪着君臣8人仰起的脸庞。

gnashed them as he foamed at the mouth, and glared, with an expression of maniacal rage, into the upturned countenances of the king and his seven companions.

"Ah, ha!" said at length the infuriated jester. "Ah, ha! I begin to see who these people *are* now!" Here, pretending to scrutinize the king more closely, he held the flambeau to the flaxen coat which enveloped him, and which instantly burst into a sheet of vivid flame. In less than half a minute the whole eight ourang-outangs were blazing fiercely, amid the shrieks of the multitude who gazed at them from below, horror-stricken, and without the power to render them the slightest assistance.

At length the flames, suddenly increasing in virulence, forced the jester to climb higher up the chain, to be out of their reach; and, as he made this movement, the crowd again sank, for a brief instant, into silence. The dwarf seized his opportunity, and once more spoke:

"I now see *distinctly*." he said, "what manner of people these maskers are. They are a great king and his seven privy-councillors, – a king who does not scruple to strike a defenceless girl and his seven councillors who abet him in the outrage. As for myself, I am simply Hop-Frog, the jester – and *this is my last jest*."

"啊，哈！"小丑火冒三丈地说，"啊，哈！小的现在可要看看他们是些什么人了！"说着便装作更仔细接近观察国王，拿着火把凑近国王身上裹着的那层麻布，瞬间便燃起了一片急炽的火焰。不消半分钟，所有的8只猩猩全被烧着了，人群里响起一片尖叫声，他们在底下怔怔地望着，吓得惊骇不已，可就是无能为力，无法对国王和大臣施与些微的帮助。

随着火势增大，瞬间就发展到不可收拾的地步，迫使小丑得顺着灯链向上爬高些以便躲开火焰。当他行动时，下面一伙人又消沉下去，片刻一片寂静。矮子就抓住机会又说道：

"这几套假面具下是什么人，我现在看得清清楚楚，"跳蛙说道，"他们其中一位是国王陛下，另外的7位是枢密顾问大臣——国王毫不犹豫地对一个手无寸铁的姑娘大打出手，他那7位大臣竟也煽动国王做这种凌弱之事。至于在下嘛，我只不过就是小丑跳蛙——这也是我最后一出滑稽戏啦。"

Owing to the high combustibility of both the flax and the tar to which it adhered, the dwarf had scarcely made an end of his brief speech before the work of vengeance was complete. The eight corpses swung in their chains, a fetid, blackened, hideous, and indistinguishable mass. The cripple hurled his torch at them, clambered leisurely to the ceiling, and disappeared through the sky-light.

It is supposed that Trippetta, stationed on the roof of the saloon, had been the accomplice of her friend in his fiery revenge, and that, together, they effected their escape to their own country: for neither was seen again.

由于黏附在身上的亚麻油和柏油都很易燃，因此矮子几乎还没发表完他简短的演说，复仇工作就已结束。那 8 具可怕的死尸烧得一团焦黑且恶臭熏天，吊在链子上来回摇摆。瘸子将火把狠狠扔在死尸上面，从容不迫地爬到殿顶，穿过天窗，消失得无影无踪了。

据说当时屈丽佩塔正守在大殿屋顶，她就是跳蛙一雪前耻的同谋，而且两人最终一同逃回故乡，再也没人见过他们。

2. The Cask of Amontillado

二. 一桶白葡萄酒

THE thousand injuries of Fortunato I had borne as I best could; but when he ventured upon insult, I vowed revenge. You, who so well know the nature of my soul, will not suppose, however, that I gave utterance to a threat. *At length* I would be avenged; this was a point definitively settled – but the very definitiveness with which it was resolved, precluded the idea of risk. I must not only punish, but punish with impunity. A wrong is unredressed when retribution overtakes its redresser. It is equally unredressed when the avenger fails to make himself felt as such to him who has done the wrong.

It must be understood, that neither by word nor deed had I given Fortunato cause to doubt my good-will. I continued, as was my wont, to smile in his face, and he did not perceive that my smile *now* was at the thought of his immolation.

He had a weak point – this Fortunato – although in other regards he was a man to be respected and even feared. He prided himself on his connoisseurship in wine. Few Italians have the true virtuoso spirit. For the most part their enthusiasm is adopted to suit the time and opportunity –

福吐纳托对我百般挑衅，我都尽量容忍，但他一旦敢侮辱我，我肯定誓报此仇。对于早就了解我脾气秉性的您来说，却未必觉得我是说说吓唬人，迟早我会报仇雪恨。对此我坚定不移，但却没考虑断然下定决心的危险。我不仅要惩罚他，还要使我置身事外。报仇者自己遭到报应，这仇就没报完。复仇者不让死敌弄清是谁在害他，这笔仇同样也没了清。

我对福吐纳托的一言一语、一举一动都可以被认为是没引起他怀疑我的不良存心。我照例还是对他笑脸相迎，而他没感觉到如今我的笑是想要他送命呢。

这个福吐纳托在某些方面虽令人尊敬，甚至有点敬畏，但还有个弱点。他自夸是品酒行家。没几个意大利人真正具备行家的气质。他们大多的热诚都用来随机应变，见风使舵，以此骗过英国和奥地利的大财主。在古画和珠宝方面，福吐

to practise imposture upon the British and Austrian *millionnaires*. In painting and gemmary, Fortunato, like his countrymen, was a quack – but in the matter of old wines he was sincere. In this respect I did not differ from him materially: I was skilful in the Italian vintages myself, and bought largely whenever I could.

It was about dusk, one evening during the supreme madness of the carnival season, that I encountered my friend. He accosted me with excessive warmth, for he had been drinking much. The man wore motley. He had on a tight-fitting parti-striped dress, and his head was surmounted by the conical cap and bells. I was so pleased to see him, that I thought I should never have done wringing his hand.

I said to him – "My dear Fortunato, you are luckily met. How remarkably well you are looking to-day! But I have received a pipe of what passes for Amontillado, and I have my doubts."

"How?" said he. "Amontillado? A pipe? Impossible! And in the middle of the carnival!"

"I have my doubts," I replied; "and I was silly enough to pay the full Amontillado price without consulting you in the matter. You were not to be found, and I was fearful of losing a bargain."

"Amontillado!"

纳托跟他的同胞一样，夸夸其谈，但涉及陈酒方面，他倒真是行家里手。这点在本质上我跟他无异——我在意大利自产葡萄酒方面还算精通，只要我打算购买就能大量买进。

在盛大热闹的狂欢节里，一天傍晚，暮色苍茫，我遇到了这位朋友。他极度亲热地招呼我，因为喝得有些多了。这家伙扮成小丑，身穿条纹紧身衣，头戴圆尖帽，上面还系着铃铛。我见到他真是高兴极了，以致抓着他的手不想放开。

我对他说："我亲爱的福吐纳托，幸会，幸会。今天你看起来真是不同凡响啊！我弄到了一大桶阿蒙蒂拉多白葡萄酒[1]，可我有点怀疑。"

"怎么呢？"他说，"阿蒙蒂拉多白葡萄酒？一大桶？不可能吧！还是在狂欢节期间弄到的！"

"所以我怀疑啊，"我答道，"我真是笨透了，竟然没咨询你，就照阿蒙蒂拉多白葡萄酒的价格付钱了。但我一直找不到你，又生怕错过这笔买卖。"

"阿蒙蒂拉多白葡萄酒！"

---

[1] 阿蒙蒂拉多白葡萄酒：西班牙产的一种白葡萄酒。

"I have my doubts."

"Amontillado!"

"And I must satisfy them."

"Amontillado!"

"As you are engaged, I am on my way to Luchesi. If any one has a critical turn, it is he. He will tell me –"

"Luchesi cannot tell Amontillado from Sherry."

"And yet some fools will have it that his taste is a match for your own."

"Come, let us go."

"Whither?"

"To your vaults."

"My friend, no; I will not impose upon your good nature. I perceive you have an engagement. Luchesi –"

"I have no engagement; – come."

"My friend, no. It is not the engagement, but the severe cold with which I perceive you are afflicted. The vaults are insufferably damp. They are encrusted with nitre."

"Let us go, nevertheless. The cold is merely nothing. Amontillado! You have been imposed upon. And as for Luchesi, he cannot distinguish Sherry from Amontillado."

Thus speaking, Fortunato possessed himself of my arm. Putting on a mask of black silk, and drawing a *roquelaire* closely about my person, I suffered him to

"我不放心。"

"阿蒙蒂拉多白葡萄酒！"

"我一定得得到确保才行！"

"阿蒙蒂拉多白葡萄酒！"

"看你一直忙，我正准备去找卢克雷西。如果有人有鉴定酒的癖好，那么只有他。他会告诉我——"

"卢克雷西不能分辨阿蒙蒂拉多白葡萄酒和雪利酒[1]。"

"可有些傻瓜硬说他的品位和你不相上下呢。"

"走，咱们出发吧。"

"去哪儿？"

"到你的地窖去。"

"我的伙计，这可不行。我不能利用你的好心就麻烦你啊。我看出你很忙啊。卢克雷西——"

"我没有安排，来吧。"

"老兄，这不行。倒不是有事没事的问题，就是冷得够呛，我觉得你会受折磨的。地窖里潮得不得了。四壁都是硝。"

"没关系，咱们还是出发吧，冷算不了什么。阿蒙蒂拉多白葡萄酒！你很可能上当啦。说到卢克雷西，他连雪利酒跟阿蒙蒂拉多白葡萄酒都辨认不出来。"

说着福吐纳托发疯般地架住我的胳膊。我戴上黑丝绸面具，把短披风紧紧包住身子，就由他催着我向公馆赶去。

---

[1] 雪利酒：西班牙南部所产的葡萄酒。

hurry me to my palazzo.

There were no attendants at home; they had absconded to make merry in honor of the time. I had told them that I should not return until the morning, and had given them explicit orders not to stir from the house. These orders were sufficient, I well knew, to insure their immediate disappearance, one and all, as soon as my back was turned.

I took from their sconces two flambeaux, and giving one to Fortunato, bowed him through several suites of rooms to the archway that led into the vaults. I passed down a Long and winding staircase, requesting him to be cautious as he followed. We came at length to the foot of the descent, and stood together on the damp ground of the catacombs of the Montresors.

The gait of my friend was unsteady, and the bells upon his cap jingled as he strode.

"The pipe," said he.

"It is farther on," said I; "but observe the white web-work which gleams from these cavern walls."

He turned towards me, and looked into my eyes with two filmy orbs that distilled the rheum of intoxication.

"Nitre?" he asked, at length.

"Nitre," I replied. "How Long have you had that cough?"

"Ugh! ugh! ugh! – ugh! ugh! ugh! –

没有一个侍从在家，都趁机溜出去祝贺节日去了。我和他们说过到第二天早晨之前我不会回家，还清楚地吩咐他们不准出门。我清楚地知道，包管我刚一转身，他们一个个马上就都消失不见了。

我从烛台上拿了两个火把，一个递给福吐纳托，恭敬地带着他穿过几套房间，走进拱廊，通向地窖。我向下穿过一条长长的回旋楼梯，请他一路跟着，多加小心。终于我们到了楼梯底下，一并站在蒙特里梭府邸地的湿地上。

我朋友的步伐摇摇晃晃，每跨一步，帽上的铃铛就叮当作响。

"那桶酒呢？"他说。

"就在前面，"我说，"可要当心墙洞上雪白的蛛网发出的光。"

他冲我转过身来，两只醉醺醺的眼睛直勾勾地盯住我的双眼。

"硝？"终于他开口问道。

"硝，"我答道，"你得了那种咳嗽有多长时间了？"

"咳！咳！——咳！咳！咳！

ugh! ugh! ugh! – ugh! ugh! ugh! – ugh! ugh! ugh!"

My poor friend found it impossible to reply for many minutes.

"It is nothing," he said, at last.

"Come," I said, with decision, "we will go back; your health is precious. You are rich, respected, admired, beloved; you are happy, as once I was. You are a man to be missed. For me it is no matter. We will go back; you will be ill, and I cannot be responsible. Besides, there is Luchesi –"

"Enough," he said; "the cough is a mere nothing; it will not kill me. I shall not die of a cough."

"True – true," I replied; "and, indeed, I had no intention of alarming you unnecessarily – but you should use all proper caution. A draught of this Medoc will defend us from the damps."

Here I knocked off the neck of a bottle which I drew from a Long row of its fellows that lay upon the mould.

"Drink," I said, presenting him the wine.

He raised it to his lips with a leer. He paused and nodded to me familiarly, while his bells jingled.

"I drink," he said, "to the buried that repose around us."

"And I to your Long life."

He again took my arm, and we proceeded.

"These vaults," he said, "are extensive."

——咳！咳！咳！——咳！咳！咳！——咳！咳！咳！"

我那可怜的朋友好久都无法回答我的问题。

"没什么。"他最后说道。

"来吧，"我断然回答，"我们回去吧，你的健康是最为宝贵的。你有钱有势，受人尊敬，得人爱戴。你像从前的我一样幸福。要是真有什么事，那真是不得了啊。我倒没有关系，我们回去吧，你若生病了，我可担待不起啊。再说，还有卢克雷西——"

"够了，"他说道，"咳嗽算不了什么的，害不死我的。我不会咳死的。"

"对——对，"我答道，"说真的，我可不是故意无端吓唬你——可总得好好当心才是啊。喝一口麦道克酒挡挡潮气吧。"

说着我就从泥地上摆着的一长排酒瓶里，拿起一瓶酒，砸了瓶颈。

"喝吧。"我说着把酒递给他。

他瞥了我一眼，将酒瓶举到唇边，还亲热地向我点点头，帽上的铃铛就又叮当响起来了。

"我为我们周围那些长眠地下的人干杯。"他说。

"我则为你万寿无疆干杯。"

他又架起我的胳膊，我们就继续往前走。

"这地窖可真够大啊。"他说。

"The Montresors," I replied, "were a great and numerous family."

"I forget your arms."

"A huge human foot d'or, in a field azure; the foot crushes a serpent rampant whose fangs are imbedded in the heel."

"And the motto?"

"Nemo me impune lacessit."

"Good!" he said.

The wine sparkled in his eyes and the bells jingled. My own fancy grew warm with the Medoc. We had passed through walls of piled bones, with casks and puncheons intermingling, into the inmost recesses of the catacombs. I paused again, and this time I made bold to seize Fortunato by an arm above the elbow.

"The nitre!" I said: "see, it increases. It hangs like moss upon the vaults. We are below the river's bed. The drops of moisture trickle among the bones. Come, we will go back ere it is too late. Your cough –"

"It is nothing," he said; "let us go on. But first, another draught of the Medoc."

I broke and reached him a flagon of De Grâve. He emptied it at a breath. His eyes flashed with a fierce light. He laughed and threw the bottle upwards with a gesticulation I did not understand.

I looked at him in surprise. He repeated the movement – a grotesque one.

"蒙特里梭家是大族，人丁兴旺。"我答道。

"我忘了你家族的图腾了。"

"巨大的一只人脚，金色的，天蓝色的背景。这只脚把一条腾起的蟒蛇踩烂了，而蛇的牙就紧咬着脚跟。"

"那么家训呢？"

"凡伤我者，必遭惩罚。"

"妙啊！"他说。

酒精使他的眼睛闪闪发亮，帽上的铃铛又叮当地响了。喝了麦道克酒[1]，我自己的幻想更加接近现实了。我们走过一堆堆尸骨和大小酒桶混在一起堆成的一长条狭弄，来到了墓窖的最深处，我停了下来，这次竟斗胆用胳膊抓住福吐纳托的上臂。

"硝！"我说，"看，越来越多了。它们挂在拱顶上像青苔一样。咱们在河床下面啦。潮气凝成的水珠滴在尸骨上呢。快走吧，我们回去吧，否则太迟了。你这咳嗽——"

"没什么，"他说，"咱们往下走吧。但先让我再喝口麦道克酒。"

我打开一壶葛拉维酒递给他。他一口气便喝光了，眼睛里射出凶狠的光芒。他笑着把酒瓶往上一扔，用了一个我难以理解的手势。

我吃惊地看着他。他重复做了那个手势——一个荒唐的手势。

---

[1] 麦道克酒：法国波尔多所产的一种红葡萄酒。

"You do not comprehend?" he said.

"Not I," I replied.

"Then you are not of the brotherhood."

"How?"

"You are not of the masons."

"Yes, yes," I said, "yes, yes."

"You? Impossible! A mason?"

"A mason," I replied.

"A sign," he said.

"It is this," I answered, producing a trowel from beneath the folds of my *roquelaire*.

"You jest," he exclaimed, recoiling a few paces. "But let us proceed to the Amontillado."

"Be it so," I said, replacing the tool beneath the cloak, and again offering him my arm. He leaned upon it heavily. We continued our route in search of the Amontillado. We passed through a range of low arches, descended, passed on, and descending again, arrived at a deep crypt, in which the foulness of the air caused our flambeaux rather to glow than flame.

At the most remote end of the crypt there appeared another less spacious. Its walls had been lined with human remains, piled to the vault overhead, in the fashion of the great catacombs of Paris. Three sides of this interior crypt were still ornamented in this manner. From the fourth the bones had been thrown down, and lay promiscuously upon the earth, forming at

"你不能理解？"他说。

"不能。"我答。

"那你就不是同行啊。"

"怎么呢？"

"你不是泥瓦匠。"

"不，我是，"我说，"不，我是。"

"你？不可能！你是泥瓦匠？"

"我是泥瓦匠。"我答。

"暗号呢？"他说

"就是这个。"我边回答边从短披风的褶皱下拿出一把泥刀。

"你真能开玩笑呀，"他喊着说，并倒退了几步，"咱们还是向前去看看白葡萄酒吧。"

"好吧。"我说着重新把泥刀放在披风下面，又伸过胳膊给他扶着。他重重地倚靠在我的胳膊上。我们继续向前走寻找白葡萄酒。我们穿过一系列拱门然后向下走，继续穿过镶嵌在向下，终于到了一个幽深的墓穴里，这里空气浑浊，使我们手里的火把顿时不见火光，只剩下零星的火星。

墓穴的尽头，又出现了更狭窄的墓穴。四壁堆着排排尸骨，一直堆到拱顶，就和巴黎那些大墓窖一样。里面这个墓穴中的三面墙仍然以相同的方式排整。第四面墙上的尸骨都被推倒了，杂乱地堆在地上，形成一个相当大的尸骨堆。在尸骨被移开的那面墙后，我们发现里头还有一个壁凹，大约深 4 英尺，宽

one point a mound of some size. Within the wall thus exposed by the displacing of the bones, we perceived a still interior recess, in depth about four feet, in width three, in height six or seven. It seemed to have been constructed for no especial use in itself, but formed merely the interval between two of the colossal supports of the roof of the catacombs, and was backed by one of their circumscribing walls of solid granite.

It was in vain that Fortunato, uplifting his dull torch, endeavored to pry into the depths of the recess. Its termination the feeble light did not enable us to see.

"Proceed," I said; "herein is the Amontillado. As for Luchesi –"

"He is an ignoramus," interrupted my friend, as he stepped unsteadily forward, while I followed immediately at his heels. In an instant he had reached the extremity of the niche, and finding his progress arrested by the rock, stood stupidly bewildered. A moment more and I had fettered him to the granite. In its surface were two iron staples, distant from each other about two feet, horizontally. From one of these depended a short chain, from the other a padlock. Throwing the links about his waist, it was but the work of a few seconds to secure it. He was too much astounded to resist. Withdrawing the key I stepped back from the recess.

"Pass your hand," I said, "over the wall;

3 英尺，高六七英尺。看上去修建当初并没打算派上什么特别用场，不过是墓窖顶下两根大柱之间的空隙罢了，后面却靠着一堵坚硬的花岗石垣墙。

福吐纳托举起他那昏暗的火把，竭力向壁龛深处仔细察看，那简直是徒劳，火光微弱，见不到底。

"往前，"我说，"白葡萄酒就在里面呢。说到卢克雷西——"

"他不过就是个假行家。"我朋友一面摇摇晃晃地向前走，一面打断我，我紧跟着他向前走着。片刻之后，他就走到壁龛的尽头了，发现岩石挡住了路而无法前行，就站在那里一筹莫展。一会儿工夫，我已经把他锁在花岗石墙上了。在墙的表面上装着两个铁环，横向相距两英尺左右。其中一个环上挂着根短铁链，另一个有把大锁。片刻之际，我就把他拦腰拴上链子上了。他惊慌失措以致忘了反抗，我拔出钥匙，就退出了壁龛。

"伸出手去，"我说道，"摸摸

you cannot help feeling the nitre. Indeed it is *very* damp. Once more let me *implore* you to return. No? Then I must positively leave you. But I must first render you all the little attentions in my power."

"The Amontillado!" ejaculated my friend, not yet recovered from his astonishment.

"True," I replied; "the Amontillado."

As I said these words I busied myself among the pile of bones of which I have before spoken. Throwing them aside, I soon uncovered a quantity of building stone and mortar. With these materials and with the aid of my trowel, I began vigorously to wall up the entrance of the niche.

I had scarcely laid the first tier of my masonry when I discovered that the intoxication of Fortunato had in a great measure worn off. The earliest indication I had of this was a low moaning cry from the depth of the recess. It was *not* the cry of a drunken man. There was then a Long and obstinate silence. I laid the second tier, and the third, and the fourth; and then I heard the furious vibrations of the chain. The noise lasted for several minutes, during which, that I might hearken to it with the more satisfaction, I ceased my labors and sat down upon the bones. When at last the clanking subsided, I resumed the trowel, and finished without interruption the fifth,

墙吧，你肯定能摸到硝。真是太潮湿了啊。让我再次求求你我们回去吧。不回去？那我必须离开你啦。可我还先得先尽心尽力照顾你一下。"

"白葡萄酒！"我的朋友还未从震惊中恢复，不由失声喊道。

"不错，"我答道，"白葡萄酒。"

我说着便在我前文提到的尸骨堆间忙着。我把尸骨分开，不久便露出了许多砌墙用的石块和灰泥。依靠这些材料和我那把泥刀的协助，我开始猛力在壁龛入口处砌起一堵墙来。

在我第一层石块还没砌好时，就发现福吐纳托深深的醉意已经醒了。首先听到壁龛深处传来的阵阵低声吼叫。这不是醉鬼的叫声。随即一阵顽固般的沉默。我砌了第二层，再砌第三层，再砌第四层。接着就听到了拼命摇晃铁链的声音。持续了好几分钟，在这期间我索性坐在尸骨堆上停下手里的活仔细倾听，令我心怀满意。终于当啷当啷的声音停止了，我才重新拿起泥刀，不停歇地砌上第五层，第六层，第七层。这时差不多砌得齐胸高了。我又停下来，将火把举到石墙上，将一线微弱的光亮照在里头那个人影上。

the sixth, and the seventh tier. The wall was now nearly upon a level with my breast. I again paused, and holding the flambeaux over the mason-work, threw a few feeble rays upon the figure within.

A succession of loud and shrill screams, bursting suddenly from the throat of the chained form, seemed to thrust me violently back. For a brief moment I hesitated – I trembled. Unsheathing my rapier, I began to grope with it about the recess: but the thought of an instant reassured me. I placed my hand upon the solid fabric of the catacombs, and felt satisfied. I reapproached the wall. I replied to the yells of him who clamored. I re-echoed – I aided – I surpassed them in volume and in strength. I did this, and the clamorer grew still.

It was now midnight, and my task was drawing to a close. I had completed the eighth, the ninth, and the tenth tier. I had finished a portion of the last and the eleventh; there remained but a single stone to be fitted and plastered in. I struggled with its weight; I placed it partially in its destined position. But now there came from out the niche a low laugh that erected the hairs upon my head. It was succeeded by a sad voice, which I had difficulty in recognising as that of the noble Fortunato. The voice said –

"Ha! ha! ha! – he! he! – a very good

突然，从那个被锁住的人的喉咙里发出一连串响亮尖厉的叫喊，似乎要拼命吓退我。一瞬间，我犹豫了，瑟瑟发抖。我拔出长剑拿在手里向壁龛里摸索起来。转念又安下心来，我将双手放在墓窖中那坚固的建筑上，觉得十分满意。再到墙跟前，我也对那个大声嚷嚷的人哇哇乱叫。他叫一声，我应一声，叫得比他响，比他有力。我这一叫，对方的大嚷大喊就停止了。

现在已经深更半夜了，我的工作也接近了尾声。我已经完成了第八层，第九层和第十层。这最后一层，也就是第十一层，也已部分完成了，只需砌上最后一块石块，再抹上灰泥就行了。我用力托起这块沉甸甸的石块，将石块的一部分放在原定位置上。可这时壁龛里传出一阵低沉的笑声，吓得我头发都竖了起来。接着传来凄惨的声音，我费了好大力气才辨认出那是福吐纳托老爷的声音。那声音说道——

"哈！哈！哈！——嘿！嘿！

joke indeed – an excellent jest. We will have many a rich laugh about it at the palazzo – he! he! he! – over our wine – he! he! he!"

"The Amontillado!" I said.

"He! he! he! – he! he! he! – yes, the Amontillado. But is it not getting late? Will not they be awaiting us at the palazzo, the Lady Fortunato and the rest? Let us be gone."

"Yes," I said, "let us be gone."

"For the love of God, Montressor!"

"Yes," I said, "for the love of God!"

But to these words I hearkened in vain for a reply. I grew impatient. I called aloud –

"Fortunato!"

No answer. I called again –

"Fortunato!"

No answer still. I thrust a torch through the remaining aperture and let it fall within. There came forth in return only a jingling of the bells. My heart grew sick – on account of the dampness of the catacombs. I hastened to make an end of my labor. I forced the last stone into its position; I plastered it up. Against the new masonry I re-erected the old rampart of bones. For the half of a century no mortal has disturbed them. *In pace requiescat!*

——的确是个天大的笑话——绝妙的玩笑，回头我们回到了公馆，准会为此笑个痛快啦——嘿！嘿！嘿！——边喝酒边笑——嘿！嘿！嘿！"

"白葡萄酒！"我说。

"嘿！嘿！嘿！——嘻！嘻！嘻！——对，白葡萄酒。但不会有些太迟了吗？福吐纳托夫人他们不会在公馆里等着咱们吗？咱们走吧！"

"对，"我说，"咱们走吧！"

"看在老天爷的分上，走吧，蒙特里梭！"

"是呀，"我说，"看在老天爷的分上。"

但我说了这些话后却怎么都听不到一个答复。我不耐烦了，便开口喊道：

"福吐纳托！"

没有回答。我再唤一遍。

"福吐纳托！"

依旧没有答复。我将火把插进还没砌上的墙孔，扔了进去。谁知只向外传来丁零当啷的响声。由于墓窖里湿气太重，使我的心里极不舒服。我强迫自己把最后一块石头放好位置，抹上灰泥。紧靠这面新墙，我又重新堆好尸骨作防御。半世纪以来没人惊扰过亡灵。愿死者安息吧！

3. The Masque of the Red Death
三． 红死魔的假面具

THE "Red Death" had Long devastated the country. No pestilence had ever been so fatal, or so hideous. Blood was its Avatar and its seal – the redness and the horror of blood. There were sharp pains, and sudden dizziness, and then profuse bleeding at the pores, with dissolution. The scarlet stains upon the body and especially upon the face of the victim, were the pest ban which shut him out from the aid and from the sympathy of his fellow-men. And the whole seizure, progress and termination of the disease, were the incidents of half an hour.

But the Prince Prospero was happy and dauntless and sagacious. When his dominions were half depopulated, he summoned to his presence a thousand hale and light-hearted friends from among the knights and dames of his court, and with these retired to the deep seclusion of one of his castellated abbeys. This was an extensive and magnificent structure, the creation of the prince's own eccentric yet august taste. A strong and lofty wall girdled it in. This wall had gates of iron. The courtiers, having entered, brought furnaces and massy hammers and welded the bolts.

"红死病"在国内肆虐已久，像这般令人谈及色变的致命瘟疫着实是史无前例。该病的症状和表现是出血——一片片血色淋漓，令人不寒而栗。表现为浑身剧痛难忍，紧接着会突发眩晕，最终毛孔大出血而亡。一旦有人身上尤其是脸上出现猩红色的斑点，就表明他已是瘟疫上身，此时，亲朋好友都不敢近身照料。从感染到发病，直至毙命，整个过程不消半个小时。

可是普罗斯佩罗王子却兴致盎然，他自诩聪慧，无所畏惧。臣民殒死过半后，他从宫中召集千名心宽体健的骑士和妇人，随他一同隐遁到了一座深墙大院式的修道院中。这座修道院幅员广阔，气势恢弘，完全出自王子那骄奢古怪的品位。修道院周围壁墙重仞，铁门星布。这批门客踏进修道院后，便用随身携带的熔炉和大铁锤把门闩紧紧焊死。他们横下心来，破釜沉舟，就算有朝一日发狂也好，绝望也罢，也无处遁身。修道院里粮草充足，衣食无忧，瘟疫之事早已被他们抛

They resolved to leave means neither of ingress or egress to the sudden impulses of despair or of frenzy from within. The abbey was amply provisioned. With such precautions the courtiers might bid defiance to contagion. The external world could take care of itself. In the meantime it was folly to grieve, or to think. The prince had provided all the appliances of pleasure. There were buffoons, there were improvisatori, there were ballet-dancers, there were musicians, there was Beauty, there was wine. All these and security were within. Without was the "Red Death."

It was toward the close of the fifth or sixth month of his seclusion, and while the pestilence raged most furiously abroad, that the Prince Prospero entertained his thousand friends at a masked ball of the most unusual magnificence.

It was a voluptuous scene, that masquerade. But first let me tell of the rooms in which it was held. There were seven – an imperial suite. In many palaces, however, such suites form a Long and straight vista, while the folding doors slide back nearly to the walls on either hand, so that the view of the whole extent is scarcely impeded. Here the case was very different; as might have been expected from the duke's love of the *bizarre*. The apartments were so irregularly disposed that the vision embraced but little more

到了九霄云外。就由得外面乱世自生自灭，再者说，劳烦牵挂也都无济于事。王子早已把寻欢作乐之事安排妥当。戏子小丑、即兴表演、芭蕾舞者、管弦乐师、靓人尤物、美酒佳酿——世间一切在此应有尽有，而高墙之外，"红死"肆虐，生灵涂炭。

外面的瘟疫兴风作浪正当时，院内已隐遁于此五六个月的普罗斯佩罗王子却煞费心思地大开化装舞会，盛况空前，以愉悦众位宾客。

真是个穷奢极侈的舞会！且待我形容一下舞会的场地。在这套皇室套房里共有 7 个房间。一般此类套房中，只要打开折叠门，推至墙边，眼前景象即可纵深看到底，整个套房一览无余。而这儿就大有不同了，如你所料，这套房间的结构同王子的品位一样怪异。不规则的内部构造让人一眼只能望到一个地方。因为每隔二三十码就会有一个急转弯，且每个转弯处都会有新奇的事物出现。左右两面墙正中各开有一扇细长的哥特式"柳叶窗"，窗

than one at a time. There was a sharp turn at every twenty or thirty yards, and at each turn a novel effect. To the right and left, in the middle of each wall, a tall and narrow Gothic window looked out upon a closed corridor which pursued the windings of the suite. These windows were of stained glass whose color varied in accordance with the prevailing hue of the decorations of the chamber into which it opened. That at the eastern extremity was hung, for example, in blue – and vividly blue were its windows. The second chamber was purple in its ornaments and tapestries, and here the panes were purple. The third was green throughout, and so were the casements. The fourth was furnished and lighted with orange – the fifth with white – the sixth with violet. The seventh apartment was closely shrouded in black velvet tapestries that hung all over the ceiling and down the walls, falling in heavy folds upon a carpet of the same material and hue. But in this chamber only, the color of the windows failed to correspond with the decorations. The panes here were scarlet – a deep blood color. Now in no one of the seven apartments was there any lamp or candelabrum, amid the profusion of golden ornaments that lay scattered to and fro or depended from the roof. There was no light of any kind emanating from lamp or candle within the suite of chambers. But in the

外廊腰缦回，紧抱整个套房。窗上的彩绘玻璃颜色各异，与各个房间的主色调浑然一体。譬如说，最东边那间的挂饰是蓝色的，那么窗户就得是晶蓝透亮的。第二间屋子的窗格玻璃与屋内的装饰和帷幔都是紫色系的。第三个房间里外通绿，所以窗扉也是绿的。第四间的家居摆设、光线照明一色橙黄。第五间通体洁白。第六间则完全被紫罗兰色包裹。第七个房间的天花板和墙壁上严严实实地布置着黑色天鹅绒面的帷幔，一直拖到同色同质的地毯上。只有这间的窗户与众不同。它不是像屋内装饰的那种黑色，而是地地道道的猩红——血一般的颜色。然而，就在这摆设充盈、挂饰奢靡的 7 间大房中，却找不到哪怕一盏灯或一架蜡台。偌大的套房里，不见一丝灯烛之光。只是在每个窗户对面的回廊中，都摆设着笨重的香炉，里面火钵发出的火光穿过外罩的彩色玻璃，幽幽地蔓延开来。整个房间被照得色彩斑斓、光怪陆离。就在最西边那个用黑色装饰的房间里，光线透过血红色的玻璃打在漆黑的帷幔上，阴气逼人，进到屋内的人无不被映衬得狰狞恐怖，因此一直没有人胆敢踏进这间屋子。

corridors that followed the suite, there stood, opposite to each window, a heavy tripod, bearing a brazier of fire that *protected* its rays through the tinted glass and so glaringly illumined the room. And thus were produced a multitude of gaudy and fantastic appearances. But in the western or black chamber the effect of the fire-light that streamed upon the dark hangings through the blood-tinted panes, was ghastly in the extreme, and produced so wild a look upon the countenances of those who entered, that there were few of the company bold enough to set foot within its precincts at all.

It was in this apartment, also, that there stood against the western wall, a gigantic clock of ebony. Its pendulum swung to and fro with a dull, heavy, monotonous clang; and when the minute-hand made the circuit of the face, and the hour was to be stricken, there came from the brazen lungs of the clock a sound which was clear and loud and deep and exceedingly musical, but of so peculiar a note and emphasis that, at each lapse of an hour, the musicians of the orchestra were constrained to pause, momentarily, in their performance, to hearken to the sound; and thus the waltzers perforce ceased their evolutions; and there was a brief disconcert of the whole gay company; and, while the chimes of the clock yet rang, it was observed that the

就在这间屋子的西墙前，矗立着一个巨型黑檀钟表。钟摆来回摆动，发出沉闷、呆滞而又单调的声音。分针每走满一圈临近整点报时之际，黄铜钟腔里就会发出一声清澈洪亮且十分悦耳的撞击声，然而整个调子和鼓点却很不对劲，以至于乐师们每到此时都不得不暂停演奏侧耳倾听；成双成对的华尔兹舞者不得不停下舞步，兴致正酣的红男绿女们也一下子乱了阵脚；就连最放荡不羁的人也会在钟声每每响起时变得面无血色，更别说那些上了年纪的人——他们双手抚额，俨然灵魂出窍，陷入冥想。然而等到钟声消逝，万籁俱寂后，人群中就会跳出一阵轻轻的笑声，人们这才反应过来；乐师们更是面面相觑，

giddiest grew pale, and the more aged and sedate passed their hands over their brows as if in confused reverie or meditation. But when the echoes had fully ceased, a light laughter at once pervaded the assembly; the musicians looked at each other and smiled as if at their own nervousness and folly, and made whispering vows, each to the other, that the next chiming of the clock should produce in them no similar emotion; and then, after the lapse of sixty minutes, (which embrace three thousand and six hundred seconds of the Time that flies,) there came yet another chiming of the clock, and then were the same disconcert and tremulousness and meditation as before.

But, in spite of these things, it was a gay and magnificent revel. The tastes of the duke were peculiar. He had a fine eye for colors and effects. He disregarded the *decora* of mere fashion. His plans were bold and fiery, and his conceptions glowed with barbaric lustre. There are some who would have thought him mad. His followers felt that he was not. It was necessary to hear and see and touch him to be *sure* that he was not.

He had directed, in great part, the moveable embellishments of the seven chambers, upon occasion of this great fête; and it was his own guiding taste which had

忍俊不禁，似乎在为刚才自己荒诞不经的神经过敏解嘲。接着大家私下悄悄发誓，下次钟鸣，绝不重蹈覆辙。然而，60 分钟 3600 秒转瞬即逝，钟声再次响起，人群再一次陷入不安、混乱和冥想之中。

但是，尽管如此，这场欢宴还是办得盛大隆重、纸醉金迷。品位古怪的王子对色彩和效果的欣赏别具一格。那些时兴的装饰他从来都是嗤之以鼻。他的想法奔放大胆，他的构思里总是闪烁着原始而豪放的光彩。有人说他歇斯底里陷入癫狂，他的门客却不以为然。不过，人们只能亲自去听、去看、去接触才能知晓他到底有无癫狂。

举办这个盛会的 7 间屋子里大部分可移动的装饰都是王子亲自设计安排的。参加舞会的人们也都配合王子的品位，生怕打扮得不够怪

given character to the masqueraders. Be sure they were grotesque. There were much glare and glitter and piquancy and phantasm – much of what has been since seen in "Hernani." There were arabesque figures with unsuited limbs and appointments. There were delirious fancies such as the madman fashions. There were much of the beautiful, much of the wanton, much of the *bizarre*, something of the terrible, and not a little of that which might have excited disgust. To and fro in the seven chambers there stalked, in fact, a multitude of dreams. And these – the dreams – writhed in and about, taking hue from the rooms, and causing the wild music of the orchestra to seem as the echo of their steps. And, anon, there strikes the ebony clock which stands in the hall of the velvet. And then, for a moment, all is still, and all is silent save the voice of the clock. The dreams are stiff-frozen as they stand. But the echoes of the chime die away – they have endured but an instant – and a light, half-subdued laughter floats after them as they depart. And now again the music swells, and the dreams live, and writhe to and fro more merrily than ever, taking hue from the many-tinted windows through which stream the rays from the tripods. But to the chamber which lies most westwardly of the seven, there are now

异。真是太像《欧那尼》[1]里展示的场景了——光影交错、溢彩流光，让人眼花缭乱、目不暇接。人群中，有奇异的四肢和装束不伦不类的；有穿那种只有疯子才想得出来的花样的；有令人赏心悦目的；还有伤风败俗的；更有不少稀奇古怪、糟糕透顶甚至令人作呕的。其实这些游荡在 7 间屋子里的人，无异于一群梦中痴人。屋里妖艳的灯光打在身上，和着乐队那听似舞步回声的奔放乐声，他们扭腰摆臀，不能自已。不一会儿，黑屋厅中那黑檀钟表再次敲响。霎时间，万籁俱寂，鸦默雀静，唯剩钟声隆隆作响。舞池中，方才的梦境随着痴人们一同凝滞，等到个把工夫，钟声消弭，人群中又逸出一阵轻轻的笑声，追着钟声荡漾开来。紧接着，又是歌舞升平，梦魇重启，透过彩色玻璃从火炉里弥漫出的光线如烟似水，抚摸着扭腰摆臀兴致正酣的人群。但是，还是没有任何一个人敢去最西边的那间屋子。夜色渐浓，血红色的窗户泻下一片红光，衬得那张乌黑的帷幔无比阴森瘆人。再等附近那黑檀钟表一阵闷响，身在这黑屋里的人听到的钟声无不比其他房间里那些正沉醉于声色犬马的人更低沉、更有力。

---

[1] 《欧那尼》：雨果的剧本。它以反暴君为主题，表现了强烈的反封建倾向。

none of the maskers who venture; for the night is waning away; and there flows a ruddier light through the blood-colored panes; and the blackness of the sable drapery appals; and to him whose foot falls upon the sable carpet, there comes from the near clock of ebony a muffled peal more solemnly emphatic than any which reaches *their* ears who indulge in the more remote gaieties of the other apartments.

But these other apartments were densely crowded, and in them beat feverishly the heart of life. And the revel went whirlingly on, until at length there commenced the sounding of midnight upon the clock. And then the music ceased, as I have told; and the evolutions of the waltzers were quieted; and there was an uneasy cessation of all things as before. But now there were twelve strokes to be sounded by the bell of the clock; and thus it happened, perhaps, that more of thought crept, with more of time, into the meditations of the thoughtful among those who revelled. And thus, too, it happened, perhaps, that before the last echoes of the last chime had utterly sunk into silence, there were many individuals in the crowd who had found leisure to become aware of the presence of a masked figure which had arrested the attention of no single individual before. And the rumor of this new presence having spread itself whisperingly around, there arose at length

可是其他屋里已是人满为患，而且人们个个精神抖擞。舞宴正欢时，钟声又一次响起——已是午夜时分。故境重现，一时间乐停音消，舞步休滞，一切照旧戛然而止。然而，这次钟声共有 12 下，这就让欢愉之中的人们陷入了更为漫长的冥想之中。也许，正因如此，人们才有工夫在最后一下钟声消逝之前察觉到一个从未引起人们注意的蒙面人。大家交头接耳，窃窃私语，后来终于喊喊喳喳起来，脸上写满了不屑和惊奇，最终演变成不安、恐惧甚至是厌恶。

from the whole company a buzz, or murmur, expressive of disapprobation and surprise – then, finally, of terror, of horror, and of disgust.

In an assembly of phantasms such as I have painted, it may well be supposed that no ordinary appearance could have excited such sensation. In truth the masquerade license of the night was nearly unlimited; but the figure in question had out-Heroded Herod, and gone beyond the bounds of even the prince's indefinite decorum. There are chords in the hearts of the most reckless which cannot be touched without emotion. Even with the utterly lost, to whom life and death are equally jests, there are matters of which no jest can be made. The whole company, indeed, seemed now deeply to feel that in the costume and bearing of the stranger neither wit nor propriety existed. The figure was tall and gaunt, and shrouded from head to foot in the habiliments of the grave. The mask which concealed the visage was made so nearly to resemble the countenance of a stiffened corpse that the closest scrutiny must have had difficulty in detecting the cheat. And yet all this might have been endured, if not approved, by the mad revellers around. But the mummer had gone so far as to assume the type of the Red Death. His vesture was dabbled in *blood* – and his broad brow, with all the

要知道，在我所描绘的这个无奇不有的舞会上，寻常人的出现是绝对不会引起此番波动的。事实上，舞会上人们的打扮已经够放荡不羁的了，不想我们说的这个人简直就是肆无忌惮，比起古怪的王子来真是有过之而无不及。就算是那些大胆的人也未尝没有为之所动。就是那些根本无动于衷的甚至可以置生死于不顾的人，也多少有些看不过去了。可见在场的人都深觉此人压根没有头脑和教养。他又高又瘦，周身裹着寿衣一般的东西。脸上的面具和僵尸的面容相差无几，就算凑近了仔细观察也难辨真假。不过正在兴头上的人们虽说心有不快，但还是默不做声能忍则忍了。话又说回来，此人的装扮确实有些过了头——他居然扮成"红死魔"的模样。罩袍上鲜血淋漓，宽宽的额头和五官上满是骇人的猩红斑点。

features of the face, was besprinkled with the scarlet horror.

When the eyes of Prince Prospero fell upon this spectral image (which with a slow and solemn movement, as if more fully to sustain its *rôle*, stalked to and fro among the waltzers) he was seen to be convulsed, in the first moment with a strong shudder either of terror or distaste; but, in the next, his brow reddened with rage.

"Who dares" he demanded hoarsely of the courtiers who stood near him – "who dares insult us with this blasphemous mockery? Seize him and unmask him – that we may know whom we have to hang at sunrise, from the battlements!"

It was in the eastern or blue chamber in which stood the Prince Prospero as he uttered these words. They rang throughout the seven rooms loudly and clearly – for the prince was a bold and robust man, and the music had become hushed at the waving of his hand.

It was in the blue room where stood the prince, with a group of pale courtiers by his side. At first, as he spoke, there was a slight rushing movement of this group in the direction of the intruder, who at the moment was also near at hand, and now, with deliberate and stately step, made closer approach to the speaker. But from a certain nameless awe with which the mad

这个鬼怪缓慢而郑重地在跳着华尔兹的人群中穿梭，像是要把自己"红死魔"的角色扮演得更加淋漓尽致。不知普罗斯佩罗王子是被吓到了还是心生厌恶，见此情景，只见他一阵抽搐，哆哆嗦嗦。然而没一会儿他就变得怒发冲冠，前额涨红。

他扯着喉咙喝问身边的门客："大胆！这是谁胆敢如此大不敬地嘲弄我们？把他给我抓起来！扯掉他的面具！我们倒要见识一下明早要在城头绞死的家伙到底长什么样子！"

虽说王子是在东边这间蓝色的屋子里吼的这番话，但他强健有力的体格让这清晰洪亮的声音直穿 7 个房间，他大手一挥，全场音乐戛然而止。

在这间蓝色的屋子里，王子身边簇拥着一帮脸色煞白的门客。他发话时，这些人正慢慢地向近处的不速之客逼近。谁知此人竟然不慌不忙、沉着镇定地向王子这边踱了过来。大家都被这狂妄之徒吓坏了，一种莫名的恐惧让所有人都怯于伸手阻拦。就这样，他径直来到了王子面前，咫尺之遥。这下屋子里的

assumptions of the mummer had inspired the whole party, there were found none who put forth hand to seize him; so that, unimpeded, he passed within a yard of the prince's person; and, while the vast assembly, as if with one impulse, shrank from the centres of the rooms to the walls, he made his way uninterruptedly, but with the same solemn and measured step which had distinguished him from the first, through the blue chamber to the purple – through the purple to the green – through the green to the orange – through this again to the white – and even thence to the violet, ere a decided movement had been made to arrest him. It was then, however, that the Prince Prospero, maddening with rage and the shame of his own momentary cowardice, rushed hurriedly through the six chambers, while none followed him on account of a deadly terror that had seized upon all. He bore aloft a drawn dagger, and had approached, in rapid impetuosity, to within three or four feet of the retreating figure, when the latter, having attained the extremity of the velvet apartment, turned suddenly and confronted his pursuer. There was a sharp cry – and the dagger dropped gleaming upon the sable carpet, upon which, instantly afterwards, fell prostrate in death the Prince Prospero. Then, summoning the wild courage of despair, a throng of the revellers at once threw

人们纷纷从屋子中央退到墙根，他则不紧不慢继续前行，步伐还是一如既往地郑重和均匀，穿过蓝屋子来到了紫屋子，踏出紫屋子进到绿屋子，蹿出绿屋子去到橙屋子，迈出橙屋子又进到了白屋子，接着他又出现在了紫罗兰色的那一间中，王子这才赶紧下令抓住他。然而，此时王子因自己的一时怯懦恼羞成怒起来，他一口气冲到第七间房里，周围人被吓得直哆嗦，莫敢尾随。他高举一把出鞘的短剑，向那个正后退的人猛冲了过去，直到只隔三四英尺。而此时那人已退到了最后一间屋子的墙根处，只见他一个转身，正面对尾随而来的王子。只听得一声惨叫一道冷光闪过，那把短剑咣当落在乌黑的地毯上，紧接着，普罗斯佩罗王子也一个跟跄，陈尸毯上。这下，那帮酒肉之众才铆足了劲，一拥而上，冲到黑色的屋子里，只见身材高大的蒙面人纹丝不动，笔挺地站在黑檀钟表那阴森的暗影中。人们一把抓住他，不想这一使劲抓住的只是一袭寿衣和一个僵尸面具——没有肉体！人们个个目瞪口呆，不知所措。

themselves into the black apartment, and, seizing the mummer, whose tall figure stood erect and motionless within the shadow of the ebony clock, gasped in unutterable horror at finding the grave-cerements and corpse-like mask which they handled with so violent a rudeness, untenanted by any tangible form.

And now was acknowledged the presence of the Red Death. He had come like a thief in the night. And one by one dropped the revellers in the blood-bedewed halls of their revel, and died each in the despairing posture of his fall. And the life of the ebony clock went out with that of the last of the gay. And the flames of the tripods expired. And Darkness and Decay and the Red Death held illimitable dominion over all.

到此"红死魔"就真的现身了，他像夜贼一般潜入院中，原本放肆浪荡的人们一个接着一个地横尸舞池，血洒成片，脸上无不布满绝望的神态。而那黑檀时钟的生命也随着奢靡舞会的结束而走到了尽头。香炉里火光消逝，只剩下黑暗、腐朽和"红死"横行天下。

4. The Pit and the Pendulum

四. 陷坑与钟摆

Impia tortorum Longas hic turba furores

Sanguinis innocui, non satiata, aluit.

Sospite nunc patria, fracto nunc funeris antro,

Mors ubi dira fuit vita salusque patent.[1]

– Quatrain composed for the gates of a market to be erected

upon the site of the Jacobin Club House at Paris

就在这方土，贪婪暴徒舞，
仇恨绵绵长，无辜鲜血淌；
大地放光明，鬼牢被夷平，
死神猖獗处，生命花将开。

——为巴黎雅各宾俱乐部原址建造的市场大门所作的四行诗

I was sick – sick unto death with that Long agony; and when they at length unbound me, and I was permitted to sit, I felt that my senses were leaving me. The sentence – the dread sentence of death – was the last of distinct accentuation which reached my ears. After that, the sound of the inquisitorial voices seemed merged in one dreamy indeterminate hum. It conveyed to my soul the idea of *revolution* – perhaps from its association in fancy with the burr of a mill wheel. This only for a brief period; for presently I heard no more. Yet, for a while, I saw; but with how terrible an exaggeration! I saw the lips of the black-robed judges. They appeared to

长久的折磨让我痛不欲生。当他们终于给我松绑，让我坐下时，我甚至都感到自己几乎灵魂出窍。我清清楚楚地听到了最后一个声音就是判决——可怕的死刑。随后，审讯的声音仿佛化了空幻迷离的嗡鸣声。这让我不由得想起"旋转"这个词，大概是它跟水车的呼呼声有几分相像吧。这念头转瞬即逝，不久耳朵里声息全无。尽管我一时间还能看得到，但眼所能及的都夸张到可怕！我看到黑袍法官那煞白的嘴唇，比我笔下这张纸还要白，而且很薄，薄到莫名其妙，就是这样薄若纸张的嘴唇，所吐之词，字字铿锵，无可商量，对人类所受炼

---

[1] 此处为法文

me white – whiter than the sheet upon which I trace these words – and thin even to grotesqueness; thin with the intensity of their expression of firmness – of immoveable resolution – of stern contempt of human torture. I saw that the decrees of what to me was Fate, were still issuing from those lips. I saw them writhe with a deadly locution. I saw them fashion the syllables of my name; and I shuddered because no sound succeeded. I saw, too, for a few moments of delirious horror, the soft and nearly imperceptible waving of the sable draperies which enwrapped the walls of the apartment. And then my vision fell upon the seven tall candles upon the table. At first they wore the aspect of charity, and seemed white and slender angels who would save me; but then, all at once, there came a most deadly nausea over my spirit, and I felt every fibre in my frame thrill as if I had touched the wire of a galvanic battery, while the angel forms became meaningless spectres, with heads of flame, and I saw that from them there would be no help. And then there stole into my fancy, like a rich musical note, the thought of what sweet rest there must be in the grave. The thought came gently and stealthily, and it seemed Long before it attained full appreciation; but just as my spirit came at length properly to feel and entertain it, the figures of the judges

狱更是深表鄙夷。我看到自己的死刑判决正从那嘴唇的一张一翕中汩汩而出。一扭一撇间吐出那宣告我命运的字眼。又是一咧一嘟，脱口而出我的名字。我浑身战栗，因为但见唇动，却未闻声音。虽说一时惊恐失措，但我分明能看到墙围上那黑幔难以察觉的微妙波动。随后我的目光就落在桌子上的 7 支长蜡烛上。乍看去，它们周身散发着仁慈的光辉，宛若能拯救我于水火之中的圣洁天使。可是转眼间，一股极度的厌恶之情涌上心头，我感到身体里的每条纤维都颤颤巍巍，像是触碰到了通电的电池。回头看那宛似圣洁天使的蜡烛，又个个变成了头顶烈焰的妖魔鬼怪，生气全无。突然间，一个念头像一段饱满的旋律那样潜入心头——我若长眠冢下，那也定是美妙而惬意的。这个念头轻悄悄地袭来，许久我才反应过来。可待我敞开胸怀准备认真体味时，眼前的法官们却变戏法一般消失得无影无踪了。烛火彻底熄灭，高挺的蜡烛也归于乌有。周遭一片漆黑，所有的知觉都随着灵魂急速向地狱堕去。紧接着，万籁俱寂，一切仿佛都凝滞，黑暗充满了整个宇宙。

vanished, as if magically, from before me; the tall candles sank into nothingness; their flames went out utterly; the blackness of darkness supervened; all sensations appeared swallowed up in a mad rushing descent as of the soul into Hades. Then silence, and stillness, night were the universe.

I had swooned; but still will not say that all of consciousness was lost. What of it there remained I will not attempt to define, or even to describe; yet all was not lost. In the deepest slumber – no! In delirium – no! In a swoon – no! In death – no! even in the grave all is *not lost*. Else there is no immortality for man. Arousing from the most profound of slumbers, we break the gossamer web of *some* dream. Yet in a second afterward, (so frail may that web have been) we remember not that we have dreamed. In the return to life from the swoon there are two stages; first, that of the sense of mental or spiritual; secondly, that of the sense of physical, existence. It seems probable that if, upon reaching the second stage, we could recall the impressions of the first, we should find these impressions eloquent in memories of the gulf beyond. And that gulf is – what? How at least shall we distinguish its shadows from those of the tomb? But if the impressions of what I have termed the first stage, are not, at will, recalled, yet, after

我昏迷过去了，但还未意识全无。至于还剩余点什么意识，我不打算详加说明，也不愿去描述。还存有些许意识。不是深度睡眠！不是精神错乱！不是昏迷晕厥！更不是身死神灭！即便在坟墓中，也不是全无意识的。否则就没有灵魂不朽的说法了。我们从深深梦魇中苏醒，就像是扯破了这薄如蝉翼细如丝的梦。大概是因为这丝网太过柔弱，即刻间我们便忘记了曾如梦魇。从梦魇到现实要经历两个阶段：先是心理和精神的苏醒，再是肉体和存在的恢复。如果踏进第二阶段后还能对第一阶段有所印象，我们就会发现这些印象极具说服力，它可以让梦境变得生动起来。而昏迷到底是什么，怎样把昏迷和死亡稍稍区别开来？但是，如果在间隔了一段时间之后，我所描述的第一个阶段中的印象没能被轻易唤起，那正当我们惊异于它从何而来时，它会否不请自来？那些从未昏迷过的人定不会看到在火光闪耀的煤焰上隐隐约约闪现着陌生的宫殿楼阁和似

Long interval, do they not come unbidden, while we marvel whence they come? He who has never swooned, is not he who finds strange palaces and wildly familiar faces in coals that glow; is not he who beholds floating in mid-air the sad visions that the many may not view; is not he who ponders over the perfume of some novel flower – is not he whose brain grows bewildered with the meaning of some musical cadence which has never before arrested his attention.

Amid frequent and thoughtful endeavors to remember; amid earnest struggles to regather some token of the state of seeming nothingness into which my soul had lapsed, there have been moments when I have dreamed of success; there have been brief, very brief periods when I have conjured up remembrances which the lucid reason of a later epoch assures me could have had reference only to that condition of seeming unconsciousness. These shadows of memory tell, indistinctly, of tall figures that lifted and bore me in silence down – down – still down – till a hideous dizziness oppressed me at the mere idea of the interminableness of the descent. They tell also of a vague horror at my heart, on account of that heart's unnatural stillness. Then comes a sense of sudden motionlessness throughout all things; as if those who bore me (a ghastly train!) had

曾相识的狰狞面孔；定不会看到可怜的绰绰影影在半空中此起彼伏；定不会流连于异样的芬芳花香；也定不会迷失于未曾为之倾倒的音乐旋律。

我常常会深深地陷入努力的回忆之中，竭力想重新搜罗起我昏迷时那段看似空白的记忆中的些许表征，有几次时段，我自以为想起来了。有一瞬间，很短的一瞬间，我魔幻般地找回了记忆，但随后明晰的理智让我明确，那种记忆只是跟表面上的不省人事有些关联而已。这记忆的影子模模糊糊地表明，当时有一些个子高高的人把我抬起来，带着我悄无声息地向下去——向下——再向下——直到一种可怕的晕眩挤压着我，压得我只能感觉得到无休止的下沉。这记忆还表明，我的心里有一种模模糊糊的恐惧，那是因为当时我的心反常地平静。然后，感觉到一切都突然静止下来了，好像是带我下去的那队可怖的家伙在向下的过程中超过了无限的界限，累得精疲力竭，不得不暂停下来。后来，我记起了平坦和潮湿，

outrun, in their descent, the limits of the limitless, and paused from the wearisomeness of their toil. After this I call to mind flatness and dampness; and then all is madness – the madness of a memory which busies itself among forbidden things.

Very suddenly there came back to my soul motion and sound – the tumultuous motion of the heart, and, in my ears, the sound of its beating. Then a pause in which all is blank. Then again sound, and motion, and touch – a tingling sensation pervading my frame. Then the mere consciousness of existence, without thought – a condition which lasted Long. Then, very suddenly, *thought*, and shuddering terror, and earnest endeavor to comprehend my true state. Then a strong desire to lapse into insensibility. Then a rushing revival of soul and a successful effort to move. And now a full memory of the trial, of the judges, of the sable draperies, of the sentence, of the sickness, of the swoon. Then entire forgetfulness of all that followed; of all that a later day and much earnestness of endeavor have enabled me vaguely to recall.

So far, I had not opened my eyes. I felt that I lay upon my back, unbound. I reached out my hand, and it fell heavily upon something damp and hard. There I suffered it to remain for many minutes,

再后来，一切都疯了——忙着冲破禁区的记忆也疯了。

刹那间，我的灵魂又恢复了听觉和知觉——耳朵里满是心脏乱跳的咚咚声，然后戛然而止，一片空白。接着，听觉、知觉和触觉又是一片混乱——一阵刺痛爬满全身。而后就意识全无，只剩下仅存的意识告诉自己我还存在着。瞬间，意识回归，令人战栗的恐惧感再次出现，心中涌起了一种迫切想要知晓真实处境的渴望。后来，一种想要堕入无觉之境的强烈愿望也油然而生。紧接着，我的精神意识彻底恢复，四肢也可以活动了。随之而来的是，审判、法官、黑幔、判决、疾病以及昏迷——一连串漫长的记忆。之后发生的事情我都完全忘记了，直到过了许久，我绞尽脑汁才隐隐约约想了起来。

直到现在，我都紧闭双眼。我可以感觉到自己周身没有绳索的束缚，面朝天地平躺着。伸出手，我分明触碰着又湿又硬的某种东西，忍受着这种感觉，我坚持了许久，

while I strove to imagine where and what I could be. I Longed, yet dared not to employ my vision. I dreaded the first glance at objects around me. It was not that I feared to look upon things horrible, but that I grew aghast lest there should be *nothing* to see. At length, with a wild desperation at heart, I quickly unclosed my eyes. My worst thoughts, then, were confirmed. The blackness of eternal night encompassed me. I struggled for breath. The intensity of the darkness seemed to oppress and stifle me. The atmosphere was intolerably close. I still lay quietly, and made effort to exercise my reason. I brought to mind the inquisitorial proceedings, and attempted from that point to deduce my real condition. The sentence had passed; and it appeared to me that a very Long interval of time had since elapsed. Yet not for a moment did I suppose myself actually dead. Such a supposition, notwithstanding what we read in fiction, is altogether inconsistent with real existence; – but where and in what state was I? The condemned to death, I knew, perished usually at the *autos-da-fe*, and one of these had been held on the very night of the day of my trial. Had I been remanded to my dungeon, to await the next sacrifice, which would not take place for many months? This I at once saw could not be. Victims had been in immediate

同时努力猜测自己身在何处又是何许人也。我很想睁开眼睛一看究竟，却终究没有胆量。我之所以对第一眼将会看到什么这一点心存畏惧，并非因为怕看到某种骇人之物，而是怕空无一物——什么都看不到。最终，心中那极度的绝望驱使我猛地一下睁开了眼睛。果不其然，糟糕透顶。长夜漫漫，黑暗将我裹挟，我拼命地呼吸。无边的黑暗压迫着我，令我窒息。凝滞的空气令人难以忍受。我依旧静躺着，竭力调动自己的思维。脑海中浮现出审判时的场景，我试图从中推断一下端倪。宣判早已结束，可对我来说，那仿佛已过去良久。然而片刻后，我就猜想自己或许已是身死神灭。尽管我们在小说里阅尽离奇之事，但我的这一猜想还是与事实大相径庭。——那我究竟身在何处，身处何境呢？我知道，被宗教法庭处以极刑的人，通常要被捆在火刑柱上烧死。就在我受审的那个晚上，就有一人被如此处决。莫非我已被押回地牢，静候数月之后才会实施下次火刑？我立刻意识到事实并非如此。因为判决之后那些人总是会被立即处死。再者说，囚禁我的那间牢房和托莱多的其他地牢一样，有石板铺地且并非暗无天日。

demand. Moreover, my dungeon, as well as all the condemned cells at Toledo, had stone floors, and light was not altogether excluded.

A fearful idea now suddenly drove the blood in torrents upon my heart, and for a brief period, I once more relapsed into insensibility. Upon recovering, I at once started to my feet, trembling convulsively in every fibre. I thrust my arms wildly above and around me in all directions. I felt nothing; yet dreaded to move a step, lest I should be impeded by the walls of a *tomb*. Perspiration burst from every pore, and stood in cold big beads upon my forehead. The agony of suspense grew at length intolerable, and I cautiously moved forward, with my arms extended, and my eyes straining from their sockets, in the hope of catching some faint ray of light. I proceeded for many paces; but still all was blackness and vacancy. I breathed more freely. It seemed evident that mine was not, at least, the most hideous of fates.

And now, as I still continued to step cautiously onward, there came thronging upon my recollection a thousand vague rumors of the horrors of Toledo. Of the dungeons there had been strange things narrated – fables I had always deemed them – but yet strange, and too ghastly to repeat, save in a whisper. Was I left to

突然，我的脑中闪现出一个可怕的想法，致使我热血沸腾，心跳加速。一时间，我又再次知觉全无，恢复之后，从脚到头，每一根纤维都震颤不已。我伸出双臂，上下左右各个方向摸去，一无所获。但我仍是怯于挪动哪怕半步，唯恐触碰到墓室的内墙。此时，周身每一个毛孔都汗如泉涌，前额还淌着冷汗，豆大一般。而焦虑带来的难以忍受的痛苦最终还是逼迫着我谨慎地向前微微挪去。我伸开双臂，瞪大眼睛，试图捕捉到一丝微弱的光线。可继续前行时，依旧是一片黑暗一片虚无。终于，呼吸畅快了许多，我清楚地意识到命运并非那般可怕，我也并非身在墓中。

就在我一步一步小心谨慎地朝前摸索时，托莱多城[1]那些繁杂而暧昧的恐怖流言一齐涌上心头，其中不乏和地牢有关的一些怪事，虽然我一直认为那都是些无稽之谈，但不可否认它确实离奇怪异甚至骇人听闻，以至于人们只是私下耳语，不敢公开谈论。莫非我就要在这地

---

[1] 托莱多城：西班牙中部的一座城市。

perish of starvation in this subterranean world of darkness; or what fate, perhaps even more fearful, awaited me? That the result would be death, and a death of more than customary bitterness, I knew too well the character of my judges to doubt. The mode and the hour were all that occupied or distracted me.

My outstretched hands at length encountered some solid obstruction. It was a wall, seemingly of stone masonry – very smooth, slimy, and cold. I followed it up; stepping with all the careful distrust with which certain antique narratives had inspired me. This process, however, afforded me no means of ascertaining the dimensions of my dungeon; as I might make its circuit, and return to the point whence I set out, without being aware of the fact; so perfectly uniform seemed the wall. I therefore sought the knife which had been in my pocket, when led into the inquisitorial chamber; but it was gone; my clothes had been exchanged for a wrapper of coarse serge. I had thought of forcing the blade in some minute crevice of the masonry, so as to identify my point of departure. The difficulty, nevertheless, was but trivial; although, in the disorder of my fancy, it seemed at first insuperable. I tore a part of the hem from the robe and placed the fragment at full length, and at right angles to the wall. In groping my way

下的黑暗世界里活活饿死？又或者前方等待着我的是更恐怖的命运？不过反正都是难逃一死，而且会死得比别人更痛苦。我对这一点深信不疑，因为看透了那些法官的伎俩。我满脑子都在琢磨自己的死法和死期，它们让我心烦意乱。

我伸出的手指终于碰到了某个坚固的障碍物。是一堵墙，像是石砌而成——光滑，黏稠，冰冷。我扶着墙继续前行，想到某些古老寓言中的启示，我每一步都迈得谨慎警觉。可这样一来，我就无法探知这地牢究竟深宽几许，因为自己很可能在兜圈子，且全然不知地绕回原点。这堵墙好像到处都长得一模一样，于是我开始寻找那把受审时放在口袋里的小刀，结果没有找到。我此时已被换上了粗布长袍。我本想把小刀插进石壁的某条隙缝，以便确定我出发的地方。尽管在头脑错乱的状态下，这些麻烦似乎无法解决，但事实上那也不过是小事一桩。我从袍子的边缘扯下一段布，把它平铺在地上，与墙面呈直角。这样，我在地牢里摸索前行时，一旦绕回原点，我就会踩到这块布。事实证明，我低估了地牢的尺寸，也低估了自己的虚弱。地面又湿又滑，我脚步蹒跚向前走去，没一会儿就一个跟跄摔倒在地。筋疲力尽的我，索性就地而卧，不愿动弹。

around the prison, I could not fail to encounter this rag upon completing the circuit. So, at least I thought: but I had not counted upon the extent of the dungeon, or upon my own weakness. The ground was moist and slippery. I staggered onward for some time, when I stumbled and fell. My excessive fatigue induced me to remain prostrate; and sleep soon overtook me as I lay.

Upon awaking, and stretching forth an arm, I found beside me a loaf and a pitcher with water. I was too much exhausted to reflect upon this circumstance, but ate and drank with avidity. Shortly afterward, I resumed my tour around the prison, and with much toil came at last upon the fragment of the serge. Up to the period when I fell I had counted fifty-two paces, and upon resuming my walk, I had counted forty-eight more; – when I arrived at the rag. There were in all, then, a hundred paces; and, admitting two paces to the yard, I presumed the dungeon to be fifty yards in circuit. I had met, however, with many angles in the wall, and thus I could form no guess at the shape of the vault; for vault I could not help supposing it to be.

I had little object – certainly no hope— in these researches; but a vague curiosity prompted me to continue them. Quitting the wall, I resolved to cross the area of the enclosure. At first I proceeded with

很快，睡意潮水般涌来。

醒来后，我向前探出一只手臂，在身边摸到了一大块面包和一罐水。我已饥肠辘辘，筋疲力尽，于是不假思索就狼吞虎咽起来。不久，我又开始了我的地牢之行。一番挣扎后，我走到了放布条的地方。摔倒之前我已经数了 52 步，爬起来后，又走了 48 步才到布条那里。这样算来，我走了共 100 步，算两步为一码，我测算绕地牢一周为 50 码。然而，由于在前行途中，我碰到了许多拐角，所以没办法想象这个地窖究竟身形几何。我忍不住猜想着这就是个地窖。

我这样做其实是漫无目的的，而且也不奢望任何转机，不过是被一种模糊的好奇心所驱使。我决定不再顺墙摸路，而从地牢中央横穿过去。起初，我一步一步都高度谨

extreme caution, for the floor, although seemingly of solid material, was treacherous with slime. At length, however, I took courage, and did not hesitate to step firmly; endeavoring to cross in as direct a line as possible. I had advanced some ten or twelve paces in this manner, when the remnant of the torn hem of my robe became entangled between my legs. I stepped on it, and fell violently on my face.

In the confusion attending my fall, I did not immediately apprehend a somewhat startling circumstance, which yet, in a few seconds afterward, and while I still lay prostrate, arrested my attention. It was this – my chin rested upon the floor of the prison, but my lips and the upper portion of my head, although seemingly at a less elevation than the chin, touched nothing. At the same time my forehead seemed bathed in a clammy vapor, and the peculiar smell of decayed fungus arose to my nostrils. I put forward my arm, and shuddered to find that I had fallen at the very brink of a circular pit, whose extent, of course, I had no means of ascertaining at the moment. Groping about the masonry just below the margin, I succeeded in dislodging a small fragment, and let it fall into the abyss. For many seconds I hearkened to its reverberations as it dashed against the sides of the chasm in its descent; at length there was a sullen plunge

慎，因为尽管地板摸上去很坚固，但却是烂泥铺面，溜滑无比。后来，我终于鼓起勇气，不再迟疑，坚定地向前迈去，尽量试图直穿而过。不想之前撕扯袍子留下的边布在腿间缠得难舍难分，就这样走了大概十一二步，不想一脚踩到了布上，迎面狠摔到了地上。

这个跟头把我摔得天旋地转，以至于没能马上认识到周遭是怎样一个让人吃惊的境况，我就那样俯卧在地上，过了几秒钟才反应过来。情况是这样的：我的下巴紧贴地牢的地板，嘴唇和头部的上半部分虽然看上去高于下巴，但却是悬空的。同时前额像是浸溺在湿冷的雾霭中，一股股霉菌的异味直蹿鼻孔。我伸出胳膊，不由一颤，发现自己倒在一个圆坑的边缘，摇摇欲坠，至于坑有多大，当时我也无从知晓。我在靠近坑沿的坑壁上一阵摸索，抠下了一小块石块。片刻，我听到了它在下落过程中撞击坑壁的声音，之后是一声入水的沉闷而大声的回响。与此同时，头顶传来了像是急速开门关门的声音，相伴而来的是一丝微弱的光线刺破黑暗，接着又瞬间归于无形。

into water, succeeded by loud echoes. At the same moment there came a sound resembling the quick opening, and as rapid closing of a door overhead, while a faint gleam of light flashed suddenly through the gloom, and as suddenly faded away.

I saw clearly the doom which had been prepared for me, and congratulated myself upon the timely accident by which I had escaped. Another step before my fall, and the world had seen me no more. And the death just avoided, was of that very character which I had regarded as fabulous and frivolous in the tales respecting the Inquisition. To the victims of its tyranny, there was the choice of death with its direst physical agonies, or death with its most hideous moral horrors. I had been reserved for the latter. By Long suffering my nerves had been unstrung, until I trembled at the sound of my own voice, and had become in every respect a fitting subject for the species of torture which awaited me.

Shaking in every limb, I groped my way back to the wall; resolving there to perish rather than risk the terrors of the wells, of which my imagination now pictured many in various positions about the dungeon. In other conditions of mind I might have had courage to end my misery at once by a plunge into one of these abysses; but now I was the veriest of cowards. Neither could I forget what I had

他们为我安排好的死法已昭然若揭。我为自己刚才的一摔而庆幸不已。试想，如果摔倒前再多走一步，我早已一命呜呼了。我逃过的这劫死法和传闻中那荒诞不经的宗教法庭死刑处置方式如出一辙。宗教法庭的暴虐下，有两种死法：一是极为可怕的肉体折磨，一是极为骇人的精神恐怖。他们为我安排的是第二种死法。百般折磨后，我已是极度的神经衰弱，以至于都可以听到自己的声音在颤颤巍巍。无论从哪个意义上讲，等待我的都将是最惨无人道的迫害。

我四肢颤抖，摸黑回到墙边，决心宁可在这个我已有大致了解的地牢里坐以待毙也不再以身犯险落得死无全尸。或许换个境况，我会鼓足勇气纵身一跃，结束这炼狱般的折磨，然而现在的我是个十足的懦夫。脑海里一直抹不去以前读到的有关陷坑的描述，它们最可怕的地方在于，不会让你轻易地一死了之。

read of these pits – that the *sudden* extinction of life formed no part of their most horrible plan.

Agitation of spirit kept me awake for many Long hours; but at length I again slumbered. Upon arousing, I found by my side, as before, a loaf and a pitcher of water. A burning thirst consumed me, and I emptied the vessel at a draught. It must have been drugged; for scarcely had I drunk, before I became irresistibly drowsy. A deep sleep fell upon me – a sleep like that of death. How Long it lasted of course, I know not; but when, once again, I unclosed my eyes, the objects around me were visible. By a wild sulphurous lustre, the origin of which I could not at first determine, I was enabled to see the extent and aspect of the prison.

In its size I had been greatly mistaken. The whole circuit of its walls did not exceed twenty-five yards. For some minutes this fact occasioned me a world of vain trouble; vain indeed! for what could be of less importance, under the terrible circumstances which environed me, then the mere dimensions of my dungeon? But my soul took a wild interest in trifles, and I busied myself in endeavors to account for the error I had committed in my measurement. The truth at length flashed upon me. In my first attempt at exploration I had counted fifty-two paces, up to the

烦乱的心绪让我久不能寐，不知过了多久才昏死过去。醒来后，我再次发现身边放着一块面包和一罐水。我正渴得唇焦舌燥呢，一口气喝光了罐子里的水。这水一定被下了药，因为我从来没喝醉过，而喝完这水我已撑持不住，昏昏欲睡。我死一般地沉沉睡去。不知过了多久，再睁开眼睛时，竟又看得到身边的物体了。借着一缕一时说不出从何而来的昏黄亮光，我终于看清了牢房的大小和形状。

我才知道自己一直没有搞清楚的这个牢房的规模。它的围墙周长不超过25码。原来一直以来我都在白费心机，真是踏破铁鞋啊！因为身处这样可怕的境地，还有什么比这地牢的大小更无关紧要的呢？可即便是此等细枝末节，我还是不肯罢休，并开始着手研究之前丈量时出错的缘由。终于我恍然大悟。刚开始测量时，在摔倒之前我已经数到了第52步，而当时，那个位置离布条也不过一两步之遥，几近绕地牢一整个周长了！随后我就睡着了。醒来后一定是又原路返了回去，这

period when I fell; I must then have been within a pace or two of the fragment of serge; in fact, I had nearly performed the circuit of the vault. I then slept, and upon awaking, I must have returned upon my steps – thus supposing the circuit nearly double what it actually was. My confusion of mind prevented me from observing that I began my tour with the wall to the left, and ended it with the wall to the right.

I had been deceived, too, in respect to the shape of the enclosure. In feeling my way I had found many angles, and thus deduced an idea of great irregularity; so potent is the effect of total darkness upon one arousing from lethargy or sleep! The angles were simply those of a few slight depressions, or niches, at odd intervals. The general shape of the prison was square. What I had taken for masonry seemed now to be iron, or some other metal, in huge plates, whose sutures or joints occasioned the depression. The entire surface of this metallic enclosure was rudely daubed in all the hideous and repulsive devices to which the charnel superstition of the monks has given rise. The figures of fiends in aspects of menace, with skeleton forms, and other more really fearful images, overspread and disfigured the walls. I observed that the outlines of these monstrosities were sufficiently distinct, but that the colors seemed faded

样一来就等于是走了两个周长。当时我思绪混乱，以至于没有意识到出发时墙在左手边，走到布条那里墙却在右手边了。

我对地牢的形状也估算错了。刚才摸索前行的途中，我在墙上摸到了许多拐角，由此判定地牢内部构造是不规则的。可见，完全的黑暗对一个刚从昏迷或沉睡中苏醒过来的人的影响是多么巨大！所谓拐角，不过是分布在墙上间隔不一的轻微凹痕。地牢大致是正方形。墙壁也并非我之前所想的那样用石板筑成，看上去倒像是用铁或其他某种金属焊接而成，接缝处，恰好形成凹陷。这个金属地牢的墙壁上，满是肆意涂抹的源于宗教迷信的阴森图画，可怕且令人厌恶。面目狰狞的骷髅魔鬼影影绰绰，与其余那些更恐怖骇人的图画连成一片，满满当当，把整堵墙搞得面目全非。我注意到那些魑魅魍魉图画的轮廓还清晰可见，只是颜色消退变得模糊不清，可能是潮湿的空气所致。我注意到了脚下石板铺就的地板。开裂的地板中央，我一眼就看到了那个我侥幸逃脱的圆形陷坑。不过，

and blurred, as if from the effects of a damp atmosphere. I now noticed the floor, too, which was of stone. In the centre yawned the circular pit from whose jaws I had escaped; but it was the only one in the dungeon.

All this I saw indistinctly and by much effort: for my personal condition had been greatly changed during slumber. I now lay upon my back, and at full length, on a species of low framework of wood. To this I was securely bound by a Long strap resembling a surcingle. It passed in many convolutions about my limbs and body, leaving at liberty only my head, and my left arm to such extent that I could, by dint of much exertion, supply myself with food from an earthen dish which lay by my side on the floor. I saw, to my horror, that the pitcher had been removed. I say to my horror; for I was consumed with intolerable thirst. This thirst it appeared to be the design of my persecutors to stimulate: for the food in the dish was meat pungently seasoned.

Looking upward, I surveyed the ceiling of my prison. It was some thirty or forty feet overhead, and constructed much as the side walls. In one of its panels a very singular figure riveted my whole attention. It was the painted figure of Time as he is commonly represented, save that, in lieu of a scythe, he held what, at a casual glance, I

整个地牢里，陷坑也仅此一个。

我看到的这一切都并非特别清晰，并且看起来非常吃力，原因在于我的身体状况在昏睡时发生了很大的变化。我现在是面朝天，伸直身体平躺在一个很矮的木架上，周身被腰带一般的皮索牢牢捆着。我的四肢和整个身体被捆绑数圈，只剩下头部还能自由转动，努力伸出左手能勉强够到身边地板上那陶盘里的食物。让我惊恐不已的是，水罐子不见了。之所以说惊恐，是因为我已渴得死去活来了。很明显，这是那些想要加害于我的人存心所为，因为陶盘里的肉已被严重变味以致刺鼻。

我抬头仔细观察这地牢的天花板。有三四十英尺高，构造与四周墙壁几乎相同。其中一块嵌板上的一幅奇异画像吸引了我的注意。那是一幅彩绘时间老人的画像，表现手法并无什么特别。不同之处在于，他手里握的不是一把镰刀。这钟表的几处外形让我忍不住多看了几

supposed to be the pictured image of a huge pendulum such as we see on antique clocks. There was something, however, in the appearance of this machine which caused me to regard it more attentively. While I gazed directly upward at it (for its position was immediately over my own) I fancied that I saw it in motion. In an instant afterward the fancy was confirmed. Its sweep was brief, and of course slow. I watched it for some minutes, somewhat in fear, but more in wonder. Wearied at length with observing its dull movement, I turned my eyes upon the other objects in the cell.

A slight noise attracted my notice, and, looking to the floor, I saw several enormous rats traversing it. They had issued from the well, which lay just within view to my right. Even then, while I gazed, they came up in troops, hurriedly, with ravenous eyes, allured by the scent of the meat. From this it required much effort and attention to scare them away.

It might have been half an hour, perhaps even an hour, (for I could take but imperfect note of time) before I again cast my eyes upward. What I then saw confounded and amazed me. The sweep of the pendulum had increased in extent by nearly a yard. As a natural consequence, its velocity was also much greater. But what mainly disturbed me was the idea that had perceptibly descended. I now observed –

眼。就在我径直仰望它时（它的位置就在我的正上方），想不到它居然在动。马上，这个想法得以证实。它的摆动幅度不大，当然也就很慢。我盯着它看了会儿，虽有几分害怕，但更多的是惊奇。直到厌烦了看它那单调的来回摆动，我才将目光转向这屋子里的其他物体。

一阵轻声的骚动引起了我的注意。我朝地板看去，发现一些体形硕大的老鼠正在地板上穿行。它们从我视线可及的右边那个陷坑里鱼贯而出。它们被肉的香味所诱引，瞪着满是贪婪的眼睛，行色匆匆，即便我盯着看，它们也依然成群结队而行。我费了九牛二虎之力才把它们吓跑。

大约过了半个小时，抑或一个小时（虽说我还有时间概念，但已不那么清楚），我再次向上看去。这一看让我惊奇不已，困惑不堪。钟摆摆动的幅度已增大了近乎一码。它的速率自然也随之变大。最让我惊慌失措的是，很明显，那钟摆在下降。我内心的恐惧已不用多说，因为现在我看到那钟摆的下端是闪着冷光的长约一英尺的月牙形钢

with what horror it is needless to say – that its nether extremity was formed of a crescent of glittering steel, about a foot in length from horn to horn; the horns upward, and the under edge evidently as keen as that of a razor. Like a razor also, it seemed massy and heavy, tapering from the edge into a solid and broad structure above. It was appended to a weighty rod of brass, and the whole *hissed* as it swung through the air.

I could no Longer doubt the doom prepared for me by monkish ingenuity in torture. My cognizance of the pit had become known to the inquisitorial agents – *the pit* whose horrors had been destined for so bold a recusant as myself – *the pit*, typical of hell, and regarded by rumor as the Ultima Thule of all their punishments. The plunge into this pit I had avoided by the merest of accidents, I knew that surprise, or entrapment into torment, formed an important portion of all the grotesquerie of these dungeon deaths. Having failed to fall, it was no part of the demon plan to hurl me into the abyss; and thus (there being no alternative) a different and a milder destruction awaited me. Milder! I half smiled in my agony as I thought of such application of such a term.

What boots it to tell of the Long, Long hours of horror more than mortal, during which I counted the rushing vibrations of

刀。钢刀两端高高翘起，我清楚地看到下方的刀刃如剃刀一般锋利。整个钟摆也形同剃刀，看上去巨大而厚重，由上到下渐变得坚实而宽阔。它附悬在一个笨重的铜棒下，在空中来回摇摆，嘶嘶作响。

我再也没有理由置疑那些善于严刑折磨的僧人们处心积虑为我安排好的生命末日。宗教法庭的那伙人已得知我发现了陷坑。这恐怖的陷坑，正是为我这样不屈于国教淫威的人而设的。它是名副其实的地狱，是传闻中宗教法庭诸多惩罚中的一种极致。我因那偶然一摔而侥幸逃脱的陷坑正是这地牢中千奇百怪死法中的一种：乘人不备，诱其深入，百般折磨。由于我没有跌进陷坑，使得那个想要把我丢进深渊的邪恶计划落了空。然而，我的死期已定，别无他选，所以前方等候我的是另外一种更为温和的死法。更为温和！我竟然用这样一个字眼，想到这里，我忍着疼痛，不由得笑了起来。

我默数着钢刀急速摆动的次数，忍受着漫长的比死亡更可怕的恐惧。说这个又有什么意思！钟摆

the steel! Inch by inch – line by line – with a descent only appreciable at intervals that seemed ages – down and still down it came! Days passed – it might have been that many days passed – ere it swept so closely over me as to fan me with its acrid breath. The odor of the sharp steel forced itself into my nostrils. I prayed – I wearied heaven with my prayer for its more speedy descent. I grew frantically mad, and struggled to force myself upward against the sweep of the fearful scimitar. And then I fell suddenly calm, and lay smiling at the glittering death, as a child at some rare bauble.

There was another interval of utter insensibility; it was brief; for, upon again lapsing into life there had been no perceptible descent in the pendulum. But it might have been Long; for I knew there were demons who took note of my swoon, and who could have arrested the vibration at pleasure. Upon my recovery, too, I felt very – oh, inexpressibly sick and weak, as if through Long inanition. Even amid the agonies of that period, the human nature craved food. With painful effort I outstretched my left arm as far as my bonds permitted, and took possession of the small remnant which had been spared me by the rats. As I put a portion of it within my lips, there rushed to my mind a half formed thought of joy – of hope. Yet

一寸一寸、一分一分地下降，每隔度秒如年的一个片刻才能感觉到它的下降，它不停地下降，再下降。几天过去了——也可能已过了好多天，钟摆就在我头顶不高处来回盘旋，生发出阴毒的微风不停地拨撩着我，那锐利的刀刃的臭味直往我的鼻孔里蹿。我祈祷着，祈求上苍让它降得快一些。我变得癫狂不安，并开始挣扎着凑向那摇摆不定的弯刀。随后我一下子冷静了下来，平躺在地板上，笑望着那闪着寒光的凶器，就像一个孩子盯着某个稀罕的玩具那般。

我又陷入了彻底的昏迷状态，不过时间很短，因为等我恢复知觉后，并没有感觉到钟摆有明显的下降。但是，或许时间很长，因为我知道那些魔鬼一看到我昏迷，可以随时让钟摆停止摆动。这次醒来，我又感到了难以言说的恶心和虚弱，貌似是长久的饥肠辘辘所致。即便当时处于极端痛苦之中，人类求生的本能还是让我对食物有着迫切的渴求。我苦苦挣扎着伸出左手，伸到了皮绳所能容忍的极限，拿到了那块老鼠吃剩的一丁点肉。就在我刚塞进嘴里一小块肉时，脑中一下子闪现了一个半成形的想法，这想法令人喜悦，充满希望。但就算有希望，那又与我何干呢？我说了，那只是个半成品。人们总有各种各

what business had I with hope? It was, as I say, a half formed thought – man has many such which are never completed. I felt that it was of joy – of hope; but felt also that it had perished in its formation. In vain I struggled to perfect – to regain it. Long suffering had nearly annihilated all my ordinary powers of mind. I was an imbecile – an idiot.

The vibration of the pendulum was at right angles to my length. I saw that the crescent was designed to cross the region of the heart. It would fray the serge of my robe – it would return and repeat its operations – again – and again. Notwithstanding terrifically wide sweep (some thirty feet or more) and the its hissing vigor of its descent, sufficient to sunder these very walls of iron, still the fraying of my robe would be all that, for several minutes, it would accomplish. And at this thought I paused. I dared not go farther than this reflection. I dwelt upon it with a pertinacity of attention – as if, in so dwelling, I could arrest here the descent of the steel. I forced myself to ponder upon the sound of the crescent as it should pass across the garment – upon the peculiar thrilling sensation which the friction of cloth produces on the nerves. I pondered upon all this frivolity until my teeth were on edge.

Down – steadily down it crept. I took a

样最终不得实现的想法。我觉得那个念头令人喜悦，充满希望，但同时我也意识到，它还未能成形就已归于虚无。我拼命想要再捉住它，把它完全展示出来，但最终都是徒劳。长久的虐待折磨几乎让我正常的思维能力消耗殆尽。我成了一个痴呆，一个傻子。

钟摆的摆动方向刚好跟我平躺的身体呈直角。我看到那新月式的钢刀被设计成要划过我心脏的位置。它将磨蹭着我那袍子的边缘，摇来摆去，一遍一遍，一下一下。尽管钟摆的巨大摆幅足有 30 英尺或更大；尽管它在下降过程中发出生猛有力的嘶嘶声；尽管这种力道足以劈开这里所有的铁墙；但若要划破我的袍子还是要多费些工夫。想到这儿，我停住了，不敢再深思下去。思绪执拗于此，不肯放开，似乎如此一来，我就能使钢刀停止降落。我强迫自己仔细想象那刀刃摩擦袍子的声音，想象那样的摩擦声对神经造成的异样的惊悚效果。我沉思于这样的细枝末节，直至牙齿开始打战。

下降——钟摆不紧不慢地下降

frenzied pleasure in contrasting its downward with its lateral velocity. To the right – to the left – far and wide – with the shriek of a damned spirit; to my heart with the stealthy pace of the tiger! I alternately laughed and howled as the one or the other idea grew predominant.

Down – certainly, relentlessly down! It vibrated within three inches of my bosom! I struggled violently, furiously, to free my left arm. This was free only from the elbow to the hand. I could reach the latter, from the platter beside me, to my mouth, with great effort, but no farther. Could I have broken the fastenings above the elbow, I would have seized and attempted to arrest the pendulum. I might as well have attempted to arrest an avalanche!

Down – still unceasingly – still inevitably down! I gasped and struggled at each vibration. I shrunk convulsively at its every sweep. My eyes followed its outward or upward whirls with the eagerness of the most unmeaning despair; they closed themselves spasmodically at the descent, although death would have been a relief, oh! how unspeakable! Still I quivered in every nerve to think how slight a sinking of the machinery would precipitate that keen, glistening axe upon my bosom. It was hope that prompted the nerve to quiver – the frame to shrink. It was *hope* – the hope that triumphs on the rack – that whispers to the

着。我心中默数着它下降和摆动的速率，不由得生发出一阵狂乱的快感。向右——向左——肆意地大幅摆动——伴随着遭受诅咒的灵魂的哀号，如老虎一般，迈着鬼鬼祟祟的步伐，直逼我的心脏而来。我的头脑被一个接着一个的想法所控制，以致时而狂笑，时而号哭。

下降——钟摆冷酷无情地下降！它就在离我的胸口上方不足 3 英寸的地方摆动。我拼命地猛烈挣扎着，试图挣脱左臂。但只有肘部以下部位可以活动。虽然十分费劲，但我可以用左手够到身边的盘子，再伸进嘴巴，再远的地方就够不到了。如果我可以挣断捆在肘部以上的皮绳子，就可以抓住钟摆，让它停止摇摆。说不定我还可以阻止一场雪崩的发生呢！

下降——钟摆不住地下降着——以不可阻挡之势下降！它每摆一次，我都会气喘吁吁，费力挣扎；它每摇一下，我都会痉挛蜷缩。伴着那索然无味的绝望中的一丝渴望，我的目光随着钟摆向外向上地摆。但当它向下摆过来时，我的眼睛又忍不住颤抖着闭上。尽管死亡是一种解脱，天哪，这种解脱又是何其痛苦！想到那钟摆再下降一点，胸膛就会被闪着寒光的锐利刀刃所切，我浑身每一根神经都颤抖不已。也正是那一丝希望让神经颤抖，身体痉挛。希望——这征服苦痛折磨的

death-condemned even in the dungeons of the Inquisition.

I saw that some ten or twelve vibrations would bring the steel in actual contact with my robe, and with this observation there suddenly came over my spirit all the keen, collected calmness of despair. For the first time during many hours – or perhaps days – I *thought*. It now occurred to me that the bandage, or surcingle, which enveloped me, was *unique*. I was tied by no separate cord. The first stroke of the razorlike crescent athwart any portion of the band, would so detach it that it might be unwound from my person by means of my left hand. But how fearful, in that case, the proximity of the steel! The result of the slightest struggle how deadly! Was it likely, moreover, that the minions of the torturer had not foreseen and provided for this possibility! Was it probable that the bandage crossed my bosom in the track of the pendulum? Dreading to find my faint, and, as it seemed, in last hope frustrated, I so far elevated my head as to obtain a distinct view of my breast. The surcingle enveloped my limbs and body close in all directions – *save in the path of the destroying crescent*.

Scarcely had I dropped my head back into its original position, when there flashed upon my mind what I cannot better describe than as the unformed half of that

希望，即使是在宗教法庭这暗无天日的地牢里，也不忘对死刑犯喃喃耳语，稍加关照。

我看到，再有10到12下，钟摆就要碰到我的袍子了。意识到这一点，我忽地从绝望中恢复过来，变得敏锐且镇定起来。多少小时以来——或许是多少天以来——我第一次开始动脑思考了。我想到，捆绑我的皮绳子，或者说腰带，是完整的一根。身上并没有别的绳索。不论这剃刀般锐利的弯刀划到哪里，皮绳都会迎刃而断。如此一来，我用左手就可以把身上缠绕的皮索解开。但那种情况太恐怖了，因为刀刃就在咫尺，紧挨着身体，一丁点的挣扎都可能是致命的。再说了，那些施暴者的走狗们怎么可能想不到我会有此一招而不加以防范呢？！还有，钟摆摆动的轨迹是否恰好经过绑在我胸口的绳索？我生怕这摇摇欲坠且貌似仅剩的希望之火归于灰烬，于是努力地抬起头，希望能清楚地看到胸口部位是什么情况，我看到自己的四肢和躯干都被皮绳五花大绑——除了那致命的弯刀即将划到的地方。

我还没来得及把头部归位，突然灵机一动，脑中闪过一个想法。我只能说，这正是之前提到的那个半成品想法的后半部分。就是那个

idea of deliverance to which I have previously alluded, and of which a moiety only floated indeterminately through my brain when I raised food to my burning lips. The whole thought was now present – feeble, scarcely sane, scarcely definite, – but still entire. I proceeded at once, with the nervous energy of despair, to attempt its execution.

For many hours the immediate vicinity of the low framework upon which I lay, had been literally swarming with rats. They were wild, bold, ravenous; their red eyes glaring upon me as if they waited but for motionlessness on my part to make me their prey. "To what food," I thought, "have they been accustomed in the well?"

They had devoured, in spite of all my efforts to prevent them, all but a small remnant of the contents of the dish. I had fallen into an habitual see-saw, or wave of the hand about the platter: and, at length, the unconscious uniformity of the movement deprived it of effect. In their voracity the vermin frequently fastened their sharp fangs in my fingers. With the particles of the oily and spicy viand which now remained, I thoroughly rubbed the bandage wherever I could reach it; then, raising my hand from the floor, I lay breathlessly still.

At first the ravenous animals were startled and terrified at the change – at the

在我正把食物送到灼痛的嘴边时飘忽而过的半个想法。现在，它完整呈现了，尽管摇摇欲坠，不甚理智，不够明确，但却完完整整。凭着那股柳暗花明的精神劲，我立刻行动起来。

几个钟头里，紧邻我躺着的这个低矮的木架，成群的老鼠窸窸窣窣，野蛮、大胆且贪得无厌、冒着红光的眼睛直勾勾地盯着我，像是在等我身死神灭之后好一拥而上瓜分我的肉体。"它们在这陷坑里一般都吃些什么？"我暗暗思考。

尽管我拼命驱逐，它们到底还是把盘子里的肉吃得仅省一点碎屑。我的手已经习惯性地在盘子周围来回挥舞，没多久，这种无意识的单调动作就无济于事了。这群贪婪毒物的利齿时不时会咬到我的手指。我拼尽全力把盘子里所剩无几的碎肉全部抹到了左手可及的皮绳上。然后，收回左手，屏住呼吸，纹丝不动地躺着。

在我的动作停止之后，起初这些贪婪的老鼠被我的这一举动吓到

cessation of movement. They shrank alarmedly back; many sought the well. But this was only for a moment. I had not counted in vain upon their voracity. Observing that I remained without motion, one or two of the boldest leaped upon the frame-work, and smelt at the surcingle. This seemed the signal for a general rush. Forth from the well they hurried in fresh troops. They clung to the wood – they overran it, and leaped in hundreds upon my person. The measured movement of the pendulum disturbed them not at all. Avoiding its strokes they busied themselves with the anointed bandage. They pressed – they swarmed upon me in ever accumulating heaps. They writhed upon my throat; their cold lips sought my own; I was half stifled by their thronging pressure; disgust, for which the world has no name, swelled my bosom, and chilled, with a heavy clamminess, my heart. Yet one minute, and I felt that the struggle would be over. Plainly I perceived the loosening of the bandage. I knew that in more than one place it must be already severed. With a more than human resolution I lay *still*.

Nor had I erred in my calculations – nor had I endured in vain. I at length felt that I was *free*. The surcingle hung in ribands from my body. But the stroke of the pendulum already pressed upon my bosom.

了以致惊恐万分。它们慌忙地后退，有的甚至退回了陷坑里。但这样的现象只持续了一会儿。我没有白白抬举它们的贪婪。看到我依然纹丝不动，有一两只胆子最大的老鼠跳上了木架，对着绳索一阵乱嗅。这算是个全体行动。一下子，从陷坑里冒出了成群结队的老鼠，它们争先恐后，爬上并淹没了木架，几百只几百只地跳上了我的身体。而钟摆那富于韵律的摆动声也丝毫没有影响它们的兴致。它们满满当当地压在我的脖子上。在我的喉咙处蠕动翻滚，冰冷的嘴巴在我嘴唇上嗅来嗅去。我差点被它们蜂拥而至的压力压得窒息。一种莫可名状的恶心从胸口油然而生，又黏又冰，使得我的心脏不由得直打寒战。不过片刻之后，我意识到，挣扎即将结束。我明显察觉到了皮绳开始松动。我知道，老鼠咬断了不止一处。凭着非人的意志力，我继续纹丝不动地平躺着。

我没估算错——也没有白白受苦。我终于感受到了自由。皮绳断了，一截一截地挂在我身上，但同时钟摆的利刃也逼到了胸膛。它已经划破了长袍的斜纹哔叽布，刺穿

It had divided the serge of the robe. It had cut through the linen beneath. Twice again it swung, and a sharp sense of pain shot through every nerve. But the moment of escape had arrived. At a wave of my hand my deliverers hurried tumultuously away. With a steady movement – cautious, sideLong, shrinking, and slow – I slid from the embrace of the bandage and beyond the reach of the scimitar. For the moment, at least, I *was free.*

Free! – and in the grasp of the Inquisition! I had scarcely stepped from my wooden bed of horror upon the stone floor of the prison, when the motion of the hellish machine ceased and I beheld it drawn up, by some invisible force, through the ceiling. This was a lesson which I took desperately to heart. My every motion was undoubtedly watched. Free! – I had but escaped death in one form of agony, to be delivered unto worse than death in some other. With that thought I rolled my eyes nervously around on the barriers of iron that hemmed me in. Something unusual – some change which, at first, I could not appreciate distinctly – it was obvious, had taken place in the apartment. For many minutes of a dreamy and trembling abstraction, I busied myself in vain, unconnected conjecture. During this period, I became aware, for the first time, of the origin of the sulphurous light which

了里面的亚麻布衣衫。又是两个来回摆动，随之而来的是刺穿每根神经的锐痛。不过同时，也到了脱身的时候。我一挥手，那些刚刚拯救了我的老鼠慌忙四散而逃。我小心谨慎地横向一缩一退，稳稳地完成了全部动作，成功地滑出了皮绳的束缚，逃离了弯刀的利刃。至少现在，我自由了。

自由！可我仍未逃出宗教法庭的魔掌！我刚从恐怖的木床上滑到地牢的石头地板上，那令人毛骨悚然的凶器就停止了摆动。我看到它被某种无形的力量向上拖去，直穿过天花板。这个教训，我已铭刻在心。毫无疑问，我的一举一动都在他们的监控之中。自由！我只不过是以一种痛苦的方式从死神手中逃脱而进入到另一种比死更痛苦的折磨中。想到这里，我开始转动眼睛，提心吊胆地打量这将我置于牢笼之境的几面铁墙。发生了一些异常的变化，刚开始我并没有清楚地意识到，但现在它就在这地牢中实实在在地发生了！有好一阵子，我恍恍惚惚，浑身哆嗦，盲目地推断和臆想。这期间就在此时。这期间，我才第一次意识到了照亮地牢的昏黄光线来自何方。它从一道宽约半英寸的缝隙中射进来，这缝隙围着地牢的地板一周。看上去墙壁和地面

illumined the cell. It proceeded from a fissure, about half an inch in width, extending entirely around the prison at the base of the walls, which thus appeared, and were, completely separated from the floor. I endeavored, but of course in vain, to look through the aperture.

As I arose from the attempt, the mystery of the alteration in the chamber broke at once upon my understanding. I have observed that, although the outlines of the figures upon the walls were sufficiently distinct, yet the colors seemed blurred and indefinite. These colors had now assumed, and were momentarily assuming, a startling and most intense brilliancy, that gave to the spectral and fiendish portraitures an aspect that might have thrilled even firmer nerves than my own. Demon eyes, of a wild and ghastly vivacity, glared upon me in a thousand directions, where none had been visible before, and gleamed with the lurid lustre of a fire that I could not force my imagination to regard as unreal.

Unreal! – Even while I breathed there came to my nostrils the breath of the vapour of heated iron! A suffocating odour pervaded the prison! A deeper glow settled each moment in the eyes that glared at my agonies! A richer tint of crimson diffused itself over the pictured horrors of blood. I panted! I gasped for breath! There could be

并非一体。事实上确实如此。我努力想透过缝隙向外瞄，可当然什么也看不到。

就在刚要放弃之时，我突然意识到地牢里发生了不可思议的神秘变化。我之前在墙上看到的那些魑魅魍魉之像的轮廓虽清晰可见，但颜色已褪去不少变得模糊不清。然而现在这颜色顷刻之间恢复起来，并且越来越不可思议光彩照人。这效果衬得那些妖魔鬼怪的图像更恐怖瘆人，估计那些比我还大胆的人都要被吓得打战。那些之前看不到的鬼怪的眼睛现在都从各个角落瞪着我，眼中充斥着野蛮可怕的躁动和快活，闪耀着火焰般血红的光芒，以至于我不能否认那火焰是虚幻的。

虚幻！——在呼吸之间，已有烧灼铁板的蒸气蹿入鼻孔！牢房里弥漫着令人窒息的味道！那些注视着我于水火之中煎熬的眼睛越发明亮了！一种更深的猩红色在恐怖的血色图画上铺漫开来。我气喘吁吁！我难以呼吸！毫无疑问，这是那帮折磨我的家伙设好的阴谋。哦，没

no doubt of the design of my tormentors – oh! most unrelenting! oh! most demoniac of men! I shrank from the glowing metal to the centre of the cell. Amid the thought of the fiery destruction that impended, the idea of the coolness of the well came over my soul like balm. I rushed to its deadly brink. I threw my straining vision below. The glare from the enkindled roof illumined its inmost recesses. Yet, for a wild moment, did my spirit refuse to comprehend the meaning of what I saw. At length it forced – it wrestled its way into my soul – it burned itself in upon my shuddering reason. – Oh! for a voice to speak! – oh! horror! – oh! any horror but this! With a shriek, I rushed from the margin, and buried my face in my hands – weeping bitterly.

The heat rapidly increased, and once again I looked up, shuddering as with a fit of the ague. There had been a second change in the cell – and now the change was obviously in the *form*. As before, it was in vain that I, at first, endeavoured to appreciate or understand what was taking place. But not Long was I left in doubt. The Inquisitorial vengeance had been hurried by my two-fold escape, and there was to be no more dallying with the King of Terrors. The room had been square. I saw that two of its iron angles were now acute – two, consequently, obtuse. The fearful difference quickly increased with a

人性的恶魔！为躲开炽热的铁壁，我退到了地牢中央。想到即将被活活烤死，陷坑的凉爽倒成了精神抚慰剂。我冲到那随时可以置人于死地的坑边，瞪圆了双眼往下看。屋顶燃烧的火焰光芒四射，照亮了陷坑里的每个角落。然而，有那么癫狂的一会儿，我内心坚决不愿接受我所看到的一切。最终它还是横冲直撞进入了我的灵魂，深深地烙进我瑟瑟发抖的心智之上。哦，不可言传！哦，太恐怖了！哦，恐怖到了极点！我跌跌撞撞逃离坑边，双手掩面，失声痛哭。

温度急剧升高。我再次抬起头，感觉像是罹患了痢疾，周身颤抖不止。地牢里再次发生变化——很明显，这次是外在形态的变化。和上次相同，刚开始我绞尽脑汁都还是搞不明白到底发生了什么。不过这一次我很快就明白了，因为连续两次化险为夷，宗教法庭要加紧报复了。这下我再也没有余地和死神周旋了。地牢内部是正方形。可现在我看到，铁壁上有两个角已经变成了锐角，还有两个成了钝角。伴随着低沉的轰隆声，牢内开始发生急速而可怕的变化。刹那间，眼前的地牢变成了菱形。且变形没有就此

low rumbling or moaning sound. In an instant the apartment had shifted its form into that of a lozenge. But the alteration stopped not here-I neither hoped nor desired it to stop. I could have clasped the red walls to my bosom as a garment of eternal peace. "Death," I said, "any death but that of the pit!" Fool! might I have not known *that into the pit* it was the object of the burning iron to urge me? Could I resist its glow? or, if even that, could I withstand its pressure And now, flatter and flatter grew the lozenge, with a rapidity that left me no time for contemplation. Its centre, and of course, its greatest width, came just over the yawning gulf. I shrank back – but the closing walls pressed me resistlessly onward. At length for my seared and writhing body there was no Longer an inch of foothold on the firm floor of the prison. I struggled no more, but the agony of my soul found vent in one loud, Long, and final scream of despair. I felt that I tottered upon the brink – I averted my eyes –

There was a discordant hum of human voices! There was a loud blast as of many trumpets! There was a harsh grating as of a thousand thunders! The fiery walls rushed back! An outstretched arm caught my own as I fell, fainting, into the abyss. It was that of General Lasalle. The French army had entered Toledo. The Inquisition was in the hands of its enemies.

停止，我不指望更不渴望它能停下来。我可以将烧得通红的铁壁扣进胸口，化作我求得永恒宁静的衣料布匹。"死亡，"我说，"我死也不会跳进那陷坑！"傻瓜！难道我不明白这炙热的铁壁为的就是逼我跳进这陷坑？难道我经得起烈焰灼烧？难道我扛得住千钧压顶？此时，菱形越来越扁，变得越来越快，以至于我都没有时间思考。菱形的中心，当然，也就是它最宽的地方，正横着那张着血盆大口的深渊。我向后退去——可不断逼近的铁壁迫使我不得不往前移动。终于，这地牢坚实的地板上已容不下我这烧痕累累、因疼痛而不住扭动的身体。我不再挣扎。一声绝望、响亮而绝望的仰天长啸，我为自己受苦受难的灵魂找到了解脱。我感觉到自己在陷坑边缘摇摇欲坠——我移开了目光——

忽然，我听到了一阵嘈杂的人声，听到了一声爆炸的巨响，像是无数喇叭齐鸣。我还听到了仿佛是雷霆万钧的刺耳的声音！灼热的铁壁一下子恢复了原状。就在我不省人事跌入深渊之际，一只手臂伸来，一把抓住了我的胳膊。是拉萨尔将军，法国军队已攻入托莱多城。宗教法庭已落入它的敌人之手。

5. Ligeia

五. 丽姬娅

And the will therein lieth, which dieth not. Who knoweth the mysteries of the will, with its vigor? For God is but a great will pervading all things by nature of its intentness. Man doth not yield himself to the angels, nor unto death utterly, save only through the weakness of his feeble will.

–Joseph Glanvill

I cannot, for my soul, remember how, when, or even precisely where, I first became acquainted with the lady Ligeia. Long years have since elapsed, and my memory is feeble through much suffering. Or, perhaps, I cannot now bring these points to mind, because, in truth, the character of my beloved, her rare learning, her singular yet placid cast of beauty, and the thrilling and enthralling eloquence of her low musical language, made their way into my heart by paces so steadily and stealthily progressive that they have been unnoticed and unknown. Yet I believe that I met her first and most frequently in some large, old, decaying city near the Rhine. Of her family – I have surely heard her speak. That it is of a remotely ancient date cannot be doubted. Ligeia! Ligeia! in studies of a

意志蕴涵其中永生不灭。有谁知晓意志的神秘及其威力呢？上帝便是一伟大意志，以其专注的特性遍泽万物。凡人若非具有意志薄弱之缺陷，绝不服从天使，亦不屈服于死神。

——约瑟夫·葛兰维尔

对于我来讲，我完全不记得最初在何时以何种方式甚至精确到于何处与丽姬娅小姐相识。这么多年过去了，况且我饱受煎熬，记忆力极差。或许可能导致我没有在脑海中追忆起这些细节的原因在于我心上人那性情脾气和博学多识以及非凡而恬静的美貌、流水欢歌般的悦耳低语，悄无声息地牢牢萦绕在我心头，我竟毫无察觉也不知晓。但我相信第一次见她是在莱茵河附近一个古老破旧的大城市里，此后就频繁来往。我倒的确听她亲口谈过她的家族。毫无疑问，那是个历史悠久的世家。丽姬娅！丽姬娅！我研究的这门学问比起其他一切都易于使人遗世忘俗，就凭单单这3个甜美的字眼——丽姬娅——她那曼妙的身影就浮现在我的眼前，其实

nature more than all else adapted to deaden impressions of the outward world, it is by that sweet word alone – by Ligeia – that I bring before mine eyes in fancy the image of her who is no more. And now, while I write, a recollection flashes upon me that I have *never known* the paternal name of her who was my friend and my betrothed, and who became the partner of my studies, and finally the wife of my bosom. Was it a playful charge on the part of my Ligeia? or was it a test of my strength of affection, that I should institute no inquiries upon this point? or was it rather a caprice of my own – a wildly romantic offering on the shrine of the most passionate devotion? I but indistinctly recall the fact itself – what wonder that I have utterly forgotten the circumstances which originated or attended it? And, indeed, if ever that spirit which is entitled Romance – if ever she, the wan and the misty-winged Ashtophet of idolatrous Egypt, presided, as they tell, over marriages ill-omened, then most surely she presided over mine.

There is one dear topic, however, on which my memory falls me not. It is the *person* of Ligeia. In stature she was tall, somewhat slender, and, in her latter days, even emaciated. I would in vain attempt to portray the majesty, the quiet ease, of her demeanor, or the incomprehensible

她早已过世。现今，随着我的描写，心头闪现着回忆，我根本就不知道她姓什么，其实她还是我的挚友和未婚妻，后来成为我研究的助手，最后变成我的爱妻呢。难道能开玩笑地指明这是我的丽姬娅？或者这是我爱情忠贞的试金石，在这一点上根本用不着进行任何调查？再不难道只是我自己的幻想——极度迷恋神龛前那种浪漫绝伦的供奉？我只是朦胧地回忆，怪不得前因后果都忘得一干二净！说真的，如果那个名为浪漫的神仙——如果她，埃及崇拜的那个苍白的蝉翼仙子——阿什脱雷思[1]，就像别人所说主管恶姻缘，那么一定是她左右着我的婚姻。

不过还真有件珍贵的事没忘记，就是丽姬娅的容颜。她身材修长，也可以算得上有点瘦弱，在她生命的末期甚至是可谓弱不禁风。要我描绘出她那雍容华贵从容悠闲的风度以及她那极其飘逸轻盈欲仙的步伐，简直是不可能。她来去像

---

[1] 阿什脱雷思：希腊的美和生育之女神。

lightness and elasticity of her footfall. She came and departed as a shadow. I was never made aware of her entrance into my closed study save by the dear music of her low sweet voice, as she placed her marble hand upon my shoulder. In beauty of face no maiden ever equalled her. It was the radiance of an opium-dream – an airy and spirit-lifting vision more wildly divine than the phantasies which hovered vision about the slumbering souls of the daughters of Delos. Yet her features were not of that regular mould which we have been falsely taught to worship in the classical labors of the heathen. "There is no exquisite beauty," says Bacon, Lord Verulam, speaking truly of all the forms and *genera* of beauty, without some strangeness in the proportion." Yet, although I saw that the features of Ligeia were not of a classic regularity – although I perceived that her loveliness was indeed "exquisite," and felt that there was much of "strangeness" pervading it, yet I have tried in vain to detect the irregularity and to trace home my own perception of "the strange." I examined the contour of the lofty and pale forehead – it was faultless – how cold indeed that word when applied to a majesty so divine! – the skin rivalling the purest ivory, the commanding extent and repose, the gentle prominence of the regions above the temples; and then the raven-black, the

幽灵一般。若非是她将玉手搭在我的肩头，吐出甜美的温柔软语，我根本没有意识到她走进了我这间房门紧闭的书斋。世上根本没一个少女可与她那秀丽的脸庞相媲美。简直就像瘾君子那光辉闪耀的梦境一般——那是销魂钩魄般的虚幻梦境，比得洛斯女儿们那睡意蒙眬时萦绕在心头的幻想还要绚丽呢。那些异教徒的古典作品中通常错误地引导我们倾慕端庄的容颜，但她并不在这一范畴之内。唯鲁拉姆男爵对各种形式、各种类型的美评论得极其恰当，"匀称中如果没有异处，则不能称为绝色"。虽然我发现丽姬娅的容貌不在端庄的古典美范畴之内——但我却认为她的美丽绝对堪称"绝色"，倒是觉察出她的脸上的确有很多"异处"，但要企图发现不端庄，从而找到心目中的"奇异"，那可真是徒劳。我仔细端详那高傲雪白的额头——简直毫无瑕疵。用这些字眼来形容如此绝妙的庄重样貌，该是多么乏味平淡啊！再细看象牙般白净的皮肤，宽阔饱满的天庭，彰显出高贵和安逸；再看那熠熠生辉的、浓密的蓬松发丝，活脱脱再现了荷马式形容词"如风信子"的整个含义！我注视着那优雅的鼻子，轮廓完美无瑕，那是只能在希伯来人优雅的浮雕里才能展现出来的。再加之那如凝脂般的鼻子，隐约有点鹰钩的鼻梁和那轮廓

glossy, the luxuriant and naturally-curling tresses, setting forth the full force of the Homeric epithet, "hyacinthine!" I looked at the delicate outlines of the nose – and nowhere but in the graceful medallions of the Hebrews had I beheld a similar perfection. There were the same luxurious smoothness of surface, the same scarcely perceptible tendency to the aquiline, the same harmoniously curved nostrils speaking the free spirit. I regarded the sweet mouth. Here was indeed the triumph of all things heavenly – the magnificent turn of the short upper lip – the soft, voluptuous slumber of the under – the dimples which sported, and the color which spoke – the teeth glancing back, with a brilliancy almost startling, every ray of the holy light which fell upon them in her serene and placid, yet most exultingly radiant of all smiles. I scrutinized the formation of the chin – and here, too, I found the gentleness of breadth, the softness and the majesty, the fullness and the spirituality, of the Greek – the contour which the God Apollo revealed but in a dream, to Cleomenes, the son of the Athenian. And then I peered into the large eyes of Ligeia.

For eyes we have no models in the remotely antique. It might have been, too, that in these eyes of my beloved lay the

相称的鼻孔，正可谓透着豪爽气概。我端详那令人爱怜的嘴巴，绝对堪称无与伦比的杰作——庄重的上唇较短，柔软且妩媚；令人迷惑的下唇；笑意盈盈的酒窝，唇色红艳欲滴；她异常冷静，又喜气洋洋地微笑着，一条条圣洁的光芒照射着牙齿，异常光亮的一排牙齿将条条圣光反射出来。我认真端详着下巴的模样——我就是在这里发现了那宽阔而圆润，柔软而威严，饱满而优雅的希腊人式的下巴，那是一种只有在阿波罗神[1]梦中才能让雅典人的儿子克里奥米尼看到的轮廓。随即我便紧紧盯住丽姬娅那对大眼睛了。

在遥远的古代从没见过这样的一双眼睛。我那爱人的双眼中可能蕴藏着范吕兰姆男爵所说的秘密。

---
[1] 阿波罗神：古希腊最著名的神祇之一，也是希腊神话十二主神之一。主管光明。

secret to which Lord Verulam alludes. They were, I must believe, far larger than the ordinary eyes of our own race. They were even fuller than the fullest of the gazelle eyes of the tribe of the valley of Nourjahad. Yet it was only at intervals – in moments of intense excitement – that this peculiarity became more than slightly noticeable in Ligeia. And at such moments was her beauty – in my heated fancy thus it appeared perhaps – the beauty of beings either above or apart from the earth – the beauty of the fabulous Houri of the Turk. The hue of the orbs was the most brilliant of black, and, far over them, hung jetty lashes of great length. The brows, slightly irregular in outline, had the same tint. The "strangeness," however, which I found in the eyes, was of a nature distinct from the formation, or the color, or the brilliancy of the features, and must, after all, be referred to the expression. Ah, word of no meaning! behind whose vast latitude of mere sound we intrench our ignorance of so much of the spiritual. The expression of the eyes of Ligeia! How for Long hours have I pondered upon it! How have I, through the whole of a midsummer night, struggled to fathom it! What was it – that something more profound than the well of Democritus – which lay far within the pupils of my beloved? What was it? I was possessed with a passion to discover. Those eyes!

不能否认，我们普通的族人的眼睛再怎样也不会这么大。连诺耶哈德谷族人中像羚羊般最圆的眼睛也不及她的双眼那么圆。可其实呢，通常只有她在欢欣愉悦的时候，这种特质才会显露无遗。此时，她就像天上玉女般美丽，世外神仙般动人——土耳其神话中的火丽那样。也许是我胡思乱想才会觉得是这样吧。她那纤长的黑色睫毛遮住了双眸。眉毛的颜色也是那么深，只是不太整齐。然而，双眼中显示出的"异点"，在性质、模样、色泽和神采上与脸庞大相径庭，归根到底，一定是神情上有"异点"。啊，神情这个词汇多没意境啊！我们掩饰了自己对灵性的一无所知，只能单单说出这等含义宽泛的字眼来。丽姬娅的眼神啊！我整整半天都在专心致志地默默揣度！整整一个仲夏之夜，我十分投入地想要领悟出蕴藏在我心上人的双眼中——比德漠克里特井还深邃的究竟是什么？会是什么呢？我一心只想揭开这个谜团。那双眼睛啊！那对又大又亮又美丽的眸子啊！在我的心目中那对双眼已然成了勒达双星，我则化身为那双眼睛最最热心的星相研究家。

those large, those shining, those divine orbs! they became to me twin stars of Leda, and I to them devoutest of astrologers.

There is no point, among the many incomprehensible anomalies of the science of mind, more thrillingly exciting than the fact – never, I believe, noticed in the schools – that, in our endeavors to recall to memory something Long forgotten, we often find ourselves *upon the very verge* of remembrance, without being able, in the end, to remember. And thus how frequently, in my intense scrutiny of Ligeia's eyes, have I felt approaching the full knowledge of their expression – felt it approaching – yet not quite be mine – and so at length entirely depart! And (strange, oh strangest mystery of all!) I found, in the commonest objects of the universe, a circle of analogies to theat expression. I mean to say that, subsequently to the period when Ligeia's beauty passed into my spirit, there dwelling as in a shrine, I derived, from many existences in the material world, a sentiment such as I felt always aroused within me by her large and luminous orbs. Yet not the more could I define that sentiment, or analyze, or even steadily view it. I recognized it, let me repeat, sometimes in the survey of a rapidly-growing vine – in the contemplation of a moth, a butterfly, a

心理学中有很多难以揣度的变态心理，其中最令人胆寒的，恐怕就是在学校讲堂里根本不会提及的，也就是在我们极力要回忆一桩本已忘怀地事情，常常发现几乎在快要回想起来之时却还是想不起。我忘情的凝视丽姬娅的眼睛，常常也是觉得在即将彻悟的时候——就是觉得那眼神马上就要被我理解了——却又怎么都不了解，结果是这么莫名其妙！真是奇怪啊，简直是怪到极致的谜团，在天下最平凡的事物中，我竟也发现了许多类似的东西。我的意思是，丽姬娅的美嵌进了我的脑海，像是供奉在神龛里那样萦绕心头。以后的日子里，每逢我见到尘世万物，一种心情就会油然而生，看到她那对水汪汪的大眼睛时，总会是这种感觉。但到底是什么心境，我始终无法说清，也没法分析，连猜测都无法猜测。重复一遍吧，有时我观察一株迅速生长的葡萄，凝视一只飞蛾，一只蝴蝶，一条虫蛹，一条流水，这种心情便突然涌现出来。看到海洋，看见陨落的流星时也曾体会过。望着年逾古稀的老人的双眼，曾经体会过。用望远镜观测天上的一两颗变幻莫测的星星，尤其是天琴座中那

chrysalis, a stream of running water. I have felt it in the ocean; in the falling of a meteor. I have felt it in the glances of unusually aged people. And there are one or two stars in heaven – (one especially, a star of the sixth magnitude, double and changeable, to be found near the large star in Lyra) in a telescopic scrutiny of which I have been made aware of the feeling. I have been filled with it by certain sounds from stringed instruments, and not unfrequently by passages from books. Among innumerable other instances, I well remember something in a volume of Joseph Glanvill, which (perhaps merely from its quaintness – who shall say?) never failed to inspire me with the sentiment; – "And the will therein lieth, which dieth not. Who knoweth the mysteries of the will, with its vigor? For God is but a great will pervading all things by nature of its intentness. Man doth not yield him to the angels, nor unto death utterly, save only through the weakness of his feeble will."

Length of years, and subsequent reflection, have enabled me to trace, indeed, some remote connection between this passage in the English moralist and a portion of the character of Ligeia. An *intensity* in thought, action, or speech, was possibly, in her, a result, or at least an index, of that gigantic volition which, during our Long intercourse, failed to give

颗大星附近的六等星，双重星，也曾领悟过。听到弦乐器的某种音响，也曾满怀这种感觉。读到书中的几节文章，也不免充斥着这种情愫。在这些数不胜数的事例中，尤其令我深深铭记的就是约瑟夫·葛兰维尔的一部书中的一段文章，读到时总不免涌出这种感觉——大概就是由于文章怪异吧。谁能说得清？——意志蕴涵其中永生不灭。有谁知晓意志的神秘及其威力呢？上帝便是一伟大意志，以其专注的特性遍泽万物。凡人若非具有意志薄弱之缺陷，绝不服从天使，亦不屈服于死神。

这么多年过去了，经过这么一番回忆，我还真能回忆起丽姬娅的某些性格特征，和那位英国伦理学家的这段名言倒有几分相关性。她全情投入地思考、行动和谈话，可能这就是那种非凡的意志产物，要不至少也是它的反映，在我们长期交往的过程中，她没有流露出其他比这更具体的表现了。我熟识的女

other and more immediate evidence of its existence. Of all the women whom I have ever known, she, the outwardly calm, the ever-placid Ligeia, was the most violently a prey to the tumultuous vultures of stern passion. And of such passion I could form no estimate, save by the miraculous expansion of those eyes which at once so delighted and appalled me – by the almost magical melody, modulation, distinctness and placidity of her very low voice – and by the fierce energy (rendered doubly effective by contrast with her manner of utterance) of the wild words which she habitually uttered.

I have spoken of the learning of Ligeia: it was immense – such as I have never known in woman. In the classical tongues was she deeply proficient, and as far as my own acquaintance extended in regard to the modern dialects of Europe, I have never known her at fault. Indeed upon any theme of the most admired, because simply the most abstruse of the boasted erudition of the academy, have I *ever* found Ligeia at fault? How singularly – how thrillingly, this one point in the nature of my wife has forced itself, at this late period only, upon my attention! I said her knowledge was such as I have never known in woman – but where breathes the man who has traversed, and successfully, all the wide areas of moral, physical, and mathematical

性中，只有她外表沉着镇定，表面矜持的丽姬娅内心中那股热情似波涛汹涌，把她折磨得异常辛苦。我也估计不出来这股热情，或者凭借着那双出奇大的双眼，那双叫我惊喜交加的眼睛；靠着她那幽幽嗓音中那份清晰镇定、抑扬顿挫，甚至是摄人心魄的语调；凭着她那一贯咄咄逼人的谈吐（与她说话时的神情相比，咄咄逼人的威势显露无遗），或许还能估计一二。

上文提及丽姬娅的学识可谓极其丰富，从没听过哪家闺秀会有的学问。她精通古典语言，就我对现代欧洲方言的知识来讲，从没发现她被难倒过。其实，任何一个十分受推崇的课题——就因为那是学院所夸耀的最深奥的学问——丽姬娅又何尝被难倒过？只不过近几年，我妻子的这一特质才显得如此不同凡响，令人惊叹，不得不使人全情投入啊！上文刚说过，我根本没听过哪家的闺秀有她这种学识，可是世上哪里又有一个男人能够涉足心理学、物理学和数理学等一切科学，而且成绩斐然呢？当初我并不了解丽姬娅的才学是这么出色，甚至到了令人咋舌的地步，直至现在才清楚。但当初我倒十分清楚她拥有至

science? I saw not then what I now clearly perceive, that the acquisitions of Ligeia were gigantic, were astounding; yet I was sufficiently aware of her infinite supremacy to resign myself, with a child-like confidence, to her guidance through the chaotic world of metaphysical investigation at which I was most busily occupied during the earlier years of our marriage. With how vast a triumph – with how vivid a delight – with how much of all that is ethereal in hope – did I *feel*, as she bent over me in studies but little sought – but less known – that delicious vista by slow degrees expanding before me, down whose Long, gorgeous, and all untrodden path, I might at length pass onward to the goal of a wisdom too divinely precious not to be forbidden!

How poignant, then, must have been the grief with which, after some years, I beheld my well-grounded expectations take wings to themselves and fly away! Without Ligeia I was but as a child groping benighted. Her presence, her readings alone, rendered vividly luminous the many mysteries of the transcendentalism in which we were immersed. Wanting the radiant lustre of her eyes, letters, lambent and golden, grew duller than Saturnian lead. And now those eyes shone less and less frequently upon the pages over which I pored. Ligeia grew ill. The wild eyes

高无上的权力可以支配我，我竟也像孩子似的安心听命，任凭她指导我研究玄妙的形而上学。婚后几年内，我孜孜不倦研究的就是形而上学。每逢我研究那没有什么人探知——不大有人通晓的学问时，她就会趴到我身上，我真是极其自豪，极其激动，怀着无限美好的憧憬，感到绝妙的美景尽在眼前，顺着那条鲜有人迹、光辉灿烂的漫漫长路，最终可抵达学问的终点，这种学识实在是弥足珍贵，总需要有人研究啊。

几年过后，眼看着这些原本切实的希望化作一阵风吹散，我心头的悲哀自不必多提！没有了丽姬娅，我只不过就像孩子独自在黑暗中摸索罢了。有她在我身边，就靠她讲解，我们埋头研究过程中所遇到的不少疑难问题便能迎刃而解。没有了她那对闪闪发亮的双眼，熠熠生辉的金字竟比铅字还无光。可现今那对眼睛越发难以投射到我研究的书上了。丽姬娅病了。惊恐的双眼散发着惨淡的光；苍白的手指变得像死尸般蜡黄；宽阔额头上的青筋随着极其微妙的感情起伏骤涨骤

blazed with a too – too glorious effulgence; the pale fingers became of the transparent waxen hue of the grave, and the blue veins upon the lofty forehead swelled and sank impetuously with the tides of the gentle emotion. I saw that she must die – and I struggled desperately in spirit with the grim Azrael. And the struggles of the passionate wife were, to my astonishment, even more energetic than my own. There had been much in her stern nature to impress me with the belief that, to her, death would have come without its terrors; – but not so. Words are impotent to convey any just idea of the fierceness of resistance with which she wrestled with the Shadow. I groaned in anguish at the pitiable spectacle. would have soothed – I would have reasoned; but, in the intensity of her wild desire for life, – for life – *but* for life – solace and reason were the uttermost folly. Yet not until the last instance, amid the most convulsive writhings of her fierce spirit, was shaken the external placidity of her demeanor. Her voice grew more gentle – grew more low – yet I would not wish to dwell upon the wild meaning of the quietly uttered words. My brain reeled as I hearkened entranced, to a melody more than mortal – to assumptions and aspirations which mortality had never before known.

That she loved me I should not have

落。我心知她肯定会死——我便会不顾性命般跟那凶恶的无常拼命。可万万没想到，我那多情的妻子与死神的搏斗竟比我还厉害。她那坚强的性格本使我信服，死神在她心里绝不可怕——可谁知绝非如此。她与死亡搏斗的那种强烈反抗力，绝非用笔墨能够形容的。我目睹这副惨状，心疼得无法形容。真想安慰安慰她，劝导劝导她。可她十分想要活下去——想活下去——只想存活——安慰劝导她，那简直是愚蠢啊。即使她那火焰般炽热的心里在翻江倒海般折腾，可不到最后关头，那看似镇定的神情也始终未曾改变。只是嗓音越发柔弱了——越发低沉了——她低声道出一番话来，那怪诞的意义，我可无法细述。我晕头晕脑地听着，恍恍惚惚的，听着那异常的声音——听着世间不曾有的痴心妄想。

她爱我，这毋庸置疑，一看便

doubted; and I might have been easily aware that, in a bosom such as hers, love would have reigned no ordinary passion. But in death only, was I fully impressed with the strength of her affection. For Long hours, detaining my hand, would she pour out before me the overflowing of a heart whose more than passionate devotion amounted to idolatry. How had I deserved to be so blessed by such confessions? – how had I deserved to be so cursed with the removal of my beloved in the hour of her making them, But upon this subject I cannot bear to dilate. Let me say only, that in Ligeia's more than womanly abandonment to a love, alas! all unmerited, all unworthily bestowed, I at length recognized the principle of her Longing with so wildly earnest a desire for the life which was now fleeing so rapidly away. It is this wild Longing – it is this eager vehemence of desire for life – but for life – that I have no power to portray – no utterance capable of expressing.

At high noon of the night in which she departed, beckoning me, peremptorily, to her side, she bade me repeat certain verses composed by herself not many days before. I obeyed her. – They were these:

Lo! 'tis a gala night
Within the lonesome latter years!
An angel throng, bewinged, bedight

知在她心中，爱情至高无上。可是，直至她临终前，我才被她那至深至爱的挚情所打动。半天时间，她一直紧紧抓着我的手，面对面向我倾诉溢满内心的情愫，心里那热恋的痴情真可谓至爱啊。我怎么配听到这首心曲呢？——我竟会这么倒霉，在心上人倾诉衷肠时，眼看着她离开人世！我不能忍受复述这个过程。这么解释好了，天哪！眼见丽姬娅比普通人强烈地爱恋着一个不该受人爱戴也不配受人爱戴的人，又看着在她生命即将香消玉殒之时，她真切地满怀希望，一心想要生存下去。这种强烈的盼望，这种满心要存活且只想存活的热切期盼，我却没有能力描写，也没有语言来诉说。

她离世的那个深夜，半夜时分，她不由分说地把我喊到她身边，要我把她几天前创作的诗再读一次。我答应了。内容如下——

看！无限欢快的夜晚，
孤独凄惨的晚年！
一群蝉翼仙子，

In veils, and drowned in tears,
Sit in a theatre, to see
A play of hopes and fears,
While the orchestra breathes fitfully
The music of the spheres.

Mimes, in the form of God on high,
Mutter and mumble low,
And hither and thither fly;
Mere puppets they, who come and go
At bidding of vast formless things
That shift the scenery to and fro,
Flapping from out their Condor wings
Invisible Wo!

That motley drama! – oh, be sure
It shall not be forgot!
With its Phantom chased forever more,
By a crowd that seize it not,
Through a circle that ever returneth in
To the self-same spot,
And much of Madness and more of Sin
And Horror the soul of the plot.

But see, amid the mimic rout,
A crawling shape intrude!
A blood-red thing that writhes from out
The scenic solitude!
It writhes! – it writhes! – with mortal pangs
The mimes become its food,
And the seraphs sob at vermin fangs
In human gore imbued.

轻纱拂面，泪水盈盈，
端坐于戏院，观看
交汇着惊恐与期盼的悲剧，
乐队间歇地演奏
缥缈虚幻的天外仙曲

丑角扮演掌控万物的天帝，
东奔西跑，反复无常，
始终嘟囔，声音低沉，
唯独傀儡，四处乱撞，
听任那无形的巨擘四处牵引。
无形的巨擘瞬息万变，
拍拍秃鹰的翅膀，降落
隐约的灾难！

此幕大戏溢彩流光！
不可遗忘
人们始终追寻"幻影"，
触手可得，却总失望，
来去地回旋，
始终身处同一地方，
剧情大多恐怖，
罪恶且疯狂。

看那只横行的爬虫，
闯入快乐的小丑群中，
遍身猩红，横冲直撞，
冲出舞台的僻角！
扭动挣扎！一阵哀号，
可怜的丑角瞬间毙命，
鲜血沾满爬虫的毒牙，
坐席上的仙女痛哭流涕。

Out – out are the lights – out all!
And over each quivering form,
The curtain, a funeral pall,
Comes down with the rush of a storm,
And the angels, all pallid and wan,
Uprising, unveiling, affirm
That the play is the tragedy, "Man,"
And its hero the Conqueror Worm.

"O God!" half shrieked Ligeia, leaping to her feet and extending her arms aloft with a spasmodic movement, as I made an end of these lines – "O God! O Divine Father! – shall these things be undeviatingly so? – shall this Conqueror be not once conquered? Are we not part and parcel in Thee? Who – who knoweth the mysteries of the will with its vigor? Man doth not yield him to the angels, *nor unto death utterly,* save only through the weakness of his feeble will."

And now, as if exhausted with emotion, she suffered her white arms to fall, and returned solemnly to her bed of death. And as she breathed her last sighs, there came mingled with them a low murmur from her lips. I bent to them my ear and distinguished, again, the concluding words of the passage in Glanvill – "*Man doth not yield him to the angels, nor unto death utterly, save only through the weakness of his feeble will.*"

She died; and I, crushed into the very

灯光转暗，进而熄灭！
好似灵柩进入棺椁，
大幕如暴雨般忽然落下，
遮住人影，引得战栗无数，
仙子摘掉面纱，起身离席，
脸色惨白，目光迷离，
台上悲剧公认名为"人生"，
主角便是"毒蛊霸王"。

"啊，上帝啊！"当我念完这首诗，丽姬娅疾风骤雨般顿时跳起，举起双手，尖叫着，"啊，天哪！啊，上帝！——难不成这情形就一成不变？——难道要让此霸王永远称霸？难道我们并非上帝的子民？有谁知晓意志的神秘及其威力呢？凡人若非具有意志薄弱之缺陷，绝不服从天使，亦不屈服于死神。"

她此时像是发泄出满腔的积怨，精疲力竭了。两只雪白的胳膊齐刷刷放下，满脸冷酷，回到床上等候死神的降临。弥留之时，口中还振振有词。我俯身贴耳一听，原来竟又是葛兰维尔那节文章中的最后一句："凡人若非具有意志薄弱之缺陷，绝不服从天使，亦不屈服于死神。"

她死了，我痛彻心扉，实在不

dust with sorrow, could no Longer endure the lonely desolation of my dwelling in the dim and decaying city by the Rhine. I had no lack of what the world calls wealth. Ligeia had brought me far more, very far more than ordinarily falls to the lot of mortals. After a few months, therefore, of weary and aimless wandering, I purchased, and put in some repair, an abbey, which I shall not name, in one of the wildest and least frequented portions of fair England. The gloomy and dreary grandeur of the building, the almost savage aspect of the domain, the many melancholy and time-honored memories connected with both, had much in unison with the feelings of utter abandonment which had driven me into that remote and unsocial region of the country. Yet although the external abbey, with its verdant decay hanging about it, suffered but little alteration, I gave way, with a child-like perversity, and perchance with a faint hope of alleviating my sorrows, to a display of more than regal magnificence within. – For such follies, even in childhood, I had imbibed a taste and now they came back to me as if in the dotage of grief. Alas, I feel how much even of incipient madness might have been discovered in the gorgeous and fantastic draperies, in the solemn carvings of Egypt, in the wild cornices and furniture, in the Bedlam patterns of the carpets of tufted

愿独自居住在那莱茵河畔沉重的破败之城中。我并不缺乏世人所说的金钱。可丽娅姬带给我的财富远比普通世人注定拥有的要多，简直多得多呢。于是我疲惫不堪地漂泊了两三个月，最终在英国一个风光旖旎且荒无人烟的蛮夷之地买了一座寺院并进行了装修。我就不提及寺名了。我是因为万念俱灰才来到这与世隔绝的荒芜之地。这座满目疮痍的富丽寺院，这个荒芜的庄园，加上很多与寺院和庄园相关且颇有些典故的凄凉物品，与我这无限悲凉的心境很是相称。虽然寺院外表面目全非，一片颓废残缺之感，但我一如孩子般任性，也许是由于幻想一线希望，期盼由此可以来慰藉心中的哀伤，故而竟大张旗鼓，将屋子装修得比皇宫还要富丽。这种愚蠢的行为，是我在童年时代就养成的习惯，似乎现在到了凄凉的晚年，竟又重新活跃开来。天哪，看那稀奇古怪的幔帐、庄严的埃及雕刻、古怪的壁沿和家具、杂乱无章的金丝地毯，我觉得疯癫病的初期症候已经显现出许多呢！我早就嗜瘾成性，工作和习性上都显现出鸦片般的梦幻特征。但我绝对不可笔锋一转来细述这件荒唐之事。还是仅仅谈谈这个鬼房间吧。最开始我一时神经错乱，在圣坛前拜了堂，领着特瑞缅因金发碧眼的罗维娜·特瑞梵依小姐作为新娘，把她

gold! I had become a bounden slave in the trammels of opium, and my labors and my orders had taken a coloring from my dreams. But these absurdities must not pause to detail. Let me speak only of that one chamber, ever accursed, whither in a moment of mental alienation, I led from the altar as my bride – as the successor of the unforgotten Ligeia – the fair-haired and blue-eyed Lady Rowena Trevanion, of Tremaine.

There is no individual portion of the architecture and decoration of that bridal chamber which is not now visibly before me. Where were the souls of the haughty family of the bride, when, through thirst of gold, they permitted to pass the threshold of an apartment so bedecked, a maiden and a daughter so beloved? I have said that I minutely remember the details of the chamber – yet I am sadly forgetful on topics of deep moment – and here there was no system, no keeping, in the fantastic display, to take hold upon the memory. The room lay in a high turret of the castellated abbey, was pentagonal in shape, and of capacious size. Occupying the whole southern face of the pentagon was the sole window – an immense sheet of unbroken glass from Venice – a single pane, and tinted of a leaden hue, so that the rays of either the sun or moon, passing through it, fell with a ghastly lustre on the objects

作为萦绕我心头的丽姬娅之替身，走进这间卧房内。

新房的结构和摆设都尽收眼底。新娘娘家一贯势利，爱慕钱财，却竟能放任这么一位可爱的姑娘，一位千金小姐进入这般陈设的房间内，他们的气节呢？上文说到，我一丝不漏地将房间中的点点细节记在心间，但对重大事件却因伤心而几乎忘怀。那种不着边际的布置秩序全无，没有一丝协调性，能会留下什么印象呢？卧房在这座城堡式寺院的高耸塔楼上，五角形，十分宽敞。有一扇窗户开在朝南的墙上——一块偌大的威尼斯不碎玻璃——只有一个青灰色的窗框，阳光和月光透过窗子照进来，映得房间里的所有东西都笼罩了一层阴森凄厉的光泽。在大窗的上半部架起一个花架，上面盘着老葡萄藤，沿着塔楼的高墙攀爬上去。毫无生气的拱形橡木天花板，异常高耸，上面精致地绘着回形图纹，既有哥特式，又有德洛伊式，简直是稀奇异常，

within. Over the upper portion of this huge window, extended the trellice-work of an aged vine, which clambered up the massy walls of the turret. The ceiling, of gloomy-looking oak, was excessively lofty, vaulted, and elaborately fretted with the wildest and most grotesque specimens of a semi-Gothic, semi-Druidical device. From out the most central recess of this melancholy vaulting, depended, by a single chain of gold with Long links, a huge censer of the same metal, Saracenic in pattern, and with many perforations so contrived that there writhed in and out of them, as if endued with a serpent vitality, a continual succession of parti-colored fires.

Some few ottomans and golden candelabra, of Eastern figure, were in various stations about – and there was the couch, too – bridal couch – of an Indian model, and low, and sculptured of solid ebony, with a pall-like canopy above. In each of the angles of the chamber stood on end a gigantic sarcophagus of black granite, from the tombs of the kings over against Luxor, with their aged lids full of immemorial sculpture. But in the draping of the apartment lay, alas! the chief phantasy of all. The lofty walls, gigantic in height – even unproportionably so – were hung from summit to foot, in vast folds, with a heavy and massive-looking tapestry – tapestry of a material which was found

荒诞不堪。从苍穹的正中,垂着一根长环金链,挂着一只偌大的撒拉森式镂空金香炉,五彩的火像蟒蛇一般,不停地在炉孔里进进出出。

几张长榻摆放在房间的 4 个角落,还有几只金烛台,几乎都是东方样式;一张矮矮的实心乌木印度卧榻作为合欢床,上面还雕着花纹,有一顶棺套似的幔帐。卧房四角分别耸立一口奇大无比的黑色花岗岩棺材,都是来自于卢克索对面的皇陵中,破旧的棺盖上不知何年何月雕满了纹饰。天哪!最为怪异的就是房中的幔帐。高耸的四壁简直无法企及,还高得不对称。通体的墙面层层叠叠地挂着巨大沉重的幔帐——其材质看似与地毯、床罩、长榻套子、乌木床罩单、半开半掩的窗户那罗纹窗帘完全相同,都是弥足珍贵的金布,遍布团团簇簇远远近近的阿拉伯式图纹,每个团簇大

alike as a carpet on the floor, as a covering for the ottomans and the ebony bed, as a canopy for the bed, and as the gorgeous volutes of the curtains which partially shaded the window. The material was the richest cloth of gold. It was spotted all over, at irregular intervals, with arabesque figures, about a foot in diameter, and wrought upon the cloth in patterns of the most jetty black. But these figures partook of the true character of the arabesque only when regarded from a single point of view. By a contrivance now common, and indeed traceable to a very remote period of antiquity, they were made changeable in aspect. To one entering the room, they bore the appearance of simple monstrosities; but upon a farther advance, this appearance gradually departed; and step by step, as the visitor moved his station in the chamber, he saw himself surrounded by an endless succession of the ghastly forms which beLong to the superstition of the Norman, or arise in the guilty slumbers of the monk. The phantasmagoric effect was vastly heightened by the artificial introduction of a strong continual current of wind behind the draperies – giving a hideous and uneasy animation to the whole.

In halls such as these – in a bridal chamber such as this – I passed, with the Lady of Tremaine, the unhallowed hours of the first month of our marriage – passed

概直径一英尺，构成了漆黑的图案。但唯独从一个角度看过去，才真正有几分阿拉伯式的意味。一番设计之后（眼下这种设计在世界上比较流行，但其实自远古时代就已出现了），这些图案就显得变幻莫测。迈步进入房内，只觉得有些稀奇；可往里深入，这种奇怪的感觉便渐渐消失；在房里四处转转，就逐渐发现周围四下流经的都是鬼魅，或者可以说是诺曼底人所信奉的传说里的一种，或是出家人噩梦里浮现的。阵阵凉风不断从幔帐后面猛烈吹过，幻影重重的感觉就此骤增 10 倍——房中也就随即平添了一种恐怖且不安的力量。

在这间卧房中，我和特瑞缅因的那位小姐无忧无虑地度过了蜜月。我不经意就发现我的妻子躲着我，因为她害怕我这种反复异常的

them with but little disquietude. That my wife dreaded the fierce moodiness of my temper – that she shunned me and loved me but little – I could not help perceiving; but it gave me rather pleasure than otherwise. I loathed her with a hatred beLonging more to demon than to man. My memory flew back, (oh, with what intensity of regret!) to Ligeia, the beloved, the august, the beautiful, the entombed. I revelled in recollections of her purity, of her wisdom, of her lofty, her ethereal nature, of her passionate, her idolatrous love. Now, then, did my spirit fully and freely burn with more than all the fires of her own. In the excitement of my opium dreams (for I was habitually fettered in the shackles of the drug) I would call aloud upon her name, during the silence of the night, or among the sheltered recesses of the glens by day, as if, through the wild eagerness, the solemn passion, the consuming ardor of my Longing for the departed, I could restore her to the pathway she had abandoned – ah, *could* it be forever? – upon the earth.

About the commencement of the second month of the marriage, the Lady Rowena was attacked with sudden illness, from which her recovery was slow. The fever which consumed her rendered her nights uneasy; and in her perturbed state of half-slumber, she spoke of sounds, and of

禀性——她根本不爱我。可我心里反倒挺高兴。我咬牙切齿般痛恨她，只有妖怪才能感觉到这种痛恨。片刻之间，我想起丽姬娅，那是我的亲人，我的仙女，我的美人，我的亡妻，唉，我心中的惋惜之情别提有多严重了！我忘情地回想着她的神圣，她的聪颖，她那高尚的绝佳性格以及她那如胶似漆的火热感情。我肆无忌惮地满腔充斥着比她还炽热的烈烈欲火。我在服用鸦片过后的噩梦中（因为我吸毒成瘾了），放声呼唤她的名字，或者在万籁俱寂的晚上，或者在白天隐秘的山场幽谷里，仿佛只要我心痒难耐地、热情似火地诚意怀念亡妻，她就能回到先前摒弃的人生之路——唉，会一直这样吗？

大概婚后的第二个月初，突然间罗维娜小姐就病倒了，病情持续了很久。高烧击毁了她的健康，折磨得她夜不能寐。半睡半醒间，她不安地与我谈论起塔楼这间卧房里的响动。我肯定这都是她胡思乱想造成的，或者可能是房中那重重幻

motions, in and about the chamber of the turret, which I concluded had no origin save in the distemper of her fancy, or perhaps in the phantasmagoric influences of the chamber itself. She became at length convalescent – finally well. Yet but a brief period elapsed, ere a second more violent disorder again threw her upon a bed of suffering; and from this attack her frame, at all times feeble, never altogether recovered. Her illnesses were, after this epoch, of alarming character, and of more alarming recurrence, defying alike the knowledge and the great exertions of her physicians. With the increase of the chronic disease which had thus, apparently, taken too sure hold upon her constitution to be eradicated by human means, I could not fall to observe a similar increase in the nervous irritation of her temperament, and in her excitability by trivial causes of fear. She spoke again, and now more frequently and pertinaciously, of the sounds – of the slight sounds – and of the unusual motions among the tapestries, to which she had formerly alluded.

One night, near the closing in of September, she pressed this distressing subject with more than usual emphasis upon my attention. She had just awakened from an unquiet slumber, and I had been watching, with feelings half of anxiety, half of vague terror, the workings of her

象的影响。她慢慢复原了——彻底痊愈了。可谁知没过多久，她再度生病，这次病情来势汹汹，使她简直日夜躺在病榻上了。她的身体本来就很虚弱，自这次病后再也不见任何起色。这段时期过去后，病势就格外沉重了，旧病复发，真是凶险，医生使用一切手段，用尽全身解数，都不能医治成功。这慢性病越发严重，简直就是套牢了她，靠人的力量怕是难以挽回了。我慢慢发现她那急躁不安的脾气越发严重了，一点小事，就会吓得要命，这种动辄过激的情绪也越发厉害了。她最初说过幔帐之中有响动——细小的声响——不寻常的动静，现在又说起，而且说得越发频繁，越发固执。

9月末的一个夜晚，她特别强调这个令她心烦意乱的问题，引起了我的注意。她从噩梦中惊醒，我看着她那瘦削的脸庞不停地抽搐，心里既是焦急，又十分忧心。我在乌木床旁边的那张印度长榻上坐下来。她半坐起身，认真地用低沉的

emaciated countenance. I sat by the side of her ebony bed, upon one of the ottomans of India. She partly arose, and spoke, in an earnest low whisper, of sounds which she then heard, but which I could not hear – of motions which she then saw, but which I could not perceive. The wind was rushing hurriedly behind the tapestries, and I wished to show her (what, let me confess it, I could not all believe) that those almost inarticulate breathings, and those very gentle variations of the figures upon the wall, were but the natural effects of that customary rushing of the wind. But a deadly pallor, overspreading her face, had proved to me that my exertions to reassure her would be fruitless. She appeared to be fainting, and no attendants were within call. I remembered where was deposited a decanter of light wine which had been ordered by her physicians, and hastened across the chamber to procure it. But, as I stepped beneath the light of the censer, two circumstances of a startling nature attracted my attention. I had felt that some palpable although invisible object had passed lightly by my person; and I saw that there lay upon the golden carpet, in the very middle of the rich lustre thrown from the censer, a shadow – a faint, indefinite shadow of angelic aspect – such as might be fancied for the shadow of a shade. But I was wild with the excitement of an immoderate dose

声音说着当时的动静，可我听不到；她也说到当时看见的异动，但我也看不出。飒飒的风从幔帐后面吹过，我很想告诉她那声音简直听不清楚，墙上的影子也几乎没有任何变化，不过是徐徐微风的杰作，可说实话，我自己也不能肯定。这么说吧，看着她的脸上一阵惨白，我的心里几乎就有了定数。尽管我竭尽全力想使她安心，但简直是徒劳。看样子估计她快晕过去了，但我的身边没有一个仆人。这时我想到卧室的那头有一瓶医生规定可以喝的淡酒，便三步并作两步地跑去拿来。谁知刚跑到香炉的火焰下，就发生了两件值得我注意的惊人的事。我感觉有什么东西轻轻走过了我的身边，虽然看不到但却能感知；又看到在香炉中的熠熠光辉中，金黄的地毯正中有个影子——那是好似天仙一般的虚影——可能被当成幻影。可我过量吞食鸦片，而且醉得晕头晕脑，对这种事完全置若罔闻，也没有告诉罗维娜。我找到酒，回到卧房这头，倒了一杯并将酒杯凑近这位不省人事的小姐嘴边。现在她已经有点清醒了，抬起手臂接过杯子，我俯身在旁边的一张长榻上坐下，怔怔地望着她。而此时，耳朵里清清楚楚地听到睡榻旁边的地毯上一阵窸窸窣窣的脚步声。一转眼，罗维娜恰巧将酒杯送到嘴边，我突然发现仿佛三四滴亮晶晶的、

of opium, and heeded these things but little, nor spoke of them to Rowena. Having found the wine, I recrossed the chamber, and poured out a gobletful, which I held to the lips of the fainting lady. She had now partially recovered, however, and took the vessel herself, while I sank upon an ottoman near me, with my eyes fastened upon her person. It was then that I became distinctly aware of a gentle footfall upon the carpet, and near the couch; and in a second thereafter, as Rowena was in the act of raising the wine to her lips, I saw, or may have dreamed that I saw, fall within the goblet, as if from some invisible spring in the atmosphere of the room, three or four large drops of a brilliant and ruby colored fluid. If this I saw – not so Rowena. She swallowed the wine unhesitatingly, and I forbore to speak to her of a circumstance which must, after all, I considered, have been but the suggestion of a vivid imagination, rendered morbidly active by the terror of the lady, by the opium, and by the hour.

Yet I cannot conceal it from my own perception that, immediately subsequent to the fall of the ruby-drops, a rapid change for the worse took place in the disorder of my wife; so that, on the third subsequent night, the hands of her menials prepared her for the tomb, and on the fourth, I sat alone, with her shrouded body, in that

红艳艳的液体从半空中不知什么无形的泉水里流淌出来,滴进了酒杯里。要不或许就是我在做梦。即使我看到了——可罗维娜却没瞅见。她毫不犹豫地将酒一饮而尽,我忍住没把此事告诉她。归根到底,我觉得无非是由于我眼见罗维娜小姐有些害怕,又吞了鸦片,恰巧又处在夜晚时分,想象力就异常活跃,只要幻想丰富肯定就会引发联想。

但我不能蒙骗自己的双眼,随着那几滴红色液体滴进酒杯,突然之间我妻子病情恶化。第三天夜晚时分,奴婢已经为她的下葬作准备了,第四天时,我独自与她那裹衾的尸体在异常稀奇的卧房中坐着,那是我和她的新房。眼前出现了一种荒诞不经的幻象,那是一种只有

fantastic chamber which had received her as my bride. – Wild visions, opium-engendered, flitted, shadow-like, before me. I gazed with unquiet eye upon the sarcophagi in the angles of the room, upon the varying figures of the drapery, and upon the writhing of the parti-colored fires in the censer overhead. My eyes then fell, as I called to mind the circumstances of a former night, to the spot beneath the glare of the censer where I had seen the faint traces of the shadow. It was there, however, no Longer; and breathing with greater freedom, I turned my glances to the pallid and rigid figure upon the bed. Then rushed upon me a thousand memories of Ligeia – and then came back upon my heart, with the turbulent violence of a flood, the whole of that unutterable wo with which I had regarded her *thus* enshrouded. The night waned; and still, with a bosom full of bitter thoughts of the one only and supremely beloved, I remained gazing upon the body of Rowena.

It might have been midnight, or perhaps earlier, or later, for I had taken no note of time, when a sob, low, gentle, but very distinct, startled me from my revery. I *felt* that it came from the bed of ebony – the bed of death. I listened in an agony of superstitious terror – but there was no repetition of the sound. I strained my

服用了鸦片才能出现的幻景，若隐若现，虚无缥缈。我眼神迷离地看着房间四角那4口石棺，盯着幔帐上那变幻莫测的花纹，凝视头顶上那香炉里四处迸射的五彩火焰。我想起几天前晚上发生的事，眼光便不由自主地落在香炉底下。当时我在那里看见的朦胧身影，如今不复存在。我大口吸着气，看着床上那苍白的僵硬的尸体。忽然间浮现出丽姬娅桩桩件件的事情，一瞬间如山洪暴发般重新涌上心头。当时看她裹着寿衾而产生的一股说不出的悲哀。夜深了，我却依然呆呆盯着罗维娜的尸体，辛酸满腹地回忆着深深迷恋的唯一亲人。

约莫深夜时分，也可能还早点，或者晚些，我并没留意看时间，一阵呜咽之声突然在耳边响起，低沉轻柔，但又极其清晰。我不禁从迷梦中醒来，发觉声音是从乌木床那边传来——就是从罗维娜临终的那张床上传来。我情不自禁地唯心起来，极其害怕却又仔细听着——谁

vision to detect any motion in the corpse – but there was not the slightest perceptible. Yet I could not have been deceived. I had heard the noise, however faint, and my soul was awakened within me. I resolutely and perseveringly kept my attention riveted upon the body. Many minutes elapsed before any circumstance occurred tending to throw light upon the mystery. At length it became evident that a slight, a very feeble, and barely noticeable tinge of color had flushed up within the cheeks, and aLong the sunken small veins of the eyelids. Through a species of unutterable horror and awe, for which the language of mortality has no sufficiently energetic expression, I felt my heart cease to beat, my limbs grow rigid where I sat. Yet a sense of duty finally operated to restore my self-possession. I could no Longer doubt that we had been precipitate in our preparations – that Rowena still lived. It was necessary that some immediate exertion be made; yet turret was altogether apart from the portion of the abbey tenanted by the servants – there were none within call – I had no means of summoning them to my aid without leaving the room for many minutes – and this I could not venture to do. I therefore struggled alone in my endeavors to call back the spirit ill hovering. In a short period it was certain, however, that a relapse had taken place; the

知并没有第二声了。我瞪着眼睛想看看尸体有没什么异动——但丝毫全无。尽管声音很微弱，但我的确听到了，这不一定是错觉所致，况且我的头脑是很清醒的。我毅然决然地盯着尸体。但能够揭秘的事却再没发生。不大一会儿我终于辨认清了尸体的腮帮和眼帘那凹陷的血管中突然泛出了一层微红，颜色非常淡，几乎分辨不出来。顿时我产生了一种难以名状的害怕之情，用普通的言语都难以形容，只得一动不动地坐着。我的心几乎停止跳动了，手脚僵硬。但是，由衷的责任感最终令我安定下来。我断定安葬之事料理得太仓促——罗维娜还活着，需要马上进行抢救。但塔楼离寺院边角的下房太远——身边没有一个仆人能差遣——如果不离开房间片刻，是没有办法让他们来帮忙的——但我绝不敢离开。因此独自一人，想方设法也要将这游魂唤醒。片刻的工夫，旧病又复发了。眼帘和腮帮上的血色退却了，留下一片惨白，竟然比云石还白；嘴唇极其褶皱，嘟成一团，简直就是一副挣扎过后的死人模样；瞬间尸体就变得软塌塌，冷冰冰，令人心生恶心；然后就又僵硬了。我大大吃了一惊，从床上站起身，现在却又一身凉意，重新躺在榻上，又醉心于幻想丽姬娅那热情鼓舞的身影来。

color disappeared from both eyelid and cheek, leaving a wanness even more than that of marble; the lips became doubly shrivelled and pinched up in the ghastly expression of death; a repulsive clamminess and coldness overspread rapidly the surface of the body; and all the usual rigorous illness immediately supervened. I fell back with a shudder upon the couch from which I had been so startlingly aroused, and again gave myself up to passionate waking visions of Ligeia.

An hour thus elapsed when (could it be possible?) I was a second time aware of some vague sound issuing from the region of the bed. I listened – in extremity of horror. The sound came again – it was a sigh. Rushing to the corpse, I saw – distinctly saw – a tremor upon the lips. In a minute afterward they relaxed, disclosing a bright line of the pearly teeth. Amazement now struggled in my bosom with the profound awe which had hitherto reigned there alone. I felt that my vision grew dim, that my reason wandered; and it was only by a violent effort that I at length succeeded in nerving myself to the task which duty thus once more had pointed out. There was now a partial glow upon the forehead and upon the cheek and throat; a perceptible warmth pervaded the whole frame; there was even a slight pulsation at the heart. The lady lived; and with

一个钟头就这样过去了，我第二次又听到了床的方向传来窸窸窣窣的响动——确有其声吗？我侧耳细听——胆战心惊。又传来啦——一声叹息之声。我急切地跑到尸体旁边，发现尸体的嘴唇在瑟瑟颤抖，能够看得一清二楚呢。不大一会儿工夫，便不抖了，随即露出珍珠般一排白牙。最初我只是害怕，现在又多了几分诧异，感觉乱七八糟的。我只感觉头晕眼花，使出浑身解数，才能勉强支撑起来，在责任感的驱动下，我又准备做起死回生的工作了。此时尸体的额头，还有腮帮和喉咙上又都泛出微红色彩，摸起来身上也有了些温度，心脏也都微微跳动了。罗维娜小姐还活着呢。我就分外热忱地工作起来：擦拭尸体的太阳穴和双手，凡是不需要钻研医书，只凭经验就可晓得的手段都用了。谁知一切都是徒劳。一瞬间，

redoubled ardor I betook myself to the task of restoration. I chafed and bathed the temples and the hands, and used every exertion which experience, and no little. medical reading, could suggest. But in vain. Suddenly, the color fled, the pulsation ceased, the lips resumed the expression of the dead, and, in an instant afterward, the whole body took upon itself the icy chilliness, the livid hue, the intense rigidity, the sunken outline, and all the loathsome peculiarities of that which has been, for many days, a tenant of the tomb.

And again I sunk into visions of Ligeia – and again, (what marvel that I shudder while I write?) again there reached my ears a low sob from the region of the ebony bed. But why shall I minutely detail the unspeakable horrors of that night? Why shall I pause to relate how, time after time, until near the period of the gray dawn, this hideous drama of revivification was repeated; how each terrific relapse was only into a sterner and apparently more irredeemable death; how each agony wore the aspect of a struggle with some invisible foe; and how each struggle was succeeded by I know not what of wild change in the personal appearance of the corpse? Let me hurry to a conclusion.

The greater part of the fearful night had worn away, and she who had been dead, once again stirred – and now more

血色全无，心脏不跳了，嘴唇又恢复了死尸般的样子，片刻间，全身冰冷，一片死灰般的颜色，格外僵硬，只留下一副骨头，长久以来早已成为死人的一切可怜特征全都露出来了。

我重新开始幻想着丽姬娅的身影——耳边却又响起了低沉的声音（简直不可思议，如今我一面写，一面还打着寒战呢!）——接着又响起了低沉的呜咽声，是从乌木床那儿发出的。但是那天深夜发生的这一切无法描述的惊悚，何必又再重复呢？何必笔头一转又来复述这出复活的恐怖戏呢？何必讲述在那黑暗的黎明到来前，这出恐怖戏一幕幕地上演。旧病接二连三地恐怖发作，结果就是越发恐怖且难以挽回的死亡。一次又一次的垂死挣扎，样子简直就像是与无形的死敌搏斗。这搏斗的结果就是死尸的面容总是显现出难以名状的怪诞表情。何必复述所有呢？还是尽快写完这篇文章吧。

这个恐怖之夜过去大半，她早已死了，却又有所动静——这次比

vigorously than hitherto, although arousing from a dissolution more appalling in its utter hopelessness than any. I had Long ceased to struggle or to move, and remained sitting rigidly upon the ottoman, a helpless prey to a whirl of violent emotions, of which extreme awe was perhaps the least terrible, the least consuming. The corpse, I repeat, stirred, and now more vigorously than before. The hues of life flushed up with unwonted energy into the countenance – the limbs relaxed – and, save that the eyelids were yet pressed heavily together, and that the bandages and draperies of the grave still imparted their charnel character to the figure, I might have dreamed that Rowena had indeed shaken off, utterly, the fetters of Death. But if this idea was not, even then, altogether adopted, I could at least doubt no Longer, when, arising from the bed, tottering, with feeble steps, with closed eyes, and with the manner of one bewildered in a dream, the thing that was enshrouded advanced boldly and palpably into the middle of the apartment.

I trembled not – I stirred not – for a crowd of unutterable fancies connected with the air, the stature, the demeanor of the figure, rushing hurriedly through my brain, had paralyzed – had chilled me into stone. I stirred not – but gazed upon the apparition. There was a mad disorder in my

以往动弹得更剧烈了，虽然看不到复活的任何希望，但却极其可怕。我早就没有任何动作了，只是呆呆坐在床头，万千情结一一涌上心头，我束手无策，深受折磨，其中那种极端恐惧并不令人害怕，也并不耗费我的心力。重复一次吧，死尸又动弹了，这次比以往更加剧烈。脸颊突然就泛出了血色，这种力量不同寻常——手脚变得不再僵硬——如果不是眼睛依旧紧闭，尸体也还缠着绷带和披挂，始终表现出一种阴森恐怖的尸体样子，我还真以为罗维娜着实挣脱了死神附加在她身上的枷锁呢。但假使当时这种想法并不完全正确，但至少有一点可以肯定，那裹衾的尸体的确从床上翻身站起，双腿软弱无力，眼睛紧闭，就像人们做噩梦的样子，跌跌撞撞地向前走，一点一点来到房间正中，真真切切，清清楚楚。

我没有颤抖——也没有任何动作——因为那人的神态、体貌和举止，使我幻想出很多难以名状的景象，在脑海中一一浮现，反倒使我麻木——全身冰凉，僵硬得好像石人。我没有什么动作——只是呆呆地盯着这个鬼怪，心里七上八下

thoughts – a tumult unappeasable. Could it, indeed, be the *living* Rowena who confronted me? Could it indeed be Rowena *at all* – the fair-haired, the blue-eyed Lady Rowena Trevanion of Tremaine? Why, *why* should I doubt it? The bandage lay heavily about the mouth – but then might it not be the mouth of the breathing Lady of Tremaine? And the cheeks-there were the roses as in her noon of life – yes, these might indeed be the fair cheeks of the living Lady of Tremaine. And the chin, with its dimples, as in health, might it not be hers? – but *had she then grown taller since her malady*? What inexpressible madness seized me with that thought? One bound, and I had reached her feet! Shrinking from my touch, she let fall from her head, unloosened, the ghastly cerements which had confined it, and there streamed forth, into the rushing atmosphere of the chamber, huge masses of Long and dishevelled hair; *it was blacker than the raven wings of the midnight!* And now slowly opened *the eyes* of the figure which stood before me. "Here then, at least," I shrieked aloud, "can I never – can I never be mistaken – these are the full, and the black, and the wild eyes – of my lost love – of the lady – of the LADY LIGEIA."

——波涛汹涌般难以平静。面前站着的这个人果真是重生的罗维娜吗？真的是罗维娜——特瑞缅因那位金发碧眼的罗维娜·特瑞梵依小姐吗？为何，为何要怀疑呢？绷带不是紧紧地围绕在唇边——这难道不是特瑞缅因那位活灵活现的小姐的嘴巴？还有脸颊——不是红扑扑的，与青春年少的她相同吗？——对，这就是活灵活现的特瑞缅因那位小姐的美丽面孔。还有下颌，两个酒窝，与健康的她一模一样，难道会不是她的？——可反过来说，难不成生病之后，身材能变高？此种想法一闪现，我简直是抓狂！一下冲到她面前！她往后一退以免别人碰到她，却任凭裹在头上的那阴森恐怖的寿衾掉落。随即那一头浓密蓬松的长发便松散开，在气息中洋洋洒洒：与深夜中乌鸦的翅膀相比还要黑呢！此时我面前的人慢慢地睁开了双眼。我厉声叫道："啊，至少我绝对不会——绝对不会弄错的——这对圆圆的，乌黑的，迷惑的双眼——是我已故妻子的——是小姐的——是丽姬娅小姐的。"

6. The Fall of the House of Usher

六. 厄舍府的倒塌

Son coeur est un luth suspendu;
Sitôt qu'on le touche il résonne.

          – De Béranger

他的心像只悬挂的琴；
轻轻弹奏便铮铮声响。

      ——贝朗瑞[1]

DURING the whole of a dull, dark, and soundless day in the autumn of the year, when the clouds hung oppressively low in the heavens, I had been passing alone, on horseback, through a singularly dreary tract of country; and at length found myself, as the shades of the evening drew on, within view of the melancholy House of Usher. I know not how it was – but, with the first glimpse of the building, a sense of insufferable gloom pervaded my spirit. I say insufferable; for the feeling was unrelieved by any of that half-pleasurable, because poetic, sentiment, with which the mind usually receives even the sternest natural images of the desolate or terrible. I looked upon the scene before me – upon the mere house, and the simple landscape features of the domain – upon the bleak walls – upon the vacant eye-like windows – upon a few rank sedges – and upon a few

一年秋天，一个阴暗低沉、寂静的日子，乌云低低地压下来，沉沉地笼罩着大地。一整天时间，我独自骑着马，在乡间一片荒芜凄凉的旷野中奔驰。暮色来临之时，使人哀伤的厄舍府终于出现在眼前。我搞不懂是什么原因，一看见那个府邸心里便充斥着无法忍受的悲伤。要说不能忍受，是因为在通常情况下即使身处蛮夷之所或恐怖境地，碰到极其严酷的自然景象，总不免生出几分诗意，甚至能产生一种喜悦感。可现在呢，这种哀伤之情却难以磨灭。我愁绪百回地看着面前的景象，那孤单的府邸和庄园中一成不变的山水景色，破旧的垣墙、像空洞的双眼般的窗户、三五枝臭气熏天的芦苇和几株苍白的枯树干——我的心中简直无比惆怅，哀愁得已经不能用世俗的情感来比喻，只有用身染阿芙蓉癖瘾者梦回

[1] 贝朗瑞：（1780~1857）法国歌谣诗人。他各个阶段的诗歌始终贯穿着各族人名团结的主题。

white trunks of decayed trees – with an utter depression of soul which I can compare to no earthly sensation more properly than to the after-dream of the reveller upon opium – the bitter lapse into everyday life – the hideous dropping off of the veil. There was an iciness, a sinking, a sickening of the heart – an unredeemed dreariness of thought which no goading of the imagination could torture into aught of the sublime. What was it – I paused to think – what was it that so unnerved me in the contemplation of the House of Usher? It was a mystery all insoluble; nor could I grapple with the shadowy fancies that crowded upon me as I pondered. I was forced to fall back upon the unsatisfactory conclusion, that while, beyond doubt, there *are* combinations of very simple natural objects which have the power of thus affecting us, still the analysis of this power lies among considerations beyond our depth. It was possible, I reflected, that a mere different arrangement of the particulars of the scene, of the details of the picture, would be sufficient to modify, or perhaps to annihilate its capacity for sorrowful impression; and, acting upon this idea, I reined my horse to the precipitous brink of a black and lurid tarn that lay in unruffled lustre by the dwelling, and gazed down – but with a shudder even more thrilling than before – upon the remodelled

未来的意境相比，才算恰当——痛苦沦为平常之事，丑陋的面纱也被除去。我的心却始终翻涌不止，凄凉地沉下去，简直是无法救赎，即使再去刺激人的想象，也不会认为这是心灵的升华。究竟是怎么回事？我思索起来。原因究竟何在，致使我在观望厄舍府时情绪竟会这般难以自控？这是个难以破解的谜团。沉思的过程中迷离的幻想涌上心头，却又无法捉摸。没有办法我退而求其次，自编自话好了——普通的自然景物拼凑起来，的确拥有控制人情绪的能量，但要分析出此种感染力，即使绞尽脑汁也是无计可施。我思索着，其实眼前景色中一草一木，一山一水的布置只需在微小之处稍加改动，可能就会将那种给人带来哀伤的情况得以缓解，也许完全消失。此种想法一萌生，我已经策马来到山中小湖的险岸边。这个小湖就依着府邸，湖面上映出暗光，但并无一丝涟漪，黑沉沉，阴暗暗，倒映出那扭曲的灰色芦苇、苍白树干、空洞双眼般的窗户。我俯视湖面，全身发抖，比方才的感觉还要诧异。

and inverted images of the gray sedge, and the ghastly tree-stems, and the vacant and eye-like windows.

Nevertheless, in this mansion of gloom I now proposed to myself a sojourn of some weeks. Its proprietor, Roderick Usher, had been one of my boon companions in boyhood; but many years had elapsed since our last meeting. A letter, however, had lately reached me in a distant part of the country – a letter from him – which, in its wildly importunate nature, had admitted of no other than a personal reply. The MS. gave evidence of nervous agitation. The writer spoke of acute bodily illness – of a mental disorder which oppressed him – and of an earnest desire to see me, as his best, and indeed his only personal friend, with a view of attempting, by the cheerfulness of my society, some alleviation of his malady. It was the manner in which all this, and much more, was said – it was the apparent heart that went with his request – which allowed me no room for hesitation; and I accordingly obeyed forthwith what I still considered a very singular summons.

Although, as boys, we had been even intimate associates, yet I really knew little of my friend. His reserve had been always excessive and habitual. I was aware, however, that his very ancient family had been noted, time out of mind, for a peculiar sensibility of temperament, displaying

可我现在仍然准备在这阴暗的府邸中停留几周。这座府邸的主人罗德里克·厄舍是我童年时代的好伙伴。我们很久未曾谋面了。但是最近，我却收到了他写来的一封信，是从这个国家一个非常遥远的地方寄来的，信中表现得十分迫切，力邀我亲自前往。在他这封亲笔信中，明显流露出一种寝食难安的意味。他提及自己得了重病——一种让他备受折磨的精神错乱，而且还说，确实很想看看我这个最好的朋友、唯一的知己，倘若可以愉悦地和我过上几天，病情可以得到缓解，等等。整封信就这样叙述了很多。他的请求明显出自真挚情意，使人都不能犹豫片刻。于是我立刻应邀前往了。虽然来了，但我却仍然觉得他的邀请有些蹊跷。

虽然我们是孩童时期的挚友，但我对这位朋友简直是了解很少。他习惯于有所保留，这已成为他的常态了。但是我十分了解，很久以前他的祖先便是以多愁善感而著名的。这么长时间以来，这种特征往往通过高贵的艺术品展露无疑，现

itself, through Long ages, in many works of exalted art, and manifested, of late, in repeated deeds of munificent yet unobtrusive charity, as well as in a passionate devotion to the intricacies, perhaps even more than to the orthodox and easily recognisable beauties, of musical science. I had learned, too, the very remarkable fact, that the stem of the Usher race, all time-honored as it was, had put forth, at no period, any enduring branch; in other words, that the entire family lay in the direct line of descent, and had always, with very trifling and very temporary variation, so lain. It was this deficiency, I considered, while running over in thought the perfect keeping of the character of the premises with the accredited character of the people, and while speculating upon the possible influence which the one, in the Long lapse of centuries, might have exercised upon the other – it was this deficiency, perhaps, of collateral issue, and the consequent undeviating transmission, from sire to son, of the patrimony with the name, which had, at length, so identified the two as to merge the original title of the estate in the quaint and equivocal appellation of the "House of Usher" – an appellation which seemed to include, in the minds of the peasantry who used it, both the family and the family mansion.

在则体现为举办了一次又一次慷慨而低调的慈善活动。他崇尚音乐的精巧复杂，而并非热衷那种众人公认的、一听即懂的优美。其实我还了解一件绝不普通的事实，那就是虽然厄舍家族历来备受推崇，但却从未产生出不衰败的旁系子孙，也就是说，除了极其微小、偶然迸发的特例之外，这个家族几乎一脉单传，始终如此。头脑中思考着这座府邸的特征和人们公认的厄舍家族的性格特点非常相匹配，思索着长久以来，府邸的特征很可能影响着厄舍家族的性格，我由此断定，或可能恰恰是由于缺少旁系亲戚，造成财富和姓氏总是代代相传，世世沿袭，才最终导致财产和姓氏合二为一，府邸的名字慢慢被遗忘，一个古怪而模糊的名字——"厄舍府"油然而生。农民全用这个称谓，因为在他们心中，貌似这个名字既涵盖了这个家族也包含了这座府邸。

I have said that the sole effect of my somewhat childish experiment – that of looking down within the tarn – had been to deepen the first singular impression. There can be no doubt that the consciousness of the rapid increase of my superstition – for why should I not so term it? – served mainly to accelerate the increase itself. Such, I have Long known, is the paradoxical law of all sentiments having terror as a basis. And it might have been for this reason only, that, when I again uplifted my eyes to the house itself, from its image in the pool, there grew in my mind a strange fancy – a fancy so ridiculous, indeed, that I but mention it to show the vivid force of the sensations which oppressed me. I had so worked upon my imagination as really to believe that about the whole mansion and domain there hung an atmosphere peculiar to themselves and their immediate vicinity – an atmosphere which had no affinity with the air of heaven, but which had reeked up from the decayed trees, and the gray wall, and the silent tarn – a pestilent and mystic vapor, dull, sluggish, faintly discernible, and leaden-hued.

Shaking off from my spirit what *must* have been a dream, I scanned more narrowly the real aspect of the building. Its principal feature seemed to be that of an excessive antiquity. The discoloration of

我上文提及，俯视湖水这一稍显稚嫩的行为，只会造成原本那种古怪的哀伤变本加厉。毫无疑问，那种迅速扩散开来的迷信感——为何不将它称为迷信呢？——只能越发浓重。我早就清楚，只有心中乱加猜测，才会感觉可怕。这是个荒诞的定律。或许就是因为这个原因，当我停止凝视水中的倒影转而抬眼观望府邸时，心里便产生了古怪的幻想。这种幻想是如此荒诞，的确，我说起它就是要解释蹂躏人的那丝丝情绪拥有多么巨大的能量。我就这样胡乱思索着，竟然确信某种气息弥散在整座府邸和整个庄园之中，甚至使得周围的一切都感染了这种气息。此种气息与空气大相径庭，那是从枯木、灰墙和死水中飘散出来的，阴暗、呆滞、灰突突的，难以辨认，像瘟疫般不可言喻。

我抛却心里那些只能称得上是所谓梦境的想法，更认真地观察着这座府邸的本来外观。似乎它的特征主要集中在年代久远，岁月沧桑使它退却了光鲜的色泽。墙上遍布

ages had been great. Minute fungi overspread the whole exterior, hanging in a fine tangled web-work from the eaves. Yet all this was apart from any extraordinary dilapidation. No portion of the masonry had fallen; and there appeared to be a wild inconsistency between its still perfect adaptation of parts, and the crumbling condition of the individual stones. In this there was much that reminded me of the specious totality of old wood-work which has rotted for Long years in some neglected vault, with no disturbance from the breath of the external air. Beyond this indication of extensive decay, however, the fabric gave little token of instability. Perhaps the eye of a scrutinizing observer might have discovered a barely perceptible fissure, which, extending from the roof of the building in front, made its way down the wall in a zigzag direction, until it became lost in the sullen waters of the tarn.

Noticing these things, I rode over a short causeway to the house. A servant in waiting took my horse, and I entered the Gothic archway of the hall. A valet, of stealthy step, thence conducted me, in silence, through many dark and intricate passages in my progress to the *studio* of his master. Much that I encountered on the way contributed, I know not how, to heighten the vague sentiments of which I have already spoken. While the objects

着微小的真菌，在屋檐下倒挂着，乱糟糟的，就像蜘蛛网一样。但是也无法找到破损得极其严重的地方，没有一堵墙是坍塌的。所有部分都协调一致，规格整齐，但有几块石头碎裂了，看上去极其不和谐。这些倒令我不禁想到地窖里那些无人问津的旧木制品，长久以来它们无法吹到外面的一丝风，看似完好无损，实则已经败絮其中了。但厄舍府除了外观的衰颓，整个府邸看来并无摇摇欲坠的迹象。倘若认真端详，就能发现一条细微的裂缝，开始于正屋顶上，弯弯曲曲沿墙向下，一直消失在浑浑噩噩的湖水中。

　　一边观察着这里的一切，我一边沿着一条不长的甬道，策马到了府邸门口。一位仆人接过了缰绳。我便迈步穿过哥特式的大厅拱门，被一个轻手轻脚的男仆悄无声息地带领着穿过那一道又一道昏暗弯曲的走廊，来到主人的起居室。不知为何，沿途的景物，竟致使我上文提及的那种模糊的哀愁更加剧烈。周围的一切东西——天花板上的雕刻、墙壁上的黑色幔帐、漆黑的地

around me – while the carvings of the ceilings, the sombre tapestries of the walls, the ebon blackness of the floors, and the phantasmagoric armorial trophies which rattled as I strode, were but matters to which, or to such as which, I had been accustomed from my infancy – while I hesitated not to acknowledge how familiar was all this – I still wondered to find how unfamiliar were the fancies which ordinary images were stirring up. On one of the staircases, I met the physician of the family. His countenance, I thought, wore a mingled expression of low cunning and perplexity. He accosted me with trepidation and passed on. The valet now threw open a door and ushered me into the presence of his master.

The room in which I found myself was very large and lofty. The windows were Long, narrow, and pointed, and at so vast a distance from the black oaken floor as to be altogether inaccessible from within. Feeble gleams of encrimsoned light made their way through the trellissed panes, and served to render sufficiently distinct the more prominent objects around; the eye, however, struggled in vain to reach the remoter angles of the chamber, or the recesses of the vaulted and fretted ceiling. Dark draperies hung upon the walls. The general furniture was profuse, comfortless, antique, and tattered. Many books and

板以及随着步伐走动而发出幻境一样"咔嗒咔嗒"声响的纹章甲胄——童年时代的我就习惯了。我必须承认，这一切都很熟悉，但我依旧很诧异，如此平常的东西，为何使我产生了那么生疏的幻想！我在一座楼梯上碰到了他家医生。他面呈刁钻与疑惑的表情，哆嗦着与我搭讪几句，便溜开了。突然男仆打开了门，带我来到他家主人面前。

我感觉这间房非常高，也很宽敞。狭长的窗子向上高耸，距离乌黑的橡木地板有些远，伸手根本碰不到。穿过玻璃格子几丝微弱的红光照射进来，映得四周比较明显的物体通体清晰。但房间远角那雕花拱顶的凹陷处，却无论如何也照射不到。深色的幔帐挂在墙上。虽然有不少家具，但几乎都不舒服，而且还都破旧过时。一些书籍和乐器散落在房间中，但并没使房间平添几分生气。我所感受到的只是忧伤的气息。周围的一切都笼罩在一种低沉幽怨的感觉和难以救赎的压抑之气。

musical instruments lay scattered about, but failed to give any vitality to the scene. I felt that I breathed an atmosphere of sorrow. An air of stern, deep, and irredeemable gloom hung over and pervaded all.

Upon my entrance, Usher arose from a sofa on which he had been lying at full length, and greeted me with a vivacious warmth which had much in it, I at first thought, of an overdone cordiality – of the constrained effort of the *ennuyé*; man of the world. A glance, however, at his countenance, convinced me of his perfect sincerity. We sat down; and for some moments, while he spoke not, I gazed upon him with a feeling half of pity, half of awe. Surely, man had never before so terribly altered, in so brief a period, as had Roderick Usher! It was with difficulty that I could bring myself to admit the identity of the wan being before me with the companion of my early boyhood. Yet the character of his face had been at all times remarkable. A cadaverousness of complexion; an eye large, liquid, and luminous beyond comparison; lips somewhat thin and very pallid, but of a surpassingly beautiful curve; a nose of a delicate Hebrew model, but with a breadth of nostril unusual in similar formations; a finely moulded chin, speaking, in its want of prominence, of a want of moral energy;

厄舍直直地在沙发上躺着，见我到来便立即起身，满怀热情地欢迎我。最初我倒认为有点过度热烈了，觉得这就是该厌世者的做作行为，可当我瞥了一眼他的脸庞，就断定他是一片真心。我们坐下来，一段时间里他没有讲一句话。我凝视着他，又同情又敬畏。我相信没有一个人在如此短的时间内会像罗德里克·厄舍这样变化这么大。我费了好大力气才判断出面前的此人就是我童年时期的朋友。但他的脸部特点始终是绝不普通。他面色惨白；眼睛大而清澈，出奇的透明；嘴唇薄且颜色偏暗，可那轮廓简直异常美丽；精巧的希伯来式鼻子，鼻孔出奇的大；下颌轮廓很好，但缺少活力，难以吸引人；头发又软又少，像蛛网一样稀疏；如此的五官，再加之太阳穴上面那颇为饱满的天庭，这样的容貌简直令人无法遗忘。容貌上的明显特点，脸上通常显现的表情，即便是微妙的夸张表情，都会表现得大有变化。虽然现在我与厄舍身处一屋，我却有一种对面不相识的感觉。面前这惨白恐怖的肤色，尤其是他那对极其明

hair of a more than web-like softness and tenuity; these features, with an inordinate expansion above the regions of the temple, made up altogether a countenance not easily to be forgotten. And now in the mere exaggeration of the prevailing character of these features, and of the expression they were wont to convey, lay so much of change that I doubted to whom I spoke. The now ghastly pallor of the skin, and the now miraculous lustre of the eye, above all things startled and even awed me. The silken hair, too, had been suffered to grow all unheeded, and as, in its wild gossamer texture, it floated rather than fell about the face, I could not, even with effort, connect its Arabesque expression with any idea of simple humanity.

In the manner of my friend I was at once struck with an incoherence – an inconsistency; and I soon found this to arise from a series of feeble and futile struggles · to overcome an habitual trepidancy – an excessive nervous agitation. For something of this nature I had indeed been prepared, no less by his letter, than by reminiscences of certain boyish traits, and by conclusions deduced from his peculiar physical conformation and temperament. His action was alternately vivacious and sullen. His voice varied rapidly from a tremulous indecision (when the animal spirits seemed utterly in

亮甚至使我惊奇的双眼，几乎把我吓到。几年间，那丝绸般顺滑、蛛丝般乱杂的头发变长了，与其说披散在头上，还不如用洋洋洒洒更恰当。不管我如何尽力，也不能从这种古怪的神情中，发现正常人的影子。

一开始我就发现我的朋友不能连续动作，而且动作一点都不协调。不久我又察觉出，他的神经竟如此紧张——他习惯性痉挛，却一直竭力克制着，最终只落得疲惫不堪，徒劳无功。说实话，我对他的这一特点早已做好了思想准备：一来由于我读了他的信；二来是我还依稀清楚他年轻时的一些禀性；再次是从他特殊的健康状况和精神表现中也能略知一二。他时而神情抖擞，时而又郁郁寡欢；他的声音前一时听起来还优柔寡断，颤颤巍巍（此时听起来则毫无生气），后一时马上就铿锵有力。那僵硬、笨重、空虚、

abeyance) to that species of energetic concision – that abrupt, weighty, unhurried, and hollow-sounding enunciation – that leaden, self-balanced and perfectly modulated guttural utterance, which may be observed in the lost drunkard, or the irreclaimable eater of opium, during the periods of his most intense excitement.

It was thus that he spoke of the object of my visit, of his earnest desire to see me, and of the solace he expected me to afford him. He entered, at some length, into what he conceived to be the nature of his malady. It was, he said, a constitutional and a family evil, and one for which he despaired to find a remedy – a mere nervous affection, he immediately added, which would undoubtedly soon pass off. It displayed itself in a host of unnatural sensations. Some of these, as he detailed them, interested and bewildered me; although, perhaps, the terms, and the general manner of the narration had their weight. He suffered much from a morbid acuteness of the senses; the most insipid food was alone endurable; he could wear only garments of certain texture; the odors of all flowers were oppressive; his eyes were tortured by even a faint light; and there were but peculiar sounds, and these from stringed instruments, which did not inspire him with horror.

To an anomalous species of terror I

不急不慢的言语，沉重、冷静、游刃有余的发音，只能从沉迷于酒精的醉汉或不可救药的烟鬼口中听到。在烟酒剧烈的刺激下，他们就是如此讲话的。

他接着讲邀我到此的目的，并说他是如何真心真意地期待着我，盼着我能给他带来慰藉。他甚至非常详细地解释他自觉生了什么疾病。他认为是一种先天性疾病，家族遗传所致，他已彻底绝望，不愿再接受治疗了。随即他又说，这不过是神经方面的小病灶，用不多时一定就可根治。这类疾病的症状，通过他那诸多的异常表现就能察觉到。他原原本本全部讲给我听。虽然他的语言和讲话方式可能有些分量，可一些语句我听了之后还是感觉既有兴趣又疑惑。神经过敏使他备受折磨。只能吃索然无味的饭菜；也只能穿特殊材质做的衣服；所有的花香都无法招架；即使是微弱的光线也会刺伤双眼；唯独特殊的声音——弦乐，才不会使他恐惧。

能够发现，异常的恐怖之情已

found him a bounden slave. "I shall perish," said he, "I must perish in this deplorable folly. Thus, thus, and not otherwise, shall I be lost. I dread the events of the future, not in themselves, but in their results. I shudder at the thought of any, even the most trivial, incident, which may operate upon this intolerable agitation of soul. I have, indeed, no abhorrence of danger, except in its absolute effect – in terror. In this unnerved – in this pitiable condition – I feel that the period will sooner or later arrive when I must abandon life and reason together, in some struggle with the grim phantasm, FEAR."

I learned, moreover, at intervals, and through broken and equivocal hints, another singular feature of his mental condition. He was enchained by certain superstitious impressions in regard to the dwelling which he tenanted, and whence, for many years, he had never ventured forth – in regard to an influence whose supposititious force was conveyed in terms too shadowy here to be re-stated – an influence which some peculiarities in the mere form and substance of his family mansion, had, by dint of Long sufferance, he said, obtained over his spirit – an effect which the *physique* of the gray walls and turrets, and of the dim tarn into which they all looked down, had, at length, brought about upon the *morale* of his existence.

把他死死捆住。"我要死了，"他说，"我是必将因这可怕的蠢病而死。是的，一定会如此死去，别无选择。我对即将发生的所有事极其害怕，所担心的并非事情本身，而是它的后果。只要想到要发生什么事，即使极其微弱也会使我寝食难安，不能忍受，还会哆哆嗦嗦。说实话，我并不痛恨危险，除非置身在它那绝对恐怖的影响中。在这种寝食难安的情境下——在那令人怜悯的环境中，我感觉这样的时刻早晚都要来临，届时我会在恐怖的幻想中失去生命和理智的。"

除此之外，我还不断从他那间断且含糊其辞的暗示中，觉察到他精神方面其他奇怪之处。他不能摆脱长久以来不敢擅离住宅的这种唯心的观点。他说长时间忍受他那府邸外观和实质上的特征，极大地影响着他的心灵。他不能摆脱这种影响。灰墙和塔楼的模样以及倒映出灰墙和塔楼那浑浑噩噩的湖水，都影响着他的神经健康。在想象这种影响的强大力量时，他用词极其模糊，我简直无法陈述出来。

He admitted, however, although with hesitation, that much of the peculiar gloom which thus afflicted him could be traced to a more natural and far more palpable origin – to the severe and Long-continued illness – indeed to the evidently approaching dissolution – of a tenderly beloved sister – his sole companion for Long years – his last and only relative on earth. "Her decease," he said, with a bitterness which I can never forget, "would leave him (him the hopeless and the frail) the last of the ancient race of the Ushers." While he spoke, the lady Madeline (for so was she called) passed slowly through a remote portion of the apartment, and, without having noticed my presence, disappeared. I regarded her with an utter astonishment not unmingled with dread – and yet I found it impossible to account for such feelings. A sensation of stupor oppressed me, as my eyes followed her retreating steps. When a door, at length, closed upon her, my glance sought instinctively and eagerly the countenance of the brother – but he had buried his face in his hands, and I could only perceive that a far more than ordinary wanness had overspread the emaciated fingers through which trickled many passionate tears.

The disease of the lady Madeline had Long baffled the skill of her physicians. A settled apathy, a gradual wasting away of

虽然一直犹豫，但他最终坦陈，追溯起来，这般蹂躏他的那独特的忧郁，很大程度上源于一个更自然且更显而易见的原因，即他疼爱的妹妹始终身染重病——说实话她不久就快要死了。一直以来，妹妹是他唯一的伴侣，是他在这世间仅存的唯一亲人。"倘使她死去，"他说，痛苦的声音让我永生难忘，"厄舍家族只剩一个了无生趣的软弱之人了。"玛德琳小姐（别人都如此称呼她）在他说话时分，远远地从房间走过，步伐不紧不慢，根本没留意到我。一眨眼便幽幽地消失了。我看着她心里不由一惊，其中还夹杂着害怕的意味。我觉得根本无法讲清其中的原因。我的目光追随着她远去的身影，一时间心中无比恍惚。最终房门在她身后关闭了，我本能地急忙转身去看她哥哥的表情，可他已用双手遮住脸庞，唯独能看见那瘦削的十指比普通时候还要惨白，泪水从指缝间滚滚流下。

玛德琳小姐的医生早已对她的疾病无计可施了。她表现出很多不同寻常的症候：与生俱来的冷淡，

the person, and frequent although transient affections of a partially cataleptical character, were the unusual diagnosis. Hitherto she had steadily borne up against the pressure of her malady, and had not betaken herself finally to bed; but, on the closing in of the evening of my arrival at the house, she succumbed (as her brother told me at night with inexpressible agitation) to the prostrating power of the destroyer; and I learned that the glimpse I had obtained of her person would thus probably be the last I should obtain – that the lady, at least while living, would be seen by me no more.

For several days ensuing, her name was unmentioned by either Usher or myself: and during this period I was busied in earnest endeavors to alleviate the melancholy of my friend. We painted and read together; or I listened, as if in a dream, to the wild improvisations of his speaking guitar. And thus, as a closer and still closer intimacy admitted me more unreservedly into the recesses of his spirit, the more bitterly did I perceive the futility of all attempt at cheering a mind from which darkness, as if an inherent positive quality, poured forth upon all objects of the moral and physical universe, in one unceasing radiation of gloom.

I shall ever bear about me a memory of the many solemn hours I thus spent alone

身体日渐衰弱，短暂且频繁发作的类痫症已经造成身体局部僵硬。但她始终与疾病顽强抗争，并未纠缠于病榻。可就是我来他家的那个夜晚，她却向死神那百般摧残的力量俯首称臣。她哥哥在午夜时分通知我这一噩耗，他那凄凉之情简直无法形容。我这才发现那恍惚间的一瞥，竟是诀别。我永远无法看到活着的玛德琳小姐了。

随后的几天，我和厄舍都闭口不谈及她的姓名。那几天中，我一腔真诚，竭尽全力想缓解朋友的悲伤。我们一起画画，一起读书，或者听他即兴演奏如怨如诉的六弦琴，恍惚置身梦境。我们就这样更加亲密了。但亲密之余，我对他内心世界的解读也就日益透彻，也就更痛苦地理解到，一切要换得他愉悦的努力都将是徒劳。他心里的忧伤仿佛天性使然，不停地散发出来，笼罩着整个世界，精神层面和物质层面都是一片惨淡。

我与厄舍府的主人共同度过了许多单独相处的庄重时刻，这将构

with the master of the House of Usher. Yet I should fail in any attempt to convey an idea of the exact character of the studies, or of the occupations, in which he involved me, or led me the way. An excited and highly distempered ideality threw a sulphureous lustre over all. His Long improvised dirges will ring forever in my ears. Among other things, I hold painfully in mind a certain singular perversion and amplification of "the wild air of the last waltz of Von Weber". From the paintings over which his elaborate fancy brooded, and which grew, touch by touch, into vaguenesses at which I shuddered the more thrillingly, because I shuddered knowing not why; – from these paintings (vivid as their images now are before me) I would in vain endeavor to educe more than a small portion which should lie within the compass of merely written words. By the utter simplicity, by the nakedness of his designs, he arrested and overawed attention. If ever mortal painted an idea, that mortal was Roderick Usher. For me at least – in the circumstances then surrounding me – there arose out of the pure abstractions which the hypochondriac contrived to throw upon his canvass, an intensity of intolerable awe, no shadow of which felt I ever yet in the contemplation of the certainly glowing yet too concrete reveries of Fuseli.

成我永久的回忆。但若要我说出他使我沉迷其中不能自拔，或者说他究竟带领我研读了什么，我还当真说不出个究竟来。活跃而异常紊乱的情绪，将所有东西都笼罩了一层硫黄般的淡淡色彩。他即兴演奏的长篇幅的挽歌始终回响在耳边。除了其他曲调，我痛苦地记得，他对那首激昂的《冯·韦伯最后的华尔兹》演奏得古怪且夸张。他靠着那精致的构思，创作出一幅幅画面，他一笔一笔地画，图案慢慢模糊不清，使我全身颤抖，却还弄不清楚什么原因致使我发抖且更加恐怖。这些画面至今仍然栩栩如生、历历在目，但我根本无法用语言形象地描绘出来。他创作的画构图非常朴素，素装容颜，这才是所谓天然去雕饰，引人注目且令人震撼。如果世间还有人的画富有真情，这人肯定是罗德里克·厄舍。至少于我来讲——在当时的环境下——看到这位忧郁症患者企图在画布上创作出浑然一体的抽象概念，心中就会产生浓浓的畏惧，使人不能忍受。而凝视福塞利那色彩强烈但情境具体的画面时，我却从未有过丝毫恐惧。

One of the phantasmagoric conceptions of my friend, partaking not so rigidly of the spirit of abstraction, may be shadowed forth, although feebly, in words. A small picture presented the interior of an immensely Long and rectangular vault or tunnel, with low walls, smooth, white, and without interruption or device. Certain accessory points of the design served well to convey the idea that this excavation lay at an exceeding depth below the surface of the earth. No outlet was observed in any portion of its vast extent, and no torch, or other artificial source of light was discernible; yet a flood of intense rays rolled throughout, and bathed the whole in a ghastly and inappropriate splendor.

I have just spoken of that morbid condition of the auditory nerve which rendered all music intolerable to the sufferer, with the exception of certain effects of stringed instruments. It was, perhaps, the narrow limits to which he thus confined himself upon the guitar, which gave birth, in great measure, to the fantastic character of his performances. But the fervid *facility* of his impromptus could not be so accounted for. They must have been, and were, in the notes, as well as in the words of his wild fantasias (for he not unfrequently accompanied himself with rhymed verbal improvisations), the result of that intense mental collectedness and

在我朋友那幻想般的观念中，倒是有一个比较具体，或许能够诉诸于文字表达，虽然解释得可能并不恰当。这幅画尺寸并不大，所画的内容是内景，也许是地窖，或者是隧道，形状是矩形，无限地延展着。雪白的墙壁矮矮的，比较光滑，没有什么图案，也没有脱落的迹象。画中的装饰陪衬揭示出，该洞穴深深地潜入地下，尽管非常宽敞，却根本看不见出口，也没有发现火把或其他人工光源，但强烈的光芒却如波涛般汹涌、四处翻滚，整张画就笼罩在一种极不恰当的恐怖光彩中。

上文我已提及他的听觉和神经方面都有疾病，除了一些弦乐之声，其他所有音乐都无法忍受。也许正是由于这个原因造成他只弹六弦琴，故而才能弹得如此空虚古怪。可是他那些慷慨激昂的即兴曲并不可归于其中。最初我曾婉转揭示，唯独在充斥着做作的极度亢奋状态下，他的精神才会无比镇定，全情投入。那些狂想曲的曲调和歌词（他经常是一边弹奏，一边即兴地押韵伴唱）必定是，也确实是他处于精神无比安定、全神贯注的状态下的杰作。我不费任何气力就能铭记住其中一首狂想曲的歌词。或许是由于他一直演唱，便撩拨了我的心弦，

concentration to which I have previously alluded as observable only in particular moments of the highest artificial excitement. The words of one of these rhapsodies I have easily remembered. I was, perhaps, the more forcibly impressed with it, as he gave it, because, in the under or mystic current of its meaning, I fancied that I perceived, and for the first time, a full consciousness on the part of Usher, of the tottering of his lofty reason upon her throne. The verses, which were entitled "The Haunted Palace", ran very nearly, if not accurately, thus:

I.

In the greenest of our valleys,
By good angels tenanted,
Once a fair and stately palace –
Radiant palace – reared its head.
In the monarch Thought's dominion –
It stood there!
Never seraph spread a pinion
Over fabric half so fair.

II.

Banners yellow, glorious, golden,
On its roof did float and flow;
(This – all this – was in the olden
Time Long ago)
And every gentle air that dallied,
In that sweet day,
ALong the ramparts plumed and pallid,
A winged odor went away.

所以深刻在心中。我从狂想曲那蕴藏的含义中，第一次体察出厄舍的心境——他完全知道，他那种高傲的理性，已经摇摇欲坠，朝不保夕了。那首名为《闹鬼的宫殿》的狂想曲，全诗内容大体如下：

I

茵茵绿意的山谷，
散步着瑰丽天使的房间，
一座无比富丽的宫殿——
流光溢彩，直插苍穹。
思想统治万物的国度里，
宫殿威严高耸。
六翼天使的翅膀，
未曾拂过这么不凡的殿堂。

II

金黄的旗帜光彩夺目，
于殿堂顶端席卷飘舞；
（所有的东西都是过往云烟，
随时光消逝）
彼时年华美好，
随风拂动。
红砖绿瓦容颜老，
幽幽芬芳飘然去。

III.

Wanderers in that happy valley
Through two luminous windows saw
Spirits moving musically
To a lute's well-tunéd law,
Round about a throne, where sitting
(Porphyrogene!)
In state his glory well befitting,
The ruler of the realm was seen.

IV.

And all with pearl and ruby glowing
Was the fair palace door,
Through which came flowing, flowing,
flowing,
And sparkling evermore,
A troop of Echoes whose sweet duty
Was but to sing,
In voices of surpassing beauty,
The wit and wisdom of their king.

V.

But evil things, in robes of sorrow,
Assailed the monarch's high estate;
(Ah, let us mourn, for never morrow
Shall dawn upon him, desolate!)
And, round about his home, the glory
That blushed and bloomed
Is but a dim-remembered story
Of the old time entombed.

VI.

And travellers now within that valley,
Through the red-litten windows, see
Vast forms that move fantastically
To a discordant melody;

III

游荡在愉悦之谷
穿透两扇明净的窗，
仙女轻歌飞舞，
琴声悠扬。
她们围绕王座盘旋
思想的君主光芒万丈，
想端坐在云上，
尽显帝王荣光。

IV

散落的珍珠和红宝石，
照得富丽殿堂那大门熠熠生光
回声仙女成群过往，
妩媚天下无双，
络绎不绝越过大门。
她们只有一个任务，
就是尽情高歌。
用风情万种的歌声，
赞美君主的聪慧。

V

然而邪恶披着一件长衫
夹带着哀伤，
侵占君主的至尊宝地；
（呜呼！我们哀悼国王凄惨地走向
死亡！）
昨天皇室风光无限，
却日渐成为遥远的神话，
随风飘逝。

VI

现在游客走入山谷，
透过血红的窗户，
看到阴森鬼魅
伴着刺耳的旋律荒诞般舞动。

While, like a rapid ghastly river,
Through the pale door,
A hideous throng rush out forever,
And laugh – but smile no more.

I well remember that suggestions arising from this ballad, led us into a train of thought wherein there became manifest an opinion of Usher's which I mention not so much on account of its novelty, (for other men have thought thus,) as on account of the pertinacity with which he maintained it. This opinion, in its general form, was that of the sentience of all vegetable things. But, in his disordered fancy, the idea had assumed a more daring character, and trespassed, under certain conditions, upon the kingdom of inorganization. I lack words to express the full extent, or the earnest *abandon* of his persuasion. The belief, however, was connected (as I have previously hinted) with the gray stones of the home of his forefathers. The conditions of the sentience had been here, he imagined, fulfilled in the method of collocation of these stones – in the order of their arrangement, as well as in that of the many *fungi* which overspread them, and of the decayed trees which stood around – above all, in the Long undisturbed endurance of this arrangement, and in its reduplication in the still waters of the tarn. Its evidence – the evidence of the sentience

恐怖的魔鬼
快速穿过苍白的殿堂大门，
步履急匆匆，无休无止，
表情僵硬，狂笑阵阵。

　　我清晰地记得，这支狂想曲隐含的意义使我们思考了很多。随着思考，厄舍的想法也就显而易见了。我提及他的想法，并不是由于其别出心裁——他人也有同样的想法，而是由于厄舍对其固执坚持。通常来讲此种想法认为万物皆具灵性。但在厄舍那混乱的古怪思维中，此想法就变得特别离奇不堪了。在特定情形下，他竟主张即使无机世界的物质也具灵性。他对这一点深信不疑、忠贞不渝。我的笔墨真是不足以描写出他的此种想法。但就像我上文所提示的，他的此种信念与他那祖传的灰色石头房子颇有关联。在他的头脑中，这些石头的组合及排列、分布在石头上的真菌、屹立在周遭的枯树——特别是那些即使经年累月也不曾改变的布局以及那死一般沉寂的湖水中的倒影都蕴涵着灵性。他评论道，湖水和石墙散发的气息从四周慢慢会聚起来，我们从中就能发现灵性的踪迹。他如此一分析把我吓得不轻。他随即又说，这无处不在的灵性造成的结局是有目共睹的，它就孕育在那悄无声息却又缠绵不绝的恐怖影响力中。长久以来，始终掌控着他家

– was to be seen, he said, (and I here started as he spoke,) in the gradual yet certain condensation of an atmosphere of their own about the waters and the walls. The result was discoverable, he added, in that silent, yet importunate and terrible influence which for centuries had moulded the destinies of his family, and which made *him* what I now saw him – what he was. Such opinions need no comment, and I will make none.

Our books – the books which, for years, had formed no small portion of the mental existence of the invalid – were, as might be supposed, in strict keeping with this character of phantasm. We pored together over such works as the "Ververt et Chartreuse" of Gresset; the "Belphegor" of Machiavelli; the "Heaven and Hell" of Swedenborg; the "Subterranean Voyage of Nicholas Klimm" by Holberg; the Chiromancy of Robert Flud, of Jean *D'Indaginé* and of De la Chambre; the "Journey into the Blue Distance of Tieck"; and the "City of the Sun of Campanella". One favorite volume was a small octavo edition of the "Directorium Inquisitorium", by the Dominican Eymeric de Gironne; and there were passages in Pomponius Mela, about the old African Satyrs and Œgipans, over which Usher would sit dreaming for hours. His chief delight, however, was found in the perusal of an

族的命运，同样又把他害成眼下这种德行。我对此种观点无须做任何评论，也不会妄加评论。

可以想象出我们读的书也和这种幻想完全吻合。长时间以来，此种书籍对病人的精神状态造成了很大的影响。我们共同认真阅读过的书有：格里塞的《绿鸟与修道院》，马基雅维利的《魔王》，斯威登堡的《天堂与地狱》，霍尔堡的《尼古拉·克里姆的地下之行》，罗伯特·弗拉德、让·丹达涅和德·拉·尚布尔合著的《手相术》，蒂克的《忧郁的旅程》，康帕内拉的《太阳城》，等等。我们比较热衷于一本名为《宗教法庭手册》的书，是 8 开小本装册，是多明我会的传教士艾梅里克·德·盖朗尼写著的。《庞波尼斯·梅拉》中提及了很多有关远古非洲的森林之神和牧羊之神的内容，往往能令厄舍长时间如梦如痴地呆坐着。不过他最喜欢的是那本弥足珍贵的 4 开本大小黑体古籍——有关一座被人遗忘的教堂的书籍——《美因茨教会合唱经本中追

exceedingly rare and curious book in quarto Gothic – the manual of a forgotten church – the *Vigiliae Mortuorum secundum Chorum Ecclesiae Maguntinae.*

I could not help thinking of the wild ritual of this work, and of its probable influence upon the hypochondriac, when, one evening, having informed me abruptly that the lady Madeline was no more, he stated his intention of preserving her corpse for a fortnight, (previously to its final interment,) in one of the numerous vaults within the main walls of the building. The worldly reason, however, assigned for this singular proceeding, was one which I did not feel at liberty to dispute. The brother had been led to his resolution (so he told me) by consideration of the unusual character of the malady of the deceased, of certain obtrusive and eager inquiries on the part of her medical men, and of the remote and exposed situation of the burial-ground of the family. I will not deny that when I called to mind the sinister countenance of the person whom I met upon the staircase, on the day of my arrival at the house, I had no desire to oppose what I regarded as at best but a harmless, and by no means an unnatural, precaution.

At the request of Usher, I personally aided him in the arrangements for the temporary entombment. The body having

思已亡占礼前夕经》。

就在那夜，厄舍突然通知我玛德琳小姐去世的消息，并说准备在下葬前将他妹妹的遗体存放在府邸主楼的地窖中，放置14天。听他如此安排，我不由得回忆起那本奇书里有类似的狂放举动以及它对这位抑郁症病人造成的可能影响。不过，他选择这么古怪的方式，肯定有他自身世俗的原因，我对此不能随便怀疑。他对我讲，只要想起去世的妹妹那不同一般的病症，想起医生那鲁莽又殷勤的询问，又想到祖坟遥远，况且那周围又都凄厉无比，所以他就如此打定了主意。我不能否认，回忆起初到厄舍家的那天，在楼梯上相遇的那人的险恶嘴脸，也就支持他的想法了。照我来看，这么做无论如何也不会伤到谁，而且再怎样也不算是有违常理。

受厄舍之邀，我亲自帮他临时安排的后事料理。尸体已经装殓，由我俩抬着前往安置它的地窖（地

been encoffined, we two alone bore it to its rest. The vault in which we placed it (and which had been so Long unopened that our torches, half smothered in its oppressive atmosphere, gave us little opportunity for investigation) was small, damp, and entirely without means of admission for light; lying, at great depth, immediately beneath that portion of the building in which was my own sleeping apartment. It had been used, apparently, in remote feudal times, for the worst purposes of a donjon-keep, and, in later days, as a place of deposit for powder, or some other highly combustible substance, as a portion of its floor, and the whole interior of a Long archway through which we reached it, were carefully sheathed with copper. The door, of massive iron, had been, also, similarly protected. Its immense weight caused an unusually sharp grating sound, as it moved upon its hinges.

Having deposited our mournful burden upon tressels within this region of horror, we partially turned aside the yet unscrewed lid of the coffin, and looked upon the face of the tenant. A striking similitude between the brother and sister now first arrested my attention; and Usher, divining, perhaps, my thoughts, murmured out some few words from which I learned that the deceased and himself had been twins, and that sympathies of a scarcely intelligible nature

窖很长时间都没有打开过，几乎令人无法呼吸，使我们没有机会仔细观察一下）。安置棺材的墓穴又小又湿，几乎难以透过一丝微弱的光线。它地处深深的地下，其上的房间部分恰恰便是我卧室之所。很明显，地窖是在远古的封建时代建造的最差用所，是用来作死牢而存在的。现今，就用来储存火药或一些易燃品，这是由于部分地板和通往外部的那条狭长走廊的四壁，全部包覆着黄铜。那扇沉重的铁门，也有同样的保护作用。开门关门时，沉重的铁门上的铰链便发出极其刺耳的嘎吱嘎吱声。

我们将令人哀伤的灵柩放在恐怖的地窖中，有稍微挪开那还未钉上的棺盖，不过瞻仰遗容时我头一次发现，他们兄妹二人的容貌真是几乎完全相同。可能厄舍看出了我的想法，低声嘟囔了几句，我这才知道，原来他和死者是孪生兄妹，两人本性中有着不可思议的相同之处，那是一种由于知晓，故而仁慈的惺惺相惜。由于心里恐惧，我们的眼光不敢长时间停留于遗体上。

had always existed between them. Our glances, however, rested not Long upon the dead – for we could not regard her unawed. The disease which had thus entombed the lady in the maturity of youth, had left, as usual in all maladies of a strictly cataleptical character, the mockery of a faint blush upon the bosom and the face, and that suspiciously lingering smile upon the lip which is so terrible in death. We replaced and screwed down the lid, and, having secured the door of iron, made our way, with toil, into the scarcely less gloomy apartments of the upper portion of the house.

And now, some days of bitter grief having elapsed, an observable change came over the features of the mental disorder of my friend. His ordinary manner had vanished. His ordinary occupations were neglected or forgotten. He roamed from chamber to chamber with hurried, unequal, and objectless step. The pallor of his countenance had assumed, if possible, a more ghastly hue – but the luminousness of his eye had utterly gone out. The once occasional huskiness of his tone was heard no more; and a tremulous quaver, as if of extreme terror, habitually characterized his utterance. There were times, indeed, when I thought his unceasingly agitated mind was laboring with some oppressive secret, to divulge which he struggled for the

她正值青春年少，疾病却掠去了她的性命，与所有身染严重病痛的人无异，她的胸口和脸庞仿佛还泛着一层薄薄的红晕，唇上显现出一抹恐怖的笑容，那微笑在死者的脸庞上凝固住，让人非常害怕。我们重新盖好棺盖，钉紧后关闭铁门，带着沉重的心情回到上面那间比地窖也好不了多少的房间。

伤心欲绝地度过了些时日，我朋友那精神错乱的毛病出现了显而易见的改变。正常的行为消失了。日常所做之事也被遗忘或忽略得一干二净。他毫无目标地从一间屋子踱步到另一间屋子，步伐急促混乱。如果最初苍白的面容还能被描绘的话，现在简直可谓是面无血色。不过双眼的光芒当真是完全消失了。再也听不到他那偶尔沙哑的声音了。他的声音变得发抖，就像极其惊悚一般。这已变成他讲话的习惯特点。有时我确实认为，他心里之所以始终焦躁不安的原因是内心里隐藏着某些使人抑郁的秘密，而他必须努力攒足力气，才能够有勇气将秘密一吐为快。我有时又只能将这所有一切仅仅看成是一种难以理

necessary courage. At times, again, I was obliged to resolve all into the mere inexplicable vagaries of madness, for I beheld him gazing upon vacancy for Long hours, in an attitude of the profoundest attention, as if listening to some imaginary sound. It was no wonder that his condition terrified – that it infected me. I felt creeping upon me, by slow yet certain degrees, the wild influences of his own fantastic yet impressive superstitions.

It was, especially, upon retiring to bed late in the night of the seventh or eighth day after the placing of the lady Madeline within the donjon, that I experienced the full power of such feelings. Sleep came not near my couch – while the hours waned and waned away. I struggled to reason off the nervousness which had dominion over me. I endeavored to believe that much, if not all of what I felt, was due to the bewildering influence of the gloomy furniture of the room – of the dark and tattered draperies, which, tortured into motion by the breath of a rising tempest, swayed fitfully to and fro upon the walls, and rustled uneasily about the decorations of the bed. But my efforts were fruitless. An irrepressible tremor gradually pervaded my frame; and, at length, there sat upon my very heart an incubus of utterly causeless alarm. Shaking this off with a gasp and a struggle, I uplifted myself upon the

解的妄想症，由于我亲眼看着他长期苦苦地向着空虚凝视，好像在倾听某种虚无缥缈的声音。毫不奇怪，他的状况把我吓着了但也感染了我。我发觉他身上这种荒诞不经而又有感召力的迷信气息，拥有强烈的感染力，这种力量正慢慢地一点一滴地进入我的内心。

我在玛德琳小姐的尸体安放在主楼地窖中的第七或第八天深夜，有着极其特殊的经历。当时我翻来覆去难以入睡，时间渐渐流逝。我紧张得几乎不能控制自己，只得极力缓解。我努力要自己确信，倘使不都是由于房间里那迷人心智的阴暗家具、破旧黑幔，也多半由于此种原因。那时，马上爆发的疾风骤雨吹得黑幔不停晃动，时而在墙壁上随风飘扬，飒飒地轻拍着床上的装饰物。可我的努力几乎是徒劳，无法压抑的战栗慢慢传遍周身，心头终于出现了恐怖得无法名状的噩梦。我大口喘着气，奋力甩开它。我起身靠在枕头上，认真观察着极其黑暗的房间，我侧耳倾听，却又不知为什么要这么做，除非天性使然。我细细听着某个低沉而模糊的声响，每当很长的间隔，当暴风雨停顿之时，声音便会响起。我无法确认它出自何方。强烈的恐惧之情

pillows, and, peering earnestly within the intense darkness of the chamber, harkened – I know not why, except that an instinctive spirit prompted me – to certain low and indefinite sounds which came, through the pauses of the storm, at Long intervals, I knew not whence. Overpowered by an intense sentiment of horror, unaccountable yet unendurable, I threw on my clothes with haste (for I felt that I should sleep no more during the night), and endeavored to arouse myself from the pitiable condition into which I had fallen, by pacing rapidly to and fro through the apartment.

I had taken but few turns in this manner, when a light step on an adjoining staircase arrested my attention. I presently recognised it as that of Usher. In an instant afterward he rapped, with a gentle touch, at my door, and entered, bearing a lamp. His countenance was, as usual, cadaverously wan – but, moreover, there was a species of mad hilarity in his eyes – an evidently restrained *hysteria* in his whole demeanor. His air appalled me – but anything was preferable to the solitude which I had so Long endured, and I even welcomed his presence as a relief.

"And you have not seen it?" he said abruptly, after having stared about him for some moments in silence – "you have not then seen it? – but, stay! you shall." Thus speaking, and having carefully shaded his

铺天盖地压过来，莫名其妙也难以忍受（由于我认为当夜我无法再入睡）。我赶忙穿好衣服，急匆匆在房间里来回踱步，竭尽全力企图把自己从所陷的可怜境地中解救出来。

我就这样刚转了几圈，临近楼梯上一阵轻微的脚步声引起了我的注意。不过不大一会儿我便辨认出那是厄舍的脚步声。随即他便轻轻叩了叩我的房门，进来时手里托着一盏灯。他的脸色仍然是死尸般惨白，眼睛里倒是显现出一种狂喜之情。显而易见，在他那整体举止中夹杂着压抑的歇斯底里。他的模样让我十分诧异。由于孤独的长夜非常难挨，所以其余所有我都视之为更优越。甚至我十分欢迎他的到来，将其视为一种慰藉。

"你没有发现吗？"他沉默地向周围看了一会儿后忽然开口说道，"难道你还没发觉？不，等等！你能够看见的。"说着，他便小心地遮好灯，信步来到一扇窗户跟前，

lamp, he hurried to one of the casements, and threw it freely open to the storm.

The impetuous fury of the entering gust nearly lifted us from our feet. It was, indeed, a tempestuous yet sternly beautiful night, and one wildly singular in its terror and its beauty. A whirlwind had apparently collected its force in our vicinity; for there were frequent and violent alterations in the direction of the wind; and the exceeding density of the clouds (which hung so low as to press upon the turrets of the house) did not prevent our perceiving the life-like velocity with which they flew careering from all points against each other, without passing away into the distance. I say that even their exceeding density did not prevent our perceiving this – yet we had no glimpse of the moon or stars – nor was there any flashing forth of the lightning. But the under surfaces of the huge masses of agitated vapor, as well as all terrestrial objects immediately around us, were glowing in the unnatural light of a faintly luminous and distinctly visible gaseous exhalation which hung about and enshrouded the mansion.

"You must not – you shall not behold this!" said I, shudderingly, to Usher, as I led him, with a gentle violence, from the window to a seat. "These appearances, which bewilder you, are merely electrical phenomena not uncommon – or it may be

忽然打开窗子。外面一片狂风骤雨。

一阵飓风凶猛袭来，仿佛要把我们吹倒。即使那个夜晚出现了狂风骤雨，但也的确是异常瑰丽，是个惊悚和美好纠缠在一起的奇妙之夜。很明显旋风就在我们附近大发威力，这是由于风向频繁且剧烈改变。乌云密布（乌云低垂好像向着府邸的塔楼压下来）但却不能阻挡我们观看云朵栩栩如生地急速浮动，从四方会聚而来，横冲直撞，但并不飘远。我是想阐明浓密的乌云并未遮蔽我们的双眼。但我们并没有看到月亮和星星，也没发现任何闪电划破夜空。可巨大的厄舍府邸外面却雾气缭绕，仿佛世间的一切都围绕在我们周围。那奇特的雾气发出微弱的光芒，但又十分清楚，致使大团的乌云下面，还有府邸周围的一切物体，都笼罩着这种光泽。

"你不能看——你也不应该看这情景！"我颤抖着和厄舍讲话，并稍稍用力将他从窗口拉回到座位上，"这些迷惑你的景象，只是普通的光电现象罢了——要不就是湖中弥漫的瘴气所致。关上窗户吧，空

that they have their ghastly origin in the rank miasma of the tarn. Let us close this casement; – the air is chilling and dangerous to your frame. Here is one of your favorite romances. I will read, and you shall listen; – and so we will pass away this terrible night together."

The antique volume which I had taken up was the "Mad Trist" of Sir Launcelot Canning; but I had called it a favorite of Usher's more in sad jest than in earnest; for, in truth, there is little in its uncouth and unimaginative prolixity which could have had interest for the lofty and spiritual ideality of my friend. It was, however, the only book immediately at hand; and I indulged a vague hope that the excitement which now agitated the hypochondriac, might find relief (for the history of mental disorder is full of similar anomalies) even in the extremeness of the folly which I should read. Could I have judged, indeed, by the wild overstrained air of vivacity with which he harkened, or apparently harkened, to the words of the tale, I might well have congratulated myself upon the success of my design.

I had arrived at that well-known portion of the story where Ethelred, the hero of the Trist, having sought in vain for peaceable admission into the dwelling of the hermit, proceeds to make good an entrance by force. Here, it will be remembered, the

气寒冷，对你的健康不利。这里有一部你喜爱的传奇，我读给你听，我们共同度过这个恐怖的夜晚吧。"

我拿起的这本古书，是兰斯劳特·坎宁爵士所著的《疯狂盛典》，但我称之为厄舍家族酷爱的一本书并非实话，不过是苦中作乐的说法罢了。说实话，我这朋友高傲至极、想象力丰富，而这部书语言粗糙、情节拖沓且缺乏幻想，是不容易勾起他的兴趣来的。但它是此时手里唯一的一本书，况且我还心怀侥幸，盼望时下这个兴奋过度的抑郁症患者，能在我所读的这绝顶荒诞的情节中寻找缓解（因为精神紊乱的病史中充斥着很多同类状况）。倘使我确实能凭借他那紧张过度、狂躁过度的模样，来判断他是否当真在听抑或假装聆听，那我就能够祝贺自己的方案成功了。

我已经念到故事最著名的那段了，盛典中的勇士埃塞尔雷德企图平和地进入隐士的居所，却终是徒劳，于是他依靠武力，强行闯了进去。记得这里的情节是这么叙述的：

words of the narrative run thus:

"And Ethelred, who was by nature of a doughty heart, and who was now mighty withal, on account of the powerfulness of the wine which he had drunken, waited no Longer to hold parley with the hermit, who, in sooth, was of an obstinate and maliceful turn, but, feeling the rain upon his shoulders, and fearing the rising of the tempest, uplifted his mace outright, and, with blows, made quickly room in the plankings of the door for his gauntleted hand; and now pulling therewith sturdily, he so cracked, and ripped, and tore all asunder, that the noise of the dry and hollow-sounding wood alarummed and reverberated throughout the forest."

At the termination of this sentence I started, and for a moment, paused; for it appeared to me (although I at once concluded that my excited fancy had deceived me) – it appeared to me that, from some very remote portion of the mansion, there came, indistinctly, to my ears, what might have been, in its exact similarity of character, the echo (but a stifled and dull one certainly) of the very cracking and ripping sound which Sir Launcelot had so particularly described. It was, beyond doubt, the coincidence alone which had arrested my attention; for, amid the rattling of the sashes of the casements, and the ordinary commingled noises of the

"埃塞尔雷德秉性凶猛刚烈，此外刚又喝过酒，凭借酒力，便不打算与隐士多费口舌。其实那隐士也生性顽固，心地狠毒。可埃塞尔雷德发觉肩膀上滴了几滴雨水，担心暴风雨来临，于是马上举起铁锤，向大门狠狠打击，不大一会儿厚厚的门板就被击出一个洞。他用戴着铁护手的手伸进去，用力一拽，"啪啦"一声，门应声而裂，随即被扯得粉碎。干枯且中空的木板的破碎之声，回荡于整个森林，使人惊慌失措。"

我读完这句话便大吃一惊，只得停下来。这是由于我貌似听见了（虽然我立刻笃定这是由于我过于激动以致幻觉蒙蔽了我）——我好像听到从府邸远角传来了模糊的回声，那回声与兰斯劳特爵士着重描写的噼啪破裂之声简直完全相同，但肯定比它低沉且压抑。毫无疑问，这种凑巧之事引起了我的注意。其实在窗扉那"噼啪噼啪"的声音下，以及混合着嘈杂之音而且更加剧烈的暴风雨中，这个声音的确不足为奇，它既不能引起我的关注，也不会搞得我意乱神迷。我继续读故事：

still increasing storm, the sound, in itself, had nothing, surely, which should have interested or disturbed me. I continued the story:

"But the good champion Ethelred, now entering within the door, was sore enraged and amazed to perceive no signal of the maliceful hermit; but, in the stead thereof, a dragon of a scaly and prodigious demeanor, and of a fiery tongue, which sate in guard before a palace of gold, with a floor of silver; and upon the wall there hung a shield of shining brass with this legend enwritten –

Who entereth herein, a conqueror hath bin;
Who slayeth the dragon, the shield he shall win.

And Ethelred uplifted his mace, and struck upon the head of the dragon, which fell before him, and gave up his pesty breath, with a shriek so horrid and harsh, and withal so piercing, that Ethelred had fain to close his ears with his hands against the dreadful noise of it, the like whereof was never before heard."

Here again I paused abruptly, and now with a feeling of wild amazement – for there could be no doubt whatever that, in this instance, I did actually hear (although from what direction it proceeded I found it impossible to say) a low and apparently

"勇敢的斗士埃塞尔雷德冲进门去，可没有发现那个令人厌恶的隐士的身影，不禁怒火中烧，独自惊叹。但却发现一条巨龙，全身鳞片，口吐火舌，驻守在一座黄金殿堂前面。白银铺设了大殿的地面，一个闪闪发亮的黄铜盾牌挂在墙上，其上刻着传奇之语——

征服者进此门
屠龙者得此盾

"埃塞尔雷德抡起铁锤，猛击龙头，龙头应声落地，在他面前滚落在地，厉声尖叫并射出一股毒气，那尖叫简直是凄惨无比且痛彻心扉，使得埃塞尔雷德必须用双手掩耳来抵御那闻所未闻的恐怖声音。"

我在这里又停下了，心里十分奇怪——毫无疑问，因为此时我的确听见了一个微弱，貌似很遥远，但却十分刺耳，拖得很长，听得出那是不同寻常的尖叫或摩擦声（尽管我不能判断出声音出自哪个方

distant, but harsh, protracted, and most unusual screaming or grating sound – the exact counterpart of what my fancy had already conjured up for the dragon's unnatural shriek as described by the romancer.

Oppressed, as I certainly was, upon the occurrence of this second and most extraordinary coincidence, by a thousand conflicting sensations, in which wonder and extreme terror were predominant, I still retained sufficient presence of mind to avoid exciting, by any observation, the sensitive nervousness of my companion. I was by no means certain that he had noticed the sounds in question; although, assuredly, a strange alteration had, during the last few minutes, taken place in his demeanor. From a position fronting my own, he had gradually brought round his chair, so as to sit with his face to the door of the chamber; and thus I could but partially perceive his features, although I saw that his lips trembled as if he were murmuring inaudibly. His head had dropped upon his breast – yet I knew that he was not asleep, from the wide and rigid opening of the eye as I caught a glance of it in profile. The motion of his body, too, was at variance with this idea – for he rocked from side to side with a gentle yet constant and uniform sway. Having rapidly taken notice of all this, I resumed the narrative of

向）。读了这位传奇作家的描绘，脑海中已经想象出巨龙那不自然的尖叫。如今耳畔传来的声音竟然和它惊人的相似。

第二次发生这么不同寻常的凑巧之事，我的心情确实像翻江倒海般互相冲击，其中最突出的要算是诧异和极度惊悚了。但我的头脑仍旧保持足够的镇定来避免我那神经敏感的朋友发觉任何问题而受到冲击。虽然过去的几分钟，他的行为的确已经发生了稀奇变化，不过我并不能断定他是不是已经留意到这些响动。他最初与我面对而坐，但此事他慢慢地转过椅子，现在面对房门。所以我只能观察到他的部分表情。他的嘴唇的确在瑟瑟发抖，仿佛无声地叨咕着什么。他的头垂到胸口。但我清楚他并没睡着，这是由于我从他的侧面瞟了一眼，发现他的眼睛呆呆的，大大地瞪着。他的身体也证明了他没有睡着。因为他始终轻轻地左摇右晃。我快速看了一下周围的一切，开始重新读兰斯劳特爵士的那篇文章，故事进展如下：

Sir Launcelot, which thus proceeded:

"And now, the champion, having escaped from the terrible fury of the dragon, bethinking himself of the brazen shield, and of the breaking up of the enchantment which was upon it, removed the carcass from out of the way before him, and approached valorously over the silver pavement of the castle to where the shield was upon the wall; which in sooth tarried not for his full coming, but fell down at his feet upon the silver floor, with a mighty great and terrible ringing sound."

No sooner had these syllables passed my lips, than – as if a shield of brass had indeed, at the moment, fallen heavily upon a floor of silver – I became aware of a distinct, hollow, metallic, and clangorous, yet apparently muffled reverberation. Completely unnerved, I leaped to my feet; but the measured rocking movement of Usher was undisturbed. I rushed to the chair in which he sat. His eyes were bent fixedly before him, and throughout his whole countenance there reigned a stony rigidity. But, as I placed my hand upon his shoulder, there came a strong shudder over his whole person; a sickly smile quivered about his lips; and I saw that he spoke in a low, hurried, and gibbering murmur, as if unconscious of my presence. Bending closely over him, I at length drank in the hideous import of his words.

"现在，斗士逃离了巨龙恐怖的暴怒，接着想到了黄铜盾牌，企图除去施加在盾牌上的魔咒。搬开横于面前的龙尸，他勇敢地通过城堡那白银地面，向着挂盾牌的墙壁走去。还未等到他完全靠近，盾牌就掉落在他脚边的白银地板上，发出恐怖的巨响。"

这些音节从我口中吐出的一瞬间，好像黄铜盾牌真的重重砸在白银地板上，我感觉到有一阵清楚且空虚，还带有明显属于金属般的沉闷叮当声响在耳畔回荡。我吓得惊魂失措，跳起身来，不过厄舍始终左摇右晃。我冲向他坐的椅子前面，见他两眼紧紧凝视自己面前，整张脸无比僵硬。然而当我将手放于他的肩头时，他竟全身剧烈战栗开来，瑟瑟发抖的嘴唇上浮出一丝惨淡的笑容。我发觉他用低沉而急促的声音嘟囔着，貌似并没意识到我的存在。我俯身靠近他，最终了解了他话语的恐怖意味。

"Not hear it? – yes, I hear it, and *have heard it*. Long – Long – Long – many minutes, many hours, many days, have I heard it – yet I dared not – oh, pity me, miserable wretch that I am! – I dared not – I *dared* not speak! We *have put her living in the tomb*! Said I not that my senses were acute? I now tell you that I heard her first feeble movements in the hollow coffin. I heard them – many, many days ago – yet I dared not – *I dared not speak!* And now – to-night – Ethelred – ha! ha! – the breaking of the hermit's door, and the death-cry of the dragon, and the clangor of the shield! – say, rather, the rending of her coffin, and the grating of the iron hinges of her prison, and her struggles within the coppered archway of the vault! Oh whither shall I fly? Will she not be here anon? Is she not hurrying to upbraid me for my haste? Have I not heard her footstep on the stair? Do I not distinguish that heavy and horrible beating of her heart? Madman!" – here he sprang furiously to his feet, and shrieked out his syllables, as if in the effort he were giving up his soul – "*Madman! I tell you that she now stands without the door!* "

As if in the superhuman energy of his utterance there had been found the potency of a spell – the huge antique pannels to which the speaker pointed, threw slowly back, upon the instant, their ponderous and ebony jaws. It was the work of the rushing gust – but then without those doors there did stand the lofty and enshrouded figure of the lady Madeline of Usher. There was

"没有听到吗？但我听到了，早就听见了。很久——很久——很久——几分钟前，几小时前，几天前我就听见了。不过我不敢——哦，怜悯怜悯我吧，我是个多么不幸的值得同情的人啊——我不敢——我不敢说。她被我们活埋啦！我不是提及我的感觉灵敏吗？那么我讲给你听，我听到她最初在空荡的棺材里发出微弱的响动。我听见了——恰在几天前——但我不敢——我没有胆量说出来。但此时——就在今夜——埃塞尔雷德——哈！哈！——隐士的门断裂了，巨龙死前如泣如诉地哀号，盾牌发出的铿锵声！——其实就是她那棺材的破碎之声，是牢狱里那铁栅栏上铰链的摩擦声，是她在墓穴的黄铜拱门里的搏斗声！啊，我究竟应该逃往哪个方向呢？难不成她不会立刻出现？难不成她没有急忙追我而来并指责我的草率？难不成我没有听出她上楼的脚步声？我没有听清她那低沉且恐怖的心跳声吗？疯子！"说着，他突然跳着起身，丧失心智地尖声大喊叫道，"疯子！告诉你，她此刻就站在门外！"

他用非人的语调尖叫着，好像有一种咒语的力量。刹那间，他指向的那扇古朴沉重的巨大黑檀木门，竟慢慢打开了。这是一阵狂风的杰作——但门外的确站着厄舍府那个身材高挑而且身上还裹着寿衣的玛德琳小姐。她那白色的袍子上沾满鲜血，憔悴的全身到处是奋力争斗的迹象。她在门槛那儿始终发

blood upon her white robes, and the evidence of some bitter struggle upon every portion of her emaciated frame. For a moment she remained trembling and reeling to and fro upon the threshold – then, with a low moaning cry, fell heavily inward upon the person of her brother, and in her violent and now final death-agonies, bore him to the floor a corpse, and a victim to the terrors he had anticipated.

From that chamber, and from that mansion, I fled aghast. The storm was still abroad in all its wrath as I found myself crossing the old causeway. Suddenly there shot aLong the path a wild light, and I turned to see whence a gleam so unusual could have issued; for the vast house and its shadows were alone behind me. The radiance was that of the full, setting, and blood-red moon, which now shone vividly through that once barely-discernible fissure, of which I have before spoken as extending from the roof of the building, in a zigzag direction, to the base. While I gazed, this fissure rapidly widened – there came a fierce breath of the whirlwind – the entire orb of the satellite burst at once upon my sight – my brain reeled as I saw the mighty walls rushing asunder – there was a Long tumultuous shouting sound like the voice of a thousand waters – and the deep and dank tarn at my feet closed sullenly and silently over the fragments of the "House of Usher."

抖，左摇右晃。接着低声呻吟，然后重重地向屋里的哥哥身上压去。这临终前剧烈而沉重的一击，将她哥哥扑倒在地，变成尸体。如他所料般被吓死了。

我从那个房间出来便逃出了厄舍府，我感觉心惊肉跳，外面仍旧风雨交加，我发现自己已经踏上那条破败的甬道。沿小路方向突然射来了一道猛烈的光芒，我转头企图找出这道如此特殊的光线到底出自哪里，因为后面除了那座巨大的府邸及其影子，再无其他东西。那光线原来出自一轮正在下落的血红色的满月，它低沉地挂在天边，映得那条难以发现的裂缝非常鲜明。我在前文提及那条裂缝，正是那条出自正屋顶、弯弯曲曲延伸到墙根的裂缝。就在我观望的时候，那裂缝急速变宽，旋风在疯狂地呼啸着，但那血红的满月，瞬间来到面前。我头晕目眩，发现坚固的墙壁崩裂为碎片，一阵嘈杂的巨响久久不停，好似万丈波涛奔腾汹涌。我脚下那幽深阴冷的湖水无声地淹没了"厄舍府"的残垣断墙。

7. The Oval Portrait
七. 椭圆的画像

THE château into which my valet had ventured to make forcible entrance, rather than permit me, in my desperately wounded condition, to pass a night in the open air, was one of those piles of commingled gloom and grandeur which have so Long frowned among the Appennines, not less in fact than in the fancy of Mrs. Radcliffe. To all appearance it had been temporarily and very lately abandoned. We established ourselves in one of the smallest and least sumptuously furnished apartments. It lay in a remote turret of the building. Its decorations were rich, yet tattered and antique. Its walls were hung with tapestry and bedecked with manifold and multiform armorial trophies, together with an unusually great number of very spirited modern paintings in frames of rich golden arabesque. In these paintings, which depended from the walls not only in their main surfaces, but in very many nooks which the bizarre architecture of the château rendered necessary – in these paintings my incipient delirium, perhaps, had caused me to take deep interest; so that I bade Pedro to close the heavy shutters of the room – since it was already night – to

我身负重伤，贴身侍从为了让我不露宿野外，冒险闯入了那座城堡。亚平宁半岛上有很多类似的城堡。这些城堡都历史悠久，一派肃穆庄严。丝毫不亚于拉德克利夫夫人想象中的城堡。所有迹象表明，城堡的主人才离开没多久。我们找了一间最小也最为朴素的房间住下。这套房间位于城堡一处偏僻的塔楼里。屋里的各种装饰都很破旧。墙上挂着壁毯，装饰着很多各式各样的奖励军章，还有数不清的现代画，画被镶在有着精美花纹的金色画框里，而且每一幅都具有灵性。无论是主墙面，还是城堡这个奇异建筑特有的凹陷且隐蔽的墙面上，到处都挂满了画作。或许是我原本就有些精神敏感，因此我对这些画作的兴趣十分浓厚。我吩咐佩德鲁把厚重的百叶窗拉上——因为此时已经入夜，将插在我床头高架烛台上的蜡烛点燃，并把床边的黑色流苏丝绒帷幔完全拉开。我希望等一切都做好之后，即使我还无法入睡，但至少能不时抬眼看看墙上的画作，读读从枕旁找到的讲解评论这些作品的小册子。

light the tongues of a tall candelabrum which stood by the head of my bed – and to throw open far and wide the fringed curtains of black velvet which enveloped the bed itself. I wished all this done that I might resign myself, if not to sleep, at least alternately to the contemplation of these pictures, and the perusal of a small volume which had been found upon the pillow, and which purported to criticise and describe them.

Long – Long I read – and devoutly, devoutly I gazed. Rapidly and gloriously the hours flew by and the deep midnight came. The position of the candelabrum displeased me, and outreaching my hand with difficulty, rather than disturb my slumbering valet, I placed it so as to throw its rays more fully upon the book.

But the action produced an effect altogether unanticipated. The rays of the numerous candles (for there were many) now fell within a niche of the room which had hitherto been thrown into deep shade by one of the bed-posts. I thus saw in vivid light a picture all unnoticed before. It was the portrait of a young girl just ripening into womanhood. I glanced at the painting hurriedly, and then closed my eyes. Why I did this was not at first apparent even to my own perception. But while my lids remained thus shut, I ran over in my mind my reason for so shutting them. It was an

我虔诚地拿起那本小册子，久久难以放手。在我的沉醉其中时，时间已悄然流逝，转眼已到了午夜。我不太满意烛台摆的位置，又不想叫醒正在酣睡的随从，于是自己费力地伸出手挪了一下，让书本能照到更多光线。

这一举动的结果大大出乎人意料。几只蜡烛的烛光照在一个壁龛上——刚刚，它隐蔽在一根床柱的阴影里。在烛光的照射下，一幅先前完全没有注意到的画呈现在眼前——画像上是一名年轻女子，她有着刚刚成熟的女人韵味。我只匆匆瞥了一眼那幅肖像，便赶忙闭上眼睛。起初，我想不通自己怎么会做出如此反应。然而下一秒我就明白自己为何会这么做了。那只是一种冲动，为了能有足够的时间思考——确定自己所看到的并不是幻觉，停止自己的想象，从而能更冷

impulsive movement to gain time for thought – to make sure that my vision had not deceived me – to calm and subdue my fancy for a more sober and more certain gaze. In a very few moments I again looked fixedly at the painting.

That I now saw aright I could not and would not doubt; for the first flashing of the candles upon that canvas had seemed to dissipate the dreamy stupor which was stealing over my senses, and to startle me at once into waking life.

The portrait, I have already said, was that of a young girl. It was a mere head and shoulders, done in what is technically termed a *vignette* manner; much in the style of the favorite heads of Sully. The arms, the bosom, and even the ends of the radiant hair melted imperceptibly into the vague yet deep shadow which formed the back-ground of the whole. The frame was oval, richly gilded and filigreed in *Moresque*. As a thing of art nothing could be more admirable than the painting itself. But it could have been neither the execution of the work, nor the immortal beauty of the countenance, which had so suddenly and so vehemently moved me. Least of all, could it have been that my fancy, shaken from its half slumber, had mistaken the head for that of a living person. I saw at once that the peculiarities of the design, of the *vignetting*, and of the

静、更理性地看待它。不久，我把眼睛睁开，目光牢牢锁定在那幅画上。

这次我看清楚了。我必须承认这一点。当烛光照到画布上时，意识里充斥着的如梦般的恍惚，仿佛一下子被驱散了。我马上惊醒过来。

我已经说过，画上是一个年轻的姑娘。只画到头部和肩膀，运用了一种被称作"虚光画"的技法，画风很有萨利最擅长的头像画的味道。画中人的双臂、胸部甚至柔亮顺滑的发丝末梢，都被自然地虚化成朦胧柔和的阴影，作为整幅画的背景。画框是椭圆形的，外层镀了厚厚的一层金，以摩尔风格进行装饰。然而从艺术价值来看，最令人欣赏的地方还是这幅肖像本身。刚刚一瞬间给予我强烈震撼的，既不是画家的技法，也不是画中人永恒的美貌，更不可能是我半梦半醒迷茫状态下的想象力了——我竟然把画上的肖像当成一位活生生的少女。然而我立即明白了，整幅画的构图、虚光和装饰画框的特点，在一瞬间让我的臆想烟消云散，绝不容许我再有丝毫遐想和疑虑。我陷入沉思之中。大约整整一个钟头的

frame, must have instantly dispelled such idea – must have prevented even its momentary entertainment. Thinking earnestly upon these points, I remained, for an hour perhaps, half sitting, half reclining, with my vision riveted upon the portrait. At length, satisfied with the true secret of its effect, I fell back within the bed. I had found the spell of the picture in an absolute *life-likeliness* of expression, which, at first startling, finally confounded, subdued, and appalled me. With deep and reverent awe I replaced the candelabrum in its former position. The cause of my deep agitation being thus shut from view, I sought eagerly the volume which discussed the paintings and their histories. Turning to the number which designated the oval portrait, I there read the vague and quaint words which follow:

"She was a maiden of rarest beauty, and not more lovely than full of glee. And evil was the hour when she saw, and loved, and wedded the painter. He, passionate, studious, austere, and having already a bride in his Art: she a maiden of rarest beauty, and not more lovely than full of glee; all light and smiles, and frolicsome as the young fawn; loving and cherishing all things; hating only the Art which was her rival; dreading only the pallet and brushes and other untoward instruments which deprived her of the countenance of her

时间，我保持着半坐半倚的姿势，凝视着那幅肖像。直到最后，我弄清了那种神奇效果背后的秘密时，才心满意足地躺下。我发现了整幅画的秘密所在——画中人的表情被描画得栩栩如生。起初我非常震惊，紧接着是迷茫，被征服，最后则是一片骇然。因为从心理产生一种敬畏之情，所以我将烛台挪回原来的位置。那幅令我激动不已的画作在视野中消失了。我匆忙找到那本评述画作的讲解小册子，待翻到介绍椭圆形画像那一页时，我看到以下这段含糊且诡异的文字：

"她是一位世间少有的美丽姑娘，她生性开朗，活泼可爱无人能比。从她与画家一见钟情并成为他的新娘那刻起，不幸便降临到她身上。他对工作满怀激情、废寝忘食，他一向不苟言笑，而且，在他看来艺术就是他的新娘。她美丽绝伦，生性开朗，活泼可爱；她魅力四射，笑容如沐春风，嬉戏时像只欢快的小鹿；她充满爱心，爱惜世上万物。然而她却憎恨艺术，因为艺术是她的情敌；她讨厌调色板、画笔和其他画具，因为是它们将爱人的笑脸

lover. It was thus a terrible thing for this lady to hear the painter speak of his desire to portray even his young bride. But she was humble and obedient, and sat meekly for many weeks in the dark, high turret-chamber where the light dripped upon the pale canvas only from overhead. But he, the painter, took glory in his work, which went on from hour to hour, and from day to day. And he was a passionate, and wild, and moody man, who became lost in reveries; so that he *would* not see that the light which fell so ghastly in that lone turret withered the health and the spirits of his bride, who pined visibly to all but him. Yet she smiled on and still on, uncomplainingly, because she saw that the painter (who had high renown) took a fervid and burning pleasure in his task, and wrought day and night to depict her who so loved him, yet who grew daily more dispirited and weak. And in sooth some who beheld the portrait spoke of its resemblance in low words, as of a mighty marvel, and a proof not less of the power of the painter than of his deep love for her whom he depicted so surpassingly well. But at length, as the labor drew nearer to its conclusion, there were admitted none into the turret; for the painter had grown wild with the ardor of his work, and turned his eyes from canvas merely, even to regard the countenance of his wife. And he

夺走。所以，当画家说想为年轻的新娘画一幅肖像时，姑娘却认为这是件再可怕不过的事了。但她温婉乖巧，最终还是顺从地在塔楼里坐了几个星期。塔楼的房间高且阴暗，只有从头顶处照下来射在灰色画布上的一丝微弱光亮。可是他，那位画家，却沉浸在自己工作的光芒中，他画了一个钟头又一个钟头，画了一天又一天。他一向满腔激情、随心所欲、喜怒无常，加上此时又沉浸在幻想中难以自拔，因此他没有看出，孤冷的塔楼上那缕暗淡的微光早已让新娘失去了往日的光鲜。她的身心都变得枯萎。所有人都看出来她很憔悴，只有他没有注意到。尽管如此她始终保持微笑，静静地坐在那儿，没有任何怨言。因为她看到了画家（他很有名）从工作中得到极大的快乐，他不分昼夜地专注于画着深爱他的姑娘。然而她却日渐消瘦、日渐虚弱了。凡是见过画像的人无不低声赞叹画得如此传神、精妙绝伦，这样的画像简直就是奇迹，不仅说明画家的画功非凡，更体现出画家对画中人的爱之热切。然而当这幅画即将完成之时，他禁止任何人登上塔楼，因为此时他的激情已经近乎疯狂，他的眼睛几乎没从画布上离开过，自然也不关心妻子的容貌。他不会注意到，那些涂抹在画布上的色彩，本来源自坐在他身边的妻子的脸庞。几个

would not see that the tints which he spread upon the canvas were drawn from the cheeks of her who sat beside him. And when many weeks bad passed, and but little remained to do, save one brush upon the mouth and one tint upon the eye, the spirit of the lady again flickered up as the flame within the socket of the lamp. And then the brush was given, and then the tint was placed; and, for one moment, the painter stood entranced before the work which he had wrought; but in the next, while he yet gazed, he grew tremulous and very pallid, and aghast, and crying with a loud voice, 'This is indeed life itself!' turned suddenly to regard his beloved: – *She was dead*!"

星期过去了，整幅画还差唇上的一抹和眼睛的一层色彩。女子的双眼重新变得炯炯有神，仿佛烛孔里的最后一闪火苗。最后，唇上的一笔和眼睛的色彩都完成了。画家迷恋地驻足于自己的作品前，突然，就在他凝视画面的时候，他开始全身发抖，脸色惨白，呆若木鸡。接着，他大声惊呼道：'这就是生命！'但是当他瞥向自己心爱的妻子时，她已经死了！"

8. The Black Cat

八. 黑猫

FOR the most wild, yet most homely narrative which I am about to pen, I neither expect nor solicit belief. Mad indeed would I be to expect it, in a case where my very senses reject their own evidence. Yet, mad am I not – and very surely do I not dream. But to-morrow I die, and to-day I would unburthen my soul. My immediate purpose is to place before the world, plainly, succinctly, and without comment, a series of mere household events. In their consequences, these events have terrified – have tortured – have destroyed me. Yet I will not attempt to expound them. To me, they have presented little but Horror – to many they will seem less terrible than *barroques*. Hereafter, perhaps, some intellect may be found which will reduce my phantasm to the common-place – some intellect more calm, more logical, and far less excitable than my own, which will perceive, in the circumstances I detail with awe, nothing more than an ordinary succession of very natural causes and effects.

From my infancy I was noted for the docility and humanity of my disposition. My tenderness of heart was even so

我现在要讲的这个故事非常荒唐，但是又很普通，我并不奢望大家会相信，因为就连我自己都不相信这些事真的是亲身经历过的，若是再希望别人相信，那我岂不是疯了？不过我此刻并没有发疯，而且确定我很清醒。既然明天就是我的死期了，我不妨趁今天将这件事告诉大家，也好让灵魂能够安生。我很想将这些日常琐事原原本本，简单明了，不加任何修饰地公之于众。因为这些事的缘故，我日夜担惊受怕，尝尽了折磨，最终一生都毁在上面。尽管如此我不想做过多的解释。因为对我而言，这些事很恐怖，但对大多数人来讲，这只不过是怪谈罢了，没什么可怕之处。或许，以后还会有一些人将这种奇谈怪论当成一件普通小事。某些人的头脑比我冷静得多，条理也更加分明，不像我这样遇事便慌张。像我这样小心翼翼，详细叙述一件事情，在他们眼里或许就是一件理所应当的寻常事罢了。

我从小就心肠软，待人温顺。那时，我的性格常被小伙伴取笑。我非常喜欢动物，父母对我十分宠

conspicuous as to make me the jest of my companions. I was especially fond of animals, and was indulged by my parents with a great variety of pets. With these I spent most of my time, and never was so happy as when feeding and caressing them. This peculiarity of character grew with my growth, and in my manhood, I derived from it one of my principal sources of pleasure. To those who have cherished an affection for a faithful and sagacious dog, I need hardly be at the trouble of explaining the nature or the intensity of the gratification thus derivable. There is something in the unselfish and self-sacrificing love of a brute, which goes directly to the heart of him who has had frequent occasion to test the paltry friendship and gossamer fidelity of mere *Man*.

I married early, and was happy to find in my wife a disposition not uncongenial with my own. Observing my partiality for domestic pets, she lost no opportunity of procuring those of the most agreeable kind. We had birds, gold-fish, a fine dog, rabbits, a small monkey, and a *cat*.

This latter was a remarkably large and beautiful animal, entirely black, and sagacious to an astonishing degree. In speaking of his intelligence, my wife, who at heart was not a little tinctured with superstition, made frequent allusion to the

爱,给了我各种各样的小宠物。我大多数时间都花在这些小动物身上,每当我给它们喂食或抚弄它们的时候,我就发自心底地高兴。随着我渐渐长大,这样的性格也随之发展,直到我成人,这依然是我的主要消遣。有的人喜欢狗,因为它们忠实聪明,我想他们根本不需要浪费唇舌来解释其中的无限乐趣。如果你饱尝了人类的薄情寡义,那么你一定会对于动物那种无私的奉献之爱铭记于心。

我结婚很早,万幸的是妻子和我脾气秉性相投,她注意到我喜欢饲养家禽,于是只要见到中意的宠物就不会丢开手。我们养了小鸟、金鱼、纯种狗、小兔子、一只小猴还有一只猫。

这只猫个头很大,非常漂亮,毛乌黑柔亮,而且聪明伶俐。我妻子原本就有些迷信,每当提到这只猫的灵性,她就会说到古老传说,说黑猫其实是女巫的化身。我倒不是想说我妻子对于这件事的执拗,

ancient popular notion, which regarded all black cats as witches in disguise. Not that she was ever *serious* upon this point – and I mention the matter at all for no better reason than that it happens, just now, to be remembered.

Pluto – this was the cat's name – was my favorite pet and playmate. I alone fed him, and he attended me wherever I went about the house. It was even with difficulty that I could prevent him from following me through the streets.

Our friendship lasted, in this manner, for several years, during which my general temperament and character – through the instrumentality of the Fiend Intemperance – had (I blush to confess it) experienced a radical alteration for the worse. I grew, day by day, more moody, more irritable, more regardless of the feelings of others. I suffered myself to use intemperate language to my wife. At length, I even offered her personal violence. My pets, of course, were made to feel the change in my disposition. I not only neglected, but ill-used them. For Pluto, however, I still retained sufficient regard to restrain me from maltreating him, as I made no scruple of maltreating the rabbits, the monkey, or even the dog, when by accident, or through affection, they came in my way. But my disease grew upon me – for what disease is like Alcohol! – and at length even Pluto,

只是刚好想到在这里说一下而已。

这只猫叫普路托，本是我喜欢的宠物和玩伴。它由我亲自喂养，无论我走到屋子里什么地方，它都会跟过来。就连我上街时，它都要跟着，无论用什么办法也赶不走它。

就这样我与猫之间的友谊维持了好几年。在这几年里，说来有些惭愧，因为我染上了酒瘾，脾气秉性完全变了。我变得越来越喜怒无常，动不动就要脾气，完全不顾别人的感受。我后来居然用恶言秽语辱骂我的妻子，甚至对她拳脚相加。当然，我养的那些小动物也感受到了我的脾气变得暴躁。我非但不照顾它们，还虐待它们。无论是兔子、小猴，还是那只狗，当它们跑到我跟前来跟我亲热，或是无意遇到我时，我总会肆意凌虐它们。只有普路托，我还存有怜惜，不忍糟蹋。怎料我的病情每况愈下——世上没有比酗酒还要命的病了——这时的普路托已经老了，脾气也比以前偏了，于是我干脆将普路托也当成自己的出气筒。

who was now becoming old, and consequently somewhat peevish – even Pluto began to experience the effects of my ill temper.

One night, returning home, much intoxicated, from one of my haunts about town, I fancied that the cat avoided my presence. I seized him; when, in his fright at my violence, he inflicted a slight wound upon my hand with his teeth. The fury of a demon instantly possessed me. I knew myself no Longer. My original soul seemed, at once, to take its flight from my body and a more than fiendish malevolence, gin-nurtured, thrilled every fibre of my frame. I took from my waistcoat-pocket a pen-knife, opened it, grasped the poor beast by the throat, and deliberately cut one of its eyes from the socket! I blush, I burn, I shudder, while I pen the damnable atrocity.

When reason returned with the morning – when I had slept off the fumes of the night's debauch – I experienced a sentiment half of horror, half of remorse, for the crime of which I had been guilty; but it was, at best, a feeble and equivocal feeling, and the soul remained untouched. I again plunged into excess, and soon drowned in wine all memory of the deed.

In the meantime the cat slowly recovered. The socket of the lost eye presented, it is true, a frightful appearance,

一天晚上，我在城里一个经常光顾的酒吧喝完酒醉醺醺地回到家，我以为这只猫会避开我，于是一下子将它抓住，它看到我满脸凶相顿时吓坏了，不自觉地在我手上轻轻咬了一口，留下两个牙印。霎时，我像被恶魔附身一样暴怒。一时间我将所有一切都抛在脑后。原本那个善良温顺的灵魂被扔到了九霄云外，酒性发作，成了凶神恶煞，不知从身体哪儿冒出来一股狠劲。我从坎肩口袋里掏出一把小刀，打开刀子，一把掐住那只可怜生灵的喉咙，残忍地挖下它的眼珠！在写下自己的暴行时，我不禁面红耳赤，浑身发抖。

一夜宿醉。第二天早上起床，似乎神志已经清醒，对于自己所犯下的罪孽后悔莫及。然而这种感觉只是一闪，转瞬即逝。我的灵魂丝毫没有触动。我继续举杯狂饮，一旦被酒精麻痹，便将自己的所作所为抛在脑后。

这时那只猫的伤势逐渐好转，被剜掉眼睛的那只眼窠十分恐怖，看来它现在已经不痛了。它像往常

but he no Longer appeared to suffer any pain. He went about the house as usual, but, as might be expected, fled in extreme terror at my approach. I had so much of my old heart left, as to be at first grieved by this evident dislike on the part of a creature which had once so loved me. But this feeling soon gave place to irritation. And then came, as if to my final and irrevocable overthrow, the spirit of PERVERSENESS. Of this spirit philosophy takes no account. Yet I am not more sure that my soul lives, than I am that perverseness is one of the primitive impulses of the human heart – one of the indivisible primary faculties, or sentiments, which give direction to the character of Man. Who has not, a hundred times, found himself committing a vile or a silly action, for no other reason than because he knows he should not? Have we not a perpetual inclination, in the teeth of our best judgment, to violate that which is *Law*, merely because we understand it to be such? This spirit of perverseness, I say, came to my final overthrow. It was this unfathomable Longing of the soul *to vex itself* – to offer violence to its own nature – to do wrong for the wrong's sake only – that urged me to continue and finally to consummate the injury I had inflicted upon the unoffending brute. One morning, in cool blood, I slipped a noose about its neck and hung it to the limb of a tree; – hung it

一样在屋里溜达，只是一看我走近，便害怕得一下子逃走。毕竟我还没有丧尽天良，所以当看到原本如此喜爱我的动物如今竟这样讨厌我，不禁有些伤心。然而这种伤心没过多久就变成了愤怒。后来，那股邪念再次出现，最终让于我走上不归路。对于这种邪念，尽管哲学上并不重视。然而我却深信不疑，这种邪念是人类内心的一股冲动，是一种隐蔽且微妙的原始本能，或者说是情绪，它决定了人类的性格。谁都会在无意中犯错或是做些蠢事，而且这样做没有任何理由，明明心里知道不能如此却偏要去做。尽管我们知道这样做触犯了法律，我们还是会模糊自己的双眼，受到想去以身试法的邪念指示。唉，这股邪念让我误入歧途最终葬送了我的一生。正是我心中这股难以捉摸的渴望，驱使着我自寻烦恼，抛弃本性，为所欲为，我竟然继续对那只无辜的动物下起毒手，最后杀害了它。一天早上，我一时发狠，用绳索将猫的脖子勒住，吊在树枝上，它泪眼汪汪地望着我，当下心里悔恨不已，可猫还是被吊死了。我之所以会这样做，是因为我明知这只猫曾深爱过我，也因为我觉得它从未惹怒过我，更因为我知道这样做是在犯罪——我罪大恶极，足以被打下地狱，足以让我原本可以永生的灵魂永世无法超生，如果可能的话，

with the tears streaming from my eyes, and with the bitterest remorse at my heart; – hung it *because* I knew that it had loved me, and because I felt it had given me no reason of offence; – hung it *because* I knew that in so doing I was committing a sin – a deadly sin that would so jeopardize my immortal soul as to place it – if such a thing wore possible – even beyond the reach of the infinite mercy of the Most Merciful and Most Terrible God.

On the night of the day on which this cruel deed was done, I was aroused from sleep by the cry of fire. The curtains of my bed were in flames. The whole house was blazing. It was with great difficulty that my wife, a servant, and myself, made our escape from the conflagration. The destruction was complete. My entire worldly wealth was swallowed up, and I resigned myself thenceforward to despair.

I am above the weakness of seeking to establish a sequence of cause and effect, between the disaster and the atrocity. But I am detailing a chain of facts – and wish not to leave even a possible link imperfect. On the day succeeding the fire, I visited the ruins. The walls, with one exception, had fallen in. This exception was found in a compartment wall, not very thick, which stood about the middle of the house, and against which had rested the head of my bed. The plastering had here, in great

即使是慈悲为怀，令人敬畏的上帝也无法赦免我的罪行。

就在我做了此等伤天害理的勾当当晚，我在睡梦中突然听到有人喊失火了，我一下子惊醒。床上的帐子已经着了火。整栋房子都烧着了。我和妻子还有一个用人好不容易才幸免于难。这场火烧得十分彻底。将我所有财产都化为乌有，从那之后，我索性自暴自弃了。

我其实没那么懦弱，会在自己犯下的罪孽和这场突来的火灾之间找联系。不过我还是要详细说说事情的来龙去脉，希望别忽略了什么环节。失火的第二天，我到废墟前凭吊。墙壁都已坍塌，唯独有一道墙矗立在那儿。走近一看原来是一堵不算厚的墙壁，位置刚好在屋子中间，我的床头就靠近这堵墙。墙上的灰泥大大削弱了火势，我想这应该是最近才粉刷过的缘故。众人密密麻麻地聚在墙面前，看来很多

measure, resisted the action of the fire – a fact which I attributed to its having been recently spread. About this wall a dense crowd were collected, and many persons seemed to be examining a particular portion of it with very minute and eager attention. The words "strange!" "singular!" and other similar expressions, excited my curiosity. I approached and saw, as if graven in *bas relief* upon the white surface, the figure of a gigantic *cat*. The impression was given with an accuracy truly marvellous. There was a rope about the animal's neck.

When I first beheld this apparition – for I could scarcely regard it as less – my wonder and my terror were extreme. But at length reflection came to my aid. The cat, I remembered, had been hung in a garden adjacent to the house. Upon the alarm of fire, this garden had been immediately filled by the crowd – by some one of whom the animal must have been cut from the tree and thrown, through an open window, into my chamber. This had probably been done with the view of arousing me from sleep. The falling of other walls had compressed the victim of my cruelty into the substance of the freshly-spread plaster; the lime of which, with the flames, and the *ammonia* from the carcass, had then accomplished the portraiture as I saw it.

人都在仔细观察着这堵墙，只听人群中不断传出"神了"之类的话，我不禁觉得好奇，便走到跟前，看见白色的墙壁上赫然有一幅猫的浮雕。这只猫被雕刻得惟妙惟肖，栩栩如生，猫的脖子上还绕着一根绞索。

我看到这个怪物的第一眼，还以为自己见鬼了，心里惊恐万分。不过仔细一想便放下心来。我清楚地记得，这只猫被吊在宅子的花园里。火警刚响，花园里便挤满了人，肯定是哪个人把猫从树上解下来，我卧室的窗子没关，他便顺着窗户把它扔了进来。他这么做或许是想叫醒我。其他几堵墙倒下来，刚好把那只因我致死的猫压在刚粉刷过的壁上，墙上的石灰经过火烤再加上尸体散发出的氨气，三者发生了某种反应，所以墙上才会出现那样的浮雕。

Although I thus readily accounted to my reason, if not altogether to my conscience, for the startling fact just detailed, it did not the less fail to make a deep impression upon my fancy. For months I could not rid myself of the phantasm of the cat; and, during this period, there came back into my spirit a half-sentiment that seemed, but was not, remorse. I went so far as to regret the loss of the animal, and to look about me, among the vile haunts which I now habitually frequented, for another pet of the same species, and of somewhat similar appearance, with which to supply its place.

One night as I sat, half stupified, in a den of more than infamy, my attention was suddenly drawn to some black object, reposing upon the head of one of the immense hogsheads of Gin, or of Rum, which constituted the chief furniture of the apartment. I had been looking steadily at the top of this hogshead for some minutes, and what now caused me surprise was the fact that I had not sooner perceived the object thereupon. I approached it, and touched it with my hand. It was a black cat – a very large one – fully as large as Pluto, and closely resembling him in every respect but one. Pluto had not a white hair upon any portion of his body; but this cat had a large, although indefinite splotch of white, covering nearly the whole region of the breast.

以上所说的这段令人惊心动魄的事实，虽然从良心上说不过去，但也并不是没有道理，而我心里从此留下一个不可磨灭的印象。几个月里我始终无法摆脱那只猫的形象的纠缠。这时，我从心里产生了一股难以名状的模糊情绪，说不清是悔恨还是理所应当。我甚至开始后悔害死这只猫，于是开始经常来往于低级场所，到处寻找一只外貌与之相似的黑猫作为内心的弥补。

一天晚上，我在一家小酒馆里喝得醉醺醺的，突然我注意到一只装有金酒或朗姆酒的大酒桶，摆在屋里格外醒目，桶上有团黑糊糊的东西。我刚刚一直全神贯注地盯着酒桶好长时间，奇怪的是竟没发现那上面有东西。我走到跟前，伸手摸摸它。原来是只黑猫，个头很大，和普路托完全一样，只有一处例外，其他地方都极为相像。普路托全身没有一根白毛，而这只猫几乎整个胸前都是一片图案模糊的白色斑点。

Upon my touching him, he immediately arose, purred loudly, rubbed against my hand, and appeared delighted with my notice. This, then, was the very creature of which I was in search. I at once offered to purchase it of the landlord; but this person made no claim to it – knew nothing of it – had never seen it before.

I continued my caresses, and, when I prepared to go home, the animal evinced a disposition to accompany me. I permitted it to do so; occasionally stooping and patting it as I proceeded. When it reached the house it domesticated itself at once, and became immediately a great favorite with my wife.

For my own part, I soon found a dislike to it arising within me. This was just the reverse of what I had anticipated; but – I know not how or why it was – its evident fondness for myself rather disgusted and annoyed. By slow degrees, these feelings of disgust and annoyance rose into the bitterness of hatred. I avoided the creature; a certain sense of shame, and the remembrance of my former deed of cruelty, preventing me from physically abusing it. I did not, for some weeks, strike, or otherwise violently ill use it; but gradually – very gradually – I came to look upon it with unutterable loathing, and to flee silently from its odious presence, as from the breath of a pestilence.

我刚摸到它，它便立即跳了起来，冲我咕噜咕噜地叫，不停地把身子往我手上蹭，表示我能注意到它很高兴。这只猫正是我要找的。我立即告诉店主要求把它买下，谁知道店主竟完全不知道这只猫的来历，而且之前也没见过它，因此也没开价。

我继续摸着这只猫，正打算要走，这只猫立刻表现出想跟我走的样子。我让它跟着，一边走一边不时弯下身子摸摸它。它刚到我家马上就很乖，我妻子一下子就喜欢上它了。

而我，不久后就对这只猫心生厌恶。这令我十分意外，我也不明白这是为什么，也不知道这其中的道理。很明显，它眷恋着我，而我反而讨厌它，还很生气。慢慢地，这种情绪竟变本加厉。我尽量和这猫保持距离，因为内心感到羞愧，再加上之前的残暴行为在我心头挥之不去，我便不敢靠近它。有好几个星期我都没打过它，更没粗暴地对待它。然而久而久之，我对这猫的厌恶感已经到了难以容忍的地步，一看到它那副样子，我就像害怕瘟疫一样，躲得远远的。

What added, no doubt, to my hatred of the beast, was the discovery, on the morning after I brought it home, that, like Pluto, it also had been deprived of one of its eyes. This circumstance, however, only endeared it to my wife, who, as I have already said, possessed, in a high degree, that humanity of feeling which had once been my distinguishing trait, and the source of many of my simplest and purest pleasures.

With my aversion to this cat, however, its partiality for myself seemed to increase. It followed my footsteps with a pertinacity which it would be difficult to make the reader comprehend. Whenever I sat, it would crouch beneath my chair, or spring upon my knees, covering me with its loathsome caresses. If I arose to walk it would get between my feet and thus nearly throw me down, or, fastening its Long and sharp claws in my dress, clamber, in this manner, to my breast. At such times, although I Longed to destroy it with a blow, I was yet withheld from so doing, partly by a memory of my former crime, but chiefly – let me confess it at once – by absolute *dread* of the beast.

This dread was not exactly a dread of physical evil – and yet I should be at a loss how otherwise to define it. I am almost ashamed to own – yes, even in this felon's cell, I am almost ashamed to own – that the

不得不说，我之所以如此痛恨这畜生是因为在我带它回家的第二天早上，我发现它竟和普路托一样，眼睛也被剜掉一个。然而，我妻子见了却更加喜欢它了。我在前面提到过，我妻子富有同情心。原本在我身上也有这种美德，它曾让我体会到真正的乐趣。

我十分讨厌这只猫，相反的，它对我却越来越亲近。几乎寸步不离地跟着我，它这股偏爱或许读者很难理解。只要我一坐下，它就会蹲在我椅子旁，或是干脆跳到我膝盖上，在我身上肆意撒娇，着实让人讨厌。我一站起来，它就在我脚边绕来绕去，差点让我摔倒。再不然，它就用又长又尖的爪子抓住我的衣服，然后一路爬到我胸前。尽管我恨不得给它来上一拳，但这时，我就是不敢下手，一是因为我想到了自己先前作的孽，而更主要的原因是——我就明说了吧——我对这个畜生十分恐惧。

这种害怕倒不是怕身体上受到伤害，可是想要说清楚确实不容易。我真不好意思承认——唉，即便现在身处死牢，我也不好意思承认，这只猫给我带来的恐惧感竟让我的

terror and horror with which the animal inspired me, had been heightened by one of the merest chimaeras it would be possible to conceive. My wife had called my attention, more than once, to the character of the mark of white hair, of which I have spoken, and which constituted the sole visible difference between the strange beast and the one I had destroyed. The reader will remember that this mark, although large, had been originally very indefinite; but, by slow degrees – degrees nearly imperceptible, and which for a Long time my Reason struggled to reject as fanciful – it had, at length, assumed a rigorous distinctness of outline. It was now the representation of an object that I shudder to name – and for this, above all, I loathed, and dreaded, and would have rid myself of the monster *had I dared* – it was now, I say, the image of a hideous – of a ghastly thing – of the GALLOWS! – oh, mournful and terrible engine of Horror and of Crime – of Agony and of Death!

And now was I indeed wretched beyond the wretchedness of mere Humanity. And *a brute beast* – whose fellow I had contemptuously destroyed – *a brute beast* to work out for me – for me' a man fashioned in the image of the High God – so much of insufferable wo! Alas! neither by day nor by night knew I the blessing of Rest any more! During the former the

臆想和幻觉更严重了。我妻子不止一次让我仔细看它胸前的这片白毛。各位应该还记得，我之前提到过，这只怪猫和被我杀掉的那只猫，唯一一点明显的不同就是这片斑记。我曾提到斑记虽然有一大片，不过开始时很模糊，然而渐渐地，不知不觉中变得异常明显了，最终显现出一个清晰的轮廓来。长时间以来，我一直不愿意承认，努力让自己将一切都当成幻觉。这时那斑记竟幻化成一样东西，一提到这个东西我便不寒而栗。也正因如此，我才特别讨厌甚至惧怕这只怪物，如果我有胆量的话，早就杀掉它了。我说，这东西的形象是够吓人的了，是个恐怖的幻象——一个绞刑台！天哪，这是多么可悲又可怕的刑具啊！这是恐怖的刑具，审判的刑具！这是让人接受惩罚的刑具，让人送命的刑具呀！

这时我的境地已经落魄到了极点。我若无其事地将一只没有理性的畜生杀死。而它的同类，另一只没有理性的畜生竟然给我——这个上帝创造出来的人，带来如此多难以忍受的灾难！天哪！我每日每夜再也无法得到片刻安宁！白天，这畜生一刻都不让我安宁；到了晚上，我时刻都有可能从可怕的噩梦中惊

creature left me no moment alone; and, in the latter, I started, hourly, from dreams of unutterable fear, to find the hot breath of *the thing* upon my face, and its vast weight – an incarnate Night-Mare that I had no power to shake off – incumbent eternally upon my *heart*!

Beneath the pressure of torments such as these, the feeble remnant of the good within me succumbed. Evil thoughts became my sole intimates – the darkest and most evil of thoughts. The moodiness of my usual temper increased to hatred of all things and of all mankind; while, from the sudden, frequent, and ungovernable outbursts of a fury to which I now blindly abandoned myself, my uncomplaining wife, alas! was the most usual and the most patient of sufferers.

One day she accompanied me, upon some household errand, into the cellar of the old building which our poverty compelled us to inhabit. The cat followed me down the steep stairs, and, nearly throwing me headLong, exasperated me to madness. Uplifting an axe, and forgetting, in my wrath, the childish dread which had hitherto stayed my hand, I aimed a blow at the animal which, of course, would have proved instantly fatal had it descended as I wished. But this blow was arrested by the hand of my wife. Goaded, by the interference, into a rage more than

醒，每当看到这东西在我面前呼着热气，我的心里就像压着一块大石，怎么也摆脱不了这真实的梦魇！

我受尽内心痛苦的煎熬，心里仅存的一点善性也被折磨得消失殆尽。我的心里只剩下了邪念，满脑子净是些卑劣龌龊的邪念。我脾气向来喜怒无常，现如今发展成仇视一切事物，仇视所有人。我盲目地放纵自己，经常无故突然发怒，完全控制不住。天哪！牵连遭殃的是我那逆来顺受任劳任怨的妻子。

因为生活拮据，我们只能住在一栋老房子里。一天，因为一点家务事，她跟我一起到房子的地窖里去。这只猫跟着我们走下陡峭的梯阶，差点把我绊倒摔在地上，我简直气疯了。怒气让我丧失了理智也忘记了自己对这只猫的恐惧，于是挥起斧子朝它砍了下去，若是当时真的如我所愿一斧砍下去，不用说，这只猫肯定当场送命。岂料，我妻子伸出手来一把挡住了我。我正在气头上，她这么一拦，更加火上浇油，于是趁势挣开她，对准她的脑门砍了一斧。可怜的妻子还没来得

demoniacal, I withdrew my arm from her grasp and buried the axe in her brain. She fell dead upon the spot, without a groan.

This hideous murder accomplished, I set myself forthwith, and with entire deliberation, to the task of concealing the body. I knew that I could not remove it from the house, either by day or by night, without the risk of being observed by the neighbors. Many projects entered my mind. At one period I thought of cutting the corpse into minute fragments, and destroying them by fire. At another, I resolved to dig a grave for it in the floor of the cellar. Again, I deliberated about casting it in the well in the yard – about packing it in a box, as if merchandize, with the usual arrangements, and so getting a porter to take it from the house. Finally I hit upon what I considered a far better expedient than either of these. I determined to wall it up in the cellar – as the monks of the middle ages are recorded to have walled up their victims.

For a purpose such as this the cellar was well adapted. Its walls were loosely constructed, and had lately been plastered throughout with a rough plaster, which the dampness of the atmosphere had prevented from hardening. Moreover, in one of the walls was a projection, caused by a false chimney, or fireplace, that had been filled up, and made to resemble the red of the

及发出呼声就当场送了命。

犯下此等伤天害理的恶行，我反而镇定下来思考毁尸灭迹的事情了。我知道无论什么时候，只要把尸首挪到外面去，难免会被邻居们发现，我盘算了各种计划。一开始想把尸首肢解成小块然后烧掉，不留一点痕迹。后来我去查看院子里的井，还打算把尸体放进货箱里，雇个搬运工若无其事地把它搬出去。最后，我想到了一条万无一失的妙计。我决定将尸首砌进地窖的墙里，据传说，中世纪时期的僧侣也是用同样的方法将殉道者砌进墙里的。

这个地窖的墙可是再合适不过了。墙壁结构很松，最近才刚刚粉刷过粗灰泥，因为地窖里阴暗潮湿，墙体至今还没干。而且有面墙因为有个假壁炉的关系向里凹进去一块，现在已经填上了，做得与地窖其他墙没什么分别。我很容易地就将这面墙的墙砖挖开，把尸体放进去，再依照原样将墙重新砌上，这

cellar. I made no doubt that I could readily displace the bricks at this point, insert the corpse, and wall the whole up as before, so that no eye could detect any thing suspicious.

And in this calculation I was not deceived. By means of a crow-bar I easily dislodged the bricks, and, having carefully deposited the body against the inner wall, I propped it in that position, while, with little trouble, I re-laid the whole structure as it originally stood. Having procured mortar, sand, and hair, with every possible precaution, I prepared a plaster which could not be distinguished from the old, and with this I very carefully went over the new brickwork. When I had finished, I felt satisfied that all was right. The wall did not present the slightest appearance of having been disturbed. The rubbish on the floor was picked up with the minutest care. I looked around triumphantly, and said to myself – "Here at least, then, my labor has not been in vain."

My next step was to look for the beast which had been the cause of so much wretchedness; for I had, at length, firmly resolved to put it to death. Had I been able to meet with it, at the moment, there could have been no doubt of its fate; but it appeared that the crafty animal had been alarmed at the violence of my previous anger, and forebore to present itself in my

样一来别人很难看出破绽。

这果然是个好主意。我用一根铁锹，没费什么力气就撬掉砖墙，再仔细将尸体沿着内侧的夹墙摆好，让它保持住不掉下来，然后轻松地把墙照原来的样子砌好。我找来了石灰、沙子和一些头发，待准备好一切之后，我调出一种跟旧灰泥差不多的新灰泥，小心翼翼地涂在砌好的墙上。等做完所有事，见一切进行得顺利，我的心才踏实下来。这面墙居然丝毫看不出改动过的痕迹。我把地上的垃圾全部清理掉。我满意地环顾四周，心里暗想："这回总算没白忙活！"

接下来要做的是找寻那个给我带来无尽灾难的祸根。我狠下心肠。岂料在我刚刚大发雷霆的时候，一不留神那个鬼精灵就不知道跑哪儿去了，此刻我正发着脾气，它当然不敢出来。这只讨厌的畜生终于不在了。我心里压着的大石也终于放下了，心里的喜悦无法用言语来形容，也难以想象。到了晚上，这只

present mood. It is impossible to describe, or to imagine, the deep, the blissful sense of relief which the absence of the detested creature occasioned in my bosom. It did not make its appearance during the night – and thus for one night at least, since its introduction into the house, I soundly and tranquilly slept; aye, *slept* even with the burden of murder upon my soul!

The second and the third day passed, and still my tormentor came not. Once again I breathed as a freeman. The monster, in terror, had fled the premises forever! I should behold it no more! My happiness was supreme! The guilt of my dark deed disturbed me but little. Some few inquiries had been made, but these had been readily answered. Even a search had been instituted – but of course nothing was to be discovered. I looked upon my future felicity as secured.

Upon the fourth day of the assassination, a party of the police came, very unexpectedly, into the house, and proceeded again to make rigorous investigation of the premises. Secure, however, in the inscrutability of my place of concealment, I felt no embarrassment whatever. The officers bade me accompany them in their search. They left no nook or corner unexplored. At length, for the third or fourth time, they descended into the cellar. I quivered not in a muscle. My heart

猫始终都没出现，就这样，从这猫来我家以后，我终于能安安稳稳地睡上一晚了。哎呀，虽然我还肩负着杀人的心理重担，可我还是睡着了。

第二天，第三天过去了，这只折磨人的猫还是没出现。此时我像重新获得自由的人那样大口呼吸着。这只鬼猫终于从屋里逃走了，再也不回来了！眼不见为净，我心里充满着无与伦比的喜悦！尽管我罪恶滔天，但我心里却异常平静。官府来调查过几次，我三言两语便敷衍过去了。甚至有一次来家里搜查，当然他们找不到任何线索。于是我认为以后我都无须担忧了。

在我将妻子杀害后的第四天，突然一群警察闯进屋里，他们进行了严密的搜查。不过，我自恃把尸体藏得天衣无缝，他们绝不会想到，因此一点也不慌张。那些警察命令我配合他们进行搜查。任何一个角落都没有放过。当搜到第三遍第四遍时，他们决定到地窖去。我依旧稳若泰山，丝毫不为所动。没有做过亏心事，夜半敲门心不惊，此时我心如止水。我从地窖这边走到那边，双臂抱胸，若无其事地来回走

beat calmly as that of one who slumbers in innocence. I walked the cellar from end to end. I folded my arms upon my bosom, and roamed easily to and fro. The police were thoroughly satisfied and prepared to depart. The glee at my heart was too strong to be restrained. I burned to say if but one word, by way of triumph, and to render doubly sure their assurance of my guiltlessness.

"Gentlemen," I said at last, as the party ascended the steps, "I delight to have allayed your suspicions. I wish you all health, and a little more courtesy. By the bye, gentlemen, this – this is a very well constructed house." [In the rabid desire to say something easily, I scarcely knew what I uttered at all.] – "I may say an excellently well constructed house. These walls are you going, gentlemen? – these walls are solidly put together;" and here, through the mere phrenzy of bravado, I rapped heavily, with a cane which I held in my hand, upon that very portion of the brick-work behind which stood the corpse of the wife of my bosom.

But may God shield and deliver me from the fangs of the Arch-Fiend! No sooner had the reverberation of my blows sunk into silence, than I was answered by a voice from within the tomb! – by a cry, at first muffled and broken, like the sobbing of a child, and then quickly swelling into one Long, loud, and continuous scream, utterly

着。警察们已完全放下戒备，打算要走，我一时得意忘形，乐不可支。为了炫耀一番，我恨不得说点什么话，哪怕只是一句也好，这样就更能让他们相信我没有任何嫌疑了。

这些人走上梯阶时，我终于忍不住开口说道："各位先生，感谢你们为我洗脱了嫌疑，我再次感谢你们。谨向各位问好，希望今后多多关照。各位先生，顺便一提，这间屋子的构造很坚固。"我一时头脑发昏，随口胡说，甚至连自己都不知道在说什么。"这栋房子的结构可是相当好。看这几面墙——各位先生，你们要离开了吗？——这几面墙可是砌得相当牢固。"说到这儿，我一时糊涂，竟装模作样地拿起一根棒子，使劲朝藏着我爱妻尸体的那面砖墙砸去。

天哪，愿主保佑，将我从恶魔的手中拯救出来吧！敲墙的回音尚未停止，只听从里面发出一个声音！——是哭声，起初瓮声瓮气，断断续续，如孩童抽泣，接着调子突然上扬，成了持续的长啸，声音异常惨烈——这是一声哀号——一声悲鸣，这声音混杂了恐惧和得意，像

anomalous and inhuman – a howl – a wailing shriek, half of horror and half of triumph, such as might have arisen only out of hell, conjointly from the throats of the dammed in their agony and of the demons that exult in the damnation.

Of my own thoughts it is folly to speak. Swooning, I staggered to the opposite wall. For one instant the party upon the stairs remained motionless, through extremity of terror and of awe. In the next, a dozen stout arms were toiling at the wall. It fell bodily. The corpse, already greatly decayed and clotted with gore, stood erect before the eyes of the spectators. Upon its head, with red extended mouth and solitary eye of fire, sat the hideous beast whose craft had seduced me into murder, and whose informing voice had consigned me to the hangman. I had walled the monster up within the tomb!

是被打入地狱的冤魂发出的痛苦惨叫，同时还混合了魔鬼见到冤魂遭受惩罚时的欢呼声。

要说我当时的想法或许有点荒唐。我迷迷糊糊，脚下踉跄，来到那面墙跟前。站在楼梯上的警察们早被吓得大惊失色，呆若木鸡地站在那儿。过了一会儿，只见十几条粗壮的胳膊一起上来忙着拆墙。整面墙倒了下来。一具腐烂不堪，凝满血块的尸体赫然呈现在所有人面前。那只可怕的畜生端坐在尸体的头上，张开血盆大口，仅剩下的眼睛里冒着火。是它搞的鬼，是它诱使我杀了妻子，现如今又用叫声唤来警察，让我落入刽子手的手里。原来我把这只怪物也一同砌进墓墙里了！

9. The Tell-tale Heart
九. 泄密的心

TRUE! – nervous – very, very dreadfully nervous I had been and am; but why *will* you say that I am mad? The disease had sharpened my senses – not destroyed – not dulled them. Above all was the sense of hearing acute. I heard all things in the heaven and in the earth. I heard many things in hell. How, then, am I mad? Hearken! and observe how healthily – how calmly I can tell you the whole story.

It is impossible to say how first the idea entered my brain; but once conceived, it haunted me day and night. Object there was none. Passion there was none. I loved the old man. He had never wronged me. He had never given me insult. For his gold I had no desire. I think it was his eye! yes, it was this! He had the eye of a vulture – a pale blue eye, with a film over it. Whenever it fell upon me, my blood ran cold; and so by degrees – very gradually – I made up my mind to take the life of the old man, and thus rid myself of the eye forever.

Now this is the point. You fancy me mad. Madmen know nothing. But you should have seen *me*. You should have seen how wisely I proceeded – with what

是的！——我经神敏感，非常非常敏感，十二万分的敏感，以前是这样，现在也是这样。可为什么偏说我是疯子呢？得了这种病，我仍然有感觉，也没变迟钝，相反的，我变得更加敏锐了。尤其是我的听觉，异常灵敏。世间万物的所有声音我都能听见。就连地狱的各种声音也听得到。这怎么能说我疯了呢？听！我现在和您说这一切的时候，是多么精神，多么镇定啊。

说不清为什么最初会有这种念头，可一旦想起来，就无论白天黑夜都难以忘怀。没有什么目的，也没什么怨恨。我爱那个老家伙。他从来没得罪过我，也没侮辱过我。我对他的财产也不感兴趣。大概是因为那只眼睛的缘故吧！没错，就是那只眼睛惹的祸！他长了一只鹰眼——淡蓝色的，蒙着一层薄膜。他只要看我一眼，我就不寒而栗。所以心里渐渐地——一点一点地——下定决心，结束他的生命，这样就永远不用再看到那只眼睛了。

看，这就是问题所在。您认为我疯了。可疯子什么也不明白。可惜您当时没有亲眼见到。真可惜没看到我做得是多么聪明——多么细

caution – with what foresight – with what dissimulation I went to work! I was never kinder to the old man than during the whole week before I killed him. And every night, about midnight, I turned the latch of his door and opened it – oh so gently! And then, when I had made an opening sufficient for my head, I put in a dark lantern, all closed, closed, that no light shone out, and then I thrust in my head. Oh, you would have laughed to see how cunningly I thrust it in! I moved it slowly – very, very slowly, so that I might not disturb the old man's sleep. It took me an hour to place my whole head within the opening so far that I could see him as he lay upon his bed. Ha! would a madman have been so wise as this, And then, when my head was well in the room, I undid the lantern cautiously-oh, so cautiously – cautiously (for the hinges creaked) – I undid it just so much that a single thin ray fell upon the vulture eye. And this I did for seven Long nights – every night just at midnight – but I found the eye always closed; and so it was impossible to do the work; for it was not the old man who vexed me, but his Evil Eye. And every morning, when the day broke, I went boldly into the chamber, and spoke courageously to him, calling him by name in a hearty tone, and inquiring how he has passed the night. So you see he would have

心周到，多么虚伪！我杀死老家伙前的那个礼拜，我对他百依百顺。每天晚上，快到半夜的时候，我悄悄扭开门锁，——啊，不发出一点声响！我把房门开了条缝，刚好将脑袋探进来，将一盏牛眼灯塞在门缝处，把灯严严实实地遮上，不留一点缝隙，连一丝灯光都漏不出，然后再把头伸进去。啊，要是您看到我是怎么巧妙地探头，肯定会失声大笑！我慢慢向屋里探着头，一点点地慢慢伸到门里，生怕把老家伙惊醒。花了将近一个钟头，才把整个脑袋完全伸到门缝里，刚好能看到他躺在床上。哈哈！——疯子会像我我一样聪明吗？我刚把头伸到房里，便小心翼翼地——啊，简直是异常小心——小心地拉开灯上的活动罩，生怕铰链发出吱呀的声响——我将活动罩掀开条缝，一道极细的灯光刚好射在他的鹰眼上。就这样整整 7 天晚上，每天都在半夜时分，然而那只眼睛总是紧闭着，无法下手，因为让我恼怒的并不是老家伙本人，而是他那只"白眼"。每当清晨，天刚刚亮，我便大摇大摆地来到他房间里，大着胆子和他讲话，亲热地喊他的名字，问他昨晚是否睡个好觉。所以您看，如果他不是个老谋深算的老家伙，是绝不会想到每天晚上，刚好 12 点钟的时候，我趁他睡着时探头进来偷看他。

been a very profound old man, indeed, to suspect that every night, just at twelve, I looked in upon him while he slept.

Upon the eighth night I was more than usually cautious in opening the door. A watch's minute hand moves more quickly than did mine. Never before that night had I *felt* the extent of my own powers – of my sagacity. I could scarcely contain my feelings of triumph. To think that there I was, opening the door, little by little, and he not even to dream of my secret deeds or thoughts. I fairly chuckled at the idea; and perhaps he heard me; for he moved on the bed suddenly, as if startled. Now you may think that I drew back – but no. His room was as black as pitch with the thick darkness, (for the shutters were close fastened, through fear of robbers,) and so I knew that he could not see the opening of the door, and I kept pushing it on steadily, steadily.

I had my head in, and was about to open the lantern, when my thumb slipped upon the tin fastening, and the old man sprang up in bed, crying out – "Who's there?"

I kept quite still and said nothing. For a whole hour I did not move a muscle, and in the meantime I did not hear him lie down. He was still sitting up in the bed listening; – just as I have done, night after night, hearkening to the death watches in the wall.

第八天晚上，我比往常还小心谨慎地打开房门。似乎连表上的长针走得也比平日快很多。那天晚上，我才第一次认识到自己的本事有多大，脑袋有多聪明。心里的得意劲溢于言表。试想，我就在房外，一点一点地打开门，他连做梦都想不到会有这样秘密的举动和阴谋。一想到这些，我不禁扑哧一笑。估计他听到了，因为他似乎吃一惊，突然翻了个身。这时您肯定以为我会就此停手了吧——才没有呢。他害怕有强盗来抢劫，所以百叶窗关得很紧，房里漆黑一片，伸手不见五指，我知道他看不到门缝，于是依旧一步一步，一步一步地小心地推开门。

我刚把头探进来，正要掀起灯上的活动罩门，大拇指按在铁皮扣上，老家伙突然坐起身，破口惊呼道："谁？"

我没有动，也不吭声。保持这个姿势整整一个钟头，然而他始终没躺下。依旧坐在床上，侧耳听着，和我每天晚上聆听墙里报死虫的鸣叫一般。

Presently I heard a slight groan, and I knew it was the groan of mortal terror. It was not a groan of pain or of grief – oh, no! – it was the low stifled sound that arises from the bottom of the soul when overcharged with awe. I knew the sound well. Many a night, just at midnight, when all the world slept, it has welled up from my own bosom, deepening, with its dreadful echo, the terrors that distracted me. I say I knew it well. I knew what the old man felt, and pitied him, although I chuckled at heart. I knew that he had been lying awake ever since the first slight noise, when he had turned in the bed. His fears had been ever since growing upon him. He had been trying to fancy them causeless, but could not. He had been saying to himself – "It is nothing but the wind in the chimney – it is only a mouse crossing the floor," or "It is merely a cricket which has made a single chirp." Yes, he had been trying to comfort himself with these suppositions: but he had found all in vain. All *in vain*; because Death, in approaching him had stalked with his black shadow before him, and enveloped the victim. And it was the mournful influence of the unperceived shadow that caused him to feel – although he neither saw nor heard – to *feel* the presence of my head within the room.

When I had waited a Long time, very

没过多久，耳边听到一声低哼，我知道这是在极度害怕时发出的声音。既不是呻吟，也不是哀叹——都不是！——每当极度恐惧的时候，才会从心里发出这样的低哼。我已经听惯了。不知道有多少个夜晚，在刚好午夜时分，四下寂静无声，我总是战战兢兢，不由得从心底发出这声呻吟，激荡出阴森的回响，然后更加害怕了。刚已说过，这早就听习惯了。我清楚老家伙此时的心情，尽管心里暗笑，但还是很同情他。我知道他突然听到细微的声响，在床上翻了个身，然后就一直睁着眼躺着，心里越想越害怕，努力让自己相信是虚惊一场，然而就是做不到。他一直自言自语："只不过是烟囱里的风声罢了——有耗子经过罢了。"或是说："不过是蛐蛐的叫声罢了。"没错，他总是这样胡乱猜想，安慰自己，但他明白这全是白费心思，因为死神即将出现，它大摇大摆地走着，一步步进逼过来，来到他这冤鬼跟前。正是那无形的死神，让他心里发毛，才觉得我的脑袋就在房间里，尽管他并没看到，也没听见任何响声。

我沉下心来，等了很久也没听

patiently, without hearing him lie down, I resolved to open a little – a very, very little crevice in the lantern. So I opened it – you cannot imagine how stealthily, stealthily – until, at length a simple dim ray, like the thread of the spider, shot from out the crevice and fell full upon the vulture eye.

It was open – wide, wide open – and I grew furious as I gazed upon it. I saw it with perfect distinctness – all a dull blue, with a hideous veil over it that chilled the very marrow in my bones; but I could see nothing else of the old man's face or person: for I had directed the ray as if by instinct, precisely upon the damned spot.

And have I not told you that what you mistake for madness is but over-acuteness of the sense? – now, I say, there came to my ears a low, dull, quick sound, such as a watch makes when enveloped in cotton. I knew that sound well, too. It was the beating of the old man's heart. It increased my fury, as the beating of a drum stimulates the soldier into courage.

But even yet I refrained and kept still. I scarcely breathed. I held the lantern motionless. I tried how steadily I could maintain the ray upon the eve. Meantime the hellish tattoo of the heart increased. It grew quicker and quicker, and louder and louder every instant. The old man's terror *must* have been extreme! It grew louder, I say, louder every moment! – do you mark

到他躺下的声音，于是决定把灯掀开一条小缝，极小，极小的一道缝。我拉开灯上的活动罩——您或许想象不出，我的动作有多么小心翼翼，鬼鬼祟祟——一点一点地掀开，终于从缝隙里射出一线朦胧的灯光，仿若游丝般，照在鹰眼上。

此刻那只眼正睁着呢，大大地睁着，我越看越恼火。我清楚地看到——整只眼是一团暗淡的蓝色，蒙着一层让人害怕的薄膜，让我心惊胆战。然而，我却看不到老家伙的脸和身体，因为不偏不倚，灯光刚好射在那个鬼地方。

看，我不是早就跟您说过，您误认为我疯了，其实我只是有些过分敏感罢了——啊，刚才说了，我耳边突然传来一阵模糊的低沉声，像是罩了一层棉花的钟表声。我倒习惯了那种声音。那正是老家伙心跳的声音。我越听越生气，仿佛被雷雷战鼓鼓舞了士气的战士。

这个时候，我仍然沉住气，纹丝不动，大气都不敢喘。我提着灯，让灯光尽量射在鹰眼上。这时，又传来那阵吓人的心跳声，扑通扑通越发严重。时间一秒秒过去，越跳越快，越跳越快，声音越来越响，越来越响。老家伙肯定被吓得够呛！刚才说过，声音越来越响，一秒比一秒地响！——听明白了吗？不是

me well? I have told you that I am nervous: so I am. And now at the dead hour of the night, amid the dreadful silence of that old house, so strange a noise as this excited me to uncontrollable terror. Yet, for some minutes Longer I refrained and stood still. But the beating grew louder, louder! I thought the heart must burst. And now a new anxiety seized me – the sound would be heard by a neighbour! The old man's hour had come! With a loud yell, I threw open the lantern and leaped into the room. He shrieked once – once only. In an instant I dragged him to the floor, and pulled the heavy bed over him. I then smiled gaily, to find the deed so far done. But, for many minutes, the heart beat on with a muffled sound. This, however, did not vex me; it would not be heard through the wall. At length it ceased. The old man was dead. I removed the bed and examined the corpse. Yes, he was stone, stone dead. I placed my hand upon the heart and held it there many minutes. There was no pulsation. He was stone dead. His eye would trouble me no more.

If still you think me mad, you will think so no Longer when I describe the wise precautions I took for the concealment of the body. The night waned, and I worked hastily, but in silence. First of all I dismembered the corpse. I cut off the head and the arms and the legs.

早就跟您说过，我神经过敏，这是真的。眼下正值午夜，老房子里寂静无声，听到这样诡异的声音，让我有种无法自持的恐惧感。但我仍然沉住气，一动不动地在原地站了片刻。怎料扑通扑通声竟越发强烈，声音越来越响！我想，那颗心准是快炸开了。此时又不禁担心——不会让邻居们听到吧！老家伙的死期到了！我哇地叫喊了一声，拉开灯上的活动罩，一个箭步迈进房门。他哎呀一声惊呼——只叫了这么一声。我一下子把他拖下地板，推倒在地，压在他身上。眼见即将大功告成，心里乐翻了。谁知道，闷闷的心跳声竟依然持续响了半天。我并没生气，隔了一面墙，这声音倒听不大清。后来响声终于停止了。老家伙死了。我挪开床，仔细检查了尸体。是的，他咽气了，一点呼吸也没有了。我把手按在他心口，放了好久。感觉不到一点心跳。那只眼睛再也不能折磨人啦。

如果您还认为我疯了的话，那么在我讲完藏匿尸体的妙计后，您就不会这么认为了。夜已过大半，我立刻动手，先悄无声息地把尸体肢解，砍掉脑袋和手脚。

I then took up three planks from the flooring of the chamber, and deposited all between the scantlings. I then replaced the boards so cleverly, so cunningly, that no human eye – not even *his* – could have detected any thing wrong. There was nothing to wash out – no stain of any kind – no blood-spot whatever. I had been too wary for that. A tub had caught all – ha! ha!

When I had made an end of these labors, it was four o'clock – still dark as midnight. As the bell sounded the hour, there came a knocking at the street door. I went down to open it with a light heart, – for what had I now to fear? There entered three men, who introduced themselves, with perfect suavity, as officers of the police. A shriek had been heard by a neighbour during the night; suspicion of foul play had been aroused; information had been lodged at the police office, and they (the officers) had been deputed to search the premises.

I smiled, – for *what* had I to fear? I bade the gentlemen welcome. The shriek, I said, was my own in a dream. The old man, I mentioned, was absent in the country. I took my visitors all over the house. I bade them search – search well. I led them, at length, to *his* chamber. I showed them his treasures, secure, undisturbed. In the enthusiasm of my confidence, I brought chairs into the room, and desired them *here*

我再把房里的 3 块地板撬起，把尸体藏在两根间柱之间。重新把木板放好，一切我都做得干净利落，极其巧妙，无论什么人都看不出有丝毫破绽，就连他的眼睛也看不出。没有什么需要清理的，因为什么污迹都没有，一点血迹都没有。我做得如此谨慎，竟没留下一点痕迹。因为全都在澡盆里了——哈！哈！

做好所有事，已经凌晨 4 点钟了——天空还和黑夜一样。钟响了 4 声，大门外突然传来一阵急促的敲门声。我若无其事地下楼开门，——现在我有什么好怕的呢？从门外进来 3 个人，他们礼貌地做着自我介绍，说是警官。有邻居听到夜里的一声惨叫，怀疑发生了命案，于是报了警，这 3 位警官就是奉命来做搜查的。

我满脸堆笑——有什么好害怕的？我和这 3 位先生客套了一番，便说，刚刚自己做了梦失声叫了出来。我说，老家伙去了乡下。我领着 3 位客人在屋里来来回回走了个遍。让他们仔仔细细地搜查。后来还把他们带到老家伙的卧室里，让给他们看所有东西都原样放着。我心里泰然自若，便热心拿了几把椅子进来，让他们在这房间里休息一

to rest from their fatigues, while I myself, in the wild audacity of my perfect triumph, placed my own seat upon the very spot beneath which reposed the corpse of the victim.

The officers were satisfied. My *manner* had convinced them. I was singularly at ease. They sat, and while I answered cheerily, they chatted of familiar things. But, ere Long, I felt myself getting pale and wished them gone. My head ached, and I fancied a ringing in my ears: but still they sat and still chatted. The ringing became more distinct: – It continued and became more distinct: I talked more freely to get rid of the feeling: but it continued and gained definiteness – until, at length, I found that the noise was *not* within my ears.

No doubt I now grew *very* pale; – but I talked more fluently, and with a heightened voice. Yet the sound increased – and what could I do? It was *a low, dull, quick sound – much such a sound as a watch makes when enveloped in cotton.* I gasped for breath – and yet the officers heard it not. I talked more quickly – more vehemently; but the noise steadily increased. I arose and argued about trifles, in a high key and with violent gesticulations; but the noise steadily increased. Why *would* they not be gone? I paced the floor to and fro with heavy strides, as if excited to fury by the

下，我心里格外得意，还大着胆子在藏尸首的地方摆了把椅子坐下。

3 位警官这下放心了。因为我的举动不容得他们不信。我也就放下心来。他们坐在那儿，开始闲聊，我也是有问必答。可没过多久，我的脸色越来越苍白，恨不得他们赶紧离开。我的头好痛，耳朵里一阵嗡嗡的响声，可惜他们还是坐在那儿，依旧聊着天。嗡嗡声变得更加清晰，不停地响着，这回听得更加清楚了，我想从这种感觉中摆脱出来，于是嘴上说得更加顺畅。谁知道这嗡嗡声不仅没停，反而更加清晰。响着，响着，我这才明白原来不是耳朵的问题。

不用说，此时我的脸色已是惨白，嘴里聊得更欢，还故意提高了嗓门。岂料声音还是越来越响——该如何是好？这时突然传出一阵模糊低沉的声音——就像罩了一层棉花的钟表声。我喘着粗气，幸好 3 位警官没有听到。我说得更快，语速更急，谁承想声音被无休止地放大。我从椅子上站起来，提高了嗓门争辩起那些鸡毛蒜皮的小事，一边说着还一边手舞足蹈的，而响声依然越来越大。为什么他们还不走呢？我脚步沉重地在房里走来走去，好像他们 3 人的话惹怒了我，

observations of the men – but the noise steadily increased. Oh God! what *could* I do? I foamed – I raved – I swore! I swung the chair upon which I had been sitting, and grated it upon the boards, but the noise arose over all and continually increased. It grew louder – louder – *louder!* And still the men chatted pleasantly, and smiled. Was it possible they heard not? Almighty God! – no, no! They heard! – they suspected! – they *knew*! – they were making a mockery of my horror!-this I thought, and this I think. But anything was better than this agony! Anything was more tolerable than this derision! I could bear those hypocritical smiles no Longer! I felt that I must scream or die! and now – again! – hark! louder! louder! louder! *louder!*

"Villains!" I shrieked, "dissemble no more! I admit the deed! – tear up the planks! here, here! – It is the beating of his hideous heart!"

谁知响声还是越来越大。啊，天哪！我该怎么办呢？我开始吐沫横飞，大声咆哮，歇斯底里地咒骂！椅子在原地摇动，磨在地板上发出嘎嘎的声响，而响声依旧掩盖了一切，而且继续不断，越来越大声。越来越响，越来越响！那 3 个人居然还聊得起劲，嘻哈着。他们难道听不见？我的老天啊！——不，不！听得到的！——他们开始怀疑了！——心里有数了！——此时正嘲笑我做贼心虚呢！——我以前这么认为，现在也这么认为。但是什么都比经受这样的折磨要好得多！什么都比受这种侮辱要好受得多！我再也受不了这种假笑了！只觉再不呼喊出来我就要死了！——瞧——又来了！——听！越来越响！越来越响！越来越响！越来越响！

"浑蛋！"我失声尖叫道，"不用再装了！我坦白了就是！——把地板撬开！——这儿，就是这儿！——他那颗可恶的心正跳着呢！"

10. William Wilson
十. 威廉·威尔逊

What say of it? what say of CONSCIENCE grim, that spectre in my path?

– Chamberlayn's "Pharronida"

说什么好呢？良知已经泯灭，如幽灵般挡在我的路上，说什么好呢？

——张伯伦《法萝妮德》

LET me call myself, for the present, William Wilson. The fair page now lying before me need not be sullied with my real appellation. This has been already too much an object for the scorn – for the horror – for the detestation of my race. To the uttermost regions of the globe have not the indignant winds bruited its unparalleled infamy? Oh, outcast of all outcasts most abandoned! – to the earth art thou not forever dead? to its honors, to its flowers, to its golden aspirations? – and a cloud, dense, dismal, and limitless, does it not hang eternally between thy hopes and heaven?

I would not, if I could, here or to-day, embody a record of my later years of unspeakable misery, and unpardonable crime. This epoch – these later years – took unto themselves a sudden elevation in turpitude, whose origin alone it is my present purpose to assign. Men usually grow base by degrees. From me, in an

现在，就让我自称为威廉·威尔逊吧。我面前的这张白纸可不想被我的真实姓名所玷污。它已经把我的家族害得够苦了，他们为此受尽了轻蔑、厌恶和憎恨。难不成那些愤慨的流言，还没把我们家族的恶名传播到天涯海角吗？哦，堕落到无以复加的浪子啊！你对人世间的一切都已经心如死水了吗？尘世间的荣誉、鲜花，以及那些金光闪闪的美好愿望都再也激不起你的兴致了吗？那片无边无际的厚厚的乌云，就这样一直横亘在你的希望和天堂之间吗？

如果可以，我今天在这里真的不愿详述我近几年所遭遇的无以言表的苦难和自己所犯下的不可饶恕的罪孽。最近这几年，我突然如坠无底深渊，现在，我要说的就是个中缘由。人的堕落往往是渐进式的。但在我这里，一瞬间，所有的德行就像披风一样从身上滑落了。我从

instant, all virtue dropped bodily as a mantle. From comparatively trivial wickedness I passed, with the stride of a giant, into more than the enormities of an Elah-Gabalus. What chance – what one event brought this evil thing to pass, bear with me while I relate. Death approaches; and the shadow which foreruns him has thrown a softening influence over my spirit. I Long, in passing through the dim valley, for the sympathy – I had nearly said for the pity – of my fellow men. I would fain have them believe that I have been, in some measure, the slave of circumstances beyond human control. I would wish them to seek out for me, in the details I am about to give, some little oasis of *fatality* amid a wilderness of error. I would have them allow – what they cannot refrain from allowing – that, although temptation may have erewhile existed as great, man was never *thus,* at least, tempted before – certainly, never *thus* fell. And is it therefore that he has never thus suffered? Have I not indeed been living in a dream? And am I not now dying a victim to the horror and the mystery of the wildest of all sublunary visions?

I am the descendant of a race whose imaginative and easily excitable temperament has at all times rendered them

那看似毫不起眼的邪恶之境路过，可能是因为步子大了点吧，突然就掉下了罪恶的深渊，比依拉加巴勒[1]那类滔天罪行还要罪恶。怎样的一种偶然啊——不知道是什么东西让这邪恶在我经过的时候扑进我的怀里。死神正在步步逼近，死亡的阴影却让我的灵魂安宁。我穿行在幽暗的深谷，渴望得到世人的同情——就算是怜悯也好啊。我只求他们能相信，在那种环境下，我多多少少是无能为力的。我只求在听了我即将讲述的情节后，他们能在我无尽的罪恶里找出一点点宿命的意味。我只求他们承认——承认那些必须承认的就够了——尽管也曾经历过很大的诱惑，可至少也有人没有被诱惑击倒，当然也就没有这么堕落。但他就真的没遭受过忍受诱惑的痛苦吗？难道我不是生活在噩梦里吗？世间所有的怪诞都那么恐怖、神秘，难道不是它们正在把我往死路上逼吗？

我的祖上富于想象，而且脾气暴躁，这使得这个家族名声在外。而我在少不更事的时候，就充分证

---

[1] 依拉加巴勒：约生于公元 205 年，是叙利亚以米沙太阳神庙祭司，218 年被选为罗马皇帝，荒淫无耻，恶名远扬，于 222 年被侍卫杀死。

remarkable; and, in my earliest infancy, I gave evidence of having fully inherited the family character. As I advanced in years it was more strongly developed; becoming, for many reasons, a cause of serious disquietude to my friends, and of positive injury to myself. I grew self-willed, addicted to the wildest caprices, and a prey to the most ungovernable passions. Weak-minded, and beset with constitutional infirmities akin to my own, my parents could do but little to check the evil propensities which distinguished me. Some feeble and ill-directed efforts resulted in complete failure on their part, and, of course, in total triumph on mine. Thenceforward my voice was a household law; and at an age when few children have abandoned their leading-strings, I was left to the guidance of my own will, and became, in all but name, the master of my own actions.

My earliest recollections of a school-life, are connected with a large, rambling, Elizabethan house, in a misty-looking village of England, where were a vast number of gigantic and gnarled trees, and where all the houses were excessively ancient. In truth, it was a dream-like and spirit-soothing place, that venerable old town. At this moment, in fancy, I feel the refreshing chilliness of its deeply-shadowed avenues, inhale the

实了自己已经完全继承了家族的特征。随着我年岁的增长，这种特征也日益明显。由于诸多原因，这也成为了我的朋友们极度焦虑的导火索，对我自己也绝对是个伤害。我变得一意孤行，沉溺于胡思乱想，沦为无法控制的情绪的奴仆。我的父母天性优柔寡断，也和我一样被先天虚弱症困扰着，所以，对于我这绝无仅有的古怪性情，他们几乎也无能为力。一些绵软无力而又搞错了头的尝试使得他们一败涂地，而我，自然是大获全胜。从那时起，我的话就成了家法。在很少有孩子能够挣脱牵线绳的年龄，我就开始自作主张了。而且，我根本就是自己当家作主，除了名义上不是。

我对学校生活的最早记忆，总是和一幢蔓生式的伊丽莎白式大房子联系在一起的。房子建在英格兰一个雾蒙蒙的村子里，那儿有很多很多浑身疙疙瘩瘩的巨树，而且所有的房子都特别古老。说实话，那真是个如梦境般的小镇，古朴庄严，令人心绪宁静。现在，我还想象得出，自己置身于浓荫如盖的街道，感受着那份沁人心脾的凉意，嗅着灌木丛的芬芳，又一次怀着莫名的

fragrance of its thousand shrubberies, and thrill anew with undefinable delight, at the deep hollow note of the church-bell, breaking, each hour, with sullen and sudden roar, upon the stillness of the dusky atmosphere in which the fretted Gothic steeple lay imbedded and asleep.

It gives me, perhaps, as much of pleasure as I can now in any manner experience, to dwell upon minute recollections of the school and its concerns. Steeped in misery as I am – misery, alas! only too real – I shall be pardoned for seeking relief, however slight and temporary, in the weakness of a few rambling details. These, moreover, utterly trivial, and even ridiculous in themselves, assume, to my fancy, adventitious importance, as connected with a period and a locality when and where I recognise the first ambiguous monitions of the destiny which afterwards so fully overshadowed me. Let me then remember.

The house, I have said, was old and irregular. The grounds were extensive, and a high and solid brick wall, topped with a bed of mortar and broken glass, encompassed the whole. This prison-like rampart formed the limit of our domain; beyond it we saw but thrice a week – once every Saturday afternoon, when, attended by two ushers, we were permitted to take brief walks in a body through some of the

喜悦战栗起来。是因为听到了教堂传来的低沉而空洞的钟声吧。每隔一个小时，沉闷的钟声就会冷不丁地敲响，打破了暗淡无光里的寂静，暮色中矗立着哥特式的尖塔，历经岁月侵蚀，沉沉而睡。

或许，细想在学校的点滴时刻或相关的事，能给我带来现在在任何情况下都体会不到的巨大的喜悦。我现在相当悲惨——悲惨，唉！千真万确——请原谅我在这里寻求些许暂时安慰，因为我所述说的都是些苍白无力的琐屑杂事。这些事情虽然特别琐细，甚至荒谬，但在我看来却格外重要。因为就是在彼时彼地，我第一次受到了来自宿命的警告，模糊不清，但却让我接下来永无出头之日。让我来回忆一下。

那房子，我说过的，很古旧而且不规则。院子很宽广，一圈高高的坚固的砖墙，顶上抹着一层灰泥，插着碎玻璃，把院子围了起来。这监狱似的壁障限制着我们的活动领地；院子的外面我们也看得到，但每周只有 3 次：星期六下午，在两个老师的监护下，我们可以集体到周边的田野散会儿步。星期天，我们中规中矩地排队到村里唯一的教

neighbouring fields – and twice during Sunday, when we were paraded in the same formal manner to the morning and evening service in the one church of the village. Of this church the principal of our school was pastor. With how deep a spirit of wonder and perplexity was I wont to regard him from our remote pew in the gallery, as, with step solemn and slow, he ascended the pulpit! This reverend man, with countenance so demurely benign, with robes so glossy and so clerically flowing, with wig so minutely powdered, so rigid and so vast, – could this be he who, of late, with sour visage, and in snuffy habiliments, administered, ferule in hand, the Draconian laws of the academy? Oh, gigantic paradox, too utterly monstrous for solution!

At an angle of the ponderous wall frowned a more ponderous gate. It was riveted and studded with iron bolts, and surmounted with jagged iron spikes. What impressions of deep awe did it inspire! It was never opened save for the three periodical egressions and ingressions already mentioned; then, in every creak of its mighty hinges, we found a plenitude of mystery – a world of matter for solemn remark, or for more solemn meditation.

The extensive enclosure was irregular in form, having many capacious recesses. Of these, three or four of the largest

堂做早晚礼拜。我们学校的校长就是教堂的牧师。满怀着深深的好奇和迷惑，我常常坐在听众席的靠背长凳上，遥望他迈着庄严缓慢的步子走上讲坛。这位可敬的人，面容故作温良，法衣闪闪发光，飘飘扬扬——就是牧师的法衣特有的那种飘扬；假发上精致地扑满了粉，僵硬且庞大。这就是刚才那个容貌酸腐的人吗？是那个穿着讨厌的制服，手里拿着教鞭，严峻地执行着学院律令的那个人吗？哦，真是矛盾得无以复加，荒谬到不可理喻！

在笨重的围墙的一角上挤出一面更笨重的大门。门上铆着大头铁螺钉做装饰，门的顶端竖着犬牙差互的铁钉，看上去很是吓人。除了上面说过的3次定期出入，大门从不打开。因此，伴随着巨大的铰链的每一次嘎吱声，我们就会看到无数奇妙的事物了——一个需要肃穆审视、慎重思考的世界。

广阔的院子呈不规则的形状，有很多地方都凹陷。其中最大的三四个凹陷连成了操场。操场很平坦，

constituted the play-ground. It was level, and covered with fine hard gravel. I well remember it had no trees, nor benches, nor anything similar within it. Of course it was in the rear of the house. In front lay a small parterre, planted with box and other shrubs; but through this sacred division we passed only upon rare occasions indeed – such as a first advent to school or final departure thence, or perhaps, when a parent or friend having called for us, we joyfully took our way home for the Christmas or Midsummer holy-days.

But the house! – how quaint an old building was this! – to me how veritably a palace of enchantment! There was really no end to its windings – to its incomprehensible subdivisions. It was difficult, at any given time, to say with certainty upon which of its two stories one happened to be. From each room to every other there were sure to be found three or four steps either in ascent or descent. Then the lateral branches were innumerable – inconceivable – and so returning in upon themselves, that our most exact ideas in regard to the whole mansion were not very far different from those with which we pondered upon infinity. During the five years of my residence here, I was never able to ascertain with precision, in what remote locality lay the little sleeping apartment assigned to myself and some

铺着上好的硬沙砾。我清楚地记得操场上没有树，没有凳子，也没有任何类似可以坐的东西。当然这是说的屋后。屋前却有个小花坛，种着黄杨及其他小灌木，不过事实上，要经过这片圣地，我们得碰上难得的机遇才行——比如第一次进校，或最后一次离校，要么就是有父母或朋友来看望，还有就是我们兴高采烈地回家过圣诞或夏至节的时候。

可是那幢房子，是多么离奇有趣、古色生香啊！对我来说，它简直就是一座魔幻宫殿。回廊迂回曲折，没有尽头，引向不可胜数的岔道。任何时候，都很难弄清两层楼的上下之分。从一间房到另外任意一间房，都肯定会有或上或下的三四级台阶。而且房子的套间也多得数不清，简直令人难以置信，一间套着一间。我们对这幢房子的确切印象，就跟想到了"无穷无尽"这个概念相差无几。在我 5 年的寄住生活里，我从未弄清楚自己和其他 20 个左右的学生所居住的这间小寝室到底位于这幢房子的哪个偏僻的角落。

eighteen or twenty other scholars.

The school-room was the largest in the house – I could not help thinking, in the world. It was very Long, narrow, and dismally low, with pointed Gothic windows and a ceiling of oak. In a remote and terror-inspiring angle was a square enclosure of eight or ten feet, comprising the sanctum, "during hours," of our principal, the Reverend Dr. Bransby. It was a solid structure, with massy door, sooner than open which in the absence of the "Dominic," we would all have willingly perished by the peine forte et dure. In other angles were two other similar boxes, far less reverenced, indeed, but still greatly matters of awe. One of these was the pulpit of the "classical" usher, one of the "English and mathematical." Interspersed about the room, crossing and recrossing in endless irregularity, were innumerable benches and desks, black, ancient, and time-worn, piled desperately with much-bethumbed books, and so beseamed with initial letters, names at full length, grotesque figures, and other multiplied efforts of the knife, as to have entirely lost what little of original form might have been their portion in days Long departed. A huge bucket with water stood at one extremity of the room, and a clock of stupendous dimensions at the other.

Encompassed by the massy walls of this venerable academy, I passed, yet not in

教室是房子里最大的一间，我不禁认为，它是全世界最大的房间。房间狭长，加上哥特式的窗子和橡树的天花板，低得让人气闷。在远处一个令人恐惧的角落里，围出了一间 10 英尺左右的密室——它是由我们校长，牧师勃兰斯比博士在"授课时间"使用的。密室结构坚固，房门厚重。即便上帝"多明尼克"不在，我们也不愿去开一下门，宁愿被酷刑折磨死，也不会去。在另外的角落里，还有两个类似的房间，虽然不那么令人敬畏，但也是相当可怖的所在。其中一间是"古典文学"老师的教坛，另一间则是"英语兼数学"老师的。散布在教室里的是横七竖八，杂乱得无法计数的桌凳，黑糊糊的，又旧又破。上面乱糟糟地堆放着翻皱的书本、刻满了缩写词的首字母，或是详细的全名，还有稀奇古怪的图形和用刀子刻了多次留下的记号。因此，早在很久以前，这里就彻底失去了其原始的模样，几乎点滴不剩。一大桶水杵在房间的一头，另一头则是一个大得令人咋舌的钟。

包围在这个古老学院的厚重的围墙里，我度过了自己一生中的第

tedium or disgust, the years of the third lustrum of my life. The teeming brain of childhood requires no external world of incident to occupy or amuse it; and the apparently dismal monotony of a school was replete with more intense excitement than my riper youth has derived from luxury, or my full manhood from crime. Yet I must believe that my first mental development had in it much of the uncommon – even much of the *outre*. Upon mankind at large the events of very early existence rarely leave in mature age any definite impression. All is gray shadow – a weak and irregular remembrance – an indistinct regathering of feeble pleasures and phantasmagoric pains. With me this is not so. In childhood I must have felt with the energy of a man what I now find stamped upon memory in lines as vivid, as deep, and as durable as the *exergues* of the Carthaginian medals.

Yet in fact – in the fact of the world's view – how little was there to remember! The morning's awakening, the nightly summons to bed; the connings, the recitations; the periodical half-holidays, and perambulations; the play-ground, with its broils, its pastimes, its intrigues; – these, by a mental sorcery Long forgotten, were made to involve a wilderness of sensation, a world of rich incident, an universe of varied emotion, of excitement the most

三个 5 年之期，倒也没觉得憋闷或厌恶。童年时代富于幻想的头脑无须拿外面世界的是是非非来填补，更无须以此自娱自乐。学校里显见的枯燥乏味的生活却比我略显成熟时的青年时代的奢华生活更能给我带来紧张刺激，就连成年后的罪恶生活也不及它。不过我必须承认，在我的心智发育的初期，一定有很多不同寻常的东西——甚至超越常规。通常，幼年时的生活很少能在成年人的记忆中留下明确的痕迹。一切都是灰蒙蒙的影像——是脆弱的、杂乱无章的记忆——混杂着淡淡的喜悦和幻影般的痛苦。但我却不同。童年时代，我必定是具备着成人一般的精力，至今还记得刻在我记忆中的点点滴滴，如同伽太基奖章上的雕刻印记一样，分明、深刻而持久。

可事实上——在世人看来的事实上——几乎没什么好回忆的！早晨醒来起床、晚上上床入睡；默读、背诵；定期的半天假外出巡游；操场上的打闹、嬉戏和恶作剧——这些早该忘记的事情，却在心智的幻境中，牵涉出疯狂躁动的场景、多是多非的世界、思绪万千却又最最惊心动魄的大杂烩。哦，童年真是黄金时代！

passionate and spirit-stirring. *"Oh, le bon temps, que ce siecle de fer!"*

In truth, the ardor, the enthusiasm, and the imperiousness of my disposition, soon rendered me a marked character among my schoolmates, and by slow, but natural gradations, gave me an ascendancy over all not greatly older than myself; – over all with a single exception. This exception was found in the person of a scholar, who, although no relation, bore the same Christian and surname as myself; – a circumstance, in fact, little remarkable; for, notwithstanding a noble descent, mine was one of those everyday appellations which seem, by prescriptive right, to have been, time out of mind, the common property of the mob. In this narrative I have therefore designated myself as William Wilson, – a fictitious title not very dissimilar to the real. My namesake alone, of those who in school phraseology constituted "our set," presumed to compete with me in the studies of the class – in the sports and broils of the play-ground – to refuse implicit belief in my assertions, and submission to my will – indeed, to interfere with my arbitrary dictation in any respect whatsoever. If there is on earth a supreme and unqualified despotism, it is the despotism of a master mind in boyhood over the less energetic spirits of its companions.

说真的，我性情中的热诚、激情和专横，很快就让我在同学当中脱颖而出。渐渐地，我自然而然地开始指使那些甚至比我年龄稍大的人，只有一个例外。这例外是一位同学，尽管我们非亲非故，但却同名同姓。这事其实并不稀奇。虽然是名门贵族之后，但我的名字却是日常常见的。根据时效原则，似乎很久以前，这名字就已为平民百姓所有。因此在我的讲述里，我自称威廉·威尔逊，一个跟真名差不多的假名字。在我们所谓的"圈子"里，只有跟我同名的那个同学，才敢和我在课堂学习方面、在操场运动和打闹的时候较劲，甚至拒绝服从我的命令，更不臣服于我的意志——事实上，他还横加干涉我在各个方面的专制。如果这世上有什么至高无上却又虚无权势的专制统治的话，那肯定是少年时代的孩子王对唯唯诺诺的伙伴的领袖精神了。

Wilson's rebellion was to me a source of the greatest embarrassment; – the more so as, in spite of the bravado with which in public I made a point of treating him and his pretensions, I secretly felt that I feared him, and could not help thinking the equality which he maintained so easily with myself, a proof of his true superiority; since not to be overcome cost me a perpetual struggle. Yet this superiority – even this equality – was in truth acknowledged by no one but myself; our associates, by some unaccountable blindness, seemed not even to suspect it. Indeed, his competition, his resistance, and especially his impertinent and dogged interference with my purposes, were not more pointed than private. He appeared to be destitute alike of the ambition which urged, and of the passionate energy of mind which enabled me to excel. In his rivalry he might have been supposed actuated solely by a whimsical desire to thwart, astonish, or mortify myself; although there were times when I could not help observing, with a feeling made up of wonder, abasement, and pique, that he mingled with his injuries, his insults, or his contradictions, a certain most inappropriate, and assuredly most unwelcome *affectionateness* of manner. I could only conceive this singular behavior to arise from a consummate self-conceit

威尔逊对我不服是我最尴尬的一件事。在大庭广众之下，我肯定会虚张声势地对付他和他的高傲。可越是这样，私下里，我也就越怕他，而且我必须承认他能够轻而易举地和我平起平坐，这证明他的确比我厉害。因为不想输给他，我就必须作出长远的斗争。但是，无论是比我厉害，还是和我平起平坐，这一点却只有我一个人知道。同学们不知出于什么原因，竟然看不出来，甚至连一点疑心都没有。说真的，他跟我较劲儿，尤其是放肆且又顽固地跟我作对，虽然尖锐，但却隐蔽。他看起来不仅缺乏必要的野心，而且欠缺我这样激情四射的性子，这恰恰让我占了上风。他跟我较劲儿，或许就是一时的激愤，以阻挠我的专横，吓唬我，或让我收敛一下。但是有时我会有一种愕然、自卑和愤怒交织在一起的感觉，因为我不自禁地发现，他在伤害我、凌辱我、反驳我的时候，会不合时宜地掺杂着一种让人极其讨厌的柔情。我只好这样劝慰自己，这种特别的举止只不过是源自他的极端自负，以保护人自居的庸俗样子而已。

assuming the vulgar airs of patronage and protection.

Perhaps it was this latter trait in Wilson's conduct, conjoined with our identity of name, and the mere accident of our having entered the school upon the same day, which set afloat the notion that we were brothers, among the senior classes in the academy. These do not usually inquire with much strictness into the affairs of their juniors. I have before said, or should have said, that Wilson was not, in the most remote degree, connected with my family. But assuredly if we *had* been brothers we must have been twins; for, after leaving Dr. Bransby's, I casually learned that my namesake was born on the nineteenth of January, 1813 – and this is a somewhat remarkable coincidence; for the day is precisely that of my own nativity.

It may seem strange that in spite of the continual anxiety occasioned me by the rivalry of Wilson, and his intolerable spirit of contradiction, I could not bring myself to hate him altogether. We had, to be sure, nearly every day a quarrel in which, yielding me publicly the palm of victory, he, in some manner, contrived to make me feel that it was he who had deserved it; yet a sense of pride on my part, and a veritable dignity on his own, kept us always upon what are called "speaking terms," while there were many points of strong

或许，就是因为威尔逊举止中的这点柔情，加上我们又同名同姓，更巧的是又在同一天入校，所以，高年级才会传开我们是兄弟的说法。高年级学生很少会认真查究低年级学生的事情。我前面说过的，应该是说过的，威尔逊和我家压根没有一点关系。但如果我们真是兄弟的话，那准是双胞胎。因为在离开勃兰斯比那个学校后，我无意中了解到，那个同名同姓的人生于1813年1月19日——这真是惊天的巧合，因为那一天，恰好也是我的生日。

看起来有点奇怪，尽管我对威尔逊的叫板和他令人无法忍受的驳斥长期感到紧张，但是我却没有对他怀恨在心。事实上，我们几乎每天都吵架，他总是在大家面前屈从于我，让我获胜，但是又通过某种方式让我觉得赢家应该是他。然而，我的自尊心和他那份真正的尊严让我们总是保持着所谓的"泛泛之交"。不过，还是有很多地方我们是性情相投的，这让我意识到，只是我们所处的位置才是阻止我们成为朋友的障碍。事实上，很难定义，

congeniality in our tempers, operating to awake me in a sentiment which our position alone, perhaps, prevented from ripening into friendship. It is difficult, indeed, to define, or even to describe, my real feelings towards him. They formed a motley and heterogeneous admixture; – some petulant animosity, which was not yet hatred, some esteem, more respect, much fear, with a world of uneasy curiosity. To the moralist it will be unnecessary to say, in addition, that Wilson and myself were the most inseparable of companions.

It was no doubt the anomalous state of affairs existing between us, which turned all my attacks upon him, (and they were many, either open or covert) into the channel of banter or practical joke (giving pain while assuming the aspect of mere fun) rather than into a more serious and determined hostility. But my endeavours on this head were by no means uniformly successful, even when my plans were the most wittily concocted; for my namesake had much about him, in character, of that unassuming and quiet austerity which, while enjoying the poignancy of its own jokes, has no heel of Achilles in itself, and absolutely refuses to be laughed at. I could find, indeed, but one vulnerable point, and

甚至描述一下我对他的感觉。这感觉错综复杂，无以言表——有几分固执的仇视，却非仇恨；几分尊重，但更多的是敬重；诸多害怕，却又好奇心重。而且，对伦理学家来说，倒没必要强调，我和威尔逊是分割不开的伙伴。

毫无疑问，我和他之间有些异乎寻常的瓜葛。所以，我对他所有的攻击——攻击很多，明的暗的都有——总是以嘲弄或揶揄——既让他痛苦，又觉得搞笑——的方式出现，而非严肃决然的敌对。但我为此所做的努力却无一成功，即便是精心制订的计划也是枉然。因为那个跟我同名同姓的人，生性谦逊，而且既宁静又严肃，即便是听出那些笑话尖酸刻薄，也严肃地不露出"阿基琉斯之踵"[1]，真是无懈可击，而且绝不会被人嘲笑。事实上，我在他身上只能找到一个弱点，就是他身上有个特异之处，或许就是先天性的疾病。任何对手都不会借这个特异之处做备用，除非像我这般

[1] 在此比喻致命点。阿基琉斯为希腊神话人物。荷马史诗中的英雄。据说他出生后，母亲为了使他能刀枪不入，便把他浸入冥河水里，但他被母亲捏住的脚踵未能浸到冥河水，成了他的致命弱点。

that, lying in a personal peculiarity, arising, perhaps, from constitutional disease, would have been spared by any antagonist less at his wit's end than myself; – my rival had a weakness in the faucal or guttural organs, which precluded him from raising his voice at any time *above a very low whisper*. Of this defect I did not fail to take what poor advantage lay in my power.

Wilson's retaliations in kind were many; and there was one form of his practical wit that disturbed me beyond measure. How his sagacity first discovered at all that so petty a thing would vex me, is a question I never could solve; but, having discovered, he habitually practised the annoyance. I had always felt aversion to my uncourtly patronymic, and its very common, if not plebeian praenomen. The words were venom in my ears; and when, upon the day of my arrival, a second William Wilson came also to the academy, I felt angry with him for bearing the name, and doubly disgusted with the name because a stranger bore it, who would be the cause of its twofold repetition, who would be constantly in my presence, and whose concerns, in the ordinary routine of the school business, must inevitably, on account of the detestable coincidence, be often confounded with my own.

The feeling of vexation thus engendered grew stronger with every circumstance

无计可施。——我对手的咽喉，或喉咙处有毛病，这使得他任何时候都提不高嗓音，比微弱的耳语好不了多少。我可不会把自己这点微弱的优势弃之不用。

威尔逊对我的报复方法很多，他聪明的心智想出一招，就让我无计可施。他的聪明才智一开始是怎么发现这样的雕虫小技就能惹恼我的呢？这个问题我永远找不到答案。不过发现了这一点之后，他就频频使用这个恼人的手段。我一直讨厌自己平庸的姓氏，还有这个就算不是平头百姓所专用，也肯定是普通透顶的名字。在我的耳朵里，这姓名无异于毒液。我到校的第一天，另一个威廉·威尔逊也到了。我对于他叫这个名字感到非常生气，也更加厌恶这个名字，因为一个陌生人竟然也可以叫威廉·威尔逊。而他，会让这个名字得到双倍喊叫，他还会经常出现在我面前，他的相关事情，在学校生活的日常事务中，总会不可避免地和我搅和在一块。

由此而引发的恼怒，随着我和对手之间出现的一次次精神或生理

tending to show resemblance, moral or physical, between my rival and myself. I had not then discovered the remarkable fact that we were of the same age; but I saw that we were of the same height, and I perceived that we were even singularly alike in general contour of person and outline of feature. I was galled, too, by the rumor touching a relationship, which had grown current in the upper forms. In a word, nothing could more seriously disturb me, (although I scrupulously concealed such disturbance,) than any allusion to a similarity of mind, person, or condition existing between us. But, in truth, I had no reason to believe that (with the exception of the matter of relationship, and in the case of Wilson himself,) this similarity had ever been made a subject of comment, or even observed at all by our schoolfellows. That *he* observed it in all its bearings, and as fixedly as I, was apparent; but that he could discover in such circumstances so fruitful a field of annoyance, can only be attributed, as I said before, to his more than ordinary penetration.

His cue, which was to perfect an imitation of myself, lay both in words and in actions; and most admirably did he play his part. My dress it was an easy matter to copy; my gait and general manner were, without difficulty, appropriated; in spite of his constitutional defect, even my voice did

上的雷同之后，变得越来越强烈。我一开始并没发现我们同庚这一惊人事实，但我看出了我们身高一样，接下来我发现，我俩体形和轮廓都出奇地相似。我痛苦万分，还因为关于我俩是亲戚的谣传在高年级风传开来了。总之，只要稍有提及我俩在性情、容貌甚至境况上的相似之处，都能让我苦恼到极致（尽管我小心翼翼地掩饰着）。可事实上，我根本没理由相信我们俩的相似性已经成为谈论的话题了，甚至不相信同学们已经发现了我俩的相似性。但我相信他们说过我俩是亲戚，威尔逊也信。他跟我一样，都看到了我俩在各个方面的相似之处是非常明显的。但是他也能发现这种情况竟然给我带来如此之多的苦恼。如我所言，这肯定要归功于他异乎常人的睿智。

他的表演，无论是言语上还是行为上，都把我模仿得恰到好处。我的穿衣打扮可以轻松模仿，步态举止也不难模仿；尽管他的嗓子天生缺陷，但我的声音也难逃此运。当然，我的高嗓门他没试着模仿，但语调上学得如出一辙，他非同常

not escape him. My louder tones were, of course, unattempted, but then the key, it was identical; *and his singular whisper, it grew the very echo of my own.*

How greatly this most exquisite portraiture harassed me, (for it could not justly be termed a caricature,) I will not now venture to describe. I had but one consolation – in the fact that the imitation, apparently, was noticed by myself alone, and that I had to endure only the knowing and strangely sarcastic smiles of my namesake himself. Satisfied with having produced in my bosom the intended effect, he seemed to chuckle in secret over the sting he had inflicted, and was characteristically disregardful of the public applause which the success of his witty endeavours might have so easily elicited. That the school, indeed, did not feel his design, perceive its accomplishment, and participate in his sneer, was, for many anxious months, a riddle I could not resolve. Perhaps the *gradation* of his copy rendered it not so readily perceptible; or, more possibly, I owed my security to the master air of the copyist, who, disdaining the letter, (which in a painting is all the obtuse can see,) gave but the full spirit of his original for my individual contemplation and chagrin.

I have already more than once spoken of the disgusting air of patronage which he

人的低语，变成了我话语的回声。

这么惟妙惟肖的模仿让我何其烦恼啊！我都不敢描绘了。因为，你不能仅仅把它当做是讽刺漫画。唯一的安慰是，他的模仿显然只有我自己注意到了。于是我不得不忍受那同姓同名者会心又异常嘲讽的笑容了。他满足于既定的计谋在我的胸腔里起效，于是暗地里为自己刺痛了我而哧哧地笑。他机智的设计获得了成功，可以轻易地就赢得公众的掌声，但他明显不在乎这些。因此，事实上全校学生都没觉察出他的手段，都没发现他的成就，也就没人跟风嘲笑。这真是个谜，提心吊胆地过了几个月，我还是没揭开谜底。或许是因为他的模仿是渐进式的，使得它不是那么容易被察觉，或者我可能更应该感谢模仿者的超高技艺保全了我，他不屑做表面文章（如画上的东西，再愚钝的人也看得出），而是只流露出他的本来面目，让我猜忌和懊恼。

我已不止一次地说起，他对我摆出一副保护人的可恶嘴脸，而且

assumed toward me, and of his frequent officious interference withy my will. This interference often took the ungracious character of advice; advice not openly given, but hinted or insinuated. I received it with a repugnance which gained strength as I grew in years. Yet, at this distant day, let me do him the simple justice to acknowledge that I can recall no occasion when the suggestions of my rival were on the side of those errors or follies so usual to his immature age and seeming inexperience; that his moral sense, at least, if not his general talents and worldly wisdom, was far keener than my own; and that I might, to-day, have been a better, and thus a happier man, had I less frequently rejected the counsels embodied in those meaning whispers which I then but too cordially hated and too bitterly despised.

As it was, I at length grew restive in the extreme under his distasteful supervision, and daily resented more and more openly what I considered his intolerable arrogance. I have said that, in the first years of our connexion as schoolmates, my feelings in regard to him might have been easily ripened into friendship: but, in the latter months of my residence at the academy, although the intrusion of his ordinary manner had, beyond doubt, in some measure, abated, my sentiments, in nearly similar proportion, partook very

常常多管闲事，干涉我的意愿。这种干涉常常是不合我意的劝告，不是公开劝告，而是暗示，拐弯抹角的。我带着反感接受了劝告，这种反感随着我一年年长大也变得越来越强烈。不过，时至今日，就让我对他做点公道的事吧。我承认，我不记得我对头的建议有哪一次是错的或者愚蠢的，虽然他年纪轻轻，看上去经验不足；如果说他的聪明才智和处世智慧没有我高明的话，那至少，他的道德感要比我高明；在他意味深长的耳语中包含着谆谆劝告，如果我当时没有常常弃它们于不顾的话，那么，今天我就该是一个比较善良、比较快乐的人。但当时，我却对他的劝告痛恨不已、轻视至极。

就这样，我终于在他那令人讨厌的监督下变得极度失控，我对他那种忍无可忍的自负日益愤恨，而且越来越公开化。我说过，在我们做同学的头几年里，我对他的感觉本可以轻易地进一步发展为友谊；但是，学校生活的最后几个月，尽管他的插手比平素无疑减轻了几分，但我心中的恨意，反而对应着增加了几分。有一次，我想他是看出来了，随后，他就躲着我，或者说假装躲着我。

much of positive hatred. Upon one occasion he saw this, I think, and afterwards avoided, or made a show of avoiding me.

It was about the same period, if I remember aright, that, in an altercation of violence with him, in which he was more than usually thrown off his guard, and spoke and acted with an openness of demeanor rather foreign to his nature, I discovered, or fancied I discovered, in his accent, his air, and general appearance, a something which first startled, and then deeply interested me, by bringing to mind dim visions of my earliest infancy – wild, confused and thronging memories of a time when memory herself was yet unborn. I cannot better describe the sensation which oppressed me than by saying that I could with difficulty shake off the belief of my having been acquainted with the being who stood before me, at some epoch very Long ago – some point of the past even infinitely remote. The delusion, however, faded rapidly as it came; and I mention it at all but to define the day of the last conversation I there held with my singular namesake.

The huge old house, with its countless subdivisions, had several large chambers communicating with each other, where slept the greater number of the students. There were, however, (as must necessarily

如果我没记错的话，就是在那个时期，我跟他大吵了一架。吵架的时候，他一反常态，毫不设防，言行大开大合，全然不是他的本性。我发现，或者说我自以为我发现，在他的口音、神情、外表中隐藏着什么，一开始让我惊愕，随后又让我兴趣迭起。我的头脑里模糊地出现了婴儿时期的场景——我的记忆尚未建立之前的那些杂乱、恼人的往事齐涌过来。我无法更好地描绘出这份让我备感压迫的情感，我只能这么说，我费了好大劲才摆脱这样的一个想法：那就是我很久以前就认识我面前站着的这个人了，在很久远的年代，久远得没有尽头。然而，这个幻觉来得快，消失得同样也快。我提到这一点，只不过是想明确我跟那个同名同姓的人的最后一次谈话究竟是在哪一天。

那幢巨大的旧房子及其数不清的房间里，有几个大房间彼此连通，那是大多数学生睡觉的地方。不过，在设计得这么蹩脚的一幢建筑里，必定会有很多小角落，小壁凹，和

happen in a building so awkwardly planned,) many little nooks or recesses, the odds and ends of the structure; and these the economic ingenuity of Dr. Bransby had also fitted up as dormitories; although, being the merest closets, they were capable of accommodating but a single individual. One of these small apartments was occupied by Wilson.

One night, about the close of my fifth year at the school, and immediately after the altercation just mentioned, finding every one wrapped in sleep, I arose from bed, and, lamp in hand, stole through a wilderness of narrow passages from my own bedroom to that of my rival. I had Long been plotting one of those ill-natured pieces of practical wit at his expense in which I had hitherto been so uniformly unsuccessful. It was my intention, now, to put my scheme in operation, and I resolved to make him feel the whole extent of the malice with which I was imbued. Having reached his closet, I noiselessly entered, leaving the lamp, with a shade over it, on the outside. I advanced a step, and listened to the sound of his tranquil breathing. Assured of his being asleep, I returned, took the light, and with it again approached the bed. Close curtains were around it, which, in the prosecution of my plan, I slowly and quietly withdrew, when the bright rays fell vividly upon the sleeper,

其他零零碎碎的结构。这些都被精打细算的勃兰斯比博士布置成了宿舍，简直就是壁橱，只能容下一个人而已。这些小小的房间里，有一间就住着威尔逊。

大约是在我第五年的学校生活就要结束的时候，就在上面提到的那次吵架后不久的一个晚上。当每个人都酣然入梦之后，我从床上爬起身，手提着灯，悄悄地穿过狭窄的走道，溜到了冤家对头的寝室。我早就密谋着要使出一个恶毒的招数，让他付出点代价，可至今也没有得逞。现在，我就要将计划付诸实施了，我一定要让他感觉到我对他的全部怨恨。到他的小屋门口，我悄无声息地潜了进去，灯被留在外面，而且扣上了罩子。我朝前挪了一步，细听着他平稳的呼吸。确信他真的睡着了，我转身出来，取了灯，又回到他的床边。床的周遭密实地挂着帐子。计划就要实行了。我慢慢地把帐子掀开，不出一点声音。明亮的灯光鲜活地照着这个睡熟的人，同时我的目光也落在了他的脸上。一望之下，我顿时全身麻木，通体冰冷。我胸口狂跳，双膝乱颤，我的灵魂被一种说不清道不明却又无法忍受的恐惧感填得满满

and my eyes, at the same moment, upon his countenance. I looked; – and a numbness, an iciness of feeling instantly pervaded my frame. My breast heaved, my knees tottered, my whole spirit became possessed with an objectless yet intolerable horror. Gasping for breath, I lowered the lamp in still nearer proximity to the face. Were these – *these* the lineaments of William Wilson? I saw, indeed, that they were his, but I shook as if with a fit of the ague in fancying they were not. What *was* there about them to confound me in this manner? I gazed; – while my brain reeled with a multitude of incoherent thoughts. Not thus he appeared – assuredly not *thus* – in the vivacity of his waking hours. The same name! the same contour of person! the same day of arrival at the academy! And then his dogged and meaningless imitation of my gait, my voice, my habits, and my manner! Was it, in truth, within the bounds of human possibility, that *what I now saw* was the result, merely, of the habitual practice of this sarcastic imitation? Awe-stricken, and with a creeping shudder, I extinguished the lamp, passed silently from the chamber, and left, at once, the halls of that old academy, never to enter them again.

After a lapse of some months, spent at home in mere idleness, I found myself a student at Eton. The brief interval had been

的。喘着粗气，我无声地把灯放低到几乎要挨着他的脸。这——这就是威廉·威尔逊的面貌吗？可是，我切切实实地看到，这就是他的面貌。可是一想到这相貌不是他的，我就像发疟疾一样颤抖起来。这副容貌怎么会把我吓成这样？我凝视着他——我的脑子被各种杂乱的念头搅成一锅粥。他不是这个样子，绝不是这个样子，他醒着的时候肯定不是这个样子的。同名同姓！同样的面容！同一天进学校！随后，他无缘无故地又锲而不舍地模仿我的步态、我的声音、我的习惯、我的行为举止！难道，真的是因为人类的能力有限，我现在所看到的就是他一贯以来讽刺性地模仿我的后果吗？敬畏袭来，我周身战栗，灭了灯，悄悄地走出房间，很快就逃离了古老的学校，再也没跨进去过一步。

有几个月的时间，我在家无所事事，随后就发现自己已成了伊顿学校的学生。短短的一段日子足以

sufficient to enfeeble my remembrance of the events at Dr. Bransby's, or at least to effect a material change in the nature of the feelings with which I remembered them. The truth – the tragedy – of the drama was no more. I could now find room to doubt the evidence of my senses; and seldom called up the subject at all but with wonder at extent of human credulity, and a smile at the vivid force of the imagination which I hereditarily possessed. Neither was this species of scepticism likely to be diminished by the character of the life I led at Eton. The vortex of thoughtless folly into which I there so immediately and so recklessly plunged, washed away all but the froth of my past hours, engulfed at once every solid or serious impression, and left to memory only the veriest levities of a former existence.

I do not wish, however, to trace the course of my miserable profligacy here – a profligacy which set at defiance the laws, while it eluded the vigilance of the institution. Three years of folly, passed without profit, had but given me rooted habits of vice, and added, in a somewhat unusual degree, to my bodily stature, when, after a week of soulless dissipation, I invited a small party of the most dissolute students to a secret carousal in my chambers. We met at a late hour of the night; for our debaucheries were to be

冲淡我对勃兰斯比学校所发生的事情的记忆，至少，再想起的时候，心情上会产生具体的变化。戏剧般的真相和悲剧都已不复存在了。我现在有机会来质疑我所感受到的事物了。我很少会关注一件事，但却想知道人类轻信他人的底限在哪里，而且我对自己所继承下来的鲜活逼真的想象力不禁莞尔。种种的质疑并未随着我到伊顿学校生活而有所减轻。一到那里，我就马上义无反顾地投身于不假思索的荒唐事所会聚成的旋涡之中，冲走了一切，只剩下往昔虚无的泡沫；也吞没了所有深刻的重要印象，记忆中只剩下先前十足的轻浮。

不过，我可不想在此描述我那悲惨的放荡生活——放荡到挑衅法律，还避开了学校的注意。3 年的愚蠢荒唐，没带来任何好处，却害得我沾染上根深蒂固的恶习。还有，就是身材长高了，高得有些不同寻常。过了一个星期的放浪形骸，我邀请了一小撮荒淫透顶的学生到我的房间参加一个秘密的盛宴。我们在深夜时分碰面，因为我们打算寻欢作乐混个通宵。我们狂饮无度，而且也找不到别的可能会更冒险刺激的诱惑了。东方拂晓已然朦胧初

faithfully protracted until morning. The wine flowed freely, and there were not wanting other and perhaps more dangerous seductions; so that the gray dawn had already faintly appeared in the east, while our delirious extravagance was at its height. Madly flushed with cards and intoxication, I was in the act of insisting upon a toast of more than wonted profanity, when my attention was suddenly diverted by the violent, although partial unclosing of the door of the apartment, and by the eager voice of a servant from without. He said that some person, apparently in great haste, demanded to speak with me in the hall.

Wildly excited with wine, the unexpected interruption rather delighted than surprised me. I staggered forward at once, and a few steps brought me to the vestibule of the building. In this low and small room there hung no lamp; and now no light at all was admitted, save that of the exceedingly feeble dawn which made its way through the semi-circular window. As I put my foot over the threshold, I became aware of the figure of a youth about my own height, and habited in a white kerseymere morning frock, cut in the novel fashion of the one I myself wore at the moment. This faint light enabled me to perceive; but the features of his face I could not distinguish. Upon my entering he

现，我们的狂奢极欲却正在如火如荼。我满面通红，醉醺醺地玩着纸牌，一边还极度无耻地叫嚷着再干一杯。突然房门被推了半开，因为动作太猛，而且门外还传来仆人急切的声音，一下子就让我分了心。他说，有个人，很急切地要我到门厅谈话。

酒精让我兴奋得跟疯了一样，这不速之客的扰乱反倒让我高兴，一点也不觉得惊讶。我立刻跟跄前往，几步就跨到了门厅。又矮又小的门厅里没有灯，这个时候也根本没有亮光能进得来，只有几线微弱的曙光从半圆形的窗户渗进来。一只脚刚踏上门槛，我就注意到一个年轻人，差不多跟我一样高，穿着件雪白的开司米晨衣，裁剪得跟我正穿着的那件一样新潮。这是我借着朦胧的光线看到的，但他的面部容貌却无法看清。我刚一进来，他就一步跨到我跟前，急不可耐地拽住了我的胳膊，对着我的耳朵低声吐出几个字："威廉·威尔逊！"

strode hurriedly up to me, and, seizing me by the arm with a gesture of petulant impatience, whispered the words "William Wilson" in my ear.

I grew perfectly sober in an instant.

There was that in the manner of the stranger, and in the tremulous shake of his uplifted finger, as he held it between my eyes and the light, which filled me with unqualified amazement; but it was not this which had so violently moved me. It was the pregnancy of solemn admonition in the singular, low, hissing utterance; and, above all, it was the character, the tone, *the key*, of those few, simple, and familiar, yet *whispered* syllables, which came with a thousand thronging memories of bygone days, and struck upon my soul with the shock of a galvanic battery. Ere I could recover the use of my senses he was gone.

Although this event failed not of a vivid effect upon my disordered imagination, yet was it evanescent as vivid. For some weeks, indeed, I busied myself in earnest inquiry, or was wrapped in a cloud of morbid speculation. I did not pretend to disguise from my perception the identity of the singular individual who thus perseveringly interfered with my affairs, and harassed me with his insinuated counsel. But who and what was this Wilson? – and whence came he? – and what were his purposes? Upon neither of

我瞬间完全清醒了。

这陌生人的模样以及亮光中他竖在我眼前的不住颤抖的手指，让我感到万分惊讶，但这还不足以让我觉得极端震撼。反而是那包含着郑重警告的古怪低沉的嘶嘶声，尤其是那几个耳语般吐出的简单熟悉的字眼所显露出的特征、音质和语调，以及蜂拥而至的庞杂记忆，如同强电流一样一下子击中了我的魂灵。没等我恢复知觉，他就已经走了。

虽然这事在我混乱的脑海里确实留下了鲜明的印象，但渐渐地它又同样鲜明地消散了。事实上，有几个星期，我认认真真地忙着去找寻答案，或者说陷入了病态的揣测。我没法欺骗自己的感觉，我的的确确认识那个总是不屈不挠地干预我私事的怪人，他还不厌其烦地暗示我一些忠言。但这个威尔逊到底是谁？他是干什么的？他从哪儿来？他的目的是什么？这些我一无所知。关于他，我唯一确定的就是，他家突遭变故，被迫离开了勃兰斯

these points could I be satisfied; merely ascertaining, in regard to him, that a sudden accident in his family had caused his removal from Dr. Bransby's academy on the afternoon of the day in which I myself had eloped. But in a brief period I ceased to think upon the subject; my attention being all absorbed in a contemplated departure for Oxford. Thither I soon went; the uncalculating vanity of my parents furnishing me with an outfit and annual establishment, which would enable me to indulge at will in the luxury already so dear to my heart, – to vie in profuseness of expenditure with the haughtiest heirs of the wealthiest earldoms in Great Britain.

Excited by such appliances to vice, my constitutional temperament broke forth with redoubled ardor, and I spurned even the common restraints of decency in the mad infatuation of my revels. But it were absurd to pause in the detail of my extravagance. Let it suffice, that among spendthrifts I out-Heroded Herod, and that, giving name to a multitude of novel follies, I added no brief appendix to the Long catalogue of vices then usual in the most dissolute university of Europe.

It could hardly be credited, however, that I had, even here, so utterly fallen from the gentlemanly estate, as to seek acquaintance with the vilest arts of the gambler by profession, and, having become an adept in

比学校，恰恰就是在我出逃的同一天的下午。不过，没过多久，我就不再思虑这些，所有的精力都集中到了既定的去牛津大学的事情上了。不久我就到了那里。我父母虚荣得昏头昏脑，给我准备了全套的用具，备好了一年的花销，让我可以尽情地享受自己钟爱的奢华生活，可以跟大不列颠那帮傲慢的豪门子弟比一比骄奢淫逸了。

我兴奋不已，因为有了堕落的本钱。我的天性变本加厉地爆发了。我甚至抛却了最基本的礼义廉耻，发了疯似的寻欢作乐。但是在此停下来细述我的放浪形骸，就显得太荒唐了。只举一例就够了。在挥霍者的群体中，我比希律王更希律王，如果把那么多稀奇古怪的荒唐事一并列出，我加在这所欧洲最荒淫的大学那串长长的罪行录上的就绝不是短短的附录。

然而，让人难以置信的是，恰恰是在这里，我彻底从绅士阶层堕落了。这都是为了能从职业赌徒那里套到最卑劣的骗术。而且我还修成了这门学科的行家里手，又常常

his despicable science, to practise it habitually as a means of increasing my already enormous income at the expense of the weak-minded among my fellow-collegians. Such, nevertheless, was the fact. And the very enormity of this offence against all manly and honourable sentiment proved, beyond doubt, the main if not the sole reason of the impunity with which it was committed. Who, indeed, among my most abandoned associates, would not rather have disputed the clearest evidence of his senses, than have suspected of such courses, the gay, the frank, the generous William Wilson – the noblest and most commoner at Oxford – him whose follies (said his parasites) were but the follies of youth and unbridled fancy – whose errors but inimitable whim – whose darkest vice but a careless and dashing extravagance?

I had been now two years successfully busied in this way, when there came to the university a young *parvenu* nobleman, Glendinning – rich, said report, as Herodes Atticus – his riches, too, as easily acquired. I soon found him of weak intellect, and, of course, marked him as a fitting subject for my skill. I frequently engaged him in play, and contrived, with the gambler's usual art, to let him win considerable sums, the more effectually to entangle him in my snares.

以此为手段来让自己本就十分丰厚的钱财不断增长，而为此埋单的就是我那些意志不坚定的大学同学。不管怎么说，事实就是这样。而这种罪恶行径全然没有男人味，也不顾尊严，无疑，这就是我作奸犯科而又觉得心安理得的主要原因——即便不是唯一的原因。但事实上，我那些自甘堕落的同伴中，谁都不愿意谈论他们清清楚楚看到的事实，更不会怀疑快乐、率直、慷慨的威廉·威尔逊。他们认为这个牛津大学最高贵、最磊落的自费生所做下的荒唐事不过是年少轻狂，所犯下的错误只室一时兴起，而他极端的恶习也不过是粗心毛躁的率性而为。

就这样，我成功地忙忙碌碌了两年，直到大学里来了个年幼的贵族暴发户。葛兰丁宁，很有钱，据说跟希律士·阿蒂克[1]一样有钱，而且也像他一样来钱很容易。我很快就发现他有点弱智，自然就把他定为施展绝技的理想对象。我经常怂恿他玩牌，还使出赌徒惯用的伎俩，刻意让他赢走相当可观的一笔钱，这样才能有效地让他落入我的陷阱。最后，我的计划就要成熟了。

---

[1] 希律士·阿蒂克:希腊修辞学家，诡辩家。曾捐献财产装饰雅典城及别的希腊城市。

At length, my schemes being ripe, I met him (with the full intention that this meeting should be final and decisive) at the chambers of a fellow-commoner, (Mr. Preston,) equally intimate with both, but who, to do him Justice, entertained not even a remote suspicion of my design. To give to this a better colouring, I had contrived to have assembled a party of some eight or ten, and was solicitously careful that the introduction of cards should appear accidental, and originate in the proposal of my contemplated dupe himself. To be brief upon a vile topic, none of the low finesse was omitted, so customary upon similar occasions that it is a just matter for wonder how any are still found so besotted as to fall its victim.

We had protracted our sitting far into the night, and I had at length effected the manoeuvre of getting Glendinning as my sole antagonist. The game, too, was my favorite ecarte! The rest of the company, interested in the extent of our play, had abandoned their own cards, and were standing around us as spectators. The *parvenu*, who had been induced by my artifices in the early part of the evening, to drink deeply, now shuffled, dealt, or played, with a wild nervousness of manner for which his intoxication, I thought, might partially, but could not altogether account. In a very short period he had become my

我在同是自费生伙计——普雷斯顿的宿舍里跟他见面（我一心揣着一个念头：这次见面是最后一次，也是决定性的一次）。普雷斯顿先生跟我们两个关系都很亲密，但是，公平地讲，他丝毫没怀疑我的安排。为了让这事更有声色，我特意召集了十来个人的一拨人马，极其小心地装成玩牌这事是偶然提及的，按部就班地引他上了钩。简略地说，赌博这件肮脏事是绝离不开下流的手段的，同样的手段经常会出现，但奇怪的是，怎么还会有人晕晕乎乎地就成了它的刀下鬼。

我们一直熬坐到深夜，最后，我终于把葛兰丁宁密谋成了我唯一的对手。游戏也是我最喜欢玩的埃卡特！其他人对我们所玩的筹码大小非常感兴趣，都扔掉自己的牌，围在我们旁边当了看客。这暴发户上半夜上了我的当，喝了很多酒。现在，洗牌、发牌、打牌，他都显得无比紧张，我想，部分是因为他喝醉了，但也不会全是因为醉酒。不一会儿的工夫，他就输给了我一大笔钱。他灌了一大口葡萄酒后，提出将原本的巨额赌注再加一倍——这正是我一直以来冷静地精密计划着的。我装出很勉强的样子，直

debtor to a large amount, when, having taken a Long draught of port, he did precisely what I had been coolly anticipating – he proposed to double our already extravagant stakes. With a well-feigned show of reluctance, and not until after my repeated refusal had seduced him into some angry words which gave a color of pique to my compliance, did I finally comply. The result, of course, did but prove how entirely the prey was in my toils; in less than an hour he had quadrupled his debt. For some time his countenance had been losing the florid tinge lent it by the wine; but now, to my astonishment, I perceived that it had grown to a pallor truly fearful. I say to my astonishment. Glendinning had been represented to my eager inquiries as immeasurably wealthy; and the sums which he had as yet lost, although in themselves vast, could not, I supposed, very seriously annoy, much less so violently affect him. That he was overcome by the wine just swallowed, was the idea which most readily presented itself; and, rather with a view to the preservation of my own character in the eyes of my associates, than from any less interested motive, I was about to insist, peremptorily, upon a discontinuance of the play, when some expressions at my elbow from among the company, and an ejaculation evincing

到我再三地拒绝引诱着他大放厥词，让我气不过，这才顺从于他。当然，结果不过是证明了这个猎物已完全掉进了我的圈套。不到一个小时，他的债就连翻了4倍。有一段时间，他的脸上连酒醉的红晕都消失不见了。但现在，让我吃惊的是，那张脸竟然变得苍白，极其吓人。我说过我非常吃惊。因为根据我的周密调查，葛兰丁宁富得无法估量。他输掉的这笔钱固然巨大，可是我想也不至于这么懊恼啊，更不会对他产生这么严重的影响啊。一个念头立刻跳出来向我举证，"他被刚刚喝下去的酒放倒了。"为了在同伙面前保持自己的人格，而不是为了什么无私的动机，我立刻紧急表态，要终止这场游戏。因为我注意到周围人的议论，也听到了葛兰丁宁蓦然发出的万分绝望的叹息。这让我一下子明白了，我已害得他倾家荡产了，这种情况下，他成了大伙同情的对象，成了魔鬼都不忍心下手的被保护者。

utter despair on the part of Glendinning, gave me to understand that I had effected his total ruin under circumstances which, rendering him an object for the pity of all, should have protected him from the ill offices even of a fiend.

What now might have been my conduct it is difficult to say. The pitiable condition of my dupe had thrown an air of embarrassed gloom over all; and, for some moments, a profound silence was maintained, during which I could not help feeling my cheeks tingle with the many burning glances of scorn or reproach cast upon me by the less abandoned of the party. I will even own that an intolerable weight of anxiety was for a brief instant lifted from my bosom by the sudden and extraordinary interruption which ensued. The wide, heavy folding doors of the apartment were all at once thrown open, to their full extent, with a vigorous and rushing impetuosity that extinguished, as if by magic, every candle in the room. Their light, in dying, enabled us just to perceive that a stranger had entered, about my own height, and closely muffled in a cloak. The darkness, however, was now total; and we could only feel that he was standing in our midst. Before any one of us could recover from the extreme astonishment into which this rudeness had thrown all, we heard the voice of the intruder.

　　我当时是怎样的一番举动？真是很难说。被我愚弄的那个人的可怜样让所有的人的头上都笼罩着尴尬阴沉的气氛。有好长一段时间，只有深深的沉默，其间我不由觉得脸上火辣辣地刺痛，因为许多轻蔑、责备的目光像喷火一样烧到了我的脸上，那是我们这一伙中一些不太放荡的人。我甚至愿意承认，一份让人无法忍受的焦虑压在我的胸口，但是突如其来的意外在一瞬间就把它取走了。又宽又重的折叠式房门突然大开，带着一股又猛又急的冲力，把房间里所有的烛火全都熄灭，如同受了巫术。蜡烛就要熄灭之前的一线亮光，刚好让我们看到一个陌生人进来了。他身高跟我相仿，紧紧地裹着件披风。但是此时正是漆黑一片，我们只能感觉得到他就站在我们中间。大家对他的粗暴感到极度震惊，都还没有回过神来，就听得这个入侵者开始说话了。

"Gentlemen," he said, in a low, distinct, and never-to-be-forgotten whisper which thrilled to the very marrow of my bones, "Gentlemen, I make no apology for this behaviour, because in thus behaving, I am but fulfilling a duty. You are, beyond doubt, uninformed of the true character of the person who has to-night won at *écarté* a large sum of money from Lord Glendinning. I will therefore put you upon an expeditious and decisive plan of obtaining this very necessary information. Please to examine, at your leisure, the inner linings of the cuff of his left sleeve, and the several little packages which may be found in the somewhat capacious pockets of his embroidered morning wrapper."

While he spoke, so profound was the stillness that one might have heard a pin drop upon the floor. In ceasing, he departed at once, and as abruptly as he had entered. Can I – shall I describe my sensations? – must I say that I felt all the horrors of the damned? Most assuredly I had little time given for reflection. Many hands roughly seized me upon the spot, and lights were immediately reproduced. A search ensued. In the lining of my sleeve were found all the court cards essential in *écarté*, and, in the pockets of my wrapper, a number of packs, facsimiles of those used at our sittings, with the single exception that mine

"先生们，"他以一种低沉、清晰、让我死也不会忘记的耳语说道，这吓得我从骨头缝里都战栗不已，"先生们，我不想为自己的行为道歉，因为这么做，是为了履行我的职责。毫无疑问，你们并不知晓这个人的真实本性，今晚这个人玩埃卡特赢了葛兰丁宁爵爷一大笔钱。因此，我要给你们提供一个快捷有效的方法去查验必要的信息。你们有空的话，就请检查一下他左边袖口的衬里，还会有几小包藏在那件绣花衬衣的大口袋里。"

他说话的时候，房间里无比安静，连一根针掉到地上都听得到。话音刚落，他立刻消失了，跟他刚才进来的时候一样突然。我还能——我还需要描述我的心情吗？我非得说自己对这该死的家伙无比害怕？确信无疑的是，我没机会作出反应了。大伙粗暴地把我当场揪住，烛火也霎时间又亮了。搜查开始了。在我袖口的衬里中搜出了埃卡特里必不可少的花牌；在衬衣口袋里，几副跟我们牌局上一模一样的复制牌也被搜了出来。不一样的是，我这几副牌，术语叫做"变更卡"，大牌的两端微凸，小牌则两边微凸。如此

were of the species called, technically, *arrondees*; the honours being slightly convex at the ends, the lower cards slightly convex at the sides. In this disposition, the dupe who cuts, as customary, at the length of the pack, will invariably find that he cuts his antagonist an honor; while the gambler, cutting at the breadth, will, as certainly, cut nothing for his victim which may count in the records of the game.

Any burst of indignation upon this discovery would have affected me less than the silent contempt, or the sarcastic composure, with which it was received.

"Mr. Wilson," said our host, stooping to remove from beneath his feet an exceedingly luxurious cloak of rare furs, "Mr. Wilson, this is your property. (The weather was cold; and, upon quitting my own room, I had thrown a cloak over my dressing wrapper, putting it off upon reaching the scene of play.) "I presume it is supererogatory to seek here (eyeing the folds of the garment with a bitter smile) for any farther evidence of your skill. Indeed, we have had enough. You will see the necessity, I hope, of quitting Oxford – at all events, of quitting instantly my chambers."

Abased, humbled to the dust as I then was, it is probable that I should have resented this galling language by immediate personal violence, had not my whole attention been at the moment

一来，受骗者在砌牌的时候，按照惯例是竖着来的，那么，他肯定会发给对手一张大牌；而赌棍则是横着砌牌，发给对手的肯定不会是一张记分的大牌。

对这一真相的任何愤慨都对我影响不大，还不如无声的鄙视或冷冷的讥讽来得厉害，那样，我才会感觉受到了影响。

"威尔逊先生，"房主弯下腰，从脚下拎起一件稀有毛皮做成的极度豪华的披风，"威尔逊先生，这是你的东西。（天气很冷，离开自己房间的时候，我披了件披风在晨衣外面，到了牌场才脱下）我觉得，还得搜搜这里（眼睛盯着披风的褶皱，脸上挂着冷笑），再给你那套把戏多找出点证据来。事实上，证据已经够多了。我希望你明白，你必须离开牛津大学——无论如何，必须马上离开我的宿舍。"

当时，我被贬得都埋到尘埃里了，本来我很有可能会对这些充满人身攻击的羞辱我的话大发脾气的，但是我的全部精力却在那个时候被一件不可思议的事情牵住了。

arrested by a fact of the most startling character. The cloak which I had worn was of a rare description of fur; how rare, how extravagantly costly, I shall not venture to say. Its fashion, too, was of my own fantastic invention; for I was fastidious to an absurd degree of coxcombry, in matters of this frivolous nature. When, therefore, Mr. Preston reached me that which he had picked up upon the floor, and near the folding doors of the apartment, it was with an astonishment nearly bordering upon terror, that I perceived my own already hanging on my arm, (where I had no doubt unwittingly placed it,) and that the one presented me was but its exact counterpart in every, in even the minutest possible particular. The singular being who had so disastrously exposed me, had been muffled, I remembered, in a cloak; and none had been worn at all by any of the members of our party with the exception of myself. Retaining some presence of mind, I took the one offered me by Preston; placed it, unnoticed, over my own; left the apartment with a resolute scowl of defiance; and, next morning ere dawn of day, commenced a hurried journey from Oxford to the continent, in a perfect agony of horror and of shame.

I fled in vain. My evil destiny pursued me as if in exultation, and proved, indeed, that the exercise of its mysterious

我穿的那件披风是用稀有到无从描述的皮子做的，但到底有多稀罕，到底值多大一笔钱，我也不敢说。它的样式也是我自己充满想象的发明。因为我对穿衣打扮的挑剔到了荒唐可笑的田地，这都是因为我虚浮轻狂的本性。所以，当普雷斯顿先生递给我他从折门附近的地板上拾起的那件披风时，我与其说是惊讶倒不如说是恐惧了。我察觉到我自己的披风已经搭在手臂上了（我肯定是无意间搭上的）。而递给我的那件，绝对就是我手臂上这件的复制品，每一点，甚至最最细微的地方都分毫不差。那个灾难性地揭露我的怪人身上，我记得是裹了件披风的。而我们这伙人中，除了我以外是没有人穿披风的。我把这事装在自己的脑子里，接过普雷斯顿递来的那件披风，悄悄地放在自己的那一件上面，带着满不在乎的满面怒容毅然决然地离开了那间公寓。第二天天亮之前，我就动身离开了牛津，踏上前往大陆的匆匆旅途，满是恐惧和羞耻交织的苦恼。

逃也没用。厄运一直紧跟着我，好像乐此不疲，而且最终证明了，事实上，这厄运对它神秘操控权的

dominion had as yet only begun. Scarcely had I set foot in Paris ere I had fresh evidence of the detestable interest taken by this Wilson in my concerns. Years flew, while I experienced no relief. Villain! – at Rome, with how untimely, yet with how spectral an officiousness, stepped he in between me and my ambition! At Vienna, too – at Berlin – and at Moscow! Where, in truth, had I not bitter cause to curse him within my heart? From his inscrutable tyranny did I at length flee, panic-stricken, as from a pestilence; and to the very ends of the earth *I fled in vain*.

And again, and again, in secret communion with my own spirit, would I demand the questions "Who is he? – whence came he? – and what are his objects?" But no answer was there found. And then I scrutinized, with a minute scrutiny, the forms, and the methods, and the leading traits of his impertinent supervision. But even here there was very little upon which to base a conjecture. It was noticeable, indeed, that, in no one of the multiplied instances in which he had of late crossed my path, had he so crossed it except to frustrate those schemes, or to disturb those actions, which, if fully carried out, might have resulted in bitter mischief. Poor justification this, in truth, for an authority so imperiously assumed! Poor indemnity for natural rights of self-agency

训练只不过是刚刚开始而已。几乎没等我的双脚踏上巴黎的土地，我就发现了新的证据：这个威尔逊又对我的事情充满了让人恶心的兴趣。几年时间很快就过去了，但我从未觉得有丝毫解脱。恶魔！——在罗马，他像个幽灵一样不合时宜地多管闲事，阻碍我实现自己的雄心壮志。在维也纳也是，在柏林，在莫斯科！说实话，在我心里，哪个角落没有对他恶毒地诅咒过？在他捉摸不定的管束下，我最终只能仓皇出逃，心惊肉跳，像是在逃避瘟疫。可纵然是逃到世界的尽头，最终也是瞎逃一场。

一次又一次地，我对着自己的灵魂悄悄地发问："他是谁？——他从哪儿来？——他的目的是什么？"但答案无处可寻。接下来，我细致入微地查看他无故地监督我的形式、方法和主要特征，但即便在这里也找不到任何的蛛丝马迹。事实上，需要注意的是，从来没有出现过以下的情况：有几次他没来得及阻止我，或是他阻止了却没能挫败我的计划，或是没能干扰到我的行动，也就说，我的计划成功实施了，结果却是让我无比痛苦的灾难。如此解释，事实上，对于一个自以为是、妄自尊大的"权威人士"来说，真是太可怜了。这点补偿，对于被执拗且无理地否决了的"独裁者"的天赐强权来说，真是太可

so pertinaciously, so insultingly denied!

I had also been forced to notice that my tormentor, for a very Long period of time, (while scrupulously and with miraculous dexterity maintaining his whim of an identity of apparel with myself,) had so contrived it, in the execution of his varied interference with my will, that I saw not, at any moment, the features of his face. Be Wilson what he might, *this*, at least, was but the veriest of affectation, or of folly. Could he, for an instant, have supposed that, in my admonisher at Eton – in the destroyer of my honor at Oxford, – in him who thwarted my ambition at Rome, my revenge at Paris, my passionate love at Naples, or what he falsely termed my avarice in Egypt, – that in this, my arch-enemy and evil genius, could fall to recognise the William Wilson of my school boy days, – the namesake, the companion, the rival, – the hated and dreaded rival at Dr. Bransby's? Impossible! – But let me hasten to the last eventful scene of the drama.

Thus far I had succumbed supinely to this imperious domination. The sentiment of deep awe with which I habitually regarded the elevated character, the majestic wisdom, the apparent omnipresence and omnipotence of Wilson, added to a feeling of even terror, with which certain other traits in his nature and

悲了。

我根本不想看到的就是我的那个痛苦的人，长期以来都在小心翼翼地利用他匪夷所思的巧妙心思维持着一个念想，那就是和我穿同样的衣服，他做到了，而且还十分巧妙地以各种各样的手段来干涉我的意愿，而我，在任何时候，都看不到他的面部特征。管他是威尔逊某某呢，他这么做，真是做作透顶，愚蠢到家了。他能否用片刻的时间想到，在伊顿学校忠告我的那个人，在牛津大学败坏我的名誉的那个人，在罗马不让我如愿的那个人，在巴黎妨碍我复仇的那个人，在那不勒斯阻挠我热恋的那个人，在埃及诬陷我是贪财鬼的那个人，被我当做凤敌的魔鬼般的那个天才，会不认识和我一起读小学的那个威廉·威尔逊？那个与我同名同姓的人，我的伙伴、冤家对头——那个勃兰斯比博士的学校里可恨可怕的对头？不可能！还是让我赶紧把这出戏最后，也是最重要的一场唱完吧。

那么久的时间，我一直被捏在这个专制独裁者的手心里。满怀着深深的敬畏，我一贯认为威尔逊品格高尚、智慧不凡、无处不在、无所不能；我甚至感到害怕，因为他某些天生和假装的特性压制着我。而这些也让我明白了，迄今为止，我是多么软弱，多么无助；这些还

assumptions inspired me, had operated, hitherto, to impress me with an idea of my own utter weakness and helplessness, and to suggest an implicit, although bitterly reluctant submission to his arbitrary will. But, of late days, I had given myself up entirely to wine; and its maddening influence upon my hereditary temper rendered me more and more impatient of control. I began to murmur, – to hesitate, – to resist. And was it only fancy which induced me to believe that, with the increase of my own firmness, that of my tormentor underwent a proportional diminution? Be this as it may, I now began to feel the inspiration of a burning hope, and at length nurtured in my secret thoughts a stern and desperate resolution that I would submit no Longer to be enslaved.

It was at Rome, during the Carnival of 18–, that I attended a masquerade in the palazzo of the Neapolitan Duke Di Broglio. I had indulged more freely than usual in the excesses of the wine-table; and now the suffocating atmosphere of the crowded rooms irritated me beyond endurance. The difficulty, too, of forcing my way through the mazes of the company contributed not a little to the ruffling of my temper; for I was anxiously seeking, (let me not say with what unworthy motive) the young, the gay, the beautiful wife of the

暗示了我虽然痛苦，但也要屈服于他的专断的意志。可后来，我把自己彻底地献给了酒精。酒精那令人发疯的效果刺激了我祖传的脾性，让我越来越焦躁，难以控制。我开始低声抱怨——踌躇——反抗。这会是一个幻觉吗？我只能这么认为：只要自己一天比一天坚定，那么折磨我的人就会一天比一天远离？实事求是地说，我现在感觉到炽热的希望给了我鼓舞。最后，在我秘密的思想里形成了一个严肃的不顾一切的决定。那就是：我不会再受到别人的奴役了。

就是在罗马，18××年的狂欢节的时候，我去那不勒斯的德·布罗利奥公爵府上参加化装舞会。在酒桌上，我毫无节制地比平时多喝了很多酒。拥挤不堪的房间里弥漫着让人窒息的乌烟瘴气，真让我烦躁得不行了。我硬生生地挤过乱哄哄的人群，太费劲了，这无疑又给我的火气上浇了不少油。因为我在急切地寻找（别让我说出是出于怎样卑鄙的动机）年老昏聩的德·布罗利奥那年轻、放荡又美丽的妻子。她先前已经恬不知耻地告诉过我一

aged and doting Di Broglio. With a too unscrupulous confidence she had previously communicated to me the secret of the costume in which she would be habited, and now, having caught a glimpse of her person, I was hurrying to make my way into her presence. – At this moment I felt a light hand placed upon my shoulder, and that ever-remembered, low, damnable *whisper* within my ear.

In an absolute phrenzy of wrath, I turned at once upon him who had thus interrupted me, and seized him violently by tile collar. He was attired, as I had expected, in a costume altogether similar to my own; wearing a Spanish cloak of blue velvet, begirt about the waist with a crimson belt sustaining a rapier. A mask of black silk entirely covered his face.

"Scoundrel!" I said, in a voice husky with rage, while every syllable I uttered seemed as new fuel to my fury, "scoundrel! impostor! accursed villain! you shall not – you *shall not* dog me unto death! Follow me, or I stab you where you stand!" – and I broke my way from the ball-room into a small ante-chamber adjoining – dragging him unresistingly with me as I went.

Upon entering, I thrust him furiously from me. He staggered against the wall, while I closed the door with an oath, and commanded him to draw. He hesitated but for an instant; then, with a slight sigh, drew

个秘密，告诉过我她会化装成什么样子。现在，我看到她的人了。我马上急匆匆地朝她所在的位置走去。此时，我却感到有一只手轻轻地搭上我的肩头，那刻骨铭心的、死不足惜的低语又在耳边响起。

我实在是愤怒到了极限，立刻转向那个打断我的人，狠狠抓住他的领子。如我所料，他打扮得跟我一模一样：穿着一件蓝天鹅绒的西班牙式风衣，腰上缠着一条猩红的腰带，上面挂着一把长剑，脸上蒙着一件黑色的丝绸面具。

"无赖！"我大叫道，气得声音都哑了，发出的每个音符，都是在怒火上再加几滴油，"无赖！骗子！该死的浑蛋！你竟敢——你真不该纠缠我到死不放！跟我来，否则，我让你血溅当场！"我不容反抗地拽起他就走，从舞厅里辟路出来。进了隔壁的小会客厅。

一进屋，我就猛地把他甩了出去，他踉跄地撞到墙上。我关门的时候还骂了一句，让他拔出剑来。他犹豫了一下，然后，轻轻地叹息一声，默默地拔出剑摆了个守势。

in silence, and put himself upon his defence.

The contest was brief indeed. I was frantic with every species of wild excitement, and felt within my single arm the energy and power of a multitude. In a few seconds I forced him by sheer strength against the wainscoting, and thus, getting him at mercy, plunged my sword, with brute ferocity, repeatedly through and through his bosom.

At that instant some person tried the latch of the door. I hastened to prevent an intrusion, and then immediately returned to my dying antagonist. But what human language can adequately portray *that* astonishment, *that* horror which possessed me at the spectacle then presented to view? The brief moment in which I averted my eyes had been sufficient to produce, apparently, a material change in the arrangements at the upper or farther end of the room. A large mirror, – so at first it seemed to me in my confusion – now stood where none had been perceptible before; and, as I stepped up to it in extremity of terror, mine own image, but with features all pale and dabbled in blood, advanced to meet me with a feeble and tottering gait.

Thus it appeared, I say, but was not. It was my antagonist – it was Wilson, who then stood before me in the agonies of his dissolution. His mask and cloak lay, where

决斗其实很简短。我因为受了各种刺激，跟疯了一样，就觉得自己的一条胳膊有着无穷无尽的能量。几秒钟的时间，我就使出全部力气，把他逼到墙壁上。他就此为我所控，我残忍粗暴地一剑又一剑刺穿他的胸膛。

那会子，有人想把门闩弄开。我慌忙赶过去阻止别人进来，然后马上回身走向垂死的对手。但是，什么样的人类语言才能贴切地描绘出那种惊讶和恐惧啊，我被眼前的景象惊呆了，吓瘫了。就在我转移视线的那短短的一瞬间，竟然足以让房间上部或者说远端的景物产生如此明显的变化。一面大镜子——一开始我还以为是幻觉——正立在原先根本什么都没有的地方。我一步步朝着它走过去，极度恐惧。我的，就是我自己的影子，面色苍白，浑身是血，步态虚浮凌乱，正迎面向我走来。

我是说，它像是我的影子，其实不是。那是我的对手——是威尔逊！他站在我的面前，强忍着灵魂和肉体分离的苦痛。他先前扔下的

he had thrown them, upon the floor. Not a thread in all his raiment – not a line in all the marked and singular lineaments of his face which was not, even in the most absolute identity, *mine own*!

It was Wilson; but he spoke no Longer in a whisper, and I could have fancied that I myself was speaking while he said:

"You have conquered, and I yield. Yet, henceforward art thou also dead – dead to the World, to Heaven and to Hope! In me didst thou exist – and, in my death, see by this image, which is thine own, how utterly thou hast murdered thyself."

面具和披风还在地上摊着。他衣服上的针脚没有一个不像我的——他脸上醒目而奇特的特征，甚至没有哪一条皱纹不像我，甚至绝对就是我自己。

他还是威尔逊，但他不再窃窃耳语，他开口了，我都以为是我自己在说话：

"你赢了，我输了。不过，自今而后，你也死了——无论是对人间、对天堂，还是对希望来说，你都死了。我在，故你在；我死，正是你亡。请看这影像吧，你把自己彻彻底底地干掉了。"

11. The Gold-bug
十一. 金甲虫

What ho! what ho! this fellow is dancing mad!
He hath been bitten by the Tarantula.

– All in the Wrong

快瞧！快瞧！这家伙跳疯了！
他被毒蜘蛛咬到了。

——一切都错了

MANY years ago, I contracted an intimacy with a Mr. William Legrand. He was of an ancient Huguenot family, and had once been wealthy; but a series of misfortunes had reduced him to want. To avoid the mortification consequent upon his disasters, he left New Orleans, the city of his forefathers, and took up his residence at Sullivan's Island, near Charleston, South Carolina.

This island is a very singular one. It consists of little else than the sea sand, and is about three miles Long. Its breadth at no point exceeds a quarter of a mile. It is separated from the main land by a scarcely perceptible creek, oozing its way through a wilderness of reeds and slime, a favorite resort of the marsh hen. The vegetation, as might be supposed, is scant, or at least dwarfish. No trees of any magnitude are to be seen. Near the western extremity, where Fort Moultrie stands, and where are some

很多年前，我结交了一位名叫威廉·勒格朗的先生并与他成为知己。他家世代是雨格诺[1]教徒，原本家境不错，不料连遭横祸，如今已经家道中落。为了避免别人落井下石，一家人离开了世代居住的新奥尔良城，来到南卡罗来纳州，在查尔斯顿附近的苏里文岛安顿下来。

这座岛十分独特，整个岛几乎全是海沙，约有 3 英里长，1/4 英里宽。在小岛和大陆之间有一条小到看不太清的海湾，海湾两边是一大片长满芦苇的烂泥塘，野鸡喜欢在那一带搭窝。不难想象，岛上草木稀少，即便有，也都长得矮小。根本看不见参天大树。岛的西部是毛特烈堡和几间简陋的小木屋，每当夏日炎炎，一些人便从查尔斯顿城里来到这里租间木屋住下，远离炎热和城市的喧嚣。靠近岛两端的地

---
[1] 雨格诺教系 16~17 世纪法国基督教新教。

miserable frame buildings, tenanted, during summer, by the fugitives from Charleston dust and fever, may be found, indeed, the bristly palmetto; but the whole island, with the exception of this western point, and a line of hard, white beach on the seacoast, is covered with a dense undergrowth of the sweet myrtle, so much prized by the horticulturists of England. The shrub here often attains the height of fifteen or twenty feet, and forms an almost impenetrable coppice, burthening the air with its fragrance.

In the inmost recesses of this coppice, not far from the eastern or more remote end of the island, Legrand had built himself a small hut, which he occupied when I first, by mere accident, made his acquaintance. This soon ripened into friendship – for there was much in the recluse to excite interest and esteem. I found him well educated, with unusual powers of mind, but infected with misanthropy, and subject to perverse moods of alternate enthusiasm and melancholy. He had with him many books, but rarely employed them. His chief amusements were gunning and fishing, or sauntering along the beach and through the myrtles, in quest of shells or entomological specimens; – his collection of the latter might have been envied by a

方可以看到一簇簇棕榈树，除了这一角和海边坚硬雪白的沙滩之外，整个小岛都长满了散发着芬芳气息的桃金娘。英国的园艺家们视它为珍宝，通常当地的桃金娘能长到15到20英尺高，一簇簇地连成一片，密得几乎无从下脚，岛上四处弥漫着灌木散发出来的芬芳气息。

在这片树丛深处，靠近小岛东部一个较偏僻的地方，勒格朗搭了一间小茅屋。我和他第一次见面时他就住在那里。隐居的生活让他身上有很多引人注意的特点，我因为十分钦佩他，所以没过多久我们就成了朋友。我看出他很有教养，且天生聪颖，只是有点愤世嫉俗，时而对人热情洋溢，时而变得郁郁寡欢，他的怪脾气不时发作。他身边有很多书，只是他很少翻阅。钓鱼狩猎是他的主要消遣，偶尔他沿着沙滩，穿过一片桃金娘丛，一路散步，或者捡些贝壳，或者采集昆虫标本——他的收藏连斯瓦默丹[1]这样的人都会羡慕。每次外出散步时，一个名叫丘比特的老黑仆总会陪在他身边。在勒格朗家败落前，丘比特就已经解放了，但他认为应该待

---

[1] 斯瓦默丹，17世纪荷兰生物学家和显微镜学家。

Swammerdamm. In these excursions he was usually accompanied by an old negro, called Jupiter, who had been manumitted before the reverses of the family, but who could be induced, neither by threats nor by promises, to abandon what he considered his right of attendance upon the footsteps of his young "Massa Will." It is not improbable that the relatives of Legrand, conceiving him to be somewhat unsettled in intellect, had contrived to instil this obstinacy into Jupiter, with a view to the supervision and guardianship of the wanderer.

The winters in the latitude of Sullivan's Island are seldom very severe, and in the fall of the year it is a rare event indeed when a fire is considered necessary. About the middle of October, 18-, there occurred, however, a day of remarkable chilliness. Just before sunset I scrambled my way through the evergreens to the hut of my friend, whom I had not visited for several weeks – my residence being, at that time, in Charleston, a distance of nine miles from the Island, while the facilities of passage and re-passage were very far behind those of the present day. Upon reaching the hut I rapped, as was my custom, and getting no reply, sought for the key where I knew it was secreted, unlocked the door and went in. A fine fire was blazing upon the hearth. It was a novelty,

在"威儿少爷"身边伺候他，无论怎样威逼利诱，他都不离开。看来或许是勒格朗的亲戚们认为他的精神不太正常，于是想办法让丘比特逐渐形成现在的脾气，在一旁照顾他，保护着他。

由于苏里文岛所在的纬度，这里几乎没有冷到彻骨的冬天，秋天也完全不用生火。尽管如此，18××年10月中旬的某天却格外的冷。太阳快下山的时候，我费力地穿过大片常青灌木丛，往我朋友那间木屋走去。那时我住在查尔斯顿，距苏里文岛有9英里远，那时的交通工具比现在要落后得多，因此几个星期都没能探望他。我来到木屋前，照例敲敲大门，但没人应门，我知道他把钥匙放在哪里，很容易就找到了，开了门，直接进屋。壁炉里还烧着柴。这有些奇怪，但我刚好需要。我把大衣脱了，坐在扶手椅上，柴火毕毕剥剥地烧着，就这么耐心等着两位屋主回来。

and by no means an ungrateful one. I threw off an overcoat, took an arm-chair by the crackling logs, and awaited patiently the arrival of my hosts.

Soon after dark they arrived, and gave me a most cordial welcome. Jupiter, grinning from ear to ear, bustled about to prepare some marsh-hens for supper. Legrand was in one of his fits – how else shall I term them? – of enthusiasm. He had found an unknown bivalve, forming a new genus, and, more than this, he had hunted down and secured, with Jupiter's assistance, a *scarabœus* which he believed to be totally new, but in respect to which he wished to have my opinion on the morrow.

"And why not to-night?" I asked, rubbing my hands over the blaze, and wishing the whole tribe of *scarabœi* at the devil.

"Ah, if I had only known you were here!" said Legrand, "but it's so Long since I saw you; and how could I foresee that you would pay me a visit this very night of all others? As I was coming home I met Lieutenant G-, from the fort, and, very foolishly, I lent him the bug; so it will be impossible for you to see it until the morning. Stay here to-night, and I will send Jup down for it at sunrise. It is the loveliest thing in creation!"

"What? – sunrise?"

"Nonsense! no! – the bug. It is of a

天刚黑，他们就回来了，热情周到地款待我。丘比特笑得嘴也合不拢，满屋子忙碌着，杀了只水鸡当做晚饭。勒格朗也恰巧犯起了热情洋溢的怪毛病——如果这不是一种病，那该称它什么好呢？他发现了一个不知是什么品种的双壳贝，此外，他还在丘比特的帮助下，一路追踪，抓到一只金龟子，这些在他看来，是绝对的新发现，他想明天听听我的看法。

"为什么不是今晚呢？"我一边问，一边在壁炉前烤手，心里却恨不得金龟子那些东西全都给我见鬼去。

"要是提前知道你来就好了！"勒格朗说，"有段日子没见你了，我哪里想到你今晚会来呢？刚才在回家的路上遇到毛特烈堡的葛××中尉，当时一糊涂，就答应把虫子借给他了，所以明天早上你才能看到。今晚你就住在这儿吧，等明天天一亮，我就派丘比特把虫子要回来。真是太好了！"

"什么？你是说日出吗？"

"胡说！不是！——我说的是

brilliant gold color – about the size of a large hickory-nut – with two jet black spots near one extremity of the back, and another, somewhat Longer, at the other. The *antennæ*? are – "

"Dey aint no tin in him, Massa Will, I keep a tellin, on you," here interrupted Jupiter; "de bug is a goole bug, solid, ebery bit of him, inside and all, sep him wing – neber feel half so hebby a bug in my life."

"Well, suppose it is, Jup," replied Legrand, somewhat more earnestly, it seemed to me, than the case demanded, "is that any reason for your letting the birds burn? The color" – here he turned to me – "is really almost enough to warrant Jupiter's idea. You never saw a more brilliant metallic lustre than the scales emit – but of this you cannot judge till tomorrow. In the mean time I can give you some idea of the shape." Saying this, he seated himself at a small table, on which were a pen and ink, but no paper. He looked for some in a drawer, but found none.

"Never mind," said he at length, "this will answer;" and he drew from his waistcoat pocket a scrap of what I took to be very dirty foolscap, and made upon it a rough drawing with the pen. While he did this, I retained my seat by the fire, for I was still chilly. When the design was complete, he handed it to me without

虫子。浑身闪着金光——大概和一个大核桃差不多——靠近背的一端，有两个漆黑的黑点，另一端还长着一个稍长的黑点。它的触须是……"

"他身上可没有锡，威儿少爷，就像我跟你说的，"丘比特突然说道，"那只甲壳虫是金色的，纯金的，从头到尾，里里外外全都是金色的，只有翅膀不是——我这辈子都还没见过这么金贵的虫子呢。"

"好吧，就算是吧，丘，"勒格朗答道，依我看，他大可不必那么认真地描述，"难道你就能看着水鸡被烤煳了？你看那颜色……"这时他回过头冲我说道——"说实话，你见过虫子之后就会同意丘比特的想法了。甲壳上泛着一层闪亮的金光，保准你从未见过——等到明天，你自己看吧。我现在可以告诉你大概的样子。"他一边说一边坐在一张小桌旁，桌子上摆着笔墨，但没有纸。他在抽屉里找，可一张纸也没有。

"算了，"临了他说，"这个也行。"说着从坎肩口袋里掏出一张小纸片，我还以为是皱皱巴巴的书写纸呢。他拿起笔开始在上面草图。他接着画，我仍然觉得冷，便依旧坐在炉火旁边。等他画完了，我没起身，他就将画递给我。我刚拿到，突然传来一阵汪汪吠叫，紧接着是

rising. As I received it, a loud growl was heard, succeeded by a scratching at the door. Jupiter opened it, and a large Newfoundland, beLonging to Legrand, rushed in, leaped upon my shoulders, and loaded me with caresses; for I had shown him much attention during previous visits. When his gambols were over, I looked at the paper, and, to speak the truth, found myself not a little puzzled at what my friend had depicted.

"Well!" I said, after contemplating it for some minutes, "this is a strange *scarabœus*, I must confess: new to me: never saw anything like it before – unless it was a skull, or a death's-head – which it more nearly resembles than anything else that has come under *my* observation."

"A death's-head!" echoed Legrand – "Oh – yes – well, it has something of that appearance upon paper, no doubt. The two upper black spots look like eyes, eh? and the Longer one at the bottom like a mouth – and then the shape of the whole is oval."

"Perhaps so," said I; "but, Legrand, I fear you are no artist. I must wait until I see the beetle itself, if I am to form any idea of its personal appearance."

"Well, I don't know," said he, a little nettled, "I draw tolerably – *should* do it at least – have had good masters, and flatter myself that I am not quite a blockhead."

"But, my dear fellow, you are joking

嚓嚓的挠门声。丘比特打开门，勒格朗养的那条纽芬兰大狗一下子蹿了进来，扑上我肩膀，和我亲密无比，因为以前我来这里做客，总是对它很友善。转眼间它就安静下来，于是我往纸上看了一眼，说实话，我真看不明白我朋友究竟画了什么。

"啊！"我静静地看了一会儿说道，"我不得不说，这只金龟子真奇特，我从来没见过这样的东西——它像头骨一样，或者说更像是个骷髅头，在我看来，再也没有比这更像骷髅头的了。"

"骷髅头！"勒格朗重复了一遍，"嗯——对——真别说，画在纸上，还真有几分相似，背上的两个黑点就像眼睛，嗯？下面的长点就像一张嘴——而且整个形状是鹅蛋形的。"

"或许是这样吧，"我说，"不过话又说回来，勒格朗，你可能画得不像。我得亲眼见了才能知道这甲虫到底长什么样子。"

"随便你吧，"他说，有点不高兴，"我画画还算可以——至少应该是这样——我曾经拜过很多名师，也相信自己并不笨。"

"那么，老兄，你就是在和我

then," said I, "this is a very passable *skull* – indeed, I may say that it is a very *excellent* skull, according to the vulgar notions about such specimens of physiology – and your *scarabœus* must be the queerest *scarabœus* in the world if it resembles it. Why, we may get up a very thrilling bit of superstition upon this hint. I presume you will call the bug *scarabœus caput hominis*, or something of that kind – there are many similar titles in the Natural Histories. But where are the *antenne*? you spoke of?"

"The *antenne*?" said Legrand, who seemed to be getting unaccountably warm upon the subject; "I am sure you must see the *antenne*? I made them as distinct as they are in the original insect, and I presume that is sufficient."

"Well, well," I said, "perhaps you have – still I don't see them;" and I handed him the paper without additional remark, not wishing to ruffle his temper; but I was much surprised at the turn affairs had taken; his ill humor puzzled me – and, as for the drawing of the beetle, there were positively no *antenne*? visible, and the whole did bear a very close resemblance to the ordinary cuts of a death's-head.

He received the paper very peevishly, and was about to crumple it, apparently to throw it in the fire, when a casual glance at the design seemed suddenly to rivet his attention. In an instant his face grew

开玩笑了，"我说，"这实在太像头颅骨了——普通人从生理学标本的角度看，我不得不说，这个头颅骨真不赖——如果你那只金龟子要真像头颅骨的话，肯定是世间罕见的怪虫。呵呵，就凭这一点，就能造出个绝顶恐怖的迷信来。我看你不妨给虫子取名叫人头金龟子，或者起个类似的名字——生物学中有很多类似的名称呢。话说，你刚刚提到的触须在哪儿啊？"

"触须！"勒格朗说道，看他的样子，一听我这么说，脸立刻莫名其妙地红了，"我敢肯定你绝对能看见。我画得和原来一模一样呢，我看画得已经够清楚了。"

"行，行，行，"我说，"或许你是画得挺清楚——但我还是没看到。"我不想惹怒他，没再继续下去，便把纸还给他。然而我万万没料到事情会到如此尴尬的地步，至于他为什么不高兴，我也十分奇怪——单从甲虫的画来讲，上面确实没有触须之类的东西，整个形状也和普通的骷髅头没两样。

他气冲冲地接过纸，刚想把它揉成一团，再丢进火里，无意中往画上瞧了一眼，这下他仿佛突然将全部注意力集中在上面了。他的脸一阵红，一阵白。坐在椅子上，仔

violently red – in another as excessively pale. For some minutes he continued to scrutinize the drawing minutely where he sat. At length he arose, took a candle from the table, and proceeded to seat himself upon a sea-chest in the farthest corner of the room. Here again he made an anxious examination of the paper; turning it in all directions. He said nothing, however, and his conduct greatly astonished me; yet I thought it prudent not to exacerbate the growing moodiness of his temper by any comment. Presently he took from his coat pocket a wallet, placed the paper carefully in it, and deposited both in a writing-desk, which he locked. He now grew more composed in his demeanor; but his original air of enthusiasm had quite disappeared. Yet he seemed not so much sulky as abstracted. As the evening wore away he became more and more absorbed in reverie, from which no sallies of mine could arouse him. It had been my intention to pass the night at the hut, as I had frequently done before, but, seeing my host in this mood, I deemed it proper to take leave. He did not press me to remain, but, as I departed, he shook my hand with even more than his usual cordiality.

It was about a month after this (and during the interval I had seen nothing of Legrand) when I received a visit, at Charleston, from his man, Jupiter. I had

细看了好久，才站起身，从桌上拿起一支蜡烛，走到屋子最远处的角落里，坐在大箱子，又不甘心地仔细看了一遍，反复检查，却始终一言不发。他的举动倒真让人吃惊，不过看来我还是得谨慎一点，最好别再说些什么火上浇油的话。过了会儿，他从衣服口袋里拿出皮夹，小心翼翼地把纸放进去，又放到写字台里，上了锁。这时他才冷静下来，但已经完全不见刚才那副热情洋溢的劲头了。看他的模样，与其说是愁眉苦脸，还不如说是满脸迷茫。夜已渐深，他的神志也渐渐变得恍惚，貌似想得出神，不管我讲什么笑话，都提不起他的兴致。以前我经常在他家过夜，原本今天打算在这里住一晚，可看主人的心情，觉得还是离开的好。他没有挽留我，但在我离开前，竟异常热情地和我握手。

这一别，竟隔了几个月的时间，始终没再见勒格朗，他却派丘比特来查尔斯顿找我。我还是头一次见到善良的老黑仆摆出一副沮丧的样

never seen the good old negro look so dispirited, and I feared that some serious disaster had befallen my friend.

"Well, Jup," said I, "what is the matter now? – how is your master?"

"Why, to speak de troof, massa, him not so berry well as mought be."

"Not well! I am truly sorry to hear it. What does he complain of?"

"Dar! dat's it! – him neber plain of notin – but him berry sick for all dat."

"*Very sick*, Jupiter! – why didn't you say so at once? Is he confined to bed?"

"No, dat he aint! – he aint' fin'd nowhar – dat's just whar de shoe pinch – my mind is got to be berry hebby' bout poor Massa Will."

"Jupiter, I should like to understand what it is you are talking about. You say your master is sick. Hasn't he told you what ails him?"

"Why, massa', t aint worf while for to git mad about de matter – Massa Will say noffin at all aint de matter wid him – but den what make him go about looking dis here way, wid he head down and he soldiers up, and as white as a gose? And den he keep a syphon all de time – "

"Keeps a what, Jupiter?"

"Keeps a syphon wid de figgurs on de slate – de queerest figgurs I ebber did see. Ise gittin' to be skeered, I tell you. Hab for to keep mighty tight eye pon him noovers.

子，于是不由得担心朋友是否遇到了什么灾祸。

"呃，丘，"我说，"这是怎么回事？——你家少爷还好吗？"

"唉，说实话，少爷，他不怎么好啊。"

"不好！真替他担心。他又抱怨什么呢？"

"唉！就是说啊！——他从来没什么可抱怨的——他病得实在是厉害。"

"病得厉害，丘比特！——你为什么不早说？他卧病在床了？"

"不，不是那样！——他哪儿都没事儿——可就糟在这儿——我可怜的威儿少爷，我都快急死了。"

"丘比特，你到底想说什么啊？你说你家少爷病了。难道他没说哪儿不舒服？"

"呦，少爷，您可犯不着为了这事发火——威儿少爷根本不说他哪儿不舒服——但他为啥总是低着头，耸着肩，一脸惨白，就这么来来回回地走呢？不光如此，还总解蜜蜂——"

"解什么，丘比特？"

"在石板上用数字解蜜蜂——我从来没见过这么奇特的数字。说真的，我快吓死了。得好好注意他耍什么花招。那天，天还没亮，他

Todder day he gib me slip' fore de sun up and was gone de whole ob de blessed day. I had a big stick ready cut for to gib him deuced good beating when he did come – but Ise sich a fool dat I hadn't de heart arter all – he look so berry poorly."

"Eh? – what? – ah yes! – upon the whole I think you had better not be too severe with the poor fellow – don't flog him, Jupiter – he can't very well stand it – but can you form no idea of what has occasioned this illness, or rather this change of conduct? Has anything unpleasant happened since I saw you?"

"No, massa, dey aint bin noffin unpleasant *since* den – 't *was* fore den I'm feared – 't was de berry day you was dare."

"How? what do you mean?"

"Why, massa, I mean de bug – dare now."

"The what?"

"De bug, – I'm berry sartain dat Massa Will bin bit somewhere 'bout de head by dat goole-bug."

"And what cause have you, Jupiter, for such a supposition?"

"Claws enuff, massa, and mouth too. I nebber did see sick a deuced bug – he kick and he bite ebery ting what cum near him. Massa Will cotch him fuss, but had for to let him go gin mighty quick, I tell you – den was de time he must ha got de bite. I did n't like de look oh de bug mouff,

就偷偷溜出去了，一去就是整整一天。我砍了根大木棍，本打算等他回来，好好教训他一顿——可我真是个笨蛋，始终下不去手——他的气色差极了。"

"啊？——什么？——明白了，明白了！——说来说去，我看你对那个倒霉的家伙还是别管得太严——别打他，丘比特——他可受不了——难道你不知道，他这病是怎么得的，或者说他为什么会变成这个样子？我跟你们分手后，你们是不是遇到了什么不高兴的事？"

"没，少爷，那次之后没遇到什么不高兴的事——恐怕在那之前就遇到了——就在您去的那天。"

"什么？什么意思？"

"呃，少爷，我说的是那只虫子——您看。"

"什么东西？"

"虫子——我敢保证，那只金甲虫肯定在威儿少爷脑门上咬了一口。"

"你为什么会这么想，丘比特？"

"好多爪子，还有好多嘴。我打出娘胎还没见过那样的虫子——一有人接近，它就开始又踢又咬的。威儿少爷一开始抓住了它，可后来又只好把它放了，说实在的——就是那会儿让它咬到了。我自己反正不喜欢那虫子嘴巴长的那样，所以

myself, no how, so I would n't take hold ob him wid my finger, but I cotch him wid a piece ob paper dat I found. I rap him up in de paper and stuff piece ob it in he mouff – dat was de way."

"And you think, then, that your master was really bitten by the beetle, and that the bite made him sick?"

"I don't tink noffin' about it – I nose it. What make him dream 'bout de goole so much, if taint cause he bit by de goole-bug? Ise heerd 'bout dem goole-bugs fore dis."

"But how do you know he dreams about gold?"

"How I know? why cause he talk about it in he sleep – dat's how I nose."

"Well, Jup, perhaps you are right; but to what fortunate circumstance am I to attribute the honor of a visit from you to-day?"

"What de matter, massa?"

"Did you bring any message from Mr. Legrand "

"No, massa, I bring dis here pissel"; and here Jupiter handed me a note which ran thus:

"MY DEAR –

"Why have I not seen you for so Long a time? I hope you have not been so foolish as to take offence at any little *brusquerie* of mine; but no, that is improbable.

"Since I saw you I have had great cause

绝对不会拿指头捏它，我找了一张纸抓它。把它包在纸里，还往它嘴里塞了张纸——就这样。"

"那么，依你的意思，少爷真的被甲虫咬了？因为这个所以病了？"

"不用我看——我心里清楚。如果他没给金甲虫咬了一口，又咋会一心想着金子呢？在这之前，我就听说过那种金甲虫。"

"但你怎么确定他想要金子呢？"

"我怎么知道？啊，因为他在梦里提到了——所以我就明白了。"

"好，丘，或许你说得对，我今天真是荣幸啊，什么风竟把你请来了？"

"咋回事，少爷？"

"勒格朗先生让你带什么口信了吗？"

"没，少爷，我只带来了一封天书。"说着他递给我一张字条，上面写着：

"我亲爱的：

"为什么这么久没来？希望你不要因为我的冒犯之处，一时生气，不，你还不至于如此。

"上次分手之后，心里一直十

for anxiety. I have something to tell you, yet scarcely know how to tell it, or whether I should tell it at all.

"I have not been quite well for some days past, and poor old Jup annoys me, almost beyond endurance, by his well-meant attentions Would you believe it? – he had prepared a huge stick, the other day, with which to chastise me for giving him the slip, and spending the day, *solus*, among the hills on the main land. I verily believe that my ill looks alone saved me a flogging.

"I have made no addition to my cabinet since we met.

"If you can, in any way, make it convenient, come over with Jupiter. Do come. I wish to see you *tonight*, upon business of importance. I assure you that it is of the *highest* importance.

"Ever yours, WILLIAM LEGRAND."

There was something in the tone of this note which gave me great uneasiness. Its whole style differed materially from that of Legrand. What could he be dreaming of? What new crotchet possessed his excitable brain? What "business of the highest importance" could he possibly have to transact? Jupiter's account of him boded no good. I dreaded lest the continued pressure

分想念。我有话想跟你说，可就是不知该如何是好，也不知是否应该和你商谈。

"前几天，我不太舒服，可怜的老丘好意关照我，却反而让我生气，差点就跟他发火。你相信吗？——有一天，我趁他不注意偷偷溜走，独自一人在岛上的山里待了一天，可他竟然准备了根大棍子，打算教训我一顿。我敢说，要不是因为我这副病恹恹的模样，肯定逃不过这顿打。

"自从我们分手后，标本柜里就没添什么新标本了。

"如果你方便的话，请务必随丘比特来我这儿。请你过来吧，希望今晚能看到你，此事关系重大。的确是非常重要的事情。

"你永远的，威廉·勒格朗上"

这张字条措辞的语气，让我感到十分不安。整体风格和勒格朗平日的文体全然不同。他在胡思乱想什么啊？他的脑子里又有什么天马行空的新奇念头了？他又有什么"非常重要的事情"要做呢？丘比特刚刚提到的明明不是什么好现象。我害怕这个朋友会遇到不好的意外，最后被折磨得神志不清，于

of misfortune had, at length, fairly unsettled the reason of my friend. Without a moment's hesitation, therefore, I prepared to accompany the negro.

Upon reaching the wharf, I noticed a scythe and three spades, all apparently new, lying in the bottom of the boat in which we were to embark.

"What is the meaning of all this, Jup?" I inquired.

"Him syfe, massa, and spade."

"Very true; but what are they doing here?"

"Him de syfe and de spade what Massa Will sis 'pon my buying for him in de town, and de debbil's own lot of money I had to gib for,em."

"But what, in the name of all that is mysterious, is your 'Massa Will' going to do with scythes and spades?"

"Dat's more dan *I* know, and debbil take me if I don't blieve 'tis more dan he know, too. But it's all cum ob de bug."

Finding that no satisfaction was to be obtained of Jupiter, whose whole intellect seemed to be absorbed by "de bug," I now stepped into the boat and made sail. With a fair and strong breeze we soon ran into the little cove to the northward of Fort Moultrie, and a walk of some two miles brought us to the hut. It was about three in the afternoon when we arrived. Legrand had been awaiting us in eager expectation.

是立刻准备和老黑仆一起上路。

我们来到码头，看到我们搭乘的小船底部放着全新的长柄镰刀和3把铲子。

"这些是做什么用的，丘？"我问道。

"这些是镰刀和铲子，少爷。"

"这我知道，可放在这儿做什么？"

"这是威儿少爷吩咐我给他从城里买的，我花了不少钱才弄到的呢。"

"可威儿少爷要这些镰刀和铲子干什么用呢？"

"我可不知道，我到死也不相信他知道，这些全都是那只虫子在捣鬼。"

看来丘比特的脑子里已经只剩下"那只虫子"了。既然从他嘴里得不到满意的答复，我便上了船，准备起程。一路顺风，没过多久船就驶进了毛特烈堡背面的小海湾，我们下了船，走了两英里路，下午3点左右，来到木屋前。看得出勒格朗早已等得不耐烦了。他热情又有些紧张地握住我的手，我不禁被吓一跳，心里立刻开始怀疑。他

He grasped my hand with a nervous *empressement* which alarmed me and strengthened the suspicions already entertained. His countenance was pale even to ghastliness, and his deep-set eyes glared with unnatural lustre. After some inquiries respecting his health, I asked him, not knowing what better to say, if he had yet obtained the *scarabæus* from Lieutenant G-.

"Oh, yes," he replied, coloring violently, "I got it from him the next morning. Nothing should tempt me to part with that *scarabæus*. Do you know that Jupiter is quite right about it?"

"In what way?" I asked, with a sad foreboding at heart.

"In supposing it to be a bug of *real gold*." He said this with an air of profound seriousness, and I felt inexpressibly shocked.

"This bug is to make my fortune," he continued, with a triumphant smile, "to reinstate me in my family possessions. Is it any wonder, then, that I prize it? Since Fortune has thought fit to bestow it upon me, I have only to use it properly and I shall arrive at the gold of which it is the index. Jupiter; bring me that *scarabæus*!"

"What! de bug, massa? I'd rudder not go fer trubble dat bug – you mus' git him for your own self." Hereupon Legrand arose, with a grave and stately air, and brought

一脸惨白像死人一样，眼窝深陷却放着异样的光彩。我询问他身体如何，一时竟想不出该说什么，就随口问到有没有从葛××中尉那儿拿回金龟子。

"要回来了，"他答道，一下子脸色通红，"转天早上就拿回来了。无论如何也不会再放掉那只金龟子了。你知道吗，丘比特的说法是真的。"

"什么说法？"我问道，心头不由得生出异样的感觉。"

"他不是说那个虫子是真金的吗？"他一本正经地说着，我不禁大惊失色。

"我就要靠这虫子发财了，"他一脸得意地接着说道，"我要重振家业了。既然如此，我看重它又有什么奇怪的？财神认为我应该得到它，那我就要好好地利用它，它可是打开金库的钥匙，我马上就会有金子了。丘比特，把金龟子拿给我！"

"啥？虫子，少爷？我看还是别去惹那虫子比较好，您还是自己去拿吧。"勒格朗听罢得意地站起身，从玻璃盒里拿出虫子给我看。

me the beetle from a glass case in which it was enclosed. It was a beautiful *scarabœus*, and, at that time, unknown to naturalists – of course a great prize in a scientific point of view. There were two round, black spots near one extremity of the back, and a Long one near the other. The scales were exceedingly hard and glossy, with all the appearance of burnished gold. The weight of the insect was very remarkable, and, taking all things into consideration, I could hardly blame Jupiter for his opinion respecting it; but what to make of Legrand's concordance with that opinion, I could not, for the life of me, tell.

"I sent for you," said he, in a grandiloquent tone, when I had completed my examination of the beetle, "I sent for you, that I might have your counsel and assistance in furthering the views of Fate and of the bug –"

"My dear Legrand," I cried, interrupting him, "you are certainly unwell, and had better use some little precautions. You shall go to bed, and I will remain with you a few days, until you get over this. You are feverish and –"

"Feel my pulse," said he.

I felt it, and, to say the truth, found not the slightest indication of fever.

"But you may be ill and yet have no fever. Allow me this once to prescribe for

这只金龟子真漂亮。在当时，生物学家还不知道这种甲虫的存在——从科学上看，这无疑是个重大的收获。靠近背上一端，有两个浑圆的黑点，另外一端还是一个长点。甲壳很硬且很光滑，外表像极了打磨后的金子。甲虫竟意外的重。我仔细琢磨了一下，怪不得丘比特会那样想了。不过，我却不明白为什么勒格朗也会这样想。

"我请你来，"我仔细看了遍甲虫，他接着大言不惭地说道，"我请你来是想让你给我出主意，帮我解出命运之神和那只虫子的奥秘……"

"亲爱的勒格朗，"我打断他的话，大声喝道，"你真的病了，还是休息一下好。你应该躺下，我在这儿陪你几天，等你病好了再走。你发着烧还……"

"你号号脉。"他说。

我按了一下，说实话，他丝毫没有发烧的症状。

"或许你病了，但是没发烧。这次，你就按我说的做吧。先去躺

you. In the first place, go to bed. In the next –"

"You are mistaken," he interposed, "I am as well as I can expect to be under the excitement which I suffer. If you really wish me well, you will relieve this excitement."

"And how is this to be done?"

"Very easily. Jupiter and myself are going upon an expedition into the hills, upon the main land, and, in this expedition we shall need the aid of some person in whom we can confide. You are the only one we can trust. Whether we succeed or fail, the excitement which you now perceive in me will be equally allayed."

"I am anxious to oblige you in any way," I replied; "but do you mean to say that this infernal beetle has any connection with your expedition into the hills?"

"It has."

"Then, Legrand, I can become a party to no such absurd proceeding."

"I am sorry – very sorry – for we shall have to try it by ourselves."

"Try it by yourselves! The man is surely mad! – but stay! – how Long do you propose to be absent?"

"Probably all night. We shall start immediately, and be back, at all events, by sunrise."

"And will you promise me, upon your honor, that when this freak of yours is over,

下，然后……"

"你搞错了，"他打断我说，"我现在心里异常激动，身体好得不得了。你要是真希望我身体好，就帮我把恢复平静。"

"我要怎么帮？"

"非常简单。我马上要和丘比特到岛那边的山里探险。这次探险，我需要信赖的人帮助。我只信得过你。不论结果如何，你现在看到的我这份激动的心情会自动消失。"

"我很愿意效劳，"我回答，"不过，你的意思是说，你去山里探险是因为这只虫子？"

"正是。"

"那么，勒格朗，我可不做这么荒唐的事情。"

"那真是遗憾——实在太遗憾了——我们只好自己去探险了。"

"你们要自己去！你这家伙一定是疯了！——哎，等下！——你们打算去多久？"

"大概一整晚吧。现在立刻动身，差不多在天亮前赶回来。"

"那么请你务必答应我，等你打消了这个怪念头，虫子的事（老

and the bug business (good God!) settled to your satisfaction, you will then return home and follow my advice implicitly, as that of your physician."

"Yes; I promise; and now let us be off, for we have no time to lose."

With a heavy heart I accompanied my friend. We started about four o'clock – Legrand, Jupiter, the dog, and myself. Jupiter had with him the scythe and spades – the whole of which he insisted upon carrying – more through fear, it seemed to me, of trusting either of the implements within reach of his master, than from any excess of industry or complaisance. His demeanor was dogged in the extreme, and "dat deuced bug" were the sole words which escaped his lips during the journey. For my own part, I had charge of a couple of dark lanterns, while Legrand contented himself with the *scarabœus*, which he carried attached to the end of a bit of whip-cord; twirling it to and fro, with the air of a conjuror, as he went. When I observed this last, plain evidence of my friend's aberration of mind, I could scarcely refrain from tears. I thought it best, however, to humor his fancy, at least for the present, or until I could adopt some more energetic measures with a chance of success. In the mean time I endeavored, but all in vain, to sound him in regard to the object of the expedition. Having

天爷哪！）一旦解决了，你就马上回来，我做你的大夫，你要按我说的去做。"

"好的，我保证。现在咱们出发吧，可没剩下多少时间了。"

我心情沉重地跟着他走了。我，勒格朗，丘比特，还有那只狗——我们4点左右出发。丘比特扛着镰刀和铲子，他硬是要拿着这些东西，在我看来，这并不是他要巴结讨好，只是他怕少爷能随手拿到罢了。他的脾气可真是偏到了家，一路上不停地嘀咕着"死虫子"这个词。我提着两盏牛眼灯；勒格朗把金龟子拴在一根鞭绳头上，得意地拎着，一边走，一边来回转着，就像在变戏法。他的这一举动明显说明他精神不正常，我都忍不住要掉眼泪了。可心想还是先顺着他的意思，至少现在只能这样，在没想出有把握成功的对策前，只好迁就他一下了。我努力想从他那儿打听出这次探险的目的，结果却白费口舌。他已经把我骗来了，更不想提其他的话题，无论问他什么，他只说一句"等着瞧吧"就算是回答了。

succeeded in inducing me to accompany him, he seemed unwilling to hold conversation upon any topic of minor importance, and to all my questions vouchsafed no other reply than "we shall see!"

We crossed the creek at the head of the island by means of a skiff; and, ascending the high grounds on the shore of the main land, proceeded in a northwesterly direction, through a tract of country excessively wild and desolate, where no trace of a human footstep was to be seen. Legrand led the way with decision; pausing only for an instant, here and there, to consult what appeared to be certain landmarks of his own contrivance upon a former occasion.

In this manner we journeyed for about two hours, and the sun was just setting when we entered a region infinitely more dreary than any yet seen. It was a species of table land, near the summit of an almost inaccessible hill, densely wooded from base to pinnacle, and interspersed with huge crags that appeared to lie loosely upon the soil, and in many cases were prevented from precipitating themselves into the valleys below, merely by the support of the trees against which they reclined. Deep ravines, in various directions, gave an air of still sterner solemnity to the scene.

我们乘着小船，渡过苏里文岛那边的小海湾，来到对面大陆的岸边，越过高地，朝着西北方向，穿过人迹罕至的荒地，继续向前走。勒格朗头也不回地向前开路，时而停下来，查看记号，看来应该是他上次留下来的。

我们就这样走了大约 2 个小时，太阳下山时才来到一片极其萧索的荒地。这里地处高原，附近有一座几乎无人能翻越的高山，茂密的树木覆盖了整座山，从山脚到山顶到处都是大块岩石，就像飘浮在土地上一样，这些山石因为多半靠着树，才没滚下山沟。山周围的深谷又给眼前的景色增添了一种阴森、肃穆的诡异气氛。

The natural platform to which we had clambered was thickly overgrown with brambles, through which we soon discovered that it would have been impossible to force our way but for the scythe; and Jupiter, by direction of his master, proceeded to clear for us a path to the foot of an enormously tall tulip-tree, which stood, with some eight or ten oaks, upon the level, and far surpassed them all, and all other trees which I had then ever seen, in the beauty of its foliage and form, in the wide spread of its branches, and in the general majesty of its appearance. When we reached this tree, Legrand turned to Jupiter, and asked him if he thought he could climb it. The old man seemed a little staggered by the question, and for some moments made no reply. At length he approached the huge trunk, walked slowly around it, and examined it with minute attention. When he had completed his scrutiny, he merely said:

"Yes, massa, Jup climb any tree he ebber see in he life."

"Then up with you as soon as possible, for it will soon be too dark to see what we are about."

"How far mus go up, massa?" inquired Jupiter.

"Get up the main trunk first, and then I will tell you which way to go – and here – stop! take this beetle with you."

我们登上高地，这里满是荆棘，很快便看出，如果不用镰刀开路，根本就无从下脚；丘比特按照少爷的吩咐为我们开路，直到一棵参天百合树前停了下来。这棵树周围有八九棵橡树，它的叶子碧绿，姿态妖娆，而且枝繁叶茂，外形庄严典雅，周围的橡树无法与之相比，我从没见过如此美丽的树。我们刚刚来到百合树前，勒格朗就扭过头问丘比特能否爬上去。老黑仆听了，似乎有些犹豫，并不做声。过了很久才走到巨大的树干前，缓缓绕着它走了一圈，仔细打量了一番。好好端详后，说道：

"行，少爷，凡是丘这辈子看到的树，我没有爬不上去的。"

"那就赶紧爬吧，天马上就全黑了。"

"得爬到多高的地方，少爷？"丘比特问道。

"先爬上树干，然后再告诉你该往哪儿爬——哎——等下！带着这只甲虫。"

"De bug, Massa Will! – de goole bug!" cried the negro, drawing back in dismay – "what for mus tote de bug way up de tree? – d-n if I do!"

"If you are afraid, Jup, a great big negro like you, to take hold of a harmless little dead beetle, why you can carry it up by this string – but, if you do not take it up with you in some way, I shall be under the necessity of breaking your head with this shovel."

"What de matter now, massa?" said Jup, evidently shamed into compliance; "always want for to raise fuss wid old nigger. Was only funnin any how. Me feered de bug! what I keer for de bug?" Here he took cautiously hold of the extreme end of the string, and, maintaining the insect as far from his person as circumstances would permit, prepared to ascend the tree.

In youth, the tulip-tree, or *Liriodendron Tulipferum*, the most magnificent of American foresters, has a trunk peculiarly smooth, and often rises to a great height without lateral branches; but, in its riper age, the bark becomes gnarled and uneven, while many short limbs make their appearance on the stem. Thus the difficulty of ascension, in the present case, lay more in semblance than in reality. Embracing the huge cylinder, as closely as possible, with his arms and knees, seizing with his hands some projections, and resting his naked

"那只虫子，威儿少爷！——金甲虫！"黑仆一边尖叫着，一边惊慌失措地向后退，"为啥还要带着虫子上树？——打死我也不干！"

"丘，你这么大个子的黑人，还怕带着一只伤不了人的小虫子，你就拎着这跟绳子上去吧——你要是不愿意带它上去，我只好用这把铲子把你的脑袋砸开花了。"

"咋了，少爷？"丘说，很明显他羞得只能照少爷的话做了，"总是跟老黑奴嚷嚷。只是开个玩笑罢了。我会害怕那只虫子！那虫子算个啥？"说罢小心谨慎地捏住绳子的一头，尽量让虫子离自己身体远远的，准备爬树了。

百合树，又称作北美鹅掌楸，是生长在美洲森林中最雄伟的一种树木，在幼苗期间，树干十分光滑，通常树身长得很高，没有一根向横处生长的树枝。到了成熟时期，树皮才开始变得凹凸不平，树干上也长出不少短枝，所以眼下看着很难爬的样子，其实倒不算难。丘比特把自己的双臂和两个膝盖尽量往巨大的树身上贴，两只手攀住树皮上的疙瘩，光脚踩着疙瘩爬上去，有一次几乎要摔下来，但最后还是左右晃着爬到头一个大树杈上，看他

toes upon others, Jupiter, after one or two narrow escapes from falling, at length wriggled himself into the first great fork, and seemed to consider the whole business as virtually accomplished. The risk of the achievement was, in fact, now over, although the climber was some sixty or seventy feet from the ground.

"Which way mus go now, Massa Will?" he asked.

"Keep up the largest branch – the one on this side," said Legrand. The negro obeyed him promptly, and apparently with but little trouble; ascending higher and higher, until no glimpse of his squat figure could be obtained through the dense foliage which enveloped it. Presently his voice was heard in a sort of halloo.

"How much fudder is got for go?"

"How high up are you?" asked Legrand.

"Ebber so fur," replied the negro; "can see de sky fru de top ob de tree."

"Never mind the sky, but attend to what I say. Look down the trunk and count the limbs below you on this side. How many limbs have you passed?"

"One, two, tree, four, five – I done pass fibe big limb, massa, pon dis side."

"Then go one limb higher."

In a few minutes the voice was heard again, announcing that the seventh limb was attained.

"Now, Jup," cried Legrand, evidently

的样子他还以为万事大吉了呢。虽然他所在的位置离地面有六七十英尺的距离，但没有什么危险。

"现在该往哪儿走，威儿少爷？"他问道。

"沿着最大的那根树枝爬上去——就是这边的这根。"勒格朗说。黑仆马上照做，显然很轻松地爬了上去。他越爬越高，越爬越高，到后来周围茂密的树叶将他又矮又胖的身子完全挡住看不见了。接着传来了他的声音，像是在高喊。

"还要爬多高？"

"爬到多高了？"勒格朗问道。

"已经不能再高了，"黑仆回答道，"在树顶上都能看见天啦。"

"别管天不天的，照我说的做吧。向下看看树身，数数这边的横枝。已经爬了几根啦？"

"1，2，3，4，5——这边，我爬了5根大横枝了，少爷。"

"那么再往上爬一根。"

过了一会儿，又听到他的声音，他已经爬上第七根横枝了。

"嘿，丘，"勒格朗喊道，听

much excited, "I want you to work your way out upon that limb as far as you can. If you see anything strange, let me know."

By this time what little doubt I might have entertained of my poor friend's insanity, was put finally at rest. I had no alternative but to conclude him stricken with lunacy, and I became seriously anxious about getting him home. While I was pondering upon what was best to be done, Jupiter's voice was again heard.

"Mos feerd for to ventur pon dis limb berry far – tis dead limb putty much all de way."

"Did you say it was a *dead* limb, Jupiter?" cried Legrand in a quavering voice.

"Yes, massa, him dead as de door-nail – done up for sartain – done departed dis here life."

"What in the name heaven shall I do?" asked Legrand, seemingly in the greatest distress.

"Do!" said I, glad of an opportunity to interpose a word, "why come home and go to bed. Come now! – that's a fine fellow. It's getting late, and, besides, you remember your promise."

"Jupiter," cried he, without heeding me in the least, "do you hear me?"

"Yes, Massa Will, hear you ebber so plain."

"Try the wood well, then, with your

声音就知道他此刻正激动万分，"我要你沿着那根横枝接着往前爬，能爬多远就爬多远。要是看到什么稀奇玩意，马上通知我。"

我本来只是有些怀疑这位仁兄神经错乱，现在倒可以断定，他已经完全疯了，便急忙想逼他立刻回去。我正暗自琢磨，该用什么方法劝他，上面突然传来丘比特的声音。

"实在太吓人了，不敢再往前爬了——这根横枝已经死了。"

"你说它是根枯枝，丘比特？"勒格朗声音有些颤抖地叫道。

"是的，少爷，已经死得一口气都没剩了。——确确实实地咽气了——归天啦。"

"该怎么办才好？"勒格朗问道，看样子他正十分苦恼。

"怎么办！"我说，暗地里庆幸总算有机会插嘴了，"回去休息。咱们走吧！——听话啊，天都晚了，再说，你总得记得答应过我什么吧。"

"丘比特，"他对我的话充耳不闻，径自叫道，"你听得见吗？"

"听得见，少爷，听得不能再清楚了。"

"你用刀子砍木头试试，看是

knife, and see if you think it very rotten."

"Him rotten, massa, sure nuff," replied the negro in a few moments, "but not so berry rotten as mought be. Mought ventur out leetle way pon de limb by myself, dat's true."

"By yourself! – what do you mean?"

"Why I mean de bug. 'Tis *berry* hebby bug. Spose I drop him down fuss, and den de limb won't break wid just de weight ob one nigger."

"You infernal scoundrel!" cried Legrand, apparently much relieved, "what do you mean by telling me such nonsense as that? As sure as you drop that beetle I'll break your neck. Look here, Jupiter, do you hear me?"

"Yes, massa, needn't hollo at poor nigger dat style."

"Well! now listen! – if you will venture out on the limb as far as you think safe, and not let go the beetle, I'll make you a present of a silver dollar as soon as you get down."

"I'm gwine, Massa Will – deed I is," replied the negro very promptly – "mos out to the eend now."

"*Out to the end!*" here fairly screamed Legrand, "do you say you are out to the end of that limb?"

"Soon be to de eend, massa, – o-o-o-o-oh! Lor-gol-a-marcy! what *is* dis here pon de tree?"

不是已经烂透了。"

"是烂了，少爷，没错，"过了一会儿，黑仆又答道，"虽然烂了，但没烂透。我一个人的话，还能再往前爬几步，说真的。"

"只你一个人！——你这是什么意思？"

"唉，我说的是那只虫子。这虫子可重了。要是我把它放下，只我一个黑仆的分量，这根横枝倒能禁得住。"

"你这个十恶不赦的浑蛋！"勒格朗嚷道，心里悬着的石头一下子落了地，"你在这儿跟我瞎扯，到底有什么用心？你要是敢把甲虫扔了，看我不让你脑袋分家。哎，丘比特，听见了吗？"

"听见了，少爷，和我这苦命的黑仆哪犯得着这么大喊大叫。"

"好！听着！——你要是还敢往前爬，遇到危险就躲开，也不扔掉手里的甲虫，等你下来以后，我送你一块银元。"

"我继续爬了，威儿少爷——正爬着呢，"黑仆立刻答道，"现在快爬到树梢了。"

"到树梢了！"此时的勒格朗几乎要失声尖叫了，"你是说，你到了横枝的梢上了？"

"马上就到那儿了，少爷——啊——啊——啊——啊——哎哟！我的老天！这树上是什么东西呀？"

"Well!" cried Legrand, highly delighted, "what is it?"

"Why taint noffin but a skull – somebody bin lef him head up de tree, and de crows done gobble ebery bit ob de meat off."

"A skull, you say! – very well! – how is it fastened to the limb? – what holds it on?"

"Sure nuff, massa; mus look. Why dis berry curous sarcumstance, pon my word – dare's a great big nail in de skull, what fastens ob it on to de tree."

"Well now, Jupiter, do exactly as I tell you – do you hear?"

"Yes, massa."

"Pay attention, then! – find the left eye of the skull."

"Hum! hoo! dat's good! why dare aint no eye lef at all."

"Curse your stupidity! do you know your right hand from your left?"

"Yes, I nose dat – nose all bout dat – tis my lef hand what I chops de wood wid."

"To be sure! you are left-handed; and your left. eye is on the same side as your left hand. Now, I suppose, you can find the left eye of the skull, or the place where the left eye has been. Have you found it?"

Here was a Long pause. At length the negro asked,

"Is de lef eye of de skull pon de same side as de lef hand of de skull, too? – cause

"啊！"勒格朗嚷道，他已经兴奋过了头，"是什么东西？"

"哟，只是个头颅骨——不知道啥人把脑袋留在树上，乌鸦把肉全啃光了。"

"你说那是个头颅骨！太好了！头是怎么钉在横枝上的？——是用什么拴着的？"

"没错，少爷，我得看看。哟，这可真是，太奇怪了——头颅骨上有个这么大的大钉子，它给钉在树上了。"

"好，丘比特，下面按我说的去做——听见了吗？"

"听见了，少爷。"

"好，听清楚了——找到头颅骨的左眼。"

"哼！呵呵！绝了！根本就没有眼睛了。"

"你可真够笨的！你分得清哪边是左，哪边是右吗？"

"分得清，分得清——当然分得清楚——这边是左手，我劈柴用的那只手。"

"可不是！你是个左撇子，你的左眼和左手在同一边。我想，这样你就能找到头颅骨上的左眼，也就是原来长着左眼的窟窿了。你找到了吗？"

过了很久，黑仆才问道：

"头颅骨上的左眼，是不是和头颅骨的左手在同一边？——因为

de skull aint got not a bit ob a hand at all –
nebber mind! I got de lef eye now – here
de lef eye! what mus do wid it?”

“Let the beetle drop through it, as far as
the string will reach – but be careful and
not let go your hold of the string.”

“All dat done, Massa Will; mighty easy
ting for to put de bug fru de hole – look out
for him dare below!”

During this colloquy no portion of
Jupiter’s person could be seen; but the
beetle, which he had suffered to descend,
was now visible at the end of the string,
and glistened, like a globe of burnished
gold, in the last rays of the setting sun,
some of which still faintly illumined the
eminence upon which we stood. The
scarabœus hung quite clear of any
branches, and, if allowed to fall, would
have fallen at our feet. Legrand
immediately took the scythe, and cleared
with it a circular space, three or four yards
in diameter, just beneath the insect, and,
having accomplished this, ordered Jupiter
to let go the string and come down from
the tree.

Driving a peg, with great nicety, into the
ground, at the precise spot where the beetle
fell, my friend now produced from his
pocket a tape measure. Fastening one end
of this at that point of the trunk, of the tree
which was nearest the peg, he unrolled it
till it reached the peg, and thence farther

在头颅骨上根本找不到手啊——算
了！我找到了——这个就是左眼！
接着我该怎么做？”

“把甲虫从左眼里扔下来，尽
量让绳子往下放——你要小心，千
万别把绳子掉了。”

“知道了，威儿少爷，把虫子
穿过那个窟窿，那太容易了——从
下面看好了！”

说话的时候根本看不到丘比特
的身影。夕阳昏昏的光线照着我们
所在的高地，他费了好大劲才放下
来的甲虫倒十分醒目，它被挂在绳
子的末端，在余晖中发出闪闪光芒，
像一个打磨光滑的金球。金龟子悬
空挂着，只要一松手就会掉在我们
脚前。勒格朗伸手抓过长柄镰刀，
在虫子的正下方，划了一个直径三
四码的圆圈，划好后便吩咐丘比特
松开绳子，从树上爬下来。

这时，我朋友在甲虫掉落的地
方不偏不倚地打进一个木桩，接着
从口袋里掏出卷皮尺，把尺的一头
钉在靠近木桩的树干上，将皮尺拉
到木桩那儿，再沿着百合树和木桩
之间形成的直线方向向前拉长了50
英尺，丘比特用长柄镰刀将周围的

unrolled it, in the direction already established by the two points of the tree and the peg, for the distance of fifty feet – Jupiter clearing away the brambles with the scythe. At the spot thus attained a second peg was driven, and about this, as a centre, a rude circle, about four feet in diameter, described. Taking now a spade himself, and giving one to Jupiter and one to me, Legrand begged us to set about digging as quickly as possible.

To speak the truth, I had no especial relish for such amusement at any time, and, at that particular moment, would most willingly have declined it; for the night was coming on, and I felt much fatigued with the exercise already taken; but I saw no mode of escape, and was fearful of disturbing my poor friend's equanimity by a refusal. Could I have depended, indeed, upon Jupiter's aid, I would have had no hesitation in attempting to get the lunatic home by force; but I was too well assured of the old negro's disposition, to hope that he would assist me, under any circumstances, in a personal contest with his master. I made no doubt that the latter had been infected with some of the innumerable Southern superstitions about money buried, and that his phantasy had received confirmation by the finding of the *scarabæus*, or, perhaps, by Jupiter's obstinacy in maintaining it to be "a bug of

荆棘砍掉。勒格朗又在那里打了一个木桩，以此为圆心，随随便便画了一个直径约 4 英尺的圆圈。然后拿起铲子，又分给我和丘比特每人一把，让我们开始挖土。

说实话，平日里我就不喜欢干活，尤其此时此刻，真恨不得能一口回绝掉。一来天马上就黑了，二来我们赶了半天路，实在累得够呛。可我偏偏想不到借口溜走，又害怕张口拒绝的话，那位老兄不定会有什么反应。要是丘比特能帮忙的话，我早就想法子让这个疯子回家了。然而我清楚老黑仆的脾气，不管什么情况，想让他或帮我或是跟少爷发生争执，是断然行不通的。南方人之间流传着地下埋有宝藏的说法，我相信勒格朗肯定听信了这些谣传，中毒太深。他找到了金龟子，就把脑子里的幻想当真了，或许是由于丘比特一口认定那是"一只真金做的虫子"，他才相信的吧。神经失常的人很容易就会轻信这种鬼话，要是和心里的想法刚好吻合的话，就尤其容易上当，于是我立刻想到这可怜的家伙曾说过，甲虫是"他金库的钥匙"。总而言之，我

real gold." A mind disposed to lunacy would readily be led away by such suggestions – especially if chiming in with favorite preconceived ideas – and then I called to mind the poor fellow's speech about the beetle's being "the index of his fortune." Upon the whole, I was sadly vexed and puzzled, but, at length, I concluded to make a virtue of necessity – to dig with a good will, and thus the sooner to convince the visionary, by ocular demonstration, of the fallacy of the opinions he entertained.

The lanterns having been lit, we all fell to work with a zeal worthy a more rational cause; and, as the glare fell upon our persons and implements, I could not help thinking how picturesque a group we composed, and how strange and suspicious our labors must have appeared to any interloper who, by chance, might have stumbled upon our whereabouts.

We dug very steadily for two hours. Little was said; and our chief embarrassment lay in the yelpings of the dog, who took exceeding interest in our proceedings. He, at length, became so obstreperous that we grew fearful of his giving the alarm to some stragglers in the vicinity; – or, rather, this was the apprehension of Legrand; – for myself, I should have rejoiced at any interruption which might have enabled me to get the

现在心里乱作一团，不知道该如何是好，最后才下定决心，既然非得行动，干脆直接动手——认认真真地挖土，这样就能拿出证据，让这个幻想家知道自己其实是在异想天开。

两盏牛眼灯全点上了，我们开始卖力干起活，要是把这股劲头儿用在正事上该有多好啊。看看微弱的灯光打在我们身上，照在工具上，我不禁暗想，我们这些人就和画中人一样，要是有人无意间闯进来，肯定觉得我们做的事情有多么神奇，多么令人费解。

我们挖了两个小时，一刻没有停歇。大家不做声，只有那条狗对我们做的事情很感兴趣的样子，汪汪地叫着，使我们感到极为不安。后来它叫得实在厉害，我们才开始担心，害怕它的叫声会惊扰了附近的路人，准确地说，这正是勒格朗担心的。我倒恨不得有人闯进来，好借机让这个流浪汉回去。丘比特冷静且顽强地从土坑里爬出来，用一条吊袜带把狗的嘴绑住，直到叫

wanderer home. The noise was, at length, very effectually silenced by Jupiter, who, getting out of the hole with a dogged air of deliberation, tied the brute's mouth up with one of his suspenders, and then returned, with a grave chuckle, to his task.

When the time mentioned had expired, we had reached a depth of five feet, and yet no signs of any treasure became manifest. A general pause ensued, and I began to hope that the farce was at an end. Legrand, however, although evidently much disconcerted, wiped his brow thoughtfully and recommenced. We had excavated the entire circle of four feet diameter, and now we slightly enlarged the limit, and went to the farther depth of two feet. Still nothing appeared. The gold-seeker, whom I sincerely pitied, at length clambered from the pit, with the bitterest disappointment imprinted upon every feature, and proceeded, slowly and reluctantly, to put on his coat, which he had thrown off at the beginning of his labor. In the mean time I made no remark. Jupiter, at a signal from his master, began to gather up his tools. This done, and the dog having been unmuzzled, we turned in profound silence towards home.

We had taken, perhaps, a dozen steps in this direction, when, with a loud oath, Legrand strode up to Jupiter, and seized him by the collar. The astonished negro

声终于停止了，他才得意地呵呵一笑，重新开始干活。

两个小时过去了，我们挖了有5英尺多深，可还是看不到金银财宝的影子。大家全都停了手，我真想让这场闹剧赶快就此结束。勒格朗有些狼狈不堪，若有所思地按了按额头，竟又开始挖起来。那个直径4英尺的圆圈早就已经挖开了，现在又稍微挖大了些，又挖深了两英尺。但还是什么都没有。淘金人此刻一脸失望，极其痛苦地从坑里爬出来，动作缓慢地将干活前脱掉的外套穿上。我一直没有做声，表示对他的同情。丘比特一看到少爷的手势，就开始收拾工具。等收拾完毕，把狗嘴上的吊袜带取下来，一行人便默默地往回走。

我们刚往回走了十几步，勒格朗突然大骂一声，大步朝丘比特走去，一把揪起他的衣领。黑仆吓了一跳，眼睛和嘴巴都张得大大的，

opened his eyes and mouth to the fullest extent, let fall the spades, and fell upon his knees.

"You scoundrel," said Legrand, hissing out the syllables from between his clenched teeth – "you infernal black villain! – speak, I tell you! – answer me this instant, without prevarication! – which – which is your left eye?"

"Oh, my golly, Massa Will! aint dis here my lef eye for sartain?" roared the terrified Jupiter, placing his hand upon his *right* organ of vision, and holding it there with a desperate pertinacity, as if in immediate dread of his master's attempt at a gouge.

"I thought so! – I knew it! hurrah!" vociferated Legrand, letting the negro go, and executing a series of curvets and caracols, much to the astonishment of his valet, who, arising from his knees, looked, mutely, from his master to myself, and then from myself to his master.

"Come! we must go back," said the latter, "the game's not up yet;" and he again led the way to the tulip-tree.

"Jupiter," said he, when we reached its foot, "come here! was the skull nailed to the limb with the face outwards, or with the face to the limb?"

"De face was out, massa, so dat de crows could get at de eyes good, without any trouble."

"Well, then, was it this eye or that

手一松，铲子掉了下来，扑通一声双膝着地。

"你这个浑蛋！"勒格朗从牙缝里挤出几个字，"你这个狼心狗肺的浑蛋！——老实说，你说！——立刻回答我，别吞吞吐吐的！——哪——哪只是你的左眼？"

"哎哟，威儿少爷！难道这不是我的左眼？"丘比特吓破了胆，哇哇地叫着，把手伸到自己的右眼上，紧紧地按着，像是害怕少爷会剜掉他的眼睛一样。

"我早就猜到了！——我早就猜到了！哈哈！"勒格朗大叫着，松手放下黑仆，独自蹦蹦跳跳地在原地转了几圈，闹了一阵，他的随从吓得睁大眼睛，从地上爬起来，默不做声地来回看着我和少爷。

"嘿！咱们得回去，"勒格朗说，"还没有结束呢。"说着便带头朝百合树走去。

我们回到树下，他说："丘比特，过来！头颅骨是脸朝外被钉在横枝上的，还是朝里钉着的？"

"脸朝外，少爷，这样乌鸦才能轻易吃掉眼睛。"

"好，那你刚才从哪边眼里把

through which you dropped the beetle?" – here Legrand touched each of Jupiter's eyes.

"Twas dis eye, massa – de lef eye – jis as you tell me," and here it was his right eye that the negro indicated.

"That will do – must try it again."

Here my friend, about whose madness I now saw, or fancied that I saw, certain indications of method, removed the peg which marked the spot where the beetle fell, to a spot about three inches to the westward of its former position. Taking, now, the tape measure from the nearest point of the trunk to the peg, as before, and continuing the extension in a straight line to the distance of fifty feet, a spot was indicated, removed, by several yards, from the point at which we had been digging.

Around the new position a circle, somewhat larger than in the former instance, was now described, and we again set to work with the spades. I was dreadfully weary, but, scarcely understanding what had occasioned the change in my thoughts, I felt no Longer any great aversion from the labor imposed. I had become most unaccountably interested – nay, even excited. Perhaps there was something, amid all the extravagant demeanor of Legrand – some air of forethought, or of deliberation, which impressed me. I dug eagerly, and now and

甲虫放下来的，这边，还是那边？"勒格朗说着，一边摸上丘比特的两只眼睛。

"这只，少爷——左眼——我就是照您的吩咐做的。"然而黑仆指着的却是他的右眼。

"行了——咱们还得重试一次。"

这时我才明白这位仁兄表面上不太正常，其实头脑还算清楚，或者说我只是自认为他清醒罢了。他把钉在甲虫下落地方的木桩取出来，往西挪了大约3英寸；再从树身最近的一点处把皮尺拉开，拉到木桩那儿，沿着直线往前拉了50英尺，绕开刚才挖的坑，重新圈个地方。

接着绕着圆点重新画了个圆圈，这比刚才那个大了一些，我们又开始挖坑。我已经筋疲力尽了，可心里却略微有了变化，不是想立刻结束这份体力活，而是感到一种莫名的兴趣——甚至有些激动。说不定，勒格朗的疯狂行为有某些地方触动了我的心——或许是他深谋远虑的劲头，又或许是他从容不迫的心态。我卖力地挖着，一边挖，一边想原来自己也希望找到那传说中的金银财宝，我那不幸的老兄就是因为发财梦才头脑不正常的。我们又挖了约一个半钟头，我满脑子

then caught myself actually looking, with something that very much resembled expectation, for the fancied treasure, the vision of which had demented my unfortunate companion. At a period when such vagaries of thought most fully possessed me, and when we had been at work perhaps an hour and a half, we were again interrupted by the violent howlings of the dog. His uneasiness, in the first instance, had been, evidently, but the result of playfulness or caprice, but he now assumed a bitter and serious tone. Upon Jupiter's again attempting to muzzle him, he made furious resistance, and, leaping into the hole, tore up the mould frantically with his claws. In a few seconds he had uncovered a mass of human bones, forming two complete skeletons, intermingled with several buttons of metal, and what appeared to be the dust of decayed woollen. One or two strokes of a spade upturned the blade of a large Spanish knife, and, as we dug farther, three or four loose pieces of gold and silver coin came to light.

At sight of these the joy of Jupiter could scarcely be restrained, but the countenance of his master wore an air of extreme disappointment He urged us, however, to continue our exertions, and the words were hardly uttered when I stumbled and fell forward, having caught the toe of my boot

想的都是这些不现实的念头，狗突然又开始大叫，惊扰到我们。刚才的叫声很明显只是因为起哄、胡闹而导致的不安，然而这次的叫声尖厉且严肃。丘比特又想绑住它的嘴，可它拼命抵抗，跳到坑里，发疯似的刨土。才一会儿，就刨出一堆尸骨，刚好是两具四肢俱全的骷髅，还夹带着几粒铜扣，以及腐烂的类似呢绒的东西。再往下铲，便挖出一把西班牙大刀，接着又看到散落的三四枚金币。

眼前的一切让丘比特分外高兴，按捺不住地激动。而少爷却一脸失望的表情，但还是催促我们继续往下挖，话音刚落，我的靴子突然钩住一个半掩在土里的大铁环，摔了一跤。

in a large ring of iron that lay half buried in the loose earth.

We now worked in earnest, and never did I pass ten minutes of more intense excitement. During this interval we had fairly unearthed an obLong chest of wood, which, from its perfect preservation and wonderful hardness, had plainly been subjected to some mineralizing process – perhaps that of the Bi-chloride of Mercury. This box was three feet and a half Long, three feet broad, and two and a half feet deep. It was firmly secured by bands of wrought iron, riveted, and forming a kind of open trelliswork over the whole. On each side of the chest, near the top, were three rings of iron – six in all – by means of which a firm hold could be obtained by six persons. Our utmost united endeavors served only to disturb the coffer very slightly in its bed. We at once saw the impossibility of removing so great a weight. Luckily, the sole fastenings of the lid consisted of two sliding bolts. These we drew back – trembling and panting with anxiety. In an instant, a treasure of incalculable value lay gleaming before us. As the rays of the lanterns fell within the pit, there flashed upwards a glow and a glare, from a confused heap of gold and of jewels, that absolutely dazzled our eyes.

I shall not pretend to describe the feelings with which I gazed. Amazement

眼下我们挖得格外认真，从没经历过如此让人兴奋的 10 分钟。片刻时间，我们顺利挖出来一只长方形木箱。这箱子完好无损，异常坚固，很明显经过什么特殊处理——大概是汞之类的矿物质。这只箱子有 3 英尺半长，3 英尺宽，2 英尺半高。四周围紧紧裹着一层铁皮，还钉着铆钉，把整只箱子截成一块块格子。左右两边靠近箱盖的地方分别有 3 个铁环，总共 6 个，能当把手供 6 个人抓着。尽管我们费了九牛二虎之力，也只能让箱子挪动几分。我们立刻看出来这么重的箱子是没法搬动的。幸好箱盖上有两个活扣。我们将两个扣子拉开——焦急得有些战栗，喘着粗气。只一眨眼，整箱金银珠宝便出现在我们面前，发着闪闪的光芒。灯光照进坑里，满箱价值连城的黄金珠宝反射出耀眼的光芒，照得我们眼花缭乱。

我睁大眼睛盯着那箱子时的复杂心情，不想再细谈了。首先自然

was, of course, predominant. Legrand appeared exhausted with excitement, and spoke very few words. Jupiter's countenance wore, for some minutes, as deadly a pallor as it is possible, in nature of things, for any negro's visage to assume. He seemed stupified – thunderstricken. Presently he fell upon his knees in the pit, and, burying his naked arms up to the elbows in gold, let them there remain, as if enjoying the luxury of a bath. At length, with a deep sigh, he exclaimed, as if in a soliloquy:

"And dis all cum ob de goole-bug! de putty goole bug! de poor little goole-bug, what I boosed in dat sabage kind ob style! Aint you shamed ob yourself, nigger? – answer me dat!"

It became necessary, at last, that I should arouse both master and valet to the expediency of removing the treasure. It was growing late, and it behooved us to make exertion, that we might get every thing housed before daylight. It was difficult to say what should be done, and much time was spent in deliberation – so confused were the ideas of all. We, finally, lightened the box by removing two thirds of its contents, when we were enabled, with some trouble, to raise it from the hole. The articles taken out were deposited among the brambles, and the dog left to guard them, with strict orders from Jupiter

感到震惊。勒格朗看起来已经兴奋到没了力气，话也变少了。一时间，丘比特脸色苍白，当然我的意思是，一般黑人的脸上能有多白，此刻他就有多白。呆若木鸡，吓得够呛。之后他双膝跪在坑里，把两条胳膊插到金子里，让金子没过胳膊肘，保持这个姿势不伸出来，就像在美滋滋地洗澡一样。最后，他深深呼出一口气，自言自语般大声喊道：

"这都亏了金甲虫！漂亮的金甲虫！可怜的小金甲虫，我那样咒骂的东西！难道你不觉得害羞吗，黑奴？——告诉我呀！"

后来我不得不提醒他们主仆二人，现在要想办法将宝贝搬走。而且夜渐深了，必须要在天亮前把宝贝搬回去。大家心里都一团乱，不知该如何是好，很难说，左思右想考虑了好久，才决定将箱子里的财宝搬出2/3，箱子变轻了，几个人努努力，总算把它搬了出来。拿出来的财宝就藏在荆棘里，让狗留下来守着，丘比特还严厉地叮嘱了一番，在我们回来之前，不管遇到什么情况，都不能离开，也不能张嘴乱叫。然后我们扛着木箱，匆匆赶路。大家都很辛苦，直到凌晨一点，才总算平安回到木屋，我们筋疲力尽，

neither, upon any pretence, to stir from the spot, nor to open his mouth until our return. We then hurriedly made for home with the chest; reaching the hut in safety, but after excessive toil, at one o'clock in the morning. Worn out as we were, it was not in human nature to do more immediately. We rested until two, and had supper; starting for the hills immediately afterwards, armed with three stout sacks, which, by good luck, were upon the premises. A little before four we arrived at the pit, divided the remainder of the booty, as equally as might be, among us, and, leaving the holes unfilled, again set out for the hut, at which, for the second time, we deposited our golden burthens, just as the first faint streaks of the dawn gleamed from over the tree-tops in the East.

We were now thoroughly broken down; but the intense excitement of the time denied us repose. After an unquiet slumber of some three or four hours' duration, we arose, as if by preconcert, to make examination of our treasure.

The chest had been full to the brim, and we spent the whole day, and the greater part of the next night, in a scrutiny of its contents. There had been nothing like order or arrangement. Every thing had been heaped in promiscuously. Having assorted all with care, we found ourselves possessed of even vaster wealth than we had at first

立刻开始工作，是绝不可能的。休息到两点钟，吃了晚饭，刚好屋里有 3 个结实的口袋，便带在身上，赶紧回到山里。4 点左右，我们才回到坑边，把剩下的金银财宝平均分成 3 份，坑也没填，就起身往木屋走，等再次把装着金银的袋子在屋里藏好时，东方树梢上已泛出几道蒙蒙的白光。

这一夜，我们早就累垮了，然而因为过于兴奋，反倒不能安稳入睡。辗转反侧三四个小时，大家像事先约定好了似的，同时起身，开始点数金银财宝。

那些财宝竟装了满满一箱，我们花了整整一天，再加大半个晚上才点完。一箱财宝随意摆放着，也没一一分类，全都胡乱堆在那儿。我们仔细地分了类，才知道这些财富要比我们料想的还要多。我们按照当时兑换的牌价，尽可能准确估计了一下，硬币的价值有 45 万多。

supposed. In coin there was rather more than four hundred and fifty thousand dollars – estimating the value of the pieces, as accurately as we could, by the tables of the period. There was not a particle of silver. All was gold of antique date and of great variety – French, Spanish, and German money, with a few English guineas, and some counters, of which we had never seen specimens before. There were several very large and heavy coins, so worn that we could make nothing of their inscriptions. There was no American money. The value of the jewels we found more difficulty in estimating. There were diamonds – some of them exceedingly large and fine – a hundred and ten in all, and not one of them small; eighteen rubies of remarkable brilliancy; – three hundred and ten emeralds, all very beautiful; and twenty-one sapphires, with an opal. These stones had all been broken from their settings and thrown loose in the chest. The settings themselves, which we picked out from among the other gold, appeared to have been beaten up with hammers, as if to prevent identification. Besides all this, there was a vast quantity of solid gold ornaments; – nearly two hundred massive finger and earrings; – rich chains – thirty of these, if I remember; – eighty-three very large and heavy crucifixes; – five gold censers of great value; – a prodigious

没有一块是银币，全都是金币，各种各样，有法国、西班牙、德国的，还有几枚是英国畿尼，除此之外还有一些从来没见过的硬币。有几枚硬币很大还很沉，已经快磨光了，完全辨认不清花纹。但没有美国货币。珠宝的价值更难估计了。其中有钻石——有些很大，非常耀眼——总共 110 颗，全都很大；18 块红宝石，发出夺目的光芒；310 块翡翠，都美得惊人；还有 21 块蓝宝石和一颗猫眼。宝石的镶嵌托都被拆掉了，胡乱地扔在箱子里。我们从别的金器里找到那些嵌托，看起来每个都被锤子砸扁了，像是不想让人认出一样。此外还有数不清的纯金首饰：将近 200 只又厚又重的戒指和耳环；价值不菲的金链子——如果我没记错的话，总共有 30 根；83 个又大又沉的十字架；5 只价值连城的金香炉；5 只大大的纯金酒钵，做工精细，雕着葡萄叶和酒仙的图案；还有两把剑柄，精细镂刻做工；以及很多小物件，我都记不清了。这些珍宝加一起总共有 350 多磅重。我还没算上 197 只昂贵的金表；其中 3 只，每只都价值 500 块；很多都是古董，要说计时的话，可不值钱了；因为零件有些都生锈了，但上面镶满了珠宝，外壳也是纯金的。当晚，我们估计那箱财宝值 150 万；可后来我们把珠宝首饰卖掉（其中几件没有卖，自

golden punch bowl, ornamented with richly chased vine-leaves and Bacchanalian figures; with two sword-handles exquisitely embossed, and many other smaller articles which I cannot recollect. The weight of these valuables exceeded three hundred and fifty pounds avoirdupois; and in this estimate I have not included one hundred and ninety-seven superb gold watches; three of the number being worth each five hundred dollars, if one. Many of them were very old, and as time keepers valueless; the works having suffered, more or less, from corrosion – but all were richly jewelled and in cases of great worth. We estimated the entire contents of the chest, that night, at a million and a half of dollars; and upon the subsequent disposal of the trinkets and jewels (a few being retained for our own use), it was found that we had greatly undervalued the treasure.

When, at length, we had concluded our examination, and the intense excitement of the time had, in some measure, subsided, Legrand, who saw that I was dying with impatience for a solution of this most extraordinary riddle, entered into a full detail of all the circumstances connected with it.

"You remember;" said he, "the night when I handed you the rough sketch I had made of the *scarabœus*. You recollect also,

己留下了），才知道原来实在低估了价钱。

我们终于点数完毕，兴奋劲也渐渐消退，心情平复了几分，勒格朗看出我迫切想知道这次神奇探险的谜底，于是便将整件事的来龙去脉原原本本地告诉了我。

"你还记得，"他说，"那天晚上，我把画好的金龟子草图递给你。你还记得当时你非常肯定我画的就

that I became quite vexed at you for insisting that my drawing resembled a death's-head. When you first made this assertion I thought you were jesting; but afterwards I called to mind the peculiar spots on the back of the insect, and admitted to myself that your remark had some little foundation in fact. Still, the sneer at my graphic powers irritated me – for I am considered a good artist – and, therefore, when you handed me the scrap of parchment, I was about to crumple it up and throw it angrily into the fire."

"The scrap of paper, you mean," said I.

"No; it had much of the appearance of paper, and at first I supposed it to be such, but when I came to draw upon it, I discovered it, at once, to be a piece of very thin parchment. It was quite dirty, you remember. Well, as I was in the very act of crumpling it up, my glance fell upon the sketch at which you had been looking, and you may imagine my astonishment when I perceived, in fact, the figure of a death's-head just where, it seemed to me, I had made the drawing of the beetle. For a moment I was too much amazed to think with accuracy. I knew that my design was very different in detail from this – although there was a certain similarity in general outline. Presently I took a candle, and seating myself at the other end of the room, proceeded to scrutinize the parchment

是一只骷髅头，当时我非常生气。你开始说得这么肯定，我还以为你在开玩笑。可后来想到昆虫背上那3个奇怪的圆点，才意识到你说的也不是没有根据。尽管如此，你笑话我画得不好，我还是很生气——人家都称赞我是个出色的画家呢——所以，当你把羊皮还给我时，我本来打算揉成一团，然后丢进火里的。"

"你说的是那张纸片吧。"我问道。

"不，那看起来很像纸，一开始我也当做是纸，可在上面一画，就知道原来那是张非常薄的羊皮。你还记得吧，那张羊皮很脏。接着说，我刚要把它揉成一团，无意中朝那张草图瞄了一眼，这一看，别提有多震惊了，说出来你也许不信，我原以为上面画着的是只甲虫，可谁想到竟然看到骷髅头像。当时我都吓呆了，大脑已经无法正常思考了。我知道这个骷髅头绝不是我画的那个——虽然外形上有几分相似。接着我拿根蜡烛，在屋子另一头坐下，又仔细地把羊皮检查了一遍。羊皮的背面，自己画的草图还在那里。开始时我觉得很奇怪，两张图的外形轮廓竟然分毫不差——我居然没有注意到这样异乎寻常的

more closely. Upon turning it over, I saw my own sketch upon the reverse, just as I had made it. My first idea, now, was mere surprise at the really remarkable similarity of outline – at the singular coincidence involved in the fact, that unknown to me, there should have been a skull upon the other side of the parchment, immediately beneath my figure of the *scarabœus*, and that this skull, not only in outline, but in size, should so closely resemble my drawing. I say the singularity of this coincidence absolutely stupified me for a time. This is the usual effect of such coincidences. The mind struggles to establish a connexion – a sequence of cause and effect – and, being unable to do so, suffers a species of temporary paralysis. But, when I recovered from this stupor, there dawned upon me gradually a conviction which startled me even far more than the coincidence. I began distinctly, positively, to remember that there had been no drawing upon the parchment when I made my sketch of the *scarabœus*. I became perfectly certain of this; for I recollected turning up first one side and then the other, in search of the cleanest spot. Had the skull been then there, of course I could not have failed to notice it. Here was indeed a mystery which I felt it impossible to explain; but, even at that early moment, there seemed to glimmer,

巧合，羊皮的一面画着个头颅骨，背面就是我画的那张金龟子图，而且头颅骨无论外形还是大小都和我画的一模一样。我刚刚提到了，遇到这样的巧合，我一时惊呆了。通常人们遇到这样的巧合，总会想得出神。我拼命想在心里理出头绪来——整件事的来龙去脉——然而就是办不到，一时想不通。等我清醒过来，才渐渐明白，却不禁吓了一跳，连那种异常的巧合都没让我如此吃惊。我完全想起来了，在画金龟子草图的时候，羊皮上并没有画。我保证没有。我记得当时想找个最最干净的东西画画，正反两面都仔细看过。要是上面有头颅骨，我绝对会注意到。这件事是个谜，没有办法解释。不过，在最开始的那一瞬间，我的内心深处隐隐闪过某种念头，就像萤火虫的光芒一闪而过，经过昨晚，一切终于真相大白。我立刻站起来，把羊皮藏好，在你们都离开后，才去思索这件事。

faintly, within the most remote and secret chambers of my intellect, a glow-worm-like conception of that truth which last night's adventure brought to so magnificent a demonstration. I arose at once, and putting the parchment securely away, dismissed all farther reflection until I should be alone.

"When you had gone, and when Jupiter was fast asleep, I betook myself to a more methodical investigation of the affair. In the first place I considered the manner in which the parchment had come into my possession. The spot where we discovered the *scarabaeus* was on the coast of the main land, about a mile eastward of the island, and but a short distance above high water mark. Upon my taking hold of it, it gave me a sharp bite, which caused me to let it drop. Jupiter, with his accustomed caution, before seizing the insect, which had flown towards him, looked about him for a leaf; or something of that nature, by which to take hold of it. It was at this moment that his eyes, and mine also, fell upon the scrap of parchment, which I then supposed to be paper. It was lying half buried in the sand, a corner sticking up. Near the spot where we found it, I observed the remnants of the hull of what appeared to have been a ship's Long boat. The wreck seemed to have been there for a very great while; for the resemblance to

"等你离开，丘比特睡着后，我便将整件事详细研究了一番。我首先要弄明白我是如何得到羊皮的。我们在大陆岸边，距离小岛东面不到一英里的地方发现了金龟子。那里离满潮标很近。我刚抓住甲虫，就被它狠咬了一口，不禁把它扔了。丘比特做事一向小心谨慎，看见虫子朝他飞过去，先在周围寻找叶子之类抓虫的东西。就在这时，我和他一下子看见了羊皮，我当时还以为是张纸呢。羊皮半掩在沙子里，一角翘起，在羊皮的附近，有几艘破船，像是长舢板。看样子已经堆在那里很长时间了，船的外形已经辨认不出来了。

boat timbers could scarcely be traced.

"Well, Jupiter picked up the parchment, wrapped the beetle in it, and gave it to me. Soon afterwards we turned to go home, and on the way met Lieutenant G-. I showed him the insect, and he begged me to let him take it to the fort. Upon my consenting, he thrust it forthwith into his waistcoat pocket, without the parchment in which it had been wrapped, and which I had continued to hold in my hand during his inspection. Perhaps he dreaded my changing my mind, and thought it best to make sure of the prize at once – you know how enthusiastic he is on all subjects connected with Natural History. At 'the same time, without being conscious of it, I must have deposited the parchment in my own pocket.

"You remember that when I went to the table, for the purpose of making a sketch of the beetle, I found no paper where it was usually kept. I looked in the drawer, and found none there. I searched my pockets, hoping to find an old letter, when my hand fell upon the parchment. I thus detail the precise mode in which it came into my possession; for the circumstances impressed me with peculiar force.

"No doubt you will think me fanciful – but I had already established a kind of *connexion*. I had put together two links of a great chain. There was a boat lying upon a

"接着刚才的说，丘比特拾起羊皮，把甲虫包在里头，交给我。然后我们就起程回家，路上我们遇到葛××中尉。我给他看虫子，他求我让他把虫子带回去。我才同意，他就把虫子塞到口袋里，不过外面没有羊皮，他看虫子那会儿，我始终拿着羊皮。他或许害怕我会改变主意，觉得还是马上拿到这个意外收获比较好吧——你知道，所有与生物学有关的东西他都非常着迷。就是那个时候，我不自觉地把羊皮放到口袋里了。

"你还记得，我当时想画下甲虫的样子，在桌子那边找了一下，却没找到。又在抽屉里找，也没找到。然后掏掏口袋，希望能找封旧信之类的，刚好一下摸到羊皮。我能如此详细地讲述得到羊皮的过程，是因为对这件事的印象尤其深刻。

"当然，你会觉得我是在异想天开——然而我早就把当中的关系弄得一清二楚了。我把一个大连环和其中的两个小环都连上了。海边

sea-coast, and not far from the boat was a parchment – *not a paper* – with a skull depicted upon it. You will, of course, ask 'where is the connexion?' I reply that the skull, or death's-head, is the well-known emblem of the pirate. The flag of the death's head is hoisted in all engagements.

"I have said that the scrap was parchment, and not paper. Parchment is durable – almost imperishable. Matters of little moment are rarely consigned to parchment; since, for the mere ordinary purposes of drawing or writing, it is not nearly so well adapted as paper. This reflection suggested some meaning – some relevancy – in the death's-head. I did not fail to observe, also, the form of the parchment. Although one of its corners had been, by some accident, destroyed, it could be seen that the original form was obLong. It was just such a slip, indeed, as might have been chosen for a memorandum – for a record of something to be Long remembered and carefully preserved."

"But," I interposed, "you say that the skull was not upon the parchment when you made the drawing of the beetle. How then do you trace any connexion between the boat and the skull – since this latter, according to your own admission, must have been designed (God only knows how or by whom) at some period subsequent to your sketching the scarabœus?"

有艘破船，离船不远的地方有张羊皮——那并不是纸——上面画着一个头颅骨。你自然会问：'这其中有什么关联呢？'我告诉，头颅骨，或者说骷髅头，是海盗的标志，这是众所周知的。海盗在抢劫的时候总会悬挂骷髅头旗。

"我刚提到那不是纸而是羊皮。羊皮结实，几乎永远都不会烂。不重要的事情可不会记在羊皮上。因为要是只画画图，写写字，用纸要好得多了。这么一想，我便想是不是骷髅头里另有玄机，有连带关系。我还注意到羊皮的外观。虽然有一角不知怎的被弄坏了，不过还是能看得出原先是长方形的。通常别人想要记下重大、需要永久保存的事情，都会用到这种羊皮。"

"但你不是说在画甲虫的时候，羊皮上还没有头颅骨吗，"我打断他问道，"那么，照你的说法，头颅骨应该是在你画上金龟子之后的一段时间里画上去的（是如何画的，谁画的，只有老天才知道），那是怎么联想到小船和头颅骨的呢？"

"Ah, hereupon turns the whole mystery; although the secret, at this point, I had comparatively little difficulty in solving. My steps were sure, and could afford but a single result. I reasoned, for example, thus: When I drew the scarabæus, there was no skull apparent upon the parchment. When I had completed the drawing I gave it to you, and observed you narrowly until you returned it. You, therefore, did not design the skull, and no one else was present to do it. Then it was not done by human agency. And nevertheless it was done.

"At this stage of my reflections I endeavored to remember, and did remember, with entire distinctness, every incident which occurred about the period in question. The weather was chilly (oh rare and happy accident!), and a fire was blazing upon the hearth. I was heated with exercise and sat near the table. You, however, had drawn a chair close to the chimney. Just as I placed the parchment in your hand, and as you were in the act of inspecting it, Wolf, the Newfoundland, entered, and leaped upon your shoulders. With your left hand you caressed him and kept him off, while your right, holding the parchment, was permitted to fall listlessly between your knees, and in close proximity to the fire. At one moment I thought the blaze had caught it, and was about to caution you, but, before I could speak, you

"是啊，这正是奇怪的地方；不过，我当时倒没细想，就解开了谜底。我仔细推敲每一步，所以答案只有一个。打个比方，我的推论是这样的：我画金龟子的时候，羊皮上明明没有头颅骨。我画好后，交给你，再到你把画还给我，这期间我始终看着你。所以头颅骨不可能是你画的，当时没有其他人。那么这就不是人力所能达到的了。不过话说回来，最后画还是在上面了。

"到了这地步，我便仔细回想当时的一切蛛丝马迹，果然全都记得一清二楚。当时天很冷（啊，这真是天大的巧合！），壁炉里生着火。我赶路走得很热，便坐在桌边。但是你却把椅子拉到炉边坐着。我正给你羊皮，你刚打算把它摊开来看，'胡尔夫'那只大狗便蹿了进来，一下子扑到你肩上。你用左手摸它，让它下去，右手拿着羊皮，随意地搭在两膝之间，刚好靠近炉火。我当时还怕火苗会烧到纸，刚想叫你，没想到你在我开口前就拿开了，正低头看画。我想到这一连串经过，便马上肯定，羊皮上显现出头颅骨是因为受热的缘故。你也知道很久之前就有一种药剂，沾了它在纸上或皮纸上写字，只有当用火烤时，才能显出字迹来。人家常常会把不纯的氧化钴在王水里溶解，然后再

had withdrawn it, and were engaged in its examination. When I considered all these particulars, I doubted not for a moment that heat had been the agent in bringing to light, upon the parchment, the skull which I saw designed upon it. You are well aware that chemical preparations exist, and have existed time out of mind, by means of which it is possible to write upon either paper or vellum, so that the characters shall become visible only when subjected to the action of fire. Zaffre, digested in *aqua regia*, and diluted with four times its weight of water, is sometimes employed; a green tint results. The regulus of cobalt, dissolved in spirit of nitre, gives a red. These colors disappear at Longer or shorter intervals after the material written upon cools, but again become apparent upon the re-application of heat.

"I now scrutinized the death's-head with care. Its outer edges – the edges of the drawing nearest the edge of the vellum – were far more *distinct* than the others. It was clear that the action of the caloric had been imperfect or unequal. I immediately kindled a fire, and subjected every portion of the parchment to a glowing heat. At first, the only effect was the strengthening of the faint lines in the skull; but, upon persevering in the experiment, there became visible, at the corner of the slip, diagonally opposite to the spot in which

加入 4 倍水将它稀释,可以得到绿色溶液。把含杂质的钴溶解在纯硝酸里,就能调出红色溶液。沾了药剂的字迹冷却后,经过很长一段时间,具体多久我说不准,颜色就会消退,不过只要一加热,便又会清楚地显现了。

"于是我仔细观察了一下骷髅头。骷髅头外面那圈,就是离纸边最近的一圈,比其他地方要看得清楚。那是羊皮受热不全,不均匀的缘故。我马上把火点着了,让羊皮的每个部分都充分受热。起先,头颅骨边缘模糊的线条变得清楚了些,可继续试验下去,在羊皮的一角,斜对着骷髅头的地方,清楚地显现出一个图形。起初我还以为是只山羊。可看清楚后,才知道原来那是只小羊羔。"

the death's-head was delineated, the figure of what I at first supposed to be a goat. A closer scrutiny, however, satisfied me that it was intended for a kid."

"Ha! ha!" said I, "to be sure I have no right to laugh at you – a million and a half of money is too serious a matter for mirth – but you are not about to establish a third link in your chain – you will not find any especial connexion between your pirates and a goat – pirates, you know, have nothing to do with goats; they appertain to the farming interest."

"But I have just said that the figure was *not* that of a goat."

"Well, a kid then – pretty much the same thing."

"Pretty much, but not altogether," said Legrand. "You may have heard of one *Captain* Kidd. I at once looked upon the figure of the animal as a kind of punning or hieroglyphical signature. I say signature; because its position upon the vellum suggested this idea. The death's-head at the corner diagonally opposite, had, in the same manner, the air of a stamp, or seal. But I was sorely put out by the absence of all else – of the body to my imagined instrument – of the text for my context."

"I presume you expected to find a letter between the stamp and the signature."

"Something of that kind. The fact is, I felt irresistibly impressed with a

"哈！哈！"我笑着说，"我当然没有资格笑话你——150万毕竟不是小数目，也不是随便说说的，你不会是想从那个连环套中想出第三个环节来吧——海盗跟山羊之间能有什么特别的联系？——要知道，他们二者没有任何关系。山羊和畜牧业倒沾点边。"

"可我说过，那图形不是只山羊。"

"行，就算是只小羊羔吧——那也差不多。"

"差不多，可并不完全相同，"勒格朗说，"你应该听说过基德船长吧，于是我把那只动物理解成一语双关，或是用象形文字写成的签名。我说它是签名，是因为注意到它在纸上的位置，让我灵光一闪。照这样推测，斜对面的骷髅头，应该是一个标记或印鉴。可除此之外，就在没有其他信息了——没有我期待的密文——没有能让我联系起来的暗语，我十分灰心。"

"你是想在标记和签名之间找到密信吧。"

"的确想找到这样的东西。说实话，我心里总有种预感，觉得很

presentiment of some vast good fortune impending. I can scarcely say why. Perhaps, after all, it was rather a desire than an actual belief; – but do you know that Jupiter's silly words, about the bug being of solid gold, had a remarkable effect upon my fancy? And then the series of accidents and coincidences – these were so very extraordinary. Do you observe how mere an accident it was that these events should have occurred upon the sole day of all the year in which it has been, or may be, sufficiently cool for fire, and that without the fire, or without the intervention of the dog at the precise moment in which he appeared, I should never have become aware of the death's-head, and so never the possessor of the treasure?"

"But proceed – I am all impatience."

"Well; you have heard, of course, the many stories current – the thousand vague rumors afloat about money buried, somewhere upon the Atlantic coast, by Kidd and his associates. These rumors must have had some foundation in fact. And that the rumors have existed so Long and so continuous, could have resulted, it appeared to me, only from the circumstance of the buried treasure still *remaining* entombed. Had Kidd concealed his plunder for a time, and afterwards reclaimed it, the rumors would scarcely have reached us in their present unvarying

快就能赚一大笔。我也说不清怎么会有这种想法。或许，与其说是相信感觉，倒不如说期望如此。丘比特说甲虫是纯金的，你知道吗，正是他这句话让我浮想联翩。之后又发生了一连串意外和巧合——全都十分离奇。那一天所有事接二连三地发生，那一天居然冷得要生火，或许是因为太冷所以才生的火吧，如果没生火的话，狗又没刚好在那时候冲进来，我根本不会看到骷髅头，现在也不会得到这笔财宝，你看多巧啊！"

"接着讲吧——我已经迫不及待了。"

"好吧，你应该听过很多传说——净是些捕风捉影的谣言，说什么基德那伙海盗把财宝埋在大西洋沿岸的某个地方。这些话必然有一定事实根据。流传了那么久都没有停止，我想，只有可能是人们还没有发现宝藏的缘故。如果基德当时藏了赃物，后来又将它取走，那么我们听到的谣言就不会像现在这样只有一个版本了。要注意，所有故事都是关于寻找宝藏的，而不是找到宝藏。如果海盗们最终取回了宝藏，那么事情会就此结束。依我

form. You will observe that the stories told are all about money-seekers, not about money-finders. Had the pirate recovered his money, there the affair would have dropped. It seemed to me that some accident – say the loss of a memorandum indicating its locality – had deprived him of the means of recovering it, and that this accident had become known to his followers, who otherwise might never have heard that treasure had been concealed at all, and who, busying themselves in vain, because unguided attempts, to regain it, had given first birth, and then universal currency, to the reports which are now so common. Have you ever heard of any important treasure being unearthed aLong the coast?"

"Never."

"But that Kidd's accumulations were immense, is well known. I took it for granted, therefore, that the earth still held them; and you will scarcely be surprised when I tell you that I felt a hope, nearly amounting to certainty, that the parchment so strangely found, involved a lost record of the place of deposit."

"But how did you proceed?"

"I held the vellum again to the fire, after increasing the heat; but nothing appeared. I now thought it possible that the coating of dirt might have something to do with the failure; so I carefully rinsed the parchment

看，这期间应该出现了什么意外——或者说他们丢了指示藏宝地点的地图——所以无法取回宝藏。这件事让海盗的手下知道了。不然的话他们根本不可能知道有宝藏的事情。他们胡乱找了一通，白白浪费力气，仍然没有结果，现在大家熟知的传言就是从他们那儿传出来的，后来就广为人知了。你听说过大西洋沿岸发现巨大宝藏的事吗？”

“从来没听说过。”

“可所有人都知道基德的宝藏多到数不清。所以我断定它们肯定还埋在某个地方。我跟你说，听了可别吓一跳，我心里抱着某种希望，很有把握。我希望这张意外得来的羊皮，就是传说中丢失的藏宝图。”

“那你后来怎么办的？”

“我把羊皮纸又放在火上，慢慢加热，但什么也没看到。我想或许是表面有灰尘的缘故，便小心翼翼地往上浇了热水，清洗一下，洗好后把它放到平底锅里，将画着头

by pouring warm water over it, and, having done this, I placed it in a tin pan, with the skull downwards, and put the pan upon a furnace of lighted charcoal. In a few minutes, the pan having become thoroughly heated, I removed the slip, and, to my inexpressible joy, found it spotted, in several places, with what appeared to be figures arranged in lines. Again I placed it in the pan, and suffered it to remain another minute. Upon taking it off, the whole was just as you see it now." Here Legrand, having re-heated the parchment, submitted it to my inspection. The following characters were rudely traced, in a red tint, between the death's-head and the goat:

"53‡‡†305))6*;4826)4‡.)4V);806*;48†8¶60))85;
1‡(;:‡*8†83(88)5*†;46(;88*96*?;8)*
‡(;485);5*†2:*‡(;4956*2(5*—4)8¶8*;4069285);
(6†8)4‡‡;1(‡9;48081;8:8†1;48†85;4)
485†528806*81(‡9;48;(88;4(‡?34;48)4‡;161;:1
88; ‡;"

"But," said I, returning him the slip, "I am as much in the dark as ever. Were all the jewels of Golconda awaiting me upon my solution of this enigma, I am quite sure that I should be unable to earn them."

"And yet," said Legrand, "the solution is by no means so difficult as you might be lead to imagine from the first hasty

颅骨的那面朝下，再把锅放在炭炉上烤。没有几分钟，锅就烧得滚烫，我把羊皮拿出来一看，心里别提有多高兴了，上面好几个地方都显现出一行行类似数字一样的东西。我又把羊皮放在锅里烤了一分钟。再拿出来时，上面的字迹就都出来了，就是你现在所见的样子。"勒格朗之前已将羊皮重新烤过，说到这里时他递给我看了下。在骷髅头和山羊之间，潦草地写着一串红色的符号：

"53‡‡†305))6*;4826)4‡.)4V);806*;48†8¶60))85;1‡(;:‡*8†83(88)5*†;46(;88*96*?;8)*‡(;485);5*†2:*‡(;4956*2(5*—4)8¶8*;4069285);)6†8)4‡‡;1(‡9;48081;8:8‡1;48†85;4)485†528806*81(‡9;48;(88;4(‡?34;48)4‡;161;:188; ‡;"

"我还是觉得很奇怪，"我把羊皮还给他说，"就算只要我解开这个谜底就能得到数不尽的宝贝，我也肯定没法把它们弄到手。"

"不过话说回来，"勒格朗道，"这个谜其实很容易，乍一看这些符号，你认为很难，其实并不难。

inspection of the characters. These characters, as any one might readily guess, form a cipher – that is to say, they convey a meaning; but then, from what is known of Kidd, I could not suppose him capable of constructing any of the more abstruse cryptographs. I made up my mind, at once, that this was of a simple species – such, however, as would appear, to the crude intellect of the sailor, absolutely insoluble without the key."

"And you really solved it?"

"Readily; I have solved others of an abstruseness ten thousand times greater. Circumstances, and a certain bias of mind, have led me to take interest in such riddles, and it may well be doubted whether human ingenuity can construct an enigma of the kind which human ingenuity may not, by proper application, resolve. In fact, having once established connected and legible characters, I scarcely gave a thought to the mere difficulty of developing their import.

"In the present case – indeed in all cases of secret writing – the first question regards the *language* of the cipher; for the principles of solution, so far, especially, as the more simple ciphers are concerned, depend upon, and are varied by, the genius of the particular idiom. In general, there is no alternative but experiment (directed by probabilities) of every tongue known to him who attempts the solution, until the

谁看了都会立马想到，这些符号是密码，也就是说，符号代表着特殊含义。不过，从我对基德的了解来看，他应该想不出什么复杂的密码。所以我断定，这些密码很简单——而且水手们头脑简单，如果没有密码书的话，他们可别想能解开。"

"你真的解开了？"

"那有什么难的，我还解开过比这难 10,000 倍的呢。由于受到周围环境的影响，再加上我本身的喜好，我向来对这类哑谜很感兴趣，我相信既然人类能够用尽心计想出一个哑谜，人类就能够用同样的心计想出正确的方法解开它。说实话，如果确定符号具有连贯性，那么要推理出其中的含义就没什么难的。

"就现在的例子来说——当然了，所有密文都有共同点——首先要知道密码使用的是什么语言。因为解谜的一项原则，尤其对于较为简单的密码来说，特定的熟语特征很重要，而且还要根据这些特征的不同进行变化。通常来讲，要想解开谜底，只有一种方法，就是用自己知晓的语言，根据一切可能进行尝试，直到猜中为止。不过，眼前

true one be attained. But, with the cipher now before us, all difficulty was removed by the signature. The pun upon the word 'Kidd' is appreciable in no other language than the English. But for this consideration I should have begun my attempts with the Spanish and French, as the tongues in which a secret of this kind would most naturally have been written by a pirate of the Spanish main. As it was, I assumed the cryptograph to be English.

"You observe there are no divisions between the words. Had there been divisions, the task would have been comparatively easy. In such case I should have commenced with a collation and analysis of the shorter words, and, had a word of a single letter occurred, as is most likely, (*a or I*, for example,) I should have considered the solution as assured. But, there being no division, my first step was to ascertain the predominant letters, as well as the least frequent. Counting all, I constructed a table, thus:

Of the character

8	here are 33.
;	there are 26.
4	there are 19.
‡)	there are 16.
*	there are 13.
5	there are 12.
6	there are 11
† 1	there are 8.

这部密码，因为有了签名，所以一切都变得简单明了了。'基德'这个单词只有在英文中才有这层双关含义。如果不是因为这个，我早就尝试法语和西班牙语了，因为常在南美洲北岸附近出没的海盗，如果要写下密码的话，肯定是用这两种语言。然而事实上，我仍然假设这部密码是用英文写成的。

"你看，所有字都是连在一起的。如果把它们分开，就容易得多了。在这种情况下，第一步应该先分析整理较短的单词，如果我能找到一个字母，大多情况下是可以找到的（比如说 a 或 I），那么我就绝对能解开谜底。然而，这部密码所有的字都连在一起，我首先需要确定出现最少和最多的字。把它们统计下来，就是这样一张表：

8 的符号共有 33 个。

；的符号共有 26 个。

4 的符号共有 19 个。

‡和)的符号分别有 16 个。

*的符号共有 13 个。

5 的符号共有 12 个。

6 的符号共有 11 个。

† 和 1 的符号分别有 8 个。

0		there are 6.
9 2		there are 5.
: 3		there are 4.
?		there are 3.
¶		there are 2.
—.		there are 1.

"Now, in English, the letter which most frequently occurs is e. Afterwards, succession runs thus: *a o i d h n r s t u y c f g l m w b k p q x z*. *E* predominates so remarkably that an individual sentence of any length is rarely seen, in which it is not the prevailing character.

"Here, then, we leave, in the very beginning, the groundwork for something more than a mere guess. The general use which may be made of the table is obvious – but, in this particular cipher, we shall only very partially require its aid. As our predominant character is 8, we will commence by assuming it as the e of the natural alphabet. To verify the supposition, let us observe if the 8 be seen often in couples – for *e* is doubled with great frequency in English – in such words, for example, as 'meet,' 'fleet,' 'speed,' 'seen,' 'been,' 'agree,' &c. In the present instance we see it doubled no less than five times, although the cryptograph is brief.

"Let us assume 8, then, as *e*. Now, of all *words* in the language, 'the' is most usual; let us see, therefore, whether there are not

0 的符号共有 6 个。

9 和 2 的符号分别有 5 个。

：和 3 的符号分别有 4 个。

? 的符号共有 3 个。

¶的符号共有 2 个。

—和.的符号分别有 1 个。

"接着看这些符号，在英文中最常见的字母是 e，按照使用频率来排序就是这样：a o i d h n r s t u y c f g l m w b k p q x z. e 用的次数最多，可无论句子有多长，都几乎看不到字母 e 不作为主要字母出现。

"说到这里，我们一开始就有了依据，而不单单是进行猜测了。这样的表很明显可以派上用场——但是在这部密码里，它只能解决一小部分问题。至于这部密码里使用最多的符号 8，我们不妨从一开始就假设这个数字代表了字母 e。为了证明这个推测是否正确，我们可以看下数字 8 是否经常连用——因为在英文中，字母 e 时常是连用的——比如，在 'meet'，'fleet'，'speed'，'been'，'agree' 等单词里，e 都是连用的。拿眼前这个例子来看，虽然密码不长，但是数字 8 的叠用次数竟有 5 次之多。

"那么我们就把 8 当做 e 了。要说，在所有英文单词里，'the' 这个单词是最常见的。那么，我们

repetitions of any three characters, in the same order of collocation, the last of them being 8. If we discover repetitions of such letters, so arranged, they will most probably represent the word 'the.' Upon inspection, we find no less than seven such arrangements, the characters being ;48. We may, therefore, assume that; represents *t*, 4 represents *h*, and 8 represents *e* – the last being now well confirmed. Thus a great step has been taken.

"But, having established a single word, we are enabled to establish a vastly important point; that is to say, several commencements and terminations of other words. Let us refer, for example, to the last instance but one, in which the combination ;48 occurs – not far from the end of the cipher. We know that the; immediately ensuing is the commencement of a word, and, of the six characters succeeding this 'the,' we are cognizant of no less than five. Let us set these characters down, thus, by the letters we know them to represent, leaving a space for the unknown –

t eeth.

"Here we are enabled, at once, to discard the '*th*,' as forming no portion of the word commencing with the first *t*; since, by experiment of the entire alphabet for a letter adapted to the vacancy, we perceive that no word can be formed of which this

可以看下有没有重复出现这样排列的 3 个符号，而且最后一个符号是数字 8。如果有这样排列的符号反复出现，那么十有八九就是 'the' 这个单词了。检查一遍，发现这种排列的符号竟出现了 7 次，且符号是;48。所以，可以假设符号；表示字母 t，数字 4 表示字幕 h，而 8 表示 e——现在最后一个字母是肯定的了。这样一来，我们就前进了一大步。

"而且，确定了一个字母，就能推断出很重要的一点，也就是说，能确定其他几个单词的首尾字母了。就拿倒数第二个;48 这 3 个符号来举例——这个单词离密码结尾很近。咱们知道后面连着的；是一个单词的首字母，'the' 字后面的 6 个符号里，出现了 5 次。不妨将这些符号用已知的代表它们的字母排列出来，留下一个空格给那个不知的字母——

t eeth。

"咱们试着在空格里填所有字母，可还是不能拼出一个以 th 结尾的单词。既然以 t 开头的单词中用不到 th，那就可以不要这两个字母，把这个单词缩成

th can be a part. We are thus narrowed into

t ee,

and, going through the alphabet, if necessary, as before, we arrive at the word 'tree,' as the sole possible reading. We thus gain another letter, *r,* represented by (, with the words 'the tree' in juxtaposition.

"Looking beyond these words, for a short distance, we again see the combination ;48, and employ it by way of termination to what immediately precedes. We have thus this arrangement:

the tree ;4(‡?34 the,

"or, substituting the natural letters, where known, it reads thus:

the tree thr‡?3h the.

"Now, if, in place of the unknown characters, we leave blank spaces, or substitute dots, we read thus:

the tree thr...h the,

"when the word 'through' makes itself evident at once. But this discovery gives us three new letters, *o, u* and *g,* represented by ‡,? and 3.

"Looking now, narrowly, through the cipher for combinations of known characters, we find, not very far from the

---

t ee,

我们接着按照之前那样，把字母一一填进去，只能拼出单词 'tree'。这样我们又得出一个新字母，（符号代表字母 r 的，而 'the tree' 这两个单词又刚好是连在一起的。

"再看这两个单词后面那段符号，又出现了;48三个符号的排列，就把它当成刚才那个单词的结尾吧。于是能列出以下几个字：

the tree ;4(‡?34 the,

"再用已知的字母代替符号，于是就有：

the tree thr‡?3h the.

"好，如果空着未知的符号，或是用点代替这些符号，就可以得出这样的单词：

the tree thr...h the,

"我们立刻能辨认出这个词是 'through'。这个发现为我们提供了 3 个新字母，o、u 和 g，代表它们的符号分别是‡,?和3。

"就这样重新将密码仔细检查一遍，找出已知的连在一起的符号，在刚开始的地方，有这样一列符号，

beginning, this arrangement,

83(88, or egree,

"which, plainly, is the conclusion of the word 'degree,' and gives us another letter, *d*, represented by †.

"Four letters beyond the word 'degree,' we perceive the combination

;46(;88.

"Translating the known characters, and representing the unknown by dots, as before, we read thus:

th rtee.

an arrangement immediately suggestive of the word 'thirteen,' and again furnishing us with two new characters, *i* and *n*, represented by 6 and *.

"Referring, now, to the beginning of the cryptograph, we find the combination,

53‡‡†.

"Translating, as before, we obtain

.good,

which assures us that the first letter is *A*, and that the first two words are 'A good.'

"It is now time that we arrange our key, as far as discovered, in a tabular form, to avoid confusion. It will stand thus:

5 represents a

† represents d

8 represents e

3 represents g

83（88，可以写成 egree，

"这个词一看就知道是 'degree' 的结尾部分，这样又知道了一个字母，即$代表字母 d。

" 'degree' 这个单词后面的一组符号中已知了 4 个字母，

;46(;88.

"用已知的字母把这些符号翻译出来，未知的还是用小点表示，就有：

th rtee.

这个排列立刻让我想到 'thirteen' 这个单词，于是又找到两个新符号，6 和*是分别表示 i 和 n。

"现在再举密码开头几组符号来看，看下面一组，

53##†.

用同样的方法翻译出来，就是

.good,

这就能肯定，第一个字母一定是 a，所以开头两个单词就是 'a good'。

"为了更加清楚易懂，现在我们将已知的线索一一列出来。就是这样的：

5 等于 a

†等于 d

8 等于 e

3 等于 g

4 represents h

6 represents i

* represents n

‡ represents o

(represents r

; represents t

‧? represents u

4 等于 h

6 等于 i

*等于 n

‡等于 o

（等于 r

；等于 t

？等于 u

"We have, therefore, no less than ten of the most important letters represented, and it will be unnecessary to proceed with the details of the solution. I have said enough to convince you that ciphers of this nature are readily soluble, and to give you some insight into the *rationale* of their development. But be assured that the specimen before us appertains to the very simplest species of cryptograph. It now only remains to give you the full translation of the characters upon the parchment, as unriddled. Here it is:

"'A good glass in the bishop's hostel in the devil's seat forty-one degrees and thirteen minutes northeast and by north main branch seventh limb east side shoot from the left eye of the death's-head a bee line from the tree through the shot fifty feet out.'"

"But," said I, "the enigma seems still in as bad a condition as ever. How is it possible to extort a meaning from all this jargon about 'devil's seats,' 'death's heads,'

"这样一来，我们就能认出十来个关键词了。解谜的具体方法也没必要再讲下去了。我已经说了不少，想你也认为解开这个密码并不难。你也了解了一些发现这些密码的方法。不过，说实在的，如今遇到的这部密码是最简单的一种。剩下的只要把羊皮上的符号全部翻译过来就可以了。你看：

"'一面好镜子在皮肖甫旅店魔椅41度13分东北偏北最大树枝第七根横枝东侧从骷髅头左眼射击从树前引一直线穿过子弹延长50英尺。'"

"但这个谜语似乎还是很难理解，"我说，"'魔椅'，'骷髅头'，'皮肖甫旅店'这些暗语的意思是什么呢？"

and 'bishop's hotels?'"

"I confess," replied Legrand, "that the matter still wears a serious aspect, when regarded with a casual glance. My first endeavor was to divide the sentence into the natural division intended by the cryptographist."

"You mean, to punctuate it?"

"Something of that kind."

"But how was it possible to effect this?"

"I reflected that it had been a point with the writer to run his words together without division, so as to increase the difficulty of solution. Now, a not over-acute man, in pursuing such an object would be nearly certain to overdo the matter. When, in the course of his composition, he arrived at a break in his subject which would naturally req uire a pause, or a point, he would be exceedingly apt to run his characters, at this place, more than usually close together. If you will observe the MS., in the present instance, you will easily detect five such cases of unusual crowding. Acting upon this hint, I made the division thus:

"A good glass in the Bishop's hostel in the Devil's seat – forty-one degrees and thirteen minutes – northeast and by north – main branch seventh limb east side – shoot from the left eye of the death's-head – a bee-line from the tree through the shot fifty feet

"说实话，"勒格朗道，"刚开始看的话，解开它似乎是不容易。我一开始就努力照着密码的原意，将全文分成原先的句子。"

"你的意思是加标点吧？"

"正是如此。"

"但要怎么做呢？"

"我想设这部密码的人将这些词连在一起没有分开，是有原因的，这样就能增加解谜的难度。要说，脑袋迟钝点的，只要一想到这点，十有八九解不开。在写密码的过程中，每到一个段落，自然需要有句号或逗号，这时，他通常会将符号紧连起来。如果你仔细看看这一份密码，很容易看出来有 5 个地方挨得特别近。根据这个提示，我把它做成分句：

" '一面好镜子在皮肖甫旅店魔椅——41 度 13 分——东北偏北——最大树枝第七根横枝东侧——从骷髅头左眼射击——从树前引一直线穿过子弹延长 50 英尺。' "

out.'"

"Even this division," said I, "leaves me still in the dark."

"It left me also in the dark," replied Legrand, "for a few days; during which I made diligent inquiry, in the neighborhood of Sullivan's Island, for any building which went by the name of the 'Bishop's Hotel;' for, of course, I dropped the obsolete word 'hostel.' Gaining no information on the subject, I was on the point of extending my sphere of search, and proceeding in a more systematic manner, when, one morning, it entered into my head, quite suddenly, that this 'Bishop's Hostel' might have some reference to an old family, of the name of Bessop, which, time out of mind, had held possession of an ancient manor-house, about four miles to the northward of the Island. I accordingly went over to the plantation, and re-instituted my inquiries among the older negroes of the place. At length one of the most aged of the women said that she had heard of such a place as Bessop's Castle, and thought that she could guide me to it, but that it was not a castle nor a tavern, but a high rock.

"I offered to pay her well for her trouble, and, after some demur, she consented to accompany me to the spot. We found it without much difficulty, when, dismissing her, I proceeded to examine the place. The

"就算你把它分开了，我还是不太明白。"我说。

"有几天时间，我也是想不明白，"勒格朗答道，"那几天里，我一直在苏里文岛周围努力寻找叫'皮肖甫旅店'的建筑。不用说，'旅店'两个字是多余的，可以忽略它。关于这方面我打听不到什么消息，于是打算扩大搜索范围，更全面地进行调查，就在那时，一天早晨，我灵光一闪，突然想到这个'皮肖甫旅店'或许和贝梭甫家族有关，很久以前，那家人曾经有过一座古老的宅子，位于苏里文岛北面4英里的地方。于是我到了庄园，重新向那里上了年纪的黑人打听。后来遇到一个八十多岁的老太太，她告诉我她听说过贝梭甫堡这个地方，她不太愿意带我去，而且还说那儿既不是城堡，也不是旅店，而是一座悬崖峭壁。

"我答应事后给她一笔钱重谢她，她犹豫了一下，还是答应带我去了。我们没费多大周折就到了那里，我把她打发走后，就开始调查。那座'城堡'其实是座满是乱石的

'castle' consisted of an irregular assemblage of cliffs and rocks – one of the latter being quite remarkable for its height as well as for its insulated and artificial appearance I clambered to its apex, and then felt much at a loss as to what should be next done.

"While I was busied in reflection, my eyes fell upon a narrow ledge in the eastern face of the rock, perhaps a yard below the summit upon which I stood. This ledge projected about eighteen inches, and was not more than a foot wide, while a niche in the cliff just above it, gave it a rude resemblance to one of the hollow-backed chairs used by our ancestors. I made no doubt that here was the 'devil's seat' alluded to in the MS., and now I seemed to grasp the full secret of the riddle.

"The 'good glass,' I knew, could have reference to nothing but a telescope; for the word 'glass' is rarely employed in any other sense by seamen. Now here, I at once saw, was a telescope to be used, and a definite point of view, admitting *no variation*, from which to use it. Nor did I hesitate to believe that the phrases, "forty-one degrees and thirteen minutes,' and 'northeast and by north,' were intended as directions for the levelling of the glass. Greatly excited by these discoveries, I hurried home, procured a telescope, and returned to the rock.

悬崖，其中一个峭壁独自突出来，像块假石头，而且高耸入云。我爬到壁顶，可不知道接下来该如何是好。

"我正想着接下来的事，猛然瞥见从岩壁东面伸出一道狭窄的岩檐，离我所在的岩顶下方约有一码的距离，向外伸出 18 英寸左右，宽度最多只有一英尺，在岩檐上的崖壁上有个壁龛，看起来很像老人们用的那种凹背椅。我肯定那里就是密码中提到的'魔椅'了，谜底就全部解开了。

"我知道，'好镜子'就是望远镜，因为对于水手来说，'镜子'一词很难有其他所指。我当下明白，要通过望远镜看一下，而且需要站在特定的地点，朝着特定的方向。我索性认为'41 度 13 分'和'东北偏北'这两个句就是在暗示望远镜对准的方向。发现这一切后，我真是异常兴奋，赶快回去拿来望远镜，重新到岩壁上。

"I let myself down to the ledge, and found that it was impossible to retain a seat upon it except in one particular position. This fact confirmed my preconceived idea. I proceeded to use the glass. Of course, the 'forty-one degrees and thirteen minutes' could allude to nothing but elevation above the visible horizon, since the horizontal direction was clearly indicated by the words, 'northeast and by north.' This latter direction I at once established by means of a pocket-compass; then, pointing the glass as nearly at an angle of forty-one degrees of elevation as I could do it by guess, I moved it cautiously up or down, until my attention was arrested by a circular rift or opening in the foliage of a large tree that overtopped its fellows in the distance. In the centre of this rift I perceived a white spot, but could not, at first, distinguish what it was. Adjusting the focus of the telescope, I again looked, and now made it out to be a human skull.

"Upon this discovery I was so sanguine as to consider the enigma solved; for the phrase 'main branch, seventh limb, east side,' could refer only to the position of the skull upon the tree, while 'shoot from the left eye of the death's head' admitted, also, of but one interpretation, in regard to a search for buried treasure. I perceived that the design was to drop a bullet from the left eye of the skull, and that a bee-line, or,

"我爬到岩檐上，只能摆出一种姿势才能安稳地坐在上面。事实证明我想的完全正确。我用望远镜看了下。'东北偏北'这句是指地平线以上的方向，所以很明显，'41度13分'只能指肉眼能看到的地平线以上的高度。我立刻用袖珍指南针确定出'东北偏北'的方向，再凭猜测，用望远镜尽量往41度的角度看去，我小心翼翼地上下挪动望远镜，后来，只看到远处有一棵大树，高出其他树木，树叶间形成一个圆形缺口，或者说是空隙，我把全部精力都集中在那儿。看到空隙间有个白色小点，起初我看的不太清，调整望远镜的焦点再看时，才发现那原来是个头颅骨。

"发现这个头颅骨，我当下十分乐观，相信谜底就要解开了，因为'最大树枝，第七根横枝东侧'那句暗语说的只能是头颅骨在树上的位置，至于'从头颅骨左眼射击'那句，也只能解释成找到宝藏的方法。我想应该就是从头颅骨右眼向下射一颗子弹，沿离树干最近的一点画一条直线，也就是说让直线穿过'子弹'，即从子弹的着落

in other words, a straight line, drawn from the nearest point of the trunk through 'the shot,' (or the spot where the bullet fell,) and thence extended to a distance of fifty feet, would indicate a definite point – and beneath this point I thought it at least possible that a deposit of value lay concealed."

"All this," I said, "is exceedingly clear, and, although ingenious, still simple and explicit. When you left the Bishop's Hotel, what then?"

"Why, having carefully taken the bearings of the tree, I turned homewards. The instant that I left 'the devil's seat,' however, the circular rift vanished; nor could I get a glimpse of it afterwards, turn as I would. What seems to me the chief ingenuity in this whole business, is the fact (for repeated experiment has convinced me it is a fact) that the circular opening in question is visible from no other attainable point of view than that afforded by the narrow ledge upon the face of the rock.

"In this expedition to the 'Bishop's Hotel' I had been attended by Jupiter, who had, no doubt, observed, for some weeks past, the abstraction of my demeanor, and took especial care not to leave me alone. But, on the next day, getting up very early, I contrived to give him the slip, and went into the hills in search of the tree. After much toil I found it. When I came home at

点向外延伸 50 英尺，就会指出特定的地方——我想，那片地下或许会埋着宝藏。"

"这些都很好理解，虽然看似巧妙，但一切清清楚楚，"我说，"你在离开'皮肖甫旅店'后做了什么？"

"这个嘛，我记下那棵树的具体方位，然后就回家了。岂料，离开'魔椅'后那个圆口竟看不到了。后来，无论我怎么看，也看不到。所以我认为，这一点正是暗语设计的巧妙之处，除非从岩壁正面的边檐上看，否则无论从什么地方看都看不到缺口，我反复试验，对这点深信不疑。

"我第一次寻找'皮肖甫旅店'时，丘比特陪在我身边，前几个星期，他肯定是看我神魂颠倒的样子便格外上心，不让我单独出去。但是，转天，我早早起来偷偷溜了出去，到山里寻找那棵树。费了很大工夫才找到。等晚上回到家里，我这个老仆竟打算狠狠教训我一顿。之后的事情你都知道了。"

night my valet proposed to give me a flogging. With the rest of the adventure I believe you are as well acquainted as myself."

"I suppose," said I, "you missed the spot, in the first attempt at digging, through Jupiter's stupidity in letting the bug fall through the right instead of through the left eye of the skull."

"Precisely. This mistake made a difference of about two inches and a half in the 'shot' – that is to say, in the position of the peg nearest the tree; and had the treasure been *beneath* 'shot,' the error would have been of little moment; but 'the shot,' together with the nearest point of the tree, were merely two points for the establishment of a line of direction; of course the error, however trivial in the beginning, increased as we proceeded with the line, and by the time we had gone fifty feet, threw us quite off the scent. But for my deep-seated impressions that treasure was here somewhere actually buried, we might have had all our labor in vain."

"But your grandiloquence, and your conduct in swinging the beetle – how excessively odd! I was sure you were mad. And why did you insist upon letting fall the bug, instead of a bullet, from the skull?"

"Why, to be frank, I felt somewhat annoyed by your evident suspicions touching my sanity, and so resolved to

"看来，"我说，"那时你第一次挖土找错了地方，都是丘比特脑子笨，没从头颅骨的左眼放下甲虫，而从右眼放了下来。"

"说得没错。这样一来，就和'子弹'的正确位置差了约 2 英寸半的距离，也就是说，跟树身最近的木桩差了约 2 英寸半。要是宝藏刚好埋在'子弹'下面，那也无妨；可是，'子弹'和树身最近的一点，只是用来确定直线的方向；当然，尽管开始时的误差微乎其微，然而直线拉得越长，错误也就越大，等直线延伸 50 英尺后，就失之毫厘，差之千里了。如果我对宝藏的埋藏地点有一丝动摇，咱们的辛苦或许就白付出了。"

"可是你当初吹法螺，还有不停挥舞甲虫的样子太奇怪了！当时我想你肯定疯了。你为什么不从头颅骨中射下子弹，而偏偏把甲虫放下来呢？"

"啊哈，说实话，当时看见你怀疑我脑子不正常，当然有点生气了，就故意弄点玄虚，算是对你的

punish you quietly, in my own way, by a little bit of sober mystification. For this reason I swung the beetle, and for this reason I let it fall it from the tree. An observation of yours about its great weight suggested the latter idea."

"Yes, I perceive; and now there is only one point which puzzles me. What are we to make of the skeletons found in the hole?"

"That is a question I am no more able to answer than yourself. There seems, however, only one plausible way of accounting for them – and yet it is dreadful to believe in such atrocity as my suggestion would imply. It is clear that Kidd – if Kidd indeed secreted this treasure, which I doubt not – it is clear that he must have had assistance in the labor. But this labor concluded, he may have thought it expedient to remove all participants in his secret. Perhaps a couple of blows with a mattock were sufficient, while his coadjutors were busy in the pit; perhaps it required a dozen – who shall tell?"

惩罚。所以我故意挥舞甲虫，还把虫子从树上吊下来。我也是听你说甲虫很重才起了吊下甲虫的念头。"

"嗯，我明白了。现在还有一件事，我想不通。该如何解释坑里发现的那两副白骨呢？"

"这问题，我也和你一样没法解释。不过似乎只有一种说法能讲得通——如果我推断得没错，那这件事还真残忍。事情很清楚，基德——如果这笔宝藏真为基德所埋的话，那么我可以肯定地说——显然有帮手帮他一起埋。等埋好后。他或许认为应该将知道这件事的人全部杀掉。说不定，他就是趁那人在坑里埋着时用锄头砸两下把他们砸晕，或许砸上十几下——这谁又知道呢？"

12. The Murders in the Rue Morgue

十二. 莫格街凶杀案

What song the Syrens sang, or what name Achilles assumed when he hid himself among women, although puzzling questions, are not beyond all conjecture.

– Sir Thomas Browne

不管海妖如何歌唱，也无论阿基里斯鬼混在女人堆里的时候用什么假名，纵然是令人费解的谜团，却也无法逃脱被拆穿的命运。

——托马斯·布朗爵士

THE mental features discoursed of as the analytical, are, in themselves, but little susceptible of analysis. We appreciate them only in their effects. We know of them, among other things, that they are always to their possessor, when inordinately possessed, a source of the liveliest enjoyment. As the strong man exults in his physical ability, delighting in such exercises as call his muscles into action, so glories the analyst in that moral activity which disentangles. He derives pleasure from even the most trivial occupations bringing his talent into play. He is fond of enigmas, of conundrums, of hieroglyphics; exhibiting in his solutions of each a degree of *acumen* which appears to the ordinary apprehension praeterratural. His results, brought about by the very soul and essence of method, have, in truth, the whole air of intuition.

The faculty of resolution is possibly

所谓"分析"这种心理活动，究其本身，大多都是经不起推敲的。我们对分析能力大小的判定，往往只是根据其结果而产生的。众所周知，一个拥有分析能力的人如果在这方面独具天赋，那他多半会情不自禁地认为这是个充满无限乐趣的源头。就像大块头喜欢炫耀自己强壮的体格，并对肌肉训练之类的运动情有独钟，善于分析的人则沉溺于破解各种谜团的脑力活动。即使是对待最不起眼的琐事，只要这有助于彰显才能，他便会对此津津乐道。同时酷爱猜谜解题，钻研象形文字，并通过这些展示他无微不至的敏锐洞察力，要知道这能力在平庸之辈看来是十分不可思议的。实际上，在他通过分析法精髓所得来的结论中，也不乏有些个例带着浓重的直觉气味。

假如通晓数学，这种反复解决

much invigorated by mathematical study, and especially by that highest branch of it which, unjustly, and merely on account of its retrograde operations, has been called, as if *par excellence*, analysis. Yet to calculate is not in itself to analyse. A chess-player, for example, does the one without effort at the other. It follows that the game of chess, in its effects upon mental character, is greatly misunderstood. I am not now writing a treatise, but simply prefacing a somewhat peculiar narrative by observations very much at random; I will, therefore, take occasion to assert that the higher powers of the reflective intellect are more decidedly and more usefully tasked by the unostentatious game of draughts than by a the elaborate frivolity of chess. In this latter, where the pieces have different and *bizarre* motions, with various and variable values, what is only complex is mistaken (a not unusual error) for what is profound. The *attention* is here called powerfully into play. If it flag for an instant, an oversight is committed resulting in injury or defeat. The possible moves being not only manifold but involute, the chances of such oversights are multiplied; and in nine cases out of ten it is the more concentrative rather than the more acute player who conquers. In draughts, on the contrary, where the moves are unique and have but little variation, the probabilities of

疑难问题的能力就会变得格外强大，尤其是精通高等教学，即所谓的解析，看起来这似乎是最理想的称呼，其实不然，实际上因为它运用的是逆算法，所以才被称为解析。然而推算本来就不等同于分析。比如一个象棋手并不会在分析上动脑筋，他只是花心思去推算。这么看来，下象棋有益于身心的说法显然是个极大的谬论。我这会儿并不是在写论文，只是很随意地在用一段毫无章法的见解去开启一篇多少有点离奇的故事。在此借机声明，比起花心思应付下象棋这件事，把反应较灵敏的智商用在看起来平庸的跳棋上显得更果敢，也更有价值。象棋这东西，每个棋子都有自己稀奇古怪的走法和变化莫测的妙用。这些事情只不过是有些复杂，却总被人误解为深不可测，说起来这真是个不寻常的错误。下象棋时，聚精会神显得尤为重要，只要稍有疏忽，一个小小的失误势必导致损兵折将，最终溃不成军。但象棋的走法不仅五花八门，简直就是错综复杂，所以出现失误的概率也就增加了不少。大多数情况下，胜利总是属于精力集中的棋手，而不是更加聪明伶俐的。与象棋不同的是，跳棋这个游戏走法单一，变化极少，因此出现失误的可能性也就小得多，所以相比较而言，棋手用不着全神贯注，当双方相遇，更加机灵

inadvertence are diminished, and the mere attention being left comparatively unemployed, what advantages are obtained by either party are obtained by superior *acumen*. To be less abstract – let us suppose a game of draughts where the pieces are reduced to four kings, and where, of course, no oversight is to be expected. It is obvious that here the victory can be decided (the players being at all equal) only by some *recherche* movement, the result of some strong exertion of the intellect. Deprived of ordinary resources, the analyst throws himself into the spirit of his opponent, identifies himself therewith, and not unfrequently sees thus, at a glance, the sole methods (sometime indeed absurdly simple ones) by which he may se duce into error or hurry into miscalculation.

Whist has Long been noted for its influence upon what is termed the calculating power; and men of the highest order of intellect have been known to take an apparently unaccountable delight in it, while eschewing chess as frivolous. Beyond doubt there is nothing of a similar nature so greatly tasking the faculty of analysis. The best chess-player in Christendom may be little more than the best player of chess; but proficiency in whist implies capacity for success in all those more important undertakings where

的一方必定不会输。说得再具体一点，现在我们不妨假设一个跳棋棋局。在每人只剩4个王棋的情况下，当然就没必要担心会出现什么失误了。这时，假如双方实力相当，显然只有善于开动脑筋，精心布置每步棋的一方才能获得胜利。当有分析能力的人遭遇束手无策的窘境，他总是专心研究对方的想法，换位思考一番，这样通常就能一下找出唯一的解决办法，有时这些方法着实简单得出奇，棋手正是靠它们诱使对方失误频频，或是忙中出错。

惠斯特牌戏素来以有助于养成所谓的推算能力而闻名。众所周知，凡是智力超群的人，似乎更容易沉溺其中，认为这里面乐趣无穷，从而把象棋划归到无聊游戏的行列中去。毋庸置疑的是，世上绝对找不出第二种拥有类似性质的玩意，它对于分析能力的要求着实很高。天底下的象棋高手至多只是在象棋方面独领风骚，但是精通惠斯特的人却能在一切更重大的尔虞我诈场合中占得先机。这里我所谓的精通是指熟练掌握这玩意，这要求了解所

mind struggles with mind. When I say proficiency, I mean that perfection in the game which includes a comprehension of all the sources whence legitimate advantage may be derived. These are not only manifold but multiform, and lie frequently among recesses of thought altogether inaccessible to the ordinary understanding. To observe attentively is to remember distinctly; and, so far, the concentrative chess-player will do very well at whist; while the rules of Hoyle (themselves based upon the mere mechanism of the game) are sufficiently and generally comprehensible. Thus to have a retentive memory, and to proceed by "the book," are points commonly regarded as the sum total of good playing. But it is in matters beyond the limits of mere rule that the skill of the analyst is evinced. He makes, in silence, a host of observations and inferences. So, perhaps, do his companions; and the difference in the extent of the information obtained, lies not so much in the validity of the inference as in the quality of the observation. The necessary knowledge is that of what to observe. Our player confines himself not at all; nor, because the game is the object, does he reject deductions from things external to the game. He examines the countenance of his partner, comparing it carefully with that of each of his

有如何在牌局中占得合理优势的诀窍。这些诀窍不仅五花八门，而且种类繁多，它们往往存在于心灵最深处，普通人对此根本就是望尘莫及。留神观察就意味着能够清晰地记忆，所以一直以来，一心一意下象棋的人玩起惠斯特来必定会很出色，并且霍伊尔牌戏谱中的规则（纯粹依据牌戏技巧而制定）非常简明易懂。普遍看来，这方面的高手必须具有两个条件，一是过目不忘，二是遵守规则。不过，当遇到规则里没有提到的情况时，具有分析能力的人就有机会大展拳脚了。他会暗中进行一系列观察和推论。也许他的牌友也在做着同样的事，此时，敌我之间相互了解程度的深浅并不取决于推论的正误，而是由观察能力的高低来决定的。因此，掌握观察之道变得很有必要。玩牌人的眼中决不会只有自己，也不会因为一心想赢牌，就忽略对于周遭事物的判断。他打量搭档的脸色，然后仔细跟对手的脸色作比较，还要研究每个人的理牌顺序，根据他们各种不同的眼神把王牌和大牌一张张推算出来。一边打牌，一边察言观色，通过观察别人表情的变化收集灵感，大家或自信、或惊讶、或得意、或懊恼。根据对方赢了一圈牌后收牌的姿势，估计赢完这一圈牌的人能不能再赢一圈同花牌。根据对方摊牌时的神态判定这家伙也许只是

opponents. He considers the mode of assorting the cards in each hand; often counting trump by trump, and honor by honor, through the glances bestowed by their holders upon each. He notes every variation of face as the play progresses, gathering a fund of thought from the differences in the expression of certainty, of surprise, of triumph, or of chagrin. From the manner of gathering up a trick he judges whether the person taking it can make another in the suit. He recognises what is played through feint, by the air with which it is thrown upon the table. A casual or inadvertent word; the accidental dropping or turning of a card, with the accompanying anxiety or carelessness in regard to its concealment; the counting of the tricks, with the order of their arrangement; embarrassment, hesitation, eagerness or trepidation – all afford, to his apparently intuitive perception, indications of the true state of affairs. The first two or three rounds having been played, he is in full possession of the contents of each hand, and thenceforward puts down his cards with as absolute a precision of purpose as if the rest of the party had turned outward the faces of their own.

The analytical power should not be confounded with simple ingenuity; for while the analyst is necessarily ingenious, the ingenious man is often remarkably

在声东击西，装腔作势。留意对方信口提及的内容，还有不经意间说出的一句话，要不就是不小心滑落或者翻开一张牌时，对方忙着掩饰脸上的焦躁不安或是漫不经心的神情。计算赢牌圈数和其中牌的搭配，对手是窘迫呢还是迟疑呢，是急切呢还是惶恐呢——所有这些都逃不过高手那近乎直觉的洞察力，事态发展的一切真相都清晰地展现在眼前。两三圈牌过后，他已经对各家手里的牌心知肚明了，从这一刻开始，他就能十拿九稳，准确无误地打出每一套牌，不知道的人还以为其他各家手里的牌都已经亮明牌面，摆在桌子上让他随便看了。

善于分析跟单纯的头脑灵活绝不能混为一谈，因为分析能力强的人必然头脑灵活，但是头脑灵活的人通常格外不善于分析。头脑灵活

incapable of analysis. The constructive or combining power, by which ingenuity is usually manifested, and to which the phrenologists (I believe erroneously) have assigned a separate organ, supposing it a primitive faculty, has been so frequently seen in those whose intellect bordered otherwise upon idiocy, as to have attracted general observation among writers on morals. Between ingenuity and the analytic ability there exists a difference far greater, indeed, than that between the fancy and the imagination, but of a character very strictly analogous. It will be found, in fact, that the ingenious are always fanciful, and the *truly* imaginative never otherwise than analytic.

The narrative which follows will appear to the reader somewhat in the light of a commentary upon the propositions just advanced.

Residing in Paris during the spring and part of the summer of 18–, I there became acquainted with a Monsieur C. Auguste Dupin. This young gentleman was of an excellent – indeed of an illustrious family, but, by a variety of untoward events, had been reduced to such poverty that the energy of his character succumbed beneath it, and he ceased to bestir himself in the world, or to care for the retrieval of his fortunes. By courtesy of his creditors, there still remained in his possession a small remnant of his patrimony; and, upon the

往往表现在创造能力或联想能力上，有些在我看来荒谬至极的骨相学家把这种能力归功于某个独立的器官，并认为此项能力是与生俱来的。在那些智商与白痴完全无异的人身上，这种与生俱来的能力往往得到体现，以至于引起了心理学作家们的广泛关注。头脑灵活和善于分析之间的差别固然大于幻想和想象的差别，但这两组对比却在同一点上极为契合。实际上并不难发现，聪明人普遍爱幻想，而真正富有想象力的人则必然善于分析。

下面这段故事在读者看来，多少可以被当做是针对上文一番议论的注释。

故事发生在18××年，正值春夏交际的时节，那时住在巴黎的我结识了当地一位名叫 C·奥古斯特·杜宾的法国绅士。这位年轻的公子哥儿出身豪门——那的确是个大户人家，不料家道中落，杜宾命运多舛，穷困潦倒，到后来意志消沉，不图进取，也没有心思重振家业。多亏债主们手下留情，他才勉强保住了一点微薄的祖业。靠这点资产带来的收益他精打细算、减衣缩食，好不容易才维持了温饱，倒也算得上是心无旁骛。实际上，看书是他唯

income arising from this, he managed, by means of a rigorous economy, to procure the necessaries of life, without troubling himself about its superfluities. Books, indeed, were his sole luxuries, and in Paris these are easily obtained.

Our first meeting was at an obscure library in the Rue Montmartre, where the accident of our both being in search of the same very rare and very remarkable volume, brought us into closer communion. We saw each other again and again. I was deeply interested in the little family history which he detailed to me with all that candor which a Frenchman indulges whenever mere self is his theme. I was astonished, too, at the vast extent of his reading; and, above all, I felt my soul enkindled within me by the wild fervor, and the vivid freshness of his imagination. Seeking in Paris the objects I then sought, I felt that the society of such a man would be to me a treasure beyond price; and this feeling I frankly confided to him. It was at length arranged that we should live together during my stay in the city; and as my worldly circumstances were somewhat less embarrassed than his own, I was permitted to be at the expense of renting, and furnishing in a style which suited the rather fantastic gloom of our common temper, a time-eaten and grotesque mansion, Long deserted through

一奢侈的享受，要知道在巴黎，没有什么事是比看书更便利的了。

我们是在蒙玛特街上一家偏僻的小图书馆里认识的。当时我俩碰巧都在找同一本稀世奇书，这件事促使我们更进一步地交流了起来。后来我们经常见面。杜宾推心置腹地把他那一段家族史娓娓道来，我对此很有兴趣，当一个法国人谈起有关自己的事情时，他总是很乐意对你掏心掏肺。他读的书涉及各个领域，这点也令我颇感惊讶。当然最令人难忘的还是他那狂放不羁的热情，以及那丰富多彩的想象力，让我觉得，自己整个灵魂都被他点燃了。那时候正在巴黎追求理想的我觉得能结识这样一个人，对自己来说无疑是一笔无价的财富。我一五一十地向他吐露了我的这个心声。后来便产生了这么一个决定，在巴黎居住的这段时间，我跟他一起住。当时我的经济状况多少比他宽裕一些，协商后决定由我出钱租下一间公寓并布置好，使其风格完全符合我们两人共有的那种古怪的忧郁气质。这间公寓坐落于市郊的圣日耳曼区，位置偏僻，样式怪异，年久失修，相传还是座荒废很长时间的鬼宅，对于这种迷信的说法，

superstitions into which we did not inquire, and tottering to its fall in a retired and desolate portion of the Faubourg St. Germain.

Had the routine of our life at this place been known to the world, we should have been regarded as madmen – although, perhaps, as madmen of a harmless nature. Our seclusion was perfect. We admitted no visitors. Indeed the locality of our retirement had been carefully kept a secret from my own former associates; and it had been many years since Dupin had ceased to know or be known in Paris. We existed within ourselves alone.

It was a freak of fancy in my friend (for what else shall I call it?) to be enamored of the night for her own sake; and into this *bizarrerie*, as into all his others, I quietly fell; giving myself up to his wild whims with a perfect abandon. The sable divinity would not herself dwell with us always; but we could counterfeit her presence. At the first dawn of the morning we closed all the messy shutters of our old building; lighting a couple of tapers which, strongly perfumed, threw out only the ghastliest and feeblest of rays. By the aid of these we then busied our souls in dreams – reading, writing, or conversing, until warned by the clock of the advent of the true Darkness. Then we sallied forth into the streets arm in arm, continuing the topics of the day, or

我俩没有深究。

假如在这里生活的状况被曝光出去，我俩准会被当成疯子——虽然可能只是两个本性不坏的疯子。我们过着完全与世隔绝的生活，不接待任何访客。当然，我对以前的朋友们都守口如瓶，并没有把公寓的地址告诉他们，而杜宾多年来在巴黎也很少与人打交道。我们就这样过着一种独来独往的生活。

我朋友有个特殊的怪癖（除了怪癖，我实在想不出别的什么词来形容）。他深深迷恋着黑夜那种独特的魅力，而我，就像染上他别的种种怪癖一样，也不由自主地陷入其中。我彻底地释放自己，沉湎于他那些不羁的幻想中。虽然夜神不会永远相伴，但我们可以想象她一直都在。破晓时分，我们把公寓里所有的大百叶窗统统关闭，点上几根细长的蜡烛，烛光伴着浓重的香料气味，投射出阴森幽暗的线条。借着缕缕微光，我们把灵魂照进梦想里——看书，写作，交谈。直到时钟响起，黑夜真正降临时，我们便会肩并肩，精神抖擞地走到街上，或者继续白天的话题，或者四处游荡，逛到老远的地方，直到深更半

roaming far and wide until a late hour, seeking, amid the wild lights and shadows of the populous city, that infinity of mental excitement which quiet observation can afford.

At such times I could not help remarking and admiring (although from his rich ideality I had been prepared to expect it) a peculiar analytic ability in Dupin. He seemed, too, to take an eager delight in its exercise – if not exactly in its display – and did not hesitate to confess the pleasure thus derived. He boasted to me, with a low chuckling laugh, that most men, in respect to himself, wore windows in their bosoms, and was wont to follow up such assertions by direct and very startling proofs of his intimate knowledge of my own. His manner at these moments was frigid and abstract; his eyes were vacant in expression; while his voice, usually a rich tenor, rose into a treble which would have sounded petulantly but for the deliberateness and entire distinctness of the enunciation. Observing him in these moods, I often dwelt meditatively upon the old philosophy of the Bi-Part Soul, and amused myself with the fancy of a double Dupin – the creative and the resolvent.

Let it not be supposed, from what I have just said, that I am detailing any mystery, or penning any romance. What I have described in the Frenchman, was merely

夜，在闪烁的灯光中，在喧嚣的城市所投下的黑影中，寻求着无限的精神刺激，这种刺激，大概只有通过默不做声的观察才能感觉得到。

尽管我早就从他那丰富的想象力中看出了一些端倪，但每当这种时候，我还是忍不住要对杜宾的分析能力刮目相看，并且佩服得五体投地。看他的样子仿佛也巴不得想要一显身手，以此来找点乐子——只要不是完全出于卖弄的目的——他毫不掩饰地承认这其中包含无限的乐趣。有时，他轻声嬉笑着对我吹牛说，大多数人跟他比起来简直是单纯得要命，一下就能被他识破，杜宾对我的心思倒真的是了如指掌，并且，他常常能够当场拿出一些令人吃惊的证据来说明这一点。每当这种时候，他总是态度冷漠，眼睛里面空白一片，整个人变得深不可测。他的声线本来就属于那种洪亮的男高音，这时竟然也会飙到最高音，若不是他语调沉稳，吐字清晰，不明真相的人听起来，还以为他是在发火呢。每当看到他这副好兴致上来的时候，我不由常常仔细回想起有关双重人格的古老学说，心里反复品味着眼前这个兼具创造能力和分析能力的双面杜宾。

看过这些，你可别以为我是在讲述什么神秘的故事，或是在写什么传奇小说。我笔下所有关于杜宾

the result of an excited, or perhaps of a diseased intelligence. But of the character of his remarks at the periods in question an example will best convey the idea.

We were strolling one night down a Long dirty street in the vicinity of the Palais Royal. Being both, apparently, occupied with thought, neither of us had spoken a syllable for fifteen minutes at least. All at once Dupin broke forth with these words:

"He is a very little fellow, that's true, and would do better for the Theatre Varietes."

"There can be no doubt of that," I replied unwittingly, and not at first observing (so much had I been absorbed in reflection) the extraordinary manner in which the speaker had chimed in with my meditations. In an instant afterward I recollected myself, and my astonishment was profound.

"Dupin," said I, gravely, "this is beyond my comprehension. I do not hesitate to say that I am amazed, and can scarcely credit my senses. How was it possible you should know I was thinking of –?" Here I paused, to ascertain beyond a doubt whether he really knew of whom I thought.

"– of Chantilly," said he, "why do you pause? You were remarking to yourself that his diminutive figure unfitted him for tragedy."

的描写，只不过是出于一种过度激动的情绪，也有可能是一种病态心理在作祟。但无论如何，在我们相处的这段时间里，如果要说到他谈吐之间的一些特点，我还是举例说明比较合适。

有一天晚上，我俩在皇宫周边一条又长又脏的街上闲逛。显然，我们当时都在想着心事，两人都一言不发，就这样，时间至少过去了一刻钟。此时，杜宾突然冷不丁地说了这么一句话：

"没错，他身材的确非常矮小，不过要是到杂耍剧院去表演，应该还算不赖。"

"这还用说吗！"我不假思索地回应道，当时正在埋头想心事的我一开始根本没意识到，我俩的想法竟会如此吻合，而杜宾他一下就看穿了我的心思。转瞬之间，我回过神来，方才感到震惊不已。

"杜宾，"我神情严肃地说道，"这可真是把我给搞晕了。跟你直说吧，我真是太震惊了，简直不敢相信自己的耳朵。你怎么会知道我在想的正是……"说到这儿我突然打住了，想弄明白他到底是不是真的知道我心里想的究竟是谁。

"……正是桑蒂伊，"他说，"怎么不往下说了？你刚才心里不是正在嘀咕，他那个矮冬瓜，根本演不了悲剧，不是吗？"

This was precisely what had formed the subject of my reflections. Chantilly was a *quondam* cobbler of the Rue St. Denis, who, becoming stage-mad, had attempted the role of Xerxes, in Crebillon's tragedy so called, and been notoriously Pasquinaded for his pains.

"Tell me, for Heaven's sake," I exclaimed, "the method – if method there is – by which you have been enabled to fathom my soul in this matter." In fact I was even more startled than I would have been willing to express.

"It was the fruiterer," replied my friend, "who brought you to the conclusion that the mender of soles was not of sufficient height for Xerxes *et id genus omne*."

"The fruiterer! – you astonish me – I know no fruiterer whomsoever."

"The man who ran up against you as we entered the street – it may have been fifteen minutes ago."

I now remembered that, in fact, a fruiterer, carrying upon his head a large basket of apples, had nearly thrown me down, by accident, as we passed from the Rue C- into the thoroughfare where we stood; but what this had to do with Chantilly I could not possibly understand.

There was not a particle of *charlatânerie* about Dupin. "I will explain," he said, "and that you may comprehend all clearly, we will first retrace the course of your

这的确是刚才那一刻我心里的所思所想。桑蒂伊之前是圣丹尼斯街上的一个皮匠，后来成了个戏迷，曾经参演过克雷比荣悲剧中的泽克西斯一角，结果出力不讨好，到头来反而遭到了一顿冷嘲热讽。

"我的天哪，快告诉我！"我冲杜宾嚷道，"快说说你用了什么神奇的伎俩，居然能看透我心里在想的正是这件事。"实际上虽然竭力掩盖，我还是不能自控地流露出十分惊讶的神情。

"就在看到那个卖水果的小贩以后，"他答道，"你便不自觉地想这个修鞋的个头太矮，根本不配饰演绎克西斯等诸如此类的角色。"

"卖水果的小贩！——你可把我搞糊涂了——我从来不认识什么卖水果的小贩啊。"

"咱俩刚才走到这条街上时，不是有个人跟你迎面遇上吗——那应该是一刻钟之前的事吧。"

我这才回想起来，刚才我们从C小街拐到这条大街上的时候，的确有个卖水果的小贩，头上顶着一大筐苹果，突然冒了出来，还差点把我撞翻。可我实在搞不懂，这人跟桑蒂伊到底有什么关系。

从杜宾的脸上看不出任何夸大其词的色彩。"回头讲给你听吧，"他说，"我一讲你就能彻底搞明白了，我们不妨先回顾一下，从现在

meditations, from the moment in which I spoke to you until that of the *rencontre* with the fruiterer in question. The larger links of the chain run thus – Chantilly, Orion, Dr. Nichols, Epicurus, Stereotomy, the street stones, the fruiterer."

There are few persons who have not, at some period of their lives, amused themselves in retracing the steps by which particular conclusions of their own minds have been attained. The occupation is often full of interest and he who attempts it for the first time is astonished by the apparently illimitable distance and incoherence between the starting-point and the goal. What, then, must have been my amazement when I heard the Frenchman speak what he had just spoken, and when I could not help acknowledging that he had spoken the truth. He continued:

"We had been talking of horses, if I remember aright, just before leaving the Rue C-. This was the last subject we discussed. As we crossed into this street, a fruiterer, with a large basket upon his head, brushing quickly past us, thrust you upon a pile of paving stones collected at a spot where the causeway is undergoing repair. You stepped upon one of the loose fragments, slipped, slightly strained your ankle, appeared vexed or sulky, muttered a few words, turned to look at the pile, and then proceeded in silence. I was not

咱俩谈话这会儿，一直追溯到之前碰见那个水果小贩的时候，你心里都在想些什么吧。那一大长串思想活动的几个主要环节应该是按照这样的顺序排列的——桑蒂伊，猎户星座，尼古斯博士，伊壁鸠鲁，石头分割术，街上的石头，水果小贩。"

在日常生活中的某些时候，大多数人总爱常常仔细回味自己的心路历程，回味思路是如何一下一下转移到某件事情上去的。仔细回味的过程往往乐趣无穷，而头一回尝试去回味的人，眼看起初的想法和最终的结论之间竟然存在天壤之别，彼此之间没有丝毫联系，难免会颇感惊奇。所以，当我听到杜宾刚才那些话，而且不得不承认他所说的句句属实的时候，心里就别提有多震撼了。杜宾继续说道：

"如果我没记错的话，咱们刚才离开 C 小街之前，一直在谈论有关马的事。这是此前咱们的最后一个话题。接着，刚拐进这条街，碰巧有个卖水果的小贩，头上顶个大筐子，匆匆地跟咱们擦肩而过，那边的人行道正在整修，旁边堆了些碎石头，他把你撞到了那堆石头上。你一不留神踩在一块散落的石子上，滑了一下，脚腕子轻微扭到了，看样子你有点发火，满脸阴沉，嘴里呢喃了几句，回头瞅瞅那堆石头，然后便默不做声地走开了。其实我

particularly attentive to what you did; but observation has become with me, of late, a species of necessity.

"You kept your eyes upon the ground – glancing, with a petulant expression, at the holes and ruts in the pavement, (so that I saw you were still thinking of the stones,) until we reached the little alley called Lamartine, which has been paved, by way of experiment, with the overlapping and riveted blocks. Here your countenance brightened up, and, perceiving your lips move, I could not doubt that you murmured the word 'stereotomy,' a term very affectedly applied to this species of pavement. I knew that you could not say to yourself 'stereotomy' without being brought to think of atomies, and thus of the theories of Epicurus; and since, when we discussed this subject not very Long ago, I mentioned to you how singularly, yet with how little notice, the vague guesses of that noble Greek had met with confirmation in the late nebular cosmogony, I felt that you could not avoid casting your eyes upward to the great *nebula* in Orion, and I certainly expected that you would do so. You did look up; and I was now assured that I had correctly followed your steps. But in that bitter tirade upon Chantilly, which appeared in yesterday's 'Musée,' the satirist, making some disgraceful allusions to the cobbler s change of name upon

并没有特别留意你的这些举动，只是近一段时间以来，观察周围事物成了我生活里不可或缺的一部分。

"你两眼直勾勾地盯着地面——愤怒地扫视人行道上的坑坑洼洼和车轮印，我知道你仍然对石头的事念念不忘。直到咱们走进那条叫做拉玛丁的小胡同，为了做实验的缘故，这条胡同由重叠紧实的砖结构铺成，这时你总算露出了笑容。我看见你嘴角微微上扬，就坚信你心里琢磨的正是石头分割术这个词儿，虽然把它跟铺路这事相提并论显得很别扭。我又想到，你心里嘀咕着'石头分割术'这词儿的时候，一定会联想到原子的事，然后就会想到伊壁鸠鲁的理论，何况不久之前，咱们刚刚才讨论过这个话题，我跟你提过，说那个著名的希腊人曾有过一些含糊不清的猜想，然而神奇的是，谁也没有想到，这些猜想竟神不知鬼不觉地与后来发现的宇宙进化星云假说不谋而合，想到这里，我就感觉你必然会抬头望一眼猎户星座的大星云，当然我心里的的确确也巴不得你这么做。结果你居然真的抬眼去看了。我这才确定，我的确对你的思路了如指掌。昨天的《博物馆报》上刊登了一大篇有关桑蒂伊的辛辣讽刺，在那篇文章里，作者使用了一堆令人发指的恶毒言语来挖苦这个皮匠，说他穿上厚底戏靴就忘了自己

assuming the buskin, quoted a Latin line about which we have often conversed. I mean the line

Perdidit antiquum litera prima sonum.

"I had told you that this was in reference to Orion, formerly written Urion; and, from certain pungencies connected with this explanation, I was aware that you could not have forgotten it. It was clear, therefore, that you would not fail to combine the two ideas of Orion and Chantilly. That you did combine them I saw by the character of the smile which passed over your lips. You thought of the poor cobbler's immolation. So far, you had been stooping in your gait; but now I saw you draw yourself up to your full height. I was then sure that you reflected upon the diminutive figure of Chantilly. At this point I interrupted your meditations to remark that as, in fact, he was a very little fellow – that Chantilly – he would do better at the *Theatre des Variété-s*."

Not Long after this, we were looking over an evening edition of the "*Gazette des Tribunaux*," when the following paragraphs arrested our attention.

"EXTRAORDINARY MURDERS. – This morning, about three o'clock, the inhabitants of the Quartier St. Roch were aroused from sleep by a succession of

姓什么，还引用了我们经常说起的一句拉丁诗。我想应该是这句——

第一个字母不发原来的音。

"我之前告诉过你，这句诗里提到的正是猎户星座，以前写作猎户星宿，后来我还不忘附上些辛辣的挖苦，我想你肯定没把这事给忘了。显而易见的是，这么一来你肯定会把猎户星座和桑蒂伊联想到一块去。看见你嘴角泛起的微笑，我就知道你一定是这样去想了。你又想起那位倒霉皮匠任人宰割的窘境。之前你走路的时候一直驼着背，可这会儿却见你伸直腰板，昂首挺胸。因此我就断定，你一定是想到了桑蒂伊矮小的身材。这时，我便打断了你的思路，说桑蒂伊的身材的确非常矮小，不过要是到杂耍剧院去演出，应该还算不赖。"

在这件事之后不久，当我们翻看《论坛报》晚刊的时候，下面这段文字引起了我们的注意。

"离奇凶杀案——今晨 3 时许，居住在圣罗克区的居民们突然被一阵凄惨的尖叫声吵醒，听起来，这阵惨叫声应该是从莫格街上一幢

terrific shrieks, issuing, apparently, from the fourth story of a house in the Rue Morgue, known to be in the sole occupancy of one Madame L'Espanaye, and her daughter Mademoiselle Camille L'Espanaye. After some delay, occasioned by a fruitless attempt to procure admission in the usual manner, the gateway was broken in with a crowbar, and eight or ten of the neighbors entered accompanied by two *gendarmes*. By this time the cries had ceased; but, as the party rushed up the first flight of stairs, two or more rough voices in angry contention were distinguished and seemed to proceed from the upper part of the house. As the second landing was reached, these sounds, also, had ceased and everything remained perfectly quiet. The party spread themselves and hurried from room to room. Upon arriving at a large back chamber in the fourth story, (the door of which, being found locked, with the key inside, was forced open,) a spectacle presented itself which struck every one present not less with horror than with astonishment.

"The apartment was in the wildest disorder – the furniture broken and thrown about in all directions. There was only one bedstead; and from this the bed had been removed, and thrown into the middle of the floor. On a chair lay a razor, besmeared with blood. On the hearth were two or

房子的4楼传来的。据悉，这幢房子里只住着一家人，包括列士巴奈太太和她女儿卡米耶·列士巴奈小姐。大伙本来打算按照礼节敲门进去的，结果，这徒劳的尝试把时间都给耽误了，最后大伙只好用铁棍把大门撬开，然后，八九个街坊外加两名警官一齐走了进去。这时候惨叫声已经停止，但正当大伙急急忙忙跑上第一段楼梯的时候，又从楼上传来了两三声气急败坏的狂吼。当大伙又奔向第二层楼梯的时候，吼声又停止了，房子里一片鸦雀无声。这时候大伙分头进行搜寻，慌忙地穿梭于各个房间中。当搜到4楼一间大里屋的时候，由于屋门从里面被反锁了，大伙只好强行进入，之后呈现在眼前的景象真是叫人惨不忍睹，在场的人个个惊慌失措，都被吓得魂不附体。

"屋内一片狼藉，家具破损不堪，散落一地。里面只有一个床架，床垫已经被挪开，丢在屋中间的地板上。有一张椅子，上面搁着一把血迹斑驳的剃刀。壁炉上散落着几大把花白的长头发，同样被鲜血浸染，看样子像是被连根拔起的。在

three Long and thick tresses of grey human hair, also dabbled in blood, and seeming to have been pulled out by the roots. Upon the floor were found four Napoleons, an ear-ring of topaz, three large silver spoons, three smaller of *métal d'Alger*, and two bags, containing nearly four thousand francs in gold. The drawers of a bureau, which stood in one corner were open, and had been, apparently, rifled, although many articles still remained in them. A small iron safe was discovered under the bed (not under the bedstead). It was open, with the key still in the door. It had no contents beyond a few old letters, and other papers of little consequence.

"Of Madame L'Espanaye no traces were here seen; but an unusual quantity of soot being observed in the fire-place, a search was made in the chimney, and (horrible to relate!) the corpse of the daughter, head downward, was dragged therefrom; it having been thus forced up the narrow aperture for a considerable distance. The body was quite warm. Upon examining it, many excoriations were perceived, no doubt occasioned by the violence with which it had been thrust up and disengaged. Upon the face were many severe scratches, and, upon the throat, dark bruises, and deep indentations of finger nails, as if the deceased had been throttled to death.

地板上还找到了 4 枚拿破仑金币，一只黄晶玉耳环，3 把大号银质汤匙，3 把小号白铜茶匙以及 2 个钱袋，钱袋里面大约装了 4000 枚金法郎，屋内一角立着一个柜子，上面的抽屉全都被拉开了，尽管里头还有很多东西，但显然已经遭到了洗劫。在床垫底下（不是床架下）发现了一只小铁匣。铁匣敞开着，钥匙还插在盖子上。匣子里面只有几封旧信函，另外还有一些无关紧要的文件。

"在房里没有见到列士巴奈太太的踪影，只是在壁炉里发现了异常多的煤灰，大伙便开始查看烟囱里的情况，说来可怕，这时竟然在里面发现了她女儿的尸体，被拖出来的时候头朝下，之前应该是被人强行从这个狭窄的烟囱管塞进去了好一大截，尸体还没有完全凉透。仔细查看后发现，上面有多处擦伤，显然是被硬塞进烟囱里的时候造成的，由于受到的外力太猛，伤口处已经皮开肉绽。另外，脸上还有多处严重的抓伤，喉部可见紫黑色的淤血，还有几条深深的指甲印，看这情形，死者应该是被掐死的。

"After a thorough investigation of every portion of the house, without farther discovery, the party made its way into a small paved yard in the rear of the building, where lay the corpse of the old lady, with her throat so entirely cut that, upon an attempt to raise her, the head fell off. The body, as well as the head, was fearfully mutilated – the former so much so as scarcely to retain any semblance of humanity.

"To this horrible mystery there is not as yet, we believe, the slightest clew."

The next day's paper had these additional particulars.

"*The Tragedy in the Rue Morgue*. Many individuals have been examined in relation to this most extraordinary and frightful affair. [The word 'affaire' has not yet, in France, that levity of import which it conveys with us,] "but nothing whatever has transpired to throw light upon it. We give below all the material testimony elicited.

"*Pauline Dubourg,* laundress, deposes that she has known both the deceased for three years, having washed for them during that period. The old lady and her daughter seemed on good terms – very affectionate towards each other. They were excellent pay. Could not speak in regard to their mode or means of living. Believed that Madame L. told fortunes for a living. Was

"在把整幢房子上上下下彻底搜查了一遍之后，并没有什么进一步的发现，于是大伙又来到屋后一个铺满砖头的小院里，只见院子里横着老太太的尸首，喉咙被完全割断了，大伙试图抬起尸首，此时她的头颅竟然掉了下来。身体连同头颅，都被划得血肉模糊——身体部分尤其惨不忍睹，简直算得上是面目全非。

"本报可以确定的是，截至目前，这件令人毛骨悚然的悬案依然找不出任何线索。"

随后一天的报纸又追加了一些特别报道。

"莫格街惨案——据悉，许多人与这件非同寻常且骇人听闻的事件有关，他们都已被传讯。（在法国，"事件"这个字眼绝非我们想象中的那么轻率。）然而，传讯的结果仍然无法为本案提供任何线索。以下，我们为您援引全部有价值的供词。

"宝兰·迪布尔，洗衣妇，供称结识遇害的母女俩已有3年，其间一直为她们洗衣服。老太太和她女儿两个人看起来相处愉快，算得上是其乐融融。她们往往出手很大方。搞不清她们的生活模式和经济来源。列太太很有可能是以算命为生。据说她们家底殷实。每次取送衣物的时候，从来看不见房子里有

reputed to have money put by. Never met any persons in the house when she called for the clothes or took them home. Was sure that they had no servant in employ. There appeared to be no furniture in any part of the building except in the fourth story.

"*Pierre Moreau,* tobacconist, deposes that he has been in the habit of selling small quantities of tobacco and snuff to Madame L'Espanaye for nearly four years. Was born in the neighborhood, and has always resided there. The deceased and her daughter had occupied the house in which the corpses were found, for more than six years. It was formerly occupied by a jeweller, who under-let the upper rooms to various persons. The house was the property of Madame L. She became dissatisfied with the abuse of the premises by her tenant, and moved into them herself, refusing to let any portion. The old lady was childish. Witness had seen the daughter some five or six times during the six years. The two lived an exceedingly retired life – were reputed to have money. Had heard it said among the neighbors that Madame L. told fortunes – did not believe it. Had never seen any person enter the door except the old lady and her daughter, a porter once or twice, and a physician some eight or ten times.

"Many other persons, neighbors, gave

别的什么人。可以肯定的是家里没有请用人。似乎整幢房子里除了 4 楼以外，其他地方都没有什么家具。

"皮埃尔·莫罗，烟商，供称在大概 4 年的时间里，列太太一直从他这儿零零星星地购买烟草和鼻烟。她是土生土长的本地人，一直定居在这儿。母女俩在她们遭遇不测的那幢房子里已经住了 6 年多。房子里面原先住着一个珠宝商，当时他把楼上的房间分别租给了各种乱七八糟的人。这房子本是列士巴奈太太的产业。当她得知租客们把房子糟蹋得够呛，便对此十分不满，后来就自己搬了进去，不肯再把房子租给外人住了。老太太平时像个孩子一样。过去的 6 年中，证人一共只见过她女儿五六次。母女俩过着完全与世隔绝的生活——据说她们很有钱。早先还听街坊说，列士巴奈太太能预知未来——但是证人却不相信这个。除了老太太和她女儿，他就只见过有个搬运工来过这房子一两次，另外还有个大夫来过大约 10 次，除此之外就再没见过别的什么人进到房子里去。

"另外还有不少人，都是街坊

evidence to the same effect. No one was spoken of as frequenting the house. It was not known whether there were any living connexions of Madame L. and her daughter. The shutters of the front windows were seldom opened. Those in the rear were always closed, with the exception of the large back room, fourth story. The house was a good house – not very old.

"*Isidore Muset, gendarme,* deposes that he was called to the house about three o'clock in the morning, and found some twenty or thirty persons at the gateway, endeavoring to gain admittance. Forced it open, at length, with a bayonet – not with a crowbar. Had but little difficulty in getting it open, on account of its being a double or folding gate, and bolted neither at bottom not top. The shrieks were continued until the gate was forced – and then suddenly ceased. They seemed to be screams of some person (or persons) in great agony – were loud and drawn out, not short and quick. Witness led the way up stairs. Upon reaching the first landing, heard two voices in loud and angry contention – the one a gruff voice, the other much shriller – a very strange voice. Could distinguish some words of the former, which was that of a Frenchman. Was positive that it was not a woman's voice. Could distinguish the words 'sacré' and 'diable.' The shrill voice was that of a foreigner. Could not be sure

邻居，他们的供词大同小异。据说这房子平时没有什么常客来拜访。搞不清楚列太太和她女儿还有没有其他在世的亲友。房子正面窗户上的百叶窗很少被打开，后面的也是一样，只有4楼上一间大里屋的窗户有时开着。房子本身是幢好房子——而且它的年代不算太久远。

"伊西陀尔·米塞，警察，供称大约凌晨3点钟的时候，有人喊他到那幢房子去看看，当时只见大门口围了有二三十个人，他们正努力设法进到门里去。最后大伙总算用一把刺刀撬开了门——而不是用铁棍。大门是双开结构，也叫折门，上下都没有门闩，所以大伙不费吹灰之力就把它打开了。惨叫声断断续续地传来。直到门被撬开后，方才突然一下没了动静。声音像是由一个人或几个人因为承受剧痛而发出的——听起来又尖又长，而不是比较短促的那一种。这时，证人带头上了楼。当大伙走到第一层楼梯口的时候，传来了两个人高声争吵的声音——其中一个人语调沙哑低沉，而另一个的嗓门则又尖又细——那是一种非常奇怪的声音。语调沙哑的那个应该是法国人，从他的话里能大概听清几个字。有一点可以肯定的是，那绝对不是女人的声音。其中能听清的部分是'真该死'和'活见鬼'。尖细嗓门的那

whether it was the voice of a man or of a woman. Could not make out what was said, but believed the language to be Spanish. The state of the room and of the bodies was described by this witness as we described them yesterday.

"*Henri Duval*, a neighbor, and by trade a silver-smith, deposes that he was one of the party who first entered the house. Corroborates the testimony of Musèt in general. As soon as they forced an entrance, they reclosed the door, to keep out the crowd, which collected very fast, notwithstanding the lateness of the hour. The shrill voice, this witness thinks, was that of an Italian. Was certain it was not French. Could not be sure that it was a man's voice. It might have been a woman's. Was not acquainted with the Italian language. Could not distinguish the words, but was convinced by the intonation that the speaker was an Italian. Knew Madame L. and her daughter. Had conversed with both frequently. Was sure that the shrill voice was not that of either of the deceased.

"*– Odenheimer, restaurateur.* This witness volunteered his testimony. Not speaking French, was examined through an interpreter. Is a native of Amsterdam. Was passing the house at the time of the shrieks. They lasted for several minutes – probably ten. They were Long and loud – very awful

个应该是外国人，弄不明白他到底是男是女。与此同时，他的话大伙也听不清，不过感觉很像是西班牙语。另外，有关这位证人对卧房内情形和尸首惨状的描述，可参阅本报昨日的相关报道。

"亨利·迪伐尔，邻居，职业是银匠，供称他是跟着头一批人进到房子里去的。证词与米塞的大致相仿。他们破门而入后立刻把门重新锁好，把围观人群挡在外面，虽然当时已经是半夜三更，但外面还是一下子就聚满了看热闹的人。证人认为那个尖细嗓门的是意大利人，总之肯定不是法国人。但他不敢确定那是不是男人的声音。可能是个女人也说不定。因为证人不懂意大利语，所以他听不出来那家伙说了些什么，不过根据腔调可以断定，说话的确实是个意大利人。证人认得列太太和她女儿，平日里常与她们母女俩交谈，所以他能肯定那个又尖又细的声音绝对不是死者发出来的。

"……奥丹海梅尔，饭店老板。这位证人自愿前来作证。原籍阿姆斯特丹的他不会说法语，因此警方借助翻译才完成了问讯。当晚他路过那幢房子时里面正有尖叫声传出，接连持续了好几分钟——大概有 10 分钟。那声音又尖又长——听

and distressing. Was one of those who entered the building. Corroborated the previous evidence in every respect but one. Was sure that the shrill voice was that of a man – of a Frenchman. Could not distinguish the words uttered. They were loud and quick – unequal – spoken apparently in fear as well as in anger. The voice was harsh – not so much shrill as harsh. Could not call it a shrill voice. The gruff voice said repeatedly '*sacré*,' '*diable*,' and once '*mon Dieu*.'

"*Jules Mignaud*, banker, of the firm of Mignaud et Fils, Rue Deloraine. Is the elder Mignaud. Madame L'Espanaye had some property. Had opened an account with his banking house in the spring of the year – (eight years previously). Made frequent deposits in small sums. Had checked for nothing until the third day before her death, when she took out in person the sum of 4000 francs. This sum was paid in gold, and a clerk went home with the money.

"*Adolphe Le Bon*, clerk to Mignaud et Fils, deposes that on the day in question, about noon, he accompanied Madame L'Espanaye to her residence with the 4000 francs, put up in two bags. Upon the door being opened, Mademoiselle L. appeared and took from his hands one of the bags, while the old lady relieved him of the other. He then bowed and departed. Did

起来阴森恐怖，甚是凄惨。后来他跟着大伙一起进入了房子。这位证人的证词与上述其他证人的证词基本相符，但唯一不同的是，他很确定那个尖细嗓门是个男人——而且是法国人，他同样没听清那家伙说了些什么。只记得那声音响亮又急促——杂乱无章——语气显然是既生气又恐惧。而且那动静与其说是尖细，倒不如用刺耳来形容更为妥切。尖细显然已经不太恰当了。另外，那个语调沙哑的人当时一再重复着'真该死'、'活见鬼'这两句话，其间还说了句'天哪'。

"茹尔·米尼亚尔，银行家，德洛雷纳街上米尼亚尔父子银行的老板。这位是其中的老米尼亚尔。他说列士巴奈太太确实有些财产。8年前的某个春天，列太太在他银行里开了个账户。此后经常投入一些小额存款。但一直都没取过，直到遇害前第三天，她才亲自提光了账户里全部的4000法郎存款。这笔钱当时是用金币支付的，由一个职员为她送到家里。

"阿道夫·勒·本，米尼亚尔父子银行的职员，供称当天正午前后，他拿出价值4000法郎的金币，分别装进了两只大钱袋，然后陪同列士巴奈太太一起把钱送到了她的府上。大门一开，列小姐就从里面走了出来，从他手里接过其中一袋金币，而老太太则把另一袋接了过

not see any person in the street at the time. It is a bye-street – very lonely.

"*William Bird*, tailor deposes that he was one of the party who entered the house. Is an Englishman. Has lived in Paris two years. Was one of the first to ascend the stairs. Heard the voices in contention. The gruff voice was that of a Frenchman. Could make out several words, but cannot now remember all. Heard distinctly 'sacré' and 'mon Dieu'. There was a sound at the moment as if of several persons struggling – a scraping and scuffling sound. The shrill voice was very loud – louder than the gruff one. Is sure that it was not the voice of an Englishman. Appeared to be that of a German. Might have been a woman's voice. Does not understand German.

"Four of the above-named witnesses, being recalled, deposed that the door of the chamber in which was found the body of Mademoiselle L. was locked on the inside when the party reached it. Every thing was perfectly silent – no groans or noises of any kind. Upon forcing the door no person was seen. The windows, both of the back and front room, were down and firmly fastened from within. A door between the two rooms was closed, but not locked. The door leading from the front room into the passage was locked, with the key on the inside. A small room in the front of the house, on the fourth story, at the head of

去。随后他鞠了个躬，就离开了。当时没见街上有别的什么人。这毕竟是条不起眼的街道——偏僻异常。

"威廉·伯德，裁缝，供称当时跟着大伙一起进入房子。他是英国人，已经在巴黎住了两年。那天他跟着第一批人冲上楼。他也听见了争吵的声音，认为语调沙哑的那个是法国人。从话中听得出几个字眼，可现在已经记不太清了。听清楚的字同样是'真该死'和'天哪'。当时，他还听见了另外一阵声响，那好像是几个人打架发出的动静——那动静里混合了摩擦声和扭打声。那个尖细嗓门的家伙声音很大——比语调沙哑的那人要大一些。显然，尖细嗓门的不是英国人。那听来更像是德国人的声音。而且可能是女人的声音。证人自己并不懂德语。

"上述 4 名证人后来又再次被传讯，他们供称大伙搜到发现列士巴奈小姐尸体的那间卧房时，房门反锁，周围一片寂静——没人听见呻吟声或是别的什么声音。大伙冲进门后，里面空无一人。卧房前后的窗子全都紧闭着，且被从里边拴得严严实实。两个隔间当中的门同样紧闭，但并没有上锁，而连接过道和前厅的门却锁着，钥匙插在内侧。4 楼上，直冲这间卧房的地方有个小房间，位于过道尽头，房门

the passage was open, the door being ajar. This room was crowded with old beds, boxes, and so forth. These were carefully removed and searched. There was not an inch of any portion of the house which was not carefully searched. Sweeps were sent up and down the chimneys. The house was a four story one, with garrets (*mansardes*.) A trap-door on the roof was nailed down very securely – did not appear to have been opened for years. The time elapsing between the hearing of the voices in contention and the breaking open of the room door, was variously stated by the witnesses. Some made it as short as three minutes – some as Long as five. The door was opened with difficulty.

"*Alfonzo Garcio*, undertaker, deposes that he resides in the Rue Morgue. Is a native of Spain. Was one of the party who entered the house. Did not proceed up stairs. Is nervous, and was apprehensive of the consequences of agitation. Heard the voices in contention. The gruff voice was that of a Frenchman. Could not distinguish what was said. The shrill voice was that of an Englishman – is sure of this. Does not understand the English language, but judges by the intonation.

"*Alberto Montani*, confectioner, deposes that he was among the first to ascend the stairs. Heard the voices in question. The gruff voice was that of a Frenchman.

虚掩着，没有上锁。房间里面堆满了旧床铺和箱子等杂物。这些东西都被仔细搬动和搜查过了。实际上，整幢房子的每一个角落都被仔细搜查了一遍。所有的烟囱也被上上下下全部扫过了。这幢房子共有4层，最上面还有个顶阁（又称阁楼）。房顶上有个天窗，被钉得严严实实——看上去已经有年头没被打开过了。从听到争吵声到闯进房门，其间一共经过了多长时间，4个证人看法不一，短到3分钟，长到5分钟，总之，打开房门的过程着实很费劲。

"阿丰索·迦西奥，殡仪馆老板，供称自己住在莫格街上。他原籍西班牙，当时随着大伙一起进入了房子，但并没有上楼。因为生来胆小，他唯恐自己被吓出个三长两短。他也听到了吵架声，认为语调沙哑的那个是法国人，同样没听清话里说了些什么。他觉得尖细嗓门的那个是英国人——并对此深信不疑。虽然不懂英语，但他说自己是根据说话腔调判断出来的。

"阿尔贝托·蒙塔尼，糖果店老板，供称他当时跟着第一批人上了楼。听见了那几种声音，认为语调沙哑的那个是法国人，话中能听

Distinguished several words. The speaker appeared to be expostulating. Could not make out the words of the shrill voice. Spoke quick and unevenly. Thinks it the voice of a Russian. Corroborates the general testimony. Is an Italian. Never conversed with a native of Russia.

"Several witnesses, recalled, here testified that the chimneys of all the rooms on the fourth story were too narrow to admit the passage of a human being. By 'sweeps' were meant cylindrical sweeping brushes, such as are employed by those who clean chimneys. These brushes were passed up and down every flue in the house. There is no back passage by which any one could have descended while the party proceeded up stairs. The body of Mademoiselle L'Espanaye was so firmly wedged in the chimney that it could not be got down until four or five of the party united their strength.

"*Paul Dumas*, physician, deposes that he was called to view the bodies about day-break. They were both then lying on the sacking of the bedstead in the chamber where Mademoiselle L. was found. The corpse of the young lady was much bruised and excoriated. The fact that it had been thrust up the chimney would sufficiently account for these appearances. The throat was greatly chafed. There were several deep scratches just below the chin, together

得出几个字眼，说话者听起来像是在规劝某人。他没听清尖细嗓门那家伙说了些什么，但因为话说得又快又乱，所以他认为那是俄国人的声音。这位证人的证词与大多数人的相符。他是意大利人，从来没跟俄国人说过话。

"几名证人再次被传讯，都一致证明，说房子4楼上各个房间的烟囱都很窄，根本容不下一个人出入。扫烟囱时用的是一种圆筒形的扫帚，就跟扫烟囱人用的那种扫帚一样。借助这种扫帚，房子里所有的烟囱管全都被上下清扫了一遍。另外，房子里没有后楼梯，因此大伙上楼时，不会有人能够趁机溜下楼逃走。列士巴奈小姐的尸体被牢牢卡在烟囱里，经过四五个人的一番共同努力，才把她从里面拖出来。

"保罗·迪马，医生，供称当天黎明时分，有人请他去验尸。当时，在发现列小姐的那间卧房里，两具尸体被停放在床架上铺着的布袋子里。其中，小姐的尸首上有多处淤伤和擦伤。这些现象足以表明，死者是被硬塞进烟囱里去的。死者喉部受到重创，颌下有几道深深的抓痕，另外还有一连串好几块淤青，显然是被手指掐过后留下的。死者的脸部已经完全不成样子，眼珠外

with a series of livid spots which were evidently the impression of fingers. The face was fearfully discolored, and the eye-balls protruded. The tongue had been partially bitten through. A large bruise was discovered upon the pit of the stomach, produced, apparently, by the pressure of a knee. In the opinion of M. Dumas, Mademoiselle L'Espanaye had been throttled to death by some person or persons unknown. The corpse of the mother was horribly mutilated. All the bones of the right leg and arm were more or less shattered. The left tibia much splintered, as well as all the ribs of the left side. Whole body dreadfully bruised and discolored. It was not possible to say how the injuries had been inflicted. A heavy club of wood, or a broad bar of iron – a chair – any large, heavy, and obtuse weapon would have produced such results, if wielded by the hands of a very powerful man. No woman could have inflicted the blows with any weapon. The head of the deceased, when seen by witness, was entirely separated from the body, and was also greatly shattered. The throat had evidently been cut with some very sharp instrument – probably with a razor.

"*Alexandre Etienne*, surgeon, was called with M. Dumas to view the bodies. Corroborated the testimony, and the opinions of M. Dumas.

突，舌头被咬断了一截。在腹部同样发现了一大块淤青，显然是被人用膝盖压住而造成的。依迪马先生来看，列士巴奈小姐明显是被掐死的，凶手的数量无法确定。另外一具老太太的尸首已经面目全非，残破不全。右腿和右臂都有不同程度的粉碎性骨折。左胫骨已经严重开裂，左侧全部的肋骨也是这个情况。尸体上到处布满了严重的淤伤，已经整个变成了青紫色。说不清楚这些伤痕都是如何造成的。大概只有当一个壮汉使劲挥舞一根大木棍或粗铁棒，或者是抢起一张椅子或别的什么又硕大又沉重的钝器，才能把人揍成这副德行。任何一个女人，不管使用什么凶器，都无法造成这么重的创伤。证人说他当时看见死者的头颅已经完全脱离了躯干，而且上面同样伴有严重的粉碎性骨折。喉咙处应该是被极其锋利的凶器所割断的——大概是把剃刀之类的东西。

"亚历山大·艾蒂安，外科医生，跟迪马医生一起被请去验尸。他的证词以及见解与迪马医生的完全吻合。

"Nothing farther of importance was elicited, although several other persons were examined. A murder so mysterious, and so perplexing in all its particulars, was never before committed in Paris – if indeed a murder has been committed at all. The police are entirely at fault – an unusual occurrence in affairs of this nature. There is not, however, the shadow of a clew apparent."

The evening edition of the paper stated that the greatest excitement still continued in the Quartier St. Roch – that the premises in question had been carefully re-searched, and fresh examinations of witnesses instituted, but all to no purpose. A postscript, however, mentioned that Adolphe Le Bon had been arrested and imprisoned – although nothing appeared to criminate him, beyond the facts already detailed.

Dupin seemed singularly interested in the progress of this affair – at least so I judged from his manner, for he made no comments. It was only after the announcement that Le Bon had been imprisoned, that he asked me my opinion respecting the murders.

I could merely agree with all Paris in considering them an insoluble mystery. I saw no means by which it would be possible to trace the murderer.

"We must not judge of the means," said

"尽管后来又传讯了其他几个证人，但警方并未从中获得更多有价值的线索。这起凶杀案就其种种细节来看，实在是让人不可思议，可谓错综复杂，如果这被确认是一起凶杀案的话，无疑它将成为巴黎市前所未有的第一奇案。警方目前完全不知所措——这种案子实属罕见，然而眼下却找不到任何线索。"

本报晚间版消息：巨大的恐慌仍旧笼罩在圣罗克区上空——涉案的那幢房子再次被仔细搜查了一遍，证人们也都重新接受了传讯，但事情仍旧毫无进展。然而，在一则附言中却提到了有关阿道夫·勒·本已遭逮捕并被关押的消息——虽然除了本报已经刊登过的相关案情，并无任何其他蛛丝马迹足以被拿来定他的罪。

杜宾对这个事件的进展似乎特别感兴趣——尽管他什么话都没说，但我根据他的举动就能判定这一点。一直到勒·本被捕入狱的消息传来，他才终于开口问我对于这件凶杀案的看法如何。

而我只能跟全巴黎人一样，认为这是件悬案。在我看来，没有什么办法可以帮助我们找到凶手。

"咱们可绝对不能指望单凭一

Dupin, "by this shell of an examination. The Parisian police, so much extolled for *acumen*, are cunning, but no more. There is no method in their proceedings, beyond the method of the moment. They make a vast parade of measures; but, not unfrequently, these are so ill adapted to the objects proposed, as to put us in mind of Monsieur Jourdain's calling for his *robe-de-chambre – pour mieux entendre la musique*. The results attained by them are not unfrequently surprising, but, for the most part, are brought about by simple diligence and activity. When these qualities are unavailing, their schemes fail. Vidocq, for example, was a good guesser and a persevering man. But, without educated thought, he erred continually by the very intensity of his investigations. He impaired his vision by holding the object too close. He might see, perhaps, one or two points with unusual clearness, but in so doing he, necessarily, lost sight of the matter as a whole. Thus there is such a thing as being too profound. Truth is not always in a well. In fact, as regards the more important knowledge, I do believe that she is invariably superficial. The depth lies in the valleys where we seek her, and not upon the mountain-tops where she is found. The modes and sources of this kind of error are well typified in the contemplation of the heavenly bodies. To look at a star by

纸传讯结果就能找出什么破案的法子来。"杜宾说道,"巴黎警方向来以足智多谋闻名于世,其实他们只不过是有些狡猾罢了。他们的办案手段乏善可陈,往往拘泥于现状。尽管他们总是宣称有一大堆办法,可用起来的时候却不得章法,不禁叫人联想到茹尔丹先生要拿睡衣,以便更舒适地欣赏音乐。虽然很多时候,他们办案的成绩令人眼前一亮,可多半是靠单纯的低头蛮干换来的。碰到这些优秀品质起不了作用的时候,他们就没那么如意了。比如维多克(法国名侦探),他善于猜测,同时具有坚忍不拔的精神。不过由于经验不足,他查案时往往只会一味地蛮干,结果总是不断犯错误。观察事物时,他隔得太近反而就看不到其中的真相。可能会有那么一两点被他完全看透,可是这么一来,他势必就无法看清问题的整体。这世上就是存在这么一些深奥异常的事。真相往往不是被隐藏在暗处。实际上,我反倒觉得,真正更有价值的信息必然就浮于表面。真相并不需要我们费多大力气去寻找,真相只是安静地待在它该待的地方。关于钻牛角尖这种错误的做法,究其过程和原因,我们可以在观察天体这件事中得到答案。假如你对着一颗星星瞥一眼——只需要斜眼瞟一下,将视网膜朝外的一面(比另一面更容易感受到微弱

glances – to view it in a side-Long way, by turning toward it the exterior portions of the *retina* (more susceptible of feeble impressions of light than the interior), is to behold the star distinctly – is to have the best appreciation of its lustre – a lustre which grows dim just in proportion as we turn our vision *fully* upon it. A greater number of rays actually fall upon the eye in the latter case, but, in the former, there is the more refined capacity for comprehension. By undue profundity we perplex and enfeeble thought; and it is possible to make even Venus herself vanish from the firmament by a scrutiny too sustained, too concentrated, or too direct.

"As for these murders, let us enter into some examinations for ourselves, before we make up an opinion respecting them. An inquiry will afford us amusement," [I thought this an odd term, so applied, but said nothing] "and, besides, Le Bon once rendered me a service for which I am not ungrateful. We will go and see the premises with our own eyes. I know G-, the Prefect of Police, and shall have no difficulty in obtaining the necessary permission."

The permission was obtained, and we proceeded at once to the Rue Morgue. This is one of those miserable thoroughfares which intervene between the Rue Richelieu and the Rue St. Roch. It was late in the afternoon when we reached it; as this

的光线）对准星星，就能把它看得一清二楚，同时也可以对它的光亮程度有个正确的认识。但如果你把视线全部集中在星星上，反而会发现它的光辉慢慢变得暗淡了下来。因为这种情况下，绝大部分光线实际照射到了眼睛上，但如果只是斜眼一瞟的话，反而更容易看清星星。有时候，把事情想得太复杂反而让人无法清醒正确地去思考，就好比假如我们观察星星时一直紧盯着它不放，或是精力太过集中，抑或是目光过于直接，那么恐怕连最亮的金星在我们眼里也会变得暗淡无光。

"至于凶杀案，咱们可以先自己进行一番深入调查，随后就能想出相应的对策来。再说，调查过程本身对咱们来说也是种消遣（我心里觉得"消遣"这字眼听起来很怪，不过嘴上什么也没说）。不仅如此，勒·本以前帮过我的忙，我可不是个忘恩负义的人。咱们就亲自去现场看看吧。警察局长葛××是我的老熟人，他肯定会放咱们进去的。"

获得许可后，我们立马动身往莫格街去了。这条街地处里舍利厄街和圣罗克街之间，街上脏乱不堪。我们的公寓离这个区相当远，所以等我们赶到那儿的时候，已经是傍晚时分了。那幢房子倒是不难找，

quarter is at a great distance from that in which we resided. The house was readily found; for there were still many persons gazing up at the closed shutters, with an objectless curiosity, from the opposite side of the way. It was an ordinary Parisian house, with a gateway, on one side of which was a glazed watch-box, with a sliding panel in the window, *indicating a loge de concierge*. Before going in we walked up the street, turned down an alley, and then, again turning, passed in the rear of the building – Dupin, meanwhile examining the whole neighborhood, as well as the house, with a minuteness of attention for which I could see no possible object.

Retracing our steps, we came again to the front of the dwelling, rang, and, having shown our credentials, were admitted by the agents in charge. We went up stairs – into the chamber where the body of Mademoiselle L'Espanaye had been found, and where both the deceased still lay. The disorders of the room had, as usual, been suffered to exist. I saw nothing beyond what had been stated in the *Gazette des Tribunaux*. Dupin scrutinized every thing – not excepting the bodies of the victims. We then went into the other rooms, and into the yard; a *gendarme* accompanying us throughout. The examination occupied us until dark, when we took our departure. On

因为仍然有一大票人站在街对面，一脸好奇地望着房子上那些紧闭的百叶窗发呆。这是幢普通的巴黎式建筑，大门的一侧设有一个带窗的瞭望小屋，窗上有块可以滑动的玻璃，上面标有"门房"两个字。进门之前，我们先沿着整条街走了一遭，随后拐进一条小巷，又拐了一个弯，来到了那幢房子的背面——这段时间里，杜宾细致地勘察了那幢房子的整体情况以及周边的一切，而在我看来，这里并没有什么蹊跷之处。

后来，我们按原路返回，又走回了房子的正前面，然后按响了门铃。亮明证件后负责看守的人把我们放了进去。随后我们走上楼——来到发现列士巴奈小姐尸体的那间卧房，死者母女俩的尸首仍然停放在里面。房间里依旧杂乱不堪，案发现场按照要求被维持原状。在我看来，这里和《论坛报》上所报道的情形并无出入。而杜宾则仔细打量了屋里的每一件东西——就连尸体都没有放过。接着我们又去了别的房间，后来还到了院子里。这期间有个警察一直陪同我们左右。调查工作持续到天黑才结束，这时我们便离开了现场。在回家的路上，

our way home my companion stepped in for a moment at the office of one of the daily papers.

I have said that the whims of my friend were manifold, and that *Je les ménagais*: – for this phrase there is no English equivalent. It was his humor, now, to decline all conversation on the subject of the murder, until about noon the next day. He then asked me, suddenly, if I had observed any thing *peculiar* at the scene of the atrocity.

There was something in his manner of emphasizing the word "peculiar," which caused me to shudder, without knowing why.

"No, nothing *peculiar*," I said; "nothing more, at least, than we both saw stated in the paper."

"The *Gazette*, "he replied, "has not entered, I fear, into the unusual horror of the thing. But dismiss the idle opinions of this print. It appears to me that this mystery is considered insoluble, for the very reason which should cause it to be regarded as easy of solution – I mean for the *outré* character of its features. The police are confounded by the seeming absence of motive – not for the murder itself – but for the atrocity of the murder. They are puzzled, too, by the seeming impossibility of reconciling the voices heard in contention, with the facts that no one was

我这位老兄还顺路到一家日报社里面待了一小会儿。

正如前文所说，我这位朋友的奇思妙想真是层出不穷，并且，我对他的这些奇怪念头总是听之任之——这个词我在英语里实在找不出恰当的同义词。杜宾性情古怪，那晚回来后，他只字未提任何有关这件凶杀案的事情，一直到第二天中午，他才突然开口，问我在案发现场有没有观察到什么特殊的东西。

他问我这话时有意强调了"特殊"这个词儿，不知什么原因，这让我感到不寒而栗。

"没……没什么特殊的吧，"我说道，"最起码，跟咱们在报上看到的描述没什么两样。"

"报上，"他回应道，"报上的描述恐怕无法表现出本案那种不同寻常的惨状。不过，暂且别去管报纸上的那些无稽之谈了。依我看，尽管大家一致觉得这件悬案是个死局，但他们做出这种判断的依据恰恰说明，想破这件案子简直就是易如反掌——我指的是本案特殊性中那些极度不寻常的部分。警方目前之所以一筹莫展，是因为找不到动机——不是杀人动机——而是杀人时下手如此狠毒的动机。还有一点令警方不解的是，大伙明明听到了争吵声，但是上楼后却没有见到人，

discovered up stairs but the assassinated Mademoiselle L'Espanaye, and that there were no means of egress without the notice of the party ascending. The wild disorder of the room; the corpse thrust, with the head downward, up the chimney; the frightful mutilation of the body of the old lady; these considerations, with those just mentioned, and others which I need not mention, have sufficed to paralyze the powers, by putting completely at fault the boasted acumen, of the government agents. They have fallen into the gross but common error of confounding the unusual with the abstruse. But it is by these deviations from the plane of the ordinary, that reason feels its way, if at all, in its search for the true. In investigations such as we are now pursuing, it should not be so much asked 'what has occurred,' as 'what has occurred that has never occurred before.' In fact, the facility with which I shall arrive, or have arrived, at the solution of this mystery, is in the direct ratio of its apparent insolubility in the eyes of the police."

I stared at the speaker in mute astonishment.

"I am now awaiting," continued he, looking toward the door of our apartment – "I am now awaiting a person who, although perhaps not the perpetrator of these butcheries, must have been in some

只是发现了被害者列士巴奈小姐的尸体，再说也不可能会有人，能从冲上楼那伙人的眼皮子底下溜走。房间里一片狼藉，尸体被头朝下塞进了烟囱里，老太太的尸首血肉模糊，令人毛骨悚然，当警方在办案时遇到这些情形，结合之前提到过的那些原因，加上其他种种不必我过多提及的因素，这时候，他们吹嘘的本领自然就无从施展了。显然，他们犯了个严重的错误，可这倒也不算罕见，他们错把仅仅有些不平常的事看得无比深奥。但是，如果想要探索事情的真相，只需要摒弃常规做法，真相就会自动浮出水面了。就拿咱们目前正在进行的调查工作来说吧，与其试图弄明白'出了什么事'，还不如想想'出了什么前所未有的事'。实际上，越是在警方看来不可思议的事，我越能利用它们去破解这件悬案，或者说已经被我破解了的这件悬案。"

我大吃一惊，一声不响地盯着杜宾。

"我正等着呢，"他一边说着，一边望着我们公寓的大门，"我正在等一个人，虽然这个人可能不是这起惨案的元凶，但他与这件事一定脱不了干系。但要是说到这些罪行

measure implicated in their perpetration. Of the worst portion of the crimes committed, it is probable that he is innocent. I hope that I am right in this supposition; for upon it I build my expectation of reading the entire riddle. I look for the man here – in this room – every moment. It is true that he may not arrive; but the probability is that he will. Should he come, it will be necessary to detain him. Here are pistols; and we both know how to use them when occasion demands their use."

I took the pistols, scarcely knowing what I did, or believing what I heard, while Dupin went on, very much as if in a soliloquy. I have already spoken of his abstract manner at such times. His discourse was addressed to myself; but his voice, although by no means loud, had that intonation which is commonly employed in speaking to some one at a great distance. His eyes, vacant in expression, regarded only the wall.

"That the voices heard in contention," he said, "by the party upon the stairs, were not the voices of the women themselves, was fully proved by the evidence. This relieves us of all doubt upon the question whether the old lady could have first destroyed the daughter and afterward have committed suicide. I speak of this point chiefly for the sake of method; for the strength of

中最令人发指的部分，恐怕就跟他没什么关系了。但愿我没有猜错，因为我可是把破案的全部希望都寄托在这一点上了。身处这个房间的我，每时每刻都在期盼着那个人的到来。但实际上，他可能不会来，不过从概率上看，他应该会来的。如果他来了，那我们就有必要把他留住。来，把枪拿上，相信咱俩都知道在必要的时候应该怎么去使用它。"

接过手枪，我对自己的行为感到难以置信，同时也不敢相信自己的耳朵，这时杜宾仍旧在继续说着，感觉很像是在演独角戏。正如我之前所说，每次遇到这种情况的时候，他总是表现得让人难以捉摸。虽然杜宾这番话是对我说的，他的声音并不算很大，但那副腔调听起来却像是在对着相隔很远的另一个人说话。这期间，他一直两眼无神，死盯着墙壁不放。

"那些吵架的声音，"杜宾说道，"就是大伙在楼梯上听到的那些，并不是那两位女士发出的，通过证人们的供词这点已经得到了确凿的证实，所以咱们可以肯定的是，不必去怀疑老太太是不是先把自己女儿杀了，然后又自尽。我之所以提到这个，主要是为了说明杀人方式的问题。因为列士巴奈太太绝

Madame L'Espanaye would have been utterly unequal to the task of thrusting her daughter's corpse up the chimney as it was found; and the nature of the wounds upon her own person entirely preclude the idea of self-destruction. Murder, then, has been committed by some third party; and the voices of this third party were those heard in contention. Let me now advert – not to the whole testimony respecting these voices – but to what was *peculiar* in that testimony. Did you observe any thing peculiar about it?"

I remarked that, while all the witnesses agreed in supposing the gruff voice to be that of a Frenchman, there was much disagreement in regard to the shrill, or, as one individual termed it, the harsh voice.

"That was the evidence itself," said Dupin, "but it was not the peculiarity of the evidence. You have observed nothing distinctive. Yet there *was* something to be observed. The witnesses, as you remark, agreed about the gruff voice; they were here unanimous. But in regard to the shrill voice, the peculiarity is – not that they disagreed – but that, while an Italian, an Englishman, a Spaniard, a Hollander, and a Frenchman attempted to describe it, each one spoke of it as that of *a foreigner*. Each is sure that it was not the voice of one of his own countrymen. Each likens it – not to the voice of an individual of any nation

对不可能会有那么大的力气，大到能把自己的女儿塞进事后发现尸体的那根烟囱里。再说，依照她自己的伤势来看，绝不会有人相信她是自杀的。因此，这件凶杀案一定是第三方所为，而大伙当时听见的吵架声正是第三方的声音。现在我来研究一下证人们的供词——没必要去推敲所有关于这些声音的供词，只需关注一下供词中各不相同的部分就可以了。你能看出有什么特殊之处吗？"

我说，证人们全都认定语调沙哑的那个是法国人，可是提到尖细嗓门的那个人时，或者，按照其中一个证人的说法是声音刺耳的那个人，此时大家的意见出现了分歧。

"那只是证据本身，"杜宾道，"并不是什么特殊之处。你显然没有看出什么门道来。但这里有一点需要我们注意，就像你所说的那样，证人们都认定语调沙哑的那个是法国人，在这个问题上大伙的看法并无分歧。可是提到尖细嗓门那个人的时候，特殊之处就出现了——特殊并不是体现在他们意见的不统一上，而是这些证人，无论是意大利人、英国人、西班牙人、荷兰人还是法国人，每当描述到这里的时候，人人都说那是个外国人发出的声音。人人都坚信那不是他们本国人的声音。没有一个人把这声音跟任

with whose language he is conversant – but the converse. The Frenchman supposes it the voice of a Spaniard, and 'might have distinguished some words *had he been acquainted with the Spanish*.' The Dutchman maintains it to have been that of a Frenchman; but we find it stated that '*not understanding French this witness was examined through an interpreter*.' The Englishman thinks it the voice of a German, and '*does not understand German*.'The Spaniard 'is sure' that it was that of an Englishman, but 'judges by the intonation' altogether, '*as he has no knowledge of the English*.' The Italian believes it the voice of a Russian, but '*has never conversed with a native of Russia*.' A second Frenchman differs, moreover, with the first, and is positive that the voice was that of an Italian; but, *not being cognizant of that tongue*, is, like the Spaniard, 'convinced by the intonation.' Now, how strangely unusual must that voice have really been, about which such testimony as this could have been elicited! – in whose *tones*, even, denizens of the five great divisions of Europe could recognise nothing familiar! You will say that it might have been the voice of an Asiatic – of an African. Neither Asiatics nor Africans abound in Paris; but, without denying the inference, I will now merely call your attention to three points. The voice is

何一种他所通晓的语言联系在一起——恰恰相反的是，法国人认为那是西班牙人的声音，'如果他懂西班牙语，或许就能听懂话里的几个字。'荷兰人坚持说那是法国人的声音，可是在他的供词里却提到说：'这位证人不懂法语，他是在翻译的帮助下接受问讯的。'英国人觉得那是德国人的声音，但他'并不懂德语'。西班牙人'确信'那是英国人的声音，但他却完全是'根据那人说话时的语调来判断的，因为他对英语一窍不通'。意大利人却以为那是俄国人的声音，但他'从来没跟俄国人说过话'。除此之外，另一个法国人的说法跟第一个法国人的说法也不一样，他坚信那是意大利人的声音，可他同样'对那种语言一无所知'，就像那个西班牙人一样，是'根据说话语调来判断的'。瞧瞧，根据上述这些供词，大概也只能得出这样的结论，那就是这人的声音真是稀奇到了让人不可思议的程度！——关于他说话时的语调，欧洲五大区域的公民居然没有一个能听出什么门道！你可能会说那可能是亚洲人的声音——或者非洲人的声音也不一定。但在巴黎，一共也找不出几个亚洲人或是非洲人。不过咱们暂且先不必否定这种可能性，我现在只想让你留意 3 点。首先，一个证人说这声音'与其说是又细又尖，倒不如干脆说是刺耳'。

十二·莫格街凶杀案

287

termed by one witness 'harsh rather than shrill.' It is represented by two others to have been 'quick and *unequal*.' No words – no sounds resembling words – were by any witness mentioned as distinguishable.

"I know not," continued Dupin, "what impression I may have made, so far, upon your own understanding; but I do not hesitate to say that legitimate deductions even from this portion of the testimony – the portion respecting the gruff and shrill voices – are in themselves sufficient to engender a suspicion which should give direction to all farther progress in the investigation of the mystery. I said 'legitimate deductions;' but my meaning is not thus fully expressed. I designed to imply that the deductions are the *sole* proper ones, and that the suspicion arises *inevitably* from them as the single result. What the suspicion is, however, I will not say just yet. I merely wish you to bear in mind that, with myself, it was sufficiently forcible to give a definite form – a certain tendency – to my inquiries in the chamber.

"Let us now transport ourselves, in fancy, to this chamber. What shall we first seek here? The means of egress employed by the murderers. It is not too much to say that neither of us believe in praernatural events. Madame and Mademoiselle L'Espanaye were not destroyed by spirits. The doers of the deed were material, and

其次，另有两个证人的描述是'语速快且杂乱无章'。最后，没有一个证人提到他能分辨出那话里的字句——或是什么听起来像是语言的东西。

"我不知道，"杜宾继续说道，"到目前为止，听了我说的这些，你自己心里是怎么理解的。但我可以很肯定地说，单凭这一部分证词，即描述沙哑语调和尖细嗓门的部分，我们就可以得到一些合理的推论，根据这些推论，完全可以进一步得到一个假设。再根据这个假设一路摸索下去，便可以对这件悬案进行更为深入的调查。刚才虽然提到了那些'合理的推论'，但我的意思并没有完全表达明白。我想指出的是，这些是唯一正确的推论，并且在此基础上我们必然会得到一个正确的假设。至于这个假设是什么，我先暂且不说。你只需要记住，在我看来这个假设拥有很强的说服力，它让我心中有了一个清晰的轮廓，即一种明确的目的性，足以使我在调查那间卧房的时候能够做到有的放矢。

"假设咱们现在已经到了那间卧房，那首先要从什么开始找起呢？自然应该是凶手逃脱的方法。毫无疑问，咱们俩都是不信邪的人。杀害列士巴奈太太母女俩的肯定不是什么妖魔鬼怪。凶手是真实存在的，所以不可能就这么凭空消失了。

escaped materially. Then how? Fortunately, there is but one mode of reasoning upon the point, and that mode *must* lead us to a definite decision. – Let us examine, each by each, the possible means of egress. It is clear that the assassins were in the room where Mademoiselle L'Espanaye was found, or at least in the room adjoining, when the party ascended the stairs. It is then only from these two apartments that we have to seek issues. The police have laid bare the floors, the ceilings, and the masonry of the walls, in every direction. No secret issues could have escaped their vigilance. But, not trusting to their eyes, I examined with my own. There were, then, no secret issues. Both doors leading from the rooms into the passage were securely locked, with the keys inside. Let us turn to the chimneys. These, although of ordinary width for some eight or ten feet above the hearths, will not admit, throughout their extent, the body of a large cat. The impossibility of egress, by means already stated, being thus absolute, we are reduced to the windows. Through those of the front room no one could have escaped without notice from the crowd in the street. The murderers must have passed, then, through those of the back room. Now, brought to this conclusion in so unequivocal a manner as we are, it is not our part, as reasoners, to reject it on account of apparent

那他到底是怎么逃走的呢？幸好，这个问题的解决办法是唯一的，依靠这个办法我们就必然能够明确地作出判断。咱们先逐一研究一下凶手可能采用的各种逃脱方法。很显然，大伙上楼的时候，凶手就在发现列士巴奈小姐尸体的卧房里，或者至少也是在隔壁的某个房间里。所以，我们只需要在这几个房间里找到出口就可以了。警方已经把地板、天花板以及石头墙全都查了个底朝天。没什么秘密出口能逃得过他们的火眼金睛。但是，我却对他们的眼力没什么信心，所以又自己勘察了一下。勘察过后，同样没有发现任何秘密出口。通向过道的两扇房门都被锁得严严实实，钥匙也都插在内侧。咱们再把注意力转向烟囱。虽然这些烟囱跟普通的烟囱宽度相等，位于火炉边上方8到10英尺的地方，可是整个烟囱里面连一只大猫的身体都容不下。既然刚才说到的两种逃脱方式都被彻底否决了，那我们只好在窗户这里做文章了。如果是从房子前面的窗户逃出去，那一定会引起街上那一群人的注意。由此看来，凶手肯定是从房子后面的窗户逃走的。事情发展到这儿，既然我们已经得出了这么明确的结论，那么作为推论者本身，我们就不能因为一些看似不可能的事再把这个结论给否定了。我们能做的只有去证明这些看似 '不可能

impossibilities. It is only left for us to prove that these apparent 'impossibilities' are, in reality, not such.

"There are two windows in the chamber. One of them is unobstructed by furniture, and is wholly visible. The lower portion of the other is hidden from view by the head of the unwieldy bedstead which is thrust close up against it. The former was found securely fastened from within. It resisted the utmost force of those who endeavored to raise it. A large gimlet-hole had been pierced in its frame to the left, and a very stout nail was found fitted therein, nearly to the head. Upon examining the other window, a similar nail was seen similarly fitted in it; and a vigorous attempt to raise this sash, failed also. The police were now entirely satisfied that egress had not been in these directions. And, *therefore*, it was thought a matter of supererogation to withdraw the nails and open the windows.

"My own examination was somewhat more particular, and was so for the reason I have just given – because here it was, I knew, that all apparent impossibilities *must* be proved to be not such in reality.

"I proceeded to think thus – a posteriori. The murderers did escape from one of these windows. This being so, they could not have refastened the sashes from the inside, as they were found fastened; – the consideration which put a stop, through its

的事',实际上它们并不是那么不可信的。

"卧房里有两扇窗户。其中一扇窗户没有被家具挡住,整体轮廓清晰可见。另一扇窗户的下半部分被床架的一端挡住了,笨重的床架紧紧顶在那半扇窗户上。上面那半扇则从里面被牢牢固定住,即使用尽浑身解数也别想把它拉开。左边窗框上钻着一个大钉眼,里面钉有一枚相当坚固的钉子,只剩一点钉头还露在外面。再看看另一扇窗户,上面同样也有一枚钉子,以同样的方式被钉在那儿,所以,就算使出吃奶的劲去拉这扇窗,结果同样也是白费工夫。警方目前完全确信,这两扇窗户绝不会是凶手逃脱的出口。因此,他们觉得拔出钉子然后打开窗户的举动很多余。

"然而我自己进行的调查从某种程度上来说更加严谨,之所以这样做的目的正如前面所说的——因为这就是我所熟知的那种情况,所有看似不可能的事,实际上经过验证后,并不是那么不可行的。

"于是我开始用逆向思维来考虑这个问题。首先认定凶手确实是从这两扇窗户中的一扇逃走的。但如果真的是这样,凶手出去后理应无法从里边重新把窗框固定好,就

obviousness, to the scrutiny of the police in this quarter. Yet the sashes were fastened. They *must*, then, have the power of fastening themselves. There was no escape from this conclusion. I stepped to the unobstructed casement, withdrew the nail with some difficulty and attempted to raise the sash. It resisted all my efforts, as I had anticipated. A concealed spring must, I now know, exist; and this corroboration of my idea convinced me that my premises at least, were correct, however mysterious still appeared the circumstances attending the nails. A careful search soon brought to light the hidden spring. I pressed it, and, satisfied with the discovery, forbore to upraise the sash.

"I now replaced the nail and regarded it attentively. A person passing out through this window might have reclosed it, and the spring would have caught – but the nail could not have been replaced. The conclusion was plain, and again narrowed in the field of my investigations. The assassins *must* have escaped through the other window. Supposing, then, the springs upon each sash to be the same, as was probable, there *must* be found a difference between the nails, or at least between the modes of their fixture. Getting upon the sacking of the bedstead, I looked over the head-board minutely at the second casement. Passing my hand down behind

像大家看到的那样。——这种分析显然很合理，所以警方就不再继续追究这个问题了。但实际上，既然窗框是被牢牢固定住的，那这个被固定的过程一定是通过某种力量自动完成的。这结论肯定不会错，我走到那扇没有被堵上的窗户旁边，下了一番工夫才把钉子拔出来，然后试图把窗框推起来重合上。正如我所预料的那样，无论我怎么推，窗户都合不起来。我这才明白，一定是在哪儿有根隐蔽的弹簧，这一点证实了我的想法，说明我假设的前提是正确的，然而，有关钉子的问题依然是迷雾重重。经过仔细的搜寻，我很快就找到了那根隐蔽的弹簧，按了几下后，我心里对这个发现十分满意，之后就没有再去推那个窗框。

"这时候，我把钉子重新放回原位，并开始用心地观察。假如一个人从这里出去，那么窗户会重新关闭，弹簧也会自动弹起，这枚钉子理应无法恢复原状。结论已经很清楚了，因此我的侦查范围又得以进一步缩小。凶手必然是从另一扇窗户逃走的。如果两扇窗户上的弹簧大致相同，那么区别一定就在钉子上，或者至少是钉法上有所不同。我踩着铺在床架上的布袋子，越过床头板仔细观察另外那半扇窗户。然后从下面把手伸到板子后面，一下就摸到了弹簧，按了一下后发现

the board, I readily discovered and pressed the spring, which was, as I had supposed, identical in character with its neighbor. I now looked at the nail. It was as stout as the other, and apparently fitted in the same manner – driven in nearly up to the head.

"You will say that I was puzzled; but, if you think so, you must have misunderstood the nature of the inductions. To use a sporting phrase, I had not been once 'at fault.' The scent had never for an instant been lost. There was no flaw in any link of the chain. I had traced the secret to its ultimate result, – and that result was *the nail*. It had, I say, in every respect, the appearance of its fellow in the other window; but this fact was an absolute nullity (conclusive us it might seem to be) when compared with the consideration that here, at this point, terminated the clew. 'There must be something wrong,' I said, 'about the nail.' I touched it; and the head, with about a quarter of an inch of the shank, came off in my fingers. The rest of the shank was in the gimlet-hole where it had been broken off. The fracture was an old one (for its edges were incrusted with rust), and had apparently been accomplished by the blow of a hammer, which had partially imbedded, in the top of the bottom sash, the head portion of the nail. I now carefully replaced this head portion in the indentation whence I had

一切都如我所料，这根弹簧跟刚才那扇窗户上的一模一样。于是我又把目光转向了钉子。果然，这枚也跟之前那枚一样坚固，而且明显是用同样的方法被钉进去的，也是只剩一点钉头还露在外面。

"这时候你大概会说我被搞糊涂了，但是，如果你真的这么想，那你一定是没弄明白归纳法的原理。引用一句体育运动里的名言，我可从来不会'阴沟里翻船'。整条线索始终没有断过，各个环节紧密连接，毫无瑕疵。我显然已经找到了这个谜题的根源——问题就出在钉子上。刚才我说过，从表面上看，这枚钉子跟另一扇窗户上的钉子一模一样。但这一切都毫无价值，此观点对我们来说可能具有决定性意义，尤其是在谜底即将被揭开的此刻。要我说的话，'这钉子上一定有什么蹊跷之处。'我伸手一摸，上面的钉头连同大约 1/4 英寸长的钉身便落入了我的指间。其余的钉身还留在钉眼里，钉子在钉眼里断成了两截。断口很陈旧，因为边缘处已经生锈，并且钉子很明显是被锤子一下砸断的，所以钉头部分也就顺势嵌入了下半扇窗框的顶端。这时我小心地把钉头重新放回刚才的缺口里面，看起来果然跟一整枚钉子没什么两样——从表面看不出一点缝隙。我又按了下弹簧，轻轻把窗框推上去几英尺，钉头仍旧牢

taken it, and the resemblance to a perfect nail was complete – the fissure was invisible. Pressing the spring, I gently raised the sash for a few inches; the head went up with it, remaining firm in its bed. I closed the window, and the semblance of the whole nail was again perfect.

"The riddle, so far, was now unriddled. The assassin had escaped through the window which looked upon the bed. Dropping of its own accord upon his exit (or perhaps purposely closed), it had become fastened by the spring; and it was the retention of this spring which had been mistaken by the police for that of the nail, – farther inquiry being thus considered unnecessary.

"The next question is that of the mode of descent. Upon this point I had been satisfied in my walk with you around the building. About five feet and a half from the casement in question there runs a lightning-rod. From this rod it would have been impossible for any one to reach the window itself, to say nothing of entering it. I observed, however, that the shutters of the fourth story were of the peculiar kind called by Parisian carpenters *ferrades* – a kind rarely employed at the present day, but frequently seen upon very old mansions at Lyons and Bourdeaux. They are in the form of an ordinary door, (a single, not a folding door) except that the

牢地嵌在窗框上的钉眼里，跟着一起被推上去了。随后我关上窗户，钉子便又重新恢复成了整整一枚的样子。

"到这一步，僵局总算是被打破了。凶手一定是从床头上这扇窗户逃走的。他逃出去之后，窗户就自动被关闭了，当然也有可能是凶手故意关上的，此时窗户便借助弹簧的力量，重新被固定好了。警方错误地认为窗户是靠钉子，而不是靠弹簧才闭合起来的——所以他们就以此为依据，不再继续深究窗户的事了。

"第二个需要解决的问题是凶手逃下楼的方式。关于这一点，在咱们绕着房子转的时候，我就已经心知肚明了。在距离那扇窗户大约5英尺半的地方，有一根避雷针。显然，任何人也别想在这根避雷针的位置上直接摸到窗户，更不用说是进到窗户里了。然而，我留意到4楼的百叶窗样式与众不同，巴黎的木匠们称之为'铁格窗'——这种样式现在很少见，不过在里昂和波尔多的某些老住宅上还时常可以见到。从外表看，它们就像是普通的门，单扇，而不是双开门结构，位于下方的另外半扇一般是格子框架，或者被做成镂空的铁栏——这

lower half is latticed or worked in open trellis – thus affording an excellent hold for the hands. In the present instance these shutters are fully three feet and a half broad. When we saw them from the rear of the house, they were both about half open – that is to say, they stood off at right angles from the wall. It is probable that the police, as well as myself, examined the back of the tenement; but, if so, in looking at these *ferrades* in the line of their breadth (as they must have done), they did not perceive this great breadth itself, or, at all events, failed to take it into due consideration. In fact, having once satisfied themselves that no egress could have been made in this quarter, they would naturally bestow here a very cursory examination. It was clear to me, however, that the shutter beLonging to the window at the head of the bed, would, if swung fully back to the wall, reach to within two feet of the lightning-rod. It was also evident that, by exertion of a very unusual degree of activity and courage, an entrance into the window, from the rod, might have been thus effected. – By reaching to the distance of two feet and a half (we now suppose the shutter open to its whole extent) a robber might have taken a firm grasp upon the trellis-work. Letting go, then, his hold upon the rod, placing his feet securely against the wall, and springing boldly from

么一来，它们倒成了绝好的攀爬扶手。眼前，列士巴奈太太家的这些百叶窗足有 3 英尺半那么宽。咱们当时从房子后面看过去，我发现那两扇百叶窗全都刚好半开着——就是说，窗面跟墙面正好形成一个直角。像我一样，警方大概也已经检查过了那幢房子背面的情况。如果他们确实检查过的话，就不会没有留心到这两扇铁格窗的宽度，实际上他们也确实注意到了这一点，但却没有看出窗子竟然有这么宽，或者就算真的看出来了，大概他们也没把这当回事。实际上，他们既然早已确信这地方不可能被凶手当做逃跑用的出口，检查到这儿的时候自然也就漫不经心了。可是我却看得很清楚，如果完全推开床头窗户上的那扇百叶窗，把它转到另一边紧挨在墙上的话，那根避雷针与窗口之间的距离便不足 2 英尺了。另外还有一点同样是显而易见的，只有身手异常敏捷并且胆量过人的家伙，在用尽浑身解数的情况下，才有可能从避雷针那个位置进到窗户里去。但现在如果我们假定这扇百叶窗处于完全敞开的状态，那它与避雷针之间的距离就只剩下 2 英尺半了，此时凶手完全可以一手紧紧抓住百叶窗上的铁网格，然后松开避雷针，两脚牢牢抵住墙壁，大胆地纵身一跃，那他正好可以跟着百叶窗一起转过来，并顺势把它关

it, he might have swung the shutter so as to close it, and, if we imagine the window open at the time, might even have swung himself into the room.

"I wish you to bear especially in mind that I have spoken of a *very* unusual degree of activity as requisite to success in so hazardous and so difficult a feat. It is my design to show you, first, that the thing might possibly have been accomplished: – but, secondly and *chiefly*, I wish to impress upon your understanding the *very extraordinary* – the almost præternatural character of that agility which could have accomplished it.

"You will say, no doubt, using the language of the law, that 'to make out my case,' I should rather undervalue, than insist upon a full estimation of the activity required in this matter. This may be the practice in law, but it is not the usage of reason. My ultimate object is only the truth. My immediate purpose is to lead you to place in juxta-position, that *very unusual* activity of which I have just spoken with that *very peculiar* shrill (or harsh) and *unequal* voice, about whose nationality no two persons could be found to agree, and in whose utterance no syllabification could be detected."

At these words a vague and half-formed conception of the meaning of Dupin flitted over my mind. I seemed to be upon the

起来。如果里面的窗户当时正好开着的话，那他便可以借助转动的铁网格直接跳进卧房里去。

"还有一点我希望你特别留心的是，刚才提到过，要完成如此惊险且难度极高的特技，凶手必须身手异常敏捷才能做到万无一失。我这么说的目的是为了让你明白，首先，跳窗这件事从理论上说是可能的——但另一方面，也是关键的一点，我希望你记住，此人的身手必须特别灵活，或者说是灵活到了令人不可思议的地步，他才能做到这一切。

"不需多想，这时你八成会引用一句法律术语跟我说，'用事实证明'，其实，我与其在这儿强调咱们要充分考量凶手所必须具备的敏捷身手，倒不如把事情看得简单一点。这在法律上或许行得通，但在分析推理时却派不上用场。但我的最终目的只有一个，那就是弄清事实真相。至于眼下，我希望你能把两件事情放到一起来考虑，就是把刚才所说的敏捷身手跟那个异常尖细或者说是刺耳的声音联系在一起，那动静听起来杂乱无章，没人能确定它究竟出自哪国人的口，而且也听不清话里到底说了些什么。"

听了杜宾这番话，我心中出现了一个模糊的轮廓，隐约间好像了

verge of comprehension without power to comprehend – men, at times, find themselves upon the brink of remembrance without being able, in the end, to remember. My friend went on with his discourse.

"You will see," he said, "that I have shifted the question from the mode of egress to that of ingress. It was my design to convey the idea that both were effected in the same manner, at the same point. Let us now revert to the interior of the room. Let us survey the appearances here. The drawers of the bureau, it is said, had been rifled, although many articles of apparel still remained within them. The conclusion here is absurd. It is a mere guess – a very silly one – and no more. How are we to know that the articles found in the drawers were not all these drawers had originally contained? Madame L'Espanaye and her daughter lived an exceedingly retired life – saw no company – seldom went out – had little use for numerous changes of habiliment. Those found were at least of as good quality as any likely to be possessed by these ladies. If a thief had taken any, why did he not take the best – why did he not take all? In a word, why did he abandon four thousand francs in gold to encumber himself with a bundle of linen? The gold was abandoned. Nearly the whole sum mentioned by Monsieur Mignaud, the

解了他的意思。似乎马上就要弄明白了，却又无法完全参透，就好比有时候，人们感觉有些话明明已经到了嘴边，却无论如何也想不起来自己要说什么。这时候，我的朋友开始继续他的长篇大论。

"你看，"他说道，"我已经把话题从逃出去的方法转移到闯进来的方法上了。我这么做的目的无非是想让你明白，逃出去和闯进来的方法是相同的，而且都是通过同一个出入点。现在，咱们不妨再把目光转回卧房内。看看这里的情形：柜子上的抽屉，据说已经遭到了洗劫，可里面仍有不少衣物，因此这种结论显然是站不住脚的。这只不过是个猜测——一个愚蠢至极的猜测——仅此而已。我们凭什么说现在抽屉里的这些衣物比原来少了呢？列士巴奈太太母女俩过着与世无争的生活——跟外人没什么来往——很少出门——自然用不着过多用来替换的衣物。抽屉里的这些，应该算是母女俩所有衣物里面的精华部分了。如果有哪个贼想要偷衣服的话，干吗不拿走最好的——或者干脆洗劫一空呢？再说了，干吗放着价值4000法郎的金币不要，反而抱走一堆衣服，这不是跟自己过不去吗？金币被留在了原地，这正是银行老板米尼亚尔先生提到的那些金币，它们几乎被原封不动地留在了地板上的两个钱袋里面。因此，

banker, was discovered, in bags, upon the floor. I wish you, therefore, to discard from your thoughts the blundering idea of motive, engendered in the brains of the police by that portion of the evidence which speaks of money delivered at the door of the house. Coincidences ten times as remarkable as this (the delivery of the money, and murder committed within three days upon the party receiving it), happen to all of us every hour of our lives, without attracting even momentary notice. Coincidences, in general, are great stumbling-blocks in the way of that class of thinkers who have been educated to know nothing of the theory of probabilities – that theory to which the most glorious objects of human research are indebted for the most glorious of illustration. In the present instance, had the gold been gone, the fact of its delivery three days before would have formed something more than a coincidence. It would have been corroborative of this idea of motive. But, under the real circumstances of the case, if we are to suppose gold the motive of this outrage, we must also imagine the perpetrator so vacillating an idiot as to have abandoned his gold and his motive together.

"Keeping now steadily in mind the points to which I have drawn your attention – that peculiar voice, that unusual

我希望你摒弃那些草率的想法，不要像警方一样，只因为供词里提到了送钱上门的事，就对作案动机的问题妄下定论。送钱上门后不到3天，收到钱的客户就遭到杀害，但是，就算比这巧合10倍的事，在生活中也是随处可见的，但又有谁去留意过这些呢。通常说来，巧合是思想家那一类人的绊脚石，以他们高深的学问必然不会了解那些有关概率的理论——可是要知道，人类科学研究中的许多重大课题之所以能够取得极为辉煌的成就，那可都是沾了这种理论的光。具体到眼前这件事上，如果金币被拿走，那么3天前送钱的事就不仅仅是巧合那么简单了。假如真是那样，反倒证实了那些关于作案动机的草率想法。不过，根据本案的实际情况，如果要认为这一切暴行的目的是为了钱，那我们必须把凶手想象成是一个优柔寡断的傻子，因为他竟然放着现成的金币不拿，好像完全忘记了自己是来干吗的。

"说到这儿，请牢记我提醒你注意的几点——奇怪的声音，敏捷异常的身手，还有就是，在如此惨

agility, and that startling absence of motive in a murder so singularly atrocious as this – let us glance at the butchery itself. Here is a woman strangled to death by manual strength, and thrust up a chimney, head downward. Ordinary assassins employ no such modes of murder as this. Least of all, do they thus dispose of the murdered. In the manner of thrusting the corpse up the chimney, you will admit that there was something excessively *outré* – something altogether irreconcilable with our common notions of human action, even when we suppose the actors the most depraved of men. Think, too, how great must have been that strength which could have thrust the body up such an aperture so forcibly that the united vigor of several persons was found barely sufficient to drag it *down*!

"Turn, now, to other indications of the employment of a vigor most marvellous. On the hearth were thick tresses – very thick tresses – of grey human hair. These had been torn out by the roots. You are aware of the great force necessary in tearing thus from the head even twenty or thirty hairs together. You saw the locks in question as well as myself. Their roots (a hideous sight!) were clotted with fragments of the flesh of the scalp – sure token of the prodigious power which had been exerted in uprooting perhaps half a million of hairs at a time. The throat of the old lady was not

绝人寰的凶杀案背后,居然找不出任何动机,这些着实令人感到吃惊——咱们不如再来研究一下杀人手段吧。房间里这个女人是被掐死的,然后又被头朝下塞进烟囱里。普通凶犯可不会采用这种杀人手段,至少,他不会采用这种藏尸灭迹的手段。单说尸首被塞进烟囱里这件事,你必须得承认这种做法着实有点极端——多数情况下,正常人绝不会做出这种事来,就算凶手是最最恶毒的人,情况也同样如此。再想想看,究竟是多么大的力气,能把尸体强行塞进这么狭窄的洞口里,以致好几个人一起用尽全身力气才勉强把尸体给拖出来!

"好了,现在我们再看看其他一些线索,它们都足以说明凶手的力量到底有多惊人。壁炉上散落着几大把花白的头发,发束很粗,它们是被连根拔起的。你一定晓得,普通情况下,哪怕是从头上一次性拔下二三十根头发都需要使出不小的力气。跟我一样,你也亲眼看到了那几把头发,发根上还带着几片血肉模糊的头皮呢,简直令人作呕——这足以说明凶手的力气到底有多大,说不定他能一口气拔下500,000根头发。老太太不但喉咙被割断,而且脑袋跟躯干也完全分了

merely cut, but the head absolutely severed from the body: the instrument was a mere razor. I wish you also to look at the *brutal* ferocity of these deeds. Of the bruises upon the body of Madame L'Espanaye I do not speak. Monsieur Dumas, and his worthy coadjutor Monsieur Etienne, have pronounced that they were inflicted by some obtuse instrument; and so far these gentlemen are very correct. The obtuse instrument was clearly the stone pavement in the yard, upon which the victim had fallen from the window which looked in upon the bed. This idea, however simple it may now seem, escaped the police for the same reason that the breadth of the shutters escaped them – because, by the affair of the nails, their perceptions had been hermetically sealed against the possibility of the windows having ever been opened at all.

"If now, in addition to all these things, you have properly reflected upon the odd disorder of the chamber, we have gone so far as to combine the ideas of an agility astounding, a strength superhuman, a ferocity brutal, a butchery without motive, a *grotesquerie* in horror absolutely alien from humanity, and a voice foreign in tone to the ears of men of many nations, and devoid of all distinct or intelligible syllabification. What result, then, has ensued? What impression have I made

家——而凶器只不过是一把剃刀。这里我希望你同样注意一下这些暴行的凶残程度。对于列士巴奈太太身上的那些淤青，我暂且不予置评。迪马先生和他那位值得钦佩的助手艾蒂安先生，声称这些淤青是由钝器造成的。到目前为止，这两位先生无疑是正确的。因为，钝器显然就是铺在院子里的那些石头，死者是从床头那扇窗户落到院子里来的。这个观点虽然现在看起来很合理，但之前却被警方忽略了，情况正如他们忽略百叶窗宽度的时候一样——由于那两枚钉子的关系，警方的思路被完全阻断了，因为他们根本就不认为窗户曾经有可能被打开过。

"现在除了以上我所说的这些事情之外，如果你能再彻底回想一下卧房内一片狼藉的情形，我们就足以把这几点综合起来，惊人的敏捷身手，超人的力量，凶残的暴行，毫无动机的杀戮，惨绝人寰的恐怖举动，以及在多个不同国家人的耳朵里都像是外国口音的声音，而且也听不清话里到底说了些什么。这么一来，能得出什么样的结论来呢？听了我这一席话，不知你心里是怎么想的？"

upon your fancy?"

I felt a creeping of the flesh as Dupin asked me the question. "A madman," I said, "has done this deed – some raving maniac, escaped from a neighboring Maison de Santé? "

"In some respects," he replied, "your idea is not irrelevant. But the voices of madmen, even in their wildest paroxysms, are never found to tally with that peculiar voice heard upon the stairs. Madmen are of some nation, and their language, however incoherent in its words, has always the coherence of syllabification. Besides, the hair of a madman is not such as I now hold in my hand. I disentangled this little tuft from the rigidly clutched fingers of Madame L'Espanaye. Tell me what you can make of it."

"Dupin!" I said, completely unnerved; "this hair is most unusual – this is no *human* hair."

"I have not asserted that it is," said he; "but, before we decide this point, I wish you to glance at the little sketch I have here traced upon this paper. It is a fac-simile drawing of what has been described in one portion of the testimony as 'dark bruises, and deep indentations of finger nails,' upon the throat of Mademoiselle L'Espanaye, and in another, (by Messrs. Dumas and Etienne,) as a 'series of livid spots, evidently the impression of fingers.'

听到杜宾问这话，我顿时有种不寒而栗的感觉，"是个疯子，"我说道，"肯定是个疯子干的，很可能是从附近疯人院里逃出来的某个丧心病狂的疯子。"

"从某些方面来看，"杜宾答道，"你的看法倒也不无道理。不过，疯子就算是发起疯来，他的声音跟大伙在楼梯上听到的那种动静也完全不一样。再说，疯子也是有国籍的，尽管他们说的话毫无逻辑性可言，但至少发音是前后一致的吧。再说了，疯子的毛发也不会像我现在手里拿的这些一样。这一小撮毛是我从列士巴奈太太紧紧握在一起的手指中间拽出来的。你来看看这是些什么毛？"

"杜宾！"我被吓得浑身无力，慌忙说道，"这毛确实非常罕见——这，这不是人的毛啊。"

"我也没说它是啊，"杜宾说，"不过，在搞清楚这个问题之前，你先看看我画在这张纸上的一幅小草图吧。我临摹的正是一部分供词中所提到的'紫黑色淤血外加几条深深的指甲印'，就是在列士巴奈小姐喉部发现的那些。另外，在迪马先生和艾蒂安先生的供词里是这样描述的：'好几块淤青，显然是被手指掐过后留下的'。

"You will perceive," continued my friend, spreading out the paper upon the table before us, "that this drawing gives the idea of a firm and fixed hold. There is no *slipping* apparent. Each finger has retained – possibly until the death of the victim – the fearful grasp by which it originally imbedded itself. Attempt, now, to place all your fingers, at the same time, in the respective impressions as you see them."

I made the attempt in vain.

"We are possibly not giving this matter a fair trial," he said. "The paper is spread out upon a plane surface; but the human throat is cylindrical. Here is a billet of wood, the circumference of which is about that of the throat. Wrap the drawing around it, and try the experiment again."

I did so; but the difficulty was even more obvious than before. "This," I said, "is the mark of no human hand."

"Read now," replied Dupin, "this passage from Cuvier."

It was a minute anatomical and generally descriptive account of the large fulvous Ourang-Outang of the East Indian Islands. The gigantic stature, the prodigious strength and activity, the wild ferocity, and the imitative propensities of these mammalia are sufficiently well known to all. I understood the full horrors of the murder at once.

"你一定会发觉，"杜宾一边继续说着，一边把那张纸平铺在我们面前的桌子上，"这张草图充分说明凶手当时又使劲又牢固地掐住了死者的脖子，并且中间显然没有任何想要松手的意思。这些印记显示出当时手指狠狠嵌入皮肉里的样子，很有可能是一直等到受害者咽了气才把手松开。现在你来试试看，按照你看到的这张草图，同时把手指头分别放在这几个指印上。"

我试了一下，可是没有成功。

"也许，我们这样试不太合理，"杜宾说道，"纸张被铺成了平面，但人的脖子却是圆筒形的。这儿正好有根木柴，看起来跟死者的脖子粗细差不多。咱们把这张草图裹在上面，然后再来试试看吧。"

我照他的话去做了，可是我的手显然更加无法跟那些印记相对应起来。"这，"我说道，"这不是人的手指印。"

"看看这个吧，"杜宾答道，"这是居维叶[1]写的一篇文章。"

这是一篇关于东印度群岛茶色大猩猩的剖析报告和概括描述。这种哺乳动物身形魁梧，力大无比，敏捷异常，天性凶残，喜好模仿，这些都是它为人们所熟知的特点。看到这里，我立刻明白这件无比可怕的凶杀案到底是怎么回事了。

---

[1] 居维叶：法国博物学家、动物学家和古生物学家。

"The description of the digits," said I, as I made an end of reading, "is in exact accordance with this drawing. I see that no animal but an Ourang-Outang, of the species here mentioned, could have impressed the indentations as you have traced them. This tuft of tawny hair, too, is identical in character with that of the beast of Cuvier. But I cannot possibly comprehend the particulars of this frightful mystery. Besides, there were *two* voices heard in contention, and one of them was unquestionably the voice of a Frenchman."

"True; and you will remember an expression attributed almost unanimously, by the evidence, to this voice, – the expression, ' *mon Dieu!* ' This, under the circumstances, has been justly characterized by one of the witnesses (Montani, the confectioner,) as an expression of remonstrance or expostulation. Upon these two words, therefore, I have mainly built my hopes of a full solution of the riddle. A Frenchman was cognizant of the murder. It is possible – indeed it is far more than probable – that he was innocent of all participation in the bloody transactions which took place. The Ourang-Outang may have escaped from him. He may have traced it to the chamber; but, under the agitating circumstances which ensued, he could never have re-captured it. It is still at large. I will not

"这些关于爪子的描述，"我读完那篇文章后说道，"恰好跟这张草图上画的对应了起来。我觉得除了这里提到的这种猩猩之外，应该没有其他动物的爪印能跟你画的这个对应起来。还有这撮茶色毛发，也跟居维叶笔下那种野兽的毛发一模一样。不过，关于这件惊悚悬案中的一些细枝末节，我还是不能理解。你想想看，当时大伙明明听见了两个人在吵架的声音，而且可以确定其中一个人是法国人。"

"说得没错，而且你应该还记得，证人们几乎全都提到了这人当时说过的一句话，他说的是'天哪！'根据其中一个证人，就是糖果店老板蒙塔尼所说，那人在当时的情形下说出这句话，听来像是在表达某种告诫或规劝的意思。所以，我就把打破这个僵局的希望全部寄托在他说的这两个字上面了。现在，我们知道有一个法国人，他了解这件凶杀案的全过程。然而有可能，确切地说我认为是极有可能，他跟这些血腥的罪行没有任何关系。这只猩猩说不定是从他那儿逃出来的，他大概也追着猩猩来到过卧房，但由于当时陆续出现的一系列混乱情况，他一直无法重新把猩猩逮住。至今，这只猩猩仍旧逍遥法外。说到这儿，我就不再继续这些猜想——因为它们也仅仅是猜想——由

pursue these guesses – for I have no right to call them more – since the shades of reflection upon which they are based are scarcely of sufficient depth to be appreciable by my own intellect, and since I could not pretend to make them intelligible to the understanding of another. We will call them guesses then, and speak of them as such. If the Frenchman in question is indeed, as I suppose, innocent of this atrocity, this advertisement which I left last night, upon our return home, at the office of *Le Monde* (a paper devoted to the shipping interest, and much sought by sailors,) will bring him to our residence."

He handed me a paper, and I read thus:

CAUGHT – In the Bois de Boulogne, early in the morning of the – inst., (the morning of the murder,) a very large, tawny Ourang-Outang of the Bornese species. The owner, (who is ascertained to be a sailor, beLonging to a Maltese vessel,) may have the animal again, upon identifying it satisfactorily, and paying a few charges arising from its capture and keeping. Call at No. –, Rue –, Faubourg St. Germain – au troisième.

"How was it possible," I asked, "that you should know the man to be a sailor, and beLonging to a Maltese vessel?"

"I do *not* know it," said Dupin. "I am not

于那些被拿来作为猜想依据的一点蛛丝马迹，在我本人看来都是极其不充分的，并且我也不敢妄想能让别人搞明白自己的这些想法。所以我们就暂且称它们为猜想吧，并继续把它们当成猜想来进行讨论。假如这个法国人真的如我所料，跟这件惨案毫无瓜葛，那么昨天在咱们回家的路上，我顺便到《世界报》（专门为航运界人士创办的，主要读者都是水手）报社登出的这则广告，应该会把他引到咱们的公寓里来。"

说着，杜宾递给我一份报纸，在上面我看到了这么一段广告：

失物招领——某天清晨（凶杀案发生的那天清晨）在布伦公园内寻得茶色巨型猩猩一只，属于婆罗洲品种。据了解，该猩猩系马耳他商船上一名水手所拥有。失主只需详细说明失物情况，一经本人核实，并收取少许捕获及赡养费后，失主即可将其领回。欢迎失主前往市郊圣日尔曼区×路×号 3 楼洽谈失物归还事宜。

"这怎么可能，"我问道，"你怎么可能知道他是个水手？而且还知道他是马耳他商船上的？"

"我并不知道啊，"杜宾说，

sure of it. Here, however, is a small piece of ribbon, which from its form, and from its greasy appearance, has evidently been used in tying the hair in one of those Long *queues* of which sailors are so fond. Moreover, this knot is one which few besides sailors can tie, and is peculiar to the Maltese. I picked the ribbon up at the foot of the lightning-rod. It could not have beLonged to either of the deceased. Now if, after all, I am wrong in my induction from this ribbon, that the Frenchman was a sailor beLonging to a Maltese vessel, still I can have done no harm in saying what I did in the advertisement. If I am in error, he will merely suppose that I have been misled by some circumstance into which he will not take the trouble to inquire. But if I am right, a great point is gained. Cognizant although innocent of the murder, the Frenchman will naturally hesitate about replying to the advertisement – about demanding the Ourang-Outang. He will reason thus: – 'I am innocent; I am poor; my Ourang-Outang is of great value – to one in my circumstances a fortune of itself – why should I lose it through idle apprehensions of danger? Here it is, within my grasp. It was found in the Bois de Boulogne – at a vast distance from the scene of that butchery. How can it ever be suspected that a brute beast should have done the deed? The police are at fault –

"我也不敢肯定这一点。可是，这儿有一小根发带，看它的形状还有满是油污的这副德行，显然是某个喜欢梳长辫子的水手拿来扎头发用的。再看发带上的结，除了水手，也没别人会这么打，而且只有马耳他商船上的水手才会打这种结。我是在避雷针下边捡到它的，这肯定不是任何一个死者身上的东西。总之现在，我根据发带判定这个法国人是一条马耳他商船上的水手，就算这个推论并不正确，那我在报上登出的这则广告也无伤大雅。假如我真的错了，报社的那位朋友也仅仅会认为我是被某些表面现象给迷惑了，而绝不会耐着性子找我问东问西。但如果我是正确的，这无疑是个莫大的进展。这个法国人虽然没有杀人，但他却了解这起凶杀案的全过程，看到广告后，他自然会犹疑再三，考虑到底要不要来认领这只猩猩。他心里大概会这么琢磨：——'我是清白的，我是个穷光蛋，我的猩猩价值不菲——尤其是对于我这种境遇窘迫的人来说——我何苦要因为一些没必要的担忧而白白放弃这只猩猩呢？它近在咫尺，一伸手就能碰到。而且猩猩是在布伦公园里被发现的——跟案发现场隔得老远呢。再说，怎么会有人把这件惨案怀疑到一只凶残的野兽头上呢？就连警方都毫无对策——他们甚至连一点点线索都找不出来。就

they have failed to procure the slightest clew. Should they even trace the animal, it would be impossible to prove me cognizant of the murder, or to implicate me in guilt on account of that cognizance. Above all, I am known. The advertiser designates me as the possessor of the beast. I am not sure to what limit his knowledge may extend. Should I avoid claiming a property of so great value, which it is known that I possess, I will render the animal at least, liable to suspicion. It is not my policy to attract attention either to myself or to the beast. I will answer the advertisement, get the Ourang-Outang, and keep it close until this matter has blown over.' "

At this moment we heard a step upon the stairs.

"Be ready," said Dupin, "with your pistols, but neither use them nor show them until at a signal from myself."

The front door of the house had been left open, and the visiter had entered, without ringing, and advanced several steps upon the staircase. Now, however, he seemed to hesitate. Presently we heard him descending. Dupin was moving quickly to the door, when we again heard him coming up. He did not turn back a second time, but stepped up with decision, and rapped at the door of our chamber.

"Come in," said Dupin, in a cheerful and hearty tone.

算他们真的查到了这只畜生身上，同样无法证明我跟这件凶杀案有什么关系，更不会因为我了解案发过程就定我的罪啊。最重要的是，我现在已经暴露了，登广告的人明确指出我就是这只野兽的主人。真搞不清他对我的了解到底有多深。要是白白放弃如此价值连城的宝贝，而又是在人家已经知道它属于我的情况下，这岂不是反倒引起了人们对这只畜生的怀疑。我的策略是既不让自己有丝毫暴露，同时也不让那野兽引起任何人的注意。我要按照这则广告上说的做，去把猩猩带回来，然后严加看管，一直等到风声过去了再说。' "

就在杜宾说这话的时候，我们突然听到楼梯处传来一阵脚步声。

"注意了，"杜宾说，"把枪拿好，但一定要留神我的手势，千万别擅自开枪，也别露出什么马脚。"

公寓的大门开着，来人没有按铃，径直走了进来，随后上了几阶楼梯。然而就在这时候，他竟犹豫不决起来，不一会儿我们又听见他下楼的声音。这时杜宾急忙跑到门口，却听到他又再次开始上楼了。这回他没有再退缩，铁了心一步步走到楼上，然后敲了敲我们卧房的门。

"请进。"杜宾说道，他的语气听起来愉快而亲切。

A man entered. He was a sailor, evidently, – a tall, stout, and muscular-looking person, with a certain dare-devil expression of countenance, not altogether unprepossessing. His face, greatly sunburnt, was more than half hidden by whisker and *mustachio*. He had with him a huge oaken cudgel, but appeared to be otherwise unarmed. He bowed awkwardly, and bade us "good evening," in French accents, which, although somewhat Neufchatelish, were still sufficiently indicative of a Parisian origin.

"Sit down, my freind," said Dupin. "I suppose you have called about the Ourang-Outang. Upon my word, I almost envy you the possession of him; a remarkably fine, and no doubt a very valuable animal. How old do you suppose him to be?"

The sailor drew a Long breath, with the air of a man relieved of some intolerable burden, and then replied, in an assured tone:

"I have no way of telling – but he can't be more than four or five years old. Have you got him here?"

"Oh no, we had no conveniences for keeping him here. He is at a livery stable in the Rue Dubourg, just by. You can get him in the morning. Of course you are prepared to identify the property?"

一个男子走了进来，打眼一看就知道他是个水手——高大，结实，肌肉健硕，一副无所畏惧的样子，给人的印象还算不错。这位水手的大半个脸被络腮胡和八字胡遮盖着，脸上的皮肤被太阳晒得漆黑。只见他手里拎着一根硕大的橡木棍，除此之外身上倒也没什么别的武器了。笨拙地鞠了一躬之后，他用法语跟我们道了句"晚上好"，虽然有一点纳沙忒尔（法国北部城市）口音，但仍然能够听得出他原本是巴黎人。

"请坐吧，我的朋友，"杜宾说，"想必你是来认领猩猩的吧。实际上，你能拥有这样一只猩猩真是叫我妒忌得要死。它真是一只令人印象深刻的极品货色，肯定值不少钱。你觉得它有几岁了？"

这位水手深深地吸了一口气，看上去一副如释重负的样子，随后他有恃无恐地回答说：

"我也说不清楚——不过最多也就四五岁吧。它现在在您这儿吗？"

"哦它不在这儿，我们可没有条件把一只猩猩养在这儿。它在附近迪布尔街上的一间马厩里。明天一早就可以去把它领走。你确定你是打算来认领它的吗？"

"To be sure I am, sir."

"I shall be sorry to part with him," said Dupin.

"I don't mean that you should be at all this trouble for nothing, sir," said the man. "Couldn't expect it. Am very willing to pay a reward for the finding of the animal – that is to say, any thing in reason."

"Well," replied my friend, "that is all very fair, to be sure. Let me think! – what should I have? Oh! I will tell you. My reward shall be this. You shall give me all the information in your power about these murders in the Rue Morgue."

Dupin said the last words in a very low tone, and very quietly. Just as quietly, too, he walked toward the door, locked it and put the key in his pocket. He then drew a pistol from his bosom and placed it, without the least flurry, upon the table.

The sailor's face flushed up as if he were struggling with suffocation. He started to his feet and grasped his cudgel, but the next moment he fell back into his seat, trembling violently, and with the countenance of death itself. He spoke not a word. I pitied him from the bottom of my heart.

"My friend," said Dupin, in a kind tone, "you are alarming yourself unnecessarily – you are indeed. We mean you no harm whatever. I pledge you the honor of a gentleman, and of a Frenchman, that we

"我很确定,先生。"

"真遗憾,我要跟它道别了。"杜宾说。

"我不会让您白忙一场的,先生,"水手说,"尽管放心好了,我一定会看在您帮我把它找回来的分上重重酬谢您的——我的意思是说,只要是合理要求我都能答应。"

"好的,"杜宾回应道,"这样很公平。让我想想看!我该要点什么呢?哦对了!这么说吧,我的要求很简单,你只要把你知道的所有关于莫格街凶杀案的事情都告诉我就行了。"

说到最后几个字的时候,杜宾的语调很低沉,而且非常镇静。说完这些,他又镇静地走到门那边,把它锁好,然后将钥匙放进口袋,又从怀里掏出手枪,不慌不忙地把它放在桌子上。

这时候水手一下涨红了脸,像快要窒息般地挣扎不休。他一下子跳了起来,攥紧了手里的木棍,但很快又跌坐了下来,浑身剧烈抖动,脸上没有半点血色。他沉默了。看到这些,我不禁打心眼里觉得这位水手很是可怜。

"我的朋友,"杜宾客气地对他说,"没必要这么惊慌失措——你也真是的。我们对你并没有任何恶意。我以一个法国绅士的人格向你保证,我们绝对无意要害你。我很

intend you no injury. I perfectly well know that you are innocent of the atrocities in the Rue Morgue. It will not do, however, to deny that you are in some measure implicated in them. From what I have already said, you must know that I have had means of information about this matter – means of which you could never have dreamed. Now the thing stands thus. You have done nothing which you could have avoided – nothing, certainly, which renders you culpable. You were not even guilty of robbery, when you might have robbed with impunity. You have nothing to conceal. You have no reason for concealment. On the other hand, you are bound by every principle of honor to confess all you know. An innocent man is now imprisoned, charged with that crime of which you can point out the perpetrator."

The sailor had recovered his presence of mind, in a great measure, while Dupin uttered these words; but his original boldness of bearing was all gone.

"So help me God," said he, after a brief pause, "I *will* tell you all I know about this affair; – but I do not expect you to believe one half I say – I would be a fool indeed if I did. Still, I *am* innocent, and I will make a clean breast if I die for it."

What he stated was, in substance, this. He had lately made a voyage to the Indian Archipelago. A party, of which he formed

确定你在莫格街上发生的这起惨案中是清白的。但不能否认的是,你跟这起惨案多多少少有一些牵连。听了我刚才说的这些话,你想必已经知道了,关于这件案子,我自有一套办法去了解与之相关的情况——那绝对是一些你连做梦也想不到的办法。现在事实就摆在眼前。你没犯什么罪,确实没有任何过失,而且原本你甚至可以肆无忌惮地趁火打劫一番,可你连这个都没做。所以没什么好隐瞒的,朋友,也没什么必要去隐瞒。再说就算从道义上来讲,你也应该把你所知道的全部一五一十地说出来。因为眼下有个无辜的家伙背了这个黑锅,被关在牢里,而只有你才能指出到底谁才是这件凶杀案的真正凶手。"

水手听完杜宾的一番话,这才慢慢回过神来,只是刚才那股天不怕地不怕的神气劲儿消失不见了。

"上帝保佑,"他稍稍缓了口气说道,"我把所有我知道的全都告诉您吧——不过我估计您能相信这些话里的一半就很不错了——要是指望您照单全收,那我一定是疯了。不管怎么说,我是清白的,就算死我也要敞开心扉说个痛快。"

他的叙述内容大致如下:不久之前,他随船到了东印度群岛,跟一伙人在婆罗洲登陆后,便深入内

one, landed at Borneo, and passed into the interior on an excursion of pleasure. Himself and a companion had captured the Ourang-Outang. This companion dying, the animal fell into his own exclusive possession. After great trouble, occasioned by the intractable ferocity of his captive during the home voyage, he at length succeeded in lodging it safely at his own residence in Paris, where, not to attract toward himself the unpleasant curiosity of his neighbors, he kept it carefully secluded, until such time as it should recover from a wound in the foot, received from a splinter on board ship. His ultimate design was to sell it.

Returning home from some sailors' frolic the night, or rather in the morning of the murder, he found the beast occupying his own bed-room, into which it had broken from a closet adjoining, where it had been, as was thought, securely confined. Razor in hand, and fully lathered, it was sitting before a looking-glass, attempting the operation of shaving, in which it had no doubt previously watched its master through the key-hole of the closet. Terrified at the sight of so dangerous a weapon in the possession of an animal so ferocious, and so well able to use it, the man, for some moments, was at a loss what to do. He had been accustomed, however, to quiet the creature, even in its

部腹地观光旅游去了。在途中，他跟一个伙伴逮到了这只猩猩。后来那个伙伴死了，猩猩就落在了他一个人手里。在返航途中，猩猩野性难驯，害他吃了不少苦头，最后终于把它带了回来，安稳地关在他在巴黎的住处里，为了避免引起街坊邻居们令人厌烦的好奇心，水手小心翼翼地把猩猩藏好，打算养到它脚上被甲板碎片划破的伤口恢复了以后再说。其实他的最终目的就是想把猩猩卖掉。

有天晚上，或者不如直接说是凶杀案发生的那天清晨，他跟几个水手快活了一夜，回到家后，发现这只野兽正待在他的卧室里，它是从隔壁一间密室里逃出来的，水手原本还以为把它关在那里很保险呢。只见猩猩拿着一把剃刀，满脸肥皂沫，它正坐在镜子前面，尝试开始刮脸，毫无疑问，它准是从前透过密室的钥匙孔看到过主人的这一举动。水手不禁被眼前发生的一切吓坏了，如此凶猛的巨兽，手持一把危险的利器，同时还能娴熟地使用它，水手愣了一会儿，不知该如何是好。之前他一直用鞭子来压制这只猛兽，哪怕是在它野性大发的时候，这招同样派得上用场，所

fiercest moods, by the use of a whip, and to this he now resorted. Upon sight of it, the Ourang-Outang sprang at once through the door of the chamber, down the stairs, and thence, through a window, unfortunately open, into the street.

The Frenchman followed in despair; the ape, razor still in hand, occasionally stopping to look back and gesticulate at its pursuer, until the latter had nearly come up with it. It then again made off. In this manner the chase continued for a Long time. The streets were profoundly quiet, as it was nearly three o'clock in the morning. In passing down an alley in the rear of the Rue Morgue, the fugitive's attention was arrested by a light gleaming from the open window of Madame L'Espanaye's chamber, in the fourth story of her house. Rushing to the building, it perceived the lightning rod, clambered up with inconceivable agility, grasped the shutter, which was thrown fully back against the wall, and, by its means, swung itself directly upon the headboard of the bed. The whole feat did not occupy a minute. The shutter was kicked open again by the Ourang-Outang as it entered the room.

The sailor, in the meantime, was both rejoiced and perplexed. He had strong hopes of now recapturing the brute, as it could scarcely escape from the trap into which it had ventured, except by the rod,

以这回他又拿起了鞭子。猩猩一见鞭子，立刻从卧室门口跳了出去，飞奔下楼，不巧的是正好有扇窗户没关，它便顺着那里跳了出去，逃窜到街上去了。

这位法国水手极度绝望地追了出去，再看那只猩猩，手里仍然握着剃刀，还不时停下脚步回头张望，对着在后面穷追不舍的主人做出各种嘲弄的姿势，等到水手眼看快要赶上来的时候，它便又开始继续逃跑。这场追逐大战就这样持续了好一阵子。这时候大概是清晨3点钟，街道上一片寂静。就在逃进莫格街后面一条小巷里的时候，猩猩发现列士巴奈太太家4楼卧房那扇开着的窗户里有灯光映出来，不由得对此产生了兴趣。于是它跑向那幢房子，一眼瞅见了那根避雷针，便依靠异常敏捷的身手爬了上去，然后一把抓住了那扇被打开并转到了靠墙位置的百叶窗，再顺着铁网格纵身一跃，最后直接跳到了床头上。这一整套把戏总共用了不到一分钟的时间就演完了。猩猩闯进房间里的时候，顺势踢开了那扇百叶窗。

这时候，水手感觉又欣喜又不安。欣喜的是，这下他看到了把这只野兽重新抓回来的希望，因为它贸然地自投罗网，显然很难从房里面脱身，除非顺着避雷针原路返

where it might be intercepted as it came down. On the other hand, there was much cause for anxiety as to what it might do in the house. This latter reflection urged the man still to follow the fugitive. A lightning rod is ascended without difficulty, especially by a sailor; but, when he had arrived as high as the window, which lay far to his left, his career was stopped; the most that he could accomplish was to reach over so as to obtain a glimpse of the interior of the room. At this glimpse he nearly fell from his hold through excess of horror. Now it was that those hideous shrieks arose upon the night, which had startled from slumber the inmates of the Rue Morgue. Madame L'Espanaye and her daughter, habited in their night clothes, had apparently been occupied in arranging some papers in the iron chest already mentioned, which had been wheeled into the middle of the room. It was open, and its contents lay beside it on the floor. The victims must have been sitting with their backs toward the window; and, from the time elapsing between the ingress of the beast and the screams, it seems probable that it was not immediately perceived. The flapping-to of the shutter would naturally have been attributed to the wind.

As the sailor looked in, the gigantic animal had seized Madame L'Espanaye by the hair, (which was loose, as she had been

回，而水手只需在此处守株待兔，到时候就可以逮它个正着。然而另一方面让水手不安的是，这畜生指不定会在屋内闯出什么祸来。想到这里，他便立刻继续追了上去。爬上避雷针倒不算一件难事，尤其对一个水手而言更是小菜一碟，但是当他爬到跟窗口一样高的地方，发现窗户离他还有一大截距离，所以只好就此作罢，此时他能做的就是尽量把头探出去，以便能够瞥一眼屋内的情况。这一眼看过去不要紧，差点没把他吓昏过去，险些失手摔下去。就在这个时候，凄惨的呼喊声打破了夜晚的寂静，同时也惊醒了莫格街居民们的美梦。当时列士巴奈太太母女俩正身着睡衣，看样子像是正在整理上文中所说的那个铁匣里的信函。这只铁匣原本就已经被挪到了房间中央，匣子敞开着，里面的东西散落一地。两个被害人当时应该都是背对着窗口坐着，因为根据那只野兽闯进房间，到喊声响起的这段时间间隔来看，她们很可能一开始并没有发现它，准是误以为百叶窗发出的啪啪声是刮风引起的。

水手朝卧房里看去，只见这只巨兽已经揪住了列士巴奈太太的头发（她刚刚梳理过的头发全都披散

combing it,) and was flourishing the razor about her face, in imitation of the motions of a barber. The daughter lay prostrate and motionless; she had swooned. The screams and struggles of the old lady (during which the hair was torn from her head) had the effect of changing the probably pacific purposes of the Ourang-Outang into those of wrath. With one determined sweep of its muscular arm it nearly severed her head from her body. The sight of blood inflamed its anger into phrenzy. Gnashing its teeth, and flashing fire from its eyes, it flew upon the body of the girl, and imbedded its fearful talons in her throat, retaining its grasp until she expired. Its wandering and wild glances fell at this moment upon the head of the bed, over which the face of its master, rigid with horror, was just discernible. The fury of the beast, who no doubt bore still in mind the dreaded whip, was instantly converted into fear. Conscious of having deserved punishment, it seemed desirous of concealing its bloody deeds, and skipped about the chamber in an agony of nervous agitation; throwing down and breaking the furniture as it moved, and dragging the bed from the bedstead. In conclusion, it seized first the corpse of the daughter, and thrust it up the chimney, as it was found; then that of the old lady, which it immediately hurled through the window headLong.

着），然后开始模仿理发师的样子，挥舞剃刀在她脸上一通乱刮。在一旁的女儿已经倒在地上，她一动不动，早就已经吓晕过去了。这时，老太太的头发被猩猩揪了下来，她一边大喊大叫，一边使劲挣扎，这一举动显然激怒了本来没什么恶意的猩猩，惹得它大发雷霆。只见猩猩大臂猛然一挥，险些没把老太太的脑袋敲下来。见了血的猩猩变得更加狂暴，它咬牙切齿，两眼透出杀气，又扑到旁边的姑娘身上，伸出吓人的爪子，一把掐住她的脖子，一直到她断了气才松开。然后它慌乱地四处张望，正巧越过床头瞅见了主人脸上那副六神无主的表情，心里准是记起了被鞭子毒打一顿的滋味，立刻没了火气，反倒开始害怕起来。猩猩心里明白这次是难逃一劫了，所以一心想要掩饰自己的残酷暴行，惴惴不安地在卧房里蹦来蹦去，不管看到什么家具，要么掀翻，要么砸烂，还把床垫扯了下来。到最后，它干脆抓起小姐，一把塞进了事后大伙发现尸体的那个烟囱里，然后又提起老太太的尸体，撒到了窗外，老太太就这么头朝下栽了出去。

As the ape approached the casement with its mutilated burden, the sailor shrank aghast to the rod, and, rather gliding than clambering down it, hurried at once home – dreading the consequences of the butchery, and gladly abandoning, in his terror, all solicitude about the fate of the Ourang-Outang. The words heard by the party upon the staircase were the Frenchman's exclamations of horror and affright, commingled with the fiendish jabberings of the brute.

I have scarcely anything to add. The Ourang-Outang must have escaped from the chamber, by the rod, just before the break of the door. It must have closed the window as it passed through it. It was subsequently caught by the owner himself, who obtained for it a very large sum at the *Jardin des Plantes*. Le Don was instantly released, upon our narration of the circumstances (with some comments from Dupin) at the *bureau* of the Prefect of Police. This functionary, however well disposed to my friend, could not altogether conceal his chagrin at the turn which affairs had taken, and was fain to indulge in a sarcasm or two, about the propriety of every person minding his own business.

"Let him talk," said Dupin, who had not thought it necessary to reply. "Let him discourse; it will ease his conscience, I am satisfied with having

当猩猩拖着血肉模糊的尸首走向窗口的时候，水手已经吓得退回到了避雷针那边，他连爬的力气都没有了，只好顺着避雷针溜下去，慌慌张张地跑回了家——因为害怕自己被牵连进这件惨案中，所以在万分惊恐之下，他宁愿自己跟这只猩猩从此以后再无瓜葛。大伙当时在楼梯上听见的话，就是这个法国人处于极度恐惧时的失声叫喊，当然这里面还夹杂着那只野兽鬼哭狼嚎一般的怪叫声。

除此之外，我没什么该补充的了。猩猩肯定是在大伙破门而入之前，顺着避雷针逃出卧房的，而且在跳窗的时候，把窗户重新合上了。后来，猩猩被主人亲自逮到，水手把它卖给了植物园，从中大捞了一笔。我们到警察局长的办公室里如实汇报了所有情况，当然杜宾还不忘在其中穿插上一些个人见解，由此，勒·本被当场释放了。局长大人尽管对我的朋友有几分欣赏，可是眼看悬案被别人破了，他实在无法抑制心中的懊恼，只好冷嘲热讽地嘟囔了几句，算是他的自我安慰吧，说什么大家只要做好自己该做的就好了，没必要多管闲事。

"让他说去吧，"杜宾说道，他觉得没必要跟局长一般见识，"只有这么高谈阔论一番，他良心上才过得去。能在他的主场把他打败，

defeated him in his own castle. Nevertheless, that he failed in the solution of this mystery, is by no means that matter for wonder which he supposes it; for, in truth, our friend the Prefect is somewhat too cunning to be profound. In his wisdom is no stamen. It is all head and no body, like the pictures of the Goddess Laverna, – or, at best, all head and shoulders, like a codfish. But he is a good creature after all. I like him especially for one master stroke of cant, by which he has attained his reputation for ingenuity. I mean the way he has 'de nier ce qui est, et d'expliquer ce qui n'est pas'."

我已经满足了。不过话说回来，警方之所以破不了这件疑案，是因为他们完全不该把这件案子当成是一件离奇的怪事，因为坦白讲，我们这位局长朋友有时过于依赖小聪明，以至于无法深入地看问题。他虽足智多谋，但却没有掌握足以制胜的法宝。就好比只有头却少了身体，像拉浮娜女神的雕塑一样——或者顶多是有头和肩膀，好像一条鳕鱼。但不管怎么说，他仍旧满有一套的。我尤其欣赏他那副装腔作势的嘴脸，也正是凭借这个，他博得了一个神机妙算的好名声。我的意思是说，他只会'睁眼说瞎话，把白的硬说成是黑的'。"

13. The Mystery of Marie Roget

十三. 玛丽·罗杰特谜案

THERE are few persons, even among the calmest thinkers, who have not occasionally been startled into a vague yet thrilling half-credence in the supernatural, by coincidences of so seemingly marvellous a character that, as mere coincidences, the intellect has been unable to receive them. Such sentiments – for the half-credences of which I speak have never the full force of thought – such sentiments are seldom thoroughly stifled unless by reference to the doctrine of chance, or, as it is technically termed, the Calculus of Probabilities. Now this Calculus is, in its essence, purely mathematical; and thus we have the anomaly of the most rigidly exact in science applied to the shadow and spirituality of the most intangible in speculation.

The extraordinary details which I am now called upon to make public, will be found to form, as regards sequence of time, the primary branch of a series of scarcely intelligible coincidences, whose secondary or concluding branch will be recognized by all readers in the late murder of Mary *Cecila* Rogers, at New York.

When, in an article entitled "The

凡是巧合，就都会有表面上看来不可思议的特质。所以有头脑的人都不太相信存在纯粹的巧合。几乎没有人——甚至在那些头脑最冷静的思考者当中——也不会偶尔地被某些巧合所震慑住，从而对超自然的现象平添了一份半信半疑的情绪，这种半截子的信任感虽说不清道不明但是却使人异常兴奋。这些情绪——就是我所提到的半信半疑的情绪，绝对不会给人带来思考的全部力量——这些情绪很少会被彻头彻尾地抑制住，除非是参考了"偶然性原理"，学术上它还被称作"概率演算"。现在的这种演算，从本质上来讲，纯粹是数学上的。因此我们就套用科学研究中最严格要求精准的特例，去解决思考当中最难以捉摸的阴暗处和精神性。

我应大家要求，将这些异乎寻常的故事详情公之于众，故事的叙述将按照时间顺序，主干是一连串让人无法理解的巧合，而故事所展开的细枝或末节，读者们可以从最近发生在纽约的"玛丽·塞西莉亚·罗杰斯凶杀案"中了解到。

大约一年前，我曾在一篇名为

Murders in the Rue Morgue," I endeavored, about a year ago, to depict some very remarkable features in the mental character of my friend, the Chevalier C. Auguste Dupin, it did not occur to me that I should ever resume the subject. This depicting of character constituted my design; and this design was thoroughly fulfilled in the wild train of circumstances brought to instance Dupin's idiosyncrasy. I might have adduced other examples, but I should have proven no more. Late events, however, in their surprising development, have startled me into some farther details, which will carry with them the air of extorted confession. Hearing what I have lately heard, it would be indeed strange should I remain silent in regard to what I both heard and saw so Long ago.

Upon the winding up of the tragedy involved in the deaths of Madame L'Espanaye and her daughter, the Chevalier dismissed the affair at once from his attention, and relapsed into his old habits of moody reverie. Prone, at all times, to abstraction, I readily fell in with his humor; and, continuing to occupy our chambers in the Faubourg Saint Germain, we gave the Future to the winds, and slumbered tranquilly in the Present, weaving the dull world around us into dreams.

《莫格街凶杀案》的文章里竭力描述过我的朋友 C·奥古斯特·杜宾爵士精神品格中的某些非常值得注意的特征，当时我没想到我将会再续这个话题。对他性格的刻画构成了我文章的思路，我在贯彻这番思路时没按常规出牌，这是为了能够举例说明杜宾的古怪行为。我本可以举出其他的一些例子，但是我没法再去验证更多例子的真实性了。然而最近的事件，其发生发展让人感到十分不可思议，某些更深层次的情节使我大为震惊，我不得不再次将其付诸纸笔。知道了我最近听说的这些事情后，如果我仍对以前的耳闻目睹保持沉默，那样做反倒真的是很古怪了。

在牵扯了列士巴奈太太和她女儿两桩人命的惨案告破后，杜宾爵士即刻将这起案件抛诸脑后，又恢复了他那随兴而起的沉思冥想的老习惯。每时每刻，他都十分容易分神，我倒也很欣然接受他的怪脾气，并且，我们仍旧居住在我们圣日耳曼区的房子里，我们把"未来"寄托在风中，安静地睡在"当下"，将身边的乏味世界编织成美梦。

But these dreams were not altogether uninterrupted. It may readily be supposed that the part played by my friend, in the drama at the Rue Morgue, had not failed of its impression upon the fancies of the Parisian police. With its emissaries, the name of Dupin had grown into a household word. The simple character of those inductions by which he had disentangled the mystery never having been explained even to the Prefect, or to any other individual than myself, of course it is not surprising that the affair was regarded as little less than miraculous, or that the Chevalier's analytical abilities acquired for him the credit of intuition. His frankness would have led him to disabuse every inquirer of such prejudice; but his indolent humor forbade all farther agitation of a topic whose interest to himself had Long ceased. It thus happened that he found himself the cynosure of the policial eyes; and the cases were not few in which attempt was made to engage his services at the Prefecture. One of the most remarkable instances was that of the murder of a young girl named Marie Rogêt.

This event occurred about two years after the atrocity in the Rue Morgue. Marie, whose Christian and family name will at once arrest attention from their resemblance to those of the unfortunate "cigar- girl," was the only daughter of the

但是，这些美梦并非完全没被打断过。我们可以很容易地推断出我朋友在"莫格街凶杀案"那出戏中扮演的角色，其精彩的表现绝对是超乎巴黎警方想象的。此事一经传播，杜宾这个名字就变得家喻户晓了。他只用了一些简单的归纳就解开了这桩谜案，但是他的归纳过程除了对我解释过以外，从来没对包括警察局长在内的任何人说明过。这样一来也难怪人们会觉得此事简直不亚于奇迹，或者说，杜宾爵士的分析能力没为它本身赢得声誉，却为他的直觉力赢得了声誉。他的坦率本可以让他对每一个有此偏见的询问之人解释清楚他们对这件事情的疑惑。但如果一个话题对他的吸引力已经失去很久了，他懒散的性格是不会允许他对这个话题的所有更进一步的煽动再次感兴趣的。因此就会发生这样的情况：他发现自己成了警方眼中引人注目的北极星，并且，试图请他在巴黎警方管辖区内参与破案的情况并不少见。其中最受人瞩目的一起，便是一个名叫玛丽•罗杰特的年轻女孩被杀的案子。

这件事情发生在莫格街那起暴行两年后。上到与玛丽家的家庭情况相当的人家，下到那些不幸的"卖雪茄的小女孩"，她作为基督徒的人道主义精神以及她的家族姓氏都能立即吸引起他们对她的关注，她还

widow Estelle Rogêt. The father had died during the child's infancy, and from the period of his death, until within eighteen months before the assassination which forms the subject of our narrative, the mother and daughter had dwelt together in the Rue Pavée Saint Andrée; Madame there keeping a pension, assisted by Marie. Affairs went on thus until the latter had attained her twenty-second year, when her great beauty attracted the notice of a perfumer, who occupied one of the shops in the basement of the Palais Royal, and whose custom lay chiefly among the desperate adventurers infesting that neighborhood. Monsieur Le Blanc was not unaware of the advantages to be derived from the attendance of the fair Marie in his perfumery; and his liberal proposals were accepted eagerly by the girl, although with somewhat more of hesitation by Madame.

The anticipations of the shopkeeper were realized, and his rooms soon became notorious through the charms of the sprightly *grisette*. She had been in his employ about a year, when her admirers were thrown into confusion by her sudden disappearance from the shop. Monsieur Le Blanc was unable to account for her absence, and Madame Rogêt was distracted with anxiety and terror. The public papers immediately took up the theme, and the police were upon the point of making

是寡妇爱丝特尔·罗杰特的独生女。她幼年丧父，从她父亲去世到暗杀发生前18个月里——我们故事的主题便是这次暗杀——母女俩一直共同居住在圣安德里的铺石街，罗杰特太太经营着一家膳宿公寓，玛丽给她帮忙。就这样过了很多年，直到玛丽22岁，她惊人的美貌引起了一个名叫莱·布兰克的香水商的注意，莱·布兰克在皇宫街的底座拥有一家店铺，他的顾客主要是经常出没于那片地区的一群不顾一切的投机商。莱·布兰克先生并不是没有意识到让美丽的玛丽照料他的香水店会给他带来的经济利益。他可观的聘金提议被姑娘急切地接受了，尽管罗杰特太太更多地是表现出几分犹豫之情。

香水店老板的预料果然变成了现实，这位活泼可爱的姑娘魅力四射，他的店铺也因此名声大噪。她被香水店老板雇用了大约一年的时间，直到有一天她突然从店里失踪了，这让她的那些仰慕者们慌了手脚。莱·布兰克先生说不清楚她去了哪里，罗杰特太太也因为焦急和害怕而被搞得六神无主。各大公众报纸立即将此事作为新闻八卦的主题，而警方也就此事展开了彻底的调查。可就在一个风和日丽的早上，

serious investigations, when, one fine morning, after the lapse of a week, Marie, in good health, but with a somewhat saddened air, made her re-appearance at her usual counter in the perfumery. All inquiry, except that of a private character, was of course immediately hushed. Monsieur Le Blanc professed total ignorance, as before. Marie, with Madame, replied to all questions, that the last week had been spent at the house of a relation in the country. Thus the affair died away, and was generally forgotten; for the girl, ostensibly to relieve herself from the impertinence of curiosity, soon bade a final adieu to the perfumer, and sought the shelter of her mother's residence in the Rue Pavée Saint Andrée.

It was about five months after this return home, that her friends were alarmed by her sudden disappearance for the second time. Three days elapsed, and nothing was heard of her. On the fourth her corpse was found floating in the Seine, near the shore which is opposite the Quartier of the Rue Saint Andree, and at a point not very far distant from the secluded neighborhood of the Barrière du Roule.

The atrocity of this murder, (for it was at once evident that murder had been committed,) the youth and beauty of the victim, and, above all, her previous notoriety, conspired to produce intense

失踪了一个星期的玛丽又重新出现在香水店她往常所站的柜台前，她的身体健康无恙，只是面容稍显哀伤。所有的询问，只要是来自那些非亲非故的人，理所当然地，都被回以"嘘"声并要求保持安静。莱·布兰克先生公开声明就像以前对此事一无所知。而玛丽以及罗杰特太太对所有问题的一致答复都是，上个星期她是在乡下的亲戚家度过的。于是事态平息了下来，普遍地被人们所遗忘。至于这个女孩本人，貌似是为了使自己摆脱大家出于好奇而产生的种种无礼举动，不久便向香水商致以了最后的道别，然后回到她母亲在圣安德里铺石街那里的住处寻求庇护了。

玛丽回家以后大约过了 5 个月，她的朋友们再次惊慌起来，因为她第二次突然地消失了。3 天过去了，她仍旧杳无音信。直到第四天，她的尸体被人发现漂浮在塞纳河上，就在圣安德里街所在的街区对面的河岸附近。浮尸地点与儒尔门周围那片僻静的地区离得不是很远。

这起谋杀案的残暴性质（显而易见，已然发生的是起谋杀案），受害者的年轻美貌，并且，尤其是她生前风流不羁的名声，这几方面的因素拼凑起来，激起了敏感的巴黎

excitement in the minds of the sensitive Parisians. I can call to mind no similar occurrence producing so general and so intense an effect. For several weeks, in the discussion of this one absorbing theme, even the momentous political topics of the day were forgotten. The Prefect made unusual exertions; and the powers of the whole Parisian police were, of course, tasked to the utmost extent.

Upon the first discovery of the corpse, it was not supposed that the murderer would be able to elude, for more than a very brief period, the inquisition which was immediately set on foot. It was not until the expiration of a week that it was deemed necessary to offer a reward; and even then this reward was limited to a thousand francs. In the mean time the investigation proceeded with vigor, if not always with judgment, and numerous individuals were examined to no purpose; while, owing to the continual absence of all clue to the mystery, the popular excitement greatly increased. At the end of the tenth day it was thought advisable to double the sum originally proposed; and, at length, the second week having elapsed without leading to any discoveries, and the prejudice which always exists in Paris against the Police having given vent to itself in several serious émeutes, the Prefect took it upon himself to offer the

人心中强烈的兴趣。我还真想不出有哪件类似的事情引起过如此广泛而又热烈的反响。连续几个星期，人们一直都在谈论着这个吸引人的话题，就连当时的重大政治话题都被忘在了一边。警察局长对此案异常卖力，而巴黎的全部警力，当然了，也被最大限度地动用以来完成任务。

最初发现尸体时，我们可以假设罪犯不可能逃远，因为这个时间段不是很长，所以警方立即着手展开调查。直到过去了一个星期，警方才认为有必要提供一笔赏金。然而尽管如此，赏金也仅限为1000法郎。与此同时，调查仍是靠着警官们充沛的精力推动，而不总是靠着审慎的洞察力。无数人被盘问过，结果却徒劳无益。由于这宗谜案的种种线索一直迟迟没有浮出水面，公众兴奋的心情反而有增无减，愈演愈烈了。在第十天要结束的时候，有人认为将原先定下的赏金加倍，这样才算是明智的做法。然而，最后，两个星期过去了，警方还是一无所获。巴黎民众长期对警方存有成见，这种常驻于心的成见经此一激终于发泄出来了——巴黎民众组织了几起性质严重的聚众闹事。警察局长把此事归咎于自己，毅然决定将提供总额达20,000法郎的赏金，给"可为凶手定罪"的人，或

sum of twenty thousand francs "for the conviction of the assassin," or, if more than one should prove to have been implicated, "for the conviction of any one of the assassins." In the proclamation setting forth this reward, a full pardon was promised to any accomplice who should come forward in evidence against his fellow; and to the whole was appended, wherever it appeared, the private placard of a committee of citizens, offering ten thousand francs, in addition to the amount proposed by the Prefecture. The entire reward thus stood at no less than thirty thousand francs, which will be regarded as an extraordinary sum when we consider the humble condition of the girl, and the great frequency, in large cities, of such atrocities as the one described.

No one doubted now that the mystery of this murder would be immediately brought to light. But although, in one or two instances, arrests were made which promised elucidation, yet nothing was elicited which could implicate the parties suspected; and they were discharged forthwith. Strange as it may appear, the third week from the discovery of the body had passed, and passed without any light being thrown upon the subject, before even a rumor of the events which had so agitated the public mind, reached the ears of Dupin and myself. Engaged in researches which

者，如果有证据可以证明被牵扯进本案的凶手不止一人，那么赏金就是给"可为其中任何一名凶手定罪"的人。在宣布了这笔奖金的公告中，还许诺任何同谋犯如果肯自愿作证检举他的同伙，对检举者的所有处罚都将予以免除。此篇公告张贴的每一处地方，除了正文以外，还附有一个市民委员会的非官方告示，说会提供 10,000 法郎加在警方提供的那笔赏金上。这样一来，全部的赏金便有 30,000 法郎之多。当我们考虑到那个女孩卑微的身份以及城里谋杀案颇为频繁的发生次数，我们就会认为这样的悬赏金额算是一笔很惊人的数目了。

现在，没人会怀疑这起谋杀案的谜底将能马上见天日了。但是尽管大家信心百倍，也确实有过那么一两次，抓捕行动看起来足以保证能解释清案情的始末，然而最终却没找到任何证据能够把这些有嫌疑的当事人牵涉进此案，所以他们都被即刻释放了。虽然看起来有些不可思议，自尸体发现后的第三个星期都已经过去了，此谜题的真相却仍未见得半点天日，甚至连有关这宗谋杀案的谣言都已经如此地搅得公众惶惶不安了——在这些谣言传到我和杜宾耳朵里之前，事情竟然

absorbed our whole attention, it had been nearly a month since either of us had gone abroad, or received a visiter, or more than glanced at the leading political articles in one of the daily papers. The first intelligence of the murder was brought us by G-, in person. He called upon us early in the afternoon of the thirteenth of July, 18–, and remained with us until late in the night. He had been piqued by the failure of all his endeavors to ferret out the assassins. His reputation – so he said with a peculiarly Parisian air – was at stake. Even his honor was concerned. The eyes of the public were upon him; and there was really no sacrifice which he would not be willing to make for the development of the mystery. He concluded a somewhat droll speech with a compliment upon what he was pleased to term the tact of Dupin, and made him a direct, and certainly a liberal proposition, the precise nature of which I do not feel myself at liberty to disclose, but which has no bearing upon the proper subject of my narrative.

The compliment my friend rebutted as best he could, but the proposition he accepted at once, although its advantages were altogether provisional. This point being settled, the Prefect broke forth at once into explanations of his own views, interspersing them with long comments upon the evidence; of which latter we were

已经发生 3 个星期了。当时我们一直致力于一些学术研究，这吸引了我们全部的注意力，差不多有一个月的时间，我们俩谁都没怎么到室外，要么就是不接待来访者，要么顶多就是匆匆瞥一眼随便哪份日报的头版政治新闻。最初的关于凶案的消息是从警察局长葛××本人那里得知的。18××年，7 月 13 日下午的早些时候，他登门造访并一直留到深夜。他说他为了查出凶犯使出了浑身解数，但终告失败，因此自尊心十分受挫。他的声誉——他说这话时，带着巴黎人特有的傲慢腔调——正危如累卵。此事甚至关系到他作为局长的尊严。公众的目光全部聚焦在他身上，只要能推动这宗谜案的侦破没什么牺牲是他不愿做的。他用了几句恭维话来结束他的另一番有些逗趣的演说，他兴高采烈地称赞了杜宾的机智，还向杜宾提了一条非常直接并且绝对是思想非常开放的建议，建议的详细内容我以为是不便透露的，好在此事与我叙述的正题并无关联。

我的朋友竭力婉拒了局长的恭维，但那条建议他却立马接受了，尽管这条建议对杜宾的好处完全是临时性的。当这点建议得到采纳时，局长立即言归正传，开始滔滔不绝地说明他自己的看法，其间缀以冗长的、对证据的评论，而这些证据我们都还没掌握到。他说了不少，

not yet in possession. He discoursed much, and beyond doubt, learnedly; while I hazarded an occasional suggestion as the night wore drowsily away. Dupin, sitting steadily in his accustomed arm-chair, was the embodiment of respectful attention. He wore spectacles, during the whole interview; and an occasional signal glance beneath their green glasses, sufficed to convince me that he slept not the less soundly, because silently, throughout the seven or eight leaden-footed hours which immediately preceded the departure of the Prefect.

In the morning, I procured, at the Prefecture, a full report of all the evidence elicited, and, at the various newspaper offices, a copy of every paper in which, from first to last, had been published any decisive information in regard to this sad affair. Freed from all that was positively disproved, this mass of information stood thus:

Marie Rogêt left the residence of her mother, in the Rue Pavée St. Andrée, about nine o'clock in the morning of Sunday June the twenty-second, 18–. In going out, she gave notice to a Monsieur Jacques St. Eustache, and to him only, of her intent intention to spend the day with an aunt who resided in the Rue des Drômes. The Rue des Drômeses is a short and narrow but populous thoroughfare, not far from the

而且毫无疑问，他的话很有见地。我时不时斗胆向他提出些问题，夜晚的时光就这样消磨过去了，让人昏昏欲睡。而杜宾呢，则稳健地坐在他常坐的扶手椅上，一直表现出一副洗耳恭听的样子。他在整场谈话中都戴着眼镜，那对绿色镜片下面，他的眼中偶尔闪烁出的光芒就像一种告知信号，足以使我确信他睡得不是一般的香，因为他一直安静地睡着，这七八个小时就在他的睡梦中迈着沉重的脚步，慢吞吞地过去了。局长结束了他七八个小时的长篇大论紧接着便起身告辞了。

第二天早上，我去警察局搞到他们查得的全部证据的完整记录，然后，又去了各家报社，那里的每份报纸，从头到尾只要刊载过任何有关这宗惨案的重要信息，我都拿了一份它的副本。剔掉所有那些一看就知道是虚假的消息后，这批资料的内容如下：

18××年6月22日，星期日，上午9点钟左右，玛丽·罗杰特离开了在圣安德里铺石街的她母亲的住所。出门的时候，她告诉一位名叫雅克·圣·尤斯塔希的先生，而且只告诉了他一个人，说她要到德罗姆街的姑妈家玩一天。德罗姆街是一条又短又窄，但却人口稠密的大街，离塞纳河的河岸不远，从罗杰特太太的膳宿公寓到那里，最短的

banks of the river, and at a distance of some two miles, in the most direct course possible, from the pension of Madame Rogêt. St. Eustache was the accepted suitor of Marie, and lodged, as well as took his meals, at the pension. He was to have gone for his betrothed at dusk, and to have escorted her home. In the afternoon, however, it came on to rain heavily; and, supposing that she would remain all night at her aunt's, (as she had done under similar circumstances before,) he did not think it necessary to keep his promise. As night drew on, Madame Rogêt (who was an infirm old lady, seventy years of age,) was heard to express a fear "that she should never see Marie again;" but this observation attracted little attention at the time.

On Monday, it was ascertained that the girl had not been to the Rue des Drômes; and when the day elapsed without tidings of her, a tardy search was instituted at several points in the city, and its environs. It was not, however until the fourth day from the period of disappearance that any thing satisfactory was ascertained respecting her. On this day, (Wednesday, the twenty-fifth of June,) a Monsieur Beauvais, who, with a friend, had been making inquiries for Marie near the Barrière du Roule, on the shore of the Seine which is opposite the Rue Pavée St.

可能路线大约有两英里远。圣·尤斯塔希是玛丽芳心相许的求婚者，寄宿在罗杰特太太的膳宿公寓，膳食同样也在那里。他本来应该在傍晚去接他的未婚妻，然后护送她回家。但是就在那天下午，天降大雨，所以，圣·尤斯塔希先生假定玛丽会在她姑妈家留宿（一如她以往遇到类似情形时那样），他觉得没必要再如约去接她。夜晚临近的时候，有人听到罗杰特太太（一名体弱多病的老妪，70岁）焦虑不安地说她恐怕再也无法见到玛丽了，不过她的这句话在当时并没有引起多少人注意。

星期一，人们查明这个女孩根本不曾到过德罗姆街。然后，一整天过去了，她还是杳无音信，一次拖拖拉拉的搜寻才在这所城市市区的几处地点以及郊区展开。不管怎样，直到她失踪的第四天才有了点儿关于她的比较靠谱的消息。就在那天（星期三，6月25日），一位叫博韦的先生和他的一个朋友正在儒尔门附近询问玛丽的下落，圆木栅门就在正对着圣安德里铺石街的塞纳河的河岸上，他们被告知一具尸体刚刚被几个渔夫拖到岸边，他们之前发现这具尸体浮在塞纳河

Andrée, was informed that a corpse had just been towed ashore by some fishermen, who had found it floating in the river. Upon seeing the body, Beauvais, after some hesitation, identified it as that of the perfumery-girl. His friend recognized it more promptly.

The face was suffused with dark blood, some of which issued from the mouth. No foam was seen, as in the case of the merely drowned. There was no discoloration in the cellular tissue. About the throat were bruises and impressions of fingers. The arms were bent over on the chest and were rigid. The right hand was clenched; the left partially open. On the left wrist were two circular excoriations, apparently the effect of ropes, or of a rope in more than one volution. A part of the right wrist, also, was much chafed, as well as the back throughout its extent, but more especially at the shoulder-blades. In bringing the body to the shore the fishermen had attached to it a rope; but none of the excoriations had been effected by this. The flesh of the neck was much swollen. There were no cuts apparent, or bruises which appeared the effect of blows. A piece of lace was found tied so tightly around the neck as to be hidden from sight; it was completely buried in the flesh, and was fasted by a knot which lay just under the left ear. This alone would have sufficed to produce

上。看过尸体以后，博韦先生很是迟疑了一阵儿才敢确认那具尸体的身份就是那个"香水西施"。而他的朋友一眼就看出来了。

死者面部发黑，满脸污血，有些污血是从嘴里流出来的。死者嘴边看不到泡沫，而人只有在溺死的情况下才口吐白沫。细胞组织并没有变色。喉咙处有淤伤以及手指的指印。两只手臂弯曲放在胸前，已经僵硬了。右手紧紧攥着拳头，左手半张着。左手的手腕有两圈擦伤，很明显是几条绳子绑在手腕上留下的绳印儿，或者是一条绳子在手腕上绕了不止一圈造成的。右手手腕的部分皮肤也被蹭破得很严重，同样，背部也满是严重的擦伤，但是肩胛骨的位置伤势尤为严重。尸体在被带往岸边的过程中是被渔夫们用一条绳子绑着的，但其实尸身上没有一处擦伤是这次捆绑导致的。死者脖子上的肉高高肿起。表面上没有任何切口或者任何由于殴打而导致的淤伤。一条蕾丝带子缠绕在她的脖子上，紧紧地系着，以至于几乎看不到。蕾丝带子完全嵌入肉里，而且被系了一个死扣，位置就处在左耳的正下方。光是这条带子就足以置人于死地了。法医的证词明确提到过死者生前是否受到过性

death. The medical testimony spoke confidently of the virtuous character of the deceased. She had been subjected, it said, to brutal violence. The corpse was in such condition when found, that there could have been no difficulty in its recognition by friends.

The dress was much torn and otherwise disordered. In the outer garment, a slip, about a foot wide, had been torn upward from the bottom hem to the waist, but not torn off. It was wound three times around the waist, and secured by a sort of hitch in the back. The dress immediately beneath the frock was of fine muslin; and from this a slip eighteen inches wide had been torn entirely out – torn very evenly and with great care. It was found around her neck, fitting loosely, and secured with a hard knot. Over this muslin slip and the slip of lace, the strings of a bonnet were attached; the bonnet being appended. The knot by which the strings of the bonnet were fastened, was not a lady's, but a slip or sailor's knot.

After the recognition of the corpse, it was not, as usual, taken to the Morgue, (this formality being superfluous,) but hastily interred not far front the spot at which it was brought ashore. Through the exertions of Beauvais, the matter was industriously hushed up, as far as possible; and several days had elapsed before any

侵犯。证词显示，她曾遭受过野蛮的暴力奸污。要不是尸体被发现时处于如此这般糟糕的状况，死者的亲友确认出死者身份本不该有任何困难的。

裙子被撕得很烂，一团乱，却乱得很不寻常。穿在外面的套裙，被从底部的裙边由下向上撕开了一截宽约一英尺的布带，一直撕到腰际，但是没有扯断。这截布带围着腰绕了3圈，然后在背后打了某种结固定住了。紧贴套裙的是一条质地优良的平纹细布衬裙，衬裙上的一截18英寸宽的布带被完全地撕了下来——撕得很均匀小心。撕下来的布带松松地绕在她的脖子上，牢牢地打了一个结。一顶无檐女帽的帽带将这截平纹细布带和那条蕾丝带子系在一起，而那顶女帽也一并连在上面。这顶无檐女帽的帽带打的那个结，不是一位女士通常会打的那种结，而是一个活结，或者说是一个水手结。

辨认完尸体的身份之后，并没有照例把尸体送到停尸房（因为这样的手续已是多余），而是匆匆埋葬在离它被打捞上岸的地点不远的地方了。博韦想尽办法，事情才被努力隐瞒下来，能瞒多久就瞒了多久。在这桩事情可能导致的任何公众情绪爆发前，事情就这样过去了几天。

public emotion resulted. A weekly paper, however, at length took up the theme; the corpse was disinterred, and a re-examination instituted; but nothing was elicited beyond what has been already noted. The clothes, however, were now submitted to the mother and friends of the deceased, and fully identified as those worn by the girl upon leaving home.

Meantime, the excitement increased hourly. Several individuals were arrested and discharged. St. Eustache fell especially under suspicion; and he failed, at first, to give an intelligible account of his whereabouts during the Sunday on which Marie left home. Subsequently, however, he submitted to Monsieur G-, affidavits, accounting satisfactorily for every hour of the day in question. As time passed and no discovery ensued, a thousand contradictory rumors were circulated, and journalists busied themselves in suggestions. Among these, the one which attracted the most notice, was the idea that Marie Rogêt still lived – that the corpse found in the Seine was that of some other unfortunate. It will be proper that I submit to the reader some passages which embody the suggestion alluded to. These passages are literal translations from *L'Etoile*, a paper conducted, in general, with much ability.

"Mademoiselle Rogêt left her mother's house on Sunday morning, June the

然而，有一家周报最终还是拿这件事当做了新闻主题。于是警方掘出尸体，开始重新验尸。但是除了上面已经被记录下来的情况外，什么都没验出来。不管怎样，死者的衣物现已交至死者的母亲及各位好友手上，他们都充分肯定说这些衣物正是那个女孩出门离家时所穿的。

与此同时，公众群情激昂也与时俱增。几个嫌疑犯被逮捕了，然后又被释放了。圣·尤斯塔希先生受到了特别的怀疑。一开始，关于星期日玛丽离家时他到底在哪儿，他没有给出清晰的解释。然而，后来他又交给葛××先生一份证词书，圆满地供述了他在当前讨论的玛丽离家的那天当中的每个钟头的活动情况。时间一天天过去了，案情仍无进展，于是无数自相矛盾的流言散布开来，而那些新闻记者们就忙着出谋划策。在这些奇谈怪论中，最引人注意的一个，当数一个认为玛丽·罗杰特仍然活着的想法——塞纳河里发现的尸体是另外某个倒霉鬼。我看把几篇文章摘录给读者倒并没有什么不妥，这些文章把以上提及的怪诞的联想具体表达了一下。以下几段文章就是从一份名叫《星报》的报纸上直译过来的——大体上讲，这份报纸办得很不错：

"18××年6月22日，星期天早晨，罗杰特小姐离开她母亲的住所，

twenty-second, 18–, with the ostensible purpose of going to see her aunt, or some other connexion, in the Rue des Drômes. From that hour, nobody is proved to have seen her. There is no trace or tidings of her at all. There has no person, whatever, come forward, so far, who saw her at all, on that day, after she left her mother's door. Now, though we have no evidence that Marie Rogêt was in the land of the living after nine o'clock· on Sunday, June the twenty-second, we have proof that, up to that hour, she was alive. On Wednesday noon, at twelve, a female body was discovered afloat on the shore of the Barrière de Roule. This was, even if·we presume that Marie Rogêt was thrown into the river within three hours after she left her mother's house, only three days from the time she left her home – three days to an hour. But it is folly to suppose that the murder, if murder was committed on her body, could have been consummated soon enough to have enabled her murderers to throw the body into the river before midnight. Those who are guilty of such horrid crimes, choose darkness rather the light. Thus we see that if the body found in the river was that of Marie Rogêt, it could only have been in the water two and a half days, or three at the outside. All experience has shown that drowned bodies, or bodies thrown into the water immediately after

表面上是想去看她住在德罗姆街的姑妈，或者其他某位亲戚。从那一刻起，再没人被证实看到过她了。任何与她有关的蛛丝马迹都没找到。不管怎样，到目前为止，还没有人站出来声称自己见到过她，就在那天，在她踏出她母亲的家门以后。现在，尽管我们没有证据能够证明在6月22日星期天上午9点钟以后玛丽·罗杰特仍旧活在人世，不过我们却有证据证明，在那天上午9点之前，她还是活着的。在星期三中午12点的时候，一名女性尸体被发现漂浮在儒尔门附近的河岸处。那么，就算我们假定玛丽·罗杰特在离开她母亲的住所3小时后就被扔进河里，那么从她离开她家到尸体浮出水面，也仅仅只有3天的时间——3天还差一个小时。假设这起凶杀案中——如果她真的惨遭杀害的话——谋杀她的凶手行凶的时间本来应该是很早的，这样才可以给凶手腾出足够的时间，使其在午夜前就能够将尸体扔进河里了，但是这样假设实在是太愚蠢了。那些犯下如此可怕罪行的人，通常更愿意选择在黑夜行凶而非在光天化日之下。因此，我们可以想到，如果河中尸体确是属于玛丽·罗杰特的，那么死尸在水中也只泡了两天半，抑或最多不超过3天。所有的经验都可以显示，溺水而亡的人的尸体，或者被残杀后马上扔进水

death by violence, require from six to ten days for decomposition to take place to bring them to the top of the water. Even where a cannon is fired over a corpse, and it rises before at least five or six days' immersion, it sinks again, if let alone. Now, we ask, what was there in this case to cause a departure from the ordinary course of nature? If the body had been kept in its mangled state on shore until Tuesday night, some trace would be found on shore of the murderers. It is a doubtful point, also, whether the body would be so soon afloat, even were it thrown in after having been dead two days. And, furthermore, it is exceedingly improbable that any villains who had committed such a murder as is here supposed, would have throw the body in without weight to sink it, when such a precaution could have so easily been taken."

The editor here proceeds to argue that the body must have been in the water "not three days merely, but, at least, five times three days," because it was so far decomposed that Beauvais had great difficulty in recognizing it. This latter point, however, was fully disproved. I continue the translation:

"What, then, are the facts on which M. Beauvais says that he has no doubt the body was that of Marie Rogêt? He ripped up the gown sleeve, and says he found

中的尸体，需要 6 到 10 天才会腐烂到浮出水面的程度。甚至用加农大炮炮轰沉尸地点的水面迫使它浮出，即使在炮轰前它浸泡了至少有五六天，它还是会再次沉下去的，如果放任不管的话。在这种情况下，我们不禁要问，此案中有种什么力量能使尸体违反自然规律提前浮出水面呢？如果尸体保持这种残毁的状态一直藏在岸上，直到星期二晚上才被扔下水，岸上就应该能发现凶手藏尸的某些痕迹。就算人死两天后才被扔下水，尸体能不能这么快就浮上来，同样也是一个值得怀疑的问题。此外，还有件事极其不可能发生，那就是会有哪个在此被怀疑制造了这样一起谋杀案的坏蛋，不用上能让尸体下沉的重物，就把尸体扔到河里呢——尽管采取这样的预防措施本来应该是件很容易的事情。"

该报撰稿人写到这里又转而争辩说尸体泡在水中肯定"不止 3 天了，而是至少有 3 天的 5 倍"，因为到目前为止尸体已经严重腐烂，以至于博韦先生在辨认尸体时遇到了很大的困难。然而，该报撰稿人的最后一个观点，却被证明是完全错误的。我继续将摘录直译过来：

"那么，博韦先生有什么证据就说他十分确信那具尸体是玛丽·罗杰特的呢？他撕开长外衣的衣袖，然后说他发现尸体身上有一

marks which satisfied him of the identity. The public generally supposed those marks to have consisted of some description of scars. He rubbed the arm and found hair upon it – something as indefinite, we think, as can readily be imagined – as little conclusive as finding an arm in the sleeve. M. Beauvais did not return that night, but sent word to Madame Rogêt, at seven o'clock, on Wednesday evening, that an investigation was still in progress respecting her daughter. If we allow that Madame from her age and grief, could not go over, (which is allowing a great deal,) there certainly must have been some one who would have thought it worth while to go over and attend the investigation, if they thought the body was that of Marie. Nobody went over. There was nothing said or heard about the matter in the Rue Pavée St. Andrée, that reached even the occupants of the same building. M. St. Eustache, the lover and intended husband of Marie, who boarded in her mother's house, deposes that he did not hear of the discovery of the body of his intended until the next morning, when M. Beauvais came into his chamber and told him of it. For an item of news like this, it strikes us it was very coolly received."

In this way the journal endeavored to create the impression of an apathy on the part of the relatives of Marie, inconsistent

些特征使他确信尸体的身份就是玛丽。公众一般会假设那些特征是由某种疤痕构成的。但其实他只摸了摸死者的胳膊，摸到了上面的汗毛——我们认为，净是些很容易就能想到的不明确的东西——就像把手伸到袖子里就能摸到胳膊一样不具有结论性。博韦先生当晚没有回家，星期三晚上 7 点捎话给罗杰特太太，说有关她女儿的那宗案子的调查仍在进行当中。如果我们考虑到罗杰特太太上了年纪，又刚经历了丧女之痛，而对她不能亲临现场有所体谅（得承认她有大量的难处），那么，当他们认为尸体属于玛丽时，总该有个人去现场参与一下调查。可是竟没人去。圣安德里的铺石街没有任何有关此事的传言和听闻，就连同住在罗杰特太太家的房客都对此事一无所知。圣·尤斯塔希先生，也就是玛丽的情人兼未婚夫，在她母亲的房子里膳宿的那位先生，他宣誓作证说，直到第二天早上博韦先生到他房里告知他，他才听说了他未婚妻的尸体已经被发现这件事。对于这样一则消息，大家竟然就这样自若地接受了，着实让人惊讶。"

这家报纸以这样的方式努力给人营造一种印象，即尽管那些人的身份是玛丽的亲属，但却对此事根

with the supposition that these relatives believed the corpse to be hers. Its insinuations amount to this: – that Marie, with the connivance of her friends, had absented herself from the city for reasons involving a charge against her chastity; and that these friends, upon the discovery of a corpse in the Seine, somewhat resembling that of the girl, had availed themselves of the opportunity to impress the public with the belief of her death. But *L'Etoile* was again over-hasty. It was distinctly proved that no apathy, such as was imagined, existed; that the old lady was exceedingly feeble, and so agitated as to be unable to attend to any duty, that St. Eustache, so far from receiving the news coolly, was distracted with grief, and bore himself so frantically, that M. Beauvais prevailed upon a friend and relative to take charge of him, and prevent his attending the examination at the disinterment. Moreover, although it was stated by *L'Etoile*, that the corpse was re-interred at the public expense – that an advantageous offer of private sculpture was absolutely declined by the family – and that no member of the family attended the ceremonial – although, I say, all this was asserted by *L'Etoile* in furtherance of the impression it designed to convey – yet all this was satisfactorily disproved. In a subsequent number of the paper, an attempt was made to throw

本不上心，这与假设这些亲属们确信尸体就是玛丽的这一推想背道而驰。文章影射的意思实际上是这样的：玛丽在她好友们的密谋协助下离开了这所城市，原因是她的贞洁问题受到了非难。而她的这些朋友看到人们在塞纳河发现的女尸与玛丽有几分相像，于是便利用这个机会给公众制造这样一种假象，即让大家相信她已经死了。不过《星报》的结论又一次下得过于草率了。事实证明，很显然并不存在漠不关心这回事，那只是凭空捏造出来的。老夫人身体本来就极度孱弱，被这么一刺激就更无法尽任何义务出席现场了，而那位圣·尤斯塔希先生，非但没有自若地接受这则消息，反而被悲痛搞得精神错乱，这则消息发狂似的扰乱着他的心绪，博韦先生只好说服一位亲友去照管他，不让他去参加挖掘现场的尸体检验。此外，尽管据《星报》宣称，说重新安葬尸体是政府花的钱——死者的家属当然会拒绝私人赠送的墓碑石刻做的厚礼——还说死者没有一位家庭成员出席了葬礼。——不管事实上如何，依我说，《星报》原本就设计好了把事情报道成"玛丽家人对女尸漠不关心"，而它以上所宣称的一切，都是为了加深公众的这一印象——然而所有这些又都被圆圆满满地证明是不真实的。随后一期的《星报》又企图质疑博韦本人

suspicion upon Beauvais himself. The editor says:

"Now, then, a change comes over the matter. We are told that on one occasion, while a Madame B- was at Madame Rogêt's house, M. Beauvais, who was going out, told her that a gendarme was expected there, and she, Madame B., must not say anything to the gendarme until he returned, but let the matter be for him. In the present posture of affairs, M. Beauvais appears to have the whole matter looked up in his head. A single step cannot be taken without M. Beauvais; for, go which way you will, you run against him. For some reason, he determined that nobody shall have any thing to do with the proceedings but himself, and he has elbowed the male relatives out of the way, according to their representations, in a very singular manner. He seems to have been very much averse to permitting the relatives to see the body."

By the following fact, some color was given to the suspicion thus thrown upon Beauvais. A visiter at his office, a few days prior to the girl's disappearance, and during the absence of its occupant, had observed a *rose* in the key-hole of the door, and the name "*Marie*" inscribed upon a slate which hung near at hand.

The general impression, so far as we were enabled to glean it from the newspapers, seemed to be, that Marie had

了。该报撰稿人写道：

"然而现在，此案又出现了新变化。我们被告知，曾经，当博韦先生正要出门时，一位 B 姓的太太恰好也待在罗杰特太太家里，博韦先生告诉她说一位警官一会儿可能要来，而她，B 太太，在他回来之前千万什么都不要对那位警官说，只管把事情交给他来处理就好了。就此案目前的情况而言，博韦先生看起来似乎把整宗案情都蓄之脑中。没有博韦先生，调查就别想向前迈开一步。因为，不管沿哪个方向进行调查，都将对他不利。出于某种原因，他决意不让除去他自己以外的任何人插手此案的调查，依照一些男性亲属的表述，他曾用一种非常高明的方式将他们推挤出调查进程。他仿佛非常不愿意家属们去看那具尸体。"

根据下面一段事实来看，本已备受怀疑的博韦先生又在其嫌疑之处被加了点儿料。在女孩失踪的前几天，有位访客去博韦先生办公室找他，当时他不在，此人发现房门的锁孔里插着一朵玫瑰花，旁边还挂着一个小留言板，板上写着"玛丽"这个名字。

就目前我们从各报所收集到的消息来看，案情给人的总体印象貌似是，玛丽已然成为一伙暴徒的受

been the victim of a gang of desperadoes – that by these she had been borne across the river, maltreated and murdered. *Le Commerciel*, however, a print of extensive influence, was earnest in combating this popular idea. I quote a passage or two from its columns:

"We are persuaded that pursuit has hitherto been on a false scent, so far as it has been directed to the Barrière du Roule. It is impossible that a person so well known to thousands as this young woman was, should have passed three blocks without some one having seen her; and any one who saw her would have remembered it, for she interested all who knew her. It was when the streets were full of people, when she went out. It is impossible that she could have gone to the Barrière du Roule, or to the Rue des Drômes, without being recognized by a dozen persons; yet no one has come forward who saw her outside of her mother's door, and there is no evidence, except the testimony concerning her expressed intentions, that she did go out at all. Her gown was torn, bound round her, and tied; and by that the body was carried as a bundle. If the murder had been committed at the Barrière du Roule, there would have been no necessity for any such arrangement. The fact that the body was found floating near the Barrière, is no proof as to where it was thrown into the water. A

害者——他们把她带到河的另一边，糟蹋了她，然后杀死了她。然而，具有广泛影响力的一家名为《商报》的出版物，却郑重其事地强烈反对这一时流行的看法。我在此从它的专栏中引述一两段文章：

"我们相信，追查行动迄今已误入歧途，因为到目前为止追查行动一直是围绕儒尔门附近的区域展开的。像这位年轻女士这样众人皆知的人物，经过了3个街区却没有谁看到过她，这样的事是不可能发生的。而且任何看到她的人都应该会对此事有印象，因为所有认识她的人都对她感兴趣。她出门离开家的时候，也正是街上全是人的时候。如果她去了圆木栅门附近，或去了德罗姆街，那么一路上她不被至少一打人认出来才怪。然而尚没有人站出来声称曾在她母亲的房门以外见过她，也完全没有任何证据——而且除了那段有提到她明确意图'她说她要出门'的证词——证明她确实出过门。她的长外衣被撕破了，缠绕着绑在她身上，还打了结，这样一来，尸体就可以像包裹一样被运载了。如果凶杀确实发生在圆木栅门，尸体就不必做这样的处理了。尸体被发现漂到了圆木栅门附近一带的水面上，但这样的事实并不能作为证据证明尸体就是在那里被抛进水里的。这个不幸女孩衬裙上的一

piece of one of the unfortunate girl's petticoats, two feet long and one foot wide, was torn out and tied under her chin around the back of her head, probably to prevent screams. This was done by fellows who had no pocket-handkerchief."

A day or two before the Prefect called upon us, however, some important information reached the police, which seemed to overthrow, at least, the chief portion of *Le Commerciel*'s argument. Two small boys, sons of a Madame Deluc, while roaming among the woods near the Barrière du Roule, chanced to penetrate a close thicket, within which were three or four large stones, forming a kind of seat, with a back and footstool. On the upper stone lay a white petticoat; on the second a silk scarf. A parasol, gloves, and a pocket-handkerchief were also here found. The handkerchief bore the name "Marie Rogêt". Fragments of dress were discovered on the brambles around. The earth was trampled, the bushes were broken, and there was every evidence of a struggle. Between the thicket and the river, the fences were found taken down, and the ground bore evidence of some heavy burthen having been dragged along it.

A weekly paper, *Le Soleil*, had the following comments upon this discovery – comments which merely echoed the

可是，就在警察局长拜访我们的前一两天，一条重要的情报到达了警方手中，这条情报看上去是可以推翻《商报》的论点的，至少是主要论点。有两个小男孩，他们是德吕克太太的儿子，当他们在圆木栅门附近的树林里闲逛时，偶然闯入了一片茂密的灌木林，灌木林里有三四块大石头，摆成的样子有几分像坐椅，既有椅背又有脚凳。上面的石头上放着一条白衬裙，第二块石头上则放着一条丝绸围巾。他们还在那里找到了一柄女用阳伞、一副手套和一块手帕。手帕上还绣有"玛丽·罗杰特"的名字。在四周的荆棘上到处都能找到裙子的碎片。泥土被踩踏过，矮树丛的枝条也被折断了，这一切都可以证明此处发生过一番搏斗。在灌木林和河流之间的篱笆被发现推倒了，地面上留下的痕迹也能证明某种重物曾经被拖着经过这里。

有一家周报，名叫《太阳报》，对这一发现作了如下评论——这些评论仅仅附和了整个巴黎新闻界的

sentiment of the whole Parisian press:

"The things had all evidently been there at least three or four weeks; they were all mildewed down hard with the action of the rain and stuck together from mildew. The grass had grown around and over some of them. The silk on the parasol was strong, but the threads of it were run together within. The upper part, where it had been doubled and folded, was all mildewed and rotten, and tore on its being opened. The pieces of her frock torn out by the bushes were about three inches wide and six inches long. One part was the hem of the frock, and it had been mended; the other piece was part of the skirt, not the hem. They looked like strips torn off, and were on the thorn bush, about a foot from the ground. There can be no doubt, therefore, that the spot of this appalling outrage has been discovered."

Consequent upon this discovery, new evidence appeared. Madame Deluc testified that she keeps a roadside inn not far from the bank of the river, opposite the Barrière du Roule. The neighborhood is secluded – particularly so. It is the usual Sunday resort of blackguards from the city, who cross the river in boats. About three o'clock, in the afternoon of the Sunday in question, a young girl arrived at the inn, accompanied by a young man of dark

意见而已:

"所有这些东西很明显已经摆在那里至少三四个星期了,它们都因为下雨而发霉发得很严重了,由于霉菌而彼此粘连在一起。其中有几样东西的周围和上面都长了草。女用阳伞上的绸面很结实,但是里面的丝线却都乱糟糟地缠在了一起。阳伞的上半部分是折叠起来的,全部已经发霉并且腐烂,而且伞一撑开伞面就扯破了。从她套裙上被矮树丛的枝杈刮下来的碎布条差不多都有3英寸宽6英寸长。有一条是套裙的褶边,还是缝补过的。还有一条是从裙摆上撕下来的,而不是褶边。它们看起来都很像被撕好的布条,挂在多刺的树林上,离地大约一英尺远。因此,毫无疑问地,这起骇人听闻的暴行的罪案现场终于被找到了。"

紧随其后的是新证据的出现。德吕克太太作证说,她开了一家路边小旅店,就在离河岸不远的地方,与圆木栅门相对。附近一带少有人烟——尤为偏僻。那里是城里的流氓们每逢星期天便去消遣的地方,他们去那儿一般得划船过河。在当前讨论的玛丽离家的那个星期天的下午3点钟左右,一个年轻女孩来到了这家小旅店,身旁陪着一个皮肤黝黑的年轻男子。他们俩在这儿

complexion. The two remained here for some time. On their departure, they took the road to some thick woods in the vicinity. Madame Deluc's attention was called to the dress worn by the girl, on account of its resemblance to one worn by a deceased relative. A scarf was particularly noticed. Soon after the departure of the couple, a gang of miscreants made their appearance, behaved boisterously, ate and drank without making payment, followed in the route of the young man and girl, returned to the inn about dusk, and re-crossed the river as if in great haste.

It was soon after dark, upon this same evening, that Madame Deluc, as well as her eldest son, heard the screams of a female in the vicinity of the inn. The screams were violent but brief. Madame D. recognized not only the scarf which was found in the thicket, but the dress which was discovered upon the corpse. An omnibus driver, Valence, now also testified that he saw Marie Rogêt cross a ferry on the Seine, on the Sunday in question, in company with a young man of dark complexion. He, Valence, knew Marie, and could not be mistaken in her identity. The articles found in the thicket were fully identified by the relatives of Marie.

The items of evidence and information thus collected by myself, from the

待了有那么一阵子。然后他们就离开了，二人顺着小路走向邻近的某个密林。这个女孩穿的衣服引起了德吕克太太的注意，因为那件衣服和她的一位已故亲戚穿过的衣服有些相似。尤其是那条围巾十分引人注意。这对男女离开后不久，一群无赖就出现了，他们吵吵嚷嚷的，吃饱喝足后也不付钱，沿着那个年轻男子和那个女孩所走的路线就走过去了，大约是黄昏时分他们才回到这家小旅店，急匆匆地过河而去，就好像很赶时间一样。

就在那天晚上，夜色刚刚降临的时候，德吕克太太和她的大儿子同时听到了从她家的小旅店附近传来的女人的尖叫声。声音凄厉而急促。德吕克太太不仅认出了灌木林里找到的围巾，还认出了死者穿着的那件衣服。一位公共马车车夫，瓦朗斯，目前也供称他曾看见玛丽·罗杰特乘船划过了塞纳河的一个渡口，就在当前被讨论的那个星期天，在一个皮肤黝黑的小伙子的陪同下。他，也就是瓦朗斯，知道玛丽这个人，所以是不会搞错那个女孩的身份的。经过玛丽家属的仔细辨认，灌木林中发现的物品被确定全部都是属于玛丽的。

我收集的这些证据和消息的简报来源于各大报纸，根据杜宾的建

newspapers, at the suggestion of Dupin, embraced only one more point – but this was a point of seemingly vast consequence. It appears that, immediately after the discovery of the clothes as above described, the lifeless, or nearly lifeless body of St. Eustache, Marie's betrothed, was found in the vicinity of what all now supposed the scene of the outrage. A phial labelled "laudanum," and emptied, was found near him. His breath gave evidence of the poison. He died without speaking. Upon his person was found a letter, briefly stating his love for Marie, with his design of self- destruction.

"I need scarcely tell you," said Dupin, as he finished the perusal of my notes, "that this is a far more intricate case than that of the Rue Morgue; from which it differs in one important respect. This is an *ordinary*, although an atrocious instance of crime. There is nothing peculiarly outré about it. You will observe that, for this reason, the mystery has been considered easy, when, for this reason, it should have been considered difficult, of solution. Thus; at first, it was thought unnecessary to offer a reward. The myrmidons of G- were able at once to comprehend how and why such an atrocity *might have been* committed. They could picture to their imaginations a mode – many modes – and a motive – many motives; and because it was not impossible

议，仅需再加入一个要点——但正是这一点貌似占据了至关重要的位置。这一点看来是这样的，就在上述衣物被发现后，紧接着，已经断气了或者说是奄奄一息的圣·尤斯塔希先生，也就是玛丽的未婚夫，被发现躺在那个被所有人假定为罪案现场的附近。在他身边找到一个标签上写有"鸦片酊"的小药瓶，而且是空的。他呼出气体的气味可以证明他服了毒。他什么也没说就死了。在他身上找到的一封信上，简短地表明了他对玛丽的爱意，以及他打算自杀的意图。

"我几乎不用跟您说您就能看出来，"杜宾仔仔细细地读完我报刊摘录笔记后说，"这是桩远比莫格街凶杀案复杂得多的案子，在一个重要方面上两桩案子是有所区别的。这只是普通犯罪，尽管它牵扯了一起手段残忍的杀人事件，但却没有什么特别出轨的行为。您会发现，正因为如此，大家才认为这桩谜案容易破解，而此时此刻，也正因如此，这桩谜案才应该被看成一桩难解之案。正因为这样，起初，警方才会认为没必要悬赏，认为葛××局长的跟班们可以马上搞清楚这起暴行本应是如何发生的以及它产生的本来原因是什么。他们甚至能给自己的想象描绘出一种犯罪手法——或者多种犯罪手法——以及一种动

that either of these numerous modes and motives *could* have been the actual one, they have taken it for granted that one of them must. But the case with which these variable fancies were entertained, and the very plausibility which each assumed, should have been understood as indicative rather of the difficulties than of the facilities which must attend elucidation. I have before observed that it is by prominences above the plane of the ordinary, that reason feels her way, if at all, in her search for the true, and that the proper question in cases such as this, is not so much 'what has occurred?' as 'what has occurred that has never occurred before?' In the investigations at the house of Madame L'Espanaye, the agents of G- were discouraged and confounded by that very *unusualness* which, to a properly regulated intellect, would have afforded the surest omen of success; while this same intellect might have been plunged in despair at the ordinary character of all that met the eye in the case of the perfumery-girl, and yet told of nothing but easy triumph to the functionaries of the Prefecture.

"In the case of Madame L'Espanaye and her daughter there was, even at the beginning of our investigation, no doubt that murder had been committed. The idea of suicide was excluded at once. Here, too,

机——或者多种动机。由于这些为数众多的手法和动机未尝不可能是凶手的真实犯罪手法和动机，所以他们便想当然地认为其中的一种手法和动机必定是真的。大家对这桩案子抱有各种猜想，而且每一种假设似乎都能说通，但是这桩谜案应该被当做难题来理解，而不应该被想得太容易，这一点必须加以说明。我以前通过观察发现，利用异于普通人水平的突出之处，理智之人才能摸索着前行，如果这个人真的拥有异于常人的见解，那么他就能在找寻真理的道路上找到方向。因此在这类案子中合适问的问题，不是'发生了什么'而是'发生了哪些以前没发生过的'。在检查列士巴奈太太那幢房子的过程中，葛××手下的警察遇到那些非比寻常的问题后都灰心丧气、困惑不已，但是对一个思维方面训练有素的人来说，'异常的情况'却成了为他提供的最有把握的成功的预兆。然而同样是那个聪明人在遇到'香水西施'这种放眼望去所有案情性质全部都很普通的案件时，倒很有可能陷入绝望，而对于警务人员来说这种案子就意味着轻松搞定。

"在列士巴奈太太和她女儿的这桩案子里，即使在调查之初，我们也能确定那是一桩谋杀案。自杀的观点立马就被排除掉了。在这起案子当中，同样地，在调查之初，

we are freed, at the commencement, from all supposition of self- murder. The body found at the Barrière du Roule, was found under such circumstances as to leave us no room for embarrassment upon this important point. But it has been suggested that the corpse discovered, is not that of the Marie Rogêt for the conviction of whose assassin, or assassins, the reward is offered, and respecting whom, solely, our agreement has been arranged with the Prefect. We both know this gentleman well. It will not do to trust him too far. If, dating our inquiries from the body found, and thence tracing a murderer, we yet discover this body to be that of some other individual than Marie; or, if starting from the living Marie, we find her, yet find her unassassinated – in either case we lose our labor; since it is Monsieur G- with whom we have to deal. For our own purpose, therefore, if not for the purpose of justice, it is indispensable that our first step should be the determination of the identity of the corpse with the Marie Rogêt who is missing.

"With the public the arguments of *L'Etoile* have had weight; and that the journal itself is convinced of their importance would appear from the manner in which it commences one of its essays upon the subject – 'Several of *the morning papers* of the day,' it says, 'speak of the

我们也能排除所有自杀的假设。在圆木栅门发现的那具尸体所处的那种境况让我们没有为这一重要问题伤脑筋的余地。有人提出，找到的这具尸体并不属于玛丽·罗杰特，但警方悬赏通缉的却是真正谋杀玛丽·罗杰特的那一个或几个凶手，而且咱们同警察局长达成的协议也完全是关于找出谋杀玛丽的真凶。咱们俩都很了解局长，不宜对他寄予太多的希望。如果我们从找到的那具尸体开始我们的调查，由此追踪到了一个杀人犯，却发现那具尸体是其他别的什么人而不是玛丽。或者说，如果我们从'玛丽还活着'开始着手调查，我们找到了她，却发现她没被杀害——出现以上任何一种情况，我们都是白费力气，因为跟我们打交道的是葛××先生。所以，要说我们自己的意图，就算不是为了伸张正义，我们第一步绝对应该要做的也是确定尸体的身份，看她是否就是失踪的玛丽·罗杰特。

"《星报》的那些观点在公众心中的分量很重，这家报纸自己也认识到了自己观点的重要性，从以下举动可以看出端倪：在它的一篇有关这件案子的评论性小短文的开篇语里——'现今有好几家早报，'它写道，'都谈到了星期一的《星报》

conclusive article in Monday's Etoile.' To me, this article appears conclusive of little beyond the zeal of its inditer. We should bear in mind that, in general, it is the object of our newspapers rather to create a sensation – to make a point – than to further the cause of truth. The latter end is only pursued when it seems coincident with the former. The print which merely falls in with ordinary opinion (however well founded this opinion may be) earns for itself no credit with the mob. The mass of the people regard as profound only him who suggests *pungent contradictions* of the general idea. In ratiocination, not less than in literature, it is the *epigram* which is the most immediately and the most universally appreciated. In both, it is of the lowest order of merit.

"What I mean to say is, that it is the mingled epigram and melodrame of the idea, that Marie Rogêt still lives, rather than any true plausibility in this idea, which have suggested it to *L'Etoile*, and secured it a favorable reception with the public. Let us examine the heads of this journal's argument; endeavoring to avoid the incoherence with which it is originally set forth.

"The first aim of the writer is to show, from the brevity of the interval between Marie's disappearance and the finding of the floating corpse, that this corpse cannot

的那篇结论性的文章。'可在我来讲，那篇文章除了作者的一腔热情以外看不出有什么结论性的东西。我们应该记住，一般来说，我们看的这些报纸的目标是宁可制造一种轰动效应——去炮制一种观点——也不愿意去深究事实的起因。只有当制造轰动效应和深究事实真相相一致时，新闻界才会贯彻后者。那种只同意平凡无奇的观点的报纸（不管这个观点是多么有根有据）是无法为自己赚得大众青睐的。只有那种提出与普通看法尖锐矛盾的观点的报纸，大众才会把它看为是意味深长的。在推理作品中，只有隽永之语才会最为直接和最为广泛地博得大家的赞赏，这一点丝毫不逊色于文学作品。可是在两种作品中，这种刻意添加的隽永论调却是价值最低的东西。

"我想说的是，正是《星报》提出的这个杂糅了可以添加隽语和闹剧的观点，说玛丽·罗杰特仍旧活着，而不说任何在此观点中真正可信的成分，这样哗众取宠的做法保证了它能被公众欣然接受。咱们来分析一下这家报纸其论述的中心论点吧，我们会尽力避开报纸上一开始就表现出的语无伦次。

"作者的首要目的是要表明从玛丽失踪到发现浮尸之间的时间间隔很短，所以尸体不可能是玛丽的。因此，将这段时间间隔缩短到可能

be that of Marie. The reduction of this interval to its smallest possible dimension, becomes thus, at once, an object with the reasoner. In the rash pursuit of this object, he rushes into mere assumption at the outset. 'It is folly to suppose,' he says, 'that the murder, if murder was committed on her body, could have been consummated soon enough to have enabled her murderers to throw the body into the river before midnight.' We demand at once, and very naturally, *why*? Why is it folly to suppose that the murder was committed *within five minutes* after the girl's quitting her mother's house? Why is it folly to suppose that the murder was committed at any given period of the day? There have been assassinations at all hours. But, had the murder taken place at any moment between nine o'clock in the morning of Sunday, and a quarter before midnight, there would still have been time enough 'to throw the body into the river before midnight.' This assumption, then, amounts precisely to this – that the murder was not committed on Sunday at all – and, if we allow *L'Etoile* to assume this, we may permit it any liberties whatever. The paragraph beginning 'It is folly to suppose that the murder, etc.,' however it appears as printed in *L'Etoile*, may be imagined to have existed actually *thus* in the brain of its inditer – 'It is folly to suppose that the murder, if murder was

的最短尺寸立即就成了这位推理者的目标。在一味贸然追赶这个目标的过程中，他匆忙以几句臆测起头。他说：'假设这起凶杀案中——如果她真的惨遭杀害的话——谋杀她的凶手行凶的时间本来应该是很早的，这样才能腾出足够的时间使其在午夜前就能够将尸体扔进河里了。'但是这样的假设实在是太愚蠢了。因此我们立即就想要知道，而且是自然而然地想要知道，为什么？为什么假设这个女孩离开她母亲家 5 分钟后就被杀害是愚蠢的？为什么假设了这桩谋杀案发生在凶案当天的某个特定的时间段倒成了愚蠢的假设了？一天当中的每时每刻都有可能发生谋杀案。但是，如果凶杀发生在星期天上午 9 点钟至午夜 12 点差一刻之间的任何时候，那么在那天仍将有足够的时间让凶手'在午夜前将尸体扔进河里'。因而，作者的这番臆测就恰好等于是说——这桩谋杀案根本就不是发生在星期天——而且，如果我们承认了《星报》的这番臆测，我们便可能许了它胡乱瞎猜的任何特权。段落开篇语'这样猜想这起谋杀案实在是太愚蠢了如此等等'，不管这句话看起来如何像它印在《星报》上的样子，在作者的脑海里实际上可能被想象成这个样子——'这样来猜想这起谋杀案实在是太愚蠢了——如果她真的惨遭杀害，谋杀她

committed on the body, could have been committed soon enough to have enabled her murderers to throw the body into the river before midnight; it is folly, we say, to suppose all this, and to suppose at the same time, (as we are resolved to suppose,) that the body was *not* thrown in until *after* midnight' – a sentence sufficiently inconsequential in itself, but not so utterly preposterous as the one printed.

"Were it my purpose," continued Dupin, "merely to *make out a case* against this passage of *L'Etoile's* argument, I might safely leave it where it is. It is not, however, with *L'Etoile* that we have to do, but with the truth. The sentence in question has but one meaning, as it stands; and this meaning I have fairly stated: but it is material that we go behind the mere words, for an idea which these words have obviously intended, and failed to convey. It was the design of the journalist to say that, at whatever period of the day or night of Sunday this murder was committed, it was improbable that the assassins would have ventured to bear the corpse to the river before midnight. And herein lies, really, the assumption of which I complain. It is assumed that the murder was committed at such a position, and under such circumstances, that *the bearing it* to the river became necessary. Now, the assassination might have taken place upon

的凶手行凶的时间本应是足够早的，这样才有时间使其在午夜前就将尸体扔进河里。我们得说，去猜测所有这些东西太愚蠢了，而且我们要是同时还假设（就按照我们决意要假设的那样），说尸体直到过了午夜才被扔到河里，这样想也是愚蠢的。'——这整句话的逻辑看起来已经够混乱的了，但其实还不如印在报上的那句话那么荒谬。

"如果我的目的，"杜宾继续说，"仅仅是想弄清这桩案子的来龙去脉以驳斥这篇阐述《星报》观点的文章，我大可以放心地撒手不管、听之任之。可是，我们现在必须要做的不是与《星报》掺和在一起，而是与事实真相打交道。刚刚讨论的那句话只有一种意图，事实也确实如此，而且这一意图我也已经说得很清楚了。但是对于一种措辞用意明显却表达失误的观点来说，我们进一步斟酌这些纯粹的措辞是至关重要的。这位记者原本打算要说的是，无论凶杀案发生在星期日的哪个时间段，不管是白天还是晚上，凶手都不可能冒险在午夜之前把尸体运到河边。说实在的，我对作者于此表达的这番假设表示抗议。作者认为要是凶案发生在这样的地点，这样的环境下，'把尸体移向河边'这一动作就变得不可避免了。然而，凶杀本来也有可能发生在河边，或者在河里。并且，如果真是

the river's brink, or on the river itself; and, thus, the throwing the corpse in the water might have been resorted to, at any period of the day or night, as the most obvious and most immediate mode of disposal. You will understand that I suggest nothing here as probable, or as coïncident with my own opinion. My design, so far, has no reference to the *facts* of the case. I wish merely to caution you against the whole tone of *L'Etoile's suggestion*, by calling your attention to its ex – parte character at the outset.

"Having prescribed thus a limit to suit its own preconceived notions; having assumed that, if this were the body of Marie, it could have been in the water but a very brief time; the journal goes on to say:

"'All experience has shown that drowned bodies, or bodies thrown into the water immediately after death by violence, require from six to ten days for sufficient decomposition to take place to bring them to the top of the water. Even when a cannon is fired over a corpse, and it rises before at least five or six days' immersion, it sinks again if let alone.'

"These assertions have been tacitly received by every paper in Paris, with the exception of *Le Moniteur*. This latter print endeavors to combat that portion of the paragraph which has reference to 'drowned bodies' only, by citing some five or six

这样的话,就在那天的任何时间段,不论是白天还是晚上,凶手都可能会采取把尸体扔进水里的方式处理尸体,因为这样做效果最显著,也最为快速。您会明白,我在这里并没有提出什么可能成为我自己的看法,或者与我的看法相一致的建议。我的目的,就我目前讲的这番话来说,是和案子的真相没什么关联。我只是希望通过请您注意一下《星报》在文章开头所提建议的片面性来劝您警惕《星报》建议的全部论调。

"在为配合它自己预先想好的观点而规定了这样的一个限制后,在假设完'如果尸体是玛丽的,那么它浸泡在水里的时间就非常短暂'后,《星报》接着又说:

"'所有的经验都可以显示,溺水而亡的人的尸体或者被残杀后马上扔进水中的尸体,需要6到10天才会腐烂到足以浮出水面的程度。甚至用加农大炮炮轰沉尸地点的水面迫使它浮出,即使在炮轰前它浸泡了至少有五六天,它还是会再次沉下去的,如果放任不管的话。'

"除了《箴言报》外,巴黎的各家报纸都默默地承认了《星报》的这些断言。但《箴言报》仅仅极力驳斥《星报》段落中提及的'溺水者尸体'那部分,通过引用五六个例子证明有些溺水者的尸体被发

instances in which the bodies of individuals known to be drowned were found floating after the lapse of less time than is insisted upon by *L'Etoile*. But there is something excessively unphilosophical in the attempt on the part of *Le Moniteur*, to rebut the general assertion of *L'Etoile*, by a citation of particular instances militating against that assertion. Had it been possible to adduce fifty instead of five examples of bodies found floating at the end of two or three days, these fifty examples could still have been properly regarded only as exceptions to *L'Etoile's* rule, until such time as the rule itself should be confuted. Admitting the rule, (and this *Le Moniteur* does not deny, insisting merely upon its exceptions,) the argument of *L'Etoile* is suffered to remain in full force; for this argument does not pretend to involve more than a question of the probability of the body having risen to the surface in less than three days; and this probability will be in favor of *L'Etoile's* position until the instances so childishly adduced shall be sufficient in number to establish an antagonistical rule.

"You will see at once that all argument upon this head should be urged, if at all, against the rule itself; and for this end we must examine the rationale of the rule. Now the human body, in general, is neither much lighter nor much heavier than the

现能够经过少于《星报》强调的时间浮起。《箴言报》想通过引用几个特例来对《星报》的断言产生对立的影响，但是在尝试反驳《星报》的一般性论断时，有些言论却使用得太有悖明智了。即使《箴言报》有可能举出 50 个例子而不是 5 个，来说明有些尸体能够在两三天后就浮出水面，这 50 个例子仍旧可能被完全地，并且仅仅地被视作是《星报》声称的'自然规律'的例外而已，直到'自然规律'本身被驳倒的时候为止。由于《星报》承认'自然规律'（而《箴言报》也并没有否定这个'规律'，它只不过是坚持了自己的'例外论'而已），《星报》的论点就保有了完整的说服力。因为这个论点没有矫揉造作地在'尸体浮出水面少于 3 天的可能性'这一问题上做过多的谈论，而且这一可能性将不会对《星报》的立场不利，直到这些被傻里傻气地举用了的例子在数量上多到足以建立一条与'自然规律'相对的'对立法则'为止。

"您肯定立刻就看懂了，如果真的想要使围绕这一中心论点展开的所有论述具有强大的说服力，就必须先要驳倒《星报》提出的'自然规律'。为了达到这个目标，我们就必须得分析一下这个规律的基

water of the Seine; that is to say, the specific gravity of the human body, in its natural condition, is about equal to the bulk of fresh water which it displaces. The bodies of fat and fleshy persons, with small bones, and of women generally, are lighter than those of the lean and large-boned, and of men; and the specific gravity of the water of a river is somewhat influenced by the presence of the tide from sea. But, leaving this tide out of question, it may be said that *very* few human bodies will sink at all, even in fresh water, *of their own accord*. Almost any one, falling into a river, will be enabled to float, if he suffer the specific gravity of the water fairly to be adduced in comparison with his own – that is to say, if he suffer his whole person to be immersed, with as little exception as possible. The proper position for one who cannot swim, is the upright position of the walker on land, with the head thrown fully back, and immersed; the mouth and nostrils alone remaining above the surface. Thus circumstanced, we shall find that we float without difficulty and without exertion. It is evident, however, that the gravities of the body, and of the bulk of water displaced, are very nicely balanced, and that a trifle will cause either to preponderate. An arm, for instance, uplifted from the water, and thus deprived of its support, is an additional weight

本原理。目前来看，人类的身体与塞纳河的河水相比，通常来说是既不会太轻也不会太重的。也就是说，人类身体的比重在正常状态下约等于身体排出的那部分淡水的比重。脂肪和肥肉较多身体骨架小的一般都是女人，她们的比重就比那些脂肪少骨架大的男人的比重要轻一些。而且河水的比重多少也会受点儿从海里涌来的潮水的影响。不过，抛开此番潮汐的问题不说，我们可以肯定地讲，很少会有人类的身体能够沉到水里，即使是在淡水之中，而且还是在放任其沉浮的情况下。几乎任何一个人掉到河里后都可以自动浮起来，只要他落入其中的水的比重与他自身的比重相比起来数值相当就行——也就是说，只要他能容忍自己的整个身体都浸入水中，尽可能地把身体少露在外面就行。对于一个不会游泳的人来说，使自己不下沉的正确姿势就跟人们在陆地上行走时的那种直立姿势一样，但头要尽量后仰，浸在水里只留嘴和鼻孔在水面上。在这种情况下，我们会发现自己毫无困难、毫不费力地就漂起来了。然而，很显然，人体的重量以及其排水量被很精细地平衡着，一点点微小的变化都会导致一边的重量超过另外一边。例如，从水中伸出一只胳膊，这样的话胳膊就失去了水的浮托，增加了额外的重量，重得足以让人

sufficient to immerse the whole head, while the accidental aid of the smallest piece of timber will enable us to elevate the head so as to look about. Now, in the struggles of one unused to swimming, the arms are invariably thrown upwards, while an attempt is made to keep the head in its usual perpendicular position. The result is the immersion of the mouth and nostrils, and the inception, during efforts to breathe while beneath the surface, of water into the lungs. Much is also received into the stomach, and the whole body becomes heavier by the difference between the weight of the air originally distending these cavities, and that of the fluid which now fills them. This difference is sufficient to cause the body to sink, as a general rule; but is insufficient in the cases of individuals with small bones and an abnormal quantity of flaccid or fatty matter. Such individuals float even after drowning.

"The corpse, being supposed at the bottom of the river, will there remain until, by some means, its specific gravity again becomes less than that of the bulk of water which it displaces. This effect is brought about by decomposition, or otherwise. The result of decomposition is the generation of gas, distending the cellular tissues and all the cavities, and giving the *puffed* appearance which is so horrible. When this

下沉至整个脑袋都浸入水中，而最小块的木材对我们的附加援助都能让我们的头伸出水面甚至能四处张望。目前来说，不会游泳的人在水中挣扎时胳膊总是向上伸着，同时头总是努力地保持像往常在岸上时的那种竖直的样子。结果就是嘴和鼻孔全浸到水里去了，并且在浸没之初，当落水者在水面之下挣扎着呼吸时，水会灌入肺中。也会有大量的水被喝进胃里，胃部和肺部原本都是空气，是空气使这些空腔脏器膨胀变大，现在这些地方灌满了水，重量就产生了差别，于是整个身体就变得比以前要重。一般来说，这样的重量差别是足以使人的身体完全沉下去的。但在以下这些情况下，那种重量差别可能还不足以使人下沉，即那些落水者是骨架小缺乏肌肉或者多脂肪的身材。这类人即使淹死了，也依然会浮在水面上的。

"如果一具尸体，假设它沉到了河底，它就会一直留在那里，直到出于某种原因致使它的比重再次变得比其取代的那部分水的比重还轻为止。这种结果可能是由尸体腐烂或者其他什么原因造成的。尸体腐烂的结果就是会产生气体，把细胞组织以及所有的空腔脏器都扩大充满了，使人看起来外表肿胀，十分可怕。当尸体的这种膨胀扩充不

distension has so far progressed that the bulk of the corpse is materially increased without a corresponding increase of *mass* or weight, its specific gravity becomes less than that of the water displaced, and it forthwith makes its appearance at the surface. But decomposition is modified by innumerable circumstances – is hastened or retarded by innumerable agencies; for example, by the heat or cold of the season, by the mineral impregnation or purity of the water, by its depth or shallowness, by its currency or stagnation, by the temperament of the body, by its infection or freedom from disease before death. Thus it is evident that we can assign no period, with any thing like accuracy, at which the corpse shall rise through decomposition. Under certain conditions this result would be brought about within an hour; under others, it might not take place at all. There are chemical infusions by which the animal frame can be preserved *forever* from corruption; the Bi-chloride of Mercury is one. But, apart from decomposition, there may be, and very usually is, a generation of gas within the stomach, from the acetous fermentation of vegetable matter (or within other cavities from other causes) sufficient to induce a distension which will bring the body to the surface. The effect produced by the firing of a cannon is that of simple vibration. This may either loosen the

断增加，以至于尸体的体积也跟着极大地增加，而尸体的质量或是重量不随之相应增大的时候，它的比重就开始小于其取代的那部分水的比重了，于是尸体便立刻上浮直至露出水面。但是腐烂的程度是受数不清的环境因素调节控制的——通过数不清的媒介来使其加速或减缓。例如，季节性的高温或者低温，矿物质含量或者水的纯度，水的深浅度，水的流动程度或者静止程度，尸体起的化学反应的程度，死者生前有无疾病，如此等等。所以，很明显，我们不好确定尸体经过腐烂分解一直到它浮出水面所用的时间周期，不好确定它的精准性。在某些情况下，要达到这一效果可能只要大约一个钟头。在其他情况下，这一上浮效果可能根本就不会产生。还有某些化学溶液可以保持动物的躯体永不受腐蚀，二氯化汞就是其中之一。然而，除了腐烂之外，还有一种导致浮尸的成因是非常常见的，那就是胃里酸臭发酵的蔬菜等物可能会产生气体（或者是在其他空腔脏器里由于别的不同原因也可能会产生气体），这些气体导致的膨胀足以将尸体带出水面。由向尸体开火的加农大炮对尸体产生的影响就仅仅是简单的震动而已。这样做可能会强行使尸体脱离它已经嵌入的水底的松软泥浆或软泥，当其他媒介已经为尸体的上升做好准备

corpse from the soft mud or ooze in which it is imbedded, thus permitting it to rise when other agencies have already prepared it for so doing; or it may overcome the tenacity of some putrescent portions of the cellular tissue, allowing the cavities to distend under the influence of the gas.

"Having thus before us the whole philosophy of this subject, we can easily test by it the assertions of *L'Etoile*. 'All experience shows,' says this paper, 'that drowned bodies, or bodies thrown into the water immediately after death by violence, require from six to ten days for sufficient decomposition to take place to bring them to the top of the water. Even when a cannon is fired over a corpse, and it rises before at least five or six days' immersion, it sinks again if let alone.'

"The whole of this paragraph must now appear a tissue of inconsequence and incoherence. All experience does *not* show that 'drowned bodies' require from six to ten days for sufficient decomposition to take place to bring them to the surface. Both science and experience show that the period of their rising is, and necessarily must be, indeterminate. If, moreover, a body has risen to the surface through firing of cannon, it will *not* 'sink again if let alone,' until decomposition has so far progressed as to permit the escape of the generated gas. But I wish to call your

时，尸体由于炮轰而产生的这番□□离就会使其有可能浮起来。或者□□动也可能会克服一部分腐烂的细□组织的黏度，使那些空腔脏器在□体的作用下膨胀。

"搞清这个问题的全部基本□理之后，我们可以很容易地用它□检验《星报》的种种断言了。'所□□的经验都可以显示，'该报称，'□水而亡的人的尸体，或者被残杀□马上扔进水中的尸体，需要6到□天才会腐烂到足以浮出水面的□度。甚至用加农大炮炮轰沉尸地□的水面迫使它浮出，即使在炮轰□它浸泡了至少有五六天，如果放□不管的话它还是会再次沉下□的。'

"现在来讲，这整个段落看□来更像是个自相矛盾和语无伦次□交结体。所有的经验都没有显示'□水而亡的人的尸体'需要6到10□才会腐烂到足以浮出水面的程度□自然科学和实际经验都可以显示□尸体上浮所需的时间是不确定的□并且是必然的绝对的不确定。此外□如果一具尸体通过加农大炮已经□到水面上来了，它是不会'如果放□任不管的话就再次沉下去的'，□会一直保持这种状态直到尸体已□极度腐烂到了会使里面产生的气□全部跑掉的程度为止。但是我希

attention to the distinction which is made between 'drowned bodies,' and 'bodies thrown into the water immediately after death by violence.' Although the writer admits the distinction, he yet includes them all in the same category. I have shown how it is that the body of a drowning man becomes specifically heavier than its bulk of water, and that he would not sink at all, except for the struggles by which he elevates his arms above the surface, and his gasps for breath while beneath the surface – gasps which supply by water the place of the original air in the lungs. But these struggles and these gasps would not occur in the body 'thrown into the water immediately after death by violence.' Thus, in the latter instance, *the body, as a general rule, would not sink at all* – a fact of which *L'Etoile* is evidently ignorant. When decomposition had proceeded to a very great extent – when the flesh had in a great measure left the bones – then, indeed, but not *till* then, should we lose sight of the corpse.

"And now what are we to make of the argument, that the body found could not be that of Marie Rogêt, because, three days only having elapsed, this body was found floating? If drowned, being a woman, she might never have sunk; or having sunk, might have reappeared in twenty-four hours, or less. But no one supposes her to

您能注意一下'溺水而亡的人的尸体'和'被残杀后马上扔进水中的尸体'之间的差别。尽管作者承认两者间是有差别的，但他还是把它们全部纳入了同一类别里。我刚才已经说明了一个溺死者的尸体的重量为什么会变得比此人的排水量还要重，也说明了他为什么根本就不可能沉下去，除非这个不会游泳的人在挣扎时把他的胳膊伸出水面，同时在他处于水面以下的时候吃力地想要呼吸——然而供他呼吸的只有水，原本应该吸进空气的肺却吸进了水。但是这样的挣扎和这样的喘息是不会发生在'被残杀后马上扔进水中'的尸体上的。因此，在第二个例子里，一般来说，尸体是根本不会下沉的——这一事实明显被《星报》忽略了。等到尸体腐烂到非常严重的程度的时候——当肌肉大范围地脱离骨架的时候——在那时，而不是在那时之前，我们才真正地再也看不到那具尸体了。

"那么现在，我们又该怎么理解另一个观点呢？也就是找到的那具尸体可能不是玛丽·罗杰特，因为找到的尸体是浮起来的，而当时才仅仅过了3天。死者系女性，如果是淹死的，她可能根本就不会沉下去。又或者如果她沉下去了，她也有可能在24小时后重新浮上来，

have been drowned; and, dying before being thrown into the river, she might have been found floating at any period afterwards whatever.

"'But,' says *L'Etoile*, 'if the body had been kept in its mangled state on shore until Tuesday night, some trace would be found on shore of the murderers.' Here it is at first difficult to perceive the intention of the reasoner. He means to anticipate what he imagines would be an objection to his theory – viz: that the body was kept on shore two days, suffering rapid decomposition – more *rapid* than if immersed in water. He supposes that, had this been the case, it *might* have appeared at the surface on the Wednesday, and thinks that only under such circumstances it could so have appeared. He is accordingly in haste to show that it *was not* kept on shore; for, if so, 'some trace would be found on shore of the murderers.' I presume you smile at the *sequitur*. You cannot be made to see how the mere *duration* of the corpse on the shore could operate to *multiply* traces of the assassins. Nor can I.

"'And furthermore it is exceedingly improbable,' continues our journal, 'that any villains who had committed such a murder as is here supposed, would have thrown the body in without weight to sink it, when such a precaution could have so easily been taken.' Observe, here, the

也许都不用那么久。但是却没人猜测说她是被淹死的。然而，如果她被扔进河里前已经死掉了，那么不管怎样，在被抛尸后的任何时候她都有可能被发现浮于水上。

"'但是，'《星报》又说，'如果尸体保持这种残毁的状态一直藏在岸上，直到星期二晚上才被扔下水，岸上就应该能发现凶手藏尸的某些痕迹。'这句话初看起来让人很难察觉出推理者的意图。他的意思是说，他早就预料到了他的设想将会成为别人反对他观点的一个理由——也就是说，尸体在岸上放了两天，腐烂得很快——腐烂的速度比浸在水中还快。依他假设，如果这具尸体是这种情况的话，那它就有可能在星期三浮出水面，并且他认为，只有在这种情况下，尸体才会漂起来。因此，于是他匆忙表示尸体并没有放在岸上。因为如果放在岸上的话，'岸上就应该能发现凶手藏尸的某些痕迹'。我想您一定会觉得这个推论好笑。您肯定想不明白，尸体放在岸上只有短短的一段时间，怎么就会增加凶手的痕迹呢？我也想不明白。

"'而且此外还有件事极其不可能发生，'我们的报纸继续道，'那就是会有哪个在此被怀疑制造了这样一起谋杀案的坏蛋不用上能让尸体下沉的重物，就把尸体扔到河里呢——尽管采取这样的预防措

laughable confusion of thought! No one – not even *L'Etoile* – disputes the murder committed *on the body found*. The marks of violence are too obvious. It is our reasoner's object merely to show that this body is not Marie's. He wishes to prove that Marie is not assassinated – not that the corpse was not. Yet his observation proves only the latter point. Here is a corpse without weight attached. Murderers, casting it in, would not have failed to attach a weight. Therefore it was not thrown in by murderers. This is all which is proved, if any thing is. The question of identity is not even approached, and *L'Etoile* has been at great pains merely to gainsay now what it has admitted only a moment before. 'We are perfectly convinced,' it says, 'that the body found was that of a murdered female.'

"Nor is this the sole instance, even in this division of his subject, where our reasoner unwittingly reasons against himself. His evident object, I have already said, is to reduce, as much as possible, the interval between Marie's disappearance and the finding of the corpse. Yet we find him urging the point that no person saw the girl from the moment of her leaving her mother's house. 'We have no evidence,' he says, 'that Marie Rogêt was in the land of the living after nine o'clock on Sunday, June the twenty-second.' As his argument

施本来应该是件很容易的事情．'您看，看这儿，看这思维逻辑，多混乱，多可笑！没有一家报纸——甚至连《星报》都没有——质疑过找到的这具尸体是被谋杀的这一点。暴力留下的痕迹太明显了。推理者的目的仅仅是想表明这具尸体不是玛丽的。他希望证明玛丽并没有被杀害——而非想证明真正的死者不是被谋杀致死的。然而他的评论只能证明后面那点。这里有一具没有系重物的尸体。那些杀人凶手要想抛尸入水就一定不会忘记系上重物。因此这具尸体就不是那些杀人凶手扔的了。这就是他证明的全部东西了，如果他的确证明了什么东西的话。死者的身份问题他在讨论时甚至都没挨着点儿边，而《星报》煞费苦心的长篇大论也只不过是否定了它一分钟前刚承认的事实。'我们完全相信，'它所表达的就是，'找到的那具尸体是一位被谋杀的女性。'

"这也不是独一例，甚至在他叙述自己主题的这块，就是在我们的大推理家说理时却无意中驳倒了他自己的这块地方，都已经不是独一例了。我前面已经说过，他的目的明显就是尽量缩短自那女孩踏出她母亲家那一刻起就再没有人看到过她了这一点。'我们没有证据能

is obviously an *ex – parte* one, he should, at least, have left this matter out of sight; for had any one been known to see Marie, say on Monday, or on Tuesday, the interval in question would have been much reduced, and, by his own ratiocination, the probability much diminished of the corpse being that of the grisette. It is, nevertheless, amusing to observe that *L'Etoile* insists upon its point in the full belief of its furthering its general argument.

"Reperuse now that portion of this argument which has reference to the identification of the corpse by Beauvais. In regard to the *hair* upon the arm, *L'Etoile* has been obviously disingenuous. M. Beauvais, not being an idiot, could never have urged, in identification of the corpse, simply *hair upon its arm*. No arm is *without* hair.. The generality of the expression of *L'Etoile* is a mere perversion of the witness' phraseology. He must have spoken of some peculiarity in this hair. It must have been a *peculiarity* of color, of quantity, of length, or of situation.

"'Her foot,' says the journal, 'was small – so are thousands of feet. Her garter is no proof whatever – nor is her shoe – for shoes and garters are sold in packages. The same may be said of the flowers in her hat. One thing upon which M. Beauvais strongly insists is, that the clasp on the garter found, had been set back to take it

够证明,'他说,'在 6 月 22 日星期天上午 9 点钟以后玛丽·罗杰特仍旧活在人世。'由于他的观点显然非常片面,至少,他本可以别让大家再看到这个问题。因为假如已知有任何一个人看到了玛丽,假定在星期一看到的,或星期二,我们当前讨论的时间间隔就将会大大缩短了,而且,根据他的理论,尸体是女店员的可能性也就大大降低了。然而,我们看到《星报》一再强调他的观点,因为它坚信这一观点可以深化其整体总论点,这真是有趣得很呢!"

"咱们再来读读这篇论证提到的有关博韦辨尸的那一部分。关于胳膊上汗毛的那段,《星报》显然不够坦率。博韦先生不是傻瓜,在认尸的时候绝对不会仅凭胳膊上的汗毛就断定这就是死者本人。没有谁胳膊不长汗毛。《星报》的这番概述是对证人证词的纯粹的扭曲。证人一定提到了汗毛的某些特征。这些特征应当是在颜色、疏密、长短、生长位置等方面的特殊之处。

"'她的脚,'这篇报纸还说了,'很小——女人的脚都很小。不管怎样她的吊袜带是当不成证据了——她的鞋子也当不成——因为鞋子和吊袜带都是批量卖的那种。她帽子上的假花也一样。有一件事是博韦先生一再强调的,那就是他发现吊袜带上的挂钩为了缩紧一点而被往

in. This amounts to nothing; for most women find it proper to take a pair of garters home and fit them to the size of the limbs they are to encircle, rather than to try them in the store where they purchase.' Here it is difficult to suppose the reasoner in earnest. Had M. Beauvais, in his search for the body of Marie, discovered a corpse corresponding in general size and appearance to the missing girl, he would have been warranted (without reference to the question of habiliment at all) in forming an opinion that his search had been successful. If, in addition to the point of general size and contour, he had found upon the arm a peculiar hairy appearance which he had observed upon the living Marie, his opinion might have been justly strengthened; and the increase of positiveness might well have been in the ratio of the peculiarity, or unusualness, of the hairy mark. If, the feet of Marie being small, those of the corpse were also small, the increase of probability that the body was that of Marie would not be an increase in a ratio merely arithmetical, but in one highly geometrical, or accumulative. Add to all this shoes such as she had been known to wear upon the day of her disappearance, and, although these shoes may be 'sold in packages,' you so far augment the probability as to verge upon the certain. What, of itself, would be no

回挪了挪。这说明不了什么问题。大部分女性都是把一对儿吊袜带买回家去试，而不是在她们买吊袜带的商店里试穿，因为她们觉得这样是合乎风化的，买回家后她们再调整袜带挂钩以适合她们腿的尺寸。'从这段文字看我们很难假设推理者在严肃认真地推理。如果博韦先生在他寻找玛丽尸体的过程中，发现了另一具女尸，其大体上的体形和外貌都与那个失踪的女孩颇为相似，那么我敢保证他（根本不会注意死者的服饰问题）会在脑海里形成一种看法，那就是他已经成功找到玛丽的尸体了。如果除了体形和轮廓这点以外，他又发现尸体的手臂汗毛很重这一特殊现象，这与他所观察到的玛丽生前的汗毛特点相同，那么这一现象就可能充分地巩固他的看法。信心的增长肯定是与多毛特征的特殊性成比例的，或者说与它的不寻常性成比例。如果玛丽的脚很小，尸体的脚也很小，就更能增加死者就是玛丽的可能性，这种可能性的增长比例就不仅仅是算术上的了，而是高度的呈几何级数递增，或者说是累积递增。除此之外，死者的那双鞋子是那么地像大家印象里玛丽失踪那天穿的鞋子，而且，尽管这种鞋子可能是'批量卖的那种'，却还是大大增加了死者是玛丽的概率，让人们近乎确定了事实就是如此。就这些东

evidence of identity, becomes through its corroborative position, proof most sure. Give us, then, flowers in the hat corresponding to those worn by the missing girl, and we seek for nothing farther. If only one flower, we seek for nothing farther – what then if two or three, or more? Each successive one is multiple evidence – proof not *added* to proof, but *multiplied* by hundreds or thousands. Let us now discover, upon the deceased, garters such as the living used, and it is almost folly to proceed. But these garters are found to be tightened, by the setting back of a clasp, in just such a manner as her own had been tightened by Marie, shortly previous to her leaving home. It is now madness or hypocrisy to doubt. What *L'Etoile* says in respect to this abbreviation of the garter's being an usual occurrence, shows nothing beyond its own pertinacity in error. The elastic nature of the clasp-garter is self-demonstration of the *unusualness* of the abbreviation. What is made to adjust itself, must of necessity require foreign adjustment but rarely. It must have been by an accident, in its strictest sense, that these garters of Marie needed the tightening described. They alone would have amply established her identity. But it is not that the corpse was found to have the garters of the missing girl, or found to have her shoes, or her

西本身而言，它们并不足以成为辨尸的证据，但是通过它那证实其他证据的身份，它们就成了最为确凿的证据。然后，要是再告诉我们，死者帽子上的那些花和失踪女孩戴的那些相似，那么我们就真的不需要再找别的证据证明死者的身份了。如果总共只有一朵花，我们就不用再找别的证据了——但如果有两三朵，或是更多呢？——证据的可靠性不是一点点加上去的，而是成百上千地乘上去的。现在让我们再来看看，死者的吊袜带是那么地像玛丽活着时穿过的，这时再继续讨论这种大众型的吊袜带就显得很傻了。但是我们发现这对儿吊袜带被缩紧了，是通过往回移挂钩缩紧的，这是种只有死者才会用的特殊的方式，而玛丽也这么干过，就在她离家前不久。这时再去质疑死者的身份，不是疯了就是太虚伪了。吊袜带以一种不同寻常的方式被缩紧了，《星报》对这一现象的说法，除了说明它在坚持自己的错误观点外其他什么也说明不了。有扣吊袜带的弹性特征本身就证明了刻意缩短袜带是件很不寻常的事。袜带可以自己调节自己的长短，必须需要外力调节是很少见的。一定是出于什么偶然的原因，在最严格的意义上来讲，使得玛丽的这对儿吊袜带必须得按上述方式缩紧。仅是吊袜带就能充分确定尸体的身份是玛丽

bonnet, or the flowers of her bonnet, or her feet, or a peculiar mark upon the arm, or her general size and appearance – it is that the corpse had each, and *all collectively*. Could it be proved that the editor of *L'Etoile really* entertained a doubt, under the circumstances, there would be no need, in his case, of a commission *de lunatico inquirendo*. He has thought it sagacious to echo the small talk of the lawyers, who, for the most part, content themselves with echoing the rectangular precepts of the courts. I would here observe that very much of what is rejected as evidence by a court, is the best of evidence to the intellect. For the court, guiding itself by the general principles of evidence – the recognized and *booked* principles – is averse from swerving at particular instances. And this steadfast adherence to principle, with rigorous disregard of the conflicting exception, is a sure mode of attaining the *maximum* of attainable truth, in any long sequence of time. The practice, *in mass*, is therefore philosophical; but it is not the less certain that it engenders vast individual error.

"In respect to the insinuations levelled at Beauvais, you will be willing to dismiss them in a breath. You have already fathomed the true character of this good gentleman. He is a *busy-body*, with much of romance and little of wit. Any one so

了。然而我们这么说，并不是因为发现死者有失踪女孩的吊袜带，或者发现死者穿着她的鞋，或者戴着她的帽子，或者有她帽子上的假花，或者和她的脚型相似，或者在胳膊上有不寻常的特征，或者有她的身材和外貌——而是因为尸体不仅符合单个特征，而且是同时符合以上的全部特征。可以证实的是，在这种情况下，如果《星报》的编辑还对死者的身份抱有怀疑，就他的情况而言，都不用去精神鉴定委员会了。他认为仿效律师们的闲谈是明智的做法，但大多数情况下，律师们只满足于重复法庭上那张长方形令状上的陈词滥调。在此我要说的是，很多被法庭驳回的证据在聪明人看来都是最好的证据。对法庭来说，它是由证据的普遍性原则来指导办事的——公认并且付诸文字的原则——是反对偏袒某个特例的。这种坚决地照章办事、严格地漠视异己的做法在任意一段长而连续的时间内都是一种可靠的获得最大限度的可得事实的办事模式。因而总体上这种模式是很明智的。但是可以确定，它会造成个案的巨大失误。

"至于强烈针对博韦先生的那段暗讽，您一定很乐意立即就对它们不予理会。您已经了解了这位善良绅士的真实个性。他是个爱管闲事的人，十分浪漫却不太精明。任何一个心智构成是这样的人在遇到

constituted will readily so conduct himself, upon occasion of *real* excitement, as to render himself liable to suspicion on the part of the over acute, or the ill- disposed. M. Beauvais (as it appears from your notes) had some personal interviews with the editor of *L'Etoile*, and offended him by venturing an opinion that the corpse, notwithstanding the theory of the editor, was, in sober fact, that of Marie. 'He persists,' says the paper, 'in asserting the corpse to be that of Marie, but cannot give a circumstance, in addition to those which we have commented upon, to make others believe.' Now, without re-adverting to the fact that stronger evidence 'to make others believe,' could *never* have been adduced, it may be remarked that a man may very well be understood to believe, in a case of this kind, without the ability to advance a single reason for the belief of a second party. Nothing is more vague than impressions of individual identity. Each man recognizes his neighbor, yet there are few instances in which any one is prepared *to give a reason* for his recognition. The editor of *L'Etoile* had no right to be offended at M. Beauvais' unreasoning belief.

"The suspicious circumstances which invest him, will be found to tally much better with my hypothesis of romantic busy-bodyism, than with the reasoner's

真正让人受刺激的场合时都容易有这样失常的举止，以至于很可能使自己受到神经过于敏感或居心不良的人的怀疑。博韦先生（正如您的报刊摘录笔记摘录的那样）与《星报》的编辑进行过几次私人会谈，他不管不顾那位编辑的理论，直言不讳地谈论他对那具尸体身份的看法从而冒犯了那位编辑，他完全是在用事实说话，认为尸体肯定就是玛丽。'他固执地，'《星报》写道，'声称尸体是玛丽的，但除了那些我们已经点评过的证据，他再也给不出具体详细的理由让其他人相信他的观点。'现在，我们先不重提那个'让其他人相信的'更强有力的证据可能永远不会被举出来，只说说我的点评：在这类案子里，一个人可能会对某件事情了解得很透彻，因此深信不疑，却没有能力说出一个理由来解释他为什么会这般深信从而说服别人成为第二个'深信者'。没有什么比辨认个体身份时谈自己的感想更说不清道不明的了。每个人都能认出自己的邻居，然而却几乎没有什么例子里有人能说出他为什么会认出。《星报》的编辑没有必要迁怒于博韦先生讲不出理由却又深信不疑的东西。

"我们会发现，用我的'浪漫的好管闲事者'的假说来说明他身上带有的可疑因素，要比那个推理者暗示的博韦有罪的观点合理得

suggestion of guilt. Once adopting the more charitable interpretation, we shall find no difficulty in comprehending the rose in the key-hole; the 'Marie' upon the slate; the 'elbowing the male relatives out of the way;' the 'aversion to permitting them to see the body;' the caution given to Madame B-, that she must hold no conversation with the *gendarme* until his return (Beauvais'); and, lastly, his apparent determination 'that nobody should have anything to do with the proceedings except himself.' It seems to me unquestionable that Beauvais was a suitor of Marie's; that she coquetted with him; and that he was ambitious of being thought to enjoy her fullest intimacy and confidence. I shall say nothing more upon this point; and, as the evidence fully rebuts the assertion of *L'Etoile*, touching the matter of *apathy* on the part of the mother and other relatives – an apathy inconsistent with the supposition of their believing the corpse to be that of the perfumery- girl – we shall now proceed as if the question of *identity* were settled to our perfect satisfaction."

"And what," I here demanded, "do you think of the opinions of *Le Commerciel*?"

"That, in spirit, they are far more worthy of attention than any which have been promulgated upon the subject. The deductions from the premises are philosophical and acute; but the premises,

多。一旦采用了这种更为厚道的说明，我们就会发现，其实不难理解锁孔上的玫瑰花、留言板上的'玛丽'、'将死者的男性亲属推挤出调查的进程'、'不愿意让家属们去看那具尸体'、嘱咐B太太一定不要同警察谈话直到他（博韦）回来为止，以及，最后，他看上去决意'不让除去他自己以外的任何人插手此案的调查进程'。在我看来，毫无疑问，博韦是玛丽的追求者之一，玛丽曾冲他卖弄风情，而他则渴望让人们以为他享有与玛丽最为亲昵的关系以及她的信任。在这点上我就不多说什么了。而且，由于有关证据充分驳斥了《星报》的断言，这番断言涉及玛丽的母亲及其他家属对她的死很冷漠的问题——这种漠不关心与假设这些亲属们确信尸体就是'香水西施'这一推想背道而驰——所以我们现在可以假装身份认证这一问题已经圆满解决了，该继续往下分析了。"

"那么，"这时我问道，"您怎么看《商报》的那些观点的呢？"

"那个啊，从本质上讲，那些观点远比任何围绕这一案件主题的、已经被叫嚣着传开了的观点更值得关注。《商报》从前提演绎出来的推论明达而又尖锐。但是就它的

in two instances, at least, are founded in imperfect observation. *Le Commerciel* wishes to intimate that Marie was seized by some gang of low ruffians not far from her mother's door. 'It is impossible,' it urges, 'that a person so well known to thousands as this young woman was, should have passed three blocks without some one having seen her.' This is the idea of a man long resident in Paris – a public man – and one whose walks to and fro in the city, have been mostly limited to the vicinity of the public offices. He is aware that he seldom passes so far as a dozen blocks from his own *bureau*, without being recognized and accosted. And, knowing the extent of his personal acquaintance with others, and of others with him, he compares his notoriety with that of the perfumery-girl, finds no great difference between them, and reaches at once the conclusion that she, in her walks, would be equally liable to recognition with himself in his. This could only be the case were her walks of the same unvarying, methodical character, and within the same *species* of limited region as are his own. He passes to and fro, at regular intervals, within a confined periphery, abounding in individuals who are led to observation of his person through interest in the kindred nature of his occupation with their own. But the walks of Marie may, in general, be

前提本身而言，最少，我们能找出两处有点瑕疵的说辞。《商报》想要间接说明的是玛丽在距她母亲家门口不远的地方被一伙卑贱的流氓抓住。'以下这种事是不可能发生的，'它极力申述，'像这位年轻的女士这样众人皆知的人物，经过了3个街区竟然会没有谁看到过她。'看来这样的观点属于一个长期定居在巴黎的人——一位公众人物——他还是一个在城市中来回奔走的人，他的活动范围大大地被限制在办公署的邻近区域内。他意识到，从他自己的办公署出来，走过了一打街区那么远，一路上是很少不被人认出来或者上前搭话的。然后，在掌握了自己熟人圈的广度以及其他人的活跃范围后，他把自己的知名度与这位'香水西施'的知名度相比较，发现两者间并没有显著的差异，于是他马上得出结论，认为玛丽在平日步行外出时会被认出来的概率应该跟他被认出的概率相同。但这个情形成立的前提是玛丽外出的路线要和他一样不会有太大变化而又很有规律，并且活动范围跟他一样是限制在某个区域之内。在每天规律性的外出时间段内，这位先生往来活动于某个特定半径的圆周范围里，他会遇到非常多的人，这些人也是跟他一样的人，有着类似的生活环境，做着类似的事情。但是我认为玛丽的外出活动，一般来说，

supposed discursive. In this particular instance, it will be understood as most probable, that she proceeded upon a route of more than average diversity from her accustomed ones. The parallel which we imagine to have existed in the mind of *Le Commerciel* would only be sustained in the event of the two individuals' traversing the whole city. In this case, granting the personal acquaintances to be equal, the chances would be also equal that an equal number of personal rencounters would be made. For my own part, I should hold it not only as possible, but as very far more than probable, that Marie might have proceeded, at any given period, by any one of the many routes between her own residence and that of her aunt, without meeting a single individual whom she knew, or by whom she was known. In viewing this question in its full and proper light, we must hold steadily in mind the great disproportion between the personal acquaintances of even the most noted individual in Paris, and the entire population of Paris itself.

"But whatever force there may still appear to be in the suggestion of *Le Commerciel*, will be much diminished when we take into consideration *the hour* at which the girl went abroad. 'It was when the streets were full of people,' says *Le Commerciel*, 'that she went out.' But not

也许是没有规律可言的。在案中这种特殊的情况里，我们就能明白，极有可能，她去姑妈家的出行路线不同于她常走的那些去香水店的路线，可能会有更多的变化。我们设想的那种已经存在于《商报》编辑脑海里的相互比较之处，只有可能在以下情况里才成立，即这两个人在整个城市中来回穿行。在这种情况下，如果认为两个人的熟人数量相等，那么他们也就有相等的机会遇到同样多的熟人。就我个人而言，我会认为，玛丽在某个时候上街，从在她自己的住处和她姑妈的住处间的众多路线里随便选一条走，那么她不仅仅可能，而且是非常有可能遇不到任何一个她认识的人，或者被认识她的人认出来。以对待这类问题该有的全面而又正确的眼光去看待它，我们在脑海里就会坚定地相信，即使是巴黎最有名的人，他的熟人的数量和巴黎的总人口比，也是严重地不成比例的。

"但是不管《商报》的观点看上去多么有说服力，只要一考虑进这个女孩外出的时间，这种说服力就会被大大削减。'在街上全是人的时候，'《商报》说，'她出门离开的家。'但实际上并非如此。当时是上午 9 点钟。除了星期天以外，

so. It was at nine o'clock in the morning. Now at nine o'clock of every morning in the week, *with the exception of Sunday*, the streets of the city are, it is true, thronged with people. At nine on Sunday, the populace are chiefly within doors *preparing for church*. No observing person can have failed to notice the peculiarly deserted air of the town, from about eight until ten on the morning of every Sabbath. Between ten and eleven the streets are thronged, but not at so early a period as that designated.

"There is another point at which there seems a deficiency of observation on the part of *Le Commerciel*. 'A piece,' it says, 'of one of the unfortunate girl's petticoats, two feet long, and one foot wide, was torn out and tied under her chin, and around the back of her head, probably to prevent screams. This was done, by fellows who had no pocket-handkerchiefs.' Whether this idea is, or is not well founded, we will endeavor to see hereafter; but by 'fellows who have no pocket-handkerchiefs' the editor intends the lowest class of ruffians. These, however, are the very description of people who will always be found to have handkerchiefs even when destitute of shirts. You must have had occasion to observe how absolutely indispensable, of late years, to the thorough blackguard, has become the pocket-handkerchief."

一周里的每个上午 9 点钟，在这个城市的街道上的确会群集很多人。在星期天上午 9 点钟的时候，人们主要是待在家中准备去教堂。没有一个观察力敏锐的人会注意不到市区中格外冷清的气氛，就在每个安息日早上的 8 点钟到 10 点钟之间。在 10 点钟到 11 点钟之间，街上就又热闹起来，但在之前说的 9 点钟的时候，由于时间太早，街上是不会有什么人的。

"还有一处也可以看出《商报》的观察不够仔细。'一截，'它写道，'从这个不幸的女孩的某件衬裙上撕下来的布带，2 英尺长，1 英尺宽，绑到她的下巴底下，还绕过了她的后脑勺，大概是为了防止她喊叫。所以，能够干出这种事的，肯定是某些没有手帕的家伙。'不管这个想法成不成立，我们以后都会尽力搞清楚的。但是通过'肯定是某些没有手帕的家伙'这句话，可以看出编辑意在说明凶手是一些社会底层的流氓。然而，他所叙述的这种人身上永远都会带着手帕，即使是连衬衣都不穿的时候也是如此。您以前一定有过这样的机会，使您能注意到，近几年来，对于十足的流氓来说，手帕变得多么的必不可少。"

"然后我们又该怎么想呢？"

"And what are we to think," I asked, "of the article in *Le Soleil*?"

"That it is a vast pity its inditer was not born a parrot – in which case he would have been the most illustrious parrot of his race. He has merely repeated the individual items of the already published opinion; collecting them, with a laudable industry, from this paper and from that. 'The things had all *evidently* been there,' he says, 'at least, three or four weeks, and there can be *no doubt* that the spot of this appalling outrage has been discovered.' The facts here re-stated by *Le Soleil*, are very far indeed from removing my own doubts upon this subject, and we will examine them more particularly hereafter in connexion with another division of the theme.

"At present we must occupy ourselves with other investigations. You cannot fail to have remarked the extreme laxity of the examination of the corpse. To be sure, the question of identity was readily determined, or should have been; but there were other points to be ascertained. Had the body been in any respect *despoiled*? Had the deceased any articles of jewelry about her person upon leaving home? if so, had she any when found? These are important questions utterly untouched by the evidence; and there are others of equal moment, which have met with no attention.

我问道,"就是《太阳报》的那篇文章。"

"真的是非常可惜,那篇文章的作者没有生成一只学舌的鹦鹉——那样的话他肯定会成为同类中最杰出的一只。他仅仅只是重复了一遍各大报纸已经发表的观点。他以一种值得赞赏的勤勤恳恳的态度,一家家报纸地收集观点。'所有这些东西很明显已经摆在那里,'它说,'至少三四个星期了,毫无疑问地,这起骇人听闻的暴行的罪案现场终于被找到了。'这些在此被《太阳报》重申的事实,实际上远远没有消除我对这个问题的疑虑,我们以后会更投入地分析它们,连同这一主题的另一个观点一起分析。

"现在,我们必须进行一下其他方面的调查。您不可能没有注意到,尸体检验得极端粗心大意。自然,死者的身份问题很容易就确定下来了,或者是早该确定下来了,但是还有其他疑点需要我们去弄清楚。死者有没有什么东西被抢了?死者出门时身上有没有戴什么珠宝饰品?如果戴了的话,那么发现尸体的时候首饰还在吗?这都是些重要的问题,却完全没有与之有关的证据。还有其他一些同等重要的问题我们还没有对其予以关注。我们必须通过自己身体力行去努力弄明

We must endeavor to satisfy ourselves by personal inquiry. The case of St. Eustache must be re-examined. I have no suspicion of this person; but let us proceed methodically. We will ascertain beyond a doubt the validity of the *affidavits* in regard to his whereabouts on the Sunday. Affidavits of this character are readily made matter of mystification. Should there be nothing wrong here, however, we will dismiss St. Eustache from our investigations. His suicide, however corroborative of suspicion, were there found to be deceit in the affidavits, is, without such deceit, in no respect an unaccountable circumstance, or one which need cause us to deflect from the line of ordinary analysis.

"In that which I now propose, we will discard the interior points of this tragedy, and concentrate our attention upon its outskirts. Not the least usual error, in investigations such as this, is the limiting of inquiry to the immediate, with total disregard of the collateral or circumstantial events. It is the mal-practice of the courts to confine evidence and discussion to the bounds of apparent relevancy. Yet experience has shown, and a true philosophy will always show, that a vast, perhaps the larger portion of truth, arises from the seemingly irrelevant. It is through the spirit of this principle, if not precisely

白这些事情。圣·尤斯塔希的自杀案也要重新调查。我并不怀疑此人，但我们还是得有系统有条理地逐步弄清楚事情的真相。毋庸置疑，我们得确定一下他交给警察局长的那份他星期天行踪的证词书的真实性。这种性质的证词书很容易被弄得神秘兮兮的。但是，如果供词里不存在造假的成分，我们就可以把圣·尤斯塔希排除出我们的调查了。不管我们有多么相信他的自杀确实存在疑点，就算在他的证词书中发现了欺骗之处，或者就算没发现欺骗之处，无论哪种情况他的自杀都不是说不通的事情，或许他的自杀必然导致了我们偏离了平时分析问题的路线。

"我现在建议的是，我们得丢掉这桩惨案中的各种内在因素，而集中精力攻它的外围。像此案进行的这种只局限于探究直接证据，而全然不顾那些间接或是偶然事件的调查，绝对是错得离谱的。限制明显与案情有关联的证据及讨论的范围，这样的行为是案件审理官员们在玩忽职守。然而实践已经证明，并且正确的理论永远都能表明，许多真相——没准能有一大半的真相——都是来自于那些看起来与案情不相关的事情。正是根据这一原理传达的精神，假如不那么咬文嚼字理解的话，现代科学才决意要把偶

through its letter, that modern science has resolved to *calculate upon the unforeseen.* But perhaps you do not comprehend me. The history of human knowledge has so uninterruptedly shown that to collateral, or incidental, or accidental events we are indebted for the most numerous and most valuable discoveries, that it has at length become necessary, in any prospective view of improvement, to make not only large, but the largest allowances for inventions that shall arise by chance, and quite out of the range of ordinary expectation. It is no longer philosophical to base, upon what has been, a vision of what is to be. *Accident* is admitted as a portion of the substructure. We make chance a matter of absolute calculation. We subject the unlooked for and unimagined, to the mathematical *formulae of the schools.*

"I repeat that it is no more than fact, that the *larger* portion of all truth has sprung from the collateral; and it is but in accordance with the spirit of the principle involved in this fact, that I would divert inquiry, in the present case, from the trodden and hitherto unfruitful ground of the event itself, to the contemporary circumstances which surround it. While you ascertain the validity of the affidavits, I will examine the newspapers more generally than you have as yet done. So far, we have only reconnoitred the field of

然性因素考虑进来。但是您可能理解不了我的意思。人类知识的发展史未曾间断地表明，正是有了那些我们该对之感恩的间接，或者次要，或者是偶然性事件，才有了那些为数众多的和最有价值的发现，任何有可能出现的有关体制的改良与进步的看法都会认为，对于会由偶然性事件衍生出的发明创造，以及那些大大地超出一般预期的发明创造，我们不只要放大放宽对它们的限制，而是要最大限度地允许它们有产生的空间，留出这样的余地最终会变得非常必要。以想象为基础已是人们常做的事情了，但是这么做却不再是明智之举。意外事件才理应被承认是基础的一部分。我们把偶然事件看成是一种纯粹的计算上的问题。我们甚至可以用学校里教的数学公式去推测那些不可预期的、无法想象的事情。

"我重申一遍，在事情的全部真相当中，有一多半是由旁证间接得来的，这不过是事实罢了。正是依照这一事实所涉及的原理所传达的精神，就眼前的这件案子来讲，我会把我的调查从案子本身这块常被踩踏寻究却至今徒劳无果的土地转移到当时其周边的环境里去。当您搞清楚那份证词书的真实性时，我会在比您之前所搜过的报圈更广的范围里去搜罗些报纸资料来好好研究一下。到目前为止，咱们只是

investigation; but it will be strange indeed if a comprehensive survey, such as I propose, of the public prints, will not afford us some minute points which shall establish a *direction* for inquiry."

In pursuance of Dupin's suggestion, I made scrupulous examination of the affair of the affidavits. The result was a firm conviction of their validity, and of the consequent innocence of St. Eustache. In the mean time my friend occupied himself, with what seemed to me a minuteness altogether objectless, in a scrutiny of the various newspaper files. At the end of a week he placed before me the following extracts:

"About three years and a half ago, a disturbance very similar to the present, was caused by the disappearance of this same Marie Rogêt, from the *parfumerie* of Monsieur Le Blanc, in the Palais Royal. At the end of a week, however, she re-appeared at her customary comptoir, as well as ever, with the exception of a slight paleness not altogether usual. It was given out by Monsieur Le Blanc and her mother, that she had merely been on a visit to some friend in the country; and the affair was speedily hushed up. We presume that the present absence is a freak of the same nature, and that, at the expiration of a week, or perhaps of a month, we shall have her among us

侦查过了调查的范围。但是，如果对这些大众出版物做一个全面的纵览之后，我们还是找不到可以确定我们调查方向的微小的关键点，那可真的实在是太奇怪了。"

我依照杜宾的建议，一丝不苟地核查了圣·尤斯塔希的证词书里提到的每件事情。结果就是，我坚定地相信证词书上所言句句属实，因而这样的结果也就印证了圣·尤斯塔希的清白。与此同时，我的朋友正在忙着做一件在我看来完全是毫无目标的精细活，他仔细审阅了各种各样的报纸文档。苦干了一个星期后，他把下面这份摘录摆到了我的面前：

"大约在 3 年半以前，曾有过一次类似于最近这种骚动的轰动一时的风波，同样也是由玛丽·罗杰特的失踪引起的，她是从皇宫街莱·布兰克先生的香水店贸然出走的。然而一星期后，她又出现在她往常所站的柜台前，就像她以前那样，只是面色有些苍白，这点不完全像平时那样。据莱·布兰克先生和她母亲说，她只是去拜访了一下她乡下的某个朋友，之后这件事便迅速地被平息了下来。我们猜测，她的这次失踪是她的又一次突发奇想，和上回失踪的性质是一样的，并且，过满一个星期，或者顶多一个月，她就会又回到我们大家中间了。"——《晚报》，6 月 23 日，星期

again." – *Evening Paper*, Monday June 23.

"An evening journal of yesterday, refers to a former mysterious disappearance of Mademoiselle *Rogêt*. It is well known that, during the week of her absence from Le Blanc's parfumerie, she was in the company of a young naval officer, much noted for his debaucheries. A quarrel, it is supposed, providentially led to her return home. We have the name of the Lothario in question, who is, at present, stationed in Paris, but, for obvious reasons, forbear to make it public." – *Le Mercurie*, Tuesday Morning, June 24.

"An outrage of the most atrocious character was perpetrated near this city the day before yesterday. A gentleman, with his wife and daughter, engaged, about dusk, the services of six young men, who were idly rowing a boat to and fro near the banks of the Seine, to convey him across the river. Upon reaching the opposite shore, the three passengers stepped out, and had proceeded so far as to be beyond the view of the boat, when the daughter discovered that she had left in it her parasol. She returned for it, was seized by the gang, carried out into the stream, gagged, brutally treated, and finally taken to the shore at a point not far from that at which she had originally entered the boat with her parents. The villains have escaped for the time, but the police are upon their trail, and some of them will soon be taken." – *Morning Paper*, June 25.

一。

"昨天一家晚间报刊,提到罗杰特小姐以前的一次神秘失踪。众所周知,在她不在莱·布兰克的香水店的那周里,她是和一名年轻的海军军官在一起,这名军官由于其放荡而广为人知。据猜测,应该是一次吵架致使她愤然回家,真是老天保佑。我们前面讨论的这位海军军官的名字叫罗塔利奥,目前驻扎在巴黎;但是,由于种种不言自明的理由,他不愿公开自己的身份。"——《信使报》,6月24日,星期二晨版。

"前天本市近郊发生了一起性质极为恶劣的暴行。一名绅士偕妻带女,在近黄昏时分雇用了6名年轻男子划船送他们过河,当时这6名青年正在离塞纳河堤不远的水中来来去去地划船闲逛。船抵达对岸后,3名乘客离开船上了岸。当女儿发觉她把她的阳伞落在船上的时候,他们已经向前走了很远,以至于都看不见船了。她回去取伞时被这伙青年抓住了,他们堵住她的嘴,强行带到船里驶入河中,野蛮地施以暴行,最终又将她送至岸边,就在离她与双亲原先上船之地不远的地方。目前这伙坏蛋在逃。不过警方正循着他们的行踪追缉,并且其中几名很快就会被逮捕归案。"——《晨报》,6月25日。

"We have received one or two communications, the object of which is to fasten the crime of the late atrocity upon Mennais; but as this gentleman has been fully exonerated by a loyal inquiry, and as the arguments of our several correspondents appear to be more zealous than profound, we do not think it advisable to make them public." – *Morning Paper*, June 28.

"We have received several forcibly written communications, apparently from various sources, and which go far to render it a matter of certainty that the unfortunate Marie Rogêt has become a victim of one of the numerous bands of blackguards which infest the vicinity of the city upon Sunday. Our own opinion is decidedly in favor of this supposition. We shall endeavor to make room for some of these arguments hereafter." – *Evening Paper*, Tuesday, June 31.

"On Monday, one of the bargemen connected with the revenue service, saw a empty boat floating down the Seine. Sails were lying in the bottom of the boat. The bargeman towed it under the barge office. The next morning it was taken from thence, without the knowledge of any of the officers. The rudder is now at the barge office." – *Le Diligence*, Thursday, June 26.

Upon reading these various extracts,

"我们曾收到过一两封检举信，写信的目的是把前几天发生的那起暴行的罪名强加给一个名叫梅奈的人身上。但是经过一番负责任的调查后，这位先生已然被证明是完全无辜的了，并且由于检举信的作者们貌似均热心有余而证据不足，所以本报认为这些信件不宜曝光。"——《晨报》，6月28日。

"我们收到数封内容很有说服力的读者来信，它们貌似来源各异，来信者均肯定地认为，一到星期天市郊就冒出来许多流氓团伙，可怜的玛丽·罗杰特一定是被这其中的一伙人害死的。本报自己的观点是，我们断然支持这些来信者的推测。我们今后将努力为这些论述的其中几遍腾出版位以便其发表。"——《晚报》，6月31日，星期二。

"星期一那天，一名工作内容与税收服务行有关的驳船船夫看见有一条空船在塞纳河上顺流而下漂了过来。船夫把这条船拖至岸边的驳船办事处。第二天早上，有人未同驳船办事处工作人员打招呼就将该船从那里取走。现在这条船的船舵仍旧留在驳船办事处。"——《交通报》，6月26日，星期四。

读过这几篇内容各式各样的摘

they not only seemed to me irrelevant, but I could perceive no mode in which any one of them could be brought to bear upon the matter in hand. I waited for some explanation from Dupin.

"It is not my present design," he said, "to *dwell* upon the first and second of those extracts. I have copied them chiefly to show you the extreme remissness of the police, who, as far as I can understand from the Prefect, have not troubled themselves, in any respect, with an examination of the naval officer alluded to. Yet it is mere folly to say that between the first and second disappearance of Marie, there is no *supposable* connection. Let us admit the first elopement to have resulted in a quarrel between the lovers, and the return home of the betrayed. We are now prepared to view a second *elopement* (if we know that an elopement has again taken place) as indicating a renewal of the betrayer's advances, rather than as the result of new proposals by a second individual – we are prepared to regard it as a 'making up' of the old *amour*, rather than as the commencement of a new one. The chances are ten to one, that he who had once eloped with Marie, would again propose an elopement, rather than that she to whom proposals of elopement had been made by one individual, should have them made to her by another. And here let me

要后，我不仅觉得它们之间风马牛不相及，而且还认为它们没有以任何方式对我们手头的这桩案子产生影响。我期待着杜宾能够做出些解释。

"我当前的设想并不是，"杜宾说道，"去仔细研究这些摘录中的前两条。我把它们摘抄下来主要是为了向您表明警方是多么地粗心大意，我从警察局长那里得知，他们都不愿意去费心调查文中提到过的那位海军军官，无论这个军官的哪一个方面都没去查。然而，如果仅仅因为缺少证据推测不出两次失踪的联系就认为没有联系，那么就太愚蠢了。咱们暂且认为《晚报》所言属实：第一次私奔的最终结果是情人之间发生了口角，被玩弄的一方愤然回家。现在咱们准备把第二次私奔（假如我们确知又发生了一次私奔的话）看做是那个爱情骗子的再度示好，而不是另一名男子初次求爱的结果——也就是说我们准备把它看做是'旧情复燃'，而不是一段新恋情的开始。这样的可能性是 10:1，10 是那个曾经和玛丽私奔的人会再次提议私奔，这种可能要大于某名男子向玛丽提议私奔，然后玛丽欣然同意的可能性。在此，请允许我提醒您注意这样一点事实，就是在第一次既定的私奔与第二次假设的私奔之间用掉的时间，比我们的海军军人们巡航的一般周

call your attention to the fact, that the time elapsing between the first ascertained, and the second supposed elopement, is a few months more than the general period of the cruises of our men-of-war. Had the lover been interrupted in his first villainy by the necessity of departure to sea, and had he seized the first moment of his return to renew the base designs not yet altogether accomplished – or not yet altogether accomplished by *him*? Of all these things we know nothing.

"You will say, however, that, in the second instance, there was no elopement as imagined. Certainly not – but are we prepared to say that there was not the frustrated design? Beyond St. Eustache, and perhaps Beauvais, we find no recognized, no open, no honorable suitors of Marie. Of none other is there any thing said. Who, then, is the secret lover, of whom the relatives (*at least most of them*) know nothing, but whom Marie meets upon the morning of Sunday, and who is so deeply in her confidence, that she hesitates not to remain with him until the shades of the evening descend, amid the solitary groves of the Barrière du Roule? Who is that secret lover, I ask, of whom, at least, most of the relatives know nothing? And what means the singular prophecy of Madame Rogêt on the morning of Marie's departure? – 'I fear that I shall never see

期多不了几个月。在他第一次干坏事带玛丽私奔后，这对情人是否是由于他必须离开去执行出海任务才被迫分手了？他是否是一回来就重新开始了那些尚未完全实施的卑鄙图谋——或者说他本人尚未完全实施的卑鄙图谋？对于以上所有问题，我们都一无所知。

"不过，您一定会说，玛丽的第二次失踪根本就不像我们想象中的那样是私奔。当然可能不是——但是难道我们就准备说并不存在什么落空的不轨图谋吗？除了圣·尤斯塔希，也许还要加上博韦，咱们就再找不出大家公认的、公开的、体面的玛丽的追求者了。没有关于其他男子追求她的传闻。那么，那个秘密情人到底是谁？尽管玛丽的亲戚（至少大部分亲戚）对此人一无所知，不过星期天上午玛丽确实赴约与此人的约会，此人深得玛丽的信任，以至于她直到傍晚时分暮色降临还不愿意离开他，两人一直待在圆木栅门一带僻静的小树林里。我要问了，这个秘密情人到底是谁呢？至少，会有谁连玛丽的大部分亲戚都对其一无所知呢？而且，玛丽离家的那天上午，罗杰特太太说的那句带有预示性的话又是

Marie again.'

"But if we cannot imagine Madame Rogêt privy to the design of elopement, may we not at least suppose this design entertained by the girl? Upon quitting home, she gave it to be understood that she was about to visit her aunt in the Rue des Drômes and St. Eustache was requested to call for her at dark. Now, at first glance, this fact strongly militates against my suggestion; – but let us reflect. That she did meet some companion, and proceed with him across the river, reaching the Barrière du Roule at so late an hour as three o'clock in the afternoon, is known. But in consenting so to accompany this individual, (*for whatever purpose – to her mother known or unknown,*) she must have thought of her expressed intention when leaving home, and of the surprise and suspicion aroused in the bosom of her affianced suitor, St. Eustache, when, calling for her, at the hour appointed, in the Rue des Drômes, he should find that she had not been there, and when, moreover, upon returning to the *pension* with this alarming intelligence, he should become aware of her continued absence from home. She must have thought of these things, I say. She must have foreseen the chagrin of St. Eustache, the suspicion of all. She could not have thought of returning to brave this suspicion; but the suspicion

什么意思呢？——'恐怕我要再也见不到玛丽了。'

"如果我们无法想象罗杰特太太暗中参与了这起私奔的策划，那么我们是否可以假设，至少玛丽对这一私奔计划是感兴趣的呢？她离家的时候，她让别人以为她此行的目的是要到德罗姆街去拜访她的姑妈，并请圣·尤斯塔希先生傍晚时分去接她。那么，乍一看，这些事实与我的假设大相径庭——但是让我们仔细回想一下。她的确是见到了某个人，在他的陪同下一起过了河，到达圆木栅门时已经很晚了，大约已经是下午 3 点钟了，我们已知的情况就是这样的。但是在她答应同那男人在一起时（不管是出于什么目的——也不管她母亲事先知不知道），她肯定想到过她离家时向别人说的她此行所向的话，肯定也想到过，当她的未婚夫圣·尤斯塔希在约好的时间去德罗姆街接她，却发现她并不在那儿的时候，圣·尤斯塔希的心中会油然生出怎样的惊慌与猜疑之情。此外，她还有可能会想到当圣·尤斯塔希带着这条令他担惊受怕的消息回到她母亲的膳宿公寓后，他一定会明白过来其实她一直都没有回家。当时她一定想到了这些事情，我敢说，她肯定预见到了圣·尤斯塔希的懊恼，预见到了众人的猜疑。她不会想回去鼓起勇气面对人们的这种猜疑的。不过如

becomes a point of trivial importance to her, if we suppose her *not* intending to return.

"We may imagine her thinking thus – 'I am to meet a certain person for the purpose of elopement, or for certain other purposes known only to myself. It is necessary that there be no chance of interruption – there must be sufficient time given us to elude pursuit – I will give it to be understood that I shall visit and spend the day with my aunt at the Rue des Drômes – I well tell St. Eustache not to call for me until dark – in this way, my absence from home for the longest possible period, without causing suspicion or anxiety, will be accounted for, and I shall gain more time than in any other manner. If I bid St. Eustache call for me at dark, he will be sure not to call before; but, if I wholly neglect to bid him call, my time for escape will be diminished, since it will be expected that I return the earlier, and my absence will the sooner excite anxiety. Now, if it were my design to return *at all* – if I had in contemplation merely a stroll with the individual in question – it would not be my policy to bid St. Eustache call; for, calling, he will be *sure* to ascertain that I have played him false – a fact of which I might keep him for ever in ignorance, by leaving home without notifying him of my intention, by returning before dark, and by

果我们假设她不打算回去了，人们对她的这种猜疑在她看来就会变得无足轻重了。

"我们可以设想一下，她会这样权衡思量——'我要去见某个人，为的是同他一起私奔，或者是为了只有我自己才知道的某些其他目的。我认为我实现这些目的的时候一定不可以被人打断——必须要有充足的时间给我们俩来躲开追寻——所以我要让大家以为我会去拜访我那住在德罗姆街的姑妈，而且要和她待上一整天——我会告诉圣·尤斯塔希，让他傍晚再去接我——用这种方法的话，我就能把我不在家的可能时间拖延到最长而不引起他人的猜疑或焦虑，也就是说，比起用其他方法我会赢得更长的时间。如果我吩咐圣·尤斯塔希到傍晚来接我，他就绝对不会提前来接我。但是，如果我一句让他在傍晚来接我的话都没吩咐，我溜掉的时间就会被缩减掉，因为大家以为我会在傍晚之前回来，我没回来势必很快会引起人们的焦虑。现如今，假如我真打算回来——如果我只是打算和当前讨论的这个人散散步——那么吩咐圣·尤斯塔希去接我就不应该出现在我的策略当中。因为，他一来接我，他就肯定会发现我耍了他——如果事实真相就是我耍了他，我可以永远不让他知道我是在骗他，通过在离开家时不告诉他我

then stating that I had been to visit my aunt in the Rue des Drômes. But, as it is my design never to return – or not for some weeks – or not until certain concealments are effected – the gaining of time is the only point about which I need give myself any concern.'

"You have observed, in your notes, that the most general opinion in relation to this sad affair is, and was from the first, that the girl had been the victim of *a gang* of blackguards. Now, the popular opinion, under certain conditions, is not to be disregarded. When arising of itself – when manifesting itself in a strictly spontaneous manner – we should look upon it as analogous with that intuition which is the idiosyncrasy of the individual man of genius. In ninety-nine cases from the hundred I would abide by its decision. But it is important that we find no palpable traces of *suggestion*. The opinion must be rigorously *the public's own*; and the distinction is often exceedingly difficult to perceive and to maintain. In the present instance, it appears to me that this 'public opinion' in respect to *a gang*, has been superinduced by the collateral event which is detailed in the third of my extracts. All Paris is excited by the discovered corpse of Marie, a girl young, beautiful and notorious. This corpse is found, bearing marks of violence, and floating in the river.

此行的目的就可以做到，然后在天黑前赶回来，那个时候我就说我去看我住在德罗姆街的姑妈了。但是，既然我的计划是永远不回来——或者几个星期后再回来——或者等到我们找到某处固定的藏匿点后再回来——那么我需要关心的唯一关键点就是争取时间了。'

"您已经观察到，从您的报刊摘录笔记来看，公众对于这桩惨案最普遍的看法是——而且从一开始就一直是这么看的——这个姑娘是被一伙流氓杀害了。现如今，某些情况下，在公众中流行的看法是不应该被忽视的。当公众看法从公众中形成以后——当公众看法以一种严格的自发性的方式从公众心中明白表示出来——我们应该把这种看法当做一种类似于直觉的东西对待，而直觉属于天才人物的特质。在 100 起案子中，99 起我会遵从于公众的抉择。但重要的是，我们不能在这种公众的看法中找到明显的受人指使过的痕迹。看法必须在严格意义上是属于公众自己的。然而这样的差别却常常是极难被感知到，并且常常也是极难遵守的。在此案中，在我看来貌似关于那伙暴徒的'公众看法'有偏激之处，详情可见我摘录的第三则间接事件。玛丽，一个年轻貌美、尽人皆知的女孩，尸体的发现刺激了整个巴黎的神经。她的尸体被发现浮于塞纳

But it is now made known that, at the very period, or about the very period, in which it is supposed that the girl was assassinated, an outrage similar in nature to that endured by the deceased, although less in extent, was perpetuated, by a gang of young ruffians, upon the person of a second young female. Is it wonderful that the one known atrocity should influence the popular judgment in regard to the other unknown? This judgment awaited direction, and the known outrage seemed so opportunely to afford it! Marie, too, was found in the river; and upon this very river was this known outrage committed. The connexion of the two events had about it so much of the palpable, that the true wonder would have been a *failure* of the populace to appreciate and to seize it. But, in fact, the one atrocity, known to be so committed, is, if any thing, evidence that the other, committed at a time nearly coincident, was not so committed. It would have been a miracle indeed, if, while a gang of ruffians were perpetrating, at a given locality, a most unheard-of wrong, there should have been another similar gang, in a similar locality, in the same city, under the same circumstances, with the same means and appliances, engaged in a wrong of precisely the same aspect, at precisely same period of time! Yet in what, if not in this marvellous train of

河上，身上伤痕累累。然而现在大家知道，恰好就在玛丽被假定杀害的这段时间中，或者在这个时间段前后的某个时间中，发生过另一起与施加在死者身上的暴行本质上有些相似的违法行为，尽管程度稍逊。这是由一伙流氓小青年干的，受害者是另一名年轻的女性。一件已为公众所知的暴行竟然会影响公众对另一件尚不清楚始末的暴行的判断，您说这妙不妙？这种判断等待着一种导向，而那起始末都为公众所知的暴行就那么及时地出现了，看起来恰好就可以担当这样一种导向！同样地，玛丽也在那条河上被发现了，而这条河又恰好是那起已知暴行发生的地方。这两件事情的联系实在是太明显不过了，大众若认识不到这种联系的重要性，不去抓紧利用这种联系，那才真叫奇怪呢。但是，事实上，这起暴行大家已知它是那样发生的，那样的暴行如果真能证明什么的话，那也只能证明几乎发生在同一时间的另一起暴行不是那样发生的。如果一伙流氓在某一特定地点干了一件令人发指的恶行，而同时又有另一伙类似的流氓，在一个类似的地点，在同样的城市里、同样的环境下，用同样的手段、同样的器具，正好干了一桩相同性质的恶行，犯罪时间又正好是相同的时间段，那可真是一个奇迹了！然而，如果不是这一奇

coincidence, does the accidentally *suggested* opinion of the populace call upon us to believe?

"Before proceeding farther, let us consider the supposed scene of the assassination, in the thicket at the Barrière du Roule. This thicket, although dense, was in the close vicinity of a public road. Within were three or four large stones, forming a kind of seat with a back and footstool. On the upper stone was discovered a white petticoat; on the second, a silk scarf. A parasol, gloves, and a pocket-handkerchief, were also here found. The handkerchief bore the name, 'Marie Rogêt.' Fragments of dress were seen on the branches around. The earth was trampled, the bushes were broken, and there was every evidence of a violent struggle.

"Notwithstanding the acclamation with which the discovery of this thicket was received by the press, and the unanimity with which it was supposed to indicate the precise scene of the outrage, it must be admitted that there was some very good reason for doubt. That it *was* the scene, I may or I may not believe – but there was excellent reason for doubt. Had the *true* scene been, as *Le Commerciel* suggested, in the neighborhood of the Rue Pavée St. Andrée, the perpetrators of the crime, supposing them still resident in Paris,

列不可思议的巧合,那么公众的那些无意中的受到过暗示的看法想要让我们相信的又是什么呢?

"在作进一步的深入探讨之前,让我们先细究一下在圆木栅门附近的灌木林中那个假定的凶杀现场。这个灌木林尽管十分茂密,却是在离公路很近的地方。灌木林里有三四块大石头,摆成的样子有几分像坐椅,既有椅背又有脚凳。在上面的石头上发现了一条白衬裙;在第二块石头上发现一条丝绸围巾。他们还在那里找到了一把女用阳伞、一副手套和一块手帕。手帕上绣有一个名字,'玛丽·罗杰特'。在四周的枝杈上到处都能看到裙子的碎片。泥土被踩踏过,矮树丛的枝条也被折断了,这一切都可以证明此处发生过一番搏斗。

"尽管新闻界看到灌木林中的这一大发现后都为其鼓掌叫好,而且大家一致认为灌木林中发现的这个地点应该显示的就是确切的暴力现场,必须得承认,我们的确有若干很好的理由来对这点看法表示怀疑。他们说这就是现场,这点我可以相信也可以不相信——然而我的确是有极佳的理由去质疑它。如果如《商报》所说,真正的凶杀现场在圣安德里的铺石街一带,那么杀人凶手呢,假如他们仍然住在巴黎,自然就会因为公众的注意力敏锐地

would naturally have been stricken with terror at the public attention thus acutely directed into the proper channel; and, in certain classes of minds, there would have arisen, at once, a sense of the necessity of some exertion to redivert this attention. And thus, the thicket of the Barrière du Roule having been already suspected, the idea of placing the articles where they were found, might have been naturally entertained. There is no real evidence, although *Le Soleil* so supposes, that the articles discovered had been more than a very few days in the thicket; while there is much circumstantial proof that they could not have remained there, without attracting attention, during the twenty days elapsing between the fatal Sunday and the afternoon upon which they were found by the boys. 'They were all *mildewed* down hard,' says Le *Soleil*, adopting the opinions of its predecessors, 'with the action of the rain, and stuck together from mildew. The grass had grown around and over some of them. The silk of the parasol was strong, but the threads of it were run together within. The upper part, where it bad been doubled and folded, was all mildewed and rotten, and tore on being opened.' In respect to the grass having 'grown around and over some of them,' it is obvious that the fact could only have been ascertained from the words, and thus from the recollections, of two

直指进通向找出杀人凶手的正确通道而被折磨得胆战心惊。那么，按照一般人的思维方式，凶手应该立刻想到有必要做些努力去转移人们的注意力。因此，既然圆木栅门一带的灌木林已经受到怀疑，那么把玛丽的身上的物品放到人们找到的那个‘凶杀现场’去的这一想法，很可能自然而然地就被凶手考虑到了。尽管《太阳报》如是推测说那些东西摆在那里至少有三四个星期，但是它们并没有真正的证据能证明灌木林中发现的那些物品置放的天数。然而现场周围的那些间接物证也不可能一直留在那里，还不会吸引别人的注意力，从那个灾难性的星期天到死者物品被男孩子们发现的那个下午，这些物品都已经在那儿躺了有 20 天了。‘它们都发霉发得很严重了，’《太阳报》又采纳了在它之前就已经有了的观点，说道，‘是因为下雨的缘故，由于霉菌而彼此粘连在一起。其中有几样东西的周围和上面都长了草。女用阳伞的绸面很结实，但是里面的丝线却都乱糟糟地缠在了一起。阳伞的上半部分是折叠起来的，全部都已经发霉并且腐烂，而且伞一撑开伞面就扯破了。’就‘其中有几样东西的周围和上面都长了草’这句话来说，显然我们只能根据字面意思来弄清事实真相，而这些叙述的真实仅是来自于两个小男孩的回忆。

small boys; for these boys removed the articles and took them home before they had been seen by a third party. But grass will grow, especially in warm and damp weather, (such as was that of the period of the murder,) as much as two or three inches in a single day. A parasol lying upon a newly turfed ground, might, in a single week, be entirely concealed from sight by the upspringing grass. And touching that *mildew* upon which the editor of *Le Soleil* so pertinaciously insists, that he employs the word no less than three times in the brief paragraph just quoted, is he really unaware of the nature of this *mildew*? Is he to be told that it is one of the many classes of *fungus*, of which the most ordinary feature is its upspringing and decadence within twenty-four hours?

"Thus we see, at a glance, that what has been most triumphantly adduced in support of the idea that the articles had been 'for at least three or four weeks' in the thicket, is most absurdly null as regards any evidence of that fact. On the other hand, it is exceedingly difficult to believe that these articles could have remained in the thicket specified, for a longer period than a single week – for a longer period than from one Sunday to the next. Those who know any thing of the vicinity of Paris, know the extreme difficulty of finding *seclusion* unless at a great distance from its suburbs.

我会这样说是因为在第三方看到这些物品之前，男孩子们可能已经把这些东西挪了地方还捡回了家。但是要知道草会长高，尤其是在一个温暖又潮湿的气候里（就比如凶案发生的那段时期的气候），仅一天就能长2或3英寸那么高。一柄阳伞躺在一块新长的草皮上，也许，在一周内，就能完全被长高的草挡住而隐匿于视线之外。《太阳报》的编辑如此执著地坚持使用'霉'这个字眼，以至于在我们刚刚引用的那段短短的段落中就用到了3次之多，他难道真的不知道'霉菌'的自然特性吗？难道没有人告诉他，霉菌是各式各样真菌中的一种，真菌最常见的特性之一就是它能在24小时之内生长与消亡？

"所以随便一瞥，我们便可看出，《太阳报》最得意的为支持它论点而举出的'这些物品在灌木林中至少有三四个星期'的理由，也是所有和那个事实相关的证据里最荒谬最没有价值的一个。另一方面，实在难以相信这些物品在文中特指的灌木林中待的时间会超过一个星期——比一个星期天到下一个的时间还长。那些对巴黎市郊稍有了解的人都知道，要想找到个'偏僻的地方'是极为困难的，除非去离市郊更远的远郊找。像这样一个未开发过乃至人迹罕至的隐秘场所，还

Such a thing as an unexplored, or even an unfrequently visited recess, amid its woods or groves, is not for a moment to be imagined. Let any one who, being at heart a lover of nature, is yet chained by duty to the dust and heat of this great metropolis – let any such one attempt, even during the weekdays, to slake his thirst for solitude amid the scenes of natural loveliness which immediately surround us. At every second step, he will find the growing charm dispelled by the voice and personal intrusion of some ruffian or party of carousing blackguards. He will seek privacy amid the densest foliage, all in vain. Here are the very nooks where the unwashed most abound – here are the temples most desecrate. With sickness of the heart the wanderer will flee back to the polluted Paris as to a less odious because less incongruous sink of pollution. But if the vicinity of the city is so beset during the working days of the week, how much more so on the Sabbath! It is now especially that, released from the claims of labor, or deprived of the customary opportunities of crime, the town blackguard seeks the precincts of the town, not through love of the rural, which in his heart he despises, but by way of escape from the restraints and conventionalities of society. He desires less the fresh air and the green trees, than the utter license of the

藏于森林或小树林中，片刻都不需想，根本不存在。让任何一个从心底热爱大自然，却被工作束缚在竞争激烈的大都市里的人——让任何一个这样的人去试试看，即使是挑工作日去试也行，让他去满足自己对于独处这一心情的渴望，让自己置身于紧紧环抱着他的自然美景当中。然而某些无赖或寻欢作乐的流氓团伙总会搞出嘈杂的噪声，侵扰他的私人空间，于是每多走一步，他就会发现逐渐增强的独处的吸引力被他们一扫而空。他决意在环抱枝叶最浓密处寻找可以独处的地方，然而最终却徒劳无获。这里是社会底层民众大量滋生的僻静角落——这里是亵渎神圣的殿堂。这位漫步者心中作呕，决意返回已被污染过的巴黎，返回那个不太令人生厌的地方，因为巴黎没有那么多处不协调的滋生堕落的巢穴。但若城市市郊在一周的工作日中都被这样困扰着，那么到了安息日又会何等不堪！现在尤其是这样，平日里城镇中的流氓总被要求不断地去工作，现在终于从中解脱出来了，或者说由于体面人的安息日也休息了，城镇流氓被剥夺了平常作案的有利机会，所以他就走向了城镇的郊区，并不是出于对田园风光的热爱——他在心底对田园风光并不感兴趣——而是为了逃离社会的束缚和俗套。他对新鲜空气和翠绿树木

country. Here, at the road-side inn, or beneath the foliage of the woods, he indulges, unchecked by any eye except those of his boon companions, in all the mad excess of a counterfeit hilarity – the joint offspring of liberty and of rum. I say nothing more than what must be obvious to every dispassionate observer, when I repeat that the circumstance of the articles in question having remained undiscovered, for a longer period – than from one Sunday to another, in any thicket in the immediate neighborhood of Paris, is to be looked upon as little less than miraculous.

"But there are not wanting other grounds for the suspicion that the articles were placed in the thicket with the view of diverting attention from the real scene of the outrage. And, first, let me direct your notice to the date of the discovery of the articles. Collate this with the date of the fifth extract made by myself from the newspapers. You will find that the discovery followed, almost immediately, the urgent communications sent to the evening paper. These communications, although various and apparently from various sources, tended all to the same point – viz., the directing of attention to *a gang* as the perpetrators of the outrage, and to the neighborhood of the *Barrière* du Roule as its scene. Now here, of course, the suspicion is not that, in consequence of

的渴望，要少于对乡下特有的那种彻底的放纵生活的渴望。在这里，无论是在路边小旅店还是林荫之下，他都不会遭受任何责难的目光，除了他的那些狐朋狗友以外，他可以在一种刻意营造的热闹气氛中纵情享受所有这些疯狂无度——无拘无束地喝朗姆酒混合后的产物。我说这话没别的意思，就是跟您讲一个每个冷静的观察者都肯定能发现的明显问题，我再说一遍，话题里的那些物品所处环境能在很长一段时间里一直保持着不被发现的状态——比一个星期天到另一个的间隔还长，而且还是处在巴黎近郊的某个灌木林里，这样的事绝不亚于奇迹。

"但是我们不需要为我们的怀疑找额外的证据，物品被移至灌木林里，为了把人们的注意力从真正的暴行现场转移过来。那么，首先，请允许我将您的注意力转移到那些物品被发现的日期上来。把这个日期同我亲自摘录的第五则消息的日期比较一下。您会发现，那几封加急的读者来信刚寄给《晚报》报社，几乎在同一时间，那些物品紧跟着就被发现了。这些读者来信，虽然各种各样而且貌似来源也各异，但用意却都趋于同一点——，把人们的注意力引向一伙流氓，说他们才是暴行的始作俑者，并且把人们的注意力引向圆木栅门的周边地区，

these communications, or of the public attention by them directed, the articles were found by the boys; but the suspicion might and may well have been, that the articles were not before found by the boys, for the reason that the articles had not before been in the thicket; having been deposited there only at so late a period as at the date, or shortly prior to the date of the communications by the guilty authors of these communications themselves.

"This thicket was a singular – an exceedingly singular one. It was unusually dense. Within its naturally walled enclosure were three extraordinary stones, *forming a seat with a back and footstool.* And this thicket, so full of a natural art, was in the immediate vicinity, *within a few rods*, of the dwelling of Madame Deluc, whose boys were in the habit of closely examining the shrubberies about them in search of the bark of the sassafras. Would it be a rash wager – a wager of one thousand to one – that *a day* never passed over the heads of these boys without finding at least one of them ensconced in the umbrageous hall, and enthroned upon its natural throne? Those who would hesitate at such a wager, have either never been boys themselves, or have forgotten the boyish nature. I repeat – it is exceedingly hard to comprehend how the articles could have remained in this thicket undiscovered, for a Longer period

说那里才是行凶现场。当然，现在我们并不是说由于读者来信的缘故，或者说并不是由于它们引导了公众注意力的缘故，那些物品才被男孩子们找到——疑点并不在这里。但是疑点曾经很可能是——并且一直很可能是——那些物品之前没被男孩子们找到，根本原因在于那些物品之前其实不在灌木林里。它们仅仅是凶手扮的'读者'在写信的当天，或在写信前不久，亲手放到那里去的。

"这片灌木林是一片独一无二的灌木林——一片非常非常特别的灌木林。它的茂密程度十分罕见。在它的天然围栏里有 3 块造型独特的石头，摆成了一个既有椅背又有脚凳的坐椅。这片灌木林，那么富有天然的艺术气息，就在紧挨着德吕克太太住处的周边地区，不过几杆远，德吕克太太家的男孩子们就养成了仔细搜查灌木林从中寻找黄樟树皮的习惯。想不想和我来个一赌定输赢？——1 对 1000 的赌注——我说用不了一天的时间，男孩子们中就至少会有一个要躲在这个多荫的娱乐中心，登上这个天然的'宝座'去坐一坐。那些在打这样一个赌时犹豫不决的人，他们肯定要么就从来没做过男孩子，要么就是忘记了男孩子的天性。我重申一遍——有一点让人极其难以理解，那就是这些物品是如何一直待在这个灌

than one or two days; and that thus there is good ground for suspicion, in spite of the dogmatic ignorance of *Le Soleil*, that they were, at a comparatively late date, deposited where found.

"But there are still other and stronger reasons for believing them so deposited, than any which I have as yet urged. And, now, let me beg your notice to the highly artificial arrangement of the articles. On the *upper* stone lay a white petticoat; on the *second* a silk scarf; scattered around, were a parasol, gloves, and a pocket-handkerchief bearing the name, 'Marie Rogêt.' Here is just such an arrangement as would *naturally* be made by a not over-acute person wishing to dispose the articles *naturally*. But it is by no means a *really* natural arrangement. I should rather have looked to see the things all lying on the ground and trampled under foot. In the narrow limits of that bower, it would have been scarcely possible that the petticoat and scarf should have retained a position upon the stones, when subjected to the brushing to and fro of many struggling persons. 'There was evidence,' it is said, 'of a struggle; and the earth was trampled, the bushes were broken,' – but the petticoat and the scarf are found deposited as if upon shelves. 'The pieces of the frock torn out by the bushes were about three inches wide and six inches long. One part was the hem

木林里而不被发现的,而且待的时间还不止一天两天。所以我们可以有很好的理由去怀疑,而完全不用管《太阳报》那独断专横的愚昧无知,我怀疑那些物品是在相当晚的时候才被摆在当初它们被找到的那个地方的。

"但是仍旧有其他的,或者有比我刚才竭力阐明的更强有力的理由能让人相信东西是后搁的。那么,现在,允许我请您注意,这些物品摆放的位置有高度的人为布置过的痕迹。上面那块状似靠背的石头上放着一条白色衬裙;下面那块状似坐垫的石头上放着一条丝绸围巾;散落在地上的,有一柄阳伞、一副手套和一块手帕,手帕上还绣着'玛丽·罗杰特'的名字。一个不那么聪明的人本想要把这些物品布置得'很自然',它们却被'很自然地'摆弄成了当前的这副样子,事情仅此而已。然而这副样子却实在是一点也不自然。我倒宁可期望看到所有的东西都躺在地上,还都被人用脚踩踏过了,那倒更像是真的。由于这片林荫地的范围很狭小,当遭遇了许多人搏斗时的搓来蹭去,衬裙和围巾几乎不可能还留在石头上而没掉落在地。'有迹象表明,'据说,'那里曾经历过一场搏斗;泥土被踩踏过了,矮树丛的枝条也被折断了'——但是衬裙和围巾竟然还好好地搁在那儿,就好像放在架子

of the frock and it had been mended. They *looked like strips torn off.*' Here, inadvertently, *Le Soleil* has employed an exceedingly suspicious phrase. The pieces, as described, do indeed 'look like strips torn off"; but purposely and by hand. It is one of the rarest of accidents that a piece is 'torn off,' from any garment such as is now in question, by the agency *of a thorn*. From the very nature of such fabrics, a thorn or nail becoming entangled in them, tears them rectangularly – divides them into two Longitudinal rents, at right angles with each other, and meeting at an apex where the thorn enters – but it is scarcely possible to conceive the piece 'torn off.' I never so knew it, nor did you. To tear a piece off from such fabric, two distinct forces, in different directions, will be, in almost every case, required. If there be two edges to the fabric – if, for example, it be a pocket-handkerchief, and it is desired to tear from it a slip, then, and then only, will the one force serve the purpose. But in the present case the question is of a dress, presenting but one edge. To tear a piece from the interior, where no edge is presented, could only be effected by a miracle through the agency of thorns, and no one thorn could accomplish it. But, even where an edge is presented, two thorns will be necessary, operating, the one in two distinct directions, and the other in

上一样。'从套裙上被矮树丛的枝杈刮下来的碎布条差不多都有 3 英寸宽 6 英寸长。有一条是套裙的褶边，还是缝补过的。它们看起来都很像被撕好的布条。'您看就在这儿，一不留神，《太阳报》就点出了那句极度可疑的短句。那些碎布条，如上所述，确实是'看起来都很像被撕好的布条'，而且是故意被撕下来的，用手撕的。刺枝儿居然能从像当前讨论的这种套裙上'撕下来'一片碎布条，这真是世间罕有的意外之一。由于这种织物的天然特性，不管是刺枝的刺儿还是钉子卷进这样的织物里，都有可能把它捅破扯出一个呈直角的破角——把织物撕出两条纵向的口子，两条口子相互呈直角，会合在刺儿扎进去的顶点处——但是我们绝不可能认为这样的碎布条会被'撕下来'。我从不知道能发生这样的事，想必您也不知道吧。要想从这样的织物上撕掉一片碎布条，必须得用不同方向的两股力同时发力，几乎在所有情况下，想撕掉布条都需要这样做。假设这件织物有两条边——假设，举个例子，这是一块手帕，我们希望把它撕出一小条，那么，为达到这一目的我们只需要一股力就行了。但是问题是在当前这个案例里，织物是一条裙子，只有一条边。想要从没有边儿的裙子中间撕出碎条来，刺枝儿就只能借助奇迹来达到这一效

one. And this in the supposition that the edge is unhemmed. If hemmed, the matter is nearly out of the question. We thus see the numerous and great obstacles in the way of pieces being 'torn off' through the simple agency of 'thorns;' yet we are required to believe not only that one piece but that many have been so torn. 'And one part,' too, '*was the hem of the frock!*' Another piece was '*part of the skirt, not the hem,*' – that is to say, was torn completely out through the agency of thorns, from the uncaged interior of the dress! These, I say, are things which one may well be pardoned for disbelieving; yet, taken collectedly, they form, perhaps, less of reasonable ground for suspicion, than the one startling circumstance of the articles' having been left in this thicket at all, by any murderers who had enough precaution to think of removing the corpse. You will not have apprehended me rightly, however, if you suppose it my design to deny this thicket as the scene of the outrage. There might have been a wrong here, or, more possibly, an accident at Madame Deluc's. But, in fact, this is a point of minor importance. We are not engaged in an attempt to discover the scene, but to produce the perpetrators of the murder. What I have adduced, notwithstanding the minuteness with which I have adduced it, has been with the view,

果了，只用一根刺枝儿是绝不可能完成的。但是，就算已经有一条边了，这两根刺枝也必须得按以下方式撕才行，即其中一个撕出两个方向的口子，另一个只朝一个方向划口子。这还是得在假设裙边不是褶边的情况下才行。如果缝上了褶边，事情就几乎不可能办到了。因此我们看到无数巨大的障碍物挡在路中间，告诉我们碎布条不可能被简单几根刺儿就'撕下来'。然而我们还得相信不止一片碎布条，而是许多碎布条都被这么撕下来的。'而且其中有一条，'同样地，'是套裙的褶边'！另一条是从'裙摆上撕下来的，而不是褶边'——也就是说，凭着刺枝儿的力量，就把它们从裙子中间完完整整地撕下来了！我得说，我们对此有怀疑，这是完全可以理解的。然而，冷静来看，也许，我们有更合理的理由怀疑以下这一惊人的事实——这些物品被完全留在了这处灌木林中，而留下它们的竟是某些谨慎到足以能想出要转移尸体的凶手。无论如何，如果您猜想我计划着否认这处灌木林为杀人现场的话，您可能没有理解清楚我的意思。这儿有可能发生过犯罪，或者更可能的是，德吕克太太的小旅馆里出了一起意外。其实，这一点都是次要的。我们并不是想要发现犯罪现场，而是要查出犯罪凶手。尽管我引证的这些点都很琐碎，但

first, to show the folly of the positive and headlong assertions of *Le Soleil*, but secondly and chiefly, to bring you, by the most natural route, to a further contemplation of the doubt whether this assassination has, or has not been, the work of a gang.

"We will resume this question by mere allusion to the revolting details of the surgeon examined at the inquest. It is only necessary to say that is published *inferences*, in regard to the number of ruffians, have been properly ridiculed as unjust and totally baseless, by all the reputable anatomists of Paris. Not that the matter might not have been as inferred, but that there was no ground for the inference: – was there not much for another?

"Let us reflect now upon 'the traces of a struggle'; and let me ask what these traces have been supposed to demonstrate. A gang. But do they not rather demonstrate the absence of a gang? What *struggle* could have taken place – what struggle so violent and so enduring as to have left its 'traces' in all directions – between a weak and defenceless girl and the gang of ruffians imagined? The silent grasp of a few rough arms and all would have been over. The victim must have been absolutely passive at their will. You will here bear in mind that the arguments urged against the thicket as the scene, are applicable in chief part,

我举出这些理由是为了表明，首先，《太阳报》过分自信而又鲁莽的断言是多么的愚蠢，其次却也是很主要的，是想让您顺着一条最自然不过的思路，去进一步思考这个疑点，即这起凶杀案究竟是不是一伙流氓干的。

"通过简单间接提一下庭审时外科医生的验尸报告里令人难以接受的细节，我们来继续讨论这个问题。我只需说，公布的关于流氓的数量推断，由于其有失诚实和毫无根据，被巴黎所有著名的解剖学家们很是奚落了一番。并不是因为此事不可以这样推断，而是因为没有依据支持这样推断——然而也不存在充分依据去支持别的推论了吗？

"让我们现在来好好回想一下文中所说的'搏斗的痕迹'。我想请问这些痕迹应该表明了什么呢？表明了作案的有一群人。但是，不是更有可能表明并没有一群人那么多吗？会有哪门子的搏斗发生——会有哪门子的搏斗如此激烈而又如此持久以至于搏斗过的'痕迹'落得哪哪儿都是——在一个柔弱无助的女孩和一伙想象中的流氓之间？几条粗壮的胳膊只需轻轻一抓，一切就都办成了。受害者不得不非常被动地服从他们的意愿。您在此得记住，我的这番极力反驳灌木林就是犯罪现场的论断，更贴切地说，我

only against it as the scene of an outrage committed by *more than a single individual*. If we imagine but *one* violator, we can conceive, and thus only conceive, the struggle of so violent and so obstinate a nature as to have left the 'traces' apparent.

"And again. I have already mentioned the suspicion to be excited by the fact that the articles in question were suffered to remain *at all* in the thicket where discovered. It seems almost impossible that these evidences of guilt should have been accidentally left where found. There was sufficient presence of mind (it is supposed) to remove the corpse; and yet a more positive evidence than the corpse itself (whose features might have been quickly obliterated by decay,) is allowed to lie conspicuously in the scene of the outrage – I allude to the handkerchief with the *name* of the deceased. If this was accident, it was not the accident of *a gang*. We can imagine it only the accident of an individual. Let us see. An individual has committed the murder. He is *alone* with the ghost of the departed. He is appalled by what lies motionless before him. The fury of his passion is over, and there is abundant room in his heart for the natural awe of the deed. His is none of that confidence which the presence of numbers inevitably inspires. He is alone with the dead. He trembles and is bewildered. Yet there is a necessity for

论断的主要部分只是为了反驳他们认为这是一个多人作案的暴力现场的看法。如果我们设想的是，总共只有一个凶手，那我们就可以认为，并且也只能这么认为，搏斗进行得如此激烈又如此难以控制，以至于不得不落下这么明显的'痕迹'。

"再有，当前讨论的那些物品被一直留在发现它们的那个灌木林里，我已经讲过这件事引出的疑点了。这些犯罪证据竟无意中被落下等着让人发现，这事看上去几乎是不可能发生的。因为罪犯十分镇定（假设是这样），镇定到足以想到要转移尸体。然而一个比尸体本身（时间拖得越久，尸体上的各种特征越可能消失不见）更无法辩驳的证据出现了，凶手使用它就暴力现场的位置问题上撒了一个很明显的谎——我指的是绣有死者姓名的手帕。就算这只是一起意外，这也绝不是一群人会出的意外。我们可以想象，这种意外只可能出在单个人的身上。让我们想想看，某人杀了玛丽，林子中只有他和出了窍的灵魂，他被躺在地上一动不动的尸体吓破了胆。他由于冲动激起的暴怒已经消退，因此大量空间从他心里腾出，他自然而然开始有余力为自己的所作所为感到害怕。他没有那种多人作案时难免产生的相互打气所带来的信心。他独自和一个死人待着，浑身发抖，不知所措。但是他还必

disposing of the corpse. He bears it to the river, but leaves behind him the other evidences of guilt; for it is difficult, if not impossible to carry all the burthen at once, and it will be easy to return for what is left. But in his toilsome journey to the water his fears redouble within him. The sounds of life encompass his path. A dozen times he hears or fancies the step of an observer. Even the very lights from the city bewilder him. Yet, in time and by long and frequent pauses of deep agony, he reaches the river's brink, and disposes of his ghastly charge – perhaps through the medium of a boat. But *now* what treasure does the world hold – what threat of vengeance could it hold out – which would have power to urge the return of that lonely murderer over that toilsome and perilous path, to the thicket and its blood chilling recollections? He returns *not*, let the consequences be what they may. He *could* not return if he would. His sole thought is immediate escape. He turns his back *forever* upon those dreadful shrubberies and flees as from the wrath to come.

"But how with a gang? Their number would have inspired them with confidence; if, indeed, confidence is ever wanting in the breast of the arrant blackguard; and of arrant blackguards alone are the supposed *gangs* ever constituted. Their number, I say, would have prevented the bewildering

须得处理掉尸体。他把尸体运到河边，却把其他犯罪证据留下了。因为很难不留下，若不留下就要一次性把东西全搬走，这是不可能做到的，而折返回来再拿落下的东西也容易些。但在他费尽力气往水边运尸体的过程中，他心里的恐惧也在不断增加。他一路上都被什么活物弄出的声响包围着。有十好几次，他都听到或者以为听到了跟踪者的脚步声。甚至市区的点点灯光都能让他疑神疑鬼。可是，道路漫长，他一路上内心极度挣扎，走走停停，终于到了河边，处理掉了自己身边那具可怕的负担——也许是通过坐船处理掉的。然而现在这个世界到底握有什么样的宝物——它能减轻什么因果报应对于凶手的威慑吗——这个宝物竟有力量诱使那个形单影只的凶手加速穿越那条充满艰难险阻的道路，返回到那片灌木林以及属于它的那些让人热血骤凝的回忆当中去？他终是没有回去，选择了听天由命。即使他愿意回去，他也不能回去了。他的唯一念头就是现在就逃。他掉转过身，再也不想面对这片可怕的灌木丛了，他逃掉了，生怕报应会降临在自己头上。

"但如果凶手是一群人又会怎样呢？他们仗着人多势众就更胆大包天。说真的，哪个彻头彻尾的流氓胸中还缺贼胆呢。这个假定的团伙是由许多单个的彻头彻尾的流氓

and unreasoning terror which I have imagined to paralyze the single man. Could we suppose an oversight in one, or two, or three, this oversight would have been remedied by a fourth. They would have left nothing behind them; for their number would have enabled them to carry all at once. There would have been no need of *return*.

"Consider now the circumstance that in the outer garment of the corpse when found, 'a slip, about a foot wide had been torn upward from the bottom hem to the waist wound three times round the waist, and secured by a sort of hitch in the back.' This was done with the obvious design of affording *a handle* by which to carry the body. But would any *number* of men have dreamed of resorting to such an expedient? To three or four, the limbs of the corpse would have afforded not only a sufficient, but the best possible hold. The device is that of a single individual; and this brings us to the fact that 'between the thicket and the river, the rails of the fences were found taken down, and the ground bore evident traces of some heavy burden having been dragged along it!' But would a *number* of men have put themselves to the superfluous trouble of taking down a fence, for the purpose of dragging through it a corpse which they might have *lifted over* any fence in an instant? Would a *number* of

组成的。他们的人数多，依我看，就可以壮胆，不会再出现我刚才设想的能麻痹单个人的那种不知所措以及毫无理由的恐惧。如果我们假设会有一两个人，或3个人，可能发生疏忽，那么第四个人肯定就是补救他们疏漏的那个。他们绝不会把任何犯罪证据留在身后。因为人多，他们足可以一次性带走所有东西。没必要再回来一趟。

"现在再来看看找到尸体时，尸体套裙的情况，'一截布带，大约一英尺宽被从底部的裙边由下向上撕开围着腰绕了3圈，然后在背后打了某种结固定住了。'这样做的意图很明显，就是想弄出一个提手好拎尸体。但是若是多人作案，他们还会想着求助于这种权宜之计吗？对于三四个人来说，尸体的四肢就不仅仅是足够他们每人抬一个，而是数量极佳地吻合上了，四肢都能派上用场。这种打扣的设计方案是单人作案时才会想到的。这不由使人想起警察局的那番描述：'在灌木林和河流之间篱笆的围栏被发现推倒了，地面上留下的明显痕迹也能证明某种重物曾经被拖着经过这里。'但如果凶手是一伙人，他们何必要给自己增添不必要的麻烦呢——何必把篱笆推倒，就为了拖一具尸体，而这具尸体还是他们自己能轻而易举地抬过篱笆的那种？他们人数这么多，您觉得他们有还可能非要拖

men have so *dragged* a corpse at all as to have left evident traces of the dragging?

"And here we must refer to an observation of *Le Commerciel*; an observation upon which I have already, in some measure, commented. 'A piece,' says this journal, 'of one of the unfortunate girl's petticoats was torn out and tied under her chin, and around the back of her head, probably to prevent screams. This was done by fellows who had no pocket-handkerchiefs.'

"I have before suggested that a genuine blackguard is never *without* a pocket-handkerchief. But it is not to this fact that I now especially advert. That it was not through want of a handkerchief for the purpose imagined by *Le Commerciel*, that this bandage was employed, is rendered apparent by the handkerchief left in the thicket; and that the object was not 'to prevent screams' appears, also, from the bandage having been employed in preference to what would so much better have answered the purpose. But the language of the evidence speaks of the strip in question as 'found around the neck, fitting loosely, and secured with a hard knot.' These words are sufficiently vague, but differ materially from those of *Le Commerciel*. The slip was eighteen inches wide, and therefore, although of muslin, would form a strong band when folded or

着尸体走吗？以至于留下了那么明显的拖痕！

"在此咱们必须得提一下《商报》上的一段观察评论。我之前已经对这篇评论多多少少地发表过一些意见了。'一条，'这张报纸写道，'从这个不幸的女孩的某件衬裙上撕下来的布带绑到她的下巴底下，还绕过了她的后脑勺，大概是为了防止她喊叫。所以，能够干出这种事的肯定是某些没手帕的家伙。'

"我之前已经说过，真正的流氓是绝不会不带手帕的。不过，我现在想请您专门留心的并不是这个问题。凶手不是因为缺少手帕才使用绷带，他的实际目的并不像《商报》所想象的那样，况且要用手帕的话也明显可以用被遗留在灌木林里的那块玛丽的手帕暂且充当一下。凶手的目的看起来并不是'防止她喊叫'，同样地，从凶手使用绷带而不使用好用得多的手帕这一点上也能看出。然而警方的证言却说当前讨论的那截布带是'松松地绕在她的脖子上，牢牢地打了一个结'。这话说得相当含糊，但却与《商报》描写的情况有着本质的不同。这截布带尽管是平纹细布的质地，却有 18 英寸宽，因此叠在一起或纵向地弄皱也能成一条结实的带子。因此发现它时，它就是皱巴巴的。我的推论是这样的。这个孤独的杀

rumpled longitudinally. And thus rumpled it was discovered. My inference is this. The solitary murderer, having borne the corpse, for some distance, (whether from the thicket or elsewhere) by means of the bandage *hitched* around its middle, found the weight, in this mode of procedure, too much for his strength. He resolved to drag the burthen – the evidence goes to show that it *was* dragged. With this object in view, it became necessary to attach something like a rope to one of the extremities. It could be best attached about the neck, where the head would prevent its slipping off. And, now, the murderer bethought him, unquestionably, of the bandage about the loins. He would have used this, but for its volution about the corpse, the *hitch* which embarrassed it, and the reflection that it had not been 'torn off' from the garment. It was easier to tear a new slip from the petticoat. He tore it, made it fast about the neck, and so *dragged* his victim to the brink of the river. That this 'bandage,' only attainable with trouble and delay, and but imperfectly answering its purpose – that this bandage was employed *at all*, demonstrates that the necessity for its employment sprang from circumstances arising at a period when the handkerchief was no longer attainable – that is to say, arising, as we have imagined, after quitting the thicket, (if the thicket it

人犯带着这个尸体，走了很远一段路（不管是从灌木林里走出来的还是从别的地方），他用绷带捆住了尸体的腰部，后来发现用这种方法运尸体，他的力气不能承受尸体的重量。于是他断然决定拖着尸体走——证据也已显示，尸体是被拖走的。要想拖着走就必须得用绳子一类的东西系在脖子上，或者系在随便一只手腕或脚腕上。最好把绳子系在脖子上，这样脑袋就可以防止绳子滑脱。于是，当时，毫无疑问地，凶手就一下子想到了尸体腰间的那条绷带。他本来可以用这条绷带，但是由于这条带子在尸体上缠了好几圈，再加上打的那个死结使他很难再解下这条带子用，而且绷带没有完全从套裙上'撕下来'，这也导致他无法使用这条带子。凶手认为再从衬裙上撕下一条新的布带要比扯下腰上的容易得多。他新撕下了一条布带缠在死者的脖子上，然后就这样一路把他的牺牲品拖到河边。这条'绷带'是费了不少脑筋，拖了不少时间，才做出来的，但也勉强认为它能回答使用带子的目的——凶手偏偏要使用这条绷带，表明当时手帕已经不在手边了，由于环境所限，使用带子的迫切性大大提升——换句话说，正如我们想象的那样，凶手必须要用带子，是在他离开灌木林之后（如果密林果真是现场的话），以及走在灌木林与塞纳

was), and on the road between the thicket and the river.

"But the evidence, you will say, of Madame Deluc, points especially to the presence of *a gang*, in the vicinity of the thicket, at or about the epoch of the murder. This I grant. I doubt if there were not a *dozen* gangs, such as described by Madame Deluc, in and about the vicinity of the Barrière du Roule at or about the period of this tragedy. But the gang which has drawn upon itself the pointed animadversion, although the somewhat tardy and very suspicious evidence of Madame Deluc, is the *only* gang which is represented by that honest and scrupulous old lady as having eaten her cakes and swallowed her brandy, without putting themselves to the trouble of making her payment. *Et hinc illéir?*

"But what *is* the precise evidence of Madame Deluc? 'A gang of miscreants made their appearance, behaved boisterously, ate and drank without making payment, followed in the route of the young man and girl, returned to the inn *about dusk*, and recrossed the river as if in great haste.'

"Now this 'great haste' very possibly seemed *greater* haste in the eyes of Madame Deluc, since she dwelt lingeringly and lamentingly upon her violated cakes and ale – cakes and ale for which she

河之间的路上的时候。

"可您要说了，德吕克太太的供词中还特别提到了一伙流氓，他们大约就在凶案发生的时间出现在了灌木林一带。这点我承认。我在想恐怕像德吕克太太描述的那种流氓团伙，会在惨案发生的那段时间前后在圆木栅门附近出现的，那还不得有一打儿之多啊。尽管德吕克太太的证词有点勉强还非常值得怀疑，但是这伙把自己置于尖锐的责难中的流氓，对这位诚实谨慎的老妇人来说，是唯一一伙吃光她的糕点，大口咽下了她的白兰地后，自己还都懒得费心去付给她饭钱的人。或许因此她就怒火中烧了呢？

"但是德吕克太太确切的证词又是怎样的呢？'一群无赖出现了，他们吵吵嚷嚷的，吃饱喝足后也不付钱，沿着那个年轻男子和那个女孩所走的路线就走过去了，大约是黄昏时分他们才回到这家小旅店，急匆匆地过河而去，就好像很赶时间一样。'

"那么这所谓的'很赶时间'，在德吕克太太眼里，可能要比实际上匆忙得多，因为她迟迟不肯把注意力移开，一直在痛惜她的那些白白葬送掉的糕点和麦芽酒——她仍

might still have entertained a faint hope of compensation. Why, otherwise, since it was *about dusk*, should she make a point of the haste? It is no cause for wonder, surely, that even a gang of blackguards should make haste to get home, when a wide river is to be crossed in small boats, when storm impends, and when night *approaches*.

"I say *approaches*; for the night had *not yet arrived*. It was only *about dusk* that the indecent haste of these 'miscreants' offended the sober eyes of Madame Deluc. But we are told that it was upon this very evening that Madame Deluc, as well as her eldest son, 'heard the screams of a female in the vicinity of the inn.' And in what words does Madame Deluc designate the period of the evening at which these screams were heard? 'It was *soon after dark*,' she says. But 'soon *after dark*,' is, at least, *dark*; and '*about dusk*' is as certainly daylight. Thus it is abundantly clear that the gang quitted the Barrière du Roule *prior* to the screams overheard by Madame Deluc. And although, in all the many reports of the evidence, the relative expressions in question are distinctly and invariably employed just as I have employed them in this conversation with yourself, no notice whatever of the gross discrepancy has, as yet, been taken by any of the public journals, or by any of the

怀有一丝微弱的希望，希望对她的糕点和麦芽酒给予点儿补偿。否则的话，既然都到了黄昏时分了，赶忙回去便是理所当然，她何必还要强调他们是赶时间呢？当然，我们没有理由去置疑，即使是一群流氓也会赶时间回家，尤其是河面宽广，过河的小船又小，暴风雨临近，暮色又将至的时候。

"我说'暮色将至'，是因为夜晚尚未到来。在一向举止庄重的德吕克太太看来格外碍眼的这伙行色猥琐的'无赖'，当他们匆匆赶时间离开时也仅仅是黄昏时分。但是我们又听说，就在当天晚上，德吕克太太和她的大儿子，'听到了小旅店附近传来了女人的尖叫声'。德吕克太太是用什么字眼形容她听到尖叫声那晚的大概时段的呢？'夜色刚刚降临'，她说的是。但是'夜色刚刚降临'说明当时至少已经入夜了，而'大约是黄昏时分'则可无疑被看做是白天的时候。由此我们可以十分明显地看出，那伙人离开圆木栅门的时间是在德吕克太太听见尖叫声的时间之前。尽管在许多对证词的报道中，我们刚才说过的那些相关措辞都被清晰明确而又无一例外地表达了出来，就像我刚才在和您的对话中引用到了它们一样，但是到目前为止，根本没有一个人注意到这个明显的不同点，不管是任意的一家大众刊物，或者是任意一

Myrmidons of police.

"I shall add but one to the arguments against *a gang*; but this *one* has, to my own understanding at least, a weight altogether irresistible. Under the circumstances of large reward offered, and full pardon to any King's evidence, it is not to be imagined, for a moment, that some member of *a gang* of low ruffians, or of any body of men, would not long ago have betrayed his accomplices. Each one of a gang so placed, is not so much greedy of reward, or anxious for escape, as *fearful of betrayal*. He betrays eagerly and early that he *may not himself be betrayed*. That the secret has not been divulged, is the very best of proof that it is, in fact, a secret. The horrors of this dark deed are known only to *one*, or two, living human beings, and to God.

"Let us sum up now the meagre yet certain fruits of our long analysis. We have attained the idea either of a fatal accident under the roof of Madame Deluc, or of a murder perpetrated, in the thicket at the Barrie du Roule, by a lover, or at least by an intimate and secret associate of the deceased. This associate is of swarthy complexion. This complexion, the 'hitch' in the bandage, and the 'sailor's knot,' with which the bonnet-ribbon is tied, point to a seaman. His companionship with the

个警局的跟班。

"我现要再为我反驳团伙作案的论述补充一点，但就这一点，至少依我自己的理解，其分量之重完全是其他论据无可抗衡的。官方加非官方提供了巨额赏金，警方又承诺对任何指正主犯的从犯都将免除所有处罚，在这样的优厚条件下，我们片刻都无法想象，这伙卑贱的流氓中的任何一员，或者随便什么犯罪团体里的任何一员，竟然都没有出卖自己的同谋。每一个身处团伙当中的人，就算不贪图赏金或不急于逃命，但肯定怕被他人出卖。一般他都会迫不及待地尽早出卖别人，这样他自己才有可能不先遭人出卖。然而秘密始终都没被泄露出去，这本身就最好地证明了，它确实是个秘密。这件邪恶之事的可怕真相只有可能同时被一两个活着的人知道，再者，就只有老天爷了。

"现在让我们来从长长的分析中总结一下咱们贫乏但又确实的结论。我们对此案有两种看法，一种看法是在德吕克太太的小旅馆里发生了一起不幸的意外，另一种看法是凶杀案发生在圆木栅门附近的灌木林里，凶手是死者的情人，或者至少是一个与死者关系亲密而又鲜为人知的同伴。此人黝黑的肤色，再加上打在死者绷带上的'死结'，以及用无边女帽的帽带系的那个'水手结'，都指出凶手的身份是一

deceased, a gay, but not an abject young girl, designates him as above the grade of the common sailor. Here the well written and urgent communications to the journals are much in the way of corroboration. The circumstance of the first elopement, as mentioned by *Le Mercurie*, tends to blend the idea of this seaman with that of the 'naval officer' who is first known to have led the unfortunate into crime.

"And here, most fitly, comes the consideration of the continued absence of him of the dark complexion. Let me pause to observe that the complexion of this man is dark and swarthy; it was no common swarthiness which constituted the sole point of remembrance, both as regards Valence and Madame Deluc. But why is this man absent? Was he murdered by the gang? If so, why are there only traces of the assassinated girl? The scene of the two outrages will naturally be supposed identical. And where is his corpse? The assassins would most probably have disposed of both in the same way. But it may be said that this man lives, and is deterred from making himself known, through dread of being charged with the murder. This consideration might be supposed to operate upon him now – at this late period – since it has been given in evidence that he was seen with Marie – but it would have had no force at the period of

名海员。死者虽然是个风流的年轻女孩，但却并不下贱，此人能与死者交上朋友，说明他的级别在普通水手之上。那些封寄给报社的言辞恳切的读者来信，也在很大程度上证实了这点。从《信使报》报道的第一次私奔时的情况来看，我们很容易把凶手的海员身份和那个最初引诱不幸的玛丽犯错误的'海军军官'放在一起相比较。

"恰逢此时我突然想到那个后来一直都销声匿迹的皮肤黝黑的年轻人。允许我在这里停下来插句别的说，这个人的肤色很深并且黑黝黝的；他的肤色不是普通的黝黑，那种黝黑在瓦朗斯和德吕克太太的记忆里单独地构成了一项值得一提的特征。但是为什么这个男人后来不露面了呢？他也被那伙人杀害了？如果是的话，为什么现场只留下了那个被杀害的女孩的痕迹呢？这两起命案的现场自然应该在同一个地方才对。那么他的尸体又跑哪儿去了？罪犯在绝大多数情况下都会使同样的手段处理掉两个他同时杀死的人的尸体。但是也许有人会说，这个男人其实活了下来，因为怕被控告犯杀人罪，所以就自行销声匿迹了。假设以上考虑现阶段在他身上还可能会发生——'现阶段'指的是最近的这段日子——因为已有人作证说看到他和玛丽走在一起——但是纵观整件事情，这样的考

the deed. The first impulse of an innocent man would have been to announce the outrage, and to aid in identifying the ruffians. This *policy* would have suggested. He had been seen with the girl. He had crossed the river with her in an open ferry-boat. The denouncing of the assassins would have appeared, even to an idiot, the surest and sole means of relieving himself from suspicion. We cannot suppose him, on the night of the fatal Sunday, both innocent himself and incognizant of an outrage committed. Yet only under such circumstances is it possible to imagine that he would have failed, if alive, in the denouncement of the assassins.

"And what means are ours, of attaining the truth? We shall find these means multiplying and gathering distinctness as we proceed. Let us sift to the bottom this affair of the first elopement. Let us know the full history of 'the officer,' with his present circumstances, and his whereabouts at the precise period of the murder. Let us carefully compare with each other the various communications sent to the evening paper, in which the object was to inculpate *a gang*. This done, let us compare these communications, both as regards style and MS., with those sent to *the morning paper*, at a previous period, and insisting so vehemently upon the guilt of Mennais. And, all this done, let us again

慮就没有什么说服力了。一个无辜的人的第一反应本应该是去把这起暴行公之于众，然后协助警方确认凶手的身份。这样的行事策略才应该是一个无辜者会采取的上策。他被看到和受害女孩在一起。他和她一起乘一条敞篷渡船过的河。即使是傻瓜也应该知道，公开指证凶手貌似才是最稳当的，以及唯一的为自己开脱罪责的方法。我们不可能假设，在那个不幸的星期天的晚上，他既是无辜的，没有参与进这起暴行，又没有意识到发生了这起暴行的。但却只能在以上这种情况下，我们才有可能想象，即使他还活着，他也是不会去公开指证凶手的。

"那么我们使用什么方法来探明真相呢？随着步步深入地分析，我们会发现可用的方法会越来越多，也变得越来越清晰具体。让我们精简出初次私奔这事的细节来好好看看吧。我们也来了解了解'海军军官'的全部历史、目前的状况，以及案发时的行踪。我们再来把每一封寄给《晚报》报社的、各式各样旨在把谋杀罪名冠于某伙流氓头上的读者来信都仔细地比较一下。比较完后，我们再就文风和笔迹，把这些读者来信同早先投寄给《晨报》报社的、一再强调梅奈先生有罪的那些揭发信进行一番比较。然后，所有这些都比较完后，我们再去把两家报纸收到的这些来信与那

compare these various communications with the known MSS. of the officer. Let us endeavor to ascertain, by repeated questionings of Madame Deluc and her boys, as well as of the omnibus driver, Valence, something more of the personal appearance and bearing of the 'man of dark complexion.' Queries, skilfully directed, will not fail to elicit, from some of these parties, information on this particular point (or upon others) – information which the parties themselves may not even be aware of possessing. And let us now trace the boat picked up by the bargeman on the morning of Monday the twenty-third of June, and which was removed from the barge-office, without the cognizance of the officer in attendance, and *without the rudder*, at some period prior to the discovery of the corpse. With a proper caution and perseverance we shall infallibly trace this boat; for not only can the bargeman who picked it up identify it, but the *rudder is at hand*. The rudder of *a sail-boat* would not have been abandoned, without inquiry, by one altogether at ease in heart. And here let me pause to insinuate a question. There was no *advertisement* of the picking up of this boat. It was silently taken to the barge-office, and as silently removed. But its owner or employer – how *happened* he, at so early a period as Tuesday morning, to be informed, without

位海军军官的手稿进行比较。我们还得多问问德吕克太太和她的儿子们，以及那个公共马车车夫，瓦朗斯，好尽力搞清楚，那天出现的那个'皮肤黝黑的年轻男子'，外貌上除了皮肤很黑以外还有哪些特征，以及他的举止谈吐又是怎样的。我们的问题，只要提得有技巧，在我们想了解的那点细节上（或者是其他方面）就绝对不会问不出名堂来，这些人里肯定会有几个知道的——可能他们自己都没有意识到他们会知道这些东西。现在让我们再来探讨一下那条被驳船船夫发现的小船，这条小船被发现于6月23日星期一的上午，后来被从驳船办事处取走，取船人没有跟办事处的值班人员打过招呼，也没拿方向舵，取船时间大约是在发现尸体之前的某段时间里。我们只要谨慎有度，锲而不舍，准会探查到这条小船的下落的。因为那条小船不仅可以让那个发现船的船夫识认，而且它的方向舵还握在我们手里。一个帆船的方向舵是绝不可能被一个心里没鬼的人遗忘的，这个我们不调查也能知道。在此请允许我停下来旁敲另一个问题。驳船办事处并没有登启示招领失船。船是无声无息被拖到驳船办事处的，又无声无息地被人取走了。但是船的主人，或说船的所有者——他是怎么在星期二上午那么早的时候，在没有公告告知的

the agency of advertisement, of the locality of the boat taken up on Monday, unless we imagine some connexion with the *navy* – some personal permanent connexion leading to cognizance of its minute in interests – its petty local news?

"In speaking of the lonely assassin dragging his burden to the shore, I have already suggested the probability of his availing himself of a boat. Now we are to understand that Marie Rogêt *was* precipitated from a boat. This would naturally have been the case. The corpse could not have been trusted to the shallow waters of the shore. The peculiar marks on the back and shoulders of the victim tell of the bottom ribs of a boat. That the body was found without weight is also corroborative of the idea. If thrown from the shore a weight would have been attached. We can only account for its absence by supposing the murderer to have neglected the precaution of supplying himself with it before pushing off. In the act of consigning the corpse to the water, he would unquestionably have noticed his oversight; but then no remedy would have been at hand. Any risk would have been preferred to a return to that accursed shore. Having rid himself of his ghastly charge, the murderer would have hastened to the city. There, at some obscure wharf, he would have leaped on land. But the boat –

情况下，就知道星期一那天租赁出去的船都停放在什么位置呢？除非我们猜测，这人与船队有某种联系——某种与他本人有关的非暂时性的联系，这种联系让他能利用职务之便了解到船舶方面的一切小小动态——某些琐碎的业内信息。

"之前提到'孤独杀手拖着他的沉重负担走到河岸'时，我就已经暗示了他很有可能为自己找条小船。现在我们应该能理解了，玛丽·罗杰特的尸体确是从船上陡然被扔下水的。事情顺理成章地就应该是这样发展的。凶手绝不会寄希望于把尸体沉在岸边的浅水区。受害者的背上和肩膀上的特殊伤痕表明它磕到了船底部的肋材。尸体被发现时并没有系着重物也证实了这一点。如果凶手从岸边抛尸，肯定会在尸体上系上重物。我们只能把它的不加重物解释为，凶手在把尸体推下水前可能忘记了预先准备重物。在把尸体投入水中的时候，他无疑会注意到他的这一疏漏。但是当时手头已经没有什么东西可以补救了。他宁愿冒任何危险，也不愿再回到那个该死的岸边了。凶手摆脱掉了自己身边的那具可怕的负担后，赶忙划回市区。在那儿，在某个僻静的码头，他肯定是纵身一跃跳上了岸。但是船怎么办——他为什么不把它拴上呢？他一定是急匆匆地太想要离开了，以至于都忘记

would he have secured it? He would have been in too great haste for such things as securing a boat. Moreover, in fastening it to the wharf, he would have felt as if securing evidence against himself. His natural thought would have been to cast from him, as far as possible, all that had held connection with his crime. He would not only have fled from the wharf, but he would not have permitted the boat to remain. Assuredly he would have cast it adrift. Let us pursue our fancies. – In the morning, the wretch is stricken with unutterable horror at finding that the boat has been picked up and detained at a locality which he is in the daily habit of frequenting – at a locality, perhaps, which his duty compels him to frequent. The next night, *without daring to ask for the rudder*, he removes it. Now *where* is that rudderless boat? Let it be one of our first purposes to discover. With the first glimpse we obtain of it, the dawn of our success shall begin. This boat shall guide us, with a rapidity which will surprise even ourselves, to him who employed it in the midnight of the fatal Sabbath. Corroboration will rise upon corroboration, and the murderer will be traced."

It will be understood that I speak of coincidences and *no more*. What I have said above upon this topic must suffice. In my own heart there dwells no faith in

去做把船拴好这类事情。除此以外，把船拴到码头上，他可能觉得这样做就像保留了一份于己不利的证据。他本能地希望，把一切与他的罪行有关的东西都从身边扔掉，扔得越远越好。他要逃离码头，也不许这条船留在这里。我们可以肯定，他非常愿意抛开这条小船，让它随波逐流。让我们来继续展开联想，——第二天早上，这个倒霉蛋却开始遭受无法形容之恐惧的折磨了，因为他得知那条小船已被人拾获，还被留在了他每天都会出现的一个他常去的地方——也许是出于工作原因迫使他频繁光顾的地方。接下来到了夜里，他把小船挪走，也没敢再去找方向舵。现在那条没有方向舵的小船在哪儿呢？我们把它当成咱们的第一个有待发掘的目标。我们找到它后只要瞥上一眼，我们胜利的曙光也就不远了。这条小船将会指引我们——以一种即便在我们自己来看都会备感惊讶的速度——到达那个在不幸的安息日的午夜使用过它的人那里。一个事实引出另一个事实，最终我们就能够追查出凶手的下落。"

读者看了自会明白，我讲的都是巧合，没有别的。以上我所讲的关于这个话题的内容一定已经够多了。在我心里从不相信存在不可思

praernature. That Nature and its God are two, no man who thinks, will deny. That the latter, creating the former, can, at will, control or modify it, is also unquestionable. I say "at will;" for the question is of will, and not, as the insanity of logic has assumed, of power. It is not that the Deity *cannot* modify his laws, but that we insult him in imagining a possible necessity for modification. In their origin these laws were fashioned to embrace *all* contingencies which *could* lie in the Future. With God all is *Now*.

I repeat, then, that I speak of these things only as of coincidences. And farther: in what I relate it will be seen that between the fate of the unhappy Mary Cecilia Rogers, so far as that fate is known, and the fate of one Marie Rogêt up to a certain epoch in her history, there has existed a parallel in the contemplation of whose wonderful exactitude the reason becomes embarrassed. I say all this will be seen. But let it not for a moment be supposed that, in proceeding with the sad narrative of Marie from the epoch just mentioned, and in tracing to its dénouement the mystery which enshrouded her, it is my covert design to hint at an extension of the parallel, or even to suggest that the measures adopted in Paris for the discovery of the assassin of a grisette, or measures founded in any similar ratiocination, would

议的怪事。万物和造物主是两码事，没有哪个能思考的人会否认这一点。后者创造了前者，还可以随意支配或改变它，这一点也是毋庸置疑的。我之所说"随意"，因为这是意志的问题，不是逻辑混乱者想当然认为的那种权力问题。并不是说造物主不能修改他的自然法则，但是我们凭空捏造出来某种潜在的可能性，认为他是按照我们这种可能性来修改他的法则的，我们这样做就是亵渎了他。在造物之初，这些法则就被拟定成囊括了一切可能在"未来"发生的意外事件。在造物主眼里，一切都是"现在"。

那么，我重申一遍，以上我说的这些事情不过是巧合罢了。更进一步讲：在我的叙述中，我们可以看到，薄命的玛丽·塞西莉亚·罗杰斯小姐的命运——就她的那段已为大家所知的命运来说——与玛丽·罗杰特在其红尘往事中某一时期的命运相比，两者之间存在着相似之处，当人们凝神研究其惊人的精确度时，头脑往往会越理越乱。我得说，所有这一切都会成为现实。但是，当我讲述玛丽在刚刚所提那一时期里的不幸遭遇时，以及当我一路追寻重重把玛丽包裹住的谜团的最终答案时，千万别以为，我暗暗打算提示大家相似之处有所增多，或是更有甚者，以为我暗暗打算间接表明，照搬以下举措——如

produce any similar result.

For, in respect to the latter branch of the supposition, it should be considered that the most trifling variation in the facts of the two cases might give rise to the most important miscalculations, by diverting thoroughly the two courses of events; very much as, in arithmetic, an error which, in its own individuality, may be inappreciable, produces, at length, by dint of multiplication at all points of the process, a result enormously at variance with truth. And, in regard to the former branch, we must not fail to hold in view that the very Calculus of Probabilities to which I have referred, forbids all idea of the extension of the parallel: – forbids it with a positiveness strong and decided just in proportion as this parallel has already been long-drawn and exact. This is one of those anomalous propositions which, seemingly appealing to thought altogether apart from the mathematical, is yet one which only the mathematician can fully entertain. Nothing, for example, is more difficult than to convince the merely general reader that the fact of sixes having been thrown twice in succession by a player at dice, is sufficient cause for betting the largest odds that sixes will not be thrown in the third attempt. A suggestion to this effect is usually rejected by the intellect at

在巴黎时为了找出杀害女店员的凶手而特意采用的举措，或根据某些其他与之类似的推理想出的举措——就会出现任何与之类似的结果。

因为，就拿以上推想的后一分枝来说，我们应该考虑到，两桩案子的实际案情哪怕只有最为细微的差别，可能也会完全把两件事的发展进程移向不同的方向，从而引发最为重大的判断失误。这就非常像在做算术时，产生了一点误差，这点误差就其个体特征而言，可能是微不足道的，但是如果把它加进了所有的运算步骤当中，那么我们最终得到的就是一个与正确答案差别很大的结果。然后，拿推想里的前一分枝来说，我们绝不能忘记我提到过的真正的"概率演算"，不容许任何有关"相似之处有所增多"的想法——我十分肯定我绝不容许这样的想法，强烈而又坚决地肯定，肯定的程度都能跟这种早已存在的且不得不存在的相似之处的肯定程度相抗衡。这是一种反常的平衡，表面上像是需要一个人的思维同数学思想完全脱离，实际上却是只有数学家才能完全把握住这种平衡。比方说，一个掷骰子的人，连续掷出了两次 6 点，因此别人也就有充分的理由压赔率最高的那注，赌他第三次绝对掷不出 6 点来，然而如果我们的读者群仅仅是一般读者的话，便没什么比给他们解释清楚这

once. It does not appear that the two throws which have been completed, and which lie now absolutely in the Past, can have influence upon the throw which exists only in the Future. The chance for throwing sixes seems to be precisely as it was at any ordinary time – that is to say, subject only to the influence of the various other throws which may be made by the dice. And this is a reflection which appears so exceedingly obvious that attempts to controvert it are received more frequently with a derisive smile than with anything like respectful attention. The error here involved – a gross error redolent of mischief – I cannot pretend to expose within the limits assigned me at present; and with the philosophical it needs no exposure. It may be sufficient here to say that it forms one of an infinite series of mistakes which arise in the path or reason through her propensity for seeking truth in detail.

一事实更困难的了。如果有人提议打猜骰子的这个赌，结果就将是，有头脑的人大抵都立刻回绝他的这一提议。头两次掷出的 6 点，无疑是在"过去"发生的事情，但它们并不会影响到发生在"未来"的第三次掷投的结果。掷出 6 点的概率似乎正好跟平时任意一次掷出的概率一样大——也就是说，掷出 6 点的几率，只受骰子所能掷出的其他不同数字的影响。这一道理看起来是无比明显的，以至于要想驳倒这点，往往更有可能会招人讥笑，而不是得到像充满敬意的关注那样的东西。这里谈到的这点误差——一个过失误差，有强烈的酿大错的意味——在本文里，限于篇幅，我不能冒昧揭破。而且从哲学上讲，这样的误差也是不需要道破的。她在意图寻找事情详细真相的过程中出现了偏差，或者说，她的推理产生偏差，这些偏差便逐渐形成了一连串层出不穷的错误，我想，我以上的这些解释大概足够可以说明问题了吧。

14. Ms. Found in a Bottle
十四. 瓶中手稿

Qui n'a plus qu'un moment à vivre
N'a plus rien à dissimuler.

– Quinault·*Atys*

人之将死，其言也诚。

——基诺《阿蒂斯》

OF my country and of my family I have little to say. Ill usage and length of years have driven me from the one, and estranged me from the other. Hereditary wealth afforded me an education of no common order, and a contemplative turn of mind enabled me to methodize the stores which early study diligently garnered up. Beyond all things, the study of the German moralists gave me great delight; not from any ill-advised admiration of their eloquent madness, but from the ease with which my habits of rigid thoughts enabled me to detect their falsities. I have often been reproached with the aridity of my genius; a deficiency of imagination has been imputed to me as a crime; and the Pyrrhonism of my opinions has at all times rendered me notorious. Indeed, a strong relish for physical philosophy has, I fear, tinctured my mind with a very common error of this age – I mean the habit of referring occurrences, even the least susceptible of such reference, to the

于国于家，我几乎无话可说。年华虚度，已使我有家难归，有国难投。世袭的财产帮我完成了不同于常人的教育，灵活多变的头脑把我早年辛勤积累的知识规整得井井有条。在所有的事情中，没有比德国伦理学家的研究更让我兴奋的了。这并非出于对他们的雄辩才华的盲目崇拜，而是因为我严谨的思维让我可以轻而易举地识破他们的虚伪。我常常被人责备，说我天赋不足，欠缺想象力也被归咎为我的罪责。我观念中的怀疑论则使我一直声名狼藉。事实上，我担心的是自己对于自然哲学的浓厚兴趣，这已经给我的思想注入了这个时代常见的谬误——那就是人们习惯于把所发生的事情归结于这门学科的原则范畴里，即便这种归结毫无关联。总体来说，每个人都跟我一样很容易被胡诌瞎扯的空想引诱，脱离真实世界的辖制。我已经想好了，我得先交代一下，否则我下面要讲的这个令人难以置信的故事就会被当

principles of that science. Upon the whole, no person could be less liable than myself to be led away from the severe precincts of truth by *the ignes fatui* of superstition. I have thought proper to premise thus much, lest the incredible tale I have to tell should be considered rather the raving of a crude imagination, than the positive experience of a mind to which the reveries of fancy have been a dead letter and a nullity.

After many years spent in foreign travel, I sailed in the year 18 –, from the port of Batavia, in the rich and populous island of Java, on a voyage to the *Archipelago Islands*. I went as passenger – having no other inducement than a kind of nervous restlessness which haunted me as a fiend.

Our vessel was a beautiful ship of about four hundred tons, copper-fastened, and built at Bombay of Malabar teak. She was freighted with cotton-wool and oil, from the Lachadive islands. We had also on board coir, jaggeree, ghee, cocoa-nuts, and a few cases of opium. The stowage was clumsily done, and the vessel consequently crank.

We got under way with a mere breath of wind, and for many days stood aLong the eastern coast of Java, without any other incident to beguile the monotony of our course than the occasional meeting with some of the small grabs of the Archipelago to which we were bound.

做语无伦次的痴人说梦，而不会被看做是一次没有虚假想象的刻骨铭心的经历。

在外游历多年之后，我于18××年从位于物阜民丰的爪哇岛的巴塔维亚港登船，开始了前往阿奇帕拉哥群岛的航程。我的身份是乘客——没有别的征兆却紧张得坐立不安，有如鬼魅缠身。

我们乘坐的是一艘400吨位左右的漂亮大船，用黄铜加固，在孟买用马拉巴尔产的柚木制造。船上载有拉克代夫岛产的棉毛和油料，还有椰壳纤维、棕榈糖、酥油、可可豆和几箱鸦片。货物装得很粗陋，所以船老是摇来晃去。

我们在微风吹拂下起锚出发，多日沿爪哇岛东海岸行进。一路上，除了偶尔遇到几只从我们的目的地阿奇帕拉哥群岛开来的小船，没有任何别的事情聊解旅途之闷。

One evening, leaning over the taffrail, I observed a very singular, isolated cloud, to the N.W. It was remarkable, as well for its color, as from its being the first we had seen since our departure from Batavia. I watched it attentively until sunset, when it spread all at once to the eastward and westward, girting in the horizon with a narrow strip of vapor, and looking like a Long line of low beach. My notice was soon afterwards attracted by the dusky-red appearance of the moon, and the peculiar character of the sea. The latter was undergoing a rapid change, and the water seemed more than usually transparent. Although I could distinctly see the bottom, yet, heaving the lead, I found the ship in fifteen fathoms. The air now became intolerably hot, and was loaded with spiral exhalations similar to those arising from *heat* iron. As night came on, every breath of wind died away, an more entire calm it is impossible to conceive. The flame of a candle burned upon the poop without the least perceptible motion, and a Long hair, held between the finger and thumb, hung without the possibility of detecting a vibration. However, as the captain said he could perceive no indication of danger, and as we were drifting in bodily to shore, he ordered the sails to be furled, and the anchor let go. No watch was set, and the crew, consisting principally of Malays,

一天傍晚，斜靠着船尾的栏杆，我望着那朵独特的云向着西北方孤零零地飘着。它引人注目，因为其色彩独特，更因为它是我们离开巴塔维亚以来第一次看到的云彩。我聚精会神地凝望着它，一直到日落时分。当时云朵突然向东西两方扯开，在海天相接的地方，幻化成一道狭长的烟霞，看起来极像一条长长的浅滩。很快，我的注意力又被暗红色的月亮和罕见的海景吸引住了。大海瞬息万变，但海水却似乎比平常明澈了。我能够清晰地看到海底，但垂下铅锤一量，才知船下水深居然有15英寻。空气此时却变得灼热难耐，热气袅袅升腾，如同烙铁上升起的蒸汽一样。夜幕降临的时候，连一丝风都没有了，寂静得让人难以想象。燃在船尾楼甲板上的蜡烛，连火苗都纹丝不动。指尖捏一根长发，也看不出有任何飘动。但船长却说他没看出有什么危险的迹象。我们还在漂浮向岸边的时候，他就命令下帆沉锚。守夜值班还没安排，那些水手——主要是马来人——就肆意地摊开了身子躺在甲板上了。我走下甲板——难以摈弃不幸的预感。说真的，种种迹象都让我想到名叫西蒙风的那种沙漠热风暴。我告诉了船长我所担心的事，但他对我的话满不在乎，连句屈尊的答复都没有，就把我自己撇在那儿了。然而，我却忐忑不安，

stretched themselves deliberately upon deck. I went below – not without a full presentiment of evil. Indeed, every appearance warranted me in apprehending a Simoon. I told the captain of my fears; but he paid no attention to what I said, and left me without deigning to give a reply. My uneasiness, however, prevented me from sleeping, and about midnight I went upon deck. As I placed my foot upon the upper step of the companion-ladder, I was startled by a loud, humming noise, like that occasioned by the rapid revolution of a mill-wheel, and before I could ascertain its meaning, I found the ship quivering to its centre. In the next instant, a wilderness of foam hurled us upon our beam-ends, and, rushing over us fore and aft, swept the entire decks from stem to stern.

The extreme fury of the blast proved, in a great measure, the salvation of the ship. Although completely water-logged, yet, as her masts had gone by the board, she rose, after a minute, heavily from the sea, and, staggering awhile beneath the immense pressure of the tempest, finally righted.

By what miracle I escaped destruction, it is impossible to say. Stunned by the shock of the water, I found myself, upon recovery, jammed in between the stern-post and rudder. With great difficulty I gained my feet, and looking dizzily around, was, at first, struck with the idea of our being

无法入睡。约莫午夜时分，我爬到了甲板上。我刚爬到甲板扶梯的上端，就被一阵类似于水车轮子飞速转动的巨大的嗡嗡声惊呆了。我还没弄清究竟是怎么回事，就觉得船身震动得厉害。紧接着，一团巨浪挟着泡沫从船梁末端向我们冲过来，把我们冲得摇摇晃晃，从船头滑过了整个甲板一直冲到船尾。

事实证明，那股极度疯狂的巨浪——从很大程度上来说拯救了我们的船只。尽管整条船都进了水，但由于桅杆已断离了甲板，船很快就吃力地从海中浮了上来，在暴风雨的重压下摇晃了一阵，最终恢复了平稳。

真是说不清楚到底是什么奇迹让我幸免于难。我被那股巨浪打晕了，苏醒过来的时候，发现自己被卡在了船尾柱和方向舵之间。费了很大的劲儿，我才抽出脚站了起来。我头晕眼花地向四周瞅了瞅，一想到我们被卷入了滚滚浪涛，就害怕

among breakers; so terrific, beyond the wildest imagination, was the whirlpool of mountainous and foaming ocean within which we were engulfed. After a while, I heard the voice of an old Swede, who had shipped with us at the moment of leaving port. I hallooed to him with all my strength, and presently he came reeling aft. We soon discovered that we were the sole survivors of the accident. All on deck, with the exception of ourselves, had been swept overboard; the captain and mates must have perished while they slept, for the cabins were deluged with water. Without assistance, we could expect to do little for the security of the ship, and our exertions were at first paralyzed by the momentary expectation of going down. Our cable had, of course, parted like pack-thread, at the first breath of the hurricane, or we should have been instantaneously overwhelmed. We scudded with frightful velocity before the sea, and the water made clear breaches over us. The frame-work of our stern was shattered excessively, and, in almost every respect, we had received considerable injury; but to our extreme joy we found the pumps unchoked, and that we had made no great shifting of our ballast. The main fury of the blast had already blown over, and we apprehended little danger from the violence of the wind; but we looked forward to its total cessation with dismay;

极了。但没想到的是，我们还被卷入了一个异常恐怖的排山倒海般的旋涡。过了一会儿，我听到了一个瑞典老头的声音，他是在船就要离港时才上来的。我使出吃奶的劲朝他高呼，不久他就跟跄着摸到了船尾。我们很快就发现自己是这次事故仅存的幸存者。除了我俩，甲板上所有的人都被扫落海中。船长和他的伙计们定是在睡梦中就死去了，因为船舱里都灌满了水。没有援助的话，我们难以奢望维持这船的安全。我们的努力一开始就被搁置了，就是因为想着船随时都会下沉。当然，我们的缆索早在风暴的第一轮袭击中像包裹用的纸捻一样断掉了，否则我们肯定当时就给翻得底朝天了。我们在海面上随波漂行，速度快得惊人。海水在我们头顶上清晰地击打着船板。船尾的支架已支离破碎，几乎每个地方都遭到了严重的破坏。但是绝对让我们高兴的是，水泵并没有坏掉，而且我们还发现压舱物也没有太大的移动。风暴的主体肆虐已经过去了，我们几乎感觉不到风灾的危险，但还是满怀着恐慌盼望它完全停息。我们绝对相信，以我们现在这种破烂不堪的境况，肯定会在随后的巨浪中死无葬身之地。不过，如此合理的推测似乎不会马上出现。整整五天五夜——其间我们只能靠花了很大力气从前甲板下的水手舱里搜

well believing, that, in our shattered condition, we should inevitably perish in the tremendous swell which would ensue. But this very just apprehension seemed by no means likely to be soon verified. For five entire days and nights – during which our only subsistence was a small quantity of jaggeree, procured with great difficulty from the forecastle – the hulk flew at a rate defying computation, before rapidly succeeding flaws of wind, which, without equalling the first violence of the Simoon, were still more terrific than any tempest I had before encountered. Our course for the first four days was, with trifling variations, S.E. and by S.; and we must have run down the coast of New Holland. –On the fifth day the cold became extreme, although the wind had hauled round a point more to the northward. The sun arose with a sickly yellow lustre, and clambered a very few degrees above the horizon – emitting no decisive light. There were no clouds apparent, yet the wind was upon the increase, and blew with a fitful and unsteady fury. About noon, as nearly as we could guess, our attention was again arrested by the appearance of the sun. It gave out no light, properly so called, but a dull and sullen glow without reflection, as if all its rays were polarized. Just before sinking within the turgid sea, its central fires suddenly went out, as if hurriedly

来的为数不多的棕榈糖来维持生命——这条废船在狂风的推动下，以无法测量的速度飞速漂行。狂风虽然没有第一阵的西蒙风暴那么惨烈，但仍然比我之前遭遇过的任何一次狂风都可怕。前四天，我们的航向是向着东南和正南，基本没有变化。我们肯定是沿着新荷兰海岸漂游过来的。到了第五天，突然冷得厉害，而且风向也更加偏北。太阳带着病恹恹的黄色光晕升起，仅仅爬上海平面一点点，也不发光。天上也没有显眼的云彩，但风却一阵猛似一阵，而且变化无常。大约在中午——我们只能靠猜测——我们的注意力再次被太阳的景象吸引了。它发出的不是光，不是正常所谓的光，而是没有发散的朦胧昏沉的光晕，似乎所有的光线都融化掉了。在沉入喧嚣的大海之前，那团光晕中心唯一的火力点也突然消失了——好像是被不可知的力量一下子熄灭了——只剩下一个边框，一个银色的边框，一下子跌落到深不可测的大海。

extinguished by some unaccountable power. It was a dim, sliver-like rim, alone, as it rushed down the unfathomable ocean.

We waited in vain for the arrival of the sixth day – that day to me has not arrived – to the Swede, never did arrive. Thenceforward we were enshrouded in pitchy darkness, so that we could not have seen an object at twenty paces from the ship. Eternal night continued to envelop us, all unrelieved by the phosphoric sea-brilliancy to which we had been accustomed in the tropics. We observed too, that, although the tempest continued to rage with unabated violence, there was no Longer to be discovered the usual appearance of surf, or foam, which had hitherto attended us. All around were horror, and thick gloom, and a black sweltering desert of ebony. Superstitious terror crept by degrees into the spirit of the old Swede, and my own soul was wrapped up in silent wonder. We neglected all care of the ship, as worse than useless, and securing ourselves, as well as possible, to the stump of the mizen-mast, looked out bitterly into the world of ocean. We had no means of calculating time, nor could we form any guess of our situation. We were, however, well aware of having made farther to the southward than any previous navigators, and felt great amazement at not meeting with the usual impediments of ice.

我们徒劳地等待着第六天的到来——对我来说，这一天尚未来到——对瑞典老头来说，第六天永远不会来到。后来，我们一直裹在浓浓的黑暗中，根本看不见离船20步以外的东西。没完没了的黑夜一直包裹着我们，并未因我们所熟悉的热带磷火的闪烁而有所减轻。我们还发现，尽管暴风持续肆虐的势头丝毫不减，但一直猛攻我们的狂涛巨浪却不见了。周围是恐怖而浓重的阴暗，犹如乌黑燥热的荒漠。因为迷信而产生的恐惧渐渐侵入瑞典老头的灵魂，而我的心里也暗自诧异。我们不再关心这条坏到无法使用的船，而是竭尽全力地抱着残存的后桅保命，悲凄地望着茫茫大海。我们无法测算时间，也无从猜测自己的处境。但我们非常清楚，我们朝着南方的漂移已经比以往任何的航海家都要远，而令我们感到万分惊奇的是，我们并没有发现常常作为障碍物出现的冰山。现在，每一刻都可能是我们的最后一刻，每个山峰般的浪头都急不可耐地想吞噬我们。巨浪超乎我的想象，我们没有当即葬身海底真是个奇迹。同伴说船上的货物不重，还提醒我说这船质量出众。但我却不禁觉得希望已彻底无望，心灰意冷地为下一刻

In the meantime every moment threatened to be our last – every mountainous billow hurried to overwhelm us. The swell surpassed anything I had imagined possible, and that we were not instantly buried is a miracle. My companion spoke of the lightness of our cargo, and reminded me of the excellent qualities of our ship; but I could not help feeling the utter hopelessness of hope itself, and prepared myself gloomily for that death which I thought nothing could defer beyond an hour, as, with every knot of way the ship made, the swelling of the black stupendous seas became more dismally appalling. At times we gasped for breath at an elevation beyond the albatross – at times became dizzy with the velocity of our descent into some watery hell, where the air grew stagnant, and no sound disturbed the slumbers of the kraken.

We were at the bottom of one of these abysses, when a quick scream from my companion broke fearfully upon the night. "See! see!" cried he, shrieking in my ears, "Almighty God! see! see!" As he spoke, I became aware of a dull, sullen glare of red light which streamed down the sides of the vast chasm where we lay, and threw a fitful brilliancy upon our deck. Casting my eyes upwards, I beheld a spectacle which froze the current of my blood. At a terrific height directly above us, and upon the very verge

钟就将光顾的死亡做好了准备。船每漂移一段，黑漆漆的海浪就翻滚得更加阴沉恐怖。有时，我们在高高的，比信天翁飞得还高的高处，喘不过气来。有时，我们急速下坠到空气凝滞、死寂无声的水中炼狱，只觉得头晕脑胀。

我们又一次掉下了深渊，突然，瑞典老头的疾呼划破了暗夜。"看！看！"他大喊，尖叫声钻进我的耳朵，"全能的上帝！看！看！"他惊呼的同时，我也注意到，一抹朦胧阴沉的红光沿着我们坠入的那个深渊的边缘洒落下来，斑斑驳驳地投到我们的甲板上。我抬眼望去，只见一个奇观，惊得我血液都凝固了。在我们的正上方不远处，沿着水涡的陡峭边缘，一艘4000吨位左右的巨轮正在打转。尽管屹立于一个比它

of the precipitous descent, hovered a gigantic ship of, perhaps, four thousand tons. Although upreared upon the summit of a wave more than a hundred times her own altitude, her apparent size still exceeded that of any ship of the line or East Indianman in existence. Her huge hull was of a deep dingy black, unrelieved by any of the customary carvings of a ship. A single row of brass cannon protruded from her open ports, and dashed from their polished surfaces the fires of innumerable battle-lanterns, which swung to and fro about her rigging. But what mainly inspired us with horror and astonishment, was that she bore up under a press of sail in the very teeth of that supernatural sea, and of that ungovernable hurricane. When we first discovered her, her bows were alone to be seen, as she rose slowly from the dim and horrible gulf beyond her. For a moment of intense terror she paused upon the giddy pinnacle, as if in contemplation of her own sublimity, then trembled and tottered, and – came down.

At this instant, I know not what sudden self-possession came over my spirit. Staggering as far aft as I could, I awaited fearlessly the ruin that was to overwhelm. Our own vessel was at length ceasing from her struggles, and sinking with her head to the sea. The shock of the descending mass struck her, consequently, in that portion of

自身高出百倍的浪尖上，但很明显它的个头仍远远超过了任何船队的，甚至是东印度公司现有的任何一条船。它庞大的船体是深深的暗黑色，未因船上刻着常见的图案而显得明亮些。一排黄铜大炮从敞开的炮口探出，锃亮的炮身表面折射出无以计数的在灯绳下晃来晃去的战灯之光。但最让我们无比惊讶和恐惧的却是它正在不可思议的巨浪和无以驾驭的飓风的口舌处，扬帆驶来。刚发现它的时候，我们只能看到船头，因为它正从阴森可怖的旋涡里缓缓爬上来。它在令人晕眩的浪尖异常恐怖地停留了一段时间，仿佛沉浸在高高在上的壮举之中，随后，就颠簸晃荡着跌落下来。

此时此刻，我不知怎的就被一种突如其来的泰然占据了灵魂。我跟跄着尽可能奔到船尾末端，无所畏惧地等待着将要来临的毁灭时刻。我们的船终于不再挣扎，船头开始沉入大海。结果，正在跌落的大家伙撞上了它，就撞在已经沉入水下的那部分骨架上。必然的结果

her frame which was already under water, and the inevitable result was to hurl me, with irresistible violence, upon the rigging of the stranger.

As I fell, the ship hove in stays, and went about; and to the confusion ensuing I attributed my escape from the notice of the crew. With little difficulty I made my way unperceived to the main hatchway, which was partially open, and soon found an opportunity of secreting myself in the hold. Why I did so I can hardly tell. An indefinite sense of awe, which at first sight of the navigators of the ship had taken hold of my mind, was perhaps the principle of my concealment. I was unwilling to trust myself with a race of people who had offered, to the cursory glance I had taken, so many points of vague novelty, doubt, and apprehension. I therefore thought proper to contrive a hiding-place in the hold. This I did by removing a small portion of the shifting-boards, in such a manner as to afford me a convenient retreat between the huge timbers of the ship.

I had scarcely completed my work, when a footstep in the hold forced me to make use of it. A man passed by my place of concealment with a feeble and unsteady gait. I could not see his face, but had an opportunity of observing his general appearance. There was about it an evidence of great age and infirmity. His knees

就是我被一股无法抗拒的力量抛起，落到了那条陌生巨轮的索具上。

我跌落的时候，大船正在低处原地挣扎，作势欲冲出深渊，船上正混乱不堪，我就此躲过了船员们的注意。没费什么力气，我就神不知鬼不觉地到了主舱门。舱门半开着，我寻了个机会藏匿其中。我为什么要这样做，自己都说不清。或许，我藏匿起来的原因就是有一种隐隐约约的惊惧，因为在第一眼看到这艘船上的水手时，就让我揪心不已。我不愿相信这伙人，因为匆匆一瞥，他们就让我觉得有诸多说不清的惊奇、疑虑和恐惧。因此，我想在这个船舱里找个藏身之处会更好一些。为此，我要挪开一小块可以活动的甲板，这样才能在庞大的船壁之间给自己找一处便于藏身的所在。

我的工程刚刚完工，船舱里就传来了脚步声，吓得我只好马上躲到甲板下。有人从我的藏身的地方经过，步履浮虚不稳。我看不见他的脸，却有机会观察他大概的体貌。我隐约找得到他已经年老体弱的证据。他的膝盖摇晃不止，只因承载了诸多岁月的负载，重压之下，全

tottered beneath a load of years, and his entire frame quivered under the burthen. He muttered to himself, in a low broken tone, some words of a language which I could not understand, and groped in a corner among a pile of singular-looking instruments, and decayed charts of navigation. His manner was a wild mixture of the peevishness of second childhood, and the solemn dignity of a God. He at length went on deck, and I saw him no more.

A feeling, for which I have no name, has taken possession of my soul – a sensation which will admit of no analysis, to which the lessons of bygone times are inadequate, and for which I fear futurity itself will offer me no key. To a mind constituted like my own, the latter consideration is an evil. I shall never – I know that I shall never – be satisfied with regard to the nature of my conceptions. Yet it is not wonderful that these conceptions are indefinite, since they have their origin in sources so utterly novel. A new sense – a new entity is added to my soul.

It is Long since I first trod the deck of this terrible ship, and the rays of my destiny are, I think, gathering to a focus. Incomprehensible men! Wrapped up in meditations of a kind which I cannot divine, they pass me by unnoticed. Concealment is utter folly on my part, for

身也哆哆嗦嗦的。他一边喃喃自语，断断续续地念叨着几个我听不出是何种语言的词句，一边在堆着奇形怪状的仪器和破烂航海图的角落里摸索着什么。他的举止中夹杂着老顽童般的暴躁，也有神明般的威严。最后，他上了甲板，而我此后就再也没有见过他。

我的心灵被一种莫可名状的感觉占据着。——这种感觉无法解释，往昔岁月中积累的学识，还不足以解释它，恐怕将来我也很难得到一个答案。像我这种头脑，还在考虑将来，真是罪过。我再也不会——我知道我再也不会——满足于自己的那些观念了。毋庸置疑，这些观念含糊不定，只因其根源本来就极端新奇。新的感觉——一种新的东西钻到我的心里了。

自我踏上这艘可怕的船以来，已经过去很久了。我想，我的命运之光也该有个明确的聚焦点了。这些人真是令人费解！走过我身边的时候，都没注意到我，他们都沉浸在某种我无法猜测的沉思之中。对我而言，这样躲躲藏藏，实在是愚

the people *will not* see. It was but just now that I passed directly before the eyes of the mate – it was no Long while ago that I ventured into the captain's own private cabin, and took thence the materials with which I write, and have written. I shall from time to time continue this journal. It is true that I may not find an opportunity of transmitting it to the world, but I will not fail to make the endeavour. At the last moment I will enclose the MS. in a bottle, and cast it within the sea.

An incident has occurred which has given me new room for meditation. Are such things the operation of ungoverned chance? I had ventured upon deck and thrown myself down, without attracting any notice, among a pile of ratlin-stuff and old sails in the bottom of the yawl. While musing upon the singularity of my fate, I unwittingly daubed with a tar-brush the edges of a neatly-folded studding-sail which lay near me on a barrel. The studding-sail is now bent upon the ship, and the thoughtless touches of the brush are spread out into the word DISCOVERY.

I have made many observations lately upon the structure of the vessel. Although well armed, she is not, I think, a ship of war. Her rigging, build, and general equipment, all negative a supposition of this kind. What she is *not*, I can easily perceive – what she *is* I fear it is

蠢，因为他们看不见。刚刚我还径直从大副眼前走过，不久前我还闯进了船长室里，在那儿拿了点可以记录所见所感的笔墨纸张等用品，而且我已经写下来了。我要把航海日记一直不断地写下去。不错，可能我找不到机会将其公布于世，但我不会放弃努力。到最后时刻，我会把手稿封进瓶子里，投入大海。

一件赋予我新的想象空间的事情发生了。难道这些都是未卜的良机？我曾经冒险走上甲板，没有引起任何注意，就在快艇底部那堆梯绳料和旧帆布之间躺下来。当我冥思苦想着自己的奇特命运的时候，不经意地捡起一把柏油刷，在身边大桶上叠得整整齐齐的翼帆的边上涂画起来。就是现在，那面翼帆正在船的上方鼓满了风张着，那把刷子在不经意间涂出了"发现"这个词。

最近，我对大船的构造进行了多次观察。尽管武装精良，但我认为它不是一艘战舰。船上的索具、构造和常用配置，都否定了战舰这一假设。我可以轻易地察觉出它不是什么船，但却担心自己难以说清它到底是什么船。也不知为什么，

impossible to say. I know not how it is, but in scrutinizing her strange model and singular cast of spars, her huge size and overgrown suits of *canvas*, her severely simple bow and antiquated stern, there will occasionally flash across my mind a sensation of familiar things, and there is always mixed up with such indistinct shadows of recollection, an unaccountable memory of old foreign chronicles and ages Long ago.

I have been looking at the timbers of the ship. She is built of a material to which I am a stranger. There is a peculiar character about the wood which strikes me as rendering it unfit for the purpose to which it has been applied. I mean its extreme *porousness*, considered independently by the worm-eaten condition which is a consequence of navigation in these seas, and apart from the rottenness attendant upon age. It will appear perhaps an observation somewhat over-curious, but this would have every characteristic of Spanish oak, if Spanish oak were distended by any unnatural means.

In reading the above sentence a curious apothegm of an old weather-beaten Dutch navigator comes full upon my recollection. "It is as sure," he was wont to say, when any doubt was entertained of his veracity, "as sure as there is a sea where the ship itself will grow in bulk like the living body

当我仔细打量着这船的奇怪的造型、独特的桅杆、巨大的船体、超大号的帆、朴实无华的船头、古色古香的船尾的时候，偶有似曾相识的念头在心中闪现，而且还夹杂着对往事的模糊记忆，记忆里是一些无从解释的古老的外国史略和很久很久以前的时代。

我一直在看船的龙骨。它是用一种我从未见过的木材造成的。这种木材有一种奇怪的特性，让我觉得震惊，它本不适合现在的使用途径——造船。我是指这种木材极其松软，这还仅仅是考虑到虫蛀情况来说的，虫蛀可是海洋航行中最常见的情况，更何况还要考虑到木头会因年代久远而腐朽。这样说就似乎显得有些杞人忧天，但假如说西班牙橡木是依靠非常规的方法膨胀起来的话，那么这种木头和西班牙橡木就具有相同的特点。

我正读着上面所写下的句子，突然一个久经风霜的荷兰老航海家的奇怪箴言插入了我的记忆中。每当有人质疑他的诚实以此取乐时，他总是会说："千真万确，在海水里。船也会变大，就跟水手的身体一样，越泡越大。"

of the seaman."

About an hour ago, I made bold to thrust myself among a group of the crew. They paid me no manner of attention, and, although I stood in the very midst of them all, seemed utterly unconscious of my presence. Like the one I had at first seen in the hold, they all bore about them the marks of a hoary old age. Their knees trembled with infirmity; their shoulders were bent double with decrepitude; their shrivelled skins rattled in the wind; their voices were low, tremulous and broken; their eyes glistened with the rheum of years; and their gray hairs streamed terribly in the tempest. Around them, on every part of the deck, lay scattered mathematical instruments of the most quaint and obsolete construction.

I mentioned some time ago the bending of a studding-sail. From that period the ship, being thrown dead off the wind, has continued her terrific course due south, with every rag of canvas packed upon her, from her trucks to her lower studding-sail booms, and rolling every moment her top-gallant yard-arms into the most appalling hell of water which it can enter into the mind of a man to imagine. I have just left the deck, where I find it impossible to maintain a footing, although the crew seem to experience little inconvenience. It appears to me a miracle of miracles that

大约一个小时前，我壮着胆子挤进了一群船员中间。虽然我就站在他们正中间，但他们对我毫不在意，看起来完全没有意识到我的存在。和我第一次在船舱里看到的那个人一样，他们全都烙着老迈的印记：头发灰白，他们的膝盖因虚弱而颤抖，肩背因衰老而弯成近乎对折，干皱的皮肤在风中簌簌作响。他们的声音很低，断断续续，颤抖不已；眼睛因岁月的侵蚀而泪光迷离；灰白的头发恐怖地和风暴融为一体，飘忽不定。在他们周围的甲板上，到处散落着稀奇古怪、式样过时的制图仪器。

我刚才提到那面翼帆已经张开了。从那时起，大船就一直被风逼着死命向前，继续着可怕的行程，一直向南。自桅杆顶端的木冠到帆的下桁，整张帆的每个部位全都鼓满了。每时每刻，桁端都可能会卷进人类所能想象的最最极度骇人的水之炼狱中。我刚刚离开甲板就发现自己站不稳了，但看起来船员们却没有遭受什么不便。在我看来，我们这艘巨轮没有当即倾覆海底，就此消失，那真是奇迹中的奇迹。我们注定要在死亡的边缘继续徘徊，而不会一击毙命，跌落深渊。

our enormous bulk is not swallowed up at once and forever. We are surely doomed to hover continually upon the brink of eternity, without taking a final plunge into the abyss. From billows a thousand times more stupendous than any I have ever seen, we glide away with the facility of the arrowy sea-gull; and the colossal waters rear their heads above us like demons of the deep, but like demons confined to simple threats and forbidden to destroy. I am led to attribute these frequent escapes to the only natural cause which can account for such effect. I must suppose the ship to be within the influence of some strong current, or impetuous under-tow.

I have seen the captain face to face, and in his own cabin – but, as I expected, he paid me no attention. Although in his appearance there is, to a casual observer, nothing which might bespeak him more or less than man-still a feeling of irrepressible reverence and awe mingled with the sensation of wonder with which I regarded him. In stature he is nearly my own height; that is, about five feet eight inches. He is of a well-knit and compact frame of body, neither robust nor remarkable otherwise. But it is the singularity of the expression which reigns upon the face – it is the intense, the wonderful, the thrilling evidence of old age, so utter, so extreme, which excites within my spirit a sense – a

在比我所见过的巨浪还要大 1000 倍的惊涛骇浪丛中，我们的大船如海鸥般灵巧，箭矢般掠过海面。巨浪如同深水恶魔，高耸着浪头漫过我们，但却只是徒有其表，貌似吓人，实则无力。我不禁把屡次逃难归结为自然因素，因为唯有自然才能有如此效力。我应该想到船是受到了强大的水流或猛烈的海底暗流。

我已经面对面地看到船长了，就是在船长室里。不过，如我所料，他没注意到我。尽管他的外表，乍一看也没什么可以证明他与常人不同的地方，但我对他仍有一种不可抑制的敬畏感，还掺杂着一些惊奇。他身高和我相仿，也就是 5 英尺 8 英寸；身材结实紧凑，既不粗壮，也不细弱。但是有一种奇特的表情挂在他的脸上——那是一种强烈的、神奇的，又令人感到恐惧的龙钟老态，衰老得如此绝对，如此极端。这让我的心头泛起一种波澜，却无法用语言来表达。他前额虽然皱纹很少，但却像是刻上了千万年的印记——灰白的头发记着过去，浑浊的双眼预见未来。舱内的地板

sentiment ineffable. His forehead, although little wrinkled, seems to bear upon it the stamp of a myriad of years. – His gray hairs are records of the past, and his grayer eyes are sybils of the future. The cabin floor was thickly strewn with strange, iron-clasped folios, and mouldering instruments of science, and obsolete Long-forgotten charts. His head was bowed down upon his hands, and he pored, with a fiery unquiet eye, over a paper which I took to be a commission, and which, at all events, bore the signature of a monarch. He murmured to himself, as did the first seaman whom I saw in the hold, some low peevish syllables of a foreign tongue, and although the speaker was close at my elbow, his voice seemed to reach my ears from the distance of a mile.

The ship and all in it are imbued with the spirit of Eld. The crew glide to and fro like the ghosts of buried centuries; their eyes have an eager and uneasy meaning; and when their fingers fall athwart my path in the wild glare of the battle-lanterns, I feel as I have never felt before, although I have been all my life a dealer in antiquities, and have imbibed the shadows of fallen columns at Balbec, and Tadmor, and Persepolis, until my very soul has become a ruin.

When I look around me I feel ashamed of my former apprehensions. If I trembled at

上厚厚地摊满了奇怪的铁扣对开本的书籍，还有一些破烂不堪的科学仪器和荒废了很久的过时航海图。船长双手托着低垂的头颅，炽热而又不安的眼睛凝视着一张纸，我觉得是份委任状，无论怎么说，那上面可有君主的签名啊。就跟我在船舱里见到的第一个船员一样，船长也喃喃自语着几句外国话，声音低微却颇有些怒气。尽管他就在我的身边，但他的声音却像从一英里外的地方传来。

大船以及船上的一切都充盈着远古的气息。船员如千年幽灵般飘来飘去，他们的眼睛里充满了渴望和不安。虽然我一生都在打点古物，在自己的灵魂也变成一片废墟之前，可能都无法忘记巴尔贝克、泰特莫、珀塞波利斯那些个倒塌圆柱的影子，但是每当他们的指尖在炫目的战灯下划过我经过的地方，我都会生出前所未有的感觉。

我看了看四周，不禁为刚才的恐惧惭愧起来。如果我对迄今为止

the blast which has hitherto attended us, shall I not stand aghast at a warring of wind and ocean, to convey any idea of which the words tornado and simoon are trivial and ineffective? All in the immediate vicinity of the ship is the blackness of eternal night, and a chaos of foamless water; but, about a league on either side of us, may be seen, indistinctly and at intervals, stupendous ramparts of ice, towering away into the desolate sky, and looking like the walls of the universe.

As I imagined, the ship proves to be in a current; if that appellation can properly be given to a tide which, howling and shrieking by the white ice, thunders on to the southward with a velocity like the headLong dashing of a cataract.

To conceive the horror of my sensations is, I presume, utterly impossible; yet a curiosity to penetrate the mysteries of these awful regions, predominates even over my despair, and will reconcile me to the most hideous aspect of death. It is evident that we are hurrying onwards to some exciting knowledge – some never-to-be-imparted secret, whose attainment is destruction. Perhaps this current leads us to the southern pole itself. It must be confessed that a supposition apparently so wild has every probability in its favor.

The crew pace the deck with unquiet and tremulous step; but there is upon their

攻击过我们的狂风感到恐惧战栗的话，我岂不是要被狂风与海洋的斗法吓得呆若木鸡？想要表达出这种斗法，龙卷风和西蒙风这样的词汇，真是微不足道，相去甚远。大船周遭，弥漫着无尽长夜的浓黑，以及连泡沫都不生的海水所发出的轰响。但是，在船两侧一里格远的地方，却可以看到巨大的冰墙，模模糊糊，时隐时现，高耸入孤寂的空中，看上去像是宇宙的围墙。

如我所料，这船正是裹在一股水流之中，如果潮汐也可以称为水流的话。现在，这股潮汐正在冲破白冰，尖声怒号着，雷霆万钧地向南方疾驰，犹如瀑布倾泻。

我觉得根本不可能把心底的恐惧表述出来。但是，想要揭开这个恐怖区域的奥秘的好奇心压制住了恐惧和绝望。这好奇心还将助我安然面对死亡中最最可怕的一面。显然，我们匆匆前行就是奔向一些激动人心的秘密，一些永无人知的秘密。到达之时，就是灭亡之际。或许这股水流正带着我们奔赴南极。不得不说，这个猜测看起来如此荒诞，但却完全可能。

船员们踱着焦躁不安的步子在甲板上走来走去。但是他们脸上的

countenances an expression more of the eagerness of hope than of the apathy of despair.

In the meantime the wind is still in our poop, and, as we carry a crowd of canvas, the ship is at times lifted bodily from out the sea! – Oh, horror upon horror! – the ice opens suddenly to the right, and to the left, and we are whirling dizzily, in immense concentric circles, round and round the borders of a gigantic amphitheatre, the summit of whose walls is lost in the darkness and the distance. But little time will be left me to ponder upon my destiny! The circles rapidly grow small – we are plunging madly within the grasp of the whirlpool – and amid a roaring, and bellowing, and thundering of ocean and of tempest, the ship is quivering, oh God! and – going down!

表情，更多的是对希望的热盼，而非绝望的冷漠。

此时，风依然自船尾吹来，由于我们张起的船帆众多，船时不时会被带出海面——哦，恐怖极了！忽而是右侧冰裂，忽而是左侧。我们围着巨大的同心圆打转，就像是绕着一个巨大的露天竞技场转个没完，直转得头晕目眩。而竞技场围墙的墙头又隐没在黑暗之中，遥不可及。但是已经没有时间让我来思量自己的命运了。同心圆迅速缩小，我们突然被涡流捕获。在大海和狂风雷霆般的怒号和轰鸣中，船不住地颤抖着，哦，上帝，它沉下去了！

（完）

附录

作者简介及生平

埃德加·爱伦·坡（1809～1849），19 世纪美国诗人、小说家和文学评论家。被誉为侦探小说鼻祖、科幻小说先驱之一、恐怖小说大师、短篇哥特小说巅峰、象征主义先驱之一，唯美主义者。其作品具有别具一格的特点。他与安布鲁斯·布尔斯和 H.P.洛夫克拉夫特并称为美国三大恐怖小说家。

爱伦·坡于 1809 年 1 月 19 日生于美国波士顿，在家中三兄妹中排名老二。他的父母均为剧团的演员。后来，他的父亲离家出走，母亲也在他很小的时候去世了。他从 1811 年沦为了孤儿，后被一富裕的烟草商收养。

爱伦·坡在学生时代就表现出对拉丁文、喜剧表演、游泳及诗歌创作的热爱和天赋。他在 1827 年应征参加了美国陆军，并在那里，出版了他的第一本书《帖木儿及其它诗》，但这本薄薄的诗集没有引起人们的注意。爱伦·坡一直有着当职业军人的梦想，在此后一直竭力谋求进入西点军校的机会。在等待西点军校消息的过程中，他出版了自己的第二部诗集，并得到了著名评论家约翰·尼尔的认可。1830 年，爱伦·坡终于如愿以偿进入西点军校，然而他在 1831 年却接受到军事法庭的审判并被开除。于是他前往巴尔的摩的姨妈家居住，在那里教他的表妹读书，并在此期间写出 6 部短篇小说，其中有两篇由《游客报》刊登。

1834 年，短篇小说《梦幻者》得以在《戈迪淑女杂志》发表，这是他首次在一份发行量大的杂志上发表作品。随后又被人推荐到《南方文学信使》月刊，大大地增加了《南方文学信使》在全国的发行量和知名度。1837 年 1 月他从《南方文学信使》辞职，举家前往纽约继续当自由撰稿人，可在经济上仍然捉襟见肘，而且找不到编辑职位。迫于生计，1839 年开始在《亚历山大每周信使》上发表第一批关于密码分析的文章。后来又在《绅士杂志》做一些编辑工作。每月提供一篇署名作品和该刊所需的大部分评论文章。1839 年底《怪异故事集》（2 卷本）由费城的利及布兰查德出版社出版，该书包括当时已写成的全部 25 部短篇小说。1841 年，爱伦·坡成为《格雷厄姆杂志》编辑，发表了他称之为"推理小说"之首篇《莫格街凶杀案》。1843 年 6 月《金甲虫》在费城《美元日报》的征文比赛中赢得 100 美元奖金并立即受到欢迎，这篇小说的大量转载以及一个剧本的改编使爱伦·坡作为一个走红的作家而闻名。1844 年继续创办之前计划的杂志《铁笔》。1846 年爱伦·坡精神压抑和贫病交加，但仍然坚持发表文章。1849 年 10 月爱伦·坡死于脑溢血。

主要作品汇总

诗歌类：

《咏乔·洛克》
Lines on Joe Locke
《致奥克塔维娅》
To Octavia
《帖木儿》 *Tamerlane*
《歌》 *Song*
《梦》 *Dreams*
《亡灵》
Spirits of the Dead
《模仿》 *Imitation*
《深眠黄土》
Deep in Earth
《一个梦》 *A Dream*
《最快乐的日子》
The Happiest Day

《新婚小调》
Bridal Ballad
《孤独》 *Alone*
《传奇》 *Romance*
《阿尔阿拉夫》
Al Aaraaf
《致河》 *To The River*
《仙境》 *Fairy-Land*

《致艾萨克·利》
To Isaac Lea
《安娜贝尔·李》
Annabel Lee

《哦，时代！哦，风尚！》
O, Tempora! O, Mores!
《一首离合诗》
An Acrostic
《诗》 *Poetry*
《致海伦》 *To Helen*
《以色拉费》 *Israfel*
《不安的山谷》
The Valley of Unrest
《睡美人》 *The Sleeper*
《海中之城》
The City in the Sea
《丽诺尔》 *Lenore*
《致路易丝·奥利维亚·亨特小姐》 *To Miss Louise Olivia Hunter*

《赞歌》
Latin Hymn//Hymn
《谜》 *Enigma*
《一个谜》 *An Enigma*
《罗马大圆形竞技场》
The Coliseum
《小夜曲》 *Serenade*
《伊丽莎白》 *Elizabeth*
《闹鬼的宫殿》
The Haunted Palace
《十四行诗——致科学》
To Science

《致玛格丽特》
To Margaret
《征服者爬虫》
The Conqueror Worm
《梦境》 *Dream-Land*
《尤拉丽——歌》 *Eulalie*
《乌鸦》 *The Raven*
《赠——的情人节礼物》
A Valentine
《诗节》 *Stanzas*
《致乐园中的一位》
To One in Paradise
《致 M.L.S》 *To M. L. S*
《尤娜路姆——一首歌谣》 *Ulalume – A Ballad*

《十四行诗——静》
Silence, a Sonnet
《钟》 *The Bells*
《致海伦》 *To Helen*
《梦中之梦》
A Dream Within A Dream
《献给安妮》 *For Annie*
《黄金国》 *Eldorado*

《致我的母亲》
To My Mother

小说类：

《梅岑格施泰因》
Metzengerstein
《失去呼吸》
Loss of Breath
《耶路撒冷的故事》
A Tale of Jerusalem
《瓶中手稿》
MS. Found in a Bottle
《与一具木乃伊的谈话》
Some Words with a Mummy
《四不象》
Four Beasts in One – The Homo-Cameleopard
《捧为名流》 Lionizing
《用 X 代替 O 的时候》
X-ing a Paragrab
《死荫——寓言一则》
Shadow – A Parable
《静——寓言一则》
Silence – A Fable
《被窃之信》
The Purloined Letter
《莫雷娜》 Morella
《欺骗是一门精密的科学》 Diddling
《故弄玄虚》
Mystification
《丽姬娅》 Ligeia

《德洛梅勒特公爵》
The Duc De L'Omelette
《生意人》
The Business Man
《人群中的人》
The Man of the Crowd
《言语的力量》
The Power of Words
《莫斯肯漩涡沉浮记》
A Descent into the Maelstrom
《莫诺斯与尤拉的对话》
The Colloquy of Monos and Una
《埃莱奥诺拉》 Eleonora
《阿恩海姆乐园》 The Domain of Arnheim
《椭圆的画像》
The Oval Portrait
《红死魔的假面具》 The Masque of the Red Death
《一星期中的三个星期天》
Three Sundays in a Week
《瘟疫王》 King Pest
《泄密的心》
The Tell-tale Heart
《金甲虫》 The Gold-Bug

《黑猫》 The Black Cat

《催眠启示录》
Mesmeric Revelation
《你就是那人》
Thou Art the Man
《气球骗局》
The Balloon-Hoax
《奇怪天使》
The Angel of the Odd
《莫格街凶杀案》
The Murders in the Rue Morgue
《瓦尔德马先生病例之真相》 The Facts in the Case of M. Valdemar
《甮甮》 Bon-Bon
《反常之魔》
The Imp of the Perverse
《陷坑与钟摆》 The Pit and the Pendulum
《斯芬克斯》
The Sphinx
《一桶白葡萄酒》
The Cask of Amontillado
《贝蕾妮丝》 Berenice
《未来之事》
Mellonta Tauta
《兰多的小屋》
Landor's Cottage
《跳蛙》 Hop-Frog

《如何写布莱克伍德式文章》 *How to Write a Blackwood Article*

《绝境》 *A Predicament*

《钟楼魔影》 *The Devil in the Belfry*

《被用光的人》 *The Man That Was Used Up*

《厄舍府的倒塌》 *The Fall of the House of Usher*

《过早埋葬》 *The Premature Burial*

《玛丽·罗杰特迷案》 *The Mystery of Marie Roget*

《幽会》 *The Assignation*

《长方形箱子》 *The Oblong Box*

《凹凸山的故事》 *A Tale of the Ragged Mountains*

《埃洛斯与沙米翁的对话》 *The Conversation of Eiros and Charmion*

《冯·肯佩伦和他的发现》 *Von Kempelen and His Discovery*

《眼镜》 *The Spectacles*

《灯塔（残稿）》 *The Light-House*

《威廉·威尔逊》 *William Wilson*

《阿·戈·皮姆的故事》 *The Narrative of Arthur Gordon Pym of Nantucket*

戏剧类：

《波利希安》选场（一至五场未完） *Scenes From 'Politian'*

随笔与评论：

《巨人舞石柱林一瞥》 *Some Account of Stonehenge*

《仙女岛》 *The Island of the Fay*

《维萨西孔河之晨》 *Morning on the Wissahiccon*

《装饰的哲学》 *The Philosophy of Furniture*

《诗歌原理》 *The Poetic Principle*

《写作的哲学》 *The Philosophy of Composition*

《本能与理性——一只黑猫》 *Instinct VS Reason – A Black Cat*

《梅泽尔的象棋手》 *Maelzel's Chess-Player*

《评霍桑的〈故事重述〉》 *Review of Hawthorne's 'Twice-Told Tales'*